An International Defence and Political Risk Consultant, James H. Jackson continues to advise a wide range of global clients on overseas trade and security matters. He is a postgraduate in military studies, with further university and professional qualifications in law, politics and as a barrister. He lectures and writes extensively on a variety of specialist subjects including low-intensity conflict and arms trade issues. He is the author of one previous acclaimed international thriller, *Dead Headers*.

'Few things give me greater pleasure than to read a tense, well-researched, fast-paced and hard-nosed thriller by a new young British thriller writer. *Dead Headers* by James Jackson falls very firmly into that category' Frederick Forsyth

'Hard-nosed and violent, [*Dead Headers*] is a terrifyingly convincing read' *Sunday Express*

Also by James H. Jackson

Dead Headers

Cold Cut

James H. Jackson

HEADLINE
FEATURE

First published in 1999
by HEADLINE BOOK PUBLISHING

First published in paperback in 2000
by HEADLINE BOOK PUBLISHING

10 9 8 7 6 5 4 3 2 1

ISBN 0 7472 5772 8

Typeset by Avon Dataset Ltd, Bidford-on-Avon, Warks

Printed and bound in France by
Brodard & Taupin

HEADLINE BOOK PUBLISHING
A division of the Hodder Headline Group
338 Euston Road
London NW1 3BH

www.headline.co.uk
www.hodderheadline.com

Acknowledgements

Special thanks to Diana, Andrei and Ram, whose insights and advice helped shape this novel.

Thanks also to:

BM, FF, AS, EH, MB, CB, GH, SO, RC, RC, CIR, RP, MP, BB, LB, TP, JP, PM, FC, FE.

Thanks to J. M. Dent for permission to quote from 'Do not go gentle into that good night' by Dylan Thomas, and to Michael Yeats for permission to quote from 'The Second Coming' by W. B. Yeats.

For Boo

And dedicated to those of my family, and their generations, who gave their lives in the twentieth century so that we could be free, sovereign, united and independent in the next. It is a legacy under threat.

Do not go gentle into that good night,
Rage, rage against the dying of the light.

'Do not go gentle into that good night',
Dylan Thomas

And what rough beast, its hour come round at last,
Slouches towards Bethlehem to be born?

'The Second Coming', W. B. Yeats

RUSSIA'S PRINCIPAL INTELLIGENCE ORGANISATIONS

1. Federal Security Service (FSB)

Headquartered at 2 Lubyanka Square, and with a staff of up to 80,000, the *Federal'naya sluzhba bezopasnost* is tasked with domestic counter-espionage, anti-subversion and counter-terrorism. Its remit covers protection of the Russian state, countering criminal gangs, military counter-intelligence and the guarding of strategic facilities. It has recourse to 150,000 support staff, continues to use hundreds of thousands of *seksoty* informers, has regained control of Border Troops and absorbed much of the former KGB's eavesdropping organisation.

2. Foreign Intelligence Service (SVR)

Headquartered at Yasenevo on Moscow's outskirts, the *Sluzhba veneshnei razvedky* inherited the assets of the KGB's First (Intelligence) Main Directorate. It employs a staff of around 12,000, and continues to mount concerted espionage and economic intelligence operations against Europe and North America. Its first Director was Yevgeni Primakov, later to become Russian Prime Minister.

3. Main Intelligence Directorate (GRU)

Headquartered in its *Stiklyashka* ('Glasshouse') next to Khodinka Airfield outside Moscow, the *Glavnoye razvedyvatel upravleniye* employs 12,000 staff, is Russia's Military Intelligence organisation, and is answerable to the General Staff. Its responsibilities embrace the running of both 'legals' (defence attachés) and 'illegals' abroad, the operation of its Lourdes electronic spying base in Cuba, and the handling of spy satellites through its Directorate of Cosmic Intelligence. It maintains control over several *Spetsnaz* Special Forces units.

4. Federal Government Communications & Information Agency (FAPSI)

Headquartered at 4 Bolshoi Kisel'ny in Moscow, the *Federal'nae agenstvo pravitelstvennoi svyazii informatsii* employs over 50,000 personnel, is the equivalent of America's NSA and Britain's GCHQ, and is involved in both domestic and foreign electronic intelligence gathering. It has absorbed the KGB's signals intelligence and cryptographic operations and the specialist GVS communications troops. It remains heavily involved in spying on Russian citizens, conducts missions as part of the FSB, and became a significant shareholder in 'Relkom', the country's leading Internet Service provider.

5. Federal Protection Service

The Kremlin's 'inner circle' of defence against attempted political overthrow or assassination, the *Federal'naya sluzhba okhrany* is operated by the President's central administration. It has inherited the protection troops of the KGB's former Ninth Directorate and possesses its own formidable intelligence apparatus.

The Key Russians:

Leonid Gresko – Director of the FSB.
Georgi Lazin – Colonel in the FSB.
Petr Ivanov – Colonel in the FSB.
Yuri Vakulchuk – Assistant to Georgi Lazin.
Boris Diakanov – Russian Mafiya Boss.
Ilya Kokhlov – Pathologist in Krasnoyarsk.

PROLOGUE

'Hell and b-b-buggery, this b-bloody cuff-link!'
The voice was English, received pronunciation, vowels fat and glottal with drink and frustration, the stammer beginning its wayward descent into outright slurring.

'Can I help?' An American, female, called through from another room. There was no response; perhaps he was angry, perhaps concentrating exclusively on the struggle with his shirt cuff. She wandered through, unwilling to pass up the opportunity to get in a dig at her tiresomely inadequate husband.

He was sitting on the bed, sweating, muttering. Pushing small things into tricky openings had been way beyond him these past few months she thought maliciously, watching from the open doorway.

'Enjoying yourself?' she asked. Stupid question. The only time he enjoyed himself was after drinking enough to blind the average human, when he would be carried, eyes glazed, from an expat party or from his favourite corner at the bar of the Hotel Normandy a few hundred yards down the hill on the waterfront.

'P-piss off, Eleanor. Go and sort yourself out instead.'

The face was pale and jowled, traced with the broken-capillaried skein of an alcoholic, ready-tuned for confrontation, eyes reddened and set by recurrent nightmares and late-evening bouts with an unparalleled variety of bottles. Those bottles often ended smashed on the sidewalk several

1

storeys below their balcony. It would not surprise her if he followed them over one night. The pet fox cub had already gone that way. She was past caring.

'We promised we'd be there on time.'

'I d-don't make p-promises.'

'Well, just damn well behave, and don't embarrass me again.'

It was pointless, she understood that, knew that he would. There were times when guests had to step over him to get to the door, other moments when he groped women furiously or furtively beneath the table oblivious to her, and their, desperate expressions. He had even goosed the wife of the British Ambassador at a recent reception. She could not go on like this, the sense of isolation and entrapment growing each day she spent in the claustrophobic apartment block in the less-than glamorous section of Ras Beirut.

There was a morose silence between the two as they climbed into the taxi which had waited for over thirty minutes. The car jolted off down Bliss Street, the driver thankful that the main argument must have occurred indoors. He drove them often, was inured to their capacity for screaming eruptions and serial bickering.

'Stop the car. I want the p-p-post office on Makdissi Street.'

'You what?' She was incredulous. 'You're kidding me?'

'Stop the car.'

The driver shrugged his shoulders and obeyed. They were bound to quarrel eventually, the quiet was simply a phoney respite, a prelude.

She rounded on him. 'Why now? Tell me, why fucking now? It's one of the few dinner invitations we've had in a month.'

'I'm a journalist. I need to p-post copy.'

'At this hour, for Chrissakes? It's with the First Secretary of the British Embassy . . .'

'I'm well aware of that,' he snapped. 'Glen Paul is my friend, remember?'

2

'I forgot you had any left.'

He jumped out and slammed the door. She leant across and wound down the window, calling after him. 'I'm not waiting, you know? You can make your own way there.' She was uncertain if he heard her as he rounded the corner, shoulders hunched, neck retracted, in anger.

Around the table, polite conversation, trill laughter, could not hide the underlying tension, the unspoken sympathy for Eleanor. She was having a ghastly time with her drunk of a husband, of course. Bad genes, probably – his father was an odd cove, an adventurer and explorer, had visited two years previously, imbibed too much at a party and died shortly afterwards in a Beirut hospital uttering the immortal words: 'God, I'm bored.' His son plainly took after him. Such a shame. He had been rather popular at the beginning, one of the more entertaining journalists on the Middle East circuit. Bit of a past, but it added to the interest, the colour; besides, who wasn't running away from something? An affable, intelligent rogue with a touching vulnerability and schoolboy stammer. A real ladies' man, was the received and given wisdom, the accepted version. He had quite swept Eleanor off her feet, you know, even though she was married at the time to that old cuckold Sam Brewer. Everyone forgave him, everyone always did – in those days. How things changed, soured – judgement, personalities, relationships, lives – out here in the fleshpots of Beirut. It was rumoured that he was heading for some sort of breakdown.

In fact, he was heading across Lebanon for the Syrian border. Another cab had been waiting for him near the post office, its driver, an Armenian from the Burj Hammoud quarter of the city, flashing his headlamps twice in recognition before the man approached and opened the rear door.

'Your clothes and papers are there on the back seat,' the Armenian spoke over his shoulder. 'Everything is correct.'

'Thank you.'

3

'The friends wish you luck.'

They headed into the slum suburbs, a second car taking him on to a rendezvous with a truck beyond the city limits. There was distance to put in before the alarm was raised, before the teams came looking. The opposition would follow the false trails which led to the docks, to a steamer departing that night for international waters and more welcoming shores. An obvious route. It was cold as the vehicle ground its way, protesting, into the snow flurries of the Chouf mountains, but by then the man was wearing thermal undergarments, thick socks, walking boots and warm padded outer clothing. He settled into his thoughts, gazing out at the shrouded peaks, past the resort at Aley, the Nahr al Metn valley running off the left, and on to the villages of Machra and Bhamdoun. He looked back only once at the city he had left behind, glittering far below through the occasional wisps of fog. He had no regrets; he was focused, determined. The driver filled water bottles for him in the natural spring fountain beside the road at Sofar – he remembered doing the same for Eleanor at this exact spot, long ago, when they were still in love – but it was their last halt that night. The road took them on to Chtaura and down into the Beqa'a Valley. Damascus lay ahead.

Dinner over, Eleanor left for home, the self-conscious attempts by her hosts to disguise their contempt for her husband and their pity for her having become intolerably awkward as the evening progressed. The efforts of other guests to engage and divert her made it worse. She sat alone in the back of the taxi, depression replaced by shivering. Why her? How could she have got it so wrong? He had changed. Had she? She thought of the concerned faces around the table. Fuck them all: their prying, their gossip, their hypocrisy, their snide remarks, their backbiting.

The apartment was dark and empty when she got back, symbol of four and a half years of marriage.

'Fuck you,' she shouted at the silent rooms. 'Fuck, fuck,

fuck, fuck . . .' before guilt, anger and remorse forced out the tears. Doubtless he would be returned drunk, comatose, wholly unrepentant the following morning.

Three days later, not far from Hakkari, a passenger clambered wearily from a cattle truck and walked the short distance across the Syrian border into Turkey. Another transport, this one carrying animal feed, was waiting for him. He lay hidden, covered in sacks, his limbs numb, as the vehicle struggled and swerved, its tyre-chains searching for grip on the icy road north. Many times they were caught in snowdrifts; many times he had to aid the cursing driver with a shovel, placing mats under the wheels to provide necessary traction. At least the weather reduced the chance of a Turkish roadblock or roving patrols.

Between Van and Patnos the engine seized, but after four hours of tinkering, swearing at his nerveless blue hands and the driver, and taking gulps from his hip-flask, the Englishman brought it back to life. A blizzard blew up in front, the driver refusing to go further in the desperate conditions, fearful for his safety, shouting incomprehensibly. It was madness to continue. The passenger took him firmly by the chin, twisted his face towards his own, and cocking fingers, fired an imaginary bullet between his eyes. There was no need for words, explanation. The driver understood – continue or I will have you shot. He revved the motor.

It was well into the following day when the exhausted pair made it to the rickety grass-roofed tea house at Dogubayazit on the southern slopes of Mount Ararat. There they parted company, the driver leaving rapidly lest he be picked up for questioning by the Turkish authorities, the Englishman pushing his way through the wooden door to thaw awhile, enjoy a Russian cigarette and wait for the bus to carry him across the featureless rockscape to the remote village of Agralik. The Armenian owner grinned at his visitor, a face remembered – it was almost ten years since it had last come through that entrance. It looked much older, crushed by fatigue.

Within three hours the bus had dropped the strange foreigner with his rucksack at the appointed destination. He would continue on foot. The Englishman felt his spirits lift, the tiredness slide away. He was so close, there would be time later to rest, to celebrate. The sun was beginning to set across the northern aspect of Ararat as he shouldered his pack and headed for a further border.

He saw the contours of the truck and moved towards it, two figures in quilted overjackets and wearing fur *shapkas* climbing from the cab as he approached. The watchtower had seen him cross the wire at the pre-agreed time and radioed back to the command blockhouse in the rear. He was expected. Hand torches flickered rapidly between them.

One of them stepped forward to greet the man Moscow Centre had codenamed 'Stanley'. They shook hands. The Russian hugs, the vodkas, speeches, would come at the reception.

'The Central Committee and Committee for State Security welcome you to the territory of the Union of Soviet Socialist Republics, Comrade Colonel.'

Cold, wet, footsore, and ready to fall asleep where he stood, Harold Adrian Russell Philby – better known as Kim Philby – traitor, Soviet agent, officer in Britain's Secret Intelligence Service, a man who had caused the deaths of hundreds, relaxed for the first time and smiled. He was home.

April 4, 1993. Cuba

There were only five in the group relaxing on the sandbar that day, hidden from view and protected from outside interference first by the miles of near-impenetrable banana plantation and tobacco crop leading down to the coast and then by the tangle of mangrove lying dense along the shoreline. Struggle through that and the visitor faced a twenty-minute rowing-boat trip across a trapped body of water – and on this day the boat was hauled up, commandeered by those who had already reached the brilliant-white coral beach on the far side. Cayo Levisa, a jewel, and you had to be a local to know how to find it.

The men were locals in a sense. They had lived in Cuba for many years, some had raised families there, all retained a residual affection for an island slowly disintegrating under the twin pressures of classic Marxist command economics and American-imposed sanctions. Decline and State bankruptcy provided a scenario with which they were well accustomed, for they were Russian. They fished for red snapper and sea bass off the Archipelago de los Colorados in the warm waters of the Gulf of Mexico, did their best to drink the entire rum production of the famed Havana Club Ronera Santa Cruz factory, had affairs with local girls, swam, drank some more, and spied for their country. All were officers in the *Glavnoye razvedyvatel upravleniye* – GRU – the Main Intelligence Directorate of the Military General Staff, and all were attached to the sprawling Lourdes electronic intelligence-gathering base set in the undulating limestone terrain above the western plains of Havana Province.

By the Year 2000, the establishment was the largest of its kind outside the Russian Federation, employed up to seventeen hundred specialists, cost several hundred million dollars a year in rent, several hundred million more to maintain, and its array of antennae, dishes and aerials pointed directly at the coast of the United States of America some one hundred miles distant across the water. Its role was both defensive and offensive, civil and military, its computers penetrating, collecting, collating, decoding and analysing military communications traffic, domestic telephone calls, facsimiles, e-mail, banking transactions and ultra-sensitive strategic and economic data on an extraordinary scale. One of its key departments concentrated solely on disruptive measures: jamming enemy command links, planting computer viruses and, if necessary, paralysing the economic nerve system of its old capitalist adversary. Recognising its central position in the framework of Russian espionage, and understanding the potential threat posed to American national interests, government officials and representatives on Capitol Hill alike repeatedly called for its closure. Yet its capabilities, and its importance to the Russians, continued to expand. Everyone spied on everyone else, even NATO allies. Germany, for example, had its ultra-secret Eismeer 'Polar Sea' listening post based on Spain's Atlantic Coast, intact since the days of Franco and the collaborative 'Delikatesse' signals intelligence operations of the 1939–40 war. Its 'yellow-stripe' transcripts all too often contained decoded communications between Langley, the Pentagon or State Department and their overseas stations. Moscow could piggy-back on such efforts: their agent at Eismeer was well placed. An espionage free-for-all, and the Russians remained well in the game.

The friends had every intention of getting drunk; it was Sunday after all, the rains would be coming soon and their private paradise was scheduled to be overrun with an 'exclusive development' of hard-currency-earning cabanas catering to fat Italians on winter charters. Between them, and carried in a number of cold-bags kept close to hand, were three containers of aguardiente, the local peasant fire water, crates of Hatuey beer and a bottle of Ponche Kuba egg liqueur included either as chaser or afterthought. It would be a celebration of their time together, of their memories, and a wake for the future.

The coastguard launch from Palma Rubia idled past on low throttle a few hundred metres offshore, its crew sunning themselves lazily, not bothering to scan the beach party through their high-powered binoculars. It was a contented scene.

'You know the best thing about this place?' one of the men asked.

'We can watch you drink too much, climb a royal palm and break your neck.' replied a companion, sprawling back in his bermudas.

'No. There isn't a filthy Chekist for miles.'

They drank a toast to it. There was an abiding hatred for the Cheka and its members, the old KGB's First Chief Directorate, since renamed the SVR, the Foreign Intelligence Service. Rivals since inception, the GRU were military men, the KGB their more powerful civilian counterparts. As economic warfare and industrial espionage gained higher priority in Moscow, so the numbers of reviled Chekists, together with their electronic eavesdropping cronies from the Agency for Government Communications and Information at the Lourdes location, grew. Resentment was mutual, suspicion widespread, livelihoods were at stake.

'Aren't you forgetting their DGI stooges?' A small man with a brooding countenance jerked a thumb over his shoulder at the patrol boat.

'Chill out, Arkady. The DGI are far too busy running Colombian shit into Florida to give a fuck about us.'

More laughter, more drinking. The DGI, Cuban Intelligence, long regarded by the KGB as a departmental subsidiary of its own Latin American desk – and thus equally loathed by the GRU – had built a well-deserved reputation for providing arms and support to a host of unsavoury Latin American revolutionary movements. In return, the Cubans received a substantial quantity of the region's finest narcotics with which to flood the American market. Politics and commerce in synergy.

'Don't blame you for being gloomy, Arkady. Just think, your tour here is over in six months and you'll be spending the rest of your life under canvas with everyone else in our heroic Russian Army.'

It was a prospect none of them relished or could bring themselves to smile at. They knew what a posting home entailed – poverty, misery and unemployment. It was an open secret that Arkady, a full Colonel, was the lucky one, had landed a job as technical supervisor at the country's new command and control centre for strategic rocket forces built into Kosvinsky mountain in the Urals. There would be no tented accommodation for him. It made the joke all the more bitter.

Arkady did not reveal to his comrades that he had little intention of returning to the Mother Country for any kind of work and whatever the lifestyle; neither did he talk of his surprise encounter with a man posing as a Canadian entrepreneur during a visit to Havana three months previously as he sat nursing his mojito cocktail at the roof-terrace bar of the Hotel Inglaterra.

'Photograph time.'

They groaned. The man had a reputation for taking hours in setting up a shot, fiddling with lenses, checking light meters, only to find upon development that the image was either unrecognisable or non-existent. He was meticulous in his ineptitude, surprising given his weekday responsibility for determining means of jamming the ultra-high frequency radios and airborne launch control systems installed on board America's fleet of E-6B TACAMO – 'Take Charge and Move Out' – intercontinental and submarine-launched ballistic missile command aircraft. The apparatus was assembled, slowly, and, amid much disparagement, the remote-timer set, the group lined up.

'Chests out, stomachs in – the reverse of the usual,' the photographer commanded enthusiastically, running back to take up position.

'Why? You'll only be getting our feet.'

They waited. Fidgeting began.

'My beer's beginning to overheat,' came the first complaint. The officer from the Sixth Operational Directorate hated warm beer.

'Patience. Get ready. And smile.'

It took three seconds, Arkady the only one remaining on his feet as the pair of sniper rifles fired from the vessel took down his friends on either side. Muzzle suppressers or the Trade Winds, there was no discernible noise of discharge. The camera shutter operated. Without turning, the Russian stooped to retrieve his beach bag, threw in the camera and walked down to the water's edge. The patrol boat came in close, he waded crotch-deep to meet it and was hauled aboard.

'Sorry 'bout your pals.' A crew-member in shorts and a sun-visor patted him on the shoulder, the rifle angled outwards in his other hand. 'Gotta say, it was easier than a Caribou shoot.'

Once owned by the US Drug Enforcement Agency, the Cougar powerboat thundered northwards at sixty-five knots. Halfway to the American coast it was met by an unmarked Bell helicopter which winched up the GRU man and carried him in to Miami International Airport. There he transferred to a Learjet and was flown up to Virginia for a lengthy debriefing at a ranch belonging to the Central Intelligence Agency. He would not be seen again at the GRU's Moscow Khoroschevskii Shausse headquarters.

Five months later, an unofficial meeting – the first of several – took place between a small group of senior military and intelligence officials from the Russian Federation and the United States within the faded pink hacienda-style walls of the Hotel Los Jazminos set above the Valle de Vinales in Cuba's Sierra de los Organos region. The unsurpassed views of rivers, caves, lakes and wondrous mogotes rock formations were not on the agenda. Conditions were intensely secret. The hotel staff were excused their duties for the duration, heavily armed guards patrolled the grounds and DGI-manned road blocks prevented any traveller from approaching the building or glimpsing its occupants. No records – written, visual or audio – were kept of the discussions. Nothing existed to show that the talks ever took place. Yet the encounter was to lead eventually to what would one day be referred to at the most select and rarefied levels of the covert intelligence world as the Cuban Sanction. Its aim: to change the fate of nations.

Book One

THINGS FALL APART

The bubble belches upwards. Then a second, a fragmented stream. I feel them roll up my cheeks, brush my temples, burst above the surface where my face cannot go. And each one carries a scream, a plea, a prayer. I am drowning, being drowned, the pressure of the hand at the back of my head holding me steady, committing routine torture, routine murder. It is a practised hand, its feel familiar to a thousand prisoners who passed this way, passed on. I, too, am crossing. Another air pocket displaced, erupting out, sink contents eructing in. Waterlogged, water-lungs. The grip is hard, pushing me to depths of pain, through it, through panic, down to grey oblivion. The hand comes from a different place, where people breathe and people talk. But I will not talk, so am here. This is his department, Administrative Measures. He is administering to me. I float through layers. Senses are amplified, the senselessness is amplified. Shrill emissions from my throat – garbled, gargled – the steel eye of the draining plug staring with metallic indifference. So like his eyes. I remember the clot of blood, the clump of rooted hair clinging to the underside of the rusted tap, the ring stain at the waterline. Men, women, children, who went before, who left something, made their mark. And I remember my family. It is too late. Water pressing in, hand pressing down. The hand of God. *The hand of Ivanov*. I have reached equilibrium. The colours have gone now, the flashing lights ceased. I no longer struggle. Only my body fights – still shaking, shaking to a kind of stillness – and I am leaving that. Behind my back, my bound hands quiver. They want to drag me to escape, conclusive and concluding, to propel me further and faster into rest. I have won, got away.

Reversal, choking, water vomited into air, lungs ripped agonised from their brackish immersion. I am back in the former world, see again the blood, the tap, the mat of hair, and I shout with the hatred of a newborn. The Death's Head has brought me here. He whispers in my ear. He will decide. It is not time. *You are going east*, he says. *Going east*. There will be more deaths, many of them mine. He is playing, as Philby played me. It is just a game.

CHAPTER 1

The roach, going solo, drawn by warmth and the promise of sweet putrefaction, lulled by a darkening of its territory, scratched its way across from a protective corner. It was a transcontinental traveller, crossing not just a cracked linoleum carriage floor, but six time zones as it traversed the vast landmass of Mother Russia, feeding on the waste and by-products of human cargo carried the length of the great Trans-Siberian Railway between Moscow and Vladivostock almost six thousand miles to the east. An easy, indolent life, cleaning up where others feared to clean, eating what others failed to eat. The nomadic member of family *Blattidae* halted, whip-antennae working furiously, body receptors and underbelly hairs testing the atmosphere, sensing changes in light and movement, the smallest anomaly. There was something.

The exoskeleton split satisfyingly, body crushed, leaking fluid beneath its dull integumen, the orthopterous insect extinguished by the nailed boot. A premature end to the adventurer's twelve-month lifespan. Others, thousands of them, nestled to take its place.

Evdokia watched the act, a rheumy gaze wandering up the leg and body to the executioner's face. A handsome man, no doubt about it – Slav-featured, cropped black hair with seams of grey, possibly forty, probably military. He had that look. During the Soviet era he would have travelled in a luxury saloon carriage reserved for senior officials and Party members. His loss was her gain, a broad-shouldered travelling companion at whom she could stare without embarrassment, a physique reminiscent of propaganda extolling the cult of the oiled bicep, a man to share her bread and pelemni with. She shifted to get comfortable and patted her face with a cloth. Outside, it was thirty centigrade below, in here it was thirty above, the carriages a superheated vein moving through a sepulchral land. Evdokia felt out of breath; there was a lack of air – oxygen – here; it was forbidden to unlock the windows. That man did not help her blood-pressure. Sixty years before she would have given him a run for his money – perhaps even for free – could have pinned him to the floor, taken him deep inside her as a gesture of worker solidarity, ridden him in heroic proletarian fashion. She was revolutionary in her day. The years passed, things changed, everything changed. She sighed.

'Anzherskaya five minutes,' the *provodnik* – reputedly a female, yet without discernible female characteristics – shouted, thumping the sides of the four-berth coupé cabins as she manouevred her bulk along the outside corridor. A chromosome twist away from the Chekovian throwback gene, she enjoyed shouting. She enjoyed extorting, stealing, controlling and persecuting. Tight little mouth, tight little palaeolithic brain; charm school was another country. Most of the passengers had jammed the locks of their sliding doors to prevent her from gaining entry. Disturbing them in different ways was the one small consolation which re-mained. Comfort-bawling. Not for her the bourgeois finesse of the *firmenny* conductors, those who pampered their elite 'spalny vagon' passengers on the Rossiya trains gliding across Siberia, providing tea, blankets and videos throughout day and night of the one hundred and fifty-six-hour journey.

The figures were bowed, huddled against the cold, outsize and distorted in several layers of bulky clothing, gloved hands thrust deep into pockets, feet stamping in vain attempts to encourage circulation. Heads were wrapped in scarves, ear-flaps pulled down from motley fur caps, faces swathed and hidden. They were the hawkers, traders, mostly old women, pushing their wares from the station platform to the occasional passing train before hastening home to re-stock and thaw out. A hard, uncomfortable existence, which would have shown in their pinched expressions had they been visible. It was approaching ten o'clock: their numbers had fallen to a handful by this hour. They waited as a few passengers, those braver souls willing to exchange, at least temporarily, the interior warmth of their carriages for the chance of a bargain struck in bitter night chill, clambered down for their brief encounters. Evdokia was among them, snuffling and wheezing her way along the line, tapping containers, enquiring at the prices, arguing, more inclined to complain than to buy.

'Babushka, you going to buy? Blinis, good quality.' It was a young man's voice, muffled. 'Meat ones in this container, cabbage in the other.'

'You should be in the army or working in a factory,' she snapped ill-temperedly.

'There's no work in the factories, no pay in the army. I'm helping out my mother, she's sick.' The shaded eyes saw Evdokia mellow; it was in the body-language. Sick mothers had that effect. In the kingdom of the stupid, sentimentality was king.

'How much for a meat blini?'

'Five thousand roubles.'

'You want me to starve? You think I got off the train to be ridiculed? I could buy seven loaves of bread for that.'

'Meat is expensive. It's the best. Have a look.' He opened the metal lid of the container, a savoury cloud of steam billowing into her face as she pushed her nose forward to inspect the warm blinis nestling between cloths padding the interior. They looked, smelt, so good. She would treat herself.

'Eighteen hundred roubles. That's my limit. The train is about to leave.'

'But my mother . . .'

They haggled furiously. Evdokia shuffled back triumphant, climbing aboard with the two purchases hot and delicious in her hand. She would eat them noisily, and at her leisure, later on. The train wailed its departure and gathered speed.

The man stood in the connecting section between the two carriages, thankful to be alone, to be away from the old woman who smelt of cabbage and drink and whose size would have done credit to the Transmash tank production line in Omsk. She was a compulsive leerer, made any excuse to engage in conversation. The other two were an improvement – a student who kept his head in a book and a drunken Belarusian wearing campaign medals and pyjamas who woke long enough to eat and drink before lapsing back into alcoholic slumber. He obviously still inhabited the dazed limbo which swept Russia between the televised showing of *The Irony of Fate* on New Year's Eve and the Orthodox Christmas a fortnight later. A miserable time of year. Thank God he would be bidding these enforced companions farewell at Krasnoyarsk. He inhaled deeply on the cigarette, a Western brand, let the nicotine swamp his nervous system, and blew the processed smoke towards the overhead light recessed behind its tin shield. Punctured with pin-prick holes to reduce illumination during wartime black-outs, the simple metal sheet was a small, visible reminder of the era of East–West confrontation. He studied it. Perhaps the causes of conflict never went: perhaps politics, pride, greed, stupidity, fear would switch dispute to war, man from wheatfield to battlefield, for the rest of eternity. The fitting should stay as it was. One never knew. Another drag. He was like that light, he thought – giving away only part of himself, a product of the Cold War, fashioned to be a tool of defence by a paranoid military and security apparat.

Below, a wheel-bogey clashed noisily with a poorly fitting length of track, jolting him against the bulkhead. Ash spilled from the cigarette. He would make himself a cup of coffee from the samovar at the far end of the corridor. Only then would he be ready to return to the compartment. The old lady would be staying up late, waiting for him to undress for bed. Savour this peace, he told himself.

'Hey, come quick!' It was the student, panicking.

He mashed the cigarette on the wall. 'What's up?'

'The old lady's choking. You've got to come. She's going to die.'

The man pushed past the youth. He wondered why he had been chosen as quasi-paramedic. Jesus, this had better not involve mouth-to-mouth.

The student was right. The old woman was going to die, die in rollicking spasms, legs splayed and shaking, arms without energy flapping by her sides, eyes like her veins pushed outwards by an unseen pressure from their bulging, deepening backdrop. He felt pity for her, her tongue flicking soundlessly, glottis blocked, the mouth working, saliva-fuelled, wanting to scream had air been present to force it out. The brain, de-oxygenated, was closing itself down, scrambling command messages, shutting off body systems behind it. The blue-blackening face, mucus-wrapped, provided its own curtains to the finale, expressed its hallucinatory awareness of the tragedy, of total helplessness. She was falling away into an inner distance. The man tried to turn the dead weight, attempting to dislodge the object inhaled into her larynx, shouting at the others to haul her over. A Heimlich manoeuvre was impossible; any type of manoeuvre was impossible with a torso this shape and size. She defecated. Shit – so much for a recovery position – a massive coronary ripping life away in the same moment as the final shock wave. Death had its own smell. He felt instinctively for a pulse. Nothing. It would be difficult to find even were she alive. No point doing massage here.

He straightened over the flesh pile. 'She's dead. Get the conductor in.' An afterthought. 'And a mop.' He was sweating. Damn heat. In this environment, she would begin to go off within the hour. Happy time for the roaches.

Alerted by the commotion, the irate *provodnik* appeared in the doorway.

What were the causes, implications, potential to impose a fine, take a bribe?

'What the fuck is going on?'

'Your first-class care has killed off another passenger.'

The conductor saw the student, shaken, attempting to light a filterless. Little bastard, no guts, probably never seen a body, never picked up a rifle, never starved in a siege. 'No smoking! It is forbidden. That's a fine, I'm telling you!'

An intervention from the powerfully built man who appeared to have taken charge. 'You have more important things to do. Run along and open the windows in your cabin. We're putting the body in there until Krasnoyarsk.'

'*Poshol ty!* You will not order me around on my train.' Her hands were on her hips. The pose spelt aggression, inability to compromise.

'You have five minutes.'

'Listen, mister . . .'

'Colonel,' he snapped. She was not yet backing down. 'Colonel Georgi Vasilevich Lazin, Federal Security Service, Member of the Strategic Facility Counter-Intelligence Department.'

It registered. The student, anticipating a shakedown, sought to mould himself into the corner. Mentioning the successor to the KGB's Second Chief Directorate, still based at the grim headquarters building at 2 Lubyanka Square, had that effect. The Service remained responsible for countering espionage, subversion and internal threats to national security, its Orwellian reputation and image only marginally improved on that of its forebear. You did not cross its senior officers: employment of a full-time Public Relations depart-ment, its promise to operate within the law, had yet to win over a generation which remembered the midnight knocks and disappearances.

The conductor's breathing became heavier, the face whitening, nervousness creeping on a voice which now sought to placate without seeming to backslide. A difficult task for a woman so unsubtle, for whom confrontation came naturally. The effect on her pleased him. The mystique, the charisma of office, had its uses, saved on energy and argument.

The climbdown. 'Colonel, we can work something out here.'

'Five minutes,' he repeated. 'Fetch a blanket. It'll make it easier to drag her along the corridor.'

She bustled away, clucking sympathetically for Evdokia without real sympathy. There would be forms to fill out, explanations required. Worst of all, she would be giving up her cabin, her travelling home, converting it to cold storage for the occasion. How the other conductors would laugh at her. Her mutterings quickly altered to a stream of expletives. In their nesting places, the roaches grew restless.

Siberia, land of ice and chains, a third of the northern hemisphere, four and a half thousand by two thousand miles of permafrost, taiga forest, steppes, some fifty thousand rivers and over a million lakes sprawling across the North Asian Continent. The United States of America would be swallowed in its immensity – as millions of prisoners throughout Russian and Soviet history had been, sent east by Kremlin dictat to labour and die in the camps. 'Sibir', the Sleeping Land, hid many corpses and many secrets. A number of those secrets were military in nature, for the territory contained some of the state's most sensitive strategic assets. Nuclear weapons production took place at Tomsk-7 and Lake Irtysh; Kamchatka and Novaya Zemlya tested the warheads; ballistic missile silos were dotted around Kansk-Eniseiski, Yablonovoya and Olovyannaya; Svobodny-18 in the eastern Amur region had been converted into a major satellite-launch site, and vast army bases stretched along the border with China.

And there was Krasnoyarsk, the destination of Colonel Georgi Lazin. It was not one city, but three, the main civilian conurbation shadowed by its secret satellites: Krasnoyarsk-26 lying forty miles to the north, known colloquially as

'Atomograd' for its key role in producing weapons-grade plutonium from its three uranium-graphite reactors, and Krasnoyarsk-45, referred to by locals as Zalenogorsk, with its space centre and electronics factories over one hundred miles to the north-east. Within this vicinity were several major components of Russia's space-defence system, including remnants of the dismantled pyramid-shaped and pyramid-sized 3-D ballistic missile-tracking and satellite-intercept control radar. As the former Soviet republics split away and formed autonomous military forces, so the surveillance and tracking systems remaining inside Russia and, allowed by treaty, had gained in importance. Behind them were the rocket forces, secure in their bunkers while the conventional military strength of tanks, infantry units and aircraft evaporated around them and the once mighty oceangoing naval fleets rusted at their moorings. The automatic buffer provided first by the old Eastern Bloc and then, nearer to home, by the CIS states, had gone. Technology – early warning – was the new buffer, dug into the hidden vastness of Siberia. German audio cassettes, South Korean televisions and a host of other consumer durables may have been produced in the converted military factories of Zalenogorsk – swords converted decisively into ploughshares – but beneath Krasnoyarsk-26 a subterranean network of factories, dwellings and research centres remained, linked by miles of tunnel which would have accommodated the Moscow Metro ten times over. It was born from an era of tension, and in Atomograd that tension had never fully disappeared. The same was true of other sites with other roles.

Lazin stamp-scraped his boots free of residual snow, proffered his pass once circulation had returned to his numbed fingers and marched purposefully towards the autopsy room. He had no real authority to be here. Responsibility for the old woman was already in the hands of the city coroner, but he felt a curious bond with someone whose life had slipped away between his fingers, whose father and siblings had died in the battle to defend Leningrad. He owed it to her to take an interest, to pay his respects, to ensure that her affairs were in order.

She was occupying the far slab, condemned veal beneath the cold fluorescent lighting, purple lips, vivid hypostasis stains reaching up from the back, a cloth covering a neck whose organs had been removed. He stood behind the glass window of the viewing section, wishing that she had been completely shrouded. The undulating pitch of an electric bandsaw biting into the vault of a skull screamed briefly through the screen, steel teeth eating circumferentially through bone, as the pathologist worked on a different cadaver – a teenager – two along. A chisel prised the vault off the base, the top of the head came away leaving the dura exposed; Lazin was transfixed. Head tilted, lateral cuts across the fragile surface, attachments divided, dura pulled away and grey brain matter revealed. More dexterity – artwork – with a scalpel. Frontal poles lifted, olfactory nerves severed. Next, the pair of optic nerves; examination of the pituitary stalk; removal of the cerebellum roof after detaching the tentorium cerebelli; and the slicing of the nine other pairs of cranial nerves. Pipette collection of cerebrospinal fluids, then cuts to the vertebral arteries and lower medulla oblongata. Brain removal; the head became an empty shell. Lazin knocked on the glass, the pathologist's face turning towards him at the sound. It was sweating and grey – a reflection of the concrete walls – made starker by the green surgical mask and framed with round, metal, regulation-issue spectacles set beneath a hairless crown. A quick movement indicated that Lazin should join him.

Death, antiseptic and haemen coiled like barbs into his sinuses. Christ, what a place to work. The pathologist was waiting for him.

'You watch the procedure?' Lazin nodded. 'I was as surprised as you, then, to find a brain in a teenager.' A smile at his own morgue humour. 'I won't shake hands.'

'Thank you.'

'I'm Kokhlov.'

'I know.'

'Of course, you're State Security. Lazin, isn't it?' He snapped off his surgical gloves and stepped from his lifeless patient towards the Colonel. Formaldehyde clung to him like aftershave. 'I can't say I'm one of your department's greatest admirers.'

'Then we have something in common.'

'Have things changed at the Lubyanka, or do your colleagues still intend to create a desert and call it peace?'

'There are a few die-hard democratic centralists left. But we now benefit from established procedures, a legal framework and full legitimacy within the constitution.' The irony did not require inflection or vocal dexterity to pick it out.

A short, economical laugh – Kokhlov was amused. 'Parliamentary deputies are bandits, the President is surrounded by pimps and gangsters, and you talk of procedures, legitimacy? I'm reassured, my rights are protected.'

'Get out a little, take a break from these bodies.'

'I enjoy their company. They don't lie to me.'

'Hello Ilya.' They hugged. The man smelt more strongly of corpse fluids.

Lazin was grateful that he had accepted the assistant's offer of a gown in the dressing room. 'Still taking your work home with you?' It was their oldest joke.

'Georgi. I'd like to say it's a pleasure.' The pathologist stood back to take a look, holding on to Lazin's arms. 'Does he send me luxury goods? No! Does he give me a bottle of finest vodka. No! He dumps a carcass on me, and not even an attractive one.'

'It's a little something I picked up on the train.'

'You're becoming more thoughtful. It won't work, I hate you *gebists*.' He used the in-house slang for a KGB member. 'How long has it been, Georgi? Three years?'

'More. It's been difficult to contact you, Ilya. I'm sorry.'

The apology was waved away. Dealing with death had given Ilya Kokhlov, former rising star in forensic pathology at the KGB's Second Chief Directorate, a pragmatic, unsentimental view of human existence, even his own. We are born, we eat, we shit, we love, we hate, we die. That was all. It was Kokhlov who had been forced to examine bodies of prisoners to assess the viability of KGB techniques in faking drownings and car accidents, Kokhlov who conducted autopsies on interrogation victims in order to gauge the pathological and physiological effects of differing drugs and 'interview paradigms'. The subsequent discovery of his links to the dissident movement and distribution of underground *samizdat* literature was a severe embarrassment, which had to be expunged. Those who spoke in his favour – including Lazin, a friend from university days – had not prospered, but they had probably ensured that he did not finish lying out on one of his own slabs. A disappearance was called for. That it was transmuted to internal exile and resettlement in the broader civilian community owed more to luck and the perceived difficulty of the case than to any real push for clemency. And so Kokhlov moved to Siberia. He stayed with the dead.

'We don't get many winter tourists. Why the State visit?'

'Because people like Ivanov want to see my balls get frostbite.'

'Ah, Ivanov. Terminally ill, I trust?'

'In rude good health.'

'Pity.'

Above anyone, it was Ivanov who represented to Kokhlov all that was most base about the old KGB and greater humanity. When the pathologist was deported east, Captain Petr Ivanov, since promoted to Colonel, was known to have made a number of unsolicited pitches to his superiors offering to tie up loose ends – blood poisoning was always such a risk in cutting open the bodies of the deceased. Poor Kokhlov, he might have got lazy, the scalpel must have slipped. But other duties had diverted Ivanov's attention: the death of a single heretic could always wait.

'I'm here to assess security procedures, liaise with local

MVD Interior Ministry teams, meet commanders of military installations, inspect their routines.'

'Stay and drink with me instead. I know their routines – there aren't any. I've carved up enough of the old drunks to realise they couldn't piss straight into a mug, let alone run a top secret installation. Routine drinking, report that. You know the main chemical we use in this place?' He did not wait for an answer. 'Sodium fluoride. It prevents alcohol in blood samples from decomposing. Which would be bad – spirits are the favourite form of suicide round here. What else is there to do? Come on, a shot.'

'Papers need to be filled out.'

'There's a better use for paper.' He gave the weary shrug of a lifelong cynic, a player and victim of the system. 'But you always were disciplined, a hard worker. It's why they hate you back at the Centre, why they send you on these meaningless excursions.'

'I was going to get out at Novosibirsk, surprise them at the Sukhoi fighter-manufacturing plant. You're making me wish I had.'

'Surprise them? Give them an order for aircraft – *that* would surprise them.' Almost an afterthought. 'You know I've asked for the Chief Investigator to call by?'

Lazin nodded to the boy on the table. 'Stab victim?'

'That wouldn't merit the interest of the Chief Investigator.' He retreated across the damp floor being slopped by a technician with a mop and bucket, beckoning to Lazin to follow. 'No, it's your old lady friend who's the story.'

'What are you talking about? Are you saying she's a drugs mule?'

'Better than that.' He had reached the trolley positioned at Evdokia's feet. 'Her pills – heart, hypertension, diuretics . . .' He gave each bottle a small shake.

'So what? They're prescription, not poison.'

'With vodka, as good as. Relaxed her so much she couldn't purge foreign objects. No wonder she choked.' Kokhlov liked his long lead-ins. 'What a mess; a walking medical timebomb.'

'Like most of our countrymen.'

He was in lecturing mode. 'We're talking completely blocked lumen in the coronary artery, thrombus and infarct around the ventricles.'

'So when she went, she really went?'

'Exploded. Rupture of the aorta, massive haemorrhaging into the pericardial sac – the worst haemopericardium I've ever seen, an avalanche of blood – disastrous cardial tamponade.'

Lazin did not need the detail. 'Why the Chief Investigator?'

'See this?' The pathologist rummaged in a kidney-shaped bowl with a pair of tweezers and extracted a bone splinter which he held up to Lazin's eyes.

'A foreign object. It's what she gagged on. A bone fragment, right?' Kokhlov pushed the tweezers forward and dropped the piece onto the Colonel's outstretched palm. There was humour behind the spectacles, oblique pathology-lab humour. 'Sure, it's a foreign object. We've had it collagen-typed. It's from a femur.'

'And?'

'A human femur.'

Sixty. Years of adventure, adrenalin and danger, and it had come to this: bad ankles, incipient deafness, a weakening bladder, and the right to a free bus pass. It didn't help that his whole being, his mind, was rooted somewhere in his mid-forties. He walked miserably along Harley Street. He might have just visited one of the country's leading ortho-paedic consultants, and been told yet again that he risked being crippled for the remainder of his life if he continued to punish his joints, but he could do without the reminders of the ageing process. He had made some concessions. He no longer indulged in his passion for free-fall parachuting every weekend; his thirty-three-mile runs between Salisbury and Poole were substituted with long walks across the Purbeck Hills; and his freelance work abroad was becoming more occasional. Yet the attitudes which had sustained him since childhood, and from the moment that he stepped through the gates of the Royal Marines training camp at Lympstone – the doggedness and sense of duty; the fearlessness which never strayed into recklessness; the sparsity of needs which reflected both the soldier and the aesthete – remained unchanged. Ben Purton, fighter, former commander of Britain's Special Boat Service, late of the Royal Marines, an elite within an elite within an elite, hated the number sixty.

He shook himself out of his moroseness. He was the lucky one. Longevity did not run in the male line; he should be grateful for the luxury of living this long. Most of his antecedents, professional soldiers like himself, had been killed before they reached their thirtieth birthdays. Some died gloriously, heroically; others died in unrecorded small-unit actions or solo missions, their bodies never identified, retrieved or buried. It was their duty, the white man's burden, the family's burden, its history and the sacrifice of its sons mapped out against British colonialism, the hidden struggles of 'The Great Game' and eventual retreat from Empire.

When war broke out in Europe in 1914, the Purtons had been established in India for several generations. Ben Purton's great-grandfather, a former army officer and rough-rider commander in General Roberts' forces which lifted the Boer Siege of Ladysmith in March 1900, had returned to the subcontinent to work for the shadowy organisation known as IPI – Indian Political Intelligence – courting maharajas, encouraging peaceful coexistence among the troublesome tribes of the North-West Frontier and compiling reports for his colleagues in London. Exciting times. Yet, for his sons, the Kiplingesque idyll was not to last. They signed up as war was declared, three eventually going off to the Western Front. At 7.20 a.m., on the morning of the 1 July 1916, a giant mine exploded on Hawthorne Ridge in front of the French village of Beaumont Hamel. It marked the beginning of the First Battle of the Somme along a forty-kilometre front. By its end four and a half months later, one hundred and fifty thousand men lay dead. Almost double that number were wounded and maimed. Among the fatalities were the three Purton boys. Two died with the Deccan Horse in the regiment's mad cavalry charge towards High Wood on 14 July 1916. Together with the Seventh Dragoon Guards, they swept up the valley with lances down and pennants flying to be cut down by shell and machine-gun fire as they sought to close with the enemy in the cornfields. The third was blown to pieces by a shell which landed in Delville Wood a week later.

The fourth and elder brother, Piers, Ben Purton's grandfather, survived the war. A fluent Russian- and Pashtuspeaker, he was already a professional soldier and espionage specialist, an officer with the Pathan Tochi Scouts of the Frontier Corps, keeping peace among the Mahsuds, Wazirs, Khyber and Malakand fiefdoms, and leading raids on his father's orders against the Fakir of Ipi and other northern anti-British rulers. Leaving behind a young wife and two children, giving up the shalwar kameez, turban and pagri of his fellow-horsemen, he had spent the major part of the conflict between the Great Powers serving in Mesopotamia and Persia for Military Intelligence before his transfer by the Committee for Imperial Defence to the intelligence Service MI 1c under its founder and chief, the eccentric, monocled, one-legged former naval officer Mansfield Cumming, the original 'C' of British Secret Intelligence. Purton's role in first arranging the murder in Persia of the German agent Preusser and then, with Harry St John Philby – father of Kim – tracking down and pursuing the guerrilla leader Wilhelm Wassmuss, impressed his masters. He was re-tasked, this time on a personal mission requested by Cumming on behalf of King George V himself. His destination was revolutionary Russia.

Tsar Nicholas II, the King's first cousin and doppelgänger, a royal in distress, had been deposed, replaced by the Provisional Government and sent eastwards with his family from their comfortable 'palace-arrest' at Tsarskoe Selo to the Siberian town of Tobolsk. Here they were installed under heavy guard at the governor's residence. The date was 19 August 1917. Behind them, after a two-day steamer trip from Tyumen up the Tura and Tobol rivers, came the King's emissary Piers Purton. Making contact with the Imperial Family through their physician, Doctor Botkin, he negotiated the British position on asylum – receiving several jewels as a 'goodwill gesture' from the Tsarina to the Fabergé-enthusiast and collector Queen Mary – and began to plan for their escape, liaising with loyal pro-monarchist officers and meeting representatives from Moscow and Petrograd. Among these was a familiar face: a young Russian whom he had met in India before the war travelling on a break from his studies in Berlin. Boris Soloviev was an officer from a powerful royalist faction, and – more importantly – had married the 'Mad Monk' Gregory Rasputin's daughter Maria, which won him the instant trust of the Empress Alexandra. Immune to Purton's advice, Alexandra ordered that all escape attempts be coordinated through Soloviev's organisation, 'The Brotherhood of St John of Tobolsk'. Was the man not son-in-law of her mentor, mystic and guardian angel, linked by marriage to the faith healer of her sick haemophiliac child Alexis? His credentials, his credibility were unassailable: perfect cover. It was a terrible mistake. Only Purton suspected, and by then Soloviev, a Bolshevik agent from the start, had betrayed every Tsarist official, sequestered every penny from every escape fund and thwarted every plan for the flight of the Imperial Family and the survival of the Russian throne. His spy in the royal household – the maid Romanova – was to marry a Communist commissar soon after her employers were taken away on 26 April 1918 to the Bolshevik stronghold in the Urals, the city of Ekaterinburg. Purton, avoiding capture, joined up with the advancing White Army of Admiral Kolchak and took part in the city's capture on 24 July 1918. By then, all that was left of the Tsar, Tsarina, their son and four daughters were ash and fragments of molten bone tipped down a mine-shaft. They had been murdered eight days previously.

Purton vowed to avenge their deaths and undermine the precarious Bolshevik government. Eager to stamp out the new regime and thwart the revolution-spreading activities of the Comintern, London supported him. He almost succeeded. In a plot hatched with another British agent, the Russian Jew Sydney Reilly, he arranged for a young revolutionary, Dora Kaplan, and three Latvian army officers to assassinate Lenin on 31 August 1918. Two bullets struck the leader, but he survived, and the uprisings in Moscow and Petrograd planned to accompany his death never materialised. Retribution was swift and ferocious yet, undeterred, Purton headed back to Siberia to organise pro-monarchist resistance. For almost four years he battled the Communists, returning home to India only once during that period. Wounded, but continuing to fight on to the last in temperatures of below −30 degrees centigrade, he was captured with other White Russians after the ten-day Battle of Volochaevka and executed without ever revealing his identity. News of his fate – along with a tattered and faded photograph of the Englishman in uniform, holding a sad-eyed spaniel in his arms – was smuggled out by one of the few who escaped alive from the carnage. Reilly, his friend, had fled the country after the failure of the 'Lockhart' plot against the Bolshevik leadership, but made several return trips. He too was to die, captured by Soviet OGPU secret policemen on 28 September 1925 outside the village of Allekul, and taken to the Lubyanka Prison, Moscow. On 5 November 1925, after interrogation and torture, he was driven into the countryside and killed with two revolver bullets fired at close range. The Great Game had ended for Piers Purton and Sydney Reilly; communism was installed.

The Purton boy was taken by his mother to London to live in a large house in Hampstead with two aunts whose husband and fiancé respectively had been killed during the War. The years at 5 Templewood Avenue passed quietly and happily for the three adults and Tom. Schooled at Westminster and Magdalen College, Oxford, he married young, served like his predecessors in the Indian Civil Service, broke with tradition by joining the Diplomatic Corps, and followed their example by entering the military when the outbreak of war drew close. It was little understood why he joined the Royal Engineers, less so how he came to die in a freak accident in 1948. Few official explanations were available for the flooding of a German mine-shaft into which the Major had apparently disappeared in order to investigate reports of discarded Nazi ammunition stockpiles. But it meant that Ben Purton and his sister Claire knew their father for only a few short years of their lives before he vanished. Selfless or selfish, dying for one's country always overlooked the feelings of those left behind. So, he had reached sixty. He wondered if his children appreciated the feat.

The beginnings of his own military career had come about by chance. Moving with his mother and sister to a family farmhouse in South Devon, Ben had grown up strong, adventurous and self-reliant, roaming the countryside or undertaking lengthy canoe and sailing dinghy trips in the foulest of weather. 'He'll grow up a poacher or a fisherman,' was the prevailing local opinion. Instead, to keep a couple of friends company, he applied for officer selection into the Royal Marines. It was the start, the beginning of the 1960s, and he had found his spiritual home. After first qualifying for the Cliff Assault Wing and later passing the arduous selection for the SBS, his official Special Forces career began in earnest. In 1963, attached to 45 Commando, he was sent to Aden on close-protection duties and survived a bomb attack on the Commissioner for the Protectorate. He went on to climb 'Coca Cola' mountain in an action to outmanoeuvre rebellious Radfan tribesmen, and his first Military Cross came with the savage heliborne mopping-up exercise which ensued among a network of heavily defended caves. One of the young Marines taking part, on his first tour from recruit training, was a teenager named Nick Howell.

British authority was under pressure elsewhere. By late summer 1964, Purton was deployed to Borneo to mount cross-border recce patrols into Kalimantan and face off Indonesian dictator President Sukarno's threat to Malaysian sovereignty. It was a vicious undeclared war, and Ben Purton, after two years of jungle warfare, counter-infiltration and countless fire fights in the Tawau and Seria regions, along the Rajang and Serudong rivers and up the Rihau Archipelago and islands off the Sumatran coast, returned to England as a Captain and with a Bar to his MC. Other wars, other operations followed – Dhofar and Northern Ireland among them – and after becoming SBS commander, transforming the service into a supremely flexible instrument of power-projection, lauded for his visionary Special Forces work, he quit. The custody fight for his three children during an acrimonious divorce with his American wife was more important. She won, taking them back to the United States while he moved out to Oman to command the Sultan's Special Forces. Here, he could use his skills in theatres and conflicts he better understood. He was one of the best operators Britain had ever produced. And now he was sixty.

His pager went, requesting that he call in and confirm the meeting in an hour. He found a payphone in Oxford Street and punched the number: an answerphone with coded details of the rendezvous.

'See you on Platform Nine.' He replaced the receiver.

The meeting was held in a room in Carlton Terrace, The Mall. Familiar faces, well-cut suits, net curtains drawn across to prevent stray camera-work from outside. Ink blotters were laid out, water carafes and glasses beside them on the polished boardroom table, but no paper or writing implements in sight.

He shook hands with the three others present – one woman, two men – and addressed the older, lean-looking individual who was plainly heading up the ensemble.

'The formality worries me. It means you're serious.'

'We're always serious, Ben. Don't worry, after this we'll go back to meeting at the Grosvenor Hotel.' The gloomy Victorian gothic pile fronting Victoria Station was an old favourite for spooks. 'Let's sit.' They pulled up chairs, centred around the senior officer, silence prevailing as he poured water for his guest. He took his time, before sitting back and running long fingers through thinning, sand-coloured hair. A cultured, diffident presence, Hugh Dryden knew Purton well, had worked with him before. 'How's your diary looking for the next month or two?'

'I'm sure you have a copy.'

'Ah yes.' He ignored the barb. 'You were planning to visit the force-protection battle lab at Lackland Air Force Base, Texas, to assess some radical counter-terrorist technologies.'

'Well researched.'

A slight nod of acknowledgement. 'The trip has been cancelled.'

Purton watched, somehow unsurprised, eyes narrowing. 'Go on.'

'There's a problem requiring direct action. We thought we should call you in.'

'I knew it wasn't a School Reunion.' Make them struggle a bit.

'It'll involve getting sand between your toes.' Sand, blood – men like Dryden were rarely discriminating. 'We'd like you to mount a little operation for us. It might require members of your usual team.'

'They're working up for a CIP job in the UAE.'

'That too has been cancelled. I'm afraid we're handing it to Hereford – they haven't got much on at the moment. There'll be compensation, of course.'

'Of course. And of course it's your prerogative to sabotage my visit to the States, to bugger up the itinerary of my men, and then to ask a favour. Hugh, you've a lot to learn about interpersonal skills.'

A modest smile. 'My Master's was in Modern History. Besides, I couldn't afford to have you distracted.'

'How do you know you can afford me at all?'

'Educated guess.'

Not much guesswork involved, Purton mused. They went

back too far for that. The relationship between the Secret Intelligence Service – SIS – and Britain's Special Forces was largely an ad hoc one, personal contacts ensuring discretion and the ready availability of a select cadre of cleared personnel for the rare occasions that they were required. Purton's own involvement was established early on with 'stay-behind' counter-Soviet sabotage exercises in the 1960s along West Germany's River Weser and with his activities in Malaysia. It continued into his freelance existence. They had used him for forty years, relied on him, depended on him – a close, symbiotic acquaintance, never quite a friendship, which had its own rituals, its own strains and uneasiness. Who needed it most, who had the upper hand, dominated, Ben Purton never fully thought through. He preferred to ignore the question, scared of his weakness, suspecting that he could never walk away, would always opt to take their commission, prove himself better than the down-faced youngsters coming up from below. If they did not require him, they would not ask. They understood that, understood him; it gave them leverage.

'What do you think?' Dryden took a sip of water.

That you're a shit, a manipulative, tricky shit. He could live with that. There was a mutual, if wary, respect between the two, a conditional trust for the controller by the controlled, depending on the mission and circumstance, under-scored by the knowledge that if things turned bad SIS could deny it all. 'I don't want to be the next Buster Crabb.'

'Meaning precisely?'

'Meaning my luck could give up before my ankles.'

The body of the retired navy frogman Lionel 'Buster' Crabb, minus head and hands, had been found a year after he had lowered himself into the water of Portsmouth Harbour to inspect the sonar arrays and mine-laying hatches beneath the hull of the Soviet cruiser *Ordzhonikidze* carrying Khruschev and Bulganin on their 1956 State visit. British Intelligence never provided an explanation, felt no urge to.

'We prefer you unscathed.'

'After my last crawl around the Kola Peninsula, Hugh, I don't take anything for granted. So many rads, I'm probably still glowing.'

'It's the best work you've done.'

'And the hottest.'

It had been an unpleasant mission, checking over fifty decommissioned and highly radioactive nuclear submarines in the Russian Northern Fleet's atomic graveyard in the Barents Sea. Unpleasantness came with the territory. It was Purton who clambered aboard the service ship *Lepse* and discovered its use as a leaking storage bay for broken uranium fuel rods from ageing Atomflot ice-breakers, Purton who had tested, and bested, the anti-swimmer defences of the great Polyarny submarine pens a few miles outside Murmansk, Purton who conducted ground-reconnaissance of Severomorsk in 1984 following an explosion at a munitions factory that tore the heart from the naval base. A regular tourist to Russia, he was.

Elegant hands were crossed on Dryden's lap, a retreat from shadow-boxing. To business. 'How would you respond to the word Yemen?' Silence. He waited. There was still no reply. 'Will you at least listen to what I have to say?'

'I'm not heading for the door.' There would be time yet for that. Ever since his first trip to the region as a young Royal Marines officer in the early 1960s, the place had meant trouble – messy, feuding, violent, lawless trouble. Modernisation, the discovery of oil, the union of north and south at first peaceful and then by civil war and annexation, had brought no improvements. The cultural differences between an Islamist, tribally oriented north and more secular, socialistic south remained as strong as ever. And now, the wily politician President Ali Abdullah Saleh, who had dominated and ridden out the upheavals with seeming impunity for over twenty years, was dead, most probably killed by the extremist Moslem Brothers faction of his own Al-Islah party. More vendettas, more fighting, more scope for intervention, political manoeuvre and counter-manoeuvre by forces within and outside the country's borders.

'Good. Progress.' Dryden being ironic or patronising, there was trouble telling. A signal to the silent partners. A briefing note was produced and passed across. Five pages. Purton scanned them rapidly as Dryden continued. 'We have been asked by the Saudis to stir up the South a little.'

'Define "stir up"; define "a little".'

'They'd like a full-blown insurgency.'

'Why?'

The rubbing of a finger. 'To relieve pressure from Yemeni fundamentalists, to demolish a source of Sunni- and Shi'ia-sponsored terrorism, to take Yemeni minds off the disputed provinces of Asir, Najir and Jizan.'

'Destabilise Yemen, so they can't destabilise Saudi?'

'Essentially. In return, Riyadh will halt funding to radical Moslem groups and black Al-Fuqra members abroad.'

'That's all we get for splitting Yemen, destroying its oil industry, ruining inward investment and allowing the Saudis to promote their pet tribal factions in the power vacuum in Sana'a?' Purton looked sceptical. 'You're holding out on me.'

'Let's just say UK plc might benefit.'

'Arms deals? The Saudis have promised arms deals?'

'We have to retain an edge. The Americans and French are nudging us out of the market.'

'A war for a trade advantage. I was beginning to lose faith in you.'

'There's more to it.'

'Always is.'

'We don't want Islamic Jihad and the Moslem Brothers taking hold in Yemen. What's bad for the peninsula is bad for us.'

'And worse for the House of Saud.'

'Domino theory never went away.' It changed its name to generalised Foreign Office paranoia.

'Remember '94?'

'Perfectly.' Sure Dryden did.

'You sent me in to shore up Ali Salem-al-Baidh's southern forces just as the north's armies were closing in on Aden. Great timing.'

The SIS man persisted. 'Better this time. The Aden governor is a hard-line bastard, a northern appointee, who's pursuing a scorched-earth policy with the Al-Amaliqa brigade. Puts the fear of God into everyone.'

'Including yourselves.'

'You've got the contacts, the credibility, the feel.' And the arse to hang out in the wind when things went wrong, Purton reflected.

'You think I should tell them they're dying for the sake of a British arms deal in Saudi?'

Dryden looked at his colleagues and then back at Purton. 'I think we need more work on this,' he said calmly.

The meeting lasted for over three hours. By its end, Ben Purton – aged sixty – was going to war.

For a man who ate such quantities of red meat, Kokhlov's work-pallor remained stubbornly fixed, beyond the world of the living. He pushed in another forkful of sausage, pulling a piece of skin from between his teeth. Lazin picked at his food.

'There are over four million people homeless out there, Georgi. They're like wildebeest, a ready food-supply for unfussy carnivores.'

'Unfussy? Christ, Ilya. Why can't they eat dogs?'

'They do. They just want variety, a balanced diet. You look shocked.'

'She offered me some of her blini.'

'Never judge until you've tried something yourself.'

'Be serious, Ilya. What's going on? There isn't mass starvation; we're not under siege. It's crazy. Why this?'

'Why, Georgi?' Kokhlov stabbed his fork towards his friend. 'I'll tell you why. Vodka, social decay, a loss of moral values, of heroes, of role models. There's taste for it, Georgi. It could be the fear of hunger, the shadow of Leningrad and

Stalingrad imprinted onto the Russian psyche. The Rostov Ripper raped, tortured and then ate some of his victims, claimed his cousin had become processed food during the Ukrainian famine.'

'He was insane.'

'And the others – misguided? Interior Ministry claims fewer than fifty people a year are eaten. It's ten times that. More. Who knows? They don't want to scare anyone.'

'Or put them off their food.' Lazin's face was grave, intense, its natural state.

Kokhlov mopped at some gravy with his bread. 'There are bodies turning up all around the country with genitals and internal organs missing. In Kemerovo a man was stuffing pelemni with human mince for the local market; Ilshat Kuzikov was caught in St Petersburg marinating huge quantities of human flesh; in Barnaul a prisoner cut a cellmate's liver out with a piece of glass and made broth with it.'

'OK, spare me the details.' Lazin pushed his plate away.

Without pausing, the pathologist scraped the meat onto his own platter. 'It's a fact of life, Georgi. Go anywhere, and you'll find yourself sitting down to dinner with someone you don't know.' He sucked on his fingers, relishing the food and the subject matter. 'Perhaps an acquaintance's aunt or uncle in the shashlyk. Nice to eat you, mister, madam.'

'You're exaggerating.'

'Am I? I'm telling you, Georgi, there are demons at work. And there's not even a crime of cannibalism in our country. It's just part of the murder act, aggravated homicide. Aggravated by what – indigestion?' He kicked an empty vodka bottle on the floor at his side. Russian superstition deemed it bad luck to leave empties on a table.

An unsubtle change of subject was called for. 'Come back to Moscow, Ilya. Things have changed.'

'Not enough for me. Ivanov would arrange an accident as soon as I stepped out of Yaroslav station into Komsomol Square.'

'Take a Yenisey train into Kazan station, then.'

'You know what I'm saying. Our friends have long memories which pre-date this regime.'

'They're too busy making money to give a damn about you.'

'I'm happy here. Can you say the same, Georgi? Sent on security checks to Siberia in midwinter? They're shitting on you; they're flushing you away. Not dependable enough; veers on the side of human rights; sees too much. Dangerous.' He saw the flash in Lazin's eyes. 'I'm sorry, old friend, but that's how it is. You going to be Gresko's golden-boy like Ivanov?'

'His bank account is the only thing that's golden,' Lazin growled.

'You'll never be part of them. You're incorruptible, straight, so they want you out. You don't play their game, so you'll stay on the outside. It's the way things are, Georgi.'

The FSB man threw another tumbler of vodka at the back of his throat, angry, knowing that Kokhlov was right, perhaps resentful that the pathologist was a partial catalyst for his own fall from grace. He was in the cold, way below freezing, denied the career that might once have been his as of right. That was life? Kokhlov's corpses became a more attractive proposition by the day.

'How's Valerya?' Strange that the question should come as Lazin thought of an autopsy room. Kokhlov asked again, breaking through his distraction. 'How's Valerya? Still got tits and a nose hard enough to pick out seams in the Achinsk-Kansk coalfield?'

Lazin groaned. 'She's worse.' His estranged wife – they had always been strangers – had troubled his existence for over twenty years. Sex was their common denominator, their only denominator; everything else – mutual respect, love, compassion, understanding, friendship – was as alien to her as a foreign tongue. On reflection, that was a poor analogy, for she had vast experience of every type of foreign tongue or object. Yet her attitude towards warmth, real human relationship, was as unproductive, barren, as her womb. They would meet infrequently, copulate and part, solitary figures until their next mating season. He had learned to live with it, without it, could survive.

'You don't need her, Georgi; you don't need to work for Security. Get out, start again. Life's too short to be surrounded by such people. My patients could tell you that.'

'You're fucking tanked.'

'Cunted. It's the bad zakuski.' The standard Russian excuse.

'I'll drink to it. *Na zdorov'je.*'

'*Na zdorov'je.*' A clink of glasses, heads tossed back in friendship. Midday meal and the pathologist was draining vodka. He was a subversive influence. 'It's a paradox,' Kokhlov wiped his mouth. 'That State Security, by oppressing and alienating the people, succeeded in destroying rather than securing the survival of the Communist administration.'

'The world is a paradox. Haven't your patients told you that too?'

'Only when I've downed too much preserving fluid.' He was probably not joking, Lazin thought. 'But, you'll stay.' He waggled his finger. 'An irredeemable secret policeman. You'll make your excuses – patriotic duty, foreign threats, Islamic militancy, whatever – and you'll stay.'

Lazin shrugged. The man had a point. It was what he knew, his waking life was his working life, and, whether out of favour or in, he was joined to it by instinct, fatalism, and by the same perverse forces which encouraged continued contact with Valerya. And he was screwed by both. 'Nothing is perfect,' he said finally.

'And in Russia nothing is bearable. We're still enslaved, Georgi.'

'Then we must unite and throw off our chains.' Marx was wrong. They would never cast off their leg-irons. It was what they were comfortable with, what they knew and understood.

Fuelled by alcohol, Ilya was warming to his theme. 'Culturally, historically, politically, physically, we're enslaved. Over one million Russian adults, Georgi – one million.' The finger was up again, moving like a metronome.

'That's more than one out of every one hundred of us is in prison, squeezed into eight hundred labour camps across the land.'

'An improvement, then.'

'Abused, raped, tortured, murdered, dying from tuberculosis . . .' Lazin poured as his friend continued. 'The West has its welfare services, we have our gulag system – the Russian safety-net.'

'It's all we can afford.'

'Because the money has been stolen.' He was waving a piece of black bread in the air now. 'And you think we're immune to it out here? Bollocks. We're all part of the same giant camp, and each prison is an offshoot, replicates the system outside: the chief thief-in-law suborns the prison authorities, runs the zone with his lieutenants, hands out patronage and receives then divides up all the takings. That's the president and his government.'

'What about parliament?'

'They're the next rung down in the hierarchy, the *Muzhiki* – guys – the common criminals who try to get by, are doing their own deals, but know ultimately that power rests with others higher up. Then there are the Goats – *Kozly* – who do the skivvying, serve up the soup, do the camp chores, warm the mattresses, make sure things run smoothly. They're the bureaucrats.'

'So, I'm the goat? What does that make you, Ilya?'

'Oh, the lowest in the prison caste system, Georgi. I'm an Untouchable. Despised, shunned, not permitted to mix with the other criminals – it's fatal for the prospects of prisoners who are seen talking to me – I'm left to rot. But I survive because I'm an Untouchable, because I'm left alone, not worth the attention.' The bread was pushed into the mouth. 'I want to keep it that way.'

'Happy times.' A glass raised in salute to the pathologist-philosopher.

A mirrored response. 'Bolshevik Revolution, Democratic Revolution and now Criminal Revolution. The names change, but we remain consistent.' Heads tossed back, tumblers smacked down.

'You think your kind liberal democracies in the West are any better, could run this place? You think they're so clean?'

'I know that the heads of their anti-organised crime units don't sit in offices decked with finest Italian marble and expensive works of modern art.'

'Listen, Ilya.' Lazin leant forwards to make his point and pour another glass. 'When did the Berlin Wall go up?'

'1961.'

'August 12, 1961. And British and American intelligence had known Kremlin and East German intentions for two years previously. A KGB Major, defecting out of Odessa in 1959, warned them it would happen; a GRU man did the same in 1960. Both advised that if the West acted tough, made a challenge, sent in bulldozers, the Communists would back down – it was simply to test Western resolve. Yet they did nothing, let it happen. Why? Because they didn't want more labourers flooding the West German market; because the Wall would stand as a monument to Communist oppression, would give America the moral high ground, allow Kennedy to stand in front of it and claim 'I am a doughnut.' And they wrung their unsoiled little hands when people died to get across to buy their better fridges and escape their cars made out of chipboard.'

'As I said, you'll make your excuses, and you'll stay.'

'If I had a choice . . .'

Kokhlov interrupted. 'If your aunt had a prick, she'd be your uncle.' He had begun to fork more cold cuts into his mouth. It would not be enough to soak up the vodka. 'Here's more history for you. The Western allies only sent six and a half thousand Nazis for trial after the War, out of over a hundred thousand indicted. Not a lot. Yet how many Communists, ogres who murdered millions, have ever been sent for trial here? And I'm not talking show-trials by their own kind. How many? Fucking zero, Georgi.' He punctured the air, a look of three parts disgust to one part alcohol on his face. 'That's because we're all fucking guilty, our country's built on bones and tears. If you start blaming, you'll never stop. That's the beauty of totalitarianism. It's so comfortable, it consumes everyone. There's so much collective guilt, no one fucking feels it. The pain's just part of the scenery, goes on for miles, goes on forever.'

'You've made me feel welcome, Ilya.'

Kokhlov grasped his forearm, staring intently at him. 'Hey. What did the cannibal do when he dumped his girlfriend?' He received no encouragement. 'Wiped his arse! Wiped his arse, you like it? An English joke.' Flecks of meat and gristle sprayed Lazin's face in the excitement. A top up. 'Come on, Georgi. *Na pososhok* – one for the stick.'

The Secret policeman cuff-swabbed his face. His mind hovered above the crowded tables of the restaurant. Busy, noisy. Mother Russia choking, shitting its pants, dying, laid out on the slab. *I'm telling you, Georgi, there are demons at work*. The Mother Country feeding on itself. He cursed Russian superstition.

Ben Purton saw him as he entered the restaurant, picked out by the stillness among the crowded tables, by the face which looked ahead as he sipped on an orange juice. He was youngish, Nautilus-honed and owned, a healthiness which exuded beach culture, West Coast America, a posture and discipline which suggested East Coast professional or British. Conflicting, hard to place.

'Hello, Max.' Purton moved around the table and gripped his shoulder, preventing him from getting up. The younger man's face creased with pleasure.

'Hey, Dad.' The accent said American, a tight nut, not one which had loosened and rolled westwards. Definitely East Coast, graduate of Amherst College, Massachusetts. 'How you doing?'

'Falling to pieces. It's a long-term trend. Short-term, pretty good. You're looking well.'

'Winter in Moscow should put an end to that.'

Purton manoeuvred into the empty seat opposite. 'When are you off?'

'One or two weeks. There's work, and I need to spend time with Adele.'

'How is she?'

'Surrounded by weirds with beards, threatening to take me to jazz-poetry sessions and a Kodály recital.'

'Should have stayed closer to home.' He was not sure if he approved of his son's choice of long-distance girlfriend. Max knew it, played on it. 'Who the hell's Kodály?'

'You think I don't want to ask?' He found his glass. 'Haven't left any books in Beirut recently, then?' A recurring joke, born from Purton's history of departing the world's trouble spots in a hurry. The question allowed slack, did not pry.

'I'm playing it quiet at the moment. Semi-retirement and all that.'

'Sure. It won't last.'

A son who understood his father. They were too alike. And the father was saving for that son, putting money aside, working for Max's retirement, not his own. 'You're probably right. What are you drinking? I think champagne's called for.' He hailed the waiter. It was worth a toast. The boy passed through about once every four months – it was not enough.

Max smiled in the direction of his father. He had been in London for a day already, time enough to orientate, reacquaint himself with Adele, re-tying and re-packaging a product which seemed more cheap and worn by the visit. Adele. Some relationships never made sense or equilibrium. Absence made the heart grow wearier, the effort greater. He was no longer sure of the original motive – sex, naturally, the thrill of overseas liaison, a low claustrophobia quotient on account of his being in one place and she in another. High maintenance affairs were not his thing, stifled him, tied him to patterns he did not enjoy. But she gave him another excuse to be in London, an easy foil to his mother's enquiries. Kath

Purton – her surname, like that of Max's sisters, now changed to Hendrick – was at once both jealous and delighted at journeys which allowed her son to build on her previous life, to pass back information on an ex-husband whom she had thought of every day for over thirty years.

He felt rested. Moments with his father were rare; he wanted to be awake to enjoy them. There was deep trust and admiration between them, an instinctive transatlantic bond of blood and mutual friendship which had surmounted the fallout from the divorce in 1975, the return of Kath and the children to her family base in Wellesley, Massachusetts. He was the only one on the American side who maintained contact, sustained the effortless informality of a son–father relationship which relied more on visceral affection, gene- and soul-sharing than on a requirement for words and protestations of familial loyalty. His sisters did not share that connection. They were too young when they left England, had been absorbed into a second family complete with half-siblings, never showed much interest in re-establishing a link. But while he had received his mother's looks, the handsome Bostonian features and easy smile which made others forgive readily what they might find unforgivable in others, he had inherited much of his father's character, interests and restlessness: the need to push himself, to explore, to find adventure while living in a culture of unmitigated self-indulgence and relentless air-conditioned superficiality. He saw his mother grow old surrounded by the die-cast bouffant coiffures of coffee-mornings, conformity, diary lunches and charity dinners. And he knew that the rebellious, irrational undercurrent which had forced her first to pursue his father in free-fall from the side of an aircraft and then later to jump from the marriage in an equally determined fashion, caused her to long for a return to a past over-romanticised by distance. It was the trait of the Irish. Big hearts, little pragmatism, idiosyncratic, wilful, at times generous, joyful and warm, at others irritatingly uncompromising, dark, unreasonable and absurdly sentimental. The same reasons why he loved the Russians: they drew you in closer than anyone else.

The six-year marriage had started well, which made its eventual foundering more painful, the upset more pronounced, the residual bitterness – between two parents whose love was equalled in strength only by incompatibility – longer-lasting. They had met in 1968, the summer of love, when America was at war. Seconded to the US Marines to pass on his jungle-fighting and escape-evasion experience to their Vietnam drafts, Purton was an immediate success. Several senior generals suggested allowing him to travel to the war-zone posing as an Australian Special Forces Adviser, but a flurry of diplomatic telexes from London buried the idea. Interest in the tough, decorated British combat veteran was being shown elsewhere. Within weeks, and much to the chagrin of American brother-officers, he had acquired a retinue of female fans – soon dubbed the 'Purtonettes' for their ability to scream in harmony in many different situations – eager to share his company and anxious to share his bed. He was unfailingly courteous, unfailingly obliging. Yet they were outclassed by Kath, whose coolness and outward indifference were matched by her sudden conversion to the hobby of sports parachuting. She had his attention, the feigned disregard lapsed, the passion increased. Long weekends spent at the family's shingle holiday home in Kennebunkport, Maine, a horse trek through Montana, a short engagement, and the two were married within six months.

At first she coped well with life in England. She was married to a rising military star, there were sailing trips to equal anything experienced back home, and the babies which arrived in quick succession took much of her attention. He was a sensitive father and caring husband, a man who exuded the aphrodisiac but conflicting qualities of danger and security, a lover with and for whom anything seemed possible or achievable. By 1970, the parties, international atmosphere and regular hours encountered during his attendance at the

Army Staff College in Camberley, convinced her that life would remain a contained, balanced act between two popular equals and partners. It was a poor call. The SBS, pulled back from foreign postings, was consolidating at Poole, and in 1971 began to modernise and broaden its range of tasks. Postponing a staff job, Ben Purton assumed the role of Operations Officer to encourage the transformation. The marriage faltered almost invisibly. Counter-terrorist assignments abroad, liaison with the SAS in Dhofar, and the necessity for discretion, contributed to the breakup. Contact and communication between them became more rare. She could never understand the Special Forces ethos, the unpredictability, the level of commitment required; he was more withdrawn, incapable of explaining, unable to comprehend her resentment or to compromise with his love of soldiering. He became commander of the SBS, she left shortly afterwards for America with Max, aged five, and the twins, aged two. In family law, pitching a bivouac and making a campfire in any kind of terrain were hardly attributes for a model single father and house-husband. This was Dorset, not a desert island. Married life was over.

'What are you laughing at?' Purton asked.

'I'm just remembering my visits over here as a teenager, Mom's face when I told her you had me abseiling down the side of the house from my bedroom window.'

'She never did appreciate the finer points of my work.' The champagne was brought and poured. They raised glasses. 'How is she?'

Max returned the glass carefully to the table. 'Older and fatter, she says, but she's lying. Pushing elderly sugar-lover around in a wheelchair doesn't help. Makes her feel everything's decaying around her.'

'Give her my love.'

'I always do.'

'And to Lucy and Anna.'

'Ditto. They're spending most of their time with concerned student types. Ought to come over here and meet

Adele's group. It'd be a love-fest for fucked-up middle-class types. Is Bess behaving herself?'

'Of course not. She's a wicked old lady.' They were the seam in his life: the Irish Terriers with which he walked, ran, returned to when the house was empty and his wife or lovers had gone. He warmed his heart and his hands on her; she was a totem, a constant. 'She's missing you.'

'I'm missing her. I'll be down to give her a Guinness soon.'

'Any chance before you go?'

'Dad, I'm sorry. Too many things to do. Adele . . .'

'Kodály recitals, I know.' Purton shook his head. 'Of all the people in all the world, you go and end up with a psychotherapist.'

'I like it – they're easy to wind up. She tells me I'm in denial, that my inability to commit is symptomatic of my inadequacies in living up to the male role-stereotype of hunter-gatherer. And all the time it's just me hedging my bets and having sex. Perfect.'

A hint of disapproval. 'I thought you were more honourable, Max.'

'Joke. I'm fond of her, Dad, but I'm not mating for life, if you know what I mean.'

'Completely.' Purton recharged the glasses. 'So what's happening in Moscow?'

'Various barter-trade opportunities, shipments of ours coming through the Russian ice-free terminal at Vyotsk, and Hunter Strachan wanting me in situ to help beat off the Irish hauliers.'

Purton knew all about Vyotsk. Close to the Finnish border, situated on the Siamaa canal, it was for many years Russia's main conduit for illicit arms exports to the outside world. He had paid it several visits.

'Are you safe out there?' he asked.

'Are you offering?' They laughed. 'Don't worry, Dad, I've got Gennady the bodyguard. Could pull the legs off a bull.'

'From what you've told me, he probably has. Plus the odd political dissident.'

'It's Russia. You take the work you can find.' He tested champagne depth with a finger. 'On the subject of unpleasantness, how are your own girlfriend problems?'

Studied avoidance. 'Let's order. I'll read the menu out. Name the category.'

'Chicken.'

Purton played it light, but each time he saw his son, his personal agony at watching Max's sight degenerate grew sharper. It was the big one, Retinitus Pigmentosa, the progressive eye disease which consumed the light-sensitive cells on the retina, destroyed night vision and the peripheral fields and ate inwards until central sight was narrowed to a pin-prick. Eventually it would go, disappearing in a blip reminiscent of an old black-and-white television set being switched to off. His son, blind. For Max, the switch had been thrown long ago, the congenital disease passed down on his mother's side. Yet a blip was exactly what it was, incidental to his existence, something to be conquered not wept over. Life was a privilege, misery too tiring, and he threw his energies into avoiding the implications, getting laid and sustaining his independence. As his physical reliance on others grew – grasping an arm or proffered shoulder – his emotional self-sufficiency compensated. It was his course, his life, his individuality; he would never be a victim, could never accept pity. It did not make it easier for his father. The issue was discussed only obliquely and in anecdotal form, and the stories of his falls and faux-pas were legion. Max claimed to do all his own stunts. Yet he never opted out. Inherited grit prevented it.

They chose and ordered.

'Is anyone sitting to the side of us?'

'Not that I noticed,' Purton replied. 'Why? Did you frighten them off?'

'Looks like it. I tried to wedge my stick into a cushion. Turned out to be a Dutch tourist's ass.'

'You sure you're going to be all right in Moscow?' Purton turned serious. Pitching it right was the problem. Trespassing on his son's territory always carried the risk of a rebuff.

'Dad.' A note of warning.

'I'm being protective, not over-protective. I'm asking. Can I help?'

'I'll be fine. I've got minders coming out of my ears.' Dodge and survive. His favoured approach.

'Only asking.' Purton concentrated on a bread roll. He wanted involvement in his son's life – to watch over him – without involvement, without Max guessing.

'I'm more worried about you, Dad. Semi-retirement sounds like bullshit.'

The receptors had picked up something in his father's manner, his speech, his aura. Purton poured his son another glass of champagne. Max would be too concerned if he learned the details. At least the life insurance was in place.

The bodies of the down-and-outs, the dispossessed of money, homes and life, were being taken out and stacked like pallets in the back of the militia trucks. Winter drove up numbers, but the stiffness of the corpses, their icy outer rags, made them easier to handle and puck-slide on board. Clever that they should find the best sites at which to die, the optimum positions for next-day retrieval. Under city regulations, public lavatories at night were plunged into darkness to dissuade undesirables from the wrong kind of long-term squatting. They should have known better. When you were that frozen, that drunk, a cocoon of night was the greatest comfort to be had. Flotsam from the varied economic crashes, out before the rubbish collection – quite a feat of organisation.

Leonid Gresko sat in the rear of his chauffeured and armoured Zil, bodyguard in front beside the driver, unmarked pursuit vehicle following with a further contingent of security men. The car dipped into a series of potholes, its rolling motion doing credit to the tractor-strength suspension and brothel-standard upholstery. Those shadowing did not enjoy such luxuries. The traffic militiaman saw the flashing blue light of the mini-cavalcade and held back other motorists, waiting drivers straining to catch a glimpse of the features blanked out by darkened glass. The blue light, signifying power of office, a symbol and privilege denied to most bureaucrats, and which the head of the FSB Federal Security Service commanded as of right. But the inheritor of Dzerzhinsky and Beria's mantle, the inhabitor of the office behind the bleak façade on 2 Lubyanka Square, had other props to cow and control those in his path: Knowledge and Fear.

An old man shook his fist as the Zil swung onto Red Square. He looked starved, haunted. Reform, democratisation and counter-democratisation to him – as to millions across the land – meant the belt being pulled another notch, the hunger pains stabbing harder and longer. Gresko saw the eyes – drink, madness, the hollowing-out of humanity. A psychological profile he understood. Perhaps he was an old soldier. They never died, simply became lost, abusive, fading into the seascape of others adrift. Every day they were joined by more. Hundreds of thousands had been cut from the services, morale and discipline cut with them. Politicians objected, but the Duma had no power or leadership, potential mutineers had desperation but no hope. Suicides went on rising. The FSB chief shot the locks of his briefcase and checked his notes. What was security when the fabric was disintegrating, when the rot had moved from the marrow of the body politic to the flesh of the nation? Soon it would not be a fist shaken, an expletive shouted, but a rocket grenade launched and culvert bomb initiated.

Statistics failed to show the depth of disenchantment with those who made and broke promises, who pledged to line the people's stomachs and instead lined their own pockets. The State was bankrupt, workers and pensioners went unpaid for two years, the predictions of a long-anticipated upturn were pushed far to the right, output maintained its free-fall, taking quality from life and life from the country. Another day. At Sosnovy Bor near St Petersburg, workers at a nuclear power station were forced at gunpoint to end their industrial unrest; in Bogotol, the open-cast coal mines turned red when demonstrators were beaten and shot. Over five hundred miners were poisoned or drowned in Kemerovo while the local power station turned off ventilation and lighting for unpaid bills. Rescue workers could find no emergency equipment: it had been sold by management for cash. The Urals were on strike; soldiers protested in every major city; the energy workers of the Kuznetski Alatai mountains rioted over back-pay. What pay? Barter and black-marketeering were the only means of survival. No wages, but you might receive a malfunctioning washing-machine, a crate of vodka or cigarettes from your factory, spares for equipment which no one wanted and nobody bought. And the leadership remained isolated – unaware or cowering, it made no difference – behind the high red walls of the fortress on Little Borovitsky Hill, advised by dollar billionaires who had grown rich on the pickings of an economic carcass, who stole, flaunted, laundered, who bought and peddled influence. Gresko slammed the case shut. Order was all that was left: precarious, precious, perilously close to collapse. It would not take much. Not much.

The Zil slowed and bounced past the gatehouse. Security was at its customary level of overkill, symbolic of paranoia and the shadow of past coup attempts. Competing yet interdependent security forces with individual command structures, agency rivalry, ensured loyalty to the top, a shared interest in maintaining the pyramidic status quo. Uniformed men of the Presidential Guard Regiment came to attention, more lined the route inside the Kremlin between the Lenin and Senate towers as the driver turned in behind the Supreme Soviet Building and pulled up to the yellow classical palace of the Senate, the offices of the President of the Russian Federation. More salutes, a formal welcome from an officer, this one a member of the elite Kremlin Commandant's Regiment responsible for guarding the inner sanctum. Close-in protection was left to the SBP *Shuzba bezopasnosti prezidenta* – Presidential Security Service – and the special-

situation 'Rus' commandos. Gresko nodded his acknowledgement and climbed from the car. Such units, fifteen
thousand strong, were controlled by the FSO Federal Protection Service. But they were only part of the mosaic which
guaranteed the survival of the Kremlin masters. Beyond them
were three further organisations with ready-armed troops,
counterbalances, checks to anyone foolhardy enough to
mount a putsch. The Defence Ministry had its Court
Divisions, the Second Taman Guards Motor Rifle units at
Alabino to the south-west of the city and the armour of the
Fourth Kantemirov Guards at Naro-Fominsk, some fourteen
thousand in number. They were backed by paratroop units,
naval infantry, a Motor Rifle Brigade at Solnechogorsk, and
the Spetsnaz formations of the 218th Air Assault Battalion
and the 117th Independent Air Assault Communications
Brigade based at Medvezhi Ozera. To rival them in size,
firepower and capability were the MVD Interior Ministry's
'VV' Troops, the Moscow contingent of the First Odon
Independent Special Designation Division stationed to the
east at Balashikha, and four special SMBM motorised militia
battalions from the surrounding areas. The MVD also
commanded armed police and paramilitary response forces
such as the highly motivated OMSN commando squad, the
700-strong combat veterans of the OMON 'Special Designation' anti-riot unit, the GNR rapid response teams of the 181
separate police precincts and the SOBR groups assigned to
each of the ten city police regions. Policing was more akin
to guerrilla warfare. Finally, the FSB, Gresko's responsibility
– the security apparatus – maintaining the cadre of troops
once managed by the KGB and incorporating Russia's finest
Special Forces groups. *The survival of the Kremlin masters*.
He smiled and entered the doors. Survival always had a
price.

They gathered in an ornate meeting room, gilt mirrors,
walls and chairs, fourteen of the nation's most powerful
officials, members of the Russian Security Council. Senior
officials, perhaps; to Gresko they were prey. He looked

around, small, bead-like eyes set wide into a porcine face taking them in, taking everything in, enemies and allies alike, matching them against files. There were no clean hands at this table, only dirt beneath the nails, oily prints across the state's assets, prints he could dust for and record. Beneath the smiles were decaying roots undermined by expensive tastes, secured by expensive surgery – he held those records also. He had *kompromat* on them all, mud that would not only stick but envelop, compromising material which could be broadcast or headlined, consigning these men to the political and luxury-denuded wilderness they most feared. When political position corresponded – less than coincidentally – to personal cashflow, none of these pigs would be happy to be kicked from the trough. In having the influence and the information to do that kicking, in prying, spying and possessing details of their credit cards and bank balances, and in discovering how little their financial wellbeing equated to the chaos and penury about them, Gresko had their full attention and compliance. It was a balance of power, a balance of threat. Occasionally he tipped it, dislodged men seemingly untainted by corruption, leaked their telephone taps or revealed details of bribes dating back to regional governorships left long ago by thrusting Moscow-bound high-fliers. He had done it recently to a deputy prime minister. It proved a point.

His gaze shifted to the Minister of Justice, oh so busy with his latest 'anti-corruption' campaign whose course and outcome were preordained. The man was in the pocket of mafiya supremo Boris Diakanov, handed over as spoils by the Solntsevo clan, benefiting from a score of import invoicing scams. The Defence Minister was chatting with the Director of the Federal Border Service. Both enjoyed lavish lifestyles, the former with links to the alcohol and tobacco concessions of the National Sports Fund and retired servicemen's leagues, the latter running unofficial tariff regimes on illegal drugs flooding in from the independent Asiatic republics. The Defence Industry Minister, enriched from privatisation, restructuring handouts and weapons sales; the Minister for Civil Defence and National Emergency, helping himself to relief money and hardship resources. Here, the Minister for Nuclear Energy enmeshed in uranium fuel-smuggling and a valuable metal price-fixing venture, skimming the frozen accounts of the Federal Nuclear Centre responsible for paying jobless scientists desperate in their twelve far-flung atomic research cities; there, the Finance Minister who had transformed the concept of self-help into the highest form of helping himself. All for none, and none for all.

The Chairman of the State Duma nodded at Gresko. The man was his agent in parliament, reported everything, ensured that the FSB knew of each deputy's particular peccadillo and perversion. He was no slouch himself: the video-footage proved it. It was how the Security Service came to win his cooperation in the first place. Fourteen of Russia's finest, as amoral and as obvious as the *nochniye babochki* – 'night butterflies' – plying their trade along Tverskaya Street, and not nearly as professional. He had them by the balls, could squeeze until they screamed, could squeeze until Russia fainted.

The President entered, flanked by his Prime Minister and Chief of Staff, followed by the Deputy Chairman and Secretary of the Committee. The group rose and applauded as he stepped forward to take his place. Gresko checked the new entrants against further files. The Russian people were kept pliant, subjugated, with alcohol; the same could be said of their president. They went on clapping. The weaker, the more senile, the more inebriated and confused the recumbent incumbent, the longer and louder the ovation. An old Kremlin tradition.

Gresko stared at the Chief of Staff – political fixer, drinks fixer, regent, gate-guardian – a rare reformer whom the President had insisted, against advice and precedent, should sit in session as observer. Scan and retrieve. The man was a survivor, had brushed off scandal, dodged crossfire, adroitly side-stepped political minefields placed in his path. His own Kremlin intelligence and counter-intelligence organisations were second to none, were proving difficult to crack. But then, they were well funded. He had established an Emergency Commission for Tax Collection to boost the government's ailing revenue collection, wrench funds from a society where evasion was a way of life, and to trickle-feed woefully bare federal coffers. Tax collection increased, the coffers remained empty. And Gresko was watching.

Papers were handed out and, at the president's direction, the Committee Secretary began to read from the prepared security overview. Gresko concentrated on the ornate plasterwork of the ceiling. Such presentations were predictably depressing. NATO continued its eastwards march, pressing in on the Rússian Federation's borders, taking over its *Dal'nye zarubezhnye* 'far abroad' regions, the countries of eastern Europe it had once considered its own fiefdom. Now the West made trouble in Russia's *Blitzhnye zarubezhnye* 'near abroad', the former republics of the USSR, attempting to drive a wedge between one-time allies with promises of investment and trade. Was the Ukraine not being prised away by blandishment and bribery? Were not the Ottoman surrogates of the United States trying to spread a Turkish empire through the Volga region, Urals and into western Siberia? Everywhere factionalism was rife; principalities claimed autonomy; unrest was spreading, the centre weakening, losing its grip and footing against the centrifugal forces of independence. In the Central Asian states – former Soviet republics – there were over twenty potential territorial or ethnic disputes alone, conflicts which could so easily insinuate across the border. Yet the Russian armed forces, pride of the Soviet Union, had become impotent scavengers. Troops potato-picked to stay alive, unable to perform against the smallest of threats; their generals were implicated in scandal and activities 'incompatible with high office'. Nothing, precisely nothing, was incompatible with high office: fraud, embezzlement, extortion, larceny on the grandest of scales. That *was* high office.

The monologue sustained its hypnotic, constant pitch. Gresko's mind drifted. When the Soviet Union unravelled, Russia had lost 5.3 million square kilometres of territory overnight and almost half of its military personnel, advanced defence technology and equipment. No programme and few units were left unscathed. The situation worsened as real defence spending fell by ninety-five percent throughout the 1990s. By the millennium, the USSR's most favoured, pampered and bloated sector had become Russia's most vulnerable and diminished. Air force squadrons flew at a quarter of their paper strength, their pilots under-trained, their aircraft obsolete. Naval fleets rusted; army regiments could find neither bootlaces nor soldiers. Only the nuclear bunkers remained equipped and funded, bolt-holes for the government, underground business centres for ministers, advisers and their contacts in 'private enterprise'. There were the two new subterranean bases under the villages of Sharapovo and Voronovo, thirty-four and forty-six miles from Moscow, the nuclear-command 'city' below the Ramenki suburbs had been refurbished and expanded, the Signal-A command and control system upgraded; the vast new strategic complexes inside Kosvinsky Mountain in the Urals and at Yamntau Mountain near the town of Beloretsk were on line. Combined with the renovation of four Cold War nuclear citadels beneath the streets of Moscow, it was a massive undertaking. The president himself enjoyed the privilege of a secret thirteen-mile escape railway running from Victory Park station near the Kremlin to his out-of-town dacha. No expense was spared when it came to ensuring the leadership's survival. But it was Gresko who held that survival in his hands. His FSB troops manned, maintained and protected these locations. This Byzantine world buried deep – the idea was attractive.

The president stirred. 'Our enemies have attempted to reach the gates of Moscow before. They have failed each time. They will fail again.' Only because those very same gates had probably been sold as scrap to a metal merchant, Gresko mused.

'Feodor Pavlovich.' The president turned to his Defence Minister. 'Address the Council on the current state of the Topol-M ballistic missile programme.'

'I am happy to report that production test launches from Plesetsk and Svobodny of both the mobile and silo-based variants are complete.'

Prolonged applause, worthy of a first night at the Bolshoi, a sense of relief at assured and continuing nuclear status. Economy shaky, but they could still wreak global destruction. A cause for celebration. Gresko's specialists were in northern Yakutia far above the Arctic Circle retrieving missile debris scattered across a swathe of frozen waste. His specialists got everyplace.

The agenda moved on – American developments in cruise missile, spaceplane and hypersonic weapons research. Always the United States, thrusting forwards, leaving the rest – Russia – in its wake, forcing the Federation to retreat and wither behind its seventeenth-century boundaries. Gresko examined a further detail of plasterwork patterning. Cracks were showing.

He was being addressed. 'Director. The situation in Tadjikistan continues to concern us.'

Concern? Panic. The Turg mountains were on fire, Russia's overworked helicopter gunships rocketed Moslem positions around the clock, Frogfoot attack aircraft bombed Taleban insurgents, but still they came. Sabotage and subversion from every point, Russia defiled, penetrated, compromised.

He summarised, voice colourless, thoughts disengaged. These people knew nothing of strategy, his strategy, of how he planned to deal with problems abroad, domestic and round this table, of Petr Ivanov. They understood little of his calling. It was a calling, and it came in tongues. *Execute, execute* they said. The power surged in his head. He controlled it, controlled it all. And he would act.

Miss Helen Temple-Furnival, fifty-three, private secretary to the headmaster, most definitely a Miss, not Mrs or – heaven forbid – a Ms. She was as set in her ways as would be expected after thirty years in one of the country's most prestigious, expensive and well-known preparatory schools for boys. Like the institution itself, she remained largely unchanged: a perceived strength in a world evolving rapidly in directions neither wholly understood nor entirely endorsed by herself or the school. Empires collapsed, governments came and went, fashions flared and faded, the surrounding Berkshire countryside succumbed to encroaching development, manners in general declined, but Helen Temple-Furnival and the products of Hawbreys Prep remained reassuringly – some might argue, alarmingly – the same.

For sure, Hawbreys, like all British boarding schools, had experienced its fair share of embarrassment and upset in its three hundred-year history. One or more matrons sacked for seducing an entire dormitory; a French teacher quietly removed for interfering with a boarder during crepe-soled rounds after lights-out, and currently employed in a similar capacity elsewhere in the Home Counties; a games teacher who encouraged boys to swim naked with him in the unheated outdoor swimming bath. The cases were hushed up in the artful manner so beloved of institutions which knew how to survive and which, since the reign of Queen Anne, had nurtured the progeny and self-perpetuation of the British upper and upper-middle classes.

But Miss Temple-Furnival was not at ease. There were unwelcome elements appearing in her school. She could cope with the nouveaux riches, their helicopters landing ostentatiously near the cricket nets to disgorge pushy over-permed mothers with strangulated vowels, their spoiled offspring winning friends through a surfeit of consumer items, aggressive fathers who collapsed with heart-failure in attempting to win the parents' race at sports day. However rude or crude, however demanding, however incapable of dealing with those either from their own social stratum or the one to which they so desperately aspired, they were not the issue. She could almost pity them, lost as they were in a societal no-man's land. Over-the-top maybe, despised by their own, sneered at by the others, hemmed in by cultural tank-traps of snobbery, raked with withering looks and loud whispers, terrified at the prospect of discovery by people who recognised them instinctively – no, indeed, they were not the worry.

She sighed. Places such as Hawbreys provided a first-rate service, a fine education and the greatest of all advantages. Primarily, notwithstanding the presence of the rich arrivistes, they allowed upmarket couples to quarrel, spouse-swap, run off and divorce as messily as possible, reassured that somewhere out in the countryside their sons and heirs would remain blissfully unaware and unconcerned, be raised as gentlemen and readied to make the same mistakes a generation on. It had worked without a hitch for centuries.

Now the Russians and East Europeans were here, and she simply would not, could not, countenance it. Hawbreys had entertained foreigners before, but never in such quantities. There was something not quite right about this influx – epidemic – of Slavs, their sinister fathers or bulky minders arriving in dark, outsize cars to pay term fees in cash up front or to make contributions, again in varied denominations, towards improving infrastructure and establishing scholarships. Such facilities had grown rapidly as a result, building work becoming part of daily life, a new excrescence appearing on the sides of the main school building at the end of almost every summer holiday. And Helen Temple-Furnival knew all about dirty money, had read of the Russian mafiya, made it perfectly clear to those who would listen, and many who did not, her views on the morality of using the English preparatory school system as a tax-dodge and currency laundry for thick-accented gangsterdom. The entreaties to her by an exasperated headmaster for a little more understanding and a little less vocal opposition failed utterly to move her.

The telephone call had concerned eleven-year-old Oleg, at five feet eleven inches a full head and shoulders above the older boys, consequently a star of the First XV Rugby team, popular and the reason behind the school's latest development: a new science block guaranteed to impress, or annoy, everyone at the Independent Schools' conference that year. It made no difference that the boy's father was some dubious apparatchik or banker from Moscow. The school's experience in dry-cleaning the offspring of both gauche criminality and the criminally gauche into something approaching respectability matched anything the financial community could do with their money, and the headmaster remained optimistic at the prospects for gaining an indoor Sports Hall from the same wealthy benefactor. Oleg was not simply a rich seam. He was the Prep's very own Urals gold mine.

The call was brief. Oleg was playing at home for the First XV against another local school – traditional rivals – and Uncle Radomir, in London for a few days, wished to surprise his favourite nephew with a visit. Summoning up reserves of charm from her 'could be patronising, but they're foreign so won't be able to tell' store, she expressed Hawbreys' pleasure at the prospect of meeting the caller and how delighted Oleg would be. Another large car crunching its way across the gravel, she suspected as she replaced the receiver.

The car did not disappoint, a gleaming, black, long-wheel-base Daimler pulling in to the redbrick front of the school in the mid-afternoon. The match had already started, the odd whistle and shouts of support drifting across the grounds from the games fields while a large man in grey homburg and dark coat clambered out, ordering his driver to remain behind. The vehicle would not be joining the line of Mercedes saloons and Range Rovers carrying parents to watch their muddied and bloodied sons and parked adjacent to the rugby pitches at the rear.

It was a fiercely contested game, most of the school turning out to clamour support from the sidelines, shrill pre-pubescent yells mingling with the barks of enthusiastic fathers and bored tweed-clad mothers dragging protesting labradors and terriers backwards and forwards as the ball was jockeyed about. The Russian stood apart from the crowd, barely noticed, before he identified and briefly introduced himself to the headmaster and his wife located amidst their small coterie of admirers. Oleg was playing well on the wing, had almost scored a try, and the head-master beamed unctuously as he talked of his great regard and hopes for the boy. He had higher, unspoken, hopes for the financial largesse of the boy's family and did not repeat Helen Temple-Furnival's suggestion that the Russian's size and success on the rugby pitch could be accounted for by an age advantage of a good three years. On the pitch, Oleg briefly looked across. There was no wave of acknowledgement. He was busy concentrating on ball play, tactics.

The final whistle: the defeated visitors sloped off disconsolately to the obligatory three cheers and polite applause, the proud victors slapping each other on the back and making their way across to accept the praise of boys and parents. The team tea was foremost in their thoughts. Oleg smiled wearily at the hero's reception, black hair hanging dankly over a wide pale face. The headmaster pushed his way towards him, accompanied by the Russian.

'Congratulations, Oleg.' The youth was being mobbed by junior formers. 'You played superbly, and we've got a surprise for you.' A blank stare from Oleg. 'Your Uncle Radomir has come all this way to see you.'

The boy's face registered confusion rather than recognition, embarrassment at the headmaster's obvious mistake.

'Hello Oleg.'

He turned helplessly to the headmaster. 'Sir, this is not . . .'

The Russian drew a pistol from his coat pocket and fired twice, the double report echoing outwards, hammering an instant stillness onto the assembled scene. Then a woman began screaming.

Human reaction to events beyond everyday comprehension, to neurological shock outside the norm, was well known to the man. Temporary paralysis, inertia, an inability to mount a coherent response, these he had witnessed through countless scenarios in which he was the killing agent. He took advantage of them now. It was the human condition, weakness, which made the adults turn their attention from him to the fallen, dying boy, which allowed him to make his way unhindered, at speed, past the sundial, across the old grass tennis court, around the lawns bordered by lime trees leading down to the swimming pool, and back to the waiting car. Those furthest from the shooting would be least affected, susceptible to other impulses – to pursue, to note details – he would vanish before group hysteria diluted from the outer edges inwards.

'Jumbo' Weatherby, one of those strange anachronisms once prevalent throughout the world of English boarding schools, was strolling in the gardens. In his seventies, approaching his delayed retirement with as much ill-temper and lack of grace as he could muster, he was Hawbreys' longest-serving master, joining the school in the 1950s and teaching French and History with wilfully fluctuating degrees of competence ever since. He was universally liked, the staff common room dominated for fifty years by his pipe smoke and contrived curmudgeonly presence, his position centre-stage ensured by the reserved high-backed leather chair from where he would rail against declining education standards, standards which he had played a not insignificant part in undermining.

Jumbo heard the shots, saw the Russian and the pistol, the man hurdling a privet hedge and dodging over an empty flower bed towards him. Interception was imminent. Used to commanding respect and instant obedience with the mere jab of his pipe, perhaps wishing to add to school folklore, he confronted the intruder with a pose customarily reserved for

64

small boys running too fast in corridors.

'What the hell d'you think you're up to, then?' he demanded.

Without replying, the assassin moved in, snatched the outstretched wrist and twisted. The pipe fell, scattering shag tobacco. Jumbo would have screamed, but a boot to the spine kicked him forwards before a single shot blew in the back of his head. It was Helen Temple-Furnival who found the body, the stained, smoke-infused sports jacket with its ripped lining floating on the surface of the ornamental fish pond, indicating the whereabouts of its owner beneath.

Later, a burnt-out Daimler was found along a track close to the perimeter of the former Greenham Common airbase. As forensics crawled over it, a man carrying an Israeli passport was checking onto an El Al flight to Tel Aviv out of Heathrow. Within four days he had returned to Moscow. Hawbreys Preparatory School for Boys did not receive its new indoor Sports Hall.

CHAPTER 2

'Fuck you,' she said. Snappish, definitely snappish. Seriously unprofessional.

He rolled his eyes. Perhaps it was lack of respect for her chosen subject, perhaps lack of respect for her. He was not sure. She took herself, her work, seriously, helping others while she could not help herself. He was never going to be one of her 'boys', as she called her patients in an 'I'm your friend as well as your psychotherapist' kind of way. This session was doomed.

The Max and Adele epic, long-running and running nowhere. Her caring Californian pretentiousness, in-your-face immediacy and formula liberalism beneath a West Coast veneer of clinic-speak, against his lazy, subtle cynicism. Perfect foils, but perfection had gone; adversarial, mutual irritation remained. Two survival mechanisms, competing, conflicting and destructive. It could never work. She wished to change him, change everybody – it was in her genes, her life, her mission statement – and he had no wish to change. Or be cared for. She was better off with the weak, the malleable, those who needed her, those who would accept unquestioningly her advice because she appeared to listen, because they had no comparable reference points. They massaged her ego, repaired her own damage and inadequacy; Max could no longer be bothered. Where once they had sparked, now they sparred; a long-distance relationship conducted by telephone – collect – where the alchemy left sediment, the solution did not mix, and absence made the heart indifferent. Yet neither had the energy to separate. It was more convenient, safer, to sleep together than apart, to share an apartment occasionally than not at all or, worse, on a permanent basis. Had been.

She juiced the oranges furiously – meaningfully – pulp spattering the transparent walls of the container. How could someone like Max make her so angry? Anger was so irrational, so . . . so . . . primal. She fed in the bananas. More symbolism. The argument and morning had started with gentle sniping and developed into a full-scale bedroom battle, a gentle skirmish on a random issue which drew on other tensions and rolled backwards and forwards across a wider front. Temporary, grudging respite and resupply, with occasional hostile encounters. No festive swapping of gifts in No-Man's Land, no give between entrenched opinions. Max was bored of it all.

'Is the kettle on?' he asked. Keep it neutral, or she will pick up on it.

'No, the coffee maker.'

'That'll do.'

'You sure I'm not cramping you? Organising you too much? Not giving you enough space?'

He sank back onto the sofa with a groan, disappearing in the open-plan immensity of Adele's Notting Hill apartment. Minimalism prevailed, walls were an afterthought. It meant fewer things for him to knock into, although the furniture – or art – had its edges. Sharp, spare and not always comfortable to be around. That was the interior, that was Adele.

'Cut me some slack. I can't deal with kitchen politics at this time of the morning.'

She slammed down a mug and began pouring. 'I just don't understand you.'

'A therapist with humility – I'll go with that.' Adele did not.

There was silence as she carried through the juice and coffee and perched on a low, cream-coloured bar stool. Prone, he could gaze up her robe, wished he had his lenses in. She had a better view of him.

'Are you going to make some effort in this relationship?'

On occasion. She was a blur of indistinct colour, unfocused. It was difficult to connect with something so amorphous. Feeling vulnerable, he sat up. Lying down, he was at a disadvantage, a subject for analysis.

'Are you suggesting it's meaningless?' He even hated the word relationship.

'What am I supposed to say? That we're content, blissfully happy? While you behave like an adolescent on heat?'

'C'mon.' Mock wheedling. 'We've had some good times.'

'Sure. In the horizontal. I need more, Max. We need more.' They could vary the positions, he thought. The glossies always suggested it.

'You know I can't settle in London.'

'You can't settle at all. It's simple – your eyesight makes you feel half a man, so you overcompensate with your dick.'

He pulled a cushion over his face. 'Eat your heart out, Mrs Freud.'

'I'm right.'

The cushion was removed. 'So what? We've all got our kinks. Why try and iron out mine?'

'It's called commitment.'

'It's called bullshit. I've explained over and over . . .'

'Unconvincingly.'

'Let me finish.' He paused, deliberately, and started again. 'I cannot change my lifestyle. I cannot change my attitude. I need to work, and work means travel.'

'And your eyes? Think about them.'

His fingers connected with the mug. 'Why? What fucking conclusion would I draw? That I should give up trying to earn a living? To play safe, to please you? There's no blueprint, Adele.' Too young for a mid-life crisis, too old for its mid-teen equivalent.

'Five years, and you'll be blind.'

'No shit? What do you suggest – that I give up masturbating?'

'That you explore the options.'

He did that in every town, every city he came to. It affirmed his remaining freedom, placed the countdown on hold, kept blindness at bay. He undressed women, unwrapped them, a gift to himself, a thrill – sometimes cheap – irresponsibility in the guise of comforter, a transient pleasure that might make him smile when eventually the darkness drew in. Lately, the unwrapping was more desperate, frantic. Adele played her own role. Looking after her man with RP gave credibility, made her the all-round carer, the all-round coper. She could talk of the disease, how brave he was being – by association, how brave she was being – in hushed tones to admiring friends. He was part of her script, up there with the texts on systemic, narrative, cognitive, transactional and behavioural therapy. And he was part of her own treatment. Selfishness posing as selflessness.

Her night smell, lightly perfumed, reached his sinuses. His bathrobe moved. 'Christ, Max. You were born with a hard-on.'

'My mother's been talking.'

'Grow up. Stop dodging.' She wanted to say that things could not function, but they had functioned well into the small hours. Post-coital emptiness would kick in later. Her hands were clenched tight, eyes concentrating on them, using them as an aide-memoire. 'Max, this is not an ultimatum.' It was an ultimatum. He had passed through several before, found them a challenge, sensual.

'Shoot.' He toyed with the towelling belt.

'You're running.' Who was not? Adele, the poor little rich girl, with baggage and too much time, coming to London to expunge demons in herself and others. 'You're running,' she repeated. And the dodging? he thought. 'And I'm tired. You're doing it because you can't face up to the future, because reality hurts.'

'Make someone smile, kill a therapist,' he murmured under his breath. Louder. 'You're tired? I feel I'm on day-release from a care home. I can't breathe, I can't move.'

A calm, over-calm sampling of the fruit juice. 'I'm not

going to go on being a fly-in, fly-out fuck, Max. It's not a life, it's not a relationship. If you don't base yourself in London, then the locks will change and you and your clothes can find a new home in a hotel.'

'Is that the full speech?'

'Getting there. It's your call. Think about it in Russia. Screw whoever you have to, wear protection, and then let me know.'

He tried to stare at the haze, could not make out her shape. 'Hunter Strachan gave me a chance. The only one who ever did, the only one who ever will. I can't invalid myself out of it.'

The robe came open as he rose and stepped towards her, her face pushing into his stomach, wet tears matting the hair around his navel. He moved a hand downwards inside the silk, cupping a small breast, feeling her shiver, extruding the nipple, leaning in against the warmth of flesh. Human silk. She was biting, small rabbit-teeth, working lower, pinching, love and hate, pulling him forward with palms circling behind. She wanted him to go, to stay, had given him more chances than Strachan ever could, and he had let her down each time. He stroked her head, running his fingers through, threading her hair, squeezing, bunching. And he thought of Moscow. Zenya would be there.

The black ravens were out there, circling, somewhere – waiting – he was sure of it. One day they would return to feed, to carry off, to vomit out to a new generation of eager young. He stared out across the Moskva to the Kremlin, a floating fairytale, its rose-red, blood-washed walls lit magnificently in the darkness, towers adorned with the luminous ruby stars of a previous regime. There was no escaping them. And the vans – black ravens – of Beria's NKVD, the Secret Police, which stole through the streets, took the executioners to the doors of men and women whose principal crime was to remain alive during tyranny, brought midnight knocks and bereavement to a hundred thousand homes, were consigned only to recent memory. Like that memory, history's amorality, its mistakes and its incubating germs of past political horror could so easily be revived, its actions relived.

The image misted in the window condensation, lines melting, details blurring back into the night. He let it fade – he was the master, the controlling influence, had the authority to drain light away on a whim, to switch it off completely. Boris Diakanov, new Russian, billionaire, Mafiya boss of bosses, owner of the Kremlin, higher source, tattooed professional *urka* of the criminal under-made-over-class, and Armani-suited killer. He understood power, raw power, in a fashion only one spawned and raised in the gulags ever could. You could buy a man or kill a man. That was it, the meaning of life. Anything else – punishment beatings, punishment shootings – were merely stages on the path to either eventuality. Yet he could be flexible. If the order was 'crucifixion', the bullet head would be scored with a cross to ensure maximum internal damage; if it were 'herbal remedy', the tip would be rubbed in garlic oil to encourage the onset of gangrene. To those who feared him, and that was everyone, he was known variously as Great White, for his position as apex predator, or *Tsisari*, Caesar, natural successor to Peter The Great and Ivan The Terrible. These were leaders who had beaten or strangled to death their own sons, forced courtiers to chew their way into cadavers or impaled passing subjects on the end of a metal-tipped staff. Strong men, great sense of humour – Tsar Ivan IV had even converted to the priesthood – worthy of respect.

The block at 2 Serafimovich Street, the 'House on the Embankment', had many ghosts, its own bad spirits. Built in 1931, reputedly on the site of a pied-à-terre belonging to Ivan The Terrible's overworked Chief Torturer, it had housed the servants of another tyranny: the generals, senior Bolsheviks, thinkers, ministers, monsters, keepers of the great Russian prison camp, and chief torturers of a later age, that of Josef Stalin. They were not in residence long. Behind the walls of each apartment were the secret corridors, the spyholes for the NKVD. And when enough information was compiled, an unguarded and incriminating remark recorded, a van would be sent for the dictator's most loyal of the loyal transformed by rubber stamp overnight into enemies of the people. In three years, half the occupants disappeared, their apartments vacated for others whose turn would come: Bukharin, Marshal Zhukov, the cream of the Party, fattened in this luxury ghetto for show trials and murder. The central location suited Diakanov well. He occupied three floors in one of its twin towers, lavishing money on it, decorating it sumptuously in the manner of inordinately rich men with inordinately poor taste. Fine art bought – or stolen – wholesale was scattered about in opulent abundance, jostling with kitsch; oil canvases used as so much wallpaper, their value made valueless by the sheer splendour of the showcase. It was not his only home. In Moscow alone he owned a cottage surrounded by pines on the exclusive river island of Serebryany Bor, an imposing mansion in Tsarskoye Selo, and a further apartment on Kutuzovsky Prospect previously let to a Soviet minister. But it was where he most liked to be, commanding the view, commanding the government. Those granted an audience in such palatial surroundings dubbed it 'The Hermitage', the winter palace of Imperial Russia: it was here that the gravitational pull of true authority, real patronage, the greatest wealth, could be found. It made him feel good, pushed the carrion-eaters of the past into distant recesses, allowed him to concentrate on birds of a finer plumage.

He ignited a Java and continued to talk into the telephone. There was no worry of eavesdropping. Communications were scrambled and a Line X technical unit of the old KGB constantly swept the system.

'You know what the fucking problem is.' The smoke was exhaled violently, a cloud punched upwards in exclamation. 'My Vietnamese elephants and turtles get intercepted in Rotterdam; you send me a bunch of shit African Greys I never asked for; the Military Macaws arrived half-dead from

Mexico, and we had to crack open the holding compound at Sheremyetevo to get back the rest of our stock. Fuck your mother!' The Tartar eyes – coals of Ghengis – were glowing a strange amber at their centres. 'You never listen. I said no Military Macaws, no Scarlet, no Gold and Blue. I want rarity – Hyacinth Macaws; those ones from Bolivia, two-foot tails . . .' He waved the cigarette around, searching for the answer. 'Yeah, Red and Greens – it's what people are shouting for. Rainbow Lorikeets – fine – Golden Conures, real fine. So what's going on? Why did you screw up?' He did not listen for an answer. 'You want to become a fucking endangered species yourself?' The hidden caller plainly did not, his apologies and excuses tumbling over each other. Extinction was always a possibility.

'Redeem yourself. Find me a Spix's. A wild one.'

Diakanov dropped the receiver back into the cradle. This was real sport. There was only one solitary Spix's Macaw – *Eyanopsitta spixii* – a male, left in the wild anywhere in the world, inhabiting a small patch of Brazilian rainforest in Bahia Province, and guarded by armed volunteers. Killing a man never needed a reason, but some sort of justification, however spurious, lent legitimacy, an order to events. After all, he was simply a straight-talking, no-bullshit entrepreneur, loved his children, loved a free market. For decades he, and before him his father, lay hidden and secure east of the Urals, consolidating, growing, oiling the creaking machinery of the disintegrating Communist state with the lubricant of black-market profiteering, making life bearable for the *narod*, the common people. Bolshevism betrayed them, but he had never let them down. He supplied them with what they needed, sustaining both oppressor and oppressed, and in permitting the survival of the first he was establishing a greater market share and rising demand from the second. *Glasnost* and *perestroika* – the well-intentioned plans of a leadership attempting to modernise and survive – followed by the end of the Communist dream, the end of the Eastern Bloc and the end of the Soviet Union. Turmoil meant opportunity, debts to be collected, money to be made. As centralised authority collapsed, Diakanov ventured from behind his redoubt, wealthy, a unifying force capable of seizing, holding and expanding unchecked into every territory. Russia had known many raiders, none quite like this. And now there were different challenges, new borders to cross, widening vistas.

He sauntered casually over to a sideboard draped with a white cloth and set with silver salvers. Niche activities always caused the most problems, dollar-for-dollar took up more of his time. Yet they kept his instincts sharp, his business acumen honed. Move in rich and move out richer. He survived and grew because he was fastest and toughest, because he could survive and grow. Dominate everything, anticipate, flow into enterprises before they became an enterprise, and you ensured that the rivals were weak or stillborn. This was his creed, his instinct. Pillaging the world's threatened wildlife, then threatening and vacuuming it up some more, was only a single manifestation. He was supplying and fuelling the near insatiable demand of wealthy Russians for exotic plants and animals – orchids, snakes, the list was as long as it was uninformed – and as the species grew rarer, so the prices rose and Diakanov's profits improved. Keepers at zoos, pounds, were bribed, few asked questions, blood stains found on the floor of empty cages were barely noticed.

One journalist did notice, but never went into print. His family holiday was interrupted, terminally, by an infestation of the deadly Brazilian Wandering Spider. Originally, four females had been infiltrated into the cottage. They were egg-carriers, aggressive, protective, sensitive to vibration, appallingly venomous, and each gave birth to a thousand offspring. Far from help, and without anti-venom, the man and his family succumbed. Others, equally reckless, met similar fates, their bodies weighted and cast into the poisonous chemical cauldron of Lake Kaskovo two hundred miles from Moscow. Occasionally, the holding chains corroded so quickly, corpses would bob to the surface of the ore-reddened water or rise to bump beneath the covering crust of orange ice. No matter. The pollutants disgorged from nearby Dzerzhinsk ate identifying features as readily as an acid bath. There were many remains down there: the investigator probing precious stones smuggling and force-fed ground diamonds; another journalist researching the link between Diakanov's hit men and highly professional *gruppa zakhvata* snatch squads from the Sixteenth Spetsnaz Brigade based at Teplyi Stan. He was himself snatched. End of questions.

Diakanov peeled away a thin white slice of buttered bread and spooned on a heavy scoop of grey-black beluga from its crushed ice mound nearby. Beside it was the fresh fine-grained, cream-grey sevruga, heaped high in its own silver bowl, a third filled with golden-sheened grains of mature oscietre. Lemon application, and the equivalent of a thick wad of foreign currency disappeared into his throat, the delicate membranes melting, chased down by a shot of industrial liquor from Talitsa. The taste for rough Siberian vodka had been acquired before that for quality sturgeon eggs, a clash of cultures, of the camps versus the good life, and neither habit could be easily relinquished. The blade he carried was a totem of both worlds, symbolic of an approach he varied for no one. It was not an affectation.

Another overloaded slice consumed. With his poachers operating in well-organised teams out of Astrakhan, his armed 'Interceptor' yachts cruising the Volga and Ural rivers out into the Caspian Sea, and a smuggling network supplying world markets through Turkey and the United Arab Emirates, he introduced to the adult sturgeon population what he had inflicted on the rest of the world's endangered species. Opposition was impossible. Over two hundred border guards and their families had been killed with car-bombs. Their senior commanders – officers holding the men's records and addresses on file – enjoyed receiving and eating the best caviar that favours could buy.

Not content with purchasing people, Diakanov also sold them. Over a quarter of a million illegal immigrants passed annually from the Third World into developed countries, chiefly Europe and the United States. A favoured route was via Moscow. Here, Diakanov's representatives would take charge, his master-forgers supplying passports and paperwork, his transport teams taking the pliant hopefuls on to Warsaw for their short night-time wade across the River Oder into Germany. After that, they could roam: border controls had long since vanished. They paid up-front for their secret journeys, some doubled up as *tsisari*'s drugs couriers. Demand was exponential.

The illegal trade in wildlife and rare plants – an estimated global market worth some eight billion dollars per year; caviar smuggling – nine billion; the human trade into Europe alone – three billion. Yet to Diakanov they remained fringe concerns. His prostitution rackets operated from Macau to Berlin, his heroin trafficking followed the old silk route across the Tien Shan and Pamir mountains along the 'Road of Life' to the trading centre at Osh for refinement and onward travel. Gem-smuggling ran from the mines above the Arctic Circle to Odessa in the Crimea, weapons and drugs by rail from Turkmenistan south through Iran to the Shahid Rajai container terminal at Bandar Abbas. Within the *vory v zakone* – thieves within the code – he was the biggest thief. When he required more 'laundries', his property developments and hotel-construction transformed skylines in Limassol and Tel Aviv; when the physical movement of cash met bottlenecks, he established two private airlines to expedite the transfers. And when the US Department of Defence produced reports claiming that the Russian mafiya was a threat to global security, it was not exaggerating.

By the millennium, annual profits for organised crime from drugs trafficking in the United States were estimated to stand at over fifty billion dollars, globally in excess of four hundred billion. With opium production tripling and cocaine supply doubling every decade, such activity was set to account for almost ten per cent of total world trade. The Russian boss expected an ever-increasing share. It was his heroin flooding the European market, his ex-military pharmaceutical labs manufacturing amphetamine sulphate and synthetic drugs on an industrial scale. Thus did he work, untouchable, supreme, above and beyond the law, above and beyond those he manipulated. More caviar, more vodka.

Irina entered, his love, the brilliant graduate from Moscow State, the girl whose cornfield hair and summer-breeze temperament had pulled out his heart and kept it from others. And his boy adored her. She was the assistant turned disciple turned mistress; she shared his secrets, life and bed, was the laughing femininity in a man's world who pricked egos and punctured vanities, imbued his existence with spirit and meaning. She was everything that he was not, gave fullness to his soul, roundness to his character. Without her presence he felt diminished, devoid. She looked straight at him, wide-eyed, numbed. There was no smile, no easy familiarity, faltering movements of shock and hesitancy betraying her confusion.

'Little one. What is the matter? What is it?' He walked towards her, arms out to comfort and clasp. She backed away, less of a recoil than a nervous reaction. His features darkened. Someone had upset her; she must be consoled. 'Come to me, Irina.' He could see the lack of colour, trembling at the sides of the mouth, motion contrasting with the stillness of the upper face, tear ducts frozen. It was horror. She wanted to tell. 'Irina, please . . .' The prehistoric amber glowed in his eyes.

The words were whispered, as if sound would break the fragility of the spell, bring reality crushing down. 'Oleg . . . in England . . . They've killed him. They've killed Oleg.'

She was in another room, alone, staring at nothing, when she heard the howls.

The pencil jerked in Hugh Dryden's mouth, a sure sign that

another cryptic line across or down in that day's *Times* crossword had been cracked. He was methodical and unemotional, completed it alone, in the summer sitting out on the canteen terrace, in winter at his desk, focused, tuned in to his own reasoning.

An electronic mail message bleated on his screen. He raised an eye to it, completed five down, folded the paper and stood. In his position, interruptions were to be expected. The journey along softly lit and silent corridors to the office of the head of Russia Division took several minutes, broken by security doors, code pads and card swipe procedures. The senior officer was waiting for him, leather-upholstered seatback against the glazed window, facing a room fixtured and fitted with designer Italian woods, metals and fabrics, all in fashionable black, all courtesy of the taxpayer. It was a far cry from the decrepitude of Century House, the old Secret Intelligence Service headquarters, with its frayed civil-service issue carpets, plastic seats, unsprung sofas and 1950s hand-me-down desks, filing cabinets and umbrella stands. Here was a post-modern temple to espionage, a ziggurat of sandstone and green glass, brooding over the Thames from Vauxhall Cross, its communications dishes clinging to spiral masts and aimed upwards at orbiting geostationary satellites. Had to impress the foreign spooks, keep up with Uncle Sam, Dryden thought as he looked out over Guy Parson's shoulder.

'Coffee?' the Russia supremo asked, getting up from his seat. He was dapper, exuded efficiency, and had a reputation for intolerance towards those with a blunter mind than his own. 'It's fresh.'

'Why not?'

A cup was poured and handed over, the two men moving across to a section dedicated to a suite of low-set leather chairs and a sofa placed around a polished table. Further black, further design.

'I see the *feng shui* consultants have been active,' Dryden observed drily.

'I can't drop a paper-clip without annoying some pedant,' his colleague replied. 'Give me formica and bakelite any day.'

'And the glow of a cigarette in a doorway, the tap of a morse key.'

'Fresh air would be enough.' Vauxhall Cross was not to everyone's taste, and Parsons was a traditionalist.

They took a moment to sip from their cups, before Dryden started. 'Presumably you haven't got me here to find a crossword solution, Guy?'

'That'll have to wait. Scan this and tell me what you think.' He extracted a red file from a ledge recessed beneath the table.

Dryden took it. 'From our friend?' Parsons nodded. *Brodets* – the wanderer – had reported in.

Assessing the value of an agent-in-place could be difficult, often impossible, the intelligence profit and loss affected by a hundred variables, a thousand intangibles, the asset's real worth either underrated or overstated, the information flawed, ignored, inconsistent, contradictory, suspect, poorly analysed, falling foul of prevailing political sentiment, overtaken by events or simply not acted on. How to measure success? The Soviet Union carried off some of the twentieth century's most remarkable and audacious espionage coups, yet it lost the Cold War. Strategic shifts in the political tectonic plates, the economic superiority of capitalism, the technological prowess of the United States, the attraction of freedom to a people long subjugated, and the inherent weaknesses of Communism: they won a victory, both real and moral, for the slayers of Marx. The Red Empire collapsed, the contribution of its agents meant nothing. The West too had its spies, men and women who supplemented the information gleaned from signals intercept and imaging satellites, whose work gave the West time, space and flexibility, the chance to fine-tune responses and prevent the Cold War turning hot. *Brodets* had more than played his part. He should have sunk into the historical depths with the rest, but stayed on, espionage debris remaining at the scene of titanic destruction.

Longevity alone placed him in a unique category, quality of information in another. Never caught or compromised, never identified or contacted, he had sent consistently accurate reports to British Intelligence for fifty years. When KGB counter-intelligence periodically rolled-up and closed down American or British agent networks, smashed hugely complex operations and executed numerous individuals from the Party's own rank-and-file, *Brodets* stayed on line. His coverage and apparent freedom to travel within a Soviet system marked by its restrictions on movement at first gained him the SIS label of 'probable provocateur.' He was dismissed as a plant, an example of more Soviet mischief-making. But the intelligence kept on arriving. A letter posted to a British diplomat in Ankara in 1954 detailed future methods of communication and suggested the use of a particular supply lighter in the Crimea with which to ferry defectors to friendly merchantmen. It was followed by Polish religious under-ground groups smuggling out Soviet military components sent to them on a goods train running between Moscow and Warsaw. An envelope left in an American press attaché's tennis locker informed the CIA of the location and move-ments of British Foreign Office defectors Guy Burgess and Donald Maclean who had fled to Moscow in May 1951. An astute move: the Agency had active plans to mount a hit on Maclean as payback for leaking atom secrets, but was content to leave Burgess to die from drink in his seedy Moscow apartment on Boshaya Progovskaya. The British wanted just to forget the whole sordid business.

The years brought new insights. A seemingly innocuous report in the late 1950s, confirming start-up in production of the Soviets' first wellington-boot factory, enabled M16 agents to identify and photograph scores of KGB officers for their files. Initial boot output was only one thousand pairs a year; Dzerzhinsky Square's intelligence men had first take. In 1960, Colonel Oleg Penkovsky, senior deputy to General Serov, head of GRU Soviet Military Intelligence, began his brief but glorious career spying for British SIS. It was an unparalleled triumph, and it was *Brodets* who verified to sceptics in Washington and London that Penkovsky was bona fide. As son-in-law to Marshal Varentsov, director of Soviet rocketry development, the Colonel could pass the precise coordinates of the USSR's land-based intercontinental ballistic missile silos to his debriefers in Coleherne Mews, London. The information confirmed what *Brodets* had already told them. More documents and photographs arrived – the files on recruits passing through the KGB training academy set behind the crumbling walls of St Nicholas monastery at Shmarkovka in Russia's Far East; the first signs of building work on an over-the-horizon radar complex at Sillinka near Vladivostock to monitor American forces on Guam – *Brodets* seemed omnipresent. And when the Soviets attempted to circumvent the START 2 arms control treaty by installing smaller, more sophisticated missiles in redundant silos, he was there to alert the West.

Each new head of SIS Russia Division had his own theory as to the informant's identity. But it was pure speculation or comic conjecture. If it were the work of one man, he must have enjoyed a critical position in the military or railway service and by now would be elderly. A wide choice of candidate. He also knew how to bear a grudge: warning was received in 1976 that an ex-KGB man, formerly of Smersh, would die during a party faithful's holiday cruise on the Black Sea. The names of ship and victim were specified, as was the date of execution. News from a shaken crew eventually filtered down. There had been a fatality during the trip, a messy one. So, *Brodets* could kill. He was a loner, the psychologists said, could murder again, was showing off, displayed multiple personality traits, probably drank, was a proto-serial murderer getting off on a power thing. He called the shots, was in control. Perhaps it was the only reason he had survived so long. He? She? They? Whoever it was chose to stay out in the Cold, had made no attempt to live among those for whom he had spied for decades.

Dryden's long, slender forefinger turned the page and traced along the text. Parsons watched without interrupting. *Brodets* – codenamed 'Cold Cut' at random by British Secret Intelligence – was again in touch. Rumblings in the 'mafiya' underworld were commented upon; a train carrying diamonds from Yakutia province – the semi-autonomous republic of Sakha – north-east Siberia, had been raided, gems taken; electricity production from the hydro-electric station at Bratsk had been stepped up by almost twenty per cent in the previous two months. A news digest which, to the uninitiated, might have seemed dull. Seasonal upsurges in criminal in-fighting and turf battles were common, raids on trains were always a problem – sometimes entire villages took part – and electrical production was erratic even in the best of years.

Dryden spoke as he read. 'Presumably you've run all the tests?'

'Fingerprints, DNA, paper and ink analysis, linguistics. No linking characteristics, always different. We haven't had any clues since he first filed a report.'

'Waste of resources even looking. If he wanted to be ID'd, he'd have made it easy for us. We should simply be grateful he's there.'

'Professional pride. I don't like having our very own Loch Ness monster leaving footprints.' Dryden finished reading and looked up. 'So?' Parsons asked.

'A loaded word, Guy. So, what do you make of it? So, is it connected to all our other thorny issues? So, can we do anything about it?'

'All the above.'

Dryden placed the file down carefully on the reflecting surface. It was the kind of table which attracted marks. 'Gut feel and considered opinion, I wouldn't go overboard on the conspiracy approach.'

'Which is why I'm flying it past you rather the Controller,

Eastern Hemisphere. I'm not looking for a pattern, Hugh, I'm just wary of coincidence.'

'Interesting that our roaming friend puts electricity production and a raid on the Baikal–Amur railway line in the same report. You think he's making a connection for us?'

'He's cryptic at the best of times. You're the one who's good at clues.'

'May as well keep the events bunched together, then. The power generation interests me. Russian defence-production isn't ring-fenced, far from it. I can't think of any project which would generate that kind of demand and over such a short period.'

Parsons picked up the file and leafed through it. 'We know the hydro-electric plant is working at less that fifty per cent, so there's enormous spare capacity.'

'I'll check with Defence Intelligence.'

'He also comments on increased landings at the nearby Padunskie Porogi airport during the autumn.'

Dryden murmured an affirmative. 'I saw that. Could be anyone.'

'I'd wager military.'

'Look at the Gromov Flight Research Institute at Zhukovsky. Underfunded, crippled, most projects grounded; even the swept-wing Su-32 technology demonstrator flights disrupted by spares and fuel shortage. And that's high priority. Defence doesn't command the resources, Guy.'

'Who'd volunteer to go to Bratsk, though? You breathe the air and go sterile it's so polluted.'

'That bad?'

'Worse.' Parsons had spotted something else. 'Note that Intourist have suspended open tours of the dam and there's a ban on photography of the control room and surrounding environs. Tell you something?'

'Tells me to keep an open mind.'

'In this business?' He returned the file to the table and raised an eyebrow at Dryden. 'Right, discount military industry for the moment. Commercial activity?'

'Why would it be so secret? We'd know the factors behind any major ramp-up in production.'

'There's the giant aluminium smelting plant, the cellulose factory. Demand might have increased.'

'With the current state of economic activity? Not a hell's chance. And an upturn wouldn't happen at this time of year. But,' Dryden tapped the red cover. 'Why would he want to lead us to it?'

'Short of anything else to do,' Parsons answered. Yet the head of Russia Division was not dismissing anything.

Cold Cut had once provided samples of rare earth metals and mono-crystals, and even complete components, from Uzbekistan's integrated High-Temperature Metals Combine located close to Tashkent. Supplying the Soviet aerospace industry, the plant was a window on the existing technological levels reached by a commercial and military-industrial complex anxious to keep pace with the West. Careful analysis allowed British and American scientists to determine many things, including the extent to which their own research was reverse-engineered into the USSR's defence systems.

No, Guy Parsons was not dismissing it at all. 'And then there's the BAM heist,' he continued. 'A lot of diamonds. Enough to depress market prices if they can circumvent De Beers on the export market.'

'That'll be the day.'

'They're from the state Almaz-juvelier export stockpile, fall outside the main De Beers–ARS agreement. There could be leakage without anyone noticing.'

'Not with that amount. We're talking well over two hundred million dollars' worth. Be difficult to hide, even with Russian cutters doing their best.' Dryden chewed on his lower lip. 'Of course, it depends on the motive of the robbers. Doesn't have to be for direct cash gain.'

'The podium's yours.' Parsons waved his hand.

'Could be elements who want to starve central government of funds, could be a hoarder, a corrupt manager and his team at the BAM rail HQ at Tynda on orders from a Moscow grandee. Could be Yakutians wanting to remove them from the market to sustain prices or sell them on a second time. Could even be an inside military-mafiya job with long-term laundering in mind.'

'Point taken. Might be anyone and everyone.' Parsons sighed. 'And still no sign of alien involvement.'

'And still no sign of alien involvement,' Dryden repeated.

'You believe Diakanov's current worries fit in with any of this?'

'Pushing it too far to get a connection between a load of diamonds falling off a train and his son getting taken down. But we're all in the dark. That includes Five and Hawbreys School. Put it under the general heading of gang rivalry.'

The Director of Russia Division shook his head. 'Diakanov doesn't deal in rivalry. After this, it'll be full-blown warfare.'

'Whoops, as they say,' Dryden responded with a thin smile. 'Very careless.' Very bloody. 'I wouldn't like to be a Russian Minister negotiating for an international loan.'

Parsons looked at him without speaking. Silent coffee drinking followed for a moment.

'Ben Purton's locked in, is he?'

'Correct,' Dryden answered.

'Any complaints?'

He drained his cup. 'None I couldn't handle.'

'And Max, his son?'

'Off on tour to Moscow.'

'All we can do is wait, then, see if our two sets of litmus paper pick anything up.'

'Lightning conductors would be a more appropriate description.'

'Whatever you say, Hugh. More coffee?' The cups were replenished and the head of Russia Division sat back in his chair. 'Yes, it's really turning into quite a family outing.'

Dryden stirred his cup. He had measured out his life in coffee spoons, in people used and discarded. He wondered distantly if the Purtons would have to be discarded. In the interests of national security, naturally. He blew on the surface and sipped. Seven across had been causing problems all morning, taunting his brain, not teasing it. Crosswords could be so exasperating.

The two saloons, both black – a Jaguar, and Volvo as escort – came in at a steady 40 mph, the vehicle in front holding the left line, the trailing car offset to the right for better visibility and reaction. They slowed, curving round to a gravelled drive leading to a three-storey lodge surrounded by shrubbery-bordered lawns. The Volvo staggered itself close by, protecting the offside, three bodyguards leaping from it, two to defend the perimeter, the third joining a suited man from the Jaguar holding the rear door open for its occupant. The man began to climb out, the robes of a Gulf leader visible beneath the armoured under-edge.

Shots, shouting. Instant response. '*Weapons front and side!*' The two men at the Jaguar caved in on the Arab, one pushing him back in and onto the floor, throwing himself on top, the other leaping into the front passenger seat, flailing for the door as the car screeched off. A bodyguard slumped beside the Volvo, his colleague – protected by the engine-block – firing an automatic before jumping in as the driver accelerated to give chase.

A simple diversion. The man on the rise watched with binoculars. Matt-black optics held in black-gloved hands to a face near-hidden by a black woollen comforter pulled low. Any moment now . . . He checked the stop-watch and brought the boom-mike down to his mouth.

The driver saw it as he rounded the turn at speed: a single BMW, side-on, blocking the route. Think, see, anticipate. He punched his foot down in short, sharp jabs, cadence-braking, maintaining control, keeping the line, palms flat and thumbs upright on the wheel ready for impact. Change down, another brake, the bonnet surged upwards, and he floored the pedal. Whoever was hiding behind the car would not have survived. The Jaguar struck behind the rear wheel-arch – optimum strike point – ramming it into a spin on its own engine axis, the pursuit Volvo following fast through the opening.

Fight or flight, they had made their decision. Adrenalin was kicking in. Keep the line, keep the line. Rear lights, turn off your fucking rear lights . . . The man on the rise was shouting into the mike, field glasses still clamped to his eyes. So, they thought they were clear.

They would not get past that roadblock – two cars parked nose-to-nose with a backup positioned behind – too dangerous to tangle in a heavyweight clash of V8 engines. They would lose momentum, could not afford to swerve, and there were possible caltrap spikes on the road beyond. Sustained fire opened up, the multiple blasts of grenade detonations. The Jaguar, in a brief wheelspin, reversed violently – allowing the Volvo to squeal by on the offside – performing a textbook J-turn and facing back the way it had come. Behind it, the Volvo had pulled side-on to the roadblock and was laying down smoke, the single bodyguard left from the pursuit-and-escort team falling as soon as he left the vehicle. By then, the attackers were moving up to cut off the Jaguar's escape, closing the kill-zone.

What are you waiting for? Get the fucking principal clear. Move out. What's the frigging PES driver playing at? Christ. An exasperated half-shout. Why didn't he switch on the Volvo's twelve-volt disruptive strobe in the windscreen when he came under frontal fire? The man on the rise concentrated intently. The final act. Seamless, smooth, hardware meets ballet.

The Volvo slammed in beside the Jag which had manoeuvred itself onto a parallel axis to the enemy, the drivers forming a

'V' with the cars before scrambling across the backseats and out to put down covering fire from their limited shelter. Two remaining bodyguards and their principal dashed across to the roadside undergrowth. The noise was reaching a crescendo, chasing them through the trees, wrenching the breath from them. They were a mile away when the shooting stopped. The principal, exhausted, grey with shock, was being carried unceremoniously across his employee's back. He felt the heat and sweat from his human transport, watched the rasps of cold white condensation from the mouth of the other man, and lay limp. There was a single shot – way behind – and he stiffened. It was the driver of the Volvo receiving a coup de grâce.

'Greeks bearing gifts, eh, Ben?'

'Something like that.'

The man on the rise gulped appreciatively from the proffered hip-flask, then repeated the process, eyes folding from the afterburn. 'Shit, you don't know how good this tastes.'

'Not any more.'

'Obliged.' A wipe of the mouth with the back of a hand, and the flask was returned.

Purton tipped it to his lips at a more modest angle. Nick Howell's thirst was legendary.

'You come to stand on the top of a mountain and see my empire die?'

'You're getting poetic, Nick.'

'I don't fucking feel like it.' He pulled the cap back from his forehead.

The face was not so much lived in as lived out of, a travelling bag which had toured every atrocity, every trouble spot which the world, in its perversity, had dreamt up. Frayed, battered, but held together, he was a hard figure with softening edges, comfortingly reliable, a soldier, friend, adviser and demolitions man for most of Purton's team operations. Ten years younger, he looked older.

'You can tell me the bad news over a pint. I'm not staying out here to freeze my tits off and get shafted at the same time. Wait one.' He repositioned the mike to speak. 'OK, not bad, bar the balls-ups and the finer detail. It's two days till the six-car, thirteen-man fire and movement drills, and you've got route dry-cleaning tomorrow. Toby, get the lads to clear the kit, return to armoury and wash up. You've got SAP and counter-surveillance this afternoon; full debrief at 1800.'

'They're looking good.'

'Should do,' Howell replied, hand clamped over an ear to listen to the report coming through the radio piece tucked behind it. 'There's over a century of combat experience down there; ten thousand jumps and fifteen gongs for bravery. Which is a crying shame you're about to tell me, because the plug's been pulled.'

'Wait for the pint.'

It was sleeting when they made it to the whitewashed inn, the interior close and warm, windows steamed by damp clothes drying from body heat and the angry fire filling the hearth. Purton fetched the drinks while Howell sat and flicked a beer mat, his nature blanched by bitterness and cynicism. Too many battles fought and friends lost, too many betrayals and disappointments, middle age compounding misanthropy. But like others who had challenged themselves in combat, there was a strength born of restless energy, a confidence born of knowing he could survive. He was comfortable with himself, uncomfortable with all but the closest; the hill-walking boy-warrior from Arbroath whose journey had turned his hair from red to white, who on the way had dropped his accent and ideals. The solitude of war and the steepest climbs were all.

Like Purton, his former commanding officer, he had been both a Royal Marine and SBS operative and they had served together in numerous theatres. In Special Forces for eighteen years, he had conducted undercover operations in Northern

Ireland and Dhofar, led recce and attack missions in the Falklands and undertaken secondments to the US Navy SEALS and 22 SAS. Money saved from work on the international security circuit went into his big idea, his pension plan: a multi-facility sports shooting range built into disused stone quarries in the Vale of Clwyd, North Wales. Its excellence was acknowledged: he erected lodges to cater for overseas visitors; spent the nights mixing cement and laying foundations. In 1997, with a government ban on handguns and sport shooting, the vision and the centre fell apart.

'How's Max?' he asked as Purton passed across a pint of Greenalls.

'Taking on the world as the tunnel-vision closes in. Says the only thing he's cut out for is gynaecology.'

'He's put in the practice.' Howell had been a surrogate uncle to Max from the start. 'I wouldn't worry about him, Ben. He's got guts, brains, and he knows his limitations. It's enough.'

'Without eyesight?'

'He doesn't need a nanny.'

A long draw on the pint. 'You're right.'

'That's what made me an NCO. Now.' Howell placed his glass emphatically to one side. 'You're here with a proposition, you've got some good news and some bad.'

'The Firm is handing the Middle East protection job to SAS. They want us on something else.'

'Always do. If they're not requesting we demolish Radovan Karadzic's secret police centre at Banja Luka, they're muscling in on our anti-Basque terror training at Euskadi.' He pulled back the glass. 'If they're playing the patriotism card, they can piss off. My boys have trained hard for this.'

'They'll get compensation.'

A snort. 'Horseshit. That's what they said when they closed down my ranges.'

'It's not about the ranges, Nick.'

'I moved up here to Denbigh, I built a clubhouse, lodges,

with my own hands. No, it's not about the ranges. It's about them fucking with my life.'

The warning signs were there. 'Go on.'

Howell shook his head. 'It's a poison, Ben. Look at our leaders, look at our land. Shit, you can bugger a sixteen-year-old boy, but you can't chase a fox. And they think they've got the moral high ground. You want me to fight for that?'

'Is that a "take me with you" plea?'

'You don't get me that easy. Where?'

'Yemen. South.'

Face unchanging. 'Fee?'

'Negotiable.'

'Bollocks. With Six it's never negotiable. Start talking before I go off the idea.'

Purton sketched out the plan. Howell stayed silent throughout, turning the beer mat relentlessly between his fingers, staring at the token decorative gesture of an emptied bottle of Moët et Chandon Dry Imperial 1959 placed on a slate sideboard.

'They're not being straight with you,' he said finally.

'You know how they operate.'

'What God abandoned, these defended . . . And saved the sum of things for pay.' Lines from a Housman poem. The remnants of the pint disappeared. 'Forty years, and you're still talking me into your crazy fucking schemes.'

'You in?'

'I was getting bored of pub quiz nights.'

'How will Molly react?'

'Cartwheels, acid-dropping, all-night raves.' Purton smiled. The idea of Howell's gentle, stolid wife doing anything more than baking and gardening was beyond conventional imagination. She was always there, normality waiting for a husband to return from an abnormal existence. She was Howell's foundation. He would never admit it. 'I'm about as welcome as a yeast infection at the moment. When do we start?'

'Monday, down at Poole. Oman in a fortnight. There's a lot to do.'

'Ah well.' Howell pushed down on the table. 'Saga holiday with violence. It'll do us good. Want to drink to it?'

'I'm driving.'

'Live dangerously.' He levered himself up and headed for the bar. Purton waited. They would have their fill of danger.

A Cane Toad – squat, ugly, warted, poisonous – Leonid Gresko sat motionless and side-on behind the stained mahogany desk in his Director's suite at FSB headquarters, Lubyanka Square. Sans shape, sans neck, sans jawline, he gazed at a booklined wall, trying to concentrate, sight and mind flicking between titles, wandering to vacant space and then down to his lap. The girl was kneeling, working hard on him – a pup with a marrow-bone – teeth, tongue, saliva, gum and cheeks distended, eyes occasionally upturned to seek encouragement or approval. He gave nothing, was saving himself for the next couple of minutes. The head bobbed, dipping and rising; he stifled a grunt, not wishing to give warning. Office politics with bite. Build up, her fingers were working frenziedly, he felt the heat, felt the tension squeezing and rising, and shifted his head back. Coming, coming, a low gasp. Come. He reached and pulled two tissues from the box beside the ink-blotter, handing them down without looking. She wiped, zipped and left him as he swung the chair to face work. He found a file with one hand and raised a glass of water with the other. Today a secretary; tomorrow, the Russian people kneeling before him. Interlude over.

The report was long, a strategic overview dotted with tactical detail, a synthesis of desk analysis and field agent reports. Its summary was sufficient to cause pleasure considerably more profound than any provided by the over-active mouth of an overworked office help. Gresko, Guardian of Mother Russia, Defender of the Borders, Keeper of the Eternal Flame. He scanned the page. If the fools in government or on the Security Council had their way, the near-abroad would crumble and vanish like the former Eastern Bloc; Russia would be exposed, marginalised, bereft of influence and power. How they wrung their hands, railed ineffectively, incapable of forming any response bar compliance, negotiating – surrendering – from a position of no position. After all, the Federation was weak militarily, weak economically. Even at its centre, around the Caspian Sea, the Republics of Kazachstan, Azerbaijan and Turkmenistan were taking steps to accelerate their independence, forging bilateral relations with other states, developing oil and gas industries, tearing out the economic heart of Russia, their ailing neighbour and former ruler. They would prosper, turning to Turkey, China, Iran, turning to anyone but their old comrades, and funded by American interests with one aim – to hasten the disintegration and burial of the old empire. Fortunes could change so rapidly, so unexpectedly, Gresko mused. Marx had been wrong; nothing was inevitable.

He massaged a statapigic jowl and continued to read. His own foreign policy was simple, a masterpiece of unofficial involvement, oblique control and sleight of a well-fleshed hand. The turncoat republics would fail. Their alternative hydrocarbon export routes were easily undermined, local insurgents could be persuaded to attack pipelines and scare off investment, 'Islamic militants' ensured oil trucked from the Caspian Basin to Europe did not get through. Kazachstan's sole oil refinery had been sabotaged five times; Iranian construction engineers were persuaded to build expensive design flaws into the new twelve hundred-kilometre pipeline carrying gas from Turkmenistan to Turkey. Reliance on Russia seemed a safer option. Gresko hummed a folk song and drummed his fingers on the desk. Yes, with patience and meticulous planning, tides could be turned.

There was much to be grateful to that discredited drunk Philby for. Bitter, depressed and largely ostracised by those whom he had spent a lifetime serving, the ageing English traitor watched from his faded Moscow flat as his beloved Soviet Union collapsed, aware that the great Communist experiment had used flawed formulae, faulty equipment and faked results. He died in May 1988, unloved and barely noticed. Yet towards the end, Leonid Gresko had spent days with this strange, enigmatic foreigner, listening to a man attempting to make sense of a life and a mission which no longer made any sense. At first he chafed at the orders of his counter-intelligence superior Oleg Kalugin to provide a supportive shoulder to this human and historical wreck. But through the whisky-tears and racking self-pity there was the glimpse of a former agent, of self-discipline, control and coldness which had allowed this entity of the Cold War to plot and betray without compunction or remorse. No one knew Kim Philby, but Gresko knew his final, redeeming plan.

The intercom tone sounded, accompanied by a blinking light.

'Yes?'

'Colonel Lazin is back in his office, sir.'

'Ask him to come in the next ten minutes.'

He flicked the switch, took a sheaf of close-printed notes and fed them into the fine-shredder, the sheets vanishing to an electro-mechanical whine, passed on to be pulped, mixed and indelibly dyed, their remnants falling through to the containers beneath. These would be collected by a guard and taken straight to the incinerator off the internal courtyard. In the past it was known for Lubyanka prisoners at the rear to find paper by-products in what passed for their food. None were exempt from the process, free from abetting the eradication of proof that a prisoner had ever lived. The cycle of life, death, of an empty cell filled, emptied, filled and emptied over and over. Method and madness. He remembered destroying his own psychiatric report in this manner. Another page was sucked from his stub fingers. Feed in, tear to pieces and transform; people, politics or paper as one, as ash. Existence was so fragile. He dropped in the last page. Like

the others it was headed with the single word 'PERIMETR'.
Then he stood and headed for the bathroom. Prostate
problems; he needed a leak.

*The old man placed another lump of ice in the canteen and
watched it melt into the water boiling above the paraffin
stove. The tea would taste bitter, but be hot. That was all he
needed. He was warm here, safe, concealed, dug in beneath
the snow bank, the six foot-deep hole reached by an 'S'-
shaped passageway sloping downwards and cut off from the
outside world by a snow block. Above, a ski-stick projected
upwards through thirty inches of snow roof, sufficient
protection and ventilation for his winter sojourn. The dull
light came from candles – reindeer fat – placed in alcoves:
enough to read and write by, to plan, enough to strip his
weapons and prepare. The ice had sunk, hissing, below the
waterline. He leant forward on the sleeping bench and added
the tea. Life had many small comforts. He was waiting.*

'So, a lady chokes to death in your arms on the train, Colonel.
Your relationships don't get easier, do they?'

Vakulchuk – sidekick and irritant – entered without
knocking. A small, spare man in an ill-fitting uniform, he
perched unbidden on the side of the desk like some paramilitary goblin.

'Yuri Andreyevich.' Lazin addressed him without looking
up. 'Captain,' he added emphatically. 'It was luck which
saved you from a lifetime as a prison guard, nepotism which
gained you your present position. So don't be clever, don't
overstretch your abilities.'

Vakulchuk grinned, arms crossed defiantly. 'The Siberian
winter has improved your temper, I see.' A grunt from the
Colonel. 'How's Kokhlov?'

'Mad. But his career's progressing better than ours.'

'I never should have tied my promotion prospects so
closely to yours.'

The jest was half-meant. Lazin felt little sympathy. The

man was lazy, but probably more loyal than the rest, a good-natured time-server, a break with the ideological zealots who had once populated and prowled these corridors, falling over themselves in their incompetence and eagerness to enforce Party insanity. Comrade Fedorovitch has made anti-Statist remarks; Comrade Petrov was overheard being slanderous; Comrade This praised Western imperialism and corruption; Comrade That has reactionary tendencies. Hearsay, gossip, each denunciation, every unneighbourly grudge, was filed or followed up.

Lazin stopped checking his papers and made eye-contact. 'You would have missed the excitement without me in your life.'

'I have children, family, a dacha to build. I have enough excitement. What I need is advancement and real pay.'

'Don't you get that for babysitting me, reporting back to the higher levels?' It was Lazin's turn to half-jest.

'You think I'd . . .'

'If you didn't, I'd think you were a poor Secret Policeman.'

A sly smile. 'There's no pleasing you, Colonel.'

Lazin indicated the pile of papers. 'After a trip like that, nothing pleases me. I visit the most godforsaken places on earth, an old woman vomits and dies on me, I deal with commanders in decaying military installations who hibernate till summer on ethyl-alcohol, and my best friend out there entertains me in a morgue.'

'Forget I ever said I wanted a promotion.'

'Where's Ivanov?'

'Rumour has it somewhere up the Director's arse.' More helpfully. 'He hasn't been seen in his office for a while. Probably on Special Assignment.'

Special Assignment. Lazin tried not to let the frustration show, tried his damnedest, but there was no fooling himself – probably no fooling Vakulchuk – that in this world of mediocrity, he shone as the best, had the instinct and the nerve to excel, and was therefore mistrusted and shunned by those above. He got results and in doing so illuminated the glaring weaknesses of the rest, showed them as fools, made him different and them fear. Sidelined to Static Security, he created a niche; passed over, he created an energy and gained departmental quasi-cult status. Georgi Lazin: one-time adviser to the Eastern Bloc's counter-espionage apparats, spycatcher, foiler of CIA technical operations on Soviet soil, senior liaison officer to Khad – the Afghan Security Police – during a war of occupation to which he objected. A decorated officer of the KGB's Second Chief Directorate, alone and successfully he had negotiated with the mujahideen for the return of five captured 'Kaskad' Eighth Directorate signals intelligence technicians alive and with balls attached. Georgi Lazin, has-been and folk-hero. Special assignments did not come to his desk.

The telephone, a requisitioned field model, marsh green as the office, rang once. Lazin reached for it. 'Lazin.' The message was short. 'Well,' he said, replacing the receiver while Vakulchuk looked on, eyebrow angled. 'Our esteemed Director is seeking an audience.'

'He's firing you. I've warned you before. I'm taking over the department. Wait and see.'

He received a frank and cruel expression in response. 'Actually, it's to discuss you. He didn't appreciate your remarks just now about Ivanov being lodged in his alimentary canal.'

Vakulchuk seemed frozen, worry seared on his face, as Lazin left the room. A troubled goblin.

At its best, the city of Brussels was a bland, self-important Mecca for technocrats, Eurocrats and bureaucrats. At its worst, it was a provincial town with delusions of pan-continental status, home to a hundred faceless buildings and ten thousand faceless civil servants, a refuge for failed national politicians, for those who could not account for the annual disappearance of ten billion euros, a repository for unelected men and women with Benelux accents and an evangelical belief that the role of the nation state and an elected parliament was dead. The Napoleonic dream of an all-pervasive, micro-managing executive lived on in its halls, corrupt, corrupting, and growing stronger. People were backward, would be dragged into the light, screaming if necessary. And always ignored. Brussels, where whistle-blowers were muzzled, and the window-jumps of senior and suicidal officers were hushed up and mopped down.

In the Year 2000, a group of officials, concerned at the fluctuating popularity of the Commission, met to brainstorm radical options for blunting the negative impact of anti-European 'saboteurs'. They would have been surprised to learn that one of their proposals, later discarded – to establish an intelligence-gathering body tasked with monitoring and actively countering disruptive and unwelcome scepticism – had become reality some years before. Article K1 of the 1997 Treaty of Amsterdam laid down specific objectives for supranational teams to combat 'racism and xenophobia'. Classing doubters of the European dream as xenophobic was an easy and logical step. They were enemies: surveillance was legitimised. But the members at that meeting did not know. Few did.

The man, at a glance – though none bothered – was probably late forties, possibly early fifties, pushing his way inconspicuously through a revolving door out onto the rue Belliard to hail a taxi. The suit was crumpled, shirt-collar pleading for starch beneath a tired but otherwise unremarkable face, all the signs of a night shift dragged too long into the morning. Even the briefcase looked fatigued. The journey was short, with little communication between driver and passenger, the cab heading out of the Eurodistrict towards the city centre, along rue de la Loi, past the Belgian parliament, Parc de Bruxelles and Royal Palace, and down the rue Royale before turning onto the historic cobblestones of Petit and Grand Sablon. It stopped in a quiet tree-lined street of modest houses with wooden shutters, an architectural expression of refinement and restraint since lost in the wider metropolis. The man checked his watch – enough time for a shower and shave – paid, and with the briefest of glances in each direction headed for a front door. Two minutes, four keys and a sophisticated alarm system later, he was past the steel-backed screen, the wrought-iron security gate beyond and into the interior, placing the case down on a hall table and struggling wearily out of his jacket. First priority was coffee and a Gauloise. Then he could think of ablutions and the imminent prospect of becoming significantly wealthier than he had been a few hours previously.

His was a small office. Security relied more on the common bonds of friendship, trust and familiarity born from long-term professional partnership than on any stipulated vetting or search procedure. Unlucky, for he felt nothing for these. Unluckier that he was head of departmental security. Shared secrets, lives and guilt: these were the buildings blocks of *Directorate-General 1(x)*, the organisation hidden on the unexplored floors of the European Commission. DG-1 itself was the premier league, dealing with the wholly legitimate aspects of international relations beyond the territorial confines of the European Union. *DG-1 (x)* was unconnected, its title merely a cover. There were thirty staff, dedicated, multilingual and with access to extensive informant networks. Most had gained their intelligence-gathering experience working within the RG, *Renseignements Generaux*, France's Secret Police, penetrating national trade unions, radical political groups and any association deemed worthy of covert monitoring at home. This often meant simply all organisations. RG was a law unto itself, and largely beyond the law, known to keep files on up to sixty thousand French media and press journalists, tapping their telephones, searching their dustbins and their closets, looking for leverage and the raw material of coercion. To RG, no area was out of bounds, nothing was illegitimate; political interference was part of its raison d'être. Democratic it was not, but it was so very French, an institution, a way of life – rather like the European Commission itself. Here, in

Brussels, the operatives' targets were different: a European Member of Parliament with a weakness for gambling, a Bavarian conservative with his fingers in too many businesses, a raw-boned and particularly uncharming Scottish parliamentarian who could not believe his luck when a shapely language student from Spain played rough and tumble without his wife's knowledge. Hard fact or drinks party innuendo, newspaper interview or radio broadcast, the information was received, the evidence collated, and profiles formed. There were follow-ups, stake-outs, recordings and photographs. Few public figures, with or without a view on the European dimension, but who might one day have a casting vote, were spared. Today's throwaway line might be tomorrow's knife-edge veto.

The doorbell rang. He splashed his face and dried it hurriedly, walking through to greet the visitor.

'Who is it?'

'Delivery for a Monsieur Dupont.'

'He is not here.'

'Then I will leave a card.'

The envelope came through; he tore it open – confirmation of a bank payment with contact details. He went to the briefcase and extracted three envelopes: two large and concertinaed, one smaller and reinforced. They contained the latest reports on senior European politicians, their foibles and peccadilloes, and a laser disk record of telephone and e-mail use. A call to the bank confirmed what the note had already told him. He pushed the packages to unseen hands waiting to receive. An easy trade, no-one got hurt, and he was richer by fifty thousand dollars.

The London cabbie adjusted his rearview mirror to achieve a better view, an optimum angle. Oh my God, he thought, I'm going to crash, I'm going to crash. She sat there, completely Gucci, from the top of her cashmere trenchcoat to the bottoms of her royal blue trouser suit, immaculate, poised, a vision, and he wanted to pull over and stare. *De trop*, darling, *de trop*; she was too beautiful for this place, this vehicle. Should he offer to wipe down the seats, wax-polish the cab, place his coat on the ground as she stepped out? She must be a supermodel. Brown is the new black, grey is the new brown, royal blue is just *her*. Whoever she was, whatever she did, strange things were happening to his jaded hormones. He was not certain if it were a curse or a blessing that she had booked him for the whole morning in order to visit rental properties around Chelsea, concentrating mainly on the expensive apartments to be found in Sloane and Molton Streets.

'Where to next, Miss?'

He saw the reflection of perfect white teeth framed in a perfect smile by perfectly formed and sensual lips.

'Nell Gwynn House please. I have a couple of places I'd like to see there.' The English was slightly accented, but the words fluent. No, he couldn't place her. He knew where he would like to place her.

'Rightio.' The wheel wobbled slightly in his hand. She could make men do foolish things, spend a great deal of money. 'Your English is very good.' He could feel himself blushing, and blushed further. It was pathetic, but he felt unworthy, inadequate, small. Keep to small talk, the usual driver-passenger banalities, and you'll be safe, Clive.

'In my work, it helps to speak English well.'

What do you do? He asked silently. And what's wrong with international body language? They drove past a flower stall, the numbed, frozen seller flapping his arms and blowing on his hands. There was little change passing into them for his over-priced winter roses. The cabbie suppressed an urge to swerve and purchase the entire stock for his designer-fantasy in the rear. She would only laugh. He did not blame her. Get a grip, he mouthed at himself, before clenching his teeth and breathing heavily through his nose.

'If it's not rude, can I ask where you come from?' he said.

'The Ukraine. And no, it's not rude at all.' He had just thought of a new holiday destination for himself and the wife. The wife? She had no right to intrude at such a private moment.

He had to ask. 'What's your job? Model? Business-woman?' She was unlike any of the buttoned-up female investment bankers he picked up in the Square Mile.

'I'm what you call a working girl.'

'Right.' There was silence. Obviously, her grasp of the English vernacular was not entirely faultless.

'I'm a prostitute,' she explained helpfully. Oh my God, emergency, he was thinking. He needed to find a cashpoint machine, had to tap into his joint-account. The explanations could be dreamt up later. 'Are you shocked?' No, simply doing some mental arithmetic. Perhaps she needed a pimp, someone to look after her.

'Aren't you a bit out of season?' was his next question.

Most of the classy international whores followed the Gulf Arabs to London for their summer break. It was a ritual, a camel-train, a trade route and root, one thousand bucks a throw, four thousand plus for a weekend, doubles, quits, cocktails and cocks – all kinds – and then the migration back to Dubai or Bahrain when the cold fronts hit the Northern Hemisphere and the warm fronts sought new climes and clients. Working your passage, sometimes overworking it, but you travelled internationally, met interesting types and improved your cashflow and linguistics. Miss World, the flip-side.

The hours and addresses passed. She left, a goddess who, for a morning at least, had fallen from bed to earth and made a cabbie happy. He again altered his rearview – for a better view of her rear – and thought of Spring. It wasn't fair. It simply wasn't fair.

She had found what she was looking for: a pink-bricked mansion block near Cadogan Square. Several of its discreet, high-ceilinged apartments were offered as short-term lets by a family trust whose aristocratic membership had been depleted by overdoses of widely varying drink-and-drug combos. Anonymity, lack of contact, suited her well. Within a week she had moved in to the fully-furnished property and out of her temporary base at a central London hotel. Her modelling assignment was over, she told the receptionist. What a glamorous lifestyle, the envious and admiring staff thought, little realising that the young woman laughing as she sought to squeeze hat-boxes into the cab would – quite literally – kill to avoid any flashbulb or the glare of publicity. She was, after all, a graduate with top honours from a certain Dzerzhinsky espionage academy near Moscow, tutored in the theory and practice of extortion and blackmail. Her looks were an international passport and access code, her body a pass key and lock-pick to boardrooms, research centres and briefcases, her brain a storage-tray for technical and strategic information. Brussels, London, Washington, assignments could take her anywhere, establishing networks, running agents, seducing informants, laundering money. An employee of Leonid Gresko, she was one of his brightest and best. She would not let her Director down.

Midnight, Ipatiev's house, the 'House of Special Purpose' as decreed by the Urals Regional Soviet. The drunk Avadeyev and his loutish, pilfering guards from the local Zlokazovsky factory had been replaced a fortnight earlier by *Letts* – outsiders – quiet, professional men, who kept themselves aloof from the occupants of the floor above.

'Wake up.' The voice was low, unemotional. Yurovsky, the cold one, the leader, shook the sleeping man. There was stirring. 'Wake up, Comrade. The cars are coming to collect you. Dress and come downstairs, we are moving you to a new location. There is not much time.'

The words urged haste, yet the tone lacked urgency. Methodical, precise, calculated – the delivery, the creature, the organisation. Jacob Yurovsky, *Cheka* to his heartless core. The man was awake now. What was the time? What new location? Cars? More likely to be horse-drawn peasant *tarantasses*, tumbrils. They were used to being shunted like baggage. Yet Christ had suffered more. They must be strong.

Ivanov watched the family descend. They did not make much sound. The father 'Nikolasha' came first, carrying the ill, transparently pale boy in his arms, followed by his wife, the German bitch, their daughters and the few remaining servants. He might have been curious, but the political education, the rallies, and the dehumanising effect of the war, had expunged any real interest, compassion or the desire to make human connection with the prisoners. They were nothing to him, would be nothing at all to anyone. For days he, Yurovsky and Comrade Goloshchekin had scoured the area for a suitable hiding place. He found it himself, hoped that it would be mentioned in the report sent back to Felix Dzerzhinsky in Moscow.

The maid, Demidova, clutching two pillows, stumbled angrily and bleary-faced down the stairs and glared at him. He ignored her. Anger never helped anyone, could not help them now. But lackeys were unforgiving creatures if their masters were inconvenienced. Demidova had been more than inconvenienced: treated with contempt for months, bullied, abused, insulted, spat at, and for months she responded with protective indignation. What was she against the Chekists sent from their base at the Hotel America? One of the girls stumbled, was supported by another. Ivanov could not remember their names.

He walked behind Yurovsky into the small basement room where they had been herded.

'You will remain here, comrades, until we come for you.'

'If we are to wait, I would like chairs for my wife and my son,' the man asked. He exuded calmness, dignity, a presence which stilled the fears of those around him.

Yurovsky nodded. Three chairs were passed through; Ivanov positioned them in a row. The man seated his wife, taking the chair beside her, the thirteen-year-old boy lolling drowsily against his father's shoulder from the third. Ivanov chucked him on the chin and playfully cuffed the peak of his military cap. The boy smiled weakly. Nice enough lad. Behind stood the four daughters – the youngest, Anastasia, holding a spaniel in her arms – and with them the cook Kharitonov, the valet Trupp, the family doctor and the parlourmaid. Demidova was fussing, placing one of the pillows behind her mistress' back.

'Where's Joy? She's not with us. Papa, we can't leave Joy.' It was one of the girls, anguished at the thought of losing one of the family pets. She looked pleadingly at her father and then at Yurovsky. 'Jimmy will really miss her.'

'Marie is right, Papa,' Anastasia joined in, bouncing the pet in her arms to emphasise the point.

'Hush now, my darlings.' The father swivelled to touch Marie tenderly on the arm. 'I'm sure Joy will be all right.'

'The other dog will be sent on later. Have no worries.' Yurovsky turned on his heel and moved out with Ivanov, shutting the door behind him. His junior looked back and saw the expression on the German woman's face. It was empty, the mind far beyond the small cellar room, perhaps reaching back to the troika rides, the dances in St Petersburg, the picnics on the Baltic, the summer cruises on the yacht. Perhaps she was in a trance, self-hypnotised – there were many strange rumours about her.

The men were waiting for them in the guard room, dressed in black, ready, completely loyal. The five Hungarians stood together speaking softly in their own tongue, the Russians were drinking vodka.

'Now.'

The door into the basement room opened as Yurovsky re-entered. Behind him the rest of the squad filed in. Ten Chekists facing ten prisoners. The family watched, the faces opposite were blank. Marie wished to ask if they had found Joy, the spaniel, but did not. There was a stillness, the transient edge between normality and action, between mundanity and grand epic gesture, when nothing happened, breath held waiting for the moment.

Yurovsky stepped forward to address the man directly, his voice as modulated and devoid of inflection as it always was.

'Your relations have tried to save you. They have failed.

We must now shoot you.' He raised the pistol.

'What ...?' The eyes, those kind, concerned eyes, widened, the man moving to rise from his seat to cover his family, an arm flung across to defend his wife, the other hugging his son close.

Eternity in a microsecond, a historic tableau framed by the flash, still-life frozen, a human life taken, captured, forced out in the expanding sound of a gunshot. Blood – so black – beginning to cascade from the forehead into the man's greying beard, the eyes now sad, now mystified, now dead, wobbling beneath the punctured cortex. He fell. His wife, the German, made the sign of the cross. Ivanov brought his revolver up and fired twice. Behind her, Olga and Tatiana looked down in wonderment, their clothes sprayed with their mother.

Smoke, blood – so much of it – displaced flesh and bone, noise. Noise so great it no longer registered to the ear, but shook through the body, butchered their bodies. And screams. Mouths opening and closing, limbs waved in hopeless gestures of supplication and panic, shrieks emitted, but not heard. *Fire, fire, fire, fire* ... The blasts were continuous, wall plaster blackened, reddened, blown away by violent impact. Ivanov's eyes watered, stung, his nostrils burned by the acrid cordite. He did not feel it; he did not feel anything. *Fire, fire, fire, fire* ... Hammers rising and falling, bodies disappearing below the sightline. He was out of ammunition, standing in something wet. He saw himself open the door, lean through and take a rifle, return, chamber a round and resume. Messy. Humans could take so long to die. It was a trance, a pagan rite, a sacrifice.

A ringing, just a ringing. The shooting had stopped, but the residue of onslaught blanketed all the senses. Ivanov closed, stabbing with his bayonet, plunging deep, damp foot placed on unrecognised bodies to withdraw the blade. Resistance, give, sucking retrieval. The spaniel was balled up, shaking, half-covered by a splintered chair and a corpse. Ivanov reversed the rifle and brought the butt down on its head. They advanced in a line towards the maid pressed into a corner. Demidova watched the oncoming blades, trapped, transfixed, head working jerkily. The defiance, the glares of contrived superiority were gone, replaced by the wild irrationality of adrenalin and flight where no flight was available. She held the pillow tight. They came on. There were no words from her, no words from anyone, only her screeching, wails punctuated by short yelps, as she ran back and forth along the wall frantic to escape the stabbing. The pillow was ripped, Ivanov bursting through while she sought to use it, use anything, in fending off the blows. Others followed. Feathers, down, ballooned out – turning festive blizzard-pink – and she kept on running and scrabbling, scrabbling. The sounds were becoming whimpers, the blood lumpy. They were not lumps, but imperial jewels, mostly rubies, hidden and stitched into the pillow and released by the butchery. Demidova died, carved up, face pushed against the wall, crying while she sank at a smear of her own and her tormentor's making.

A quiet groan. Was it a groan? Ivanov tried to shake the deafness from his ears. It was the boy, twitching, still lying across his father, clutching at the buttons of the torn, smoking greatcoat, seeking a comforting hand. The heir. He walked across and stamped down. Again. Yurovsky knelt and fired into the thirteen-year-old's ear. There was more screaming. The girl, Anastasia, had come round from her faint, was half-sitting in the pool produced by her siblings. The Chekists turned their attention to her. The end. Ivanov saw a small emerald cross, spattered, around the neck of the Empress. It had become the property of the State. He wrenched it from its chain – the body still trembled slightly in life's aftermath – gave it a cursory wipe and pocketed it.

It was before daybreak on 17 July 1918 when the bodies of the Russian Imperial Family – Tsar, Tsarina and their five children – and their handful of staff from the royal suite, were slung onto trucks for the short trip to the abandoned mine near the 'Four Brothers' pines fifteen miles beyond

Ekaterinburg's city limits. There they were dismembered with axes and saws, the limb bones placed and partially melted in drums of sulphuric acid, the remaining body parts and smaller bones burned on towering pyres of wood and gasoline. The residue was thrown into a nearby flooded shaft. Orders carried out, the family transferred successfully. Ivanov joined his colleagues on the third and final day of their labours. He had been busy, throwing Elizabeth Fyodorov, the Tsar's sister-in-law, down the well next to Ipatiev's house. She survived for two days, until he pumped down gas to finish her off.

Within a week, Ekaterinburg fell to the White Russian forces advancing from the south, the Bolsheviks retreating to regroup and re-arm. Into the city clattered the first units of cavalry, a detachment of officers galloping hard for Ipatiev's house up on the hill. They dismounted, drew swords and pistols and approached the front door. It was locked.

'Stand back.' He was medium height, well-muscled, dark, close-cropped hair, oak-brown eyes set in a field of radiating stress lines and mounted above an aquiline nose. A young man grown old by war. He was different from the others: a presence, a natural commander. The door was kicked in. 'The top rooms,' he ordered, taking two lieutenants to check downstairs.

He knew, understood as soon as he entered. The room, sixteen feet by eighteen, was scrubbed, over-scrubbed, a place of execution, of evidence washed and slopped away, an abattoir stripped clean. At one end, the wall was pitted and pock-marked more heavily than the others, plaster removed, plaster scorched, gouged in places by the multiple strikes of heavy blades. He approached and placed his fingers in the bullet holes, wanting to feel, to witness, to experience; Doubting Thomas without the doubt. He leant against the wall, smelling it, looking for the Romanov shadow, for evidence that the family existed, were once living beings.

'Captain?'

He turned. The man was holding a model battleship.

'We found it under the boy's bed, left behind.' It was the Tsarevich's favourite toy, one with which he would play for hours on his sickbed.

'Anything else?'

'There are corsets left in the cupboards of the other rooms.'

A dog's bark could be heard faintly. 'Collect them, collect everything.'

He pushed his way out towards the sound, making for the rear of the house and the courtyard. The spaniel was three-quarters starved, barely able to stand, and close to death, its eyes near-hidden by the folds of loose skin puckered on its face. The stub-tail wagged at the sound of human presence.

'Come on you little thing. I've got you,' the officer said gently, picking her up in his arms. She was 'Joy', the spaniel belonging to Alexis.

The officer knelt in the snow, frostbitten hands tied behind his back, a gun to his head. It was so cold, so cold, and so many dead. He had mapped out his life in battles, won or lost, and this had been lost. Yet it was worth it, worth every moment. He would be forgotten, but he was a soldier. There were others to remember. He thought back to the basement room in Ekaterinburg, to the broken wall and the charred fragments of earthly existence found down the mine. For four years he had fought in their memory; now he was facing their fate and their oblivion. How was his wife, his son? They were far away in time, in space. Would they remember him? Would they receive the letter and photograph smuggled out in the last days of battle? And Natasha, friend and sometime lover, working in Moscow as secretary to Zinoviev at the Communist International, minute-taker of the meetings with Lenin, Trotsky, Kamenov and that Georgian bureaucrat Stalin, privy to their plans to export Bolshevism around the globe – what of her? Her survival chances . . . He stared into the grey half-light. Everything had gone, even the spaniel, that bundle of life taken from the place of death, his constant companion since he picked her up, placed her inside his jacket and rode away with her from the House of Special Purpose, the house on the hill. A green hill far away. The words fell into his mind, English hymns, English singing, another country. *Pray for us now* . . .

'I have been ordered by the Extraordinary Commission for Combating Counter-revolutionaries and Sabotage to shoot you, Comrade.'

'You are no better than the Okhrana,' he replied.

The Tsar's feared Secret Police were gone, replaced by the Cheka. Regimes, rulers and politics could change, one dictatorship substituted for another, but the organs of control, the shadow world, the means for man to persecute fellow-man, stayed constant. History was not a cycle, but a fault running beneath the human race. He was tired, so very tired.

The weapon was cocked. 'This is the People's justice.'

'Then the People have been misled.' The cultivated Russian voice betrayed no tremor. He was never misled, always aware that if the support of the people were claimed or assumed they were invariably the ones being starved and shot. 'I am the lucky one.'

A misfire. Another click, another malfunction. Swearing from the executioner.

He waited calmly. 'Nothing you Bolsheviks touch will ever work. This is your legitimacy, your state, your foundation for a better world? You will kill millions, enslave millions, and then you will vanish. Your only legacy will be poison and scorched earth.'

A spin of the chambers. Aim. More dry-firing. 'The Cheka is obliged to defend the Revolution.' The man was quoting his chief, Felix Dzerzhinsky, purveyor of organised evil.

'I am glad to die.'

The commissar took the replacement revolver proffered by an underling.

'Long live the October Revolution!'

He fired once. A satisfactory and terminal conclusion. It would be repeated many times before recidivist bourgeois

111

and imperialist tendencies were crushed and the authority of the Central Committee entrenched. He, the chief executioner, leader of the Cheka's *Mokrie dyela* operations – those in which blood was to be shed – a man who had proved his loyalty and credentials long ago through participating in the murder of the Romanovs, would remain in the vanguard. Ivanov fingered the emerald cross in his pocket and stepped across the body, snow beginning to melt around it, blood steaming and puddling from the head. It was English blood, the blood of an agent of His Majesty's British Intelligence Service, the blood of a man named Piers Purton.

He ground the cigarette into the compacted snow, killed its short hiss, watched the brief steam-wisp from beneath his foot, and waited. Nature or nurture, forces had conspired to forge Petr Ivanov into a creature devoid of compassion, humour or the ability to interact with other humans where it did not involve violence or its very real threat. A cadaverous, watchful man, a light drinker in a world where alcohol proof corresponded with proof of manhood, his was a cramped soul with room only for control and calculation; life energy expended on the energy and industry of death. His psychological baggage was not that of conscience or squeamishness – a fanatical loyalty to the concept of order and centralised authority were more persuasive motivators – but of the grim recent past of family and nation. He was a born oppressor, born of an oppressor. If his mother was the Soviet Union, his father and grandfather had both been its suitors, lovers, unwavering servants and ultimately victims of its capriciousness, devoured by the fury on which they themselves had fed.

Grandfather was a founding Chekist, murderer of the Romanovs, feared enforcer for the security apparat – whether Cheka, GPU, OGPU 'State Political Administration' or NKVD 'People's Commissariat for Internal Affairs' – confidant and contemporary of its most terrifying head, Stalin's henchman Lavrenti Beria. On Beria's command, Grandpa

Ivanov had liquidated the sharp-faced Georgian's predecessor, Nikolai 'Bloody Dwarf' Yezhof; on Beria's command he toured the land seizing under-age girls for the architect of Stalin's Terror to rape, torture and kill; on Beria's command he assassinated enemies, inflicted genocide on the kulak peasantry and disappeared those who displeased his master. It was on Beria's command also that he himself was disappeared. No reason was given, none were required: boredom, paranoia, jealousy at a lieutenant's growing reputation for barbarity: all might have played a part. Beria survived until 1953 when, upon Stalin's death, he was outwitted by Khruschev, Malenkov and their political cronies, summoned to a meeting at the Kremlin, arrested and later shot.

By then, Petr Ivanov's father Konstantin was already working for State Security, far enough removed from the centre not to be viewed by Beria as a direct threat, his skills honed in the wartime Smersh – *Smert Shpionam* or 'Death to Spies,' one of Stalin's Special Branches. His abilities as judge, juror and executioner were put to good use in the organisation's first and fifth Departments, passing sentence on 'traitors and defeatists' and leading army punishment squads against dissenters in the ranks. It was said the Soviet soldier fought so fiercely because he feared those behind more than he feared the enemy in front. Konstantin Ivanov personified all that was feared. Smersh was absorbed into the KGB in 1946, its operatives given new directives. The Cold War temperature was plummeting, competition with the West increasing, and the Soviet stamp of authority had to be branded on the new Eastern Bloc territories. Assigned to 'Administrative Measures', Ivanov was the branding tool, the instrument of institutionalised terror, touring the Communist map and visiting the internment centres swelling with dissidents, liberals, Social Democrats, practising Christians, 'anti-State agitators,' bourgeois recidivists and counter-revolutionaries. Some were as young as eight. His favourite trips were to East Germany. Here, in the concentration and extermination camps established by the Nazis, he beat, tortured, skinned, electrocuted, hanged and drowned. At Sachsenhausen, in the Berlin suburb of Oranienberg, he cut into the flesh of victims on pathology tables once used by SS scientists; in Waldheim camp he kicked chairs from beneath the feet of youths standing with ropes around their necks, ten at a time; in Buchenwald, Forgau, Fuenfeichen and Bautzen he shot, stabbed, castrated, and injected with aminazin, sulfazin, sodium aminate and the ever-terminal potassium chloride. In the 'U-boat' torture dungeons beneath the former Hohenschoenhausen meat factory, he chain-whipped inmates until the rubber walls of the cells appeared to sweat blood; others were filled with water before their bellies were stamped on. Yet he was saving himself – for the twenty thousand young prisoners of the *jugendlager* at Ketschendorf. Over a third of them died, many coughing up their lives in the bloody froth of tuberculosis. Many also succumbed at the hands of Konstantin Ivanov. They were lucky: the rest were selected for transportation east to fuel the industrialisation of the Soviet Union, to fuel the furnaces, lay the tracks and dig the mines for a heroic Communist future. The Facilitator, building a better world. The East German Stasi secret police called him 'The Hangman.' To the inmates he was simply *Totenkopf* – 'Death's Head' – for a visit by Konstantin Ivanov meant an upsurge in brutality, a spate of mass killings and nights of endless screaming while provincial underlings sought to prove their worth, loyalty and dedication, supported assiduously by the man from Moscow. Even as an old man, he was not averse to under-takings in the style of his former department. On a chilly winter's morning in January 1984, Boris Bakhlanov, Russian defector, one-time Smersh employee, a man unwise enough to write of his former activities, was discovered face-down and drowned in a shallow, icy pond in London's Wimbledon. A strange suicide. Konstantin's was stranger still. In July 1990, while on a summer cruise for retired and honoured apparatchiks around the Black Sea, he was found by a steward in his blazing cabin having apparently set himself alight with petrol and alcohol.

Petr Ivanov was the proud progeny of this line. A Colonel in the KGB's Second Chief Directorate and now the FSB, he was – like his forebears – drawn to secret police work, attracted to power and its many forms of abuse. A change of regime, the ending of Communism, had done nothing to engender within him a spirit of democracy. In his department, he was neither alone nor in a minority. When, in November 1989, the Berlin Wall was breached as a prelude to its eventual demolition and the October 1990 reunification of the two Germanies, it was Ivanov who led a special assignment squad to the GDR to trace sensitive records and to kidnap or liquidate senior Stasi officials suspected of opening a dialogue with Western intelligence agencies. A bankrupt Soviet Union could not afford to buy their loyalty or silence – Ivanov was the cheaper solution. While legendary Cold War spy chief Markus Wolf, former head of East Germany's Foreign Intelligence Service, hid out in Moscow and dined during Christmas 1990 with the then KGB chief Vladimir Kryuchkov, he was unaware of the presence of several of his countrymen and work-colleagues undergoing different entertainment in cells not a mile from where he sat. Ivanov was a diligent host. He was a professional at whatever assignment he undertook.

He had lit another cigarette when he saw the man approach, negotiate a path flooded and iced-over for the skaters, and pick his way across the snow to his clump of silver birches. He smelt coffee on his breath.

'You're late. I don't pay you to stuff your face on Tretyakov Gallery pastries.' It was unfair. He had just eaten a large breakfast of eggs and fried potatoes at the American Bar & Grill in Triumfalnaya Square. Sustained by the Americans. There was irony.

The man extracted a hip-flask, proffered it and took a gulp when it was declined. 'You pay me to do a job, which I have done.'

'I have seen the international press reaction. Most encouraging. It can only get worse.' Much worse.

The assassin looked at the thin, fleshless face, skin cling-wrap taut and fish-white, mouth an anaemic slash set below the featureless nose and hollowed eyes. A skull with few extras, the domed forehead and thinned hair scraped short against a crown hidden by black sable. Truly the son of Konstantin Ivanov.

The Death's Head spoke again. 'Let us walk.'

From any distance they were two unrecognised and unrecognisable Muscovites, behatted, coat-wearing, indistinguishable from the rest, save that one man was large enough to wrestle a brown bear. A young skater, red-faced from exertion and cold, pushed past, blades scraping and travelling. They watched.

In an environment where Russia's armed forces had become toothless, in which anti-state gangsterdom and lawlessness were rife, military units which remained effective, capable of responding flexibly to a range of terrorist and low-intensity scenarios, were greatly prized and in high demand. They were the *spetsgruppy* – Special Groups – and those absorbed, inherited or home-grown by the FSB Federal Security Service were the best available. There was the counter-terrorist 'Alpha' group – used to overcome the anti-Yeltsin coup plotters in 1993 – backed by regional offshoots and its Beta training unit; the 'Zenit' special security organisation, and finally the 'Vega' squad tasked specifically with combating air and nuclear-based terrorism. They came under the aegis of the Service's Special Operations Directorate, to which Ivanov was attached. And they reported directly to FSB head Leonid Gresko.

The individual walking with Ivanov in Gorky Park belonged to none of these. His team had once been answerable only to the foreign intelligence wing of the KGB, the First Chief Directorate, before being passed to the Interior Ministry and losing most of its 180-man contingent in mass resignations. Its name was 'Vympel' – Banner, in English –

and it was used for infiltration, sabotage, disruption and assassination on enemy territory. A former operative, and now freelance, the man had performed many missions for Ivanov. His most recent involved the murder of a Russian boy at a boarding school situated in the English countryside.

They stopped awhile, talking softly, grey forms in a grey light. Ivanov unbuttoned the top of his greatcoat and withdrew an envelope.

'These are the details. Total deniability applies. See that it is done.'

The man pocketed the orders and walked away. Ivanov placed another cigarette in his mouth and felt for a lighter. The small emerald cross was there. To him it was nothing religious, no aid to prayer or meditation, but a talisman, a memory, a family jewel. It was a reminder of how much could be seized by force, how fragile was authority, how easily a life and a nation might be taken with the barrel of a gun. There was tradition to be maintained.

CHAPTER 3

The building was heroic-grey, its massive bulk set along the broad sweep of Kuznetsky Most and surrounded by its architectural clones. In the heart of Moscow's administrative district, it was a short walk from Leonid Gresko's office in Lubyanka Square, a longer one from the President's. Stalin and his henchman Beria had kept apartments here once, launch pads for their extracurricular, extra-Kremlin activities, bolt-holes from the hurly-burly world of dictatorship. Uncle Joe painting the town red – with whatever came to hand. The entrance hall was modest, deceptively so, one of the city's more unhelpful potato-fed, potato-faced grandmothers sitting motionless in the gloom of the interior, her role in office and life to man four antiquated telephones and to glare malevolently at visitors. In front of her were three elevators, without call-buttons, and a locked steel security door which could be opened only from inside. Those seeking an audience on the floors above would, after reporting first to the impassive gate-guardian, get collected and taken through the doorway for a full and thorough search and accompanied out to an elevator for its pre-set journey to an upper level. Having endured this less-than-Western ideal of a public relations exercise, some chose to cancel appointments and head straight for the exit. Had they opted to stay, they would have been only dimly aware of the formidable security apparatus arrayed beyond: cameras on every sealed corridor, heavily armed guards standing in front and behind every blast-proof entrance to every floor. Imagination was generally enough. The corporate headquarters of Boris

119

Diakanov, crime boss, was always going to be a fortress.

The meeting was underway, not so much a committee as a council – of war. Diakanov sat at the head, black-suited in mourning, Irina at his side, his senior lieutenants spread out around the length of the baize-covered table. Natural light had been excluded by the heavy, brocaded curtains drawn across the row of great windows at the far end of the room; the double-glazing contained copper-matrix and active-noise devices to overload external eavesdropping; the room was electronically swept and the doors locked. They were secure. Above their heads an intricate turn-of-the-century chandelier bathed the panelling in gentle iridescence, colours falling on the sombre oil portraits of historic Russian conquerors, merchants and traders, piratical figures who had gained fame and market share through sheer force of character and through sheer force. To Diakanov they were not merely heroes, but antecedents – family – quirk of fate alone preventing ties to him by blood. Blood was why he was here today.

'What do we do?' He stared about him, his dark eyebrows coming together to emphasise the rage, the grief. There was silence. Some looked down; most gazed straight ahead. It was best not to catch his eye. 'I asked a question.'

Behind, incongruous, attached in brackets to the wall was a baseball bat signed by the Chicago Cubs and presented to him by the head of one of the United States' most successful crime syndicates. He called it his 'Untouchables' bat, for the Hollywood evocation of Capone's table-manners appealed to his sense of humour. Unfortunately, *tsisari*'s humour was known to be of a practical, hands-on variety. He did not discourage comparisons with the Chicago mobster of the prohibition era – both were businessmen; both filled market needs; both transcended rigid ethnic divisions to dominate respective empires, one from the Hotel Metropole the other from palatial residences in and around Moscow. But there were major differences Diakanov enjoyed pointing to. Capone ruled a city whereas he ruled a nation; Capone was jailed, while he would never be troubled by such irrelevances. He was the true Untouchable. Such comments were made in lighter moments; today was not a lighter moment.

'My son – dead!' The flat of his hand hit the table. Water trembled in a glass twenty feet away on the green swathe. He waited and slammed down the palm a second time. 'Dead!' Liquid slopped from the nearer tumblers and clung together in glass beads on the surface. 'And no one has answers. You, Konon.' He pointed at a bespectacled, glum-looking individual halfway along. 'You have suggestions?'

The man stiffened, uncomfortable – fearful – at being singled out. 'Our contacts in the Security Service are examining every aspect for us, chief.'

No institution was immune to the pervasive corruption of Russian criminality. Officers moonlighted, passed across databases, leaked secretly acquired evidence and enjoyed the patronage of the new gangster emperors. The private sector paid better, and in foreign denominations. Even KGB General Valery Monastiretsky, one-time head of the state's FAPSI electronic eavesdropping service, had been charged with diverting millions of dollars to his numbered bank account. Diakanov was the information beneficiary; a pity the man became greedy. No one was irreplaceable. Except his beloved Oleg, his only son. He was irreplaceable.

'What are we paying them?'

'Two thousand dollars a month.' That was ten times the average FSB employee's government salary. Refusals of such generosity were rare.

'Double it, recruit more agents – I want their departments turned over. Offer a bonus for anyone who gets a lead.' Konon nodded. He was an old KGB hand who had crossed to free enterprise five years earlier, exchanged his battered Volga for a brand new Mercedes, his wife for a carousel of hostesses and hookers. There were moments when he regretted it.

Diakanov closed his eyes, reaching out to squeeze Irina's hand for several seconds. The eyes opened a fraction. 'Who?'

Deadpan, frightening. 'That is all I want. Who killed my son in cold blood? There is no limit to what I will pay.' There was no limit to what he would do to the murderer. Traitor? 'All resources will be assigned to this. You.' Another aide was singled out. 'Who is it?'

'I do not know, ch . . .'

'Get out! You fucking whore, get out!' He was on his feet, striding round, dragging the man over the back of his chair. 'I could slit your fucking throat. My son is dead, and you say nothing! Nothing!' The man was choking, clutching to relieve pressure, Diakanov screaming in close-up. Face-to-face, both distorted, one with incandescence, the other through lack of oxygen. The assembled court watched silently. Their boss was under great strain, appeared to be screwing a pistol into the ear of their colleague. 'Oleg died like this, like this.' The pistol was pushed deeper, the angle of the chair became more pronounced, balance maintained only by the grip on a constricted throat. 'And you sit here, alive!' Pistol extracted, brought down rhythmically on the face. 'Fed by me . . . clothed by me . . . housed by me . . . paid by me . . . for nothing!' Five blows; heavy blood-spill. The minutes-taker placed down his pen.

A stillness followed the shot, the violence of the noise detaching the onlookers from the scene, sealing them in worlds of self-contained echo from where they watched slow-motion, unable to move. A spell.

It broke. Agonised wheezing as the man, barely conscious, scrabbling on his back to keep up, one hand flailing for support, the other still protecting his windpipe, was pulled across the floor by his tie. A kick was administered and he disappeared through the opened door. Soundproofing failed to prevent the noise of vomiting reaching the remaining group. They pretended not to glance at the dark stains radiating across the table from the vacated position, nor at the baseball bat cradled on the wall and the shattered ceiling frieze.

Diakanov resumed his place, physical anger temporarily

dissipated, worked through, diversions forgotten. Meeting declared open.

'Next on the agenda?'

A sharp dresser, tie and suit made more vivid by overlaid flecks of drying blood, the Georgian neighbouring the empty seat spoke up unprompted. 'The FSB has become involved in searching for the group responsible for attacking the diamond train near the mouth of the Baikal mountain tunnel at Daban.'

The matter was close to Diakanov's heart. Siberia was his personal fiefdom, the BAM railway running across its northern wastes through Buryatiya, Amur Oblast and Sakha, a profit artery feeding many of the ventures which he operated from Moscow. Building started in the 1930s, and scores of men – slaves – had died for every sleeper laid. If the winter did not get them, the deadly encephalitis-carrying *Ixodes tic* of the summer, or TB, starvation, executions and near-indescribable levels of human brutality generally finished the job. Diakanov senior had survived it, prospered, for he was a harder man than any guard, took a cut from the mining and forestry concerns, ran protection in the dismal rotting towns spread along the railway's length, pilfered, plundered and extorted from the state, organised and sold labourers to the highest bidders. Commissars who crossed him had their tongues cut out and reproductive organs removed. His son continued with similar methods, a matching philosophy. And now a shipment of uncut precious stones had been stolen, diamonds for whose safe passage Diakanov was responsible. Commission vanished, face lost, standing reduced. Robbed in his backyard. The implications would not be wasted on his own men or on the thrusting criminal syndicates waiting to bring him down. Scavengers. He would have to make an example.

'There's an army base there. Were they asleep or paid off?' he asked.

The Georgian, survivor of the gulag, and a better knifeman than Diakanov, kept the sight line level. 'Shot, chief.

Six guards at the tunnel entrance to meet the train and check the papers were all killed.'

'How quickly did the base respond?'

'Two hours later when a new detail went out. A radio report was sent an hour before claiming everything was fine.'

Another individual spoke. 'We can assume it was false.'

'You will assume nothing.' A visible swallow; sweat squeezed the colour out of the man's face. 'And the guards at the other end of the tunnel?' Diakanov turned back to the Georgian. 'Didn't the driver report to them when he came through?'

'They were dead too, chief. The driver's radio was smashed. The attackers strapped a bomb to him, attached it to a tacograph-type device. If he slowed or stopped before he reached Ust-Kut, three hundred kilometres west, or outside a certain time, it would have exploded.'

'He'll wish it did. Where is he now?'

The man named Konon checked his notes. 'Co-driver was taken away by the attackers. Driver himself is under militia protection at Taishet.'

'Good. Have him handed over to us as soon as it can be arranged.'

'Yes chief.'

'What does this say to you?' He did not wait for a response; the committee were relieved. 'It says professionalism, it says conspiracy.' He stood, and tension climbed with it. 'Eastern Siberia, at night, a covert transit of gems, near a base for railway troops. There's no obvious escape route, snow blanks the evidence. And guards die. What an operation. That takes careful planning.' He clapped a hand on the shoulder of a seated boyar. 'That takes careful preparation.' The man was basalt. Diakanov shifted on to another lieutenant. 'So, it says inside involvement.' The baseball bat was eyed uneasily, but the chief had moved back to the head of the table. 'Someone talked, opened their mouth too wide. I want to know who; I want to widen it some more. Speak to contacts at the BAM railway headquarters in Tynda, speak to the stooges in the Ministry of Rail control room. Anyone.' A different tack. 'Are FSB involved, or just the investigators from Rail Troops?'

'They've sent a colonel,' Konon replied. 'Gresko's given him full authority on the case. He wants to demonstrate that State Security cannot tolerate such blatant acts against government property.'

They were not alone in that, Diakanov thought grimly. Parallel armies would hunt down these hidden opponents; his was the strongest, and the most vengeful. In recent years, the FSB had opted to imprison traitors rather than to execute them summarily. *Tsisari* preferred an older value system, a code of justice which worked.

Still standing, he leant forward and gripped the chair-back. 'This colonel. One of ours?'

A long pause from Konon. 'Not yet, Chief.'

'Work on him, and get our men at GRU involved. The military must be covered: they were closest to the scene when it happened.'

It was fortuitous that the Sixteenth Spetsnaz Brigade based in Moscow's south-west suburb of Teflyi Stan, from whose ranks Diakanov hired hands for the more violent aspects of his business dealings, also provided troops to guard the headquarters of GRU Military Intelligence. Officers coerced or willing to cooperate could readily palm microfilms and documents for onward transfer to the mafiya. There was no one to challenge the Spetsnaz, no one to guard the guardians.

'You know your roles. I want everything, every piece of information, every question the FSB man asks, every answer he is given. You understand?' Perfectly, and they showed it. 'Irina wishes to address you.'

She kept her voice low. The redness remained in her eyes. Oleg had not been her son, but those present recognised the surrogate bond between the two. 'We are being tested – by other groups and factions. They cannot face us, so they hide, resort to these measures.'

'They would not dare . . .' one of Diakanov's key cheer-lead courtiers began.

Irina interrupted. 'They have dared.'

'First Oleg, then the train.' Diakanov, seated once more, kept his eyes half-closed. 'There are enemies searching for weakness in us, in me. My son was murdered – as a decoy? As a trial of our resolve? We have no weaknesses. We have no pity. I want these cowards discovered. On my soul, I want them bled.'

A murmur of agreement.

Boris Diakanov, an Untouchable? He had always believed that in building and consolidating his empire, by pushing outwards and devouring the weak, he would be kept safe, that political and commercial influence was creating an unassailable position which none could challenge. Money was security, and he possessed more of both than any. Yet he had deceived himself, deceived everyone, and Oleg was buried by that deception. He would find his son's killers, discover who had taken three hundred million dollars' worth of gems from a Siberian train. *We have no weaknesses*. The lie exposed. He was weak, vulnerable, the one at risk of being devoured. Certainties had gone. Without them he felt an alien emotion, gnawing deep, making him falter. At first he did not recognise, suspect it. Then he knew. He was scared.

The Georgian coughed. He had a suggestion. 'Boss, do you think there should be a meeting of the Senate?'

There was no response. The Senate was the federation of notoriously uncooperative dons from the most powerful Russian crime organisations.

They met only if business was seriously threatened or when turf battles and simmering internecine feuds began to move from low- to high-impact street warfare. The tolerance threshold for in-fighting was high. Diakanov was President, ensuring that Moscow dominated the truly ugly specimens from St Petersburg, encouraging dispute resolution through negotiation and acknowledged superior firepower. Government troops were ever present to guard the approaches to their rare conferences; senior hostages were exchanged beforehand. Trust was grudging.

'The syndicates have sent their condolences,' the Georgian continued.

'And their wreaths and capos to the funeral. So what?'

'They have also stressed that they want stability.'

'Because they know I could turn them into bonemeal with a telephone call.' He was looking dangerous. A dozen rectums tightened involuntarily.

The Georgian persisted. 'I would suggest that the optimum way of testing loyalty is to meet them face-to-face. See what they are offering.'

'You hear that?' A shadow of a smile. No one relaxed. 'I used to take. Now I have to wait to be offered.' He laughed. It was not echoed. 'Set it up.' He scanned the faces slowly. 'Trust . . . trust.' The head was nodding. Irina leant over and whispered in his ear, distracting him, acting as a pressure-valve. He translated for the rest. 'What is the name of this investigating colonel?'

'Lazin, chief. His name is Georgi Lazin.'

He rarely enjoyed coming to London. Pollution, gridlock, meetings with his Harley Street orthopaedic consultant and the antiquated Underground system reinforced his general prejudice against the capital every time. It was cleaner than in the seventies, the grime largely removed, the bleak barbarism of Corbusier-inspired tower blocks beginning to disappear. Yet faces were greyer, commuting got harder, stress levels rose and the cosmopolitan mantle the city had brought upon itself gave inhabitants and visitors alike a greater excuse to be rude. Everything was relative to Moscow, he supposed. He wondered how Max was faring.

The car was parked east of Aldgate, on the undeveloped peripheries of the City, where squalor was a badge of honour, child benefit was smoked, and state support fed the betting shops and pay-as-you-view satellite channels. Gritty, absorbing, real-life drama, television executives would call it.

Depressing was what it was. Purton wandered slowly back, aware that a chassis on blocks might await his return. The afternoon had found him at the Kelvin Hughes office in the nearby Minories searching for Indian Ocean and Red Sea tidal tables and pilot charts. A mobile phone-call later and he was sitting with a former Royal Marine turned private-client stockbroker in a bar off Cornhill. The man was miserable, should never have left the service. After three hours they parted, the stockbroker drunk, unsteady and still angry; Purton sober and pleased to be heading for Poole.

The streets were quiet, the car untouched, darkness and the snow-carrying chill encouraging people indoors. He had immobilised the alarm and was inserting the key when the two made their approach, silent but for an air-cushioned sole brushing against a discarded beer bottle. They must have been waiting in the alleyway behind.

'Hey man, we want to talk to you.' White, aggressive.

'Got any money? Y'know what I mean?' Black, aggressive.

No other voices. Ebony and ivory, working in perfect harmony, the impressive culmination to years of progressive teaching and social work. Not as progressive as what he had in mind. No 'please', no *Big Issue*, but they wanted his wallet all the same. They would have to earn it.

A hand clamped down on his neck. There was a muscular forearm behind it. Don't tense, keep them relaxed. He was just another pensioner. Pickings.

'We've got blades, man. You want to be cut?' His preference was unlikely to be a consideration. 'Spread your legs and lean against the car.' Must have learned the procedure from a thousand police shake-downs.

He shuffled his feet wider. Better balance.

'Get your fucking wallet out. Cards, chequebook, everything, man. Slowly, fucker, 'cos I'll stab your kidneys.'

'OK, OK. I'm doing it. OK . . .' He did his best to sound frightened, to sound convincing. Don't overdo it, Purton; acting isn't your suit.

Things were going well for the pair. The white's voice, crackling with adrenalin, came in. 'What's your card PIN number?'

'I don't kn—'

'Tell him, motherfucka.' The breath of the man holding his neck was close; hand-pressure increased. Uncomfortable. Worse, undignified.

He didn't want this. Stall. 'There's no need . . .'

'Sure there is. Tell him or you're dead.' To use his number, they would have to incapacitate him anyway. 'You got a death wish? You want to be ID'd by your teeth?'

Purton breathed slowly. He was sixty, law-abiding, and the only concerned member of the public in the area. It was too bad.

'You hear him?' The more distant team member was losing patience. Nervy. 'You want to fucking die?'

'No.' This was all so unnecessary.

'Give it to us, then.'

'Fine.'

'Sh—'

The shriek of surprise was cut off by the impact of a key bundle flailed down onto the bridge of the closer man's nose. Purton felt flesh give beneath the strike, strips torn away by the metal attachments fixed to one end of the 5.5-inch hardened plastic kubotan. He turned the instrument, striking fast into the stomach and solar plexus, seizing a hand held defensively and uselessly outwards, levering on the base of the thumb, pressing down and twisting into an outside arm lock. He brought the weapon hard down above the elbow. It gave. There was a scream and the body fell away to join the knife on the ground. A human-blade combination which had lost its effectiveness.

He switched to the second attacker now backing away up the alley, and moved in, the sound of muffled, bubbling sobs following behind. 'My arm. Jesus, my arm. My arm is fucking broken, man.' An interlude for groaning. 'Oh God, my nose.' Long, wet sniffs. 'You're a fucking racist.' Pain was giving the voice, part-hissed through clenched teeth, a higher pitch.

No, thought Purton. He could hurt the other just as much.

The swagger had gone, the knife held more to fend off than to lunge. It was an eight-inch, double-bladed thrusting type, matt-black, difficult to follow in travel. Dangerous. There would be no simple cut or slash here; parrying would be harder. In the dull moon-glare of a cracked overhead security light, there was a face in shock, fear competing with hatred for the prey which had fought back. The far end was blocked by a security gate set into high walls. Impassable.

'Going somewhere?'

'I'm going to cut you. I'll kill you.' The threats were becoming repetitive, and irritating.

'Have you wet yourself? I can smell something.' Divert, unnerve with conversation. 'Question. Which emergency service?'

'What?'

'Police or ambulance? Drop the knife, and I won't hurt you.'

Rage and terror were more pronounced. 'You don't scare me.' Unconvincing.

Purton took a step forward. 'Then I'm a bad judge of character. I'm old-fashioned too. I don't like law-breakers.'

'Stay away. You fucking hear me? Back off.'

'Or you'll call the authorities? Fine. Give up the weapon. We'll go and see them. Come on.'

'Piss off.'

'Please.' Purton edged to one side and reached for a steel lid perched on top of an overflowing dustbin. Retrieval, the makings of an improvised weapons package. The odds had moved further in his favour. Another step. 'What's your excuse – deprived, abused, addicted? Don't know who your father is, bored with your latest pair of sneakers?'

'You're fucking mad, man. Fucking mad.' Stress did not improve syntax.

'Sometimes I think I am. I just want to do what's right. I'm giving you a chance. A choice.' He lowered the circular lid, took a pace back. The knife quivered, shifted in the hand. Decision made, no compromise. Purton closed.

'Wanker. *Shit.*' The youth probably had. He retreated further. 'Fucking stay away. Tosser. You fucking tosser.' Purton concentrated. Panic from his opposite. 'Christ . . .'

'Not round here.'

The mugger shrank against the steel door. 'Fuck off, man, fuck off.' A whining edge had entered his shouts.

'Still going to cut me?' Purton watched the cornered man, scanned for nuances, signs of desperation feeding through to imminent action. The grip on the knife tightened. Commitment? What he wanted was overcommitment. *Create space, create space*, his unarmed-combat instructors would have shouted. He ignored them. 'Bad choice of place this. No one to hear, no one to help. It's why you picked me.'

'You're fucking dead.'

'I doubt it. One last time. Lay down the knife.'

A change of expression – anticipation, relief, triumph – poorly masked, a quick aversion of the eyes. It was enough. Purton glanced back and saw the third man coming for him. Taller and better built than his cornered colleague, he must have been acting as lookout. Tricky.

The knife was fast, its holder emboldened by the new arrival, his attack made purposeful by the need for peer approval and a trophy. Purton was waiting. Deflecting the blow with a quick flick of the lid, he stepped in and drove his knee between the man's legs, coshing the kubotan into an exposed temple and forcing the face onto a second knee-anvil. The steel crashed into the back of a head pitched forward in semi-conscious agony. One to go.

'Not bad, lawman.'

They eyed each other. The element of surprise was gone. 'His reactions were slow. Must have been the glue in his brain.'

Laughter. 'You're funny.'

'Famous for it.' He did not feel amused. His opponent had the physique of a boxer, the stance and confidence of a street-fighter. An expertly handled combat knife was in one hand, knuckle-spikes slipped over the fingers of the other. This was no amateur. Careful.

'Well, funny bastard. Man-to-man, I'm going to gut you.'

'Is it worth a prison sentence?'

'Oh yeah.' A large smile. Perhaps he should not have asked.

'Think about your future.'

'I am.' They swayed, danced, sizing, measuring distance and timing. 'It's longer than yours.' Wise-guy as well as a thug. 'Where your fucking laws to help you now? They're shit. You think they'll protect you?' He made a quick jab; Purton jumped back.

'Assault contrary to Section 39, Criminal Justice Act 1988. Causing another to apprehend the immediate infliction of a battery.'

The smile had gone. 'What you saying?'

'Don't underestimate the English legal system.' He feinted forward, the man dodged. The knife came out, connecting and glancing off the metal shield. Purton's foot – steel-tipped – struck a knee-cap and stamped down on an unprotected instep before withdrawing. There was a pained yell, an arm dropped involuntarily for the injured leg. 'That's a Battery, also Section 39.'

Purton shifted, watching the knife-hand, and punched the baton up under the chin. The head jerked back. He stepped in, swept his leg behind the attacker and chest-punched the heavyweight backwards. 'Contrary to Offences Against the Person Act 1861, Section 47. Actual Bodily Harm. But it has to hurt. What do you think?'

His studded sole rose and fell on the hand, on the face, on the sternum. Assorted noises accompanied each impact. 'This is counter to Section 18, Offences Against the Person Act 1861, because . . .' The foot thudded down. 'There needs to be intent.' The pugilist's torso jumped to another blow. 'And

I fully intend to cause grievous bodily harm.' It was vital in the circumstance, the only way to neutralise the enemy.

A victory for age and experience. He emptied the contents of two dustbins over the groaning leader. 'Of course, in a court of law, I can plead self-defence. But the force has to be reasonable in the circumstances. And I've probably been less than reasonable.' He shook more garbage out over the disappearing figure, his tone becoming conspiratorial. 'So, let's keep this our own little secret. All your prints are on the knives; you're bound to have criminal records; and your reputations would all suffer if it emerged you were whipped by an old person.' He knelt down. 'Grunt if you agree.' Affirmation came from beneath the evil-smelling pile. 'Good lad.'

He limped back to the car, panting slightly, stepping across the prostrate body of his first, temporarily fainting victim. The key needed to be wiped free of facial tissue before it would insert. He climbed behind the wheel. No lights had come on in the residential street nearby; people knew better than to get involved. A stirring on the ground. He lowered the window.

'Say it loud, eh?'

A regrettable incident to mar an otherwise successful day. He would not call the police. Publicity, or tabloid newspaper interest in any court case, were far from welcome in his business. Purton settled back for the drive to Poole. At least he had the charts. London was a dreadful place.

White cold, evaporating human warmth and spirit into minus fifty centigrade of permafrost and measureless tundra. This was the Special Assignment: frostbite, an ice-shrivelled penis and the threat of hypothermia as an added attraction. Lazin was too frozen to curse, too depressed to wish it on his gnome-like assistant Vakulchuk, to wish it on anyone. Except Petr Ivanov, perhaps. But then, the death's head colonel would never have been sent on an operation such as this: he could sidestep anything, enjoyed the patronage of the most senior figures in the Security apparat, including that of its boss, Leonid Gresko. Lazin scrambled angrily over a section of track. He thought of the small *izba* inherited from his father on the shores of Lake Plescheevo, dreamt of driving up the M8 highway in springtime to Pereslavl-Zalesky. Then he remembered back to the briefing. Pleasure, pure pleasure – he had sensed it in Gresko's face. It showed in his smile, in the stagnant pools of grey sweat sitting in the folds of skin. It showed in his eyes. *They want you out of Moscow, Georgi.* Perhaps his pathologist friend, Kokhlov, was right. He slipped and steadied himself with a gloved hand. It was treacherous here, everywhere. They would like to see him stumble badly. Balance was precarious.

'What are we looking for, Colonel?'

'If I knew that, I wouldn't be out here.' If he had any friends left at FSB headquarters, he would not be out here.

Midwinter, a trainload of rough diamonds goes missing in Siberia, and an under-resourced official was sent as a token gesture – as a gesture of tokenism – to take notes and lose his balls and fingertips in the process. It did not surprise him that prehistoric mammoths were dug from this natural deep-freeze – the cold had plainly got to them also. He looked around, the area etched by feeble guard-lights leading to the tunnel entrance, picked out in places by the directed beams of soldiers' torches. More than snow would have covered over the traces. He had already checked the small station behind, a solitary structure set in its own snow field. Nothing.

Lazin stopped and pumped his arms up and down. It sent the arctic stream faster round his body.

'Coffee?'

A thermos, double-insulated, was thrust towards him. A sip to test temperature, then a stronger gulp, taste, aroma and the heat of warmer climes flooding into his interior and nervous system. His eyes watered; the water froze quickly into stinging crystals.

The Major returned the flask to inside his shapeless, fur-lined overcoat, the lower part of his face obscured once again by the balaclava pulled upwards. Signs hidden. 'You want us to go on?'

Lazin did not reply immediately. He was staring at the Major's *unti* boots, the thigh-length reindeer-skin footwear favoured by local trappers and anyone with common sense. They must be warm. 'The train stopped here?'

'They always do. Nothing moves in or out without documentation being checked.'

'Except, this time, the documentation was checked by bandits. Where were the bodies of the tunnel guards found?'

'Behind the bank over there.' He pointed. 'We had to dig them out. An arm snapped off one.'

'All shot?'

'Back of the head. They were good men.' The voice was unsentimental. Siberia did that to people.

'You had photographs taken for forensics?'

'Naturally.'

'Any sign of the fifteen guards or co-driver from the train?'

'Nothing. Not even blood.'

'They would have been alive when they left here – too difficult to drag so many corpses away.' He squinted into the darkness, eyebrows crackling. 'I want the area searched methodically, five hundred-metre radius. If you've got enough men, send them to the western end of the tunnel to start there. Anything unusual – footprints, damaged perma-frost, snow vehicle tracks, lost buttons – I want them reported.'

'And the Chekist troops are too busy enjoying saunas to join in, I assume?' The dislike for the FSB and its military units was obvious, the sarcasm profound.

'Not this Chekist, Major.' Lazin could barely threaten to make life unpleasant for the officer, to send him to Siberia. 'I'm sure your men will be grateful that I've added variety to their regime.' The Major's reply was chewed up in the lining of the balaclava. Lazin kept it businesslike. 'What were weather conditions like up here the night of the theft?'

'Ice mist, poor visibility, the usual. We are fifteen hundred metres above sea level, Colonel.' As if he needed reminding. The Baikal mountains at this time of year were no place for a creature of any kind to be. He tried to imagine it as a favourite summer destination for mountaineers and trekkers, but failed. The chill factor was eating at his brain.

'The airport at Nizhneangarsk?' He would check anyway.

'I am a railway soldier, Colonel. Refer to your notes.'

Fair enough. They could have come by skidoo or ski, by earlier train, and exited the area by a thousand points. From Nizhneangarsk fifty-five miles to the east, there were express trains to Moscow, to anywhere. Before that, lying only thirty miles distant, was Severobaikalsk and the frozen expanse of Lake Baikal, an ice cover which could take the weight of an escaping army. Time had passed, time in which the uncut stones could have been spirited abroad, hidden in a remote logging cabin or fisherman's cottage, lodged down a disused mica mine in the Akikan Valley to await the summer and a leisurely boat trip to a new destination. Siberia had swallowed hundreds of thousands of human souls, a graveyard that left no trace. What was a consignment of diamonds against that?

The following day, and they were yet to become soulmates. Lazin's questions into the types of bribes, the protection and trading scams run by the railway troops were unlikely to endear him to the Major. He had pulled his file: diligent, but unimaginative, to be commended, to be passed over on account of his lack of contacts and distance from the promotion boards. A Major after nineteen years' service, unlikely to be made up to Colonel in the 'Forces for the Construction and Maintenance of Railways' corps, never to reach the hallowed portals of the Academy of Rear Services and Transport. Rear-echelon soldier, rear-echelon achiever. On the other hand, strategic location could give the man leverage as well as a tidy pensions package – the low profile and poor prospects were perfect cover. He would contact Moscow Centre on the secure communications net and ask Vakulchuk to instigate investigations into the man's personal finances and personal friendships. It might turn something up.

'Tell me, Major. Why do you think there were so few men on board the train guarding the load that night?'

The office in the single-storey concrete barrack block was airless, overheated, as claustrophobic as the rail journey he had made to Krasnoyarsk. He thought of Evdokia – the old lady – choking, dying, a lost statistic in a lost region.

There was a stillness in the Major, sadness or depression, closed in like the weather. His father had been a camp guard on the infamous Solovetsky islands in the White Sea, another facilitator for another grand, mad, failed ego-economics trip of Josef Stalin. Lazin waited for a reply. So, the Major was the spawn of a camp guard and was now the commandant of his own camp, albeit of soldiers, not of *zeks*. Often hard to differentiate: the bullying and the buggery were the same. Inherit the sins of the father or improve on them? The military base at Daban was a small leap, but a leap nevertheless. It was not his fault that he had the bearing and pallor of a prisoner. Here in Siberia, officials, soldiers and prisoners shared the same desperation. It was worse in the areas of the BAM.

'I am under suspicion, Colonel?' The man was rummaging for cigarettes.

'Along with three hundred thousand other godforsaken souls in the BAM region and an equal number living in Moscow and elsewhere.'

The Prima was found, tapped out and lit. 'Then you have an impossible task.'

'Flawless deduction. You should have joined Federal Security.'

'They start with the answer,' the Major replied. 'Deduction doesn't play a part.' The Soviets and their security organs had turned everyone into cynics.

'You didn't answer my question. Why so few guards on the train?'

A shrug. 'The camp here mans both ends of the tunnel. It's not creative, it's not difficult and I'm not paid to advise on security.' He drew deeply on the cigarette, words exhaled with a smokescreen. 'But I can tell you what you know. That the train came from Tynda, that it carried surplus rough stones which fall outside the main Russian-De Beers agreement, that it was authorised direct from the Economics Ministry, and countersigned by the Precious Stones Committee. They wanted it kept quiet.' Someone certainly did.

'Do you have any theories?' Lazin asked.

'You're the secret policeman. Russian mafiya, Yakutian mafiya, Russian government, Yakutian government. It's all the same.'

'How much warning did you have that the train was passing through?'

'Three hours. It's on record. We're informed of special consignments organised by individual ministries only a short time before they reach us. We check the papers and wave them by.'

'What papers do you enjoy checking then, Major? Foreign denomination? Your overseas bank statements?'

'It's a tight operation here, Colonel.'

'I don't doubt it.'

The Major saw the look on his face. 'You're searching in the wrong place.'

'It's what I'm paid to do.'

He was being paid, poorly paid, to go through the motions, keep officialdom pampered, the in-trays filled. There was no other reason to be assigned to the desolation of the *Baikalo-Amurskaya-Magistral* 'BAM' Railway. It was the gulag route to Eastern Siberia, the single-tracked rail link that split from the Trans-Siberian at the old *Ozerlag* prison transit camp at Taishet, itself almost three thousand miles of wilderness east of Moscow, and ran for a further two thousand miles from the great Lake Baikal to Sovietskaya Gavan and the Pacific

Coast. On the way it traversed rivers, mountains, swamp and virgin taiga, plugging the uranium, gold, iron and precious stones deposits into the Soviet system, extracting the resources of the Lena Basin and bleeding the souls of a million prisoners. Running parallel to the Trans-Siberian six hundred miles to its south, BAM's stop-start construction continued for half a century and was to herald the arrival of vast industrial enterprises, boom times. They never came. Nothing did. When official completion occurred in 1991, the scheme was already dead, standing as a monument not only to human endeavour, but to the waste, stupidity and failings of central Communist planning. Unemployed navvies moved on, their temporary prefabricated housing requisitioned by those condemned to stay in half-built towns with moribund economies. Despair, depression and drink were their cohabitants and main community activities. That, and stealing from the railway.

They viewed each other in silence, the Major smoking. Lazin appreciated uncomfortable atmospheres. Bonhomie was another expression for dropping one's guard, coming to some sort of arrangement. He did not care for arrangements of any sort.

'There was nothing unusual about the call from the tunnel guards?'

'We have been over this. None at all.'

'Except that they were already dead. That's unusual.'

A shallow drag on the cigarette. 'If the operator in the communications room had noticed anything, he would have reported it. There were no duress codes given, the log-book shows that.'

'It's a small camp, people recognise each other's voices.'

'Not on this occasion. Slurred voices, a bad line.'

'Fortuitous.'

'Bad luck,' the Major countered. 'Colonel, you will be drinking a lot of coffee if you intend to sit around asking questions.'

'I'm addicted to caffeine.'

'The nervous system will suffer. Ultimately health.'

A threat? Too early to tell. Plainly the man did not relish an outsider trampling on the boundaries of his remote little kingdom. Lazin would push him, note the response. Of course there would be defensiveness; of course the Major was guilty of something. Who was not? It was the basis of that guilt which the Security officer intended to probe.

He stood. 'You are right; I have other things to address. I wish to talk to some of the men individually – standard procedure – and assess chains of command, access to rail movement information. The sooner it is done, the sooner I move on along the line. Your cooperation is noted.' He reached the door. 'Is there anything you wish to add?'

The remains of the cigarette were being ground beneath a toe-cap on the littered floor. 'Only that you are one security man a long way from Lubyanka Square.' The threat was more explicit this time. No smile. 'Colonel.'

He was a light sleeper and the coffee consumed late into the evening had infused his body into a state of only semi-slumber. Several sleep-cycles had been missed, and the erratic, surging thought-patterns would ensure that by morning he would feel exhausted. It was lucky that he had never felt the desire to be comfortable, materially or physically – different mattresses in different places were as good as coming home to his cramped, empty apartment off Belorusskaya Square with the smell of communal living seeping through its walls and the views over Butyrskaya prison. Escape the neighbours, come to Siberia. Upon returning, he would doubtless find his living space absorbed into a New Russian's expanded quintuplex condominium. Anything was possible in the current environment. He shifted on the pillow, his brain leading off down a jumbled path of past surveillance missions and memories of lost Moscow vistas, his head connecting with a lump representing the loaded pistol lying two inches beneath the thin horsehair padding. It had been used many times recently – against the

Chechens, Georgians, Uzbeks; against anyone who no longer feared the authority provided by his office. Physically and psychologically, Communism was a safer place for a secret policeman. Few would risk the wrath of the State in challenging the KGB and its representatives. There were still over a quarter of a million informers, well over, but now they had many loyalties, reported to whoever paid them most or had most on them. And that was not the government. Security organisations proliferated, every business, every bank, every crime syndicate or wealthy individual ran intelligence and counter-intelligence arms; he found himself investigating – fighting even – those with whom he had once worked. He stayed. Perhaps it was just less confusing that way, perhaps it was lack of imagination, a sense of duty. Duty? To what? To whom? Rather, it was obeisance to habit – a habit with serious and far-reaching effects on both finances and well-being. *The nervous system will suffer*. He rolled uncomfortably, willing the tension to ebb out and sleep to flood in. Useless, he was becoming less drowsy and more alert by the second.

A noise – breath – a change in room temperature so slight as to be barely registered. He listened. Nothing, it had gone. His nostrils flared, eyes flickered and strained, trying to catch a scent, a shadow. Imagination, paranoia, age: they tripped up the mind at night. Something lingered; there was a taste in the back of his mouth, a presence unconsciously picked up. Adrenal glands opened, instinctive, automatic, already propelling sweat from subcutaneous pores into the bedclothes. It had to be something. His fingers worked their way beneath the pillow, burrowing for the hardware. Connection; he felt less naked, but still trapped, the arm sliding back into position over a torso now oiled with perspiration for fight or flight. Safety off. There were two doors into the airless room: one he had blocked with a chair and kit-bag to prevent ingress from the corridor, the other – locked – led to an empty and adjacent sleeping quarter. Summer was when they filled up: rail-troop manoeuvres and fishing trips for

141

officers always led to increased bookings. He raised the pistol beneath the covers.

'One step and you get a full magazine.'

The entity remained, unmoving. 'Then you will never hear what I have to say.' It had a voice, low, indistinct. Lazin adjusted the muzzle towards the source. He would not switch on the side-light yet: it would pick him out for an accurate body shot. Standoff.

'You took a risk in coming here.'

'As have you.'

A silence. 'What do you want?' Get the man talking, hear the voice, pick up on identifying features. It could be useful.

'I want you to apply the safety-catch and lower your weapon. If I wished to kill you, by now you would be staring lifelessly at the ceiling.'

'Done.' He did neither.

'It will do you no good trying to identify me. That will only divert your real investigations. Some people might prefer it that way.'

'Who?'

The voice had its own script, independent of Lazin's questions. 'What do you know of Tyumen?'

'Oil capital of western Siberia, about seven hundred thousand inhabitants. I've passed it on the Trans-Siberian railway. Why?'

'1996. Thirty-six youths in the province apparently hanged themselves that year.'

'People lose faith, people get drunk. This is Russia.'

'Police preferred initially to call the incidents suicides to keep down the crime figures. They eventually conceded that the cabalistic signs, diabolical drawings, cryptic writings and altars found in the surrounding villages of Roshchino and Antipovo where several of the hangings occurred, suggested the deaths were cult murders, ritualistic satanic sacrifice.'

'And how has it been since then for Black Magic?'

'Positive.' The voice betrayed a tautness, urgency; the

story-telling held a message. 'I am not here to humour you, Colonel.'

'And I am Federal Security Service, not the local police.'

'Then you should be able to use your imagination, find patterns from random events. You're investigating a diamond theft. It's a side-effect, not a symptom, not the illness. Probe deeper, search around the wound. It's national security you're concerned with. Be concerned. Look at the other deaths.'

Lazin moved slowly up onto his elbow, pistol cradled. 'I'm listening.'

'1998. What did it mean to you?'

'A lack of decent sex, the economy free-falling, my career and salary doing the same. Nothing unusual.'

'1998. Three times 666. The Year of the Devil.'

'If you play ouija; if you're superstitious.'

'The Russian psyche is based on superstition, Colonel. The Orthodox Church is tainted; American evangelism is corrupting and foreign; Communism collapsed. What is left, but occultism?'

'Common sense.'

'And does common sense, your rational mind, explain the upsurge in cult-style killings in Siberia from 1998 onwards? Right along the BAM, settlements, mining towns, railheads. Children have gone missing, teenagers have written notes saying they've left town . . .'

'The region's dying; industry has left – it never came. There are no prospects. Of course youngsters move on.'

'That's what the militia say; the parents don't say anything. They're too frightened. And then bodies – pieces of bodies – are found. Parts of different torsos were discovered last month in the kerosene tubes along the BAM section running across the Verkhnezeskaya plains.'

Two metres high and sunk into the ground, the condensing tubes stopped rail subsidence by preventing the permafrost from melting. Midwinter, it was pure chance that they were checked at all. The voice was continuing. 'Others, mutilated and half-eaten, were stored down the Neryungri coal mine

143

on the way to Yakutsk.' So? People got hungry. 'They moved on all right.'

The man was mad, possibly dangerous. 'And this is Devil worship?'

A quiet snort. 'On that scale? Oh no, Colonel. Made to seem like devil worship, the odd serial murder, or even suicide. Gives the militia something to put in their reports. Political sensitivity between the Sakha Republic and Russia ensures no one investigates too deeply, no one coordinates. Do we want to know we're eating each other in our brave new world? Do we even want to find a conspiracy? Life is difficult enough. Where's the incentive?'

'I thought you were insane or foolish. But you're both. You expect an underpaid Colonel in the FSB to take an interest, to have that incentive.'

'You're here, in Daban, at this time of year. That's either bad luck or devotion to duty.'

'I'm a winter person.'

'Some people have disappeared; some are left as warnings.' Or revenge, Lazin thought.

'You're saying these aren't random?'

'I would not wish to prejudice your investigation.'

'They are not part of my investigation.' Lazin replied carefully. 'It's a civil matter.' And yet.

Political killings disguised as motiveless killings. There was quite a pedigree. He wondered why the image of Colonel Petr Ivanov had come to him now. But the voice was talking again.

'A man was found three weeks ago – as a stew. He had been a senior official with *Almazy Rossii-Sakha*, the state diamond group, working out of Yakutsk. Then there were the two young children of a railway officer working for BAM administration based in Tynda.' An intake of breath. 'The kids, a girl and a boy, had been raped and dismembered. Not necessarily in that order. Their father collapsed, is in an asylum. His role has been filled by central appointment.'

Lazin sank back on the mattress. Dear God, or his nearest

equivalent. There were few times when he thought that the life of a secret policeman was preferable to that of a criminal investigator. This was one such moment. If man were created in the image of the Creator, creation was damned. There was no future, no salvation. A giant practical joke, with torture and misery thrown in to polish the act. He hoped there was not a God.

'You want me to go on?'

He wanted him, it, to leave. 'Only if there is a point to what you are telling me.'

'That is for you to decide. The night of the robbery, there were other trains moving along the single track, laid up in passing loops. Check the sidings. Always check the sidings. Whatever the rolling-stock, they had disappeared the following morning. No one asked where, or why.'

'Moscow sent me for that reason.'

'Then you are naïve.'

'Why do you trust me?'

'I don't. Which is why you will die if you attempt to turn on the light.' Lazin felt scrutinised in the dark, as if decisions were being taken. Mutual assessment, making contact without making contact. 'You're an outsider; you ask questions; and the base commander did not appreciate your arrival. It's the only guarantee there is that you're clean.'

'And there's no guarantee that I will be effective.'

'Or live.'

Thirty seconds passed. Lazin thought the man might have left, but there was still a presence. Why had the night visitor not acted sooner? Why had he waited for a roving Federal Security officer before reporting his theories and fears? Perhaps he simply needed to share the burden with another, with someone anonymous, someone passing through. The idea that the owner of the voice was insane came again to him: it happened frequently with men stationed in these solitary outposts. Comforting in a way, easier to dismiss. The voice sensed his thoughts.

'You want to know where those missing train guards can

be found?' A step towards proving sanity. A handing over of the torch which could burn them both.

'You know the question to ask, so you also know the answer.' Lazin replied.

'But not your actions.'

'Why do you wish to help?' Charity was not in the Russian vocabulary. It was a Western luxury which had yet to become an import. And then they would impose a tariff.

'Why do men repent on Judgement Day?' came the response. Lazin would check the personnel files. The man was no reserve soldier or transport guard. 'You have asked enough. I will do my best to aid you. but I cannot show myself. I am already under suspicion. If you are not part of the conspiracy, then you are also under sentence.' There was no choice but to take the flame.

Conspiracy, the voice spoke of conspiracy. 'You're a brave man,' Lazin said. And a paranoiac who creeps about in the dark.

'No, Colonel,' the voice answered. 'I am a dead one.'

Ilya Kokhlov, pathologist, chief morbid anatomist, was removing an eye. He cut around the conjunctiva, separated the optic nerve and extrinsic ocular muscles, and extracted the globe like a wet lychee with a pair of forceps. Behind him, bent over another porcelain slab, a technician used spring-loaded shears to access a chest, dividing the costal cartilages and severing the sternal attachments to the diaphragm. The first stage of wholesale evisceration. The third dissection station was occupied by a corpse so badly burned that its blackened and unrecognisable head was largely detached from the rest of the fused body. A busy morning in the butcher's shop.

'Leave some bronchus on the lung,' Kokhlov said over his shoulder. 'I want to inflate it with formal-saline.'

'Fine.' The technician raised the sternum upwards. 'We've got fluid in the pleural sacs.'

'Collect it. And none of your fancy Letulle stuff, Dmitri.

Basic Virchow will do. Nice, easy, separate organ removal. Understood?'

'Understood.'

'And don't forget to swab the thoracic.'

Dmitri sighed. 'As if I would.'

They had worked together a long time. Ilya might be eccentric, but he was a consummate professional, one of the best in his field. At one moment he might be making medical students faint by feeding air into a corpse's anterior jugular vein and making the head move, or insisting that they throw intestine at the wall to test its age and adhesive quality, the next he would be solving the most bizarre of murder cases. The senior technician was no slouch himself, an expert in assessing time of death through changes in rectal temperature – without the aid of a thermometer. Dmitri's rule of thumb. His shoulders were often lightly dusted with a fine layer of dandruff whose source was the subject of some conjecture among the post-mortem staff.

An assistant entered the raised viewing room to the side and waved through the glass. The intercom crackled. 'Ilya, your friend, Colonel Lazin, is on the line.'

Kokhlov looked up and gestured he would take the call, making a figure three with his fingers and pointing in the direction of Body Preparation. A hands-free conference was possible from the dissection room itself, but Lazin would not be contacting him for small-talk. Privacy was required.

'I'll put it through.' The tannoy switched off and the assistant disappeared. Kokhlov peeled off his surgical gloves, threw them onto the bulging pile of trash beneath the shelves and walked for the door.

'Anything on the thymus?' he asked.

'Nope.' Dmitri was making small dissections with a scalpel. 'How do you want the heart cooked?'

'Cut into the left atrium and take a close look at the mitral and tricuspid valves.' Dmitri grunted and peered closer. Kokhlov went through.

It was a long conversation. Dmitri had removed the heart

and was incising the sternomastoids prior to lifting out everything in the neck. A delicate operation. He grinned at his returning boss.

'Before you say anything, I'm not about to crush the hyoid bone.'

'Fuck the hyoid bone. We've got real work.'

'From the KGB? Life is never dull round here.' He sliced downwards, almost affectionately. 'Quiet, but never dull.'

'You want to hear?'

'Go on. What's the job?' The senior technician placed the blade to one side.

Kokhlov looked gleeful, the stained teeth camouflaged in an open-mouthed smile against corpse-tinted features. 'Hunting. We're hunting for cannibals.'

Lazin vented the windproof with the zip-pulls beneath his armpits. Temperatures precipitously below freezing and he was sweating like a stag in rut. At least the layers were carrying the moisture away from his body: thermal undergarments covered by the stacked insulation of woollen shirt, pullover, fibrepile fleece, down-duvet suit and a windproof PTFE membrane, complete with air pockets, all restricting his movement. All keeping him alive. His companions, three of them – rail guards he had picked at random from the Daban Camp – were faring no better, struggling under heavy loads, cursing on their cross-country skis. But they were fit, strong and mountain-trained. Lazin felt old, aware of the need to drive them, drive himself. The complaints were becoming less intermittent.

'Colonel, we have marched for five hours. It's time for a rest.' The face behind the balaclava was angry. Vodka-stops had been denied.

Lazin trudged on without turning to face the malcontent. They were lucky that he had not forced them into harness to haul a pulk. 'The canyon is an hour away. No easing up until we're there. Eat some chocolate.' Mutterings to the rear.

The two glaciers loomed sheer, ice-columns supporting

the heavy twilight of a winter's day, natural gateways to the canyon. They pushed themselves through, diminutive, lost in the measureless snow sea, framed in white, backed by white, made insignificant by white, their shallow tracks left reaching out far behind.

His timing was accurate. They shrugged off their packs, grateful, footsore. 'You two set up camp. We're spending the night here. You,' Lazin pointed at the senior NCO, 'come with me. We will make a preliminary reconnaissance of the mine entrance. Conduct radio checks and bring your mask and the counter. It will take us twenty minutes to get there.'

A uranium mine, or at least its initial workings. There were few better places to hide bodies. Permafrost prevented burial in the ground, but there was a shaft which led only to abandoned and unvisited tunnels and the threat of radioactive dust inhalation: definitely the first choice for a professional. It was a small affair, the surrounding snow-humped slag mounds lower than usual for deserted mines, for it had been closed before it could ever compete with its more viable and significant sisters further east in the Kodar mountains. Here, there were no ruins, no derelict remains of enforced habitation. The slave workers lived under canvas. When they died – and most did – they were tossed into one of the earlier exploratory passages. Additional corpses would go unnoticed among the grim geological layers, buried deep in graves unmarked on any map or record.

The counter showed acceptable background readings, the needle quivering within its safety zone as Lazin passed the device across the expelled rocks leading to a lower entrance. There were no signs of recent disturbance or visitation. He knelt and scraped away loose snow with a mitten. Nothing to suggest that cadavers had been dragged this way, or that live humans were made to march up the incline. He stood.

'Arms out to your side. Do it. Now.'

A woollen underglove held the pistol, finger curled on the trigger. Lazin moved slowly. He had thought that his random selection technique would reduce the chance of an unpleasant surprise. Plainly, some modifications to the approach were required.

'Are these your orders?' he asked.

'Part of them.' The barrel was held low, aimed mid-body. 'You either cooperate fully or you die here.' Rather than at the mine entrance.

Lazin preferred to cause maximum inconvenience. He felt cold, consigned already to ice eternity. It was no point looking around for warmth or support. The radio mouthpiece was held in the other hand, the sergeant speaking briefly into it, gaze and gun-hand unwavering. 'I have him. Move up when you hear the signal.' When you hear the shots. The mouthpiece was lowered. 'Turn . . .'

At first Lazin thought the soldier had phlegm in his throat, or that a rapid intake of air rendered him breathless, speechless. He waited. The eyes wobbled, tilted heavenward, the mouth emitting a shallow sigh before one hundred and ninety pounds fell forward on itself. It was more than something caught in the throat: an ice-pick lay embedded to its shaft between the shoulder-blades.

'Always check the rear.' The man, swathed in furs and white arctic coveralls, face shrouded in a hood of snow fox, placed his boot in the small of the sergeant's back and worked the pick free. The pistol was reclaimed and aimed away. 'This one's to the back of your head.' The shot whiplashed the canyon, cracking the brittle silence with myriad echoes. 'This one's in your ear.' The next raced after its predecessor.

'I could have questioned him.'

'From the after-life? Through a psychic?' The eyes, tinted by goggles, almost hidden in an epicentre of age and weather-dug ravines, were intelligent and remote. Control and self-sufficiency reflected from the soul of a survivor. The body was old, stooped but strong, thin yet sinewy beneath the hunter's clothes, comfortable in the natural wilderness. 'There was a time, Colonel Lazin, when I would have done the same as our friend here to anyone from your department.'

Colonel Lazin? His department? He was not wearing uniform. 'You know who I am?'

'Call it intuition.' Lazin called it inexplicable. 'News travels.'

'You are not indigenous.'

'Few are. Remember Stalin?' A veteran of the camps? Some preferred to live on close to their sites of torment. It was both madness and therapy, a link to the certainties and past they knew, to an existence so harsh that it stamped itself indelibly on their beings.

Lazin looked at the hunting rifle jutting diagonally above a shoulder. 'Are you a trapper?'

'Of sorts.'

'You have a name?'

'I am more comfortable with numbers. And fewer questions.' The figure gestured at the body. 'We'll move Trotsky later. His brethren will be making their way towards us. I hope that you are armed.'

'Pistol.'

'Useless. Still, we have advantages. Let us prepare. The closer to the mine, the less distance you'll have to carry them later.' The old man did not suffer from lack of confidence.

They edged forward, snake-bellying on dead ground towards the temporary camp, the elderly hunter surprisingly agile and tactically informed. Lazin followed, happy to let another lead on this terrain. The two slithered up an ice bank, stopped, listened, spread out, and swung themselves over simultaneously into fresh cover. The advance began again. Then the shooting came.

Pinned down. Automatic fire was heavy, the fight one-sided, the trapper unconcerned. In these temperatures, the chances of malfunction were high. Weapons sweated, condensation froze, gun oil congealed, breech mechanisms could block. Rapid shots meant an increase in barrel temperature, and with it the risk of metal fracture or firing pin and extractor damage. The theory. Unfortunately, these were

151

Kalashnikovs – rugged, reliable – and Lazin did not welcome drawing the attention of their operators.

He rolled into a fresh position, loosed three rounds towards the enemy and threw himself into a crawl as lead thumped into the vacated snow berm.

'You must have located them!' he yelled across to the hunter lying camouflaged behind an ice ridge at high right.

'Indeed I have.'

The old man was spotting for tell-tale vapour clouds forming above the firing positions. Rail troops never made good soldiers; neither did paid executioners. He sighed, taking his time, and made an adjustment to the rifle, sliding the long, insulated and white-masked barrel through an opening. 'Ice-crete, you need a minimum of thirty centi-metres to protect against small-arms fire.' He spoke to himself. 'Ice alone, at least a hundred centimetres; snow-crete about one-thirty; packed snow, approximately two hundred.' The butt shuddered twice in his shoulder, the twin reports, divided by the bolt action, sharp and loud in contrast to Lazin's earlier diversions. Spent round extraction. 'And if the snow is wind-driven, you need around three hundred centimetres.' He squeezed the trigger again – more shock-waves – the noise reverberating outwards in a miniature powder blizzard. 'So, I'd say you're under-protected.' The rifle was withdrawn. Silence.

They waited for return fire. Nothing. Lazin initiated the half-crouch, half-crawl around the three hundred-metre stretch to the enemy position. Although largely hidden from line-of-sight, ducking into gullies and pulling himself behind rocks, he felt exposed, a billowing, sweating, clambering target picked out against a blank crystalline sea. He was expecting an ambush, his limbs slow, cold and heavy. Nerves and muscles twitching, he leapt into the turn, pistol extended, covering the angles, keeping low. A small skid down an incline, edging up past an ice wall, and the path was blocked. The body, near-headless, skull blown away by a rifle shot above the eye, contents littered bloodily in a five-metre radius, sprawled haphazardly on its back, assault rifle thrown casually to the side. Two down.

'The third one's been hit. There's a trail.' The figure was beckoning. He must have moved around on the opposite side, travelling fast. Lazin trudged up towards him. 'He's heading back to the mouth of the canyon. It's more than a flesh wound, so he'll be weak.' Without waiting for orders, the hunter pushed off on his skis. 'I'll cut him off.' The quarry was close.

'I want him alive,' Lazin shouted.

The snow alternated red-pink, spattering in places, the blood flowing more freely where ground undulations necessitated greater effort. Lazin crouched, watching the track disappear into a rise.

'He's sitting against a rock, minus his weapon, attempting to work his radio.' The trapper re-materialised with a progress report. 'It's a shoulder wound. Right side.' A bullet entry exposed in these conditions would have made any activity a supreme feat of endurance, movement a continuum of jarring pain. They had to prevent him calling in support.

'I'm taking him.'

'Sooner than you think.' An unconcerned nod uphill.

Staggering, ungainly, drunk from blood-loss, the soldier had moved from behind cover and was descending in exaggerated strides towards them.

Lazin raised his pistol. 'Stop and put your left hand up,' he called out to the swaying form. 'Your uninjured arm,' he repeated. 'Slowly.' The legs churned into a lumbering run, gloved hand brought briefly up to face, arm arched back and thrown forwards. 'Grenade! Down!' He shot twice, missed, and dropped heavily onto impacted ice, eyes up, searching for the fall of the explosive.

The man had halted, the pin falling from his mouth. He was staring, uncomprehending, at the mitten on his left hand, at a grenade which had failed to leave it. The injured arm was forgotten, a red river streaming from the shoulder, dividing into separate flows across the smock. A splash of brightness, incongruous, riveting. Lazin watched. The man's eyes were wide, confused, mouth open and pink as the ground. He began to shake his hand; the grenade remained fast. Bewilderment. The seconds slowed, movements stretched, time lengthened within the pocket of space between them. Metal – the grenade handle – attached in frozen marriage to the condensation of the mitten fibre. There were no shouts, no screams. A frantic lack of struggle. Detonation.

Earth scrapes, smoking, gouged and dull where shrapnel and flesh had hit at high velocity. The boots lay splayed in their own island, leg segments partially attached, the rest gone, clothing charred and scattered, drifting in small and blackened fragments or caught in the jagged edges of natural ice sculptures.

'Less to tip down the mine,' the ancient trapper opined, retrieving the grenade ring and attaching it to the front of his windproof as trophy and cold-weather zip-pull. 'Basic mistake,' he muttered. 'Should have tied the thing to a stick to throw.'

Lazin looked around. 'I still have work to do in the shaft.'

'If there isn't a manhunt out for you.' The hunter kicked at something wet and shapeless.

'I don't have a choice.'

The old man paused. 'The bodies? There are over a dozen of them.'

'You've been down there?' Lazin was incredulous.

'And checked.' He slapped the back of his head. 'You know the technique. The KGB invented it.'

'It needs more than the word of a stranger. Even one who saved my life.'

The old man rummaged beneath two layers of clothing. 'Photographs. Colour. You wouldn't get better in a pathology room. Numbered and measured.'

Lazin took the clear plastic packet. He could see the details in the top print, an unsightly and over-generous exit wound high at the front of the skull vault, caught in the light. It was enough. He turned back to the trapper. 'The dust in the mine is probably radioactive.'

'It didn't kill those men.' The rifle sling was eased to a more comfortable position across the shoulders.

Like the night visitor, there were so many questions which needed to be asked, which required an answer.

'Thank you,' he said simply.

The face remained hidden, the eyes gave nothing. 'The odds have to be reduced.'

Take the turn gently, gently . . . There was a bench here somewhere, his kneecap had connected with it last time, had connected with most of the things hereabouts. It was trips such as this which made Max wonder why he bothered. Moscow, midwinter, not the place for a near-blind sucker. What was he proving? To whom? For years he had fought to show that he was as good as anyone – better – could move and shake, duck and dive. And here he was, the potential to fall at the first fence, the first bench, prone to ending prone, failing to kid himself or the rest, a victim not of fading eyesight but of his own stubbornness. Christ, Sheremyetevo airport got worse each time. He placed the stick out in front and walked it tentatively forwards. *I do not need help; I do not need help*. The day would arrive when he was guided by the arm or by a dog, when he would sit in his new world, alone in the darkness. Enjoy the struggle, he told himself. It is a luxury. Appreciate the stumbles, the occasional black eye. They will be but a memory.

Passport control. Long queues and chaos. Certain things never changed here: Russian bureaucracy, bullshit and a capacity for rubbing travellers' noses in it. 'Stand behind the line until you are called . . . look towards the glass.' So, they were still doing their covert photography. He shuffled forward, careful lest a young child crossed his path. They had been stepped on before. A group of Africans were talking excitedly – their first time here. The enthusiasm would diminish when they underwent the gratuitous interrogations and strip-searches. Russians did not like *tychyomy*.

The arm circled his chest, gripping him backwards against a mountainous body. 'Maximilian.' The voice started as a rumble near the diaphragm, swelling upwards in an effortless bass and emerged in a deep-hued growl.

Max attempted to disengage from the hold. 'Shit, Gennady, how did you get here? You're on the wrong side of the gate.' His Russian was flawless.

'I have friends,' the bodyguard explained simply, allowing his client to turn and face him.

'Spare me the detail. How are you keeping?' They hugged, Russian-style, the air expelled from Max a second time.

'I'm well, I'm well.' The slab-like features split into a beatific smile, the Russian pushing him back to take a better look. Max felt like a rag doll. 'And you look good.' Gennady gave an appreciative nod. 'The Russian girls will be crazy for you.'

'Not after you've broken my spinal column.'

'Come.' His arm was taken. 'We'll pick up your case on the other side.'

A knock on a bare-faced door and they were given entry to a labyrinth of darkened corridors and staircases, Gennady shouting friendly obscenities at those security men he recognised. Few other passengers had made it to the retrieval hall when the luggage arrived; they might take another three hours to trickle through.

The two cases were heavy. To Gennady, they might have been empty. Lodging the first beneath an armpit, the second held easily on the same side, he resumed his hold on Max's arm and guided him effortlessly through the milling crowds.

'Stop.'

Max halted on command, was prevented from going further by the benign lock on his arm. Gennady was one guide he was not going to argue with. The baggage trolley passed. They continued their journey.

He was caught out each time, was never fully prepared for the cold of a Moscow winter. No cliché did justice to it: chilling to the marrow, cutting like a knife. Forget it. It turned him inside out, made him transparent, froze him from within. The voice seized, the heart took a hit and the eyes blistered. Gennady did not notice, propelled his shaking charge by the elbow. *Months of this, months of this*. Fuck. Max swore silently behind teeth clamped shut by trembling jaw muscles. *I'll become a fucking ice-cube*. He shuffled to keep up; in thirty seconds his extremities had lost colour, feeling, and size. The car was reached just in time. Whistling, Gennady tossed the cases into the back of the designer four-by-four, and opened the door for a grateful Max who slid inside and waited as the prize-fighting shape ambled about pouring vodka on the windscreen and scraping away the rapidly formed layers of ice. He drained the remnants and climbed inside.

'Are we happy?'

'I'll tell you when I'm sure I've still got my balls. Let's drive. Where's Hunter?' His boss moved around.

'At the Ukraina.' Max's spirits sank. Views were fine – and you could not do better than one of Stalin's jerry-built 'Seven-Sisters' wedding-cake constructions – but he preferred the decorative and service culture of the city's Western-owned or managed hotels. Strachan was different. The mid-life crisis which encouraged him to test himself in the hostile environments of Moscow's less comfortable hotels and hostelries was a vivid example. At least it was not the Sputnik or Ural.

'And I'm booked in there?'

'Of course.' Strachan had a malicious sense of humour.

Resigned, Max belted himself in. 'Let's go then.'

Gennady rummaged around on the back seat, found what he was searching for, and threw a general's peaked hat up against the rear window. It was a well-tested routine; a symbol of authority would keep the bribe-taking traffic police off their tails. No one liked to mix it with a general or his acquaintances.

Leningradsky prospekt into the city was choked with slow-moving rush-hour traffic, the way lit by a forest of illuminated hoardings advertising foreign electronics and beverages, cars and trucks weaving and honking to maintain position in the free-for-all that was the Moscow driving scene. Economic misfortune had not dampened the experience. The bodyguard swerved, braked and cursed, lowering his window to roar abuse at the timid or his equals, accelerating hard to exploit gaps and weaknesses. This man is here to ensure my safety, Max reminded himself. But this man had also reversed two hundred metres down Tverskaya ulitsa against oncoming traffic. He was jolted by another hard-braking manoeuvre, the assorted Nefto Agip air-fresheners clattering in protest.

'Cool it, Gennady. The car electronics won't take it,' Max tried, appealing to the man's innate fondness for his gadgetry, mobile communications, jammers, and radio and radar intercept devices. The Russian was too absorbed in muttering expletives, looking over his shoulder to ward off contenders to a potential opening. The car accelerated, Max stiffened.

'Welcome to the criminal-syndicalist state, bubba.' Dry, familiar, the distressed-leather voice carried from beneath the black cavalry hat pulled over Hunter Strachan's face.

'After Gennady's driving, I'm ready for anything,' Max replied, heading for an armchair positioned on the far side of the overblown but curiously empty Socialist-sized room, working his way around suitcases and carriers clumped on the floor.

His boss did not move from the prone position, reptile-booted feet and expensively clad legs stretched across the double bed. Even without a face, the reclining figure exuded contradictory elements of energy and indolence. But there were many contradictions in Hunter Strachan. He had flown Huey helicopters, Cessna Bird Dog and Bronco spotter aircraft for the First Air Cav in Vietnam, survived fifteen hundred assault missions, been shot down four times, wounded twice, evaded capture, and then volunteered for further tours of duty. He had even piloted H-13 observation helicopters in near-suicidal missions to draw and locate enemy fire: fewer than twenty per cent of the unit survived the first six months. He could talk for hours of skimming at over a hundred knots in eighty-ship formations just above tree-level, of landing blind in hot LZs and watching fireball-red tracer race towards him, of seeing fellow 'slick' aviators impaled with giant sapling arrows or land on ten-feet sharpened stakes. It was not therapy – he had been through that way back, drink and valium too – now it was the reminiscences of a risk-taker and rehabilitated veteran.

A lapsed convert to Vietnamese Caodaism, he was a frontiersman at heart, a loner who had flown ramshackle aircraft for ramshackle regimes throughout Asia and Africa, ploughing the tax-free proceeds into an international truck haulage company which spread from its original hubs in Texas and New Mexico to some of the least glamorous and seemingly untenable locations on the earth's surface. Russia was his latest love. There had been others, Mexico among them, a land where drugs were government, government were drugs, and his sometime beauty-queen daughter had been abducted and murdered by cocaine *narcotraficante* billionaire Amado Carrillo Fuentes. It was punishment for Strachan's refusal to carry anything more illegal than migrant 'poyong' fruit-pickers from Tijuana into California. *El Señor de los Cielos* – Lord of the Skies – they called the Mexican, the man who owned a fleet of converted Boeing freighter aircraft, an economy and a president. Underworld rumours persisted that he sent cocaine to St Petersburg hidden in shipments of frozen shrimp for onward European distribution by Boris Diakanov's teams, that *tsisari* despatched military hardware to the Colombian port of Turbo in return. A profitable relationship. Carrillo died in July 1997, the apparent victim of an an accident in Mexico City hospital while undergoing surgery for liposuction. Lord of the Skies, outmanoeuvred and sucked dry – perhaps under anaesthetic. Diakanov transferred his business to the Arrelano-Felix cartel. He had moved on; Strachan had moved on.

The hat was pushed up, legs crossed, a lined Marlboro country face tilting forward to acknowledge Max's presence with a lopsided grin. Pockets of scar tissue ran from beneath an ear along the jawline while another dimpled the skin from the side of the nose to the corner of the mouth – the effects of flying plexiglass from a shattered helicopter canopy.

'So whaddya think of my suite? Apparently it's got plumbing.'

'Spoil yourself.' Max gazed around. 'I don't think running water has been budgeted for my floor. Except through the ceiling.'

'You'll be out too much to notice. Everyone's looking forward to seeing you, Max. We're those two regular American refugees wintering out in Moscow again.'

'Regular? Fucking crazy.' But his boss had a point. No one sat through this kind of climate without good reason.

Strachan rubbed his face and squinted. 'How the eyes?'

'Not as good as my sense of smell.'

'As long as you're hungry and can cuss in Russian, I've got a job for you. OK,' he shifted his legs over the side, gravity pulling his frame into a sitting position behind. 'A quick résumé, then we'll go through your itinerary. Economy's still shit, but we're keen to import, they're desperate to export. Perfect synergy if we search for the deals.'

'I'm your man.'

'You're the best counter-trade negotiator I've got. So nail them. Demand for spirits defies any cycle, fancy leather stuff and English furniture is popular, and perfume's doing well – even in Siberia where they think it's flavoured alcohol.'

'They've always liked to party.'

'It's why I love 'em, and the girls have the world's tightest rhythm sections.'

'Any trouble getting our supplies through to the warehouses?'

'Nothing that me and the guys from Russian Airborne can't handle.' Strachan went through to the bathroom to relieve himself, a built-up sole failing to disguise the limp in a leg shortened by combat. He left the door ajar and continued to speak, ceramic tiling lending the voice an echo. 'The convoy I ran in last month was attacked. Small arms, no explosions. Probably local gangsters wanting to test our response.'

'Which was?'

The contents of the minibar continued to empty into the pan. 'With overkill. Works every time.' Running water, and Strachan reappeared drying his hands on a towel. He straddled a chair. 'Should have seen my parachute colonel jump from the cab, stand in the middle of the highway and take three of them down with a Dragunov on the overhead walkway. After that, it was a straight run all the way to the bonded warehouse at Moshaisk.' He enjoyed his brawls. 'And before you ask, all the problems with the TIR's have been sorted out, with a little help from the Hunter Strachan Christmas bonus and incentive scheme.'

There was no easy way of getting goods safely into Russia. A standard twenty-foot container could carry approximately eleven hundred cases of branded whisky, each with twelve bottles selling individually at the distillery price of three to four pounds sterling: approximately forty pounds a case, forty-four thousand a container. Once stolen and black-marketed, the contents might be worth up to two hundred thousand pounds. And the mafiya had a thirst. Bribe the correct officials in the correct government ministries in Moscow and you could gain permission to import; bribe again and you could avoid the strip stamp system or paying duty until in country; bribe once more – this time the customs officers and 'security men' supervising the eighty or so Russian Customs warehouses – and your supplies might reach their destination. On the way, they risked delay, diversion or theft. So, Hunter Strachan had built himself an autonomous, self-contained and massively guarded distribution network. Sure, he purchased the 'consultancy services' of key government ministers, had a three-way deal with Defence and Interior to use elite airborne troops as escort;

certainly he paid the odd stipend to Boris Diakanov for protection against peripheral scavengers. But in introducing smooth-running and guaranteed haulier services to a chaotic world, he provided a secure conduit for Western companies and extra income to senior figures in the Russian hierarchy. Loud-mouthed, often foul-mouthed, Strachan bestrode the scene in his cavalry blues, hard-hitting, hard-talking and hard-drinking, winning respect by showing none, facing down the natives because he understood them, was tougher than most. Order, discipline and drive: he had, and hid well. And Max saw.

'Nice to see they're still so big on law and order,' he observed.

'Not for long. Y'see the news about Diakanov's boy?'

'Couldn't miss it. In Britain, it's all the Press are talking about. What's going to happen?'

'Fuck knows, and fuck ain't telling. But if the Great White is badly mauled, his rivals will tear him to shreds. We're talking feeding frenzy.'

'Has it started?'

'Nope. Though if it's just a scratch, it'll be him doing the feeding. There's tension. You'll pick it up.'

'Great. It'll do wonders for business confidence.'

'Diakanov will contain it. I've got money riding on him.'

'Difficult odds.'

Strachan removed his hat and inspected it. 'You know what he did to competitors two years ago? They were found hanging from beneath the ski-jump on the Sparrow Hills. The last thing that went over their heads before they died were their wives going into orbit on wooden crates. Kinda like ET, without the bicycle.' He was working the stetson rim between his fingers. '*Tsisari*'s filled couriers up with heroin and used them for target practice because he likes to see white cloudbursts come out of them. There are railway sleepers made out of entire families because he's sent so many people into the Novo-kuznetsk steel mill. Sure, I'm confident he'll stay boss.'

'No wonder they call the Kuzbass region Siberia's Crematorium. I'm growing to like his surreal sense of humour.'

'Swell. Because you're going to meet him.'

'Christ, my mouth. Why?'

''Cos he can help us out with Junktim bonds, and we need him sweet on future switch deals. Trade is king, and he's a god. He likes to put faces to names.'

'Or remove them.'

'Exactly.' Strachan gripped the sides of his chair. 'Dialogue's preferable. Anything to maintain presence on the ground. I said it was a criminal-syndicalist state – makes the Sam Giancana-JFK connection look like amateur night.' He saw Max touch his ear and point to the wall. 'Relax. The guys with headphones are part of it. Everyone knows the system stinks.'

Strachan glided – limped – through that system, different enough to be untouched, close enough to be comfortable, to thrive in it. An old snake, a proud, unrepentant former member of Charlie Company, the 'Snakes', 229th Air Assault Battalion of 'The First Team'. Skin, friends and emotion shed, he kept going. The hunting ground was Russia. There were no panaceas, no illusions.

'Know what kills a country?' he asked.

Max had heard the lecture many times. 'Corruption.'

'Corruption.' His chairman, CEO and MD nodded. 'And to fight it you need political will, effective laws, a clear-cut strategy for investigation and prosecution, and public support.' Max went through the checklist silently. 'Out here, public support is the only one you'll find.'

'And the leadership doesn't give a shit.'

An appreciative grin, scar tissue disappearing into the creases. 'Finding anyone straight is as rare as a Jew getting membership of the Santa Monica Beachclub. You're my quickest student.'

Not really. It was a matter of learning by repetition. God, how he wanted to see Zenya. But there was a reception planned for that evening, a mixed Russian–European affair at the Intourist hotel, toasts, bonhomie and an assault course of statuesque hookers to avoid. Tomorrow, deals and meetings: more toasts, more bonhomie, and hard-nosed bargaining. There were new bulk customers to find, representations to be made, vodka – always vodka – to be drunk. They would pour it down you, before, during and after negotiation, then bring in fresh teams and fresh glasses for resumed talks. Old tricks, old habits, and Max and his Virginia cowboy boss were old hands.

'Where can I find you this week?'

'Up at the Finnish border with the next convoy, making sure the engineers don't steal more parts from the Maz and Kamaz rigs.' The hat was repositioned. 'It's take, take, take. Peasant mentality, see? Nothing's changed.' A moment's reflection, and a return to the agenda. 'I've also got appointments at EuroSib over our thirty-wagon block trains for eastwards transit. You can nose around exhibitors at the Economic Achievements Park, see if they need our services. Economic Achievements, Christ.' He shook his head, rose and went to extract a refrigerated soda. Ring-pull removed, he tipped it to his lips and turned. 'And we've got the dinner at the Kremlin with three hundred Western businessmen and a bunch of American politicos, courtesy of the Mayor of Moscow.'

'Who's leading the American delegation?'

A scowl. 'Senator Paddy O'Day. Catholic and an asshole – it's one and the same.' The angle of the can increased. Strachan's hatred of politicians, particularly those involved in foreign policy-making, had a long history and a longer way to run. 'They're fact-finding. How to find cheap furs; how to fuck whores on an expense account; how to screw somebody else's country now they've screwed their own. And we're paying five hundred dollars each for the privilege of meeting them, lining the Mayor's pockets and hearing him say that Russia's becoming the place again to invest.'

'We'll have to eat off the floor. Didn't you buy most of their Soviet-era silver?'

'A small symbol of capitalism's triumph.' He changed the subject. 'How's your ma?'

'She says older and fatter.' It was a friend of his mother's who had contacted Strachan five years previously with news of a young, fluent Russian-speaking graduate on the market. The trader and haulier took him on, trained him up, one of the few willing to assume the risk. Max had been saved from a life as a telephone-receptionist, or as a visually challenged tomato- or banana-costumed leafleteer on a city street. He was grateful.

'And your pa?'

'Just older. And retired.'

Howell was on his knees examining the charts spread out across the floor, chewing on a cigarette, brushing away occasional ash-falls with an abrupt back-handed flick. Purton watched from an easy chair, a stained coffee mug in his hand. It was the most comfortable room in the house, but still spartan – functional – dominated by two bookcases of military histories, biographies and poetry, a small cluster of family photographs covering a side-table: Piers Purton, his grandfather, wearing the uniform of a Captain in the White Russian army and holding the Tsarevich Alexis's surviving spaniel Joy; Purton's father, Tom, again in uniform, but for a different conflict, with the reserved, understated pose of a professional some time during 1940. The male line shared the same square build, square jaw and ice-blue eyes; the women were elegant, strong, capable of dealing with crises, colonial revolts, husbands away on active service. Max and his sisters smiled in colour from their frames – inheritors of their mother's softer, oval features. On a wall hung a print of canoe-borne SBS teams landing at night to plant charges during the Falklands campaign; the other featured a painting of 'Finn', the Irish Terrier, who had followed his master to France in 1916 and served on the Western Front carrying messages for trapped units across No Man's Land. Blinded by gas, wounded from shellfire, he saved an entire battalion near Pozières Ridge before falling to a German sniper bullet. There were reports of troops weeping openly.

Purton turned as a draught eddied in from the hall. Bess, a direct descendant of Finn, wandered through, intent on finding company, perturbed that she had been excluded. She enjoyed visits, the chance to nuzzle her way into human interaction. Her nose bobbed in greeting above the armrest, eyes understanding, intelligent, warm with Celtic mysticism and canine empathy, and disappeared as she shuffled across to the familiar figure crouching studiously over the maps. A low, rolling growl of welcome, genuine pleasure, tail working, gave Howell warning before a whiskered muzzle thrust in his ear. She slumped heavily across the charts, head turned away, intent on causing disruption.

'Give up, Nick. She always gets her way.'

'Don't all women?' He patted her flank fondly, climbed to his feet, pre-planning on hold. 'We've got the basics. It's enough to go on.' He checked his watch. 'Our Saudi's late.'

'He doesn't know Poole. You want a cup?' Howell nodded and headed through for the kitchen, Purton following. Bess entrenched herself more firmly on her territorial gains. 'So, we're agreed on sea and land infiltration from Oman?'

'Gives us flexibility,' Howell replied, helping himself to coffee. 'Sure London is keeping its distance?'

'That's what Six is promising. Hands off, no meddling. It's our show.' And lives. A grunt of scepticism from the NCO. 'Last thing they want is a connection to be made between us and them.'

'Renegades on a frolic of their own. I can see the headlines now.' The cigarette butt was propelled into the sink.

'It's what you wanted. We'll firm up when we're there, but we may as well capitalise on the airstrip north of Al-Mahra.'

'Be foolish not to if it's still deserted.' Howell tried the cup and perched up near the sink. 'With the funds the Saudis are throwing at us, we'll be able to buy every bloody LZ in the country.'

'Shouldn't have to. The rest of the kit we can move up by boat and stockpile across the Yemen border at the fishing village of Al Fatk. I was there in '94. According to Ahmed Badr, it's still pro-rebel.'

'Bet they'll be surprised to see you again.'

A rueful smile. 'Hope I don't have to leave in such a hurry.'

'Are we using the same cover?'

'Makes sense. Ahmed Badr Arabian Treks. It's a tour company I can recommend. He's got the paperwork.'

'And the weaponry. Guarantees a decent tour. Al Fatk – where to from there?'

'We send men and equipment out to the coastal areas of Ra's Sharwayn, Ra's Fartwak and Ra's Sharmah, as far from government posts as possible, and begin training.'

Howell rolled his eyes. 'Training? Our Saudi asks us to mount an insurgency, reignite the South's independence movement, and then tells us to put guerrillas in the field after only four weeks.'

'They're not novices, Nick. We'll be selecting from the National Opposition's best.'

''Scuse my lack of confidence.'

Purton poured for himself. 'There'll be three weeks' post-course for small-unit work and fire exercises. And we can trial them on limited-scope operations.'

'Limited is the word I was looking for.'

'We're not hired to question their schedule. They need spectaculars in a hurry.'

'And they'll get spectacular fuck-ups, Ben. We're trying to produce people who can place a bomb on a car, not wash the damn thing.'

He was right. Everything from weapons handling, fire and tactical movement, patrolling and ambush through observation positions, rendezvous, reception and resupply procedures to demolition, sabotage, sniping and vehicle use, would have to be taught. They could do it in eight weeks, establish the first elements of an opposition Special Forces squadron. Four weeks was paring back below basics.

'You're paid six hundred pounds a day to be optimistic.'

'You're paid a thousand. For that, I'd drive straight into Sana'a to topple the northern government.'

'How's the shopping list?' Purton steered the conversation.

Howell blew on the coffee and sipped, becoming more enthusiastic. 'Ready, right down to tents, weapons mounts, IR beacons, sand channels, NVGs, GPS, tactical radio, cam nets, shoulder-launched anti-tank rounds and custom-loaded ammo. We also need a dhow, at least two Ribs, and a fleet of Landcruisers.'

'The initial five million will cover it. We've got the budget.' And the war.

'I ought to buy my own army more often.' The happiness was fleeting. He looked up. 'Ben, I've got a bad feel about this one.'

They walked back to the sitting room to wait, the discussion stalled. Howell lit another cigarette, Purton smoked passively. They were to strike a blow against radical Islam, for the British government, for the Saudi government. *Domino Theory*. Black and white. He would like to believe it. There was the sound of a vehicle turning in to the narrow driveway outside.

A fur-gloved hand scuffed snow crystals from the coat, purchased grip and pulled wide. The garment cracked open like bone. Fabric gaping and rigid; below it, body gaping and rigid. Someone's son, someone's husband, someone's father or brother, unyielding and alone in the ice desert, without identity, without arms. The old trapper looked down into the frosted eyes, as if searching for a reflected negative of the killers. But he knew who they were, understood what it was that produced them. A chest cavity marked the heart's exit, life's exit. Another corpse to lie in the sleeping land, because the man was in the way, knew too much or knew too

little. At least they had left him his face; at least Colonel
Lazin remained alive. Stub candles were here, littered, half-
burnt, crude symbology discarded, haphazard scraps of
undeciphered verse abandoned or pinned to clothing. Diver-
sions, just as the cadaver itself was diverting. There was
little to be done, but take note, take photographs. He would
cover the grave and trudge on. Wanderers always trudged
on.

The project: a thousand-year Love Reich of touchy-freely
fascism and moral conceit. Arrogance was out, smugness in;
sense out, sensibility in. *All you need is hugs* – hugs, candlelit
vigils, yellow ribbons, keening, and the occasional universal
peace dance. Farewell logic, welcome correctness – political
and emotional – with all its attendant hypocrisies and
cynicism. The new century, where politics met media in a
vacuum free of thought, news-entertainment was just that,
sound bites displaced debate, democracy. The three-minute
culture had long since gone, usurped by its three-second
cousin. Leaders won legitimacy through glib prefixes –
'People's', 'New', 'Cool', 'Youth', 'Pine Fresh' – electorates
were markets, elections marketing strategies. All hail to the
lowest common denominator, getting lower by the day; praise
the vapid and the victims, for they *felt*. Image manipulation,
reality manipulation.

For Nigel Ferris, Member of Parliament and Junior
Foreign Office minister, it was the perfect situation. And for
that situation he was the perfect vessel – empty. *We are*
Straw Men, Hollow Men.

'Oh, it's you.'

'Hello darling.' A generic form of address. Not endear-
ment, but applied to all, a Groucho-Club affectation used
seamlessly from hair salon to political salon. Today it was
aimed at his wife.

'Where are you?' Her voice filled the car on the speaker.
Harassed, almost accusatory, the words were accompanied
by the background clutter of children shouting, of toys being

thrown. 'Sean! I've told you before . . .' A hand over the receiver and her mouth turned away muffled part of the scolding. 'Go on, take it outside . . .' A whining response, becoming a chorus of primary-age disaffection. 'Do it now!' Tears, a foot stamping, shouts, a door slammed. She sighed, a short, hyperventilated breath. To her, an embrace caught on camera, the lighting of a scented candle, a public face as fixed as The Joker's, and the wearing of non-exploitative fabrics, were all that it took to cure the world. She had yet to find a cure for domestic life.

'Coping?' Ferris asked.

'What does it sound like?'

He smiled. A ring of confidence, of unassailable self-belief. Jackie was so much better with the theory of child-raising than the practice. A career woman, she had chosen to have children late to prove that she owned her body and her destiny, wanted to make a statement, led campaigns against pre-school gender-stereotyping. The statement at first became muddled and then disappeared beneath the avalanche of soiled nappies, beneath the three-year-old daughter's dollies and prams and beneath the five-year-old son's obsession with tractors and trucks. Yet public percep-tion of Nigel and Jackie Ferris remained inviolate. He was a communicator, on-message, a rising star whose role at the Foreign Office allowed him to project and package himself, human rights and ersatz compassion in favourable, press-digestible news plants. And if some thought him conceited, then the occasional picture displaying vulner-ability, the evidence of a man willing to choke up or weep in public, were generally enough to silence the more reactionary of critics. The smile was fixed by charm school, the tone honeyed by elocution lessons, expressions given sincerity by media experts, the couple's colour-coordination chosen by lifestyle consultants, the presentation, the persona, the emotions buffed, polished, spun and doctored. Like his wife: warm, honest, humane and competent, that was Nigel Ferris, for that was how he seemed. Nothing left untouched; everything touched up. Quite a team, quite a product.

'Did you see my statement at the Foreign Office?'

'No.' Flat, uninterested. She was obviously on the cordless, tracking the children round the house.

'I claimed that the place is dominated by white upper-middle-class males who don't represent the modern multicultural reality.'

'The answer's still no.' He decided not to mention the Opposition spokesman's accusation that he was merely being a chip off the old shoulder. 'When are you getting back?' she asked.

'Later tonight. I've got a whole lot of flesh to press and Commonwealth people to meet. Depends on how long the drink lasts. The kids will be asleep.'

A weary sigh. 'I wouldn't bet on it.'

'Tell them I'll take them out tomorrow if they behave.'

'I thought you were in favour of sanctions.' His anti-apartheid stance throughout the 1980s, the public relations advice he proffered the ANC, had done much to enhance his international profile and credibility. His wife would not let him forget it.

'Don't believe everything you read in the papers.'

'I never do – you put the stories there.'

'OK. I'll catch up with you later. I'm coming up to a traffic jam in Piccadilly. Love you. Ciao.'

The line went dead as he pulled the Rover hire-car into the fast lane and accelerated past a long-distance lorry. He would not use his own BMW today, nor the chauffeured government car service vehicle. This was unofficial business. Traffic was moving unusually well on the M1, a motorway better known for its roadworks and cone-induced bottlenecks. He took advantage of the rare situation, scanning ahead for the law and the correct junction number, and pushed his foot down. *We are Straw Men, Hollow Men*. Three cars back, an indistinguishable grey saloon settled into cruise mode. Its occupants, including a tall, languid, female employee of

Leonid Gresko, head of Russia's FSB Security Service, tailed. Watched.

In Georgetown, Washington DC, Senator Patrick O'Day yawned, switched the bedside lamp to dim, checked the clock, broke wind, and hoped that his wife was still asleep. She had her back to him, straight black hair in a bob which had retained its severity since Harvard Law School resting deep in a pillow, body sealed in the shimmer of a silk nightdress. He was not certain if he loved her or if she loved him, but there was mutual dependence, acceptance on both sides of faults and of past, present or future infidelities which might have left more judgemental types speechless. If that was love, so be it. He yawned again and stared at her, gift-parcelled by a faggoty Italian designer whose name he did not recognise. Perhaps he should have been content with the wedding dowry she brought to the marriage, money which papered over the cracks, bought influence and friends, suited him, booted him, gave him style and a plutocratic gravitas which wrung the smell of peat from the family line. She was a class act, in a world in which acting was about all that was required.

He swung his feet to the ground, waiting while they searched for slippers before he stood and shuffled to the bathroom. She twitched and pulled the covers closer. The kitchen was next – cranberry juice, mineral water, and two bananas were consumed – and twenty minutes after leaving his wife's side, hamstring stretches and circulation jumps complete, he stepped into the below-zero darkness of an early-morning snow vortex. Grey tracksuit, grey windcheater, black woollen hat pulled down hard on the ears, gloves, and thick socks rolled up from the air-cushioned running shoes, the figure left the safety of the door, edged down the steps, and broke into a strong, steady pace along Q Street, kicking up miniature and momentary powder storms from the treads. He kept east of Wisconsin Avenue, the route taking him past the dark crenellations of the Two Worlds Church, the soft impact of feet the only accompaniment on streets lined with heavily shuttered red-brick mansions and low villas broken by the stark branches of winter trees picked out in the pale yellow light of globed street lamps. A patch of ice lay in front; he dodged it without breaking step and headed for the park, a solitary runner lost in a sound-deadened world bounded with phantom, slumbering houses. The turn into 30th, a corner marked by the conical tower of a white-painted urban folly; a short burst up to R Street and a lengthening stride on the edge of Oak Hill. Usually, he would enter near the cemetery, sustain his pace beside the tennis courts and children's playground, pass through the wooded tracks and along Lover's Lane to Massachusetts Avenue, before doubling back beside the quiet-flowing waters of Rock Creek. This morning, the circuit was different. There was no need for the canned mace he carried for potentially violent encounters with vagrants. Cold would keep the cut-throats away, and he was bypassing the area.

Panting heavily now, trailing vapour puffs, the lungs attempting to cope with the chill hits made on a warming body, O'Day lowered his head and surged forward, feet racing, heart racing. Behind, his tracks were being eradicated by fresh fall. Another trail had appeared alongside. Gasping, several blocks on, the white edifice of Dunbarton Court looming to the left, the closed gates of Tudor Place Gardens on the right, the Senator leaned heavily on his knees, lowering the noise, steadying the pulse before attempting to squint and listen into the gloom. Nothing. He jogged on the spot, flapped his arms and stopped again. Then he retraced a hundred metres and ducked into an alleyway. He knew the exact location, had visited it many times; light was unnecessary. Across the street, an image-intensifier on a camcorder captured the movements from an electrically heated pane fitted to a first-storey window.

'Visuals are indistinct.'

'No matter.'

Sound and sight, the target location was checked and

wired. Cameras, lights, anticipated action. Once inside, the Senator would take his regular slot as unwitting star of the small screen. Patrick O'Day, influential member of the Senate Foreign Relations Committee, intermittent and powerful ranker on the Select Intelligence Committee, strong advocate of reallocating defence resources to aid and social programmes, and – although considered a dove – a key exponent of aggressive anti-drugs measures overseas. Narcotics brought destruction and despair to inner-city constituencies; he was tireless in promoting the issue to the top of the national security agenda. Patrick O'Day, friend of the President. The sensor operator scratched his balls and waited. Show-time.

While in the employ of Boris Diakanov, bodyguards were felt superfluous. The reputation of the crime chief alone was enough to guarantee the personal safety of his senior captains. Or so Konon had thought. Theory was comforting, but since the brutal murder of young Oleg, the practice was showing obvious deficiencies. And if the boss's son had been hit . . . Konon sipped his coffee contemplatively, ignoring the pimps and prostitutes cruising the ground floor of the Kosmos Hotel, the businessmen from the shabbier end of the spectrum gorging their faces at the single-price restaurant. Naturally, with tension rising, Diakanov had refused Konon recourse to armed protection. How could it be other? It was to do with face; surround yourself with suited paramilitaries and it meant you were running scared. Yet the policy was less than even-handed. It did not preclude *tsisari* himself from benefiting from a private army. Ah, but he needed a praetorian guard: that too was a question of face. Inconsistency meant nothing in this world. Konon stared mournfully into his cup. He missed the certainties and routine of his old KGB days, when he could blind himself to immorality because he had a cause, when the security guard in the entrance hallway on Furkasovsky pereulok would salute him in the morning and salute him out at night. What price that?

Face it, he was not cut out to be a gangster, had never broken bones, rocks or teeth. He was an administrator, and a good one, worth every tainted dollar bill which his new master paid. He looked about him. A ghastly hotel – unattractive, Soviet-quality, Soviet block, banished to the north-eastern outskirts of the city near a park where relics of space exploration and technological prowess provided shelter for lunatics and catatonics who stared uncomprehendingly at the startled visitor. Madmen living among decay. The VDNKh – USSR Economic Achievements Exhibition – madmen living among past lies. Japanese electronics now filled buildings stripped of their former displays. He could not think of a better metaphor. So the name had been changed, foreign cars put into the Space Pavilion, but the utter waste of eighty years of untruths could not be disguised. Perhaps they should solder the remaining rocket parts together, wire up the museum exhibits, and send them into orbit to represent the cutting edge of current Russian research.

He checked his watch. The contact was late. Another cup of coffee was called for. He was pleased that he had stayed in touch with former colleagues: it kept everyone smiling. For the FSB Security Service officers it meant cash and long-coveted consumer durables; for Diakanov it meant information and influence. And for Konon it meant an excuse to keep up friendships and maintain position in the Diakanov hierarchy. Win-win. Today's meeting was to check Security Service progress in investigating the Siberian diamond robbery. His source had promised to trade a variety of tantalising and revelatory detail.

The murmur quieted, at first not enough to draw his attention, a faint change in tempo, almost indiscernible, unlikely to impinge on the consciousness of a man deep in thought. The numbers of people in the vicinity seemed to have thinned out. Konon brought the cup to his lips. It was most unusual for his contact to be late; by nature he was punctilious. Moscow traffic grew worse by the day. New

Russians, new problems. Odd given the tragi-comic financial climate. He sighed. *Odd*. Was he imagining it or had the bar become emptier? Emptier – it was empty. A shrug and another look at his watch.

He was no amateur, had boxed at the KGB academy in his youth, and behind the bureaucrat's façade was a man who enjoyed toiling on his dacha, splitting logs and hunting. But age, drink and rich food could slow anyone, catch anyone. There was time only to throw black coffee into the eyes of the nearest assailant, to lash out ineffectively with a foot, before they were on him. They had the advantage in height, speed and numbers; he the disadvantage of being seated. Inequality and overpowering violence marked the onslaught, the four men systematically beating Konon to the ground, clubs, coshes and then a stainless-steel bar stool rising and falling, joining in a brutal flurry. He did not make much noise, did not whimper or scream, and after the odd futile attempt, ceased to fend off the blows. Passive resistance, an acceptance of fate – the perpetrators were not over-interested in reasons. They had orders; thinking belonged to others. Two caught the lolling torso by the lapels and began to drag him, trailing a blood-slick, into the lobby. Potential spectators had long since vanished, decided to opt for room-service: so much easier. Even the security staff were absent, on their rounds, on leave, detained, sick or afflicted by migraine. They were missing quite a performance. The beating went on, kicking became predominant, a man swore as his boots lost traction on the now slippery surface and he fell. Fatigue was setting in. The bar stool, tarnished red, was lifted and positioned, delicately. Accuracy was essential. It was readied by two pairs of hands, and the heaviest of the quartet climbed on. Resistance gave and the stool sank. Beneath, the body was quivering.

The men had gone, security, staff and hotel guests returned. A few prostitutes were discernible: where there was a crowd, there was trade. And in the centre, a focus for attention, alone in his own bloody radius, hemmed in by a voyeuristic throng, was Konon, his battered face turned upwards and punctured by a bar stool thrust deep in an eye socket.

'You want a fuck?' a high-cheeked girl whispered in the ear of a male onlooker. Death was a well-known aphrodisiac, she reasoned. But he was too engrossed to notice her. Shit, assumption disproved. She sauntered away.

In a far corner of the restaurant, Max continued to eat his open sandwich. He could hear the excitable noises, the sound of camera shutters, and assumed that a member of Moscow's criminal royalty had appeared for a reception of paid sycophants. Or a senior government minister was gracing the hotel with his presence. It all amounted to much the same. Another bite. The food was foul, but he was hungry after three hours of talks hammering out a barter trade. German security equipment for Russian ship fittings. Chew and swallow. He could get the food down; keeping it there might be a problem. Gennady, his minder, would have wolfed this delicacy were he not on temporary leave. A militia siren penetrated the babble.

The men, sweating and elated, pounded the short distance to the Mercedes, its engine kept turning and warm by the driver who waited as his passengers jumped in to blasts of iced air. Acceleration. A door, half open, slammed from the momentum. Sitting low in a steam-windowed Moskovich, its bodywork dented and rusted in the hands of a multitude of previous owners, was Colonel Petr Ivanov. Konon had wanted to discuss the diamond theft with him; Diakanov was raging, demanding results. But the FSB officer did not feel talkative, preferred to watch from a distance until the hired help bludgeoned his former colleague to death. The place was so drab, could benefit from a bit of colour. He turned down the heating and reached for the mobile phone beside him, punching the programmed number with a gloved finger.

'Did you get the footage?' He paused for the reply. 'Good.' It was a pity that Konon had to go, he reflected. They were once in the same department together; their wives were friends. But Leonid Gresko had ordered it; there was no choice, no discretion. A second number was called. He counted the rings, a stickler for punctuality and professionalism. The receiver was picked up. 'They've just left,' he said. 'When they reach Lyublinsky District, you know what to do.' He hung up and started the engine, his mind already turned to the operation taking place in St Petersburg.

Four hundred miles to the north-west in the Petrograd sector of the city of St Petersburg, Viktor Gribanov lay back in a doctor's chair wearing darkened eye-protectors and a hospital gown. He was a vain man, surprising given a complexion which resembled gravel and a visage as featureless as the M1 motorway stretching east from Poland, but money and ugliness had conspired to send him on a constant and lifelong quest for facial enhancement. But vanity was a lesser sin, for with two older brothers he was co-founder and joint leader of one of the city's leading crime syndicates, ruling the docks with legendary ruthlessness and jostling to dominate the Baltic smuggling routes with the rival Lessiovski, Nechiporenko and Orlov mafiagentsia clans. The competition was fierce, fractious and often bloody, yet in recent years a semblance of peace had been imposed through a de facto division of labour and profit, and by order of Boris Diakanov, boss of bosses, to whom they owed grudging fealty. Of late, it was less grudging: the murder of *tsisan*'s son had unnerved them all. They could not protest their innocence more loudly, their desire to track down the perpetrators more strongly. A quarrel with Diakanov, worse – a vendetta – would be harmful for business, terminally damaging to life expectancy. Gribanov sniffed – cocaine was playing havoc with his moods and sinuses – and waited. He was the safest of all the St Petersburg set, his tenure secure, his position well known by the patron in Moscow. Indeed, it was the Gribanovs who were quickest in accepting Diakanov's offer to join the Senate, to use its distribution networks. Viktor himself had been instrumental in negotiating a deal by which Diakanov became majority owner of the family's non-core business: a computer-hacking operation which plundered the world's financial markets of fifty million dollars a year. Diakanov's team of programmers had grown the venture tenfold. Using the global telephone network, there were few limits to what it could achieve. The ultimate in computer trading, in getting something for free. A sweetener which *tsisari* appreciated.

Gribanov liked to pamper himself; there was little else to do during these long winters. Time away in the sun meant time for the rest – those in other families, those in his own – to get ahead, to move in on the key concessions. Loyalty could be fluid and short-lived here in St Petersburg.

'Are you content with what we discussed, sir?' His cosmetic specialist gazed down from behind the surgical mask, the shape of his head a shadowed smudge through the goggle lenses. 'We're agreed. It's just those three small wrinkles to be treated.'

Gribanov gave a slight nod. He was a veteran of such visits to the discreet clinic tucked away near the military sanatorium in the old Kamenoostrovsky Palace, a short walk across the parks and pleasure gardens from his own dacha on 2-ya Beryozovaya alleya. This was Stone Island – Kamenny ostrov – the exclusive, secluded and landscaped preserve of the city's power and moneyed elite, refuge for the Russian president when in town, and home to only the highest-achieving *krutoy* and wealthiest of mafiya heads. Gribanov was among them, had made it. Geographically, not far from the waterfront warehouses to which he was born; materially, psychologically, another continent.

The specialist busied himself with the equipment, his assistant performing checks stage left and out of view. Gribanov did not enjoy small talk, but let the man chatter; he was good at what he did, had performed every conceivable type of laser cosmetic surgery on him, could assume a certain familiarity. Over the previous three years, Gribanov's tattoos had been removed with Q Switched Ruby and Alexandrite lasers, broken veins eradicated with pulsed dye and copper bromide lasers and his face smoothed and made wrinkle-free with CB Erbium YAG and CO_2 laser pulses. Burn, peel and rejuvenate: a light-show to freshen the image and palate of any jaded gangster.

The goggles were pulled off roughly. He winced against the sharpness of the overhead lighting. This was a liberty, an insult. He made to sit up, but two figures now stood either side of him, pinning his arms to the rests and binding them down with nylon restraints. The pneumatic chair-pedal was depressed, Gribanov's body tilting backwards into full horizontal.

'What's the meaning of this?' he shouted.

'Natural selection.'

'What the fuck? Get me out of here.'

'I think not.' A face – up-ended – moved into his field of vision, putting him into shadow. It was the head of Petr Ivanov's hired mechanic. Today, he would be trying his hand at the cutting-edge of laser technology.

'You'll fucking pay for this.'

'We have. It's a great privilege.'

Fear generated heat. Gribanov's face, already as ill-defined as melted butter, appeared to melt some more. 'Hey, this is no way to negotiate.'

'Lucky, we're not negotiating.' A finger was run along the side of the criminal's sweating features. Past attempts at beautification had plainly been a matter of faith. 'All that money gone to waste,' the man murmured.

'Look, you want cash? No problem. I can get you cash. Any currency.'

'You're starting positively.' The hand gently pinched and slapped a cheek.

'Jesus, what is this?' A frightened man trying not to be frightened, attempting to maintain the dignity of rank in a position which was less than dignified. 'Who are you working for? I'll talk to them. OK? We'll deal.' The arm of the laser was pulled into position above him, the pen-sized device at its end pointing directly downwards. The words were flowing faster. 'Stop it! Stop it! Fuck . . . God.' A type of squealing, charisma of office – authority of office – stripped away. 'Listen, my brothers will arrange something; they'll organise it.'

'They'll have to. You'll be indisposed. Now. . .'

'Please . . .'

'Now,' the man repeated. 'We want every detail of the Gribanov bank accounts, how the money is moved, duress codes, authorisation sequences and anything which you believe might be of interest.'

'You think I can tell you all this?'

'There's an incentive.'

'This is the biggest fucking mistake of your tiny fucking lives,' he yelled.

'Yours also.' The man nodded at a colleague, before turning back. 'Looks can kill, Viktor.' He gripped the laser.

'Get me out, get me out!' Screaming, and a rocking, struggling movement to escape. 'There'll be war. You fucking understand me? You'll be buried, you hear? Totally fucking buried. I'm telling you. Let me go. You want war? This is war, OK?'

'Then this is the opening shot, Viktor.'

It was usual during cosmetic surgery for the laser to make a slight popping noise as it was fired. Today there was no such sound, for the device was turned to full power, constant beam. The only popping seemed to emanate from Gribanov himself. Smoke rose from a socket. The eyes have it. Meltdown.

850 miles east of Moscow, lying buried in the Urals, the Russian nuclear command bunker at Kosvinsky Mountain.

'Low-frequency communication from General Staff at Chekov, sir.'

The technician hurried towards the general leaning on the bridge rail overlooking the control centre. The senior officer breathed hard, slapped his palms down with an air of finality,

181

turned and held out his hand. Below him, surrounded by the winking lights and glowing consoles of communications suites, satellite uplink stations and data retrieval centres, lay the mountain's operational heart, hub of Russia's strategic nuclear rocket forces.

He took the sheet of paper, checked the first row cipher, and nodded. 'Get back to your station.' The man saluted and trotted away. The general was left alone to his thoughts, walking slowly and purposefully to the raised dais and climbing into the chair in front of his personal console. He reached for one of five telephones set vertically in the binnacle.

'The mountain is fully secure?' He waited for the reply, replaced the receiver, and snatched up another. 'Positions are taken?' Affirmation.

For a few seconds he watched the central twenty-foot screen, its sides flanked by a pair of smaller and angled displays, dominating the electronic pit beneath him. The globe lay spread out, flattened like two lungs, ready for nuclear dissection. He also was ready. Palm scan – acceptance – key insert, a flick of a switch and a flat panel of illuminated numerals lit up on the desk. It did not take long to cross-reference the printout against the codebook taken from the safe, to enter the strategic authorisations. The screen began to flash. He pulled the microphone arm close and spoke into it. 'Waiting for acceptance, Captain.'

A red light came on; cyrillic figures moved horizontally across the twelve-inch visual display, and a hush fell across the chamber. 'The situation is go,' the general intoned. 'The order is OU. Confirm, OU.' *Otvetniy udar* – launch on attack. Confirmation was received. 'National leadership *Chegets* and Kazbek codes are no longer functional.' Any missile launch orders sent from the three *Chegets* – the nuclear command briefcase 'footballs' in the possession of the Russian President, his Defence Minister and Chief of the General Staff – were now invalidated and overridden. 'We have preliminary sanction codes from General Staff; national command authority has been transferred. I am deactivating the *Kasvaz* C2 and *Vyuga* fall-back strategic communication system as of this moment.' He depressed a lever; a bank of lights went down and an alarm sounded briefly. 'We have control; we are autonomous. Mission, I am handing off.'

He rose to retake his position at the rail and plugged in a headset for the performance. Against every law of nature, yet done so naturally, so definitively. Above it all, Man as God, Man as Destroyer. To dust they shall return. Sweat was beginning to glint on the general's face.

Down in the pit, pace and pulses were quickening, tension climbing. '*Perimetr* activated. Dead Hand is functional. I repeat, Dead Hand is functional.'

'Status of 15PO11 transmitter payload?'

'Positive.'

'Check. Systems at standby. Ready for launch.'

'Switch to automatic.'

A finger punched a sequence of lit buttons which changed to orange on the monitor. 'Mode achieved.'

The launch and payload managers sat at twin consoles, peering intently, waiting.

Parabolic lines appeared on the giant screen, moving outwards from left to right, their numbers growing. 'Warning. *Krokus* system is identifying incoming. We have multiple tracks, ICBM and SLBM, MX and Trident. Trajectory computations underway. Estimated time to MIRV and MARV separation ten minutes. Preliminary target indications appearing.'

'Read out.'

'General Staff Command Bunker at Chekov; Kapustin Yar; Tyuratam; Semipalatinsk and Sary Shagan; Novosibirsk; Petropavlosk and Bratsk. Radar and multi-spectral updates imminent.' Bratsk, site of the giant hydroelectric dam, had only recently become of special strategic significance, a centre for highly classified military research. It was the only target whose activities those present were unfamiliar with. The others were always expected to be at the top end of the list for an American pre-emptive first strike.

'Thank God. Just a warning shot.' A laugh, which was not reciprocated by the rest.

'Heavy jamming, Elint satellites non-operational, Hen House units blank. Phased arrays at Baranovichi, Olnegorsk, Pechora and Mishelevka giving sporadic returns. Triumph point-defence malfunctioning.'

'What's new?' Even in peacetime, the radars were less than reliable, their coverage poor. The situation had worsened with the demise of early warning bases stationed on territories once belonging to the former Soviet Union: the Skrunda site in Latvia gone, Mykolayiv and Mukacheve in Ukraine taken over, Lyaki in Azerbaijan, Balqash in Kazakhstan – dismantled. And now Russia dismantled, gone.

'ABM system down.' Accepting, almost indifferent. The last line of defence – the anti-ballistic missile system – no longer operational. 'Pushkino command radar is not giving a readout.' Farewell Moscow. 'SH-11 missiles are failing to fly. I repeat, SH-11's are failing to fly.'

'Check.'

A different voice. 'OK, we have further plume and post-boost detection; TACAMO intercepts. Signals intelligence from Lourdes verifies American launch commands. We've managed to scramble some of their communications, delayed operability of several US Minuteman III and MX silos.'

As if it mattered, the mission controller thought, jaws masticating furiously on a stick of gum. Mouth still dry. The world was about to split physically down its seams, its continents splinter into a million glowing fragments, its lakes, rivers and seas evaporate into space steam, and Lourdes had reduced by a fraction the amount of megaton throw-weight to land on Russian soil. Medals, surely, for the boys in Cuba? He wondered how his old friend Arkady had fared in the United States, a man sentenced to death in absentia for his part in the killings of four compatriots on a beach prior to defecting in 1993. The long arm of Russian martial law: he would doubtless be in a suburban semi, unhappy, nostalgic, and about to be terminated by firing squad, a long-range, silo-based, rocket-equipped, nuclear-tipped, firing-squad. Serious retribution.

'Impact data, detonation algorithms, I want them *now*,' the ground environment controller shouted.

Rings rippled outwards from the displayed impact points, associated data – estimated blast radii, fallout patterns, emp warnings and fatality estimates – nudging up onto a side screen. Further lines, many of them, were forming across the main panel, speeding towards Russian territory. The end of the world looked like a child's frenzied drawing. Starbursts.

'We have separation of multiple re-entry vehicles. Going terminal. The ten units are from MX missiles. Additional impacts, earth penetration expected, at Sharapovo, Voronovo, Vnukovo-2 and Ramenki.' The operators watched in awe. Other targets were read out. Not long to go; finality to this particular evolutionary branch. 'CEP patterns are shown.'

'Blasts registered.' New readouts were flickering up. 'Satellite surveillance overloaded. Main comms link down . . . We have been targeted; we have been targeted. Authority will be passed to Yamntau mountain if command position becomes untenable.'

Untenable? Their command position? The world was becoming fucking untenable – unrecognisable – a specialist thought, loosening his collar. In this position, it never helped to have a sense of irony or imagination. Beside him, a systems manager closed his eyes, mumbled a quick prayer, and stared again at the situation. That's what the Americans would have called it: 'a situation'. We have a situation. Superpower rivalry over who could best master the art of ultimate understatement, the skill of apocalyptic euphemism. He suppressed a smile. The central command post, Russian Strategic Nuclear Forces, was burning.

'*Perimetr* level two has been achieved.' The mission manager's voice was calm. The process was beyond his control, beyond anyone's. Fate, computers and surrealism had taken charge. '*Perimetr* level one has been achieved.'

* * *

The sombre, undulating call of a klaxon hung over the snow-clad expanse of concrete and cleared ground which constituted the missile launch complex of Yedrovo, set anonymously, like its sister Vypolzozo, in the Valday hills almost a hundred miles from Moscow. The site appeared deserted, devoid of human life, shouts, the stampede of men and women hurrying to prepare for emergency action. Its masts and blockhouses stood stark against a strangely iridescent sky, a wisp of steam escaping as a silo cover slid back across the launch position of an SS-17 Intercontinental Ballistic Missile. On the far side of the compound, in a hardened bunker set deep below ground, personnel gathered to watch the unfolding process on a closed-circuit television monitor. Their computer consoles were unmanned, for the chain of command was broken – vaporised – the launch code process circumvented. Perimetr was on automatic, Dead Hand operational. They were watching Doomsday passively, in real-time and for real.

Parameters met, calculations concluded. Critical point, critical mass. 'We have a launch. We have a *Perimetr* launch.' A tone of normality announcing the abnormal, the unique, the end. No going back – that was never an option built into the system. Dr Strangelove celebrated. 'Long live Russia,' a solitary enthusiast bellowed from behind an electronic support station. Foolish. No one joined in. Simply silence, a desolation. A minute or so before, Russia had ceased to exist as an entity, a living, breathing nation. There was a moment to reflect, to think. But as the general watched from his position at the metal rail, the brains of those present were refusing to accept what had been initiated.

'Barring fratricidal detonation, we are due to receive a direct nuclear impact in ... forty ... four-zero seconds.' Professional to the last.

The SS-17 unsheathed itself from the silo, sliding upwards, accelerating, the white-fire plume trailing meteoric, roaring, behind. It rose, heading south-east, a climbing, quickening sun thrusting determinedly away from earth on an irregular axis to bring heat to different continents. It flew, not towards targets within the United States or China – its old power adversaries – but in a profile which traversed the great landmass of Russia itself. And in its nose-cone was not the paraphernalia of an advanced thermonuclear weapon, but a compact ultra high-frequency transmitter device. Perimetr was functioning, sending signals across the mountains and steppes, bypassing satellites and land-lines which were disrupted, distrusted or destroyed. The messages were received by computers, decoded by computers, processed and acted upon by computers. Silo covers were rolling back. The first missiles were launching. The Perimetr transmitter was still live, mankind dead.

The general cleared his throat. 'Congratulations, ladies and gentlemen. You have just incinerated the entire populations of the planet. Several times over. You may stand down.'

After the warmth and claustrophobia of the mountain citadel, the crisp, searing air of the Urals in winter made the Major pause and blink, allowing him short, shallow breaths for acclimatisation. He preferred to be beneath the ground, his kingdom, an environment to which the survival instincts of all burrowing creatures were best suited. He had penetrated further than most. Kosvinsky Mountain was his responsibility, his life, and the culmination of a long career in the security service, and he was as assiduous in tending the complex as he was in protecting his own personal interests and advancement. A veteran of the KGB's Directorate 15, charged with guarding Russia's strategic nuclear facilities and command posts, he had spent a significant part of his subterranean existence patrolling and overseeing the vast network of strongholds which formed the backbone of his country's intercontinental ballistic missile response. His knowledge and memory of these labyrinths were at once

187

encyclopaedic and photographic, his suspicion of the military personnel manning them profound. The downgrading of the KGB, its loss of status and pervasive control, its redesignation as the Federal Security Service and, worse, the downwards spiral of its pay conditions to rival those of the army, were not conducive to a sense of well-being. Whatever the posturing, the successful launch of ballistic missiles, the simulation exercises involving *Perimetr* and the strategic command system, there was no disguising the parlous and perilous state of affairs. He would have to watch out for himself. Leonid Gresko had promised much. Sit tight and wait; there will be a spring after this long winter.

He changed down a gear and slewed the four-wheel-drive military vehicle to gain better traction in the pits made by an earlier convoy of trucks. It bucked, engine grinding, but maintained its grip on the surface. A Mil helicopter had made a cold-weather landing at the small emergency airstrip; as security chief for the mountain, he was paying a courtesy call. FSB contacts often passed through. No one would interfere.

The helicopter had moved across to an empty pan, rotors gently turning, closed up like the mountain. A guard saluted from behind double panes of glass. The Major failed to acknowledge, negotiating the angled gate approach and speeding past the upraised barrier. He pulled in behind a snow-tractor, reached for a briefcase and stepped out, adjusting the fur hat and patting down his coat. A face stared from the helicopter's cargo window, framed by the bubble perspex, unmoving. It reminded him of the image of a cosmonaut he had once seen, focusing on deep space, looking through him, beyond. He might have been a worthless speck of floating debris, a long-dead stellar fragment, for the distant eyes did not seem to register. He cleared his throat, shrugged deeper into the coat-collar and picked his way over to the steps. The cargo door slid back, far enough for access, and he climbed up to enter.

'Vodka?'

'Not while I'm on duty.'

'Don't mind if I do.' Answering his own invitation, Hunter Strachan threw the shot down his throat and capped the bottle. 'So, the *Perimetr* test went off without a hitch?'

'Everyone was pleased, even the general.'

'I never gave up on miracles. Did the technical enhancements work?'

'Perfectly. It's all in the report.'

'Told you American software was good.' He tugged at the peak of his cavalry stetson. 'My people are going to sleep more sound knowing that our cities won't glow because of your computer problems.'

It was American expertise and advice which was steadily modernising the creaking Russian strategic nuclear command system. In 1993, the defection of a GRU officer from a sun-warmed beach in Cuba had provided US intelligence with the most accurate assessment of its superpower rival's decaying missile capabilities. Decay meant faults; decay meant early launch based on flawed information; decay meant an undermining of deterrence and loss of central control. And loss of central control made the West nervous. The Cuban Sanction, the crypto-secret allocation of funding and technical assistance made available to Russia's Strategic Rocket Forces after a meeting held in May 1993 at Cuba's Hotel Los Jazminos between a select group of intelligence officers, was its response. Leonid Gresko, current head of the FSB Federal Security Service, played a pivotal role, had been a motivating factor, throughout the negotiations. The scenario was nightmarish: malfunctions which caused Russia's nuclear command equipment to switch spontaneously to combat mode, power cuts from unpaid bills leaving missile silos without communications or maintenance. When, in 1997, Russian Defence Minister Igor Rodionov admitted that 'the system could fall apart', America was already acting.

The aid came. And below it, far below, unknown to the United States President, the legislators, or even to the Director of the Central Intelligence Agency, were the deeper contacts spawned by the Cuban Sanction. They fed and grew on dread, that to raise funds Russia might sell nuclear missile technology on to China and lesser wannabe league players, that the Kremlin could spread its vulnerable arsenal back into neighbouring Belarus, that while its conventional armies dissolved its nuclear dependency would continue to increase. The logic was appalling but clear: while Russian reliance on its strategic missile forces remained, it was better to see those forces upgraded, functioning and secure. New facilities were dug into mountains, bunkers were overhauled, command centres rebuilt, the highly advanced static and mobile SS-25 Topol Intercontinental Ballistic Missile introduced, and a satellite launch base constructed at Svobodny. The programme went on, grew. Hunter Stranchan was one of its manifestations.

The briefcase was passed across, Strachan flicking the catches and thumbing cursorily through the documents inside. 'My, my, you have been busy.' The Agency would be pleased.

'It's what I'm paid for.' Strachan was always the highest bidder in the loyalty auction.

'Too true.' He pulled a thick envelope from inside his coat pocket and tossed it on to the Major's lap. 'Buy your wife something nice.' Like a divorce. He smiled – deceptive benevolence, scar tissue rippling like concertinaed chamois – but the security man was busy checking the foreign denomination inside.

Strachan waited, bored. He had purchased too many individuals to see them as individuals. They were a human mass: weak, stupid, desperate or greedy, in varied combinations, predictable and unchallenging. Russians – their asking price, souls, were pathetically cheap. Endearing in a way, the tussle with their pride, the shallow justifications, the turmoil of conscience and genuine love for the Mother Country. Irritating in another. He had cut his teeth on Operation Giraffe in the early 1990s, the American–German espionage effort run from a command villa in the Dahlem suburb of Berlin, aimed at stripping the departing Soviet forces of their most sensitive and advanced military secrets. For three years, they systematically bribed, blackmailed and thieved countless items from disaffected Russian soldiers and Red Army commanders, struck deals in bars and flea-markets. Lada cars were swapped for tanks, stereo systems for codebooks, microwave ovens for helicopter gunsights, petty cash for missile warning systems. A commercial free-for-all, and Hunter Strachan played his part. It was his commercial trucks which hauled the tons of stolen hardware across to American bases in southern Germany for onward transit to the United States without arousing suspicion. It was Strachan, who, posing as an import-export specialist, flew the most advanced version of Russia's Mi-24 attack-helicopter out of an army aviation camp to be spirited away for technical evaluation.

The currency-count was coming to an end. This was no different. The Agency had entrusted him with establishing transport and haulage links across the territories of the former Soviet Union, to act as a forward indicator, as early warning, to courier men and material around the republics, service agent networks, take payments in and information out. Unbeatable cover. He could roam, barter and buy, and with political patronage and secure hub-and-spoke operations, the CIA amassed in-theatre assets on a scale which it only dreamt of during the controlled and difficult years of the Cold War. Strachan, a prime mover.

'Everything is in order.' The formality of the official receiving unofficial payment.

'We have a deal then,' Strachan replied.

No movement. 'You have something else for me.'

'I surely do.'

He ducked beneath the canvas bench and slowly manoeuvred out a heavy metallic case between his spread feet. Blood rushed to his eyes, the cargo floor swerved towards him, the vision red, a flashback of la Drang Valley and a grunt's head rolling out while he helped a crew chief stash mine casualties

– flesh pieces – in the rear. The crew chief had pinned a detached leg to the deck with his foot for the return to the Cav's 'Golf Course' landing area near An Khe. The medics laughed, simply laughed, when they landed. Strachan shook the image out of his brain.

'Is something wrong?'

'It's heavy.' He pushed it across. 'I trust you can evade security?'

'I am security, Mr Strachan.' There would be no X-ray or explosive checks to pass. 'These are the diamonds?'

'Some of them. Rough. And five pounds of anti-tampering plastic explosive. We don't want the ice melting away, do we?'

'They will be safe below the mountain. You have my word.' And your balls, the American thought.

'OK, time to crank up,' he announced, standing. 'So, unless you want to stay on the ship . . .'

The Major had made it back to his off-roader and stowed the case, crouching from the downwash as the rotors gathered speed behind. Strachan opened the throttle, humming 'Doin' a what comes naturally', and peered out from the cockpit window.

'Stay deep, little guy,' he muttered. 'It's going to get mighty hot out here on the surface.' Rotors checked, cyclic tested, he pulled back on the collective.

The helicopter rose and headed away. The Major felt a need to get back below ground.

Book Two

ANARCHY IS LOOSED

Breathing is laboured, rasping, the coughs and nightmares of the *zeks* turning the prison hut into a cave for the ill and the insane. The man moans gently. He will be dead by morning, and we will take his food. Nothing is' wasted, not even a life. Lips babble, are licked by dry tongues; someone is whispering in half-trance, someone is crying. A few hours of broken sleep for broken minds, the atmosphere rank with sweat and faeces, the smell of juices digesting empty stomachs. We lie on our wood platforms – death litters – and wait, for orders, beatings, reveille, eternity. There is no warmth, no comfort. The thin blankets crack with ice. We listen for tuberculosis, for the low rattle that means a corpse's rations, for the innuendo or footfall which herald a nail to the throat, the sharpened edge of a can lid in the groin. Fate is improvised like the weaponry, changeable by the second. It is not a matter of luck – here, no one is lucky. And I am a '58' – a political – the damned. We live in misery, create misery, feed on misery. The gulag system.

Movement, boots thundering, the disorientating yellow intrusion of paraffin light. We are bathed in it – all become yellow – inmates, cowards, lice-scurrying to the shadow beyond. A killing has been commanded. The man is held down, too weak to struggle, too starved to care. An axe swings up, the executioner brings it high. Log-splitting, human splitting, the tool is flexible. Descent. But I am standing. *Pravda* – 'Truth' – the propagandist newspaper distributed to read, absorb, eat, is rolled in my hand. I strike out, feel it connect, the windpipe give. *Pravda byvaet bol'no . . . Pravda byvaet bol'no.* The Truth often hurts. I laugh, exhilarated, for I am fighting. My fingers seize the axe, batter it back and forwards. Figures run; I stamp on a prostrate form. This is the Truth, I am shouting. The blade has found a new home, between two eyes. On his wooden slats, the intended sacrifice stares mournfully. I am extending a life, shortening my own. He will not thank me. I have cheated him.

CHAPTER 4

Four chairs, four men were seated, tied, facing inwards, Diakanov was standing centre stage, centre circle. The warehouse was empty, half-lit, the illuminated theatre filling only a fraction of the echoing, vaulted space encompassing the grimed concrete and the black suits of *tsisari*'s praetorian guards stationed around its walls. Lyublinsky District, midwinter, frozen and grim, a heavy industrial graveyard on the outskirts of Moscow. It was no warmer inside, perhaps colder given the scene of captor and captives.

'You remember that snow cover was disappointing in November?' Diakanov stared around at the straining faces. There was no reply from the quartet; masking tape across their mouths prevented a response. Undeterred, the boss continued. The theme would become clearer. 'And that means two things: the winter rye crop gets frost-damage and the Moscow reservoirs don't get filled. Water and bread, the two staples, get fucked, and the people suffer. Shortages mean price rises. That's a drawback; for me an opportunity. I provide the goods, meet demand, quote my price. I even put pressure on the West to send surplus stocks of corrupted meat to fill our shops, and again I charge.' The select audience stayed silent with his lecture on supply-and-demand economics. Perhaps they were old-school Communists, protectionists. They could not protect themselves. Diakanov cocked his head and looked at them. Soon they would be only too willing to join in, to venture up what they knew. 'Everything has a price.' He leant over and ripped the tape from the face of a mute observer. 'What was yours?'

The man feared, but hid it convincingly, a nerve twitching sporadically beneath an eye. He understood violence, could not afford to be sentimental over either its giving or receiving. He was the youngest, had most to prove. The gloved hand cupped his chin and squeezed hard. 'I am asking you a question.' The face puckered between the fingers, grotesque; the pressure did not ease. 'It is simple. You talk and I will listen. Who paid you to kill one of my senior officers in the Kosmos Hotel this morning? Are they linked to the death of my son?' Nothing. Diakanov withdrew his hand, the face dropped. 'You see this?' Eight eyes swivelled to stare. 'And this?' The Mafiya chief was hunched, holding up both trouser legs, displaying a star tattooed on either knee. 'You know why they are here?' They did – the symbols of the hardest men of the *vor v zakonye*, thieves in law, within the code, leaders who had survived the worst of the penal system. They would kneel to no one. Diakanov straightened. 'My father was a thief, his father before him and my relations stretching back three hundred years. They went to Siberia under the Tsars and under the Bolsheviks and ended up running it. They were fair, honourable, dignified men – real men.' He paused. 'Men who were trusted; men who were untainted; men who were steel.' He nodded at two lieutenants positioned beyond the circle. One carried the beloved baseball bat – Imperial Bat-in-Waiting – the other a heavy-calibre automatic. Both came forward. Diakanov selected the pistol; the duo retreated to their positions. *Tsisari* was turning, talking. 'In many ways my father was old-fashioned, didn't like narcotics, was slow to move into new business areas. He preferred conciliation, arbitration. Times have changed, people have changed, are different.' He checked the firing mechanism, removed the safety. His father had carried tattoos of Stalin and Lenin on his chest and back to dissuade highly politicised execution squads from firing bullets through such icons. A quaint tradition, its effectiveness unproven. Diakanov preferred pornographic imagery on his torso – a more contemporary religion. 'I am different.'

The action was sudden, intense, drama focused on one spot in the immensity of its setting, drawing the attention of the peripheral players. Arm upright and extended, Diakanov advanced towards the figure and screwed the Makarov's barrel into the sweating forehead. The man flinched, shoulders rising, head sinking, neck shrinking into his collar. The body was shaking violently, pretence outweighed by human biology.

'Tell me!' Diakanov screamed.

The face was creased in denial and terror, eyes unseeing, lips folded tight to button the man into some remote self-sealed security.

'Who the fuck killed Konon?' Again. 'Who killed Konon?' Echoes, as loud as their source, bounced away and back in distorted repetition. Slower, defined in shouts, Diakanov reciting, moving behind and adjusting the gun against the back of the head. 'You know what I'm going to do?'

Terrorized. 'What? It's . . . I don't . . .'

A slap with the barrel. 'Who paid you? Who is behind this?'

'No . . . I don't know . . . I . . .' A thin wail starved of courage. 'Please, I don't . . .'

The muzzle blast lent the head a brief halo of light and smoke, matter erupting in a cascade of sound across the shirt front, more following as the face tilted and tipped its contents. The mafiya called it bespoke Versace.

Diakanov bent next to an ear of the slumped form. 'That was foolish.' That was a hair-trigger. The feet continued to flutter. It was best that Irina was not here. Her position in his security apparatus was purely nominal, an excuse to allow her at his side. Today she remained at home, aware only that he was on official business. Business which was far from complete.

He began to notice the others, bodies tied, struggling to friction-rub their way to safety. Maggots, escaping into darkness. He covered them with the automatic in a sweeping, exaggerated arc; their movements became more pronounced.

A chair up-ended, its occupant writhing, strange moans through masking tape that lent the face a jaunty square smile in black. Diakanov attempted to simulate the expression; the man's eyes grew wilder. He was placed back on the chair by a bored-looking staffer who had witnessed too many similar performances. His chief made a further selection. A finger pointed. The chain rattled down, its hook taken and attached between the handcuffs binding the victim's arms behind his back. Chair removed, he crouched, red-faced and squealing, trussed and ready for the gymnastics section.

The Great White watched the preparations. He had taken the call in his office – a Federal Security Service code was given – and listened while the anonymous voice reported an incident involving his senior capo Konon at the Kosmos Hotel. His body was currently lying in its own blood-lake, the killers driving off to join the highway, heading south-east for the industrial suburbs. There were four of them, he was told, and they could be found at a certain warehouse waiting for payment. The line cut off, security ringing through to confirm that it was recorded, but untraced. He ordered a team, special tactics – very special – and went to buckle into undersuit body armour. If it were a trap, his Spetsnaz moonlighters would soon flush out and finish off the ambushers. If it were genuine, a lead, then he was determined to follow it through personally. Revenge was always personal. They were expecting payment. He would be paying more than a passing visit, more than in kind.

Additional details of the murder were reported back, footage from hotel security videos seized, while he shrugged on his jacket, the kevlar protection undervest redefining the contours of the covering pullover. Definitely four men seen leaving the hotel, matching the description already received. To kill in Moscow without his permission or sanction by the Senate was inadvisable, to kill one of his trusted capos: that was suicide. He had lost face, a son, a share of diamonds under his protection, and now a core member of his controlling committee, was obliged to act. Respect came from strength; reassertion of both was essential. To do nothing would be to display infirmity, to move down the food-chain, to risk being consumed by ally or crypto-enemy. In this life one was not retired gracefully, and former friends enjoyed voracious appetites. Who had turned on him? Who was testing him? He would show no weakness, no mercy.

A signal – the head momentarily inclined – and the man rattled upwards bellowing through the adhesive gag. The sound hung over them, dominating the interior, muffled, continuous screams from the spiralling figure as his arms dislocated backwards from their sockets. Hands clasped behind, Diakanov waited below, rocking on his toes to encourage circulation. He had seen worse, heard worse. There was no reason why, with the minimum of effort, the acrobat could not internalise his pain. After all, it was early in the proceedings; he should save his energy.

'You want to be human decorations like your friend?' Diakanov turned back to the two remaining and restrained survivors. They were scarcely conscious through shock, uncomprehending eyes sliding in front of brains that were processing their own betrayal and the bloody cameos occurring before them. One choked on vomit behind his taped mouth, bile pulsing from the nose as the head jerked. The tape was pulled away. Release. Diakanov stood back.

'Shelepin . . .' An agony of retching; laboured, liquid breathing. 'Maxim Shelepin.'

'Continue.'

More coughs, heaving. 'We were approached, paid . . . asked to do a hit for him at the Kosmos.'

'Did you meet him?'

'No.' Saliva unwound to the concrete. 'But I recognised his lieutenant. We've worked for him before. Same format.'

Shelepin? But he was part of the Moscow syndicate, sat on the mafiya Senate. He would not dare to strike without backing. Yet he had dared, struck, so there was backing. Which interests did he represent? The Orlovs, those St Petersburg upstarts, who had always caused trouble? The

Lessiovskis? A splinter group of disgruntled, over-ambitious Moscow factions? Specialist cabals wishing to broaden their operating scope? Never. Loyalties shifted, responsibilities overlapped, their command structures were too porous and linked vertically to the Senate: dissent would be quickly reported and quashed. Had he linked with Chechens or Georgians frustrated at difficulties in holding market share in the consolidating criminal oligopoly, or teamed with Kazachs eager to claw back the smuggling routes into Asia? Why had he, *tsisari*, boss of All Russias, not sensed such threats, foreseen these machinations? Motives could be so complex. They would not move without resources, hidden capital to sustain them through a prolonged underworld conflict. Were the stolen diamonds part of that hidden capital? He was blind, deaf, unable to counter what he could not predict. They were attacking him, so assumed they were safe, secure, beyond retribution. None were beyond retribution. Shelepin – too small on his own, must be. A tough man, reliable. Suspicions existed that he had once tapped into the communal *Obschack* fund established to support those gang members serving prison sentences – his son had two years to go in a penal colony – but the rumours were proved unfounded. Diakanov used his computer and banking experts to maintain an intermittent check on the man's accounts, would be doing so again. Perhaps it was why the little Shelepin had turned on him, pre-empting further investigation, hiding larger discrepancies or non-payment of annuities. Diakanov would demonstrate the true meaning of pre-emption.

The chain was released, the spinning body falling twenty feet before the drop was halted, torso trampolining out of the shoulders. A single shriek. He probably had children, Diakanov thought, enjoyed taking them on the train at weekends to ski in the woods out beyond Moscow. It was what Oleg had missed most about being at school in England: the tree-lined runs glistening like white rivers beneath the moon, the tobogganing, the building of snowmen – snow women in Russian – when the powder became easier. He was so young, and so dead. The funeral was over, the tables of his wake cleaned, the portion of food left for his spirit cleared, the candles snuffed.

'Who killed my son?'

'It was not me . . . us. We had nothing to do with it. *Nothing*. Only the Kosmos. We're sorry.' The talkative one, the one able to talk, was breathing hard, staring down, avoiding eye-contact, somehow seeking anonymity. 'We're sorry.'

'I know.' The baseball bat was offered up. Diakanov exercised his wrist, flexing, rotating the handle. Another gag removed, the man grimaced, skin red around the mouth. The disjointed, broken string-puppet remained taped; round and round, before unwinding anti-clockwise. *Tsisari* gave a prod of encouragement. Strange murmuring from the suspended mannequin, arms elevated upwards in the unnatural beginnings of a swallow-dive. Both hands clutching the bat, lined up. 'And the diamonds. Who stole them?'

'I don't know, I d . . .'

The bat struck the figure flat across the stomach, the force propelling him away, boar-grunting.

'Please. Believe me. We were in Moscow. If we knew, we'd tell you.'

Diakanov adjusted his foot position, shuffled, tried a different grip. 'I ask again. Who took the rough stones?' He would go for the knees.

The talker stared from his chair. 'I beg you. We were not involved. It's Shelepin who ordered the hotel hit, I'm telling you, I swear.' He glanced at his colleague close by for encouragement, but the man was still, resigned, head bowed. 'We'll work for you, anything you say.'

'No.' Bat met bone emphatically. 'I have enough staff.' He began to work methodically.

Exercise relieved tension, was good for the soul. His smuggling syndicate in Vladivostock had sent news that morning of its success in shooting five adult Siberian tigers in the Alchan Valley. The resources of the authorities and their anti-poaching Tiger Group were outclassed by the technology and speed of his own teams. It was the same everywhere: government impotent, mafiya omnipotent. The big cats would be skinned, eviscerated, their organs and body parts packaged for transport to China and its natural medicines market. Fewer than three hundred Amur tigers remained in the Lazovsky Zapovednik reserve. Enough to maintain the price, enough to last five years. Diakanov swung the bat, connected with flesh, was building up a sweat. The tiger was worthy of his attention; humans were so disappointing, so soft. Becoming softer. He looked forward to getting away, to the spring, when he could take *Krista*, his rare five-year-old silver-grey gyrfalcon up into the hills to hunt. Oleg had loved her, would always clamour to accompany them in the off-roader, watching as she circled, folded and stooped, falling on her prey at over two hundred miles an hour, the sound of a ripped sail accompanying her sky-dive. The act was familiar. She would end the day with blood matting the front of her broad white chest, sated, fierce, imperious.

Blood covered the front of this man's chest. Diakanov brought the bat high above his head and down. *For Oleg, for Oleg, for Oleg.* It was over. He threw the instrument clattering to the ground and took the white towel proffered by an aide. Hands wiped, towel discarded, a second was used to mop his face. It followed the first, landing beneath the leaking human container hanging in its restraints, absorbing only part of the fluids pooling beneath. Prisoner N549, his mentor from the camps, would have advised him against such behaviour. But he was dead, his advice with it. Diakanov did not need such doubters. Toilet complete, rage expended, he could concentrate on the two more senior figures he had saved until last.

'Gentlemen, I hope that you share my interest in wildlife.'

'Mrs Cherkashin. A word.'

Her face, pinched by grief and deserted faith, registered the dullness of a mother who had lost her children, a wife who had lost a husband, a human who had lost everything. Neutrality of emotion was all that remained. Lazin repeated the request, more slowly. Shock tended to render the mind an arid place.

'The government cannot even pay my pension, but it can afford to send investigators to spy.'

'I am not equipped to spy, Mrs Cherkashin. Only to listen.'

'The Federal Security Service is becoming a caring institution?' A mirthless laugh which had more in common with a bronchial cough. 'I suppose the Bolsheviks fell eventually – anything is possible.'

He noticed her eyes, dark and stagnant, giving away nothing. Not even suspicion or hostility made their way to the surface; she had sunk far below. The dacha was modest, once loved, set in an outlying village near Tynda, a refuge for a woman who no longer enjoyed the privilege of an official apartment in town, who no longer enjoyed anything. Icicles hung morosely, uncleared, from the eaves, catching the scene in the jaws of a glass trap, pushing down on her, on the house. Duckboards cluttered the yard waiting for the spring thaw; Lazin could not imagine spring reaching here. Spiritless desolation. He had walked around for a while, kicked at snow ridges, allowed the cold to clear and cauterise his brain.

The night-visitor had sent him, the disembodied voice at the Rail Troops' camp where he lay in bed holding a pistol on the ghost. He was prepared for a meandering, meaningless investigation, one which covered the bases, went through the motions, and allowed him to leave a 'Case Open' file for others to pick up or shred at will. Leonid Gresko, Director, initiated the process expecting failure – Lazin expected it himself – for there could be no alternative in a cold wasteland where theft at ministerial level was a way of life, croneyism, cover-up and institutionalised corruption a lifestyle choice. He was there because somebody had to be, because the Federal Security Service needed to be busy, or at least give that impression: the secret to maintaining an empire. Results were incidental, optional. Then this phantom who spoke of death, of cannibalism and the murder of innocents, of bodies hidden down the shaft of an abandoned uranium mine, men taken from a freight train carrying diamonds and executed. And Lazin had picked up the trail, trails, which started somewhere and ended nowhere – paths that crossed close enough to the truth and led to a concerted attempt on his life. It was saved by a stranger, the apparition of an ancient, who knew his name and his motives, allowed him to proceed to further dangers, to pursue an unknown agenda without revealing his own. Results were no longer incidental or optional. The evidence handed over by the unidentified snow-traveller, the narrowness of escape from an ice-bound and deep-set grave, pushed him on to explore areas uncovered in his conversation with the Voice. The wife of a BAM railway official was one; they had got her children prior to seizing the sanity of her husband. A survivor, she might hold a fragment of the truth.

Reaching Severobaikalsk, the small BAM railway town thirty miles east of the camp, he had contacted Moscow Centre to inform superiors of his experience at the hands of the Major and his troops and to await orders. He envisaged an immediate recall. Proceed with caution came the reply. The Major would be investigated. Lazin checked the message: he was the target of attempted murder, of a conspiracy involving forces answerable to the Ministry of Transport Construction, shot at by men who were more poorly paid than civilian labourers and therefore, commensurately, more easily bought. He requested backup, an officer with local knowledge. The communication, direct from Leonid Gresko, was repeated. There would be no abort for his Special Assignment. Again, proceed with caution. He was on his own; the trapper had vanished.

'I can sense you are not a bad man.' She was ending the stand-off unilaterally.

'I am flattered.'

'Don't be. I'm a good judge of character. You wish to ask

me painful questions and will do so whether I protest or not.'

'I have a job.'

'Said Stalin to the kulaks when he exiled them to starve.'

'May I enter?'

'State Security with manners. I said anything is possible.'
She stood aside and nodded him through.

The stove pushed the heat out in a weakening radius
about the room. The interior might have been tidy once,
the semi-rural living space of a proud urban family with a
future and security, transformed by dust and mourning into
a shell with little to offer. Glass pickling bottles jostled on
the floor with boxes and scavenged household items, filling
the space where furnishings had sat prior to sale or barter.
A chair was pushed beneath a wall-light, sewing strewn
about in different stages of repair. Survival not aesthetics
dominated. A shelf had been converted to a shrine – the
pictures of two children bordering a larger photograph taken
while they fished with their father, decked in black, the
happy images framed by lit candles. She saw him looking
at them.

'It's *Maslenitsa* soon. I would have made the family
pancakes. They loved that.' The ancient pagan rites of seeing
off the winter were followed enthusiastically throughout
Russia. There was no one to celebrate its departure from this
dacha. She went over to the chair and lowered herself wearily.
'I don't bother much with food or cooking any more.' He
waited. 'Sometimes I put the pictures flat. They are not
memories, only reminders of what happened.'

The impossibility of articulating sorrow, respect, and the
sour fury of witnessing this barren aftermath of tragedy,
kept him silent. There was no point to the horror, no words
to express it. He went to sit on a box, upright, disciplined,
wanting to put his arms around her. Uniform and a stern
bearing could be relied upon to overcome most forms of
awkwardness. Familiarity only got in the way.

'Before the children disappeared and were found, did
you notice changes in your husband's behaviour?' Pause.

'Was he depressed, irrational? Did he seem under greater pressure?'

'You sound like a policeman. Why should this concern State Security? You know he had an alibi.'

'I am investigating him as a victim, not as a suspect, Mrs Cherkashin. He could never have been the murderer.'

'But he saw himself as one. He went mad because of guilt. He felt he could have saved them; he believed he was responsible for killing them.' She glanced at the pictures and quickly away. 'For a year before they died, he was different, could not sleep, paced about at night. He would get angry when I asked, told me he could sort it out himself.'

'Do you know what he meant?'

'No.' She was staring ahead, speaking softly. 'And he refused to explain. We were so close, but he wanted to protect the family, did not wish to burden me. He was the man, I the woman. I had no right to enquire.'

'Did he ever talk about his work?'

'Occasionally, of characters in the office, of visits by important Moscow figures. We laughed about some of the people stepping from their VIP carriages. But the numbers arriving fell off. Gorbachev . . .' The name of the one-time President of the Soviet Union was reviled throughout the BAM Zone. He had declared the railway a monument to stagnation, cut off its investment, redirected central funds to his campaign for economic perestroika. Restructuring meant disintegration; the BAM left marooned in its Stalinist past and in a Siberia whose development was no longer a priority. 'My husband loved the railways, claimed the BAM was the most advanced system in Russia. It hurt him physically, mentally, to see its business fall away.'

'Financially?'

'Everyone suffered.' But the subtext implied that the bureaucrats were the last to be affected.

Decline was structural and inevitable, its cause going far beyond the pat established bogeyman of Mikhail Gorbachev. For every reason which lay behind the BAM's original construction, there lay a counter and more convincing argument to explain its diminishing attractiveness. Modern container ships ensured that cargo could reach European destinations from the Pacific faster and more cheaply by sea; the trans-Siberian railway and land links opened from Hong Kong via China's north-western Urumqi region, Kazakhstan, Moscow and onwards to the West ensured there was little requirement for the spare capacity offered by the BAM; marauding gangs encouraged freight carriers to take to the sea rather than chance it with rail. Men like Misha Cherkashin were left bitter, abandoned, presiding over a prestige project without prestige, without a role, riding a wholly Siberian elephant – white – through a devastated economic landscape.

Lazin settled into the interrogation. Was she aware of any other killings? No. It was true her husband was part of the BAM administration liaising with ministries and commercial groups requiring low-profile special freight transportation? Yes. Were rough diamonds part of his remit? Yes. Before their killings, had the children spoken of strangers in the neighbourhood, noticed anything unusual? No. Lazin alternated the subjects, interspersed them with attempts to draw out further detail, kept the tone formal, bloodless, while he felt his own soul haemorrhaging. Had she ever been aware of surveillance against her family? In what way? she asked. He explained. No, came the reply. Were there official papers she knew about? No. What were her thoughts on her husband's work colleagues? She told him. Any give her a bad feeling? Too many to mention. Try. He noticed what a handsome woman she was, could be, when the pall lifted, found himself asking questions about her own life and background. She replied each time in the same still manner, careful, balancing responses lest the grief overwhelmed her, exploded the fragility of her contrived state. Had she been happy? Of course.

'You're a brave woman.'

'Bravery is simply a lack of imagination, Colonel. Isn't

that why soldiers go into battle?'

A good enough reason. 'Sometimes.'

'Or bravery is madness. It's why my husband sits in a straitjacket saying nothing.'

'Was he ever threatened?' Lazin asked.

She was speaking in a near-monotone again. 'Misha? I used to think not. Only bribes, the usual. Small-scale: the bottles of vodka left in plastic bags below his desk, caviar. Private enterprise is more important to the region, so there were unofficial bodies to deal with.'

'Mafiya?'

'I don't know.' She shifted her gaze from the floor. 'Something made him fearful. I dismissed it, didn't press him, put it down to general work worries. He was spending fewer hours in the office – there was nothing to do.'

'Did he confide in anyone?'

'He might have reported his worries. An FSB man like yourself came to the dacha one weekend.'

'Like me?'

'He did not mention who he was to me, but told Misha that he was a Colonel in the Federal Security Service.'

'Why did he come here rather than the office?'

'It was a weekend; he said it was easier. They went away together for the day to talk. I remember being angry because Misha had promised to take the children out.'

'Did you discover the man's name?'

A small shake of the head. 'Neither did Misha.'

'How was your husband when he returned?'

'Uncommunicative. It was becoming his way by then. He was worried for the future.' With hindsight that was prescient.

'Could you identify the man, this Colonel?'

'Naturally. I have met him since. He offered condolences when the children were taken and killed, more condolences when Misha was institutionalised. He asked if there was anything I wanted.' She gestured around the room. 'What could I possibly want?' There was no smile.

'Tell me more about him.'

'I can tell you he scared me. I could tell he scared Misha. He ordered me not to speak with anyone about his visits.'

'Yet you speak to me.'

'I read somewhere that human contact can be beneficial.' She had every cause to doubt it, thought Lazin. Perhaps there was an elemental trace of colour in the wan face. Did she love Misha? he wanted to ask. 'I'm used to being questioned. It was only when it ended that I felt the pain, pain which dried me. I gave everything up, the police gave little. They left and I was on my own, totally on my own.'

'What questions did this Security officer ask?'

'There were few. But I was assessed all the same. I felt it, felt his eyes. He has not returned in a while.' A slight shudder. 'I thank God.'

'Could you describe him, Mrs Cherkashin?' A nod. 'How?'

'Without light. Just darkness. He was like a dead man, a corpse.' Petr Ivanov had visited.

The pirates were on board, Purton beneath a canvas awning sharpening a Sykes-Fairburn combat knife, Howell tying and untying knots, slouched on a sea-chest, watching the terns pick their way among the *jaliboots* pulled up on the Salalah foreshore. Their dhow was a 'boom', decrepit, patched, low in the water, one hundred and sixty feet in length, a pregnant beam of thirty-five, her teak hull and decks worn by monsoon winds and countless trading voyages from Bahrain to Bombay. Hired, along with her crew, she was to be the Forward Operations Base, a platform for the planned insurgency into the Yemen. But, for the moment, she sat across the border in Oman, waiting for supplies, the *matériel* of war. Away from land, planning and preparation would be less easily observed. Agents might be anywhere.

Howell sniffed, unravelled a bowline, and squinted up at the yard, skeletal bare without sails against the transparency of the sky, cutting diagonally across a mainmast which rose sixty-five feet above the deck.

'Glad the boat's solid.'

Purton continued to strop the blade. 'Small-arms-proof with that amount of hardwood.' Anything else, and protection was limited.

'Fine by me.'

He jumped from the chest and began to prowl. Forward, untutored in Western impatience, two crew members sprawled contentedly against coils of coir rope, one asleep, the other chewing *qat*. A third levered a rusting can from the sea on a cord as a precursor to ritual ablutions, a fourth had finished squatting on the sanitation box slung over the stern. Facilities were primitive to non-existent; men slept, prayed, ate, washed, and excreted in the open. Only the Captain enjoyed the comforts of a damp, mildewed mattress. He was ashore, haggling for supplies, an impassive old-style trader raised on a pearling *shu'ai* in the Gulf who had gravitated in adulthood towards carrying pilgrims and cargo and undertaking smuggling runs with alcohol and hashish, the contraband staples. Ahmed Badr claimed he was reliable, had proved himself in the past, was happy to work with *nazrani* – Christians. It was enough.

Howell leant over the side. 'Want to get some climbing practice in up the Capstan Plateau?'

'We don't want to attract attention.'

His NCO stooped and switched on the battery-operated radio – Arabic music – and started to shuffle unrythmically across the plank. Purton shook his head, tested the blade. Time passed slowly on the water. It pumped up the tension.

'You've seen the recruits, Ben. Think they're up to it?'

'It's your job to beast them till they are.'

The face was expressive. 'Five weeks, Ben. That's the concession to us – an extra week. They'll have barely woken up by then.' He spun and jigged some more.

'As long as they can point and fire.'

The knife scraped. He was preparing for war, returning to an historical land where tribal feuds, coups, counter-coups and political blood-letting had assumed epic proportions. Civil war was a custom, losing presidents to bomb, bullet, booby-trap or a prostitute's dagger an entertaining diversion. After decades of sporadic fighting and mutual mistrust, the south's People's Democratic Republic of Yemen and north's Yemen Arab Republic, undertook in 1990 to join together in unholy matrimony. A troubled relationship. The PDRY, until 1967 the British protectorate of Aden, was a Marxist satellite of the Soviet Union, a base for the Red Navy, an access point to the Bab al-Mandab straits and island of Socotra, and a launch pad for Communist influence in the Gulf. The YAR, conversely, neighbour to Saudi Arabia, a buffer against Moscow's intentions, remained staunchly wedded to its own political values and desire to dominate the south. The discovery of oil, with production beginning in 1987, furthered this ambition. Different outlooks, different traditions, equalled fallout, hostilities, and a crushing in 1994 of southern attempts at insurrection and secession. Opposition groups fled into exile, the Republic of Yemen was established, and a fragile unity restored. Ben Purton, adviser to the South, escaped into Oman.

Howell was performing knee-bends. 'You'd think the Yemenis would have grown tired of all the aggro. Five thousand years to get it out of their system.'

'It's in their blood.'

'Just like us. What about the Saudis, Ben? What's their real calling – smacking Moslem fanatics, punishing Sana's for its past support of Saddam? Doesn't wash, not for something this big.'

Purton ran a finger flat against the second edge. 'Almost ninety per cent of the country's oil exploration blocks are in the south, its gas reserves are second only to Qatar in the region. Get us to stir things up, keep light and low-sulphur petroleum off the market . . .'

'And you increase Saudi influence for the whole area.' Howell had transferred to squat-jumps.

'If you sat in Riyadh, you'd want to see Yemen split.

Large population, worrying democratic tendencies, cultural links to Jordan and Iraq.'

'Well, they've come to the best.' He was perspiring. 'Give me a cut from the Wadi Medden gold mines, and they'll have my loyalty for life.' The first sign of growing old: when motives no longer mattered. Purton finished with the knife, wiped and sheathed it and reached into a kit-bag for a length of piping. It emerged, wrapped in an oily rag. 'Christ, it's the lucky mascot.' Howell stopped exercising. 'Now, I know it's serious.'

'Set her up.' A nod at an empty paint tin. The NCO retrieved it, tapped the sides and lined it up on the rail.

'It's a fucking antique,' he grumbled.

Purton was chambering a round. 'It's a classic.' He turned the breech. '1954 Special Forces model, upgraded from .32 to 9mm. Nick, I'm rusty.' Howell stepped back a pace. Cradled across his commander's forearm lay a Welrod, the single-shot, silenced pistol used by British agents throughout every theatre of conflict during World War Two. The weapon was designed for one task only: assassination.

Phut. The barrel, extended by an eight-inch suppressor, remained motionless, barely made a sound, the can splitting noisily and blasting from view.

'Needs a slight left adjustment,' Howell intoned, taking a further precautionary step to the side. The Welrod was for extreme close-range; there were no sights fitted. An approaching vessel caught the NCO's attention. 'Head shed on his way across. In a high fucking hover.' Purton stowed the armoury and climbed to his feet.

The launch drew alongside, fenders draped, and a stocky Arab in white jumped fluidly across to the dhow. He shouted orders back before approaching, expansive smile and out-stretched arms, his transport accelerating away in a growling spume to a position a hundred metres off the bow.

Hugs, kisses, the affectionate friendship of Gulf Arabs, sunglasses and teeth catching the light beneath the headdress. Tea was offered and accepted, Howell placing a canteen on the boat's rudimentary gas stove. They sat on the deck, the infectious delight of Ahmed Badr in being among his old companions propelling them into an hour of anecdotes and war stories. A wealthy merchant's son and exile from South Yemen, he had fled Aden's Marxist utopia in 1967 and later joined a Saudi-funded unit mounting agitprop and deep penetration intelligence-gathering missions against his former homeland. Training came from the Omani Sultan's Armed Forces and a British liaison officer: Ben Purton. The link was made, had lasted decades and seen them through countless military actions. Following the family tradition, Badr became a trader based in Salalah, powerful, rich, yet it was he who led a small convoy of vehicles to the southern Yemen city of Mukalla in 1994 and spirited out Ali Salem al-Beedh's opposition leadership, repeating the extraction for Purton whom he had originally approached on behalf of the rebels. His liberation fight was ongoing.

'You never give up.' Purton aligned his slouch-hat to the sun's new angle. 'Thanks for recommending us to the Saudis.'

'They control the funds and you have the credibility.'

'I haven't won a campaign for them yet.'

Ahmed Badr gave a resigned shrug. '1994 was unfortunate, but we are better prepared this time. I insisted you both came in at the start. We want an offensive. Not,' he struggled for the words, 'crisis management. There are many volunteers, but they require proper refresher courses.' He patted Howell on the shoulder.

'How's the adventure business going, Ahmed?' the NCO asked.

'Expanding,' Badr replied. 'It's allowed us to insert teams into the Hadramawt and Al-Mahra under the guise of tourism. They're ready.'

'Have you managed to get your hands on the two Ribs we asked for?'

'They will be arriving tomorrow.'

'Our coxswains land in Muscat in four days; they'll need to work up a crew.' One was the ex-Royal Marine Purton had met for lunch in the City of London. He wondered if the three attackers from the dark alleyway had recovered, were reformed. 'Do they meet the specs?'

'Completely, Ben. I acquired them second-hand from a diving support team on the oil rigs. Six-metre rigid inflatables – Defenders – deep V-hulls, two ninety-horsepower four-stroke engines each, can carry up to seventeen men.'

'The rest of the kit?'

'Will be flown direct from Saudi.'

Everything was in order, in place. The chaos, the fog of war, would come with the fighting. It always did. They stood and watched as the launch pulled away, carrying Ahmed Badr back to his native domain of logistics and diplomacy.

'Verdict?'

Howell's face wrinkled. 'If our side gets dicked? It's not the first time, and it's not our business. We bug out before we end up in a Yemeni jail. Glad Ahmed's there for us.' He slapped his commander on the back.

Purton leant on the gunwale, staring after the boat diminishing into the distance. He was not thinking of battle. He was thinking of Max.

Badr ducked into the low, white room. The man did not rise to greet him.

'Did you hear?' the Arab asked.

'Every word,' the seated Russian replied. 'Moscow is encouraged you are expediting matters.'

Badr appeared pleased and unclipped the transmitter. He was an exceptional deal-maker.

Baroness Orczy eat your heart out. The old man contemplated his hands, allowed himself a wry inward smile. He might have overdone it on the campaign medals, the Communist hero pins, but they were his passport, their weight on his chest corresponding to weight of influence, ease of access. Age was persuasive. None could challenge a snow-haired veteran, suspect anything but dotage. They would never get close, penetrate the barrier. He was among them, but viewed them from afar. And every official or engineer, every subtle or pronounced change in Russian life, he observed. This was his kingdom. The train was drawing in to the deserted station. He stood. Trapper, hunter, soldier, spy, aware of the eyes on him, aware that he had them fooled.

Corruption and conspicuous consumption, the great and the bad – a prelude to the fall of Rome. At least he had discovered his chair; that was a start. There were too many functions at which he found himself searching myopically for a seat while proceedings had started, the delegates too engrossed to notice the young man floundering among them wearing a resigned smile on his face. Max scanned around, taking in the colours, dazzling lights, the tables burdened with the Kremlin's finest plate and crystal and set beneath the ancient, soaring canopy of Granovitaya Palata. It was a rare privilege – a site of tsarist ceremonial for four hundred years and of Communist state receptions for seventy more, jewels and rich silks making way for ill-fitting nylon suits swathing Soviet figures as svelte as tractors – and now given over to entertaining the new rulers and occupiers. Business as usual. The conversation was a deluge, small talk and business deals lost in a general clamour, a high-volumed murmur that swept above the sharper tones of dining, of glasses sipped and replaced, of silver connecting with bone china. To his right, Strachan engaged in conversation with a well-heeled, well-oiled and well-built Russian matron whose husband was doubtless powerless and scowling across the table. By now, a hand would be on her knee, or higher. *You don't know the people as I do*, he was fond of telling Max. Possibly, he was right. The haulier's execrable Russian, mixed with American colloquialisms, cut through the background clutter. 'I'm telling you, darlin'. The best two sounds in the world are the hiss of a Huey's turbine firing up and the noise the waves make on China Beach during R&R.' He did not touch on the worst sounds: the screams or grunts falling on excreta-

215

covered punji stakes as they off-loaded into a hot LZ, the frantic cries of aircrew in the headset when other slicks took hits in ambush crossfire. *We're going down, we're going down*. Then a crackling, haunted silence. Tonight, Strachan kept to party-mode. It was lost on his listener, but she smiled politely, displaying first-class Western dentistry superimposed on distinctly rougher indigenous art. The smile got bigger – he was leaning in towards her.

Foie gras aux truffes and lamb en croûte, mass catering for an internationally oriented elite, standard fare when senior US Senators came to town. They were at a top table, beyond Max's line-of-sight, being diplomatic, saying the right things, generating goodwill and passing on the President's personal best wishes. They had been given the use of Air Force 3, lending official status, promoting the importance of bilateral ties and trade. The worst of the late 1990s was over – cautious enthusiasm was in. Paid to eat, paid to bolster the fortunes of the Kremlin hierarchy. Not a bad life. Max chewed on his food and resumed dialogue with a woman with ready cash and a ready expression who represented a Sports fund. He was tired. The days had been taken up with countless meetings, over lunch or bare wood, his stomach lined with cod-liver oil to counteract the native trick of over-generosity with alcohol. Evenings were equally hazardous, spent in hotel bars, drinking with businessmen, taken to the sixth floor of the Intourist to watch unimaginative floor shows, avoiding a particularly persistent hooker named Thumper who stuck her tongue in his ear and told him that she had fucked everyone else in the group. Why not a full house? He chose to visit a theatrical celebration of the life and works of Vladimir Visotski at Taganka instead. Far less depressing. Speeches would be soon.

Leonid Gresko viewed the American politicians from above the rim of his glass. He sat close to them, radiating unpleasantness and the occasional uninterested half-smile, an anonymous figure to most of those present, ugly enough to be respected, uncommunicative enough to be left alone.

Matters were accelerating, several more senior political figures and Duma representatives ensnared in the past week. Blackmail was so much more effective than purchase: if one bought a man's loyalty, he held the initiative, would eventually raise the price; if one possessed photographs, recordings, waved hard-copy of his flaws and aberrations beneath his nose, then ownership and compliance were assured for a lifetime. Everyone had weaknesses: the skill was to exploit them. Only that morning, a member of the Upper House had begged, cried, when told of the LSD-pushing habits of his son. College entrance was at stake, future career prospects threatened, family pride about to be stripped. Tears were unbecoming in the male. Gresko took another sip. He could smooth away the unpleasantness, he told the man, at minimal cost – that of future support. A simple argument, rapidly accepted. The professional in quid pro quo. His own men had supplied the boy with drugs.

He watched the wet lips, the stained teeth, mouths closing on food and wine, chattering. So many receptions in so many countries, they lost shape or meaning. He had moved among them for over thirty years, from the moment he swaggered from Leningrad State University into the KGB's First Chief Directorate and a career in overseas espionage. They marked out his progress like stepping-stones: assignments abroad under cover of university administrator and international city liaison official, his sideways manoeuvre into the Presidential Administration and its Main Control Department, his cultivation of reformers and reactionaries, his appointment as head of the Federal Security Service. Parties and the party-line. He saw through them all. A man spoke to him, but he did not hear. The face was smiling, came nearer, transformed itself into that of Kim Philby. A reminder. A trick. *I can* play those. Gresko gaped up at the chandelier – its lights blew and picked out the shape of a pentangle. He blinked.

The Mayor of Moscow stood to speak. He had good cause to be cheerful: the assembled diners were paying in dollars.

Platitudes and politics combined in a meaningless welcoming speech, a segue of sustained applause and brief acoustic feedback which drew predictable laughter, and Senator Patrick O'Day, leader of the American delegation, rose to respond. Gresko concentrated.

The opening lines were in Russian – he had been coached well – warm, flattering, tables slapped appreciatively by the gathering. A smattering of cordial good humour, fraternal greetings from the President of the United States, talk of Valentine's Day and love between nations as a humanising bond, and a strategic appeal for greater contact at all levels to build on existing Russo-American relations. *We're back*, was the message, the firm pledge. Slick, professional, underlaid with the charm of a born communicator. Gresko was impressed. It was no surprise that the man was a key player on Capitol Hill, a close friend of the American President, an arm-twister and ball-breaker, an ally capable of rallying support and carrying the day for the most contentious government legislation. Prohibition hoodlums as antecedents added to the allure: money, style and an exotic family history had never been handicaps on Pennsylvania Avenue. But then, chronic alcoholism, serial sexual deviation, unimpeachable evidence of impeachable criminality, and sworn depositions concerning the erectile coefficient of an incumbent's penis, were hardly obstacles to holding high office in the White House or Kremlin either. The Senator was telling a joke; explosive applause. He had won them over, a tall, silver-streaked titan dominating the hall, playing to every individual, drowning them in charisma. Gresko saw their faces, upturned, admiring, expectant, business leaders hearing what they wanted to hear. And now the gravitas, arms resting on the podium, comfortable and authoritative. Expressions changed, heads nodding sagely, contemplatively, on cue. The FSB Chief thought of the dossier detailing O'Day's remarks at the annual Wehrkunde Conference in Munich, the world's most prestigious forum for discussing international security and defence matters. The Senator was a stalwart of the meetings, a heavyweight and networker without compare, bringing Washington savvy, capable of articulating American foreign policy and winning points, influence and arguments against all detractors and doubt. Gresko had no doubt. This was the man, his target. *You are mine Senator; you are mine.*

A standing ovation, the crowd on its feet to signal support for the message, whatever it might have been. The Russian hosts were pleased; it was a boost for the status quo, a vote of confidence in the current system and regime. Fireworks were to follow. They would surely follow, the Director of the Federal Security Service mused. So many businessmen and women from whom to choose: the first victim, the first sacrifice. He liked to think of it as natural wastage. End to the status quo. He wiped his mouth with a napkin. Philby had disappeared. The voices were calling from within.

Sand was blowing off Dasoudi beach, powdering the empty bars and tawdry discotheques, drifting along avenues to join the dust on silent mannequins in silent shops, covering the basil planted outside half-completed apartment blocks. The forlorn, deserted atmosphere of Limassol in winter. Cyprus without the tourists, gap-toothed streets containing urbanised subsistence families from the Troodos at varying stages of economic mutation: street sellers and vegetable-stall holders slowly upgrading to supermarket ownership and motel operation. Not wholly deserted. Here and there a couple of low-slung Russians, the men with hairstyles reminiscent of European footballers circa 1975, dressed in beige nylon and viscous suits in pastel shades, the women, fat-thighed and mud-packed in make-up, wandering desultorily along the coastal front, shopping and finding relief from a former lifetime of malnutrition and penury. This was Yermasoyias – 'Little Russia' to the natives – the city area populated since the end of the Soviet Union by the murkier elements of Moscow and St Petersburg society, host to gangsters, smugglers, money launderers, rogue bankers and the support staff of a host of global criminal enterprises. Every third shop was a furrier's, catering to the inward migration of moneyed peasant-stock, each subterranean nightclub a staging-post for package whores and decked in ersatz red velveteen and glitter balls. There was no accounting for acquired tastelessness, no explanation for the dark Mercedes saloons heading north to the port of Kyrenia in the Turkish sector or south for Famagusta. It was where Boris Diakanov had arrived a few days earlier.

He spat the pistachio shell into the bowl and observed the table-dancer gyrating earnestly beyond the double doors in the dining section of his split-level suite. She took the eye contact as cue to increase the tempo, grinding her pelvis, shaking her backside rhythmically to the beat of a rock track on low volume, sliding a finger beneath her crotch, masturbating unconvincingly, and extracting the digit to suck at different angles and with varied cameo expressions: pouting, pensive, profane, profound, prudish or professional. An actress without real stage presence, a career relying more on the occasional dollar handout than on any real talent. The show was boring him. At least she was off-camera. He turned back to the video screen to continue the conference.

'If you want to deal, you have to deal.'

'That's a fair bid for a logging concession,' the Australian countered. 'It's more than we paid for the last one.'

'And I have to pay more to the regional administration in Sakha than the last one. You are making big profits from cutting down our taiga, Mr Anderson. Should I remind you that I have many Asian concerns waiting to deforest Siberia, expecting a decision? You recall that they have burnt out most of their own resources?'

'We deal in replenishable woods, Mr Diakanov.'

'Your second joke. The first was your price. The Malaysians have offered more – attacking the east Amazon is not enough for them – and the South Koreans want to expand from only taking ginseng from my areas. I like them, Mr

Anderson. They appreciate trade, they buy from my musk deer farms.'

'We assumed—'

'Assume nothing,' Diakanov cut in. Keep the man on the defensive, dominate the negotiations. 'Replenishable? Then use those stocks, don't trouble me. If you wish to continue . . .' He trailed off, let it float.

'Boris, I don't want misunderstandings, just a little good faith.'

'You use my connections, you use my ice-breaking tugs out of Sovetskaya Gavan, you use the North Korean labour I have organised. And you talk of good faith.'

'Wait one, Boris.' The Australian's face disappeared from the screen, mute whispering replacing empty visuals. Diakanov rolled another nut into his mouth, crushing it beneath his tongue. They would capitulate, always did.

Russia's Far East was his, the furthest extension of the BAM railway emerging from the Siberian wastes into the fog-bound gulf of Sovetskaya Gavan close to Japan's northern Hakkaido island, from where he could monitor and control the movement of trade with the Pacific nations and charge any business seeking to enter what he considered his very own personal enterprise zone. Its prosperity was his prosperity, its bays the pot of gold at one end of his economic rainbow.

A decision was reached, the Australian returned. 'Very well, we're agreeing to the conditions, but we'd rather pay in instalments. It'll help our cashflow.'

'Do the paperwork and talk to my lawyers.'

Diakanov chopped his hand downwards. An aide responded and the link was cut. The table-dancer moved feverishly on her platform. A satcom technician walked from his console and bent to deliver a message. *Tsisari* listened and grunted, sitting upright in his chair, framing himself for the video camera.

'Twenty seconds.' A pause. 'Ten, nine . . .' The countdown was called across from the master station. Diakanov rested his forearms on the sides of the chair, waiting. Forgotten, the dancer's choreography faltered with her enthusiasm, disappointment and resentment registering strongly before she was blanked out by the closing of the doors.

'Three, two, one . . . connection is made.' A second monitor, set below the first, threw up the live imagery of a lunch party underway. By invitation only, starting early, ending late, and Diakanov was gatecrashing through technology. He had given up a place at the Kremlin high table that night for this, trusted that it would not disappoint.

'*Tsisari*. Boris Fedorovich. Greetings.' The diamond tooth of Maxim Shelepin winked from Krylatskoye in Russia, the small, pugnacious face set with a smile of respect and formal supplication. Behind him, men in tailored Savile Row seated around the table and caught by the wide-angle lens, applauded. Shelepin enjoyed the good life, insisted that his cohorts were well dressed. An exclusive enclave within an exclusive enclave.

Diakanov took his time to respond, flaming the end of a cigarette into life and inhaling. 'My greetings to you all.' A burst of clapping. Diakanov counted the seconds, counted the individuals in the room. All present, all drinking fine wine, all owing ultimate allegiance to him. It meant so little.

Shortly after the discussion with four killers in a Moscow warehouse, a meeting at which Shelepin's name had been volunteered in connection with the murder of Konon, news came through of a separate fatality. Viktor Gribanov, a St Petersburg trusty, and a lynch-pin of Diakanov's authority in the region, had, it seemed, undergone laser cosmetic surgery of the most extreme and terminally altering kind. Anxious to prevent leakage of funds, *tsisari* assigned his banking and computer specialists to trace and check the deceased's accounts. The results were ominous: currency equivalent to over a hundred million dollars had vanished, codes were broken, deposit boxes plundered by officials apparently working on behalf of a man who by that stage was lying unrecognisable on a mortuary slab. His brothers, who failed to identify the mortal and rearranged remains of their beloved sibling, were organising for war, immune to orders for a period of calm reflection, issuing threats to former colleagues and rivals on the Senate whom they suspected of the heinous crime. Scores were to be settled, long-held grudges acted upon. Then came the breakthrough, Diakanov's team picking up a trace and following part of the dispersed finances to an offshore account in the Cayman Islands used exclusively as a switching point by Maxim Shelepin's bankers. From there it was wired to the Maldives and disappeared. But other discrepancies were noticeable in the don's ventures closer to home. The remaining Gribanovs demanded reprisals.

Diakanov drew on the cigarette, its glowing tip placing embers below Shelepin's head; smoke exhalation, and the face clouded. A pyre. Irina was in Moscow ensuring that his family were cared for, that wife and children were taken to a safe compound. There was no room for non-combatants on the front line.

'A toast to you, Boris Fedorovich,' Shelepin was saying. Diakanov's attention drifted back. Vodka shots up-ended into several throats. From the corner of his eye he saw his communications specialist hold up a hand, fingers splayed. Five minutes.

In the dining room of his mansion, Maxim Shelepin watched the real-time picture of Diakanov, boss of bosses, transmitted from the Limassol base. *Tsisari* had made him rich, given him the protection to thrive and grow beneath the aegis of the Senate, the firepower to clear his four industrial regions of rivals. He took convincing, but the violence of the newer gangs and the erosion of his business base to younger, hungrier mobsters made the eventual deal an imperative and foregone. For sure he resented the dominant male – who with balls would not? – complained bitterly of the franchising structure, but they had an understanding, and understanding was how Senate members survived. There would, could, never be a challenge to Diakanov's supremacy: life was too comfortable, yet altogether too fragile. He broke a piece of black bread, folded in salmon, dripped lemon, and pushed it into his mouth. A pity about Viktor Gribanov. He had never liked the brothers, distrusted their hold on the St Petersburg docks, but they at least meant stability and a safe conduit for black-market chemicals to his network of international buyers. Rumours were circulating of trouble in the baroque city: his friends, the Lessiovskis, suspected a Gribanov brother himself was to blame for the slaying. Inter-family greed could be so unhealthy. Then there were the Orlovs, longstanding enemies. Everyone was nervous. Shelepin decanted more iced liquor into his glass. In Cyprus, Diakanov was spitting a pistachio shell to a point off-screen.

'We have heard no additional news from St Petersburg,' Shelepin ventured. The cigarette went up to Diakanov's lips, smoke drawn in, blown out. A nut followed, was split, the case expelled. 'The Lessiovskis are anxious to aid in the investigation.'

'Their loyalty is commendable.'

'It is not in doubt, Boris Fedorovich.' Shelepin thought that he could see a strange amber light in Diakanov's eyes. He dismissed it as technical artifice, an electronic flaw in the micro-circuitry. 'We are all concerned at the developments.' There were nods of agreement from those around him. 'If there is anything I can do . . .'

'I am sure you will play a central role, Maxim,' came the reply.

The diamond tooth flashed. 'Then I am honoured. My resources are wholly at your disposal.'

And currently being cashed in. Diakanov looked down and marked off the last member of the seating-plan on the clipboard. Ash fell from the cigarette – earth thrown across their bodies. A hand signal. Two minutes.

'If you would like me to take a delegation to St Petersburg?'

'That will no longer be necessary.' Or possible. Besides, *tsisari* mused, the city had already suffered from one of

Shelepin's recent representations: the reconfigured body of Viktor Gribanov bore witness to it.

Shelepin was breaking more bread, when he stopped. A glance at his dining companions who failed to register a change in atmosphere. He shifted in his chair and returned to the camera. 'Do you have orders?'

'To stay where you are.' To continue eating and drinking; movement would be inconvenient. Diakanov pulped the tobacco embers. Shelepin tore at the bread. The Last Supper. A telephone rang beside him.

'Excuse me.' Shelepin waited for Diakanov's assent – it was given – and raised the handset to his ear. 'Yes?' In Cyprus, a nut cracked between Diakanov's teeth.

Shelepin's expression did not change, but his immobility spread to the others, stress suffusing the room. 'You, check the door.'

The voice had become as colourless as his face, the carat-smile replaced by a small tremble of the lips. He clung to the receiver, grip tightening, skin drawn thin across the knuckles, to prevent his hand from shaking. Responsibility was lonely, death lonelier. The lieutenant extracted a pistol and lumbered to the far side of the room, opening the doors and stepping through to investigate. He re-entered as an aerosol, the 12-gauge blast slamming the headless torso backwards across the table, flailing limbs raking crystal, porcelain and food in a bloody wake across those present. A plate dropped and shattered in the silence; the men of the Shelepin clan spattered, mildly drunk, and wholly traumatised, did not move.

A gesture from Diakanov to raise the volume. In Russia, the finale. Figures in combat fatigues and balaclavas – his operatives – appeared on screen and spread out on one side of the dining room. The viewer shrugged: finding trustworthy staff could be such a problem. Shelepin stared out towards him, only now lowering the telephone from his ear.

'Bad news, I guess?' the boss of bosses said. 'Be my Valentine, Maxim.' The don said nothing, adjusted his tie, and moved round to face the visitors. He would show courage.

The table dancer was hustled from the apartment. They had barely allowed her time to leave with her clothes, let alone her dignity, and she angrily clutched the carrier bags bulging with the oils, unctions and exotic paraphernalia of her trade as she tottered over the rugs in six-inch heels. A professional, she was being treated like an amateur, pushed out as she was getting into her stride, getting astride, halted in early-to-mid flow. Ingrates, impotent tycoons, misogynists. Was that shooting, shouting, she could hear? The man preferred to watch Westerns on satellite television than to linger over her high, tight ass? Got to be strange. A hand took her by the elbow and pulled her roughly away. On the other side of the doors, Boris Diakanov watched as the jacketed Kalashnikov rounds struck home.

Out in the street, the table-dancer rearranged her clothes, dropping her bags, running fingers through breeze-blown hair, shutting her eyes and cupping hands to light a cigarette. Christ, this wind was a pain. Less tedious than some of the tricks she had turned recently. She strained backwards to look up to the top storeys and mouth off. In his apartment, Diakanov studied the screen. It was interesting how the staccato crack of rifle fire was amplified by the sound equipment at the expense of the deeper, more resonant subsonic tones; extra bass was required.

The end. Credits roll. Time to leave the dining room in the red-brick mansion at Krylatskoye. He applauded his men briefly – the team leader gave a thumbs-up sign – and shifted attention to the upper monitor. His favourite game-show was about to start. A fresh bowl of pistachios was placed beside him. He did enjoy the viewing choice afforded by satellite television.

'Prisoner 2351, wait here.'

Felix Shelepin shambled in, feigning to ignore the guard, and sat on the rotten wooden slats of the lower bunk. The prison authorities were scared of him, terrified of his father Maxim. Guards had families, lived out beyond the wire, outside the security of uniform, rule-book and group protection. They were vulnerable to organised crime: it was best not to antagonise the offspring of senior mafiosi, even if they came from regions far from the tuberculosis-ridden hell of the Perm penal camps. Shelepin ruled the low wooden huts, had his own personal cook, the warmest clothes, the pick of the youngest inmates. His excesses were part of camp-lore. Generally, those with little time left to serve bore the brunt of the prison governor's capricious brutality – lifers had nothing to lose in fighting back. But he circled warily around Felix, a triple-murderer serving only for extortion.

Shelepin rubbed his hands. The prisoners were out working in the snow or doing drill, the inadequate stove cooling, ice hanging from metal hooks on the wall. It was the usual scenario for a meeting with the governor: concessions asked for and granted in secret, information passed, favours returned. Between them they ran a slick, profitable organisation, where viciousness was the currency and debts were paid with shallow graves and a lack of ceremony.

The door opened, snow flurrying through while the guard looked and stepped aside. The two prisoners, identically padded in quilted grey jackets, came in fast, rushing Shelepin as he sprang to meet them. He was strong, might have shaken them off, but they were used to heavy labour, had toiled while he caroused, knew that failure would mean death. And they had a third party. He followed behind and lunged forward, the shank driving straight through Shelepin's throat and pinning him to the side of the upper bunk. Legs spasmed, a prisoner swore, heaving to restrain the bucking body. The movements slowed; they held him in position. A gust entered the room: the governor stood, hands behind his back, waiting while the blade was twisted out. Satisfied, he left for his rounds. Orders had once been issued which consigned this mafiya spawn to prison, gave leverage over his father, kept the young man secure and fresh for such an occasion. Today, the orders were changed, he was to be paroled into the after-life. Every Felix had his day. The governor wiped his nose and marched with his armed escort to inspect a group of road-building convicts. It was an honour to be of service to Boris Diakanov, rewarding in so many ways.

Cigarette finished, the performer – Tallulah was her stage name – stooped to collect up her bags and swung off with angry sexuality along the depopulated seafront. The hip swivel was wasted here. She had walked, jiggled, five hundred metres, stopped to reapply lipstick and was window-browsing for second-hand cheesecloth when the bomb exploded. The glass before her quivered, the shock rever-berating outwards in an echoing report from its inland location, a smoke pall rising skywards in its instant after-math. Makarios III Avenue. Her pane-reflection stilled, registering the open mouth, disbelief and beginnings of panic. She knew the sound. The local Aeroporos and Fanieros clans were forever indulging in blood-feuds. What she could not guess was that a banking operation had been obliterated by a single detonation, or that it belonged to the Russian for whom she had danced so vigorously, yet so unrewardingly, some minutes before.

Max smelled her skin, warm, sweet in the darkened room. He might have been imagining, was drowsy from the lateness of the hour and the soporific effects of Kremlin drink in the higher proof percentiles. Alcohol played some mean games. He had left Strachan downstairs in an empty side-lobby of the Ukraina, singing stanzas from an Air Cav song, talking of Viet Clap to no one in particular and trying to urinate into a discarded glass on the grounds that he was the piss-tube champion of Pleiku.

'Hello, Max.'

She came close. He let his stick fall and held out his arms without saying a word. His fingers felt her face, her lips kissing them, held her head between his palms, caressing the hair back, stroking, rediscovering. They stood together, swaying in silence, breathing, his nose pushed into her neck and shoulder, taking in her presence, exulting in the tenderness. He wanted to cry, for every minute wasted, for every hour lost to absence, distraction and distance. But she pressed him tight, comforted, pulled him back into happiness, away from Adele, from four months of emotional void, an embrace as familiar as the memories it drew out of their student lives together in Volgograd.

Zenya was twenty-one then, a student teacher, Max, the same age, on an undemanding one and a half-year post-university sabbatical to the city's State Pedagogic Institute. Ten hours' teaching of English a week left him with time to spare, and Zenya – the prettiest and most intelligent of his charges – filled it with a passion and intensity which hijacked the soul of a boy who had come of age making love and making out with innumerable, unmemorable one-night to one-month stands. Some had been blessed with cute butts, others cursed with neuroses and blister-packs of valium, yet more with bubble-gum in their craniums and a refreshing desire to discover his being through his fly-zip. He was indiscriminate, searching, claustrophobic, escaping eventually to Russia while thousands of its own citizens sought to escape in the opposite direction. And in the bleak student block at the foot of Mamaev Kurgan, where the heroic Motherland statue dominated the city from its hilltop Stalingrad memorial, in the grimy, crowded rooms where he bribed the Ingush *kommandant* to open an illegal bar, and among his friends who squeezed in to watch the floor's only television – acquired for dollars from a policeman fencing stolen property – he felt at ease, at home. It seemed familiar.

She was shy at first, approaching him during a break, when students milled out between classes to smoke and drink coffee in the small couryard formed by two sandstone wings at the Institute's entrance on Lenin Avenue. She enjoyed his teaching, lived in the same hostel and wondered which contemporary American writers he could recommend. He wrote down names and said he would be delighted to lend his personal copies, more delighted to have a drink. His teeth were excellent. She blushed and smiled, astonished at her own forwardness, gratified by his response, embarrassed with her provincial ways. He was the first American she or her classmates had ever met, from a land long demonised by State propaganda, the source of blue jeans, cola, plotless action films and predigested culture. It was irresistible; it was freedom. And here was its ambassador: a diplomatic representation was called for. There was no doubt he was good-looking, charming, strangely vulnerable – afflicted with an eye-condition – yet able to command a room and hold attention. She was petite, elfin, a fairy-child, so different from the pampered East Coast elite to which he was accustomed.

They shared books, *pertsovka*, walks and finally bed. It took three months to become her lover, his longest-ever courtship. And in that time he released himself from past constraints and inhibitions and bound himself with new unspoken covenants to a girl who expanded his vision, brought colour and hope to horizons dimmed by the threat of blindness. They broke into the nearby Red October factory to take saunas, picnicked on the sands of 'Crete' beach at the far bank of the Volga, journeyed to dances in outlying and unheated village halls where locals shuffled to the beat dressed in boots and fur coats, and introduced new levels of carnality and noise to the log cabins set in the forests reaching down to the Kazach border. The teaching contract came to an end, rampant inflation ensured that the Institute could no longer justify or afford its renewal, and he returned to the United States. Zenya stayed, had little choice, the gravitational pull of place and background forcing each to accept that such relationships were finite and condemned from the start. It did not make parting easier. He sought a career which might send him to Russia, she left teaching and gained a position in Moscow as translator and interpreter on the chance he might succeed. Hunter Strachan's transportation business was the closest he got, allowing quarterly visits, a staggered resumption of contact and the thrill and pain which each visit and subsequent farewell entailed. There were affairs, there was Adele, token attempts at commitment, committed attempts at tokenism, but for Max they were pretence while Zenya was real, alive, his life.

His lips brushed her eyelids and tasted salt. 'Don't cry,' he whispered. 'Hey, my sprite. I don't want you to cry.'

'I'm happy, Max.'

She found his mouth with hers, drifted over it, kissed it lightly, more firmly, each working against the other, then together, probing. Hands moved randomly, circling, pulling at buttons and sleeves, fumbling in intensity, clutching to fuse two pelvic opposites, clumsiness and eroticism feeding and flowing in parallel. Jacket off, the tie had gone. Her hands mapped out his chest and abdomen, kneading, feeling, needing, sliding round to the hips, buttocks and back to the groin, mirroring his actions, smoothing and outlining the contours. She was damp, wet, through her jeans, through his trousers. More clothes were shrugged off, struggled from, dropped; nipples sugar-stiff with saliva, nails clenched into skin.

Love whimpers growing, rhythmic, pleasure shuddering agonised on a threshold of anguish, her self-absorption absorbing him, compelling him deeper, harder. Her hands were talons, at once gripping and tearing, trying to dominate, to orchestrate, to win. The fairy-child had turned predator, huntress. He forced in a tongue, overrode resistance, penetrated, locked in as she clamped his head down. Total unity, total connection. He burnt through her climax, rode it, felt the inner ripples surge outwards, hypoxia squeals, as she rolled and straddled, sweat streaming, hair dank in his face, fingers interlocking to stretch him out. He tasted salt again, her breath short and shallow in his ear, her teeth nipping. She pumped, thighs pistoning, pressure rising in his head, nasal moans only half-heard through the torrent. Human hogs, grunting, snapping, fucking, loving. A gathering tightness. Oh yes, oh shit, oh Christ, oh Momma.

The panting had died, the heartbeats level, calm in the eye of their first night. They lay close, limbs cat-cradled, talking, nuzzling and laughing quietly. Honesty and nakedness, the two went together. Bullshit. It simply made the untruths more convincing, when bedrooms gave legitimacy, and humans thought with their hormones and spoke through their genitals. Adam lied; Eve lied; he lied. But not now, not with Zenya. Where Adele dictated, she nurtured; where Adele cramped him, she gave space; where Adele drained him, she inspired; where Adele judged, she accepted. Max stared into the darkness, aware that the bedside lamp was on, giving her – denying him – a chance to see. Touch, smell and hearing; it was enough.

'What are you thinking?'

'After that? I don't think I'm capable of thought,' he murmured.

'Something must be in there.' She spider-walked her fingers across his forehead. 'Tell me.'

'OK, I'm thinking how lucky we were not to be interrupted by students from the Physical Culture Institute crawling onto the balcony and pinching our clothes and chickens.' It had been a recurrent problem at the hostel in Volgograd.

'Even they wouldn't be stupid enough to do it twenty-five storeys up.'

'They were fairly committed Communists.'

'Then, perhaps you have a point.'

'I still get flashbacks. That, and the Arab students slaughtering goats in the communal showers.'

She soothed his head. 'How was the dinner? You and your important Kremlin friends. Did they like you?'

'I didn't tip anything on my lap or put my coffee spoon in the cigars, and I helped raise money for the Mayor's luxury holiday fund, so I guess I passed the test.'

'Of course you did.'

'Sure. I start with the advantage of having the sympathy vote.' He leant over and kissed her. 'And I'm overwhelmed by your ongoing and highly personal efforts to find a miracle cure.' Her methods would have raised Lazarus.

The creases to her face told him she was smiling. 'It worked for me.'

'I'm reserving judgement.' He lay back. 'The results could be flawed, faked even. I suggest we go for an extra set of tests.'

'Which approach do you favour?'

'Anything capable of surprising.' His head disappeared below the covers. An hour later, side-light remaining on, picking out their forms, they were asleep. Two bodies, luminous against the sheets.

In his room, sober, Hunter Strachan worked at a computer. Communicating.

Two bodies, luminous against the porcelain. Ilya Kokhlov watched from behind the viewing glass, taking a break from his office while his technicians moved around below cutting, extracting, weighing and bottling. A production line, nothing more. The negative pressurisation was plainly faulty, yet no one complained. Even at his desk he could smell death, carried it with him, was immune to the odours seeping from the pathology patients. Faulty was a norm, smooth-running a cause for suspicion. A breast, incised from its inner aspects, lay dissected, open on a trestle.

Dmitri looked up and grinned. He was back with his shears – the bearded gladiator's weapon of choice – standing back to appreciate his work at the third slab. The body of a middle-aged man, overweight, pockets of flesh dimpling outwards like the skirts of a hovercraft, lay face down, muscles pulled away from a longitudinal cut running along the vertebrae laminae and exposing the spine. Dmitri had already sawed through the laminar processes either side of the vertebrae, removed a dorsal section and exposed the cord in its spinal canal. It was hard work. The shears were to raise the vertebrae and facilitate removal of the cord once the cauda equina was clamped. An art getting it out undamaged.

For the moment, the man retained his spine. Kokhlov was not certain if he could say the same for himself. How could Georgi Lazin have done this to him? Friendship was about leaving people alone, not arriving unannounced in their post-mortem room, not asking for favours which involved personal risk, enmeshed former colleagues in new dangers and old enmities. Kokhlov had left it all behind, been exiled willingly from Moscow, made a life beyond the KGB, where his employers did not provide the bodies and his routine discoveries of 'unnatural causes' were just as routinely recorded as 'natural'. There was nothing natural about that existence: even the suicide victims were those seeking final escape from their persecutors, were stampeded into darkness. Prisoners in KGB camps stretched beyond endurance, inmates at the Serbsky Institute subject to constant physical and psychological torture, dissidents hounded or drugged until they neither knew themselves or their names. And Kokhlov cut them up and covered up, brave lives ending as thickened, muddied liquids sluiced away down the guttering of his pathology suite. So many. They were braver than he. He made a stand once, used up his reserves, was grateful to have lost only privileges, income, apartment and hair. Why could he not be left alone to quietly live and die in Krasnoyarsk?

Kokhlov flicked the intercom switch. 'It's not an ice-hockey fight. Gentler traction on the neck if you want to get those lungs out.' A thumbs-up sign. 'I'll examine the abdominal viscera later, Andrei. What's the fluid situation in the peritoneal?' Without turning, the man performed an upwards spiralling motion with his arm. 'Thought as much. Incidentally, the larvae you found in yesterday's stomach have hatched. A magical birth. I knew you'd be pleased.'

He made his way back to the office, a small, cluttered affair with anatomical drawings, weight charts and photographs illustrating particular stages of human decomposition, and cleared a space in which to sit. Flat surfaces were at a premium, covered either by papers or glass jars containing pickled gherkins – his favourite – or with organs. Mistakes were possible. In one container, a bust of Lenin floated ethereally and detached in its preservative, ready, as Kokhlov told inquisitive guests, 'for when the next bastards come in and tell us to dust him off.' Anything was possible with a totalitarian mindset, even regeneration. The Soviets had invented animatronics: there was no other explanation for the walking, talking corpses who filled the upper echelons of the Communist politburo during its final decades. Extraordinary decades – spectacle fronting hidden decay – the level of deceit, the scale of the lie reaching unsurpassed heights. And, generation by generation, the killing went on, and, generation by generation, the killers such as Colonel Petr Ivanov went on. He, like his father and grandfather before, had traversed the Communist Bloc and its aligned states, instilling fear and faith, parcelling the occasional gift back to Moscow Centre for analysis and comment. It was Kokhlov who often took delivery. Limbless bodies from Afghanistan, displaying the effectiveness of later-model plastic anti-personnel mines on captives forced to walk across them by *Khad* interrogators; bodies from Iraq's 'special prisons' at Radwaniyah and Abu Ghraib where victims were electrocuted to death or exposed to lethal doses of nerve agent; bodies from the secret police mortuaries of East Germany or from the labour camps operated by North Korea in eastern Siberia. Disfigured humankind.

The notes had taken long hours to compile, verify and complete; the phone calls went late into the night. He bullied, cajoled and pleaded, contacted old friends, offered future favours, played on the liberal-mindedness of those pathologists who knew his past and sympathised with his approach, played the national security line with the unco-operative impressed by his apparent closeness to the FSB. Kokhlov relished scaring the bureaucrats – out of practice, yet he had not lost the knack. The KGB had taught him something. Coercing others meant that for a while he could forget his own fear. But exhaustion had replaced the caffein-ated adrenalin, and the fear was returning. He held its source, the papers, in his hand; three thin sheets. Evidence. Terrible acts, spread out across several years, details recorded and recounted to him by post-mortem specialists and morbid anatomists across Siberia and into Russia. Stories of cadavers chewed on and hacked at, mass murders involving missing organs and entrails, children half-eaten, fragments of human bone, the odd suspect – scapegoat – too drunk to remember, but pliant enough to confess. The press were bored of cannibalism, low-life would always be low-life; the incidents earned a few lines or none at all, executions and tuberculosis in the camps ensured an end to follow-up questioning. No one linked the deaths: for the most part the victims were miners, railway workers, truckers, oil men in remote loca-tions, the occasional unfortunate offspring of professional managers unlucky enough to live in insalubrious districts or the BAM zone. Randomness – awful, inexplicable. Kokhlov ran a finger down the dates and locations. Khilok, in the Yabolonovy Mountains, where a group of hikers were found dismembered; human remains discovered in the sulphur baths at Usole-Sibirskoe; youngsters ritually strangled during a black mass near Kuibyshev off the trans-Siberian route. Low-grade militia matters, not worthy of newspaper interest. Yet officers of the Federal Security Service thought them interesting, had made inquiries, threatened unspecified action if the pathologists spoke to others of the cases or failed to submit their reports first to the FSB. Obfuscation, gagging. Why? There was not a pattern, but a shadow across these events. And he knew instinctively that it belonged to the Death's Head – his enemy, Lazin's enemy – Ivanov, and behind him the brooding darkness of Leonid Gresko. He had seen evil close, expected it. Officially practised, sanctioned cannibalism, a cult in high office, went beyond his imagination.

The preparation room was empty when he entered, and

far colder than the overheated office. He wandered through to the body lockers, arranged for short-term and long-term stay, four degrees centigrade or minus twenty, and selected the room temperature section. Deep frozen was difficult to work with. Masked and gloved-up, he stretched his fingers and approached. The load rolled out effortlessly on the runners; he reached for the zipper.

'Well, my pretty. Excuse the indignity, but I'd like to ask a favour.' He leant over. 'No, no. Don't spray Proteus bacteria at me. Resistance is useless.'

Tomorrow he would change the host, move his papers from corpse to corpse until Lazin came to collect them. They might search a safe, never a dead patient. He understood their mentality – why work over an individual if you did not get the satisfaction of seeing it bleed, hearing it yelp? His uncomplaining assistant – he checked the name again – would guard it well. And then he saw himself, was staring prone from the trolley, up at his own face peering in, before the zip rose, clouding the view with a milky plastic transparency and his double's arm pushed him back into the blackness. He felt the motion of the wheels below, the weight of others entombed and gently decaying above. *Get me out of here, Georgi. Get me out.* But Lazin did not respond; Ivanov was the janitor, had put locks on the doors. Breathe, breathe deep. Kokhlov gripped the sides of the unit, head down, nauseous. A panic attack, a premonition. He needed a drink.

The screams and shots halted abruptly as the head of Russia Division thumbed the remote, the screen image hiccuping and turning blank. They were seated in a briefing room at Vauxhall Cross, padded chairs and projection equipment strewn around the walls and in front of tinted windows, low-energy strip lights making up for the anaemic ambient effects of the winter sun outside.

'Seen enough?'

'Haven't you?' Dryden answered.

'Can't get enough of it, Hugh. It's compulsive viewing.

The St Valentine's Day Massacre, a modern interpretation of the theme. That's the glory of wide-band transmission.' And GCHQ's ability to intercept and decode it, thought Dryden. Britain's electronic eavesdroppers at Cheltenham had automatically accessed and downloaded Boris Diakanov's video conference call from a commercial satellite. Secure communications meant nothing to a facility which swallowed over a billion pounds of taxpayers' money each year. 'So,' Parsons replaced the control and leant back. 'What do you make of it?'

'I'd hate to see *tsisari* when he's really angry.'

'My view entirely. Worrying enough as it is. And the script can only get more violent – not the crowd-pleasing variety either: Boris's son; Gribanov carved up with lasers in St Petersburg; Maxim Shelepin and assorted extras in our home snuff movie here. People are scared and they've every right to be.'

'So, it'll be vegetables rather than flowers at the dachas this year.' Dryden jotted down a memo. When Russians were insecure, they turned to gardening for therapy, when really troubled they grew food rather than flowers. It was the best diviner and leading indicator of public and political mood there was. 'Fallout?'

'Not yet.'

'Are you making specific predictions?'

Parsons gave an economical smile. 'That wouldn't do at all. I was hoping you'd save me the embarrassment.'

'Presumably the Foreign Secretary and that dreadful shit Nigel Ferris will be clamouring for briefings shortly?' It was a shame that MI5, the Security Service, no longer kept watch on the likes of the Junior Minister.

'Presumably.'

Dryden rubbed his chin. 'Escalation will be rapid. It always is with sectarian warfare and mafiya turf battles.'

'And,' Parsons added, angling himself forwards, 'if you'll forgive the expression, so far we've seen a great deal of tit, but not a lot of tat.'

'Which means the smaller gangs will be deciding where they stand, or who they want to be buried with. If they're going to die anyway, they might as well go for the top and bring down Diakanov.'

The Russia head examined a cuff-link. 'To where and to whom will the ripples spread?'

'Depends on how quickly the fighting is contained, who *tsisari* brings on side, whether the authorities become involved.'

'They will if renascent business confidence is affected,' Parsons suggested.

Dryden cocked his head, body-language uncommitted. 'It's used to taking punishment, business expects to tough it out. That's the frontier spirit for you. A shoot-out is a non-event unless it involves rocket-propelled grenades.'

'So, executives with their noses in the Kremlin foie gras would need quite a shock to notice.' Parsons was thinking aloud.

'If they can't make money, or stop breathing: that's when they'd consider an exodus.'

'Ah, the businessman as human being. An interesting viewpoint.' The eyebrow lowered. 'We'll stay plugged in to the banks and lending agencies, then. It's about all we can do at present. I want contingencies for Armageddon, however.'

'Consider them in place.'

'With ministers like Ferris in Whitehall, the Chief doesn't like being caught out. Says he needs his own PR machine just to survive.' Parsons gave a thinly camouflaged sigh. 'We slew the Soviet dragon and now there are a thousand snakes in the garden to deal with.' Dryden was not certain if he was talking of Russia, but pulled a sympathetic face.

'Cold War was always easier than thaw. It's why we're still in business.'

The Division head turned to a different file. 'Which leads me neatly to our next item. Defence Intelligence has been taking a look at the Bratsk dam, Hugh.'

The subject had trickled from his mind in recent days. 'The *Brodets* lead?'

'The very same.' Parsons pushed a sheet of paper across. 'Note production schedules for Sukhoi's aircraft manufacturing plant in Irkutsk.'

Dryden scanned down. 'Heavy transports from a fighter plant?'

'Exactly. Explained by the decision to produce Beriev's turbofan-powered Be-200 amphibian there. Quite a break with precedent, a long way from the group's home base at Taganrog, and done apparently for purely commercial reasons. Logical to put seaplanes at Irkutsk with Lake Baikal only forty miles away. Beriev has even become part of the Sukhoi Aviation Military-Industrial Complex. Rationalisation is the buzz-word.'

'My God. They're learning common sense.' Dryden continued reading.

'Strategic deception is one thing they'll never have to learn.'

A quizzical glance. 'You've got my attention.'

Parsons stood and went to the window, gazing out and talking. 'DIS has American satellite imagery showing some strange shapes, bigger than the Be-200. They dismissed them, filed them as early examples of a larger 70-tonne A-40 Albatross maritime patrol aircraft, or possible wing-in-ground effects airframes. Collapse of the USSR meant the Albatross was killed off.'

'But remains hanging round their necks,' Dryden ventured.

Parsons was concentrating on a point far upriver. 'There were other pictures showing aircraft similar to Tupolev's Tu-160 Blackjack supersonic strategic bomber and smaller Tu-26 Backfire. Nothing to worry about we were told; snapshots of the elephants' graveyard. Very comforting.'

'And wrong, I assume?'

'Defence intelligence has returned to the pictures and reassessed them in the light of a parallel analysis of the Bratsk dam.'

'Have they reached conclusions?'

'Made suggestions. What they're unaware of is that one

of my sources was killed during the Winter Festival in Irkutsk at the beginning of last year.'

'Troika rides have their downside.'

'As do midnight wanders along the ul Chkalova near the Angara river bridge.'

'Or having Leonid Gresko, head of the FSB, as our main Russian adversary.'

The small, neat figure turned from the window. 'Local militia say the area is terrible for street-crime.'

'And as we all know, the Lake Baikal hydrofoil doesn't operate from there in winter, so there was no reason for his being in the area. Ergo, he was dumped.'

'Ergo, he found something before he was murdered and dumped. You're right – it has all the hallmarks of Gresko's thugs. It was kind of them to draw my attention to it, particularly as our man was keeping an eye on staff from TsAGI, the Central Aero and Hydrodynamic Institute. They've been swarming round Irkutsk in droves.'

'I thought you favoured cock-ups over conspiracies, Guy.'

The head of Russia Division returned from his window position. 'But I'm ambivalent about coincidence. At least we know the DIS study is objective.' He turned the folder and nudged it across. 'Take a look at Bratsk. Places what's going on in perspective.'

Five minutes passed before Dryden reached the end of the summary. 'Liquid hydrogen?' He tapped his fingers on the page. 'They have been busy.' There was no indication of amusement.

'That's what scares me.'

Strolling on walkways high above the main electrolysing plant in Bratsk, the two men, besuited, engaged in conversation, were dwarfed by the immensity of the industrial processes mapped out by pipes, tanks and insulated electrical elements below. They came to a viewing stand and halted. Grandeur, scale, everywhere, workers diminished by distance as small and white as lice, some static, clustered, others breaking away to travel the acreage in slow-time and motion. The visitor from Irkutsk was impressed. He had never liked Bratsk, a polluted hell-hole – even the locals joked that the best form of contraception was to breathe the atmosphere – but the strategic vision here, its importance to the viability of Russia's most secret military programme, a programme for which he held ultimate responsibility, ensured that trips were unavoidable.

'Was the aerostat up last night?'

'And functioning flawlessly. Local commanders claim its input has transformed the area defence situation.' Similar in concept to the American Defence Elevated Netted Sensor, the balloon carried a high-powered, large-aperture radar capable of detecting and tracking low-flying aircraft or cruise missiles and providing targeting data for the region's SAM systems.

'How reassuring. I trust that other news is equally positive.'

His host waved an arm. 'A further consignment of fuel will reach Angarsk in a week, ready for the next test-flight.'

'Production problems are solved?'

'Our concerns are only with transport and logistics, and those are funding issues, not technical.'

They watched awhile. Here, the re-emergence was being acted out, a birth to project power far beyond Russia's shrunken borders. Change, order, discipline, self-belief, strength. The will and the iron, together. They were coming, hidden behind the chaos, concealed within the redundant factories, the Border Troops, the political system. Audacious, meticulous, monumental – it was reality, it was ready. Coursing through the pipes, processed from water taken from the Bratsk reservoir and supercharged with electricity, was the future, Russia's future, hydrogen.

As an aviation fuel, hydrogen had many advantages. Available from water, its supply – unlike that of hydrocarbons – was limitless. It provided almost three times the calorific energy of kerosene for a given weight, it was efficient and 'lean-burning', produced a small flame with a low heat signature less detectable by military infrared scanners, and its by-products were largely water vapour and insignificant quantities of nitrous oxide. There were drawbacks: its lower fuel density increased the liquid volume to be carried in flight by a factor of four over kerosene; to prevent premature evaporation it required on-board storage in low-pressure centre-line tanks kept at -252 degrees centigrade; it needed to pass through heat exchangers prior to entering the engine combustion chambers in a gaseous state. A challenge, particularly when pumps, valves and engine systems had to work effectively and repeatedly at astronomically low temperatures. Difficulties in handling LH2 had thus restricted its use to fuelling rockets for satellite launch and space exploration. But scientists and designers dreamt of wider applications. For them, these issues – advantages and disadvantages – were outweighed by liquid hydrogen's greatest asset. It would burn faster and produce a far superior jet velocity than any conventional fuel and, in doing so, could propel an aircraft to speeds higher than anything yet achieved within the earth's atmosphere.

Russia's known work in the cryoplane field had started early. In April 1988, it began flying a converted Tupolev Tu-155 experimental airliner with its starboard Trud turbofan capable of running on liquefied natural gas, hydrogen or methane. Tests were positive. A Mil Mi-8TG helicopter was adapted to use cryogenic fuels, and in 1994, the Russian government, confirming its commitment to liquefied natural gas – a resource of which there remained deposits for an estimated two hundred years – announced plans for Tupolev to reconfigure Tu-154Ms into Tu-156 LNG freighters. Goals were clear, if budgets limited. Cooperation with Germany in civil cryoplane technology increased from 1990, both sides developing hydrogen-fuelled powerplants and working together on the Dornier 328 JET testbed concept. The way ahead for Russian civil aviation seemed clear.

Military aerospace continued to decline. Projects were

proposed and disposed, started and abandoned. By the late 1990s, Western intelligence were reporting six Russian combat aircraft design programmes underway, all under-funded, all compromised by the collapse in integrated research, production flaws, antiquated avionics and poor cockpit environments. None were likely to be purchased in quantity. While America flew its F-22 Raptor, the most advanced air-supremacy fighter ever to enter service – combining stealth, vectored thrust and supercruise in one package – Russian designs floundered. Innovation was not enough to save them: only orders could do that, and they were not forthcoming. For the West, the Cold War was won, the former enemy was in disarray. It was the received opinion; it was the opinion which Leonid Gresko, director of the Federal Security Service, wished to be received.

The military cryoplane programme centred at Irkutsk was an immense undertaking, unknown to the Kremlin leadership and kept from any of the parliamentarians, self-serving and unaware in Moscow. At first, supersonic Tu-26 Backfire bombers and larger long-range Tu-160 Blackjacks were used to test liquid hydrogen components. Then came unmanned models, scores of them, screeching through the sound barrier, accelerating on hypersonic shock waves to reach higher Mach numbers, leaving a noise of pulsing thunder rumbling thousands of feet above the steppes. While Russia's defence base disintegrated, the project remained intact and ongoing, development funded and camouflaged by numerous illicit sources. Protection was charged to enterprises throughout Siberia, contraband and narcotics seized by Border Troops were sold on, and freedom-to-operate deals struck with mafiya heads served to raise additional sums. The Federal Security Service was the clearing house, the prime instru-ment: its resources, informants and longstanding tradition of persecution and press manipulation allowed it to blackmail, extort and cover-up at will. Suppression had been its raison d'être since inception. When an unmanned scramjet crashed, its troops cordoned off the area to collect apparent debris from a satellite launch at Svobodny; sightings of rapidly moving aerial objects were dismissed as the ramblings of irrational UFO-freaks.

There was nothing irrational or unreal about the two white, diamond-shaped airframes sitting squat in their hidden hangars at Irkutsk. For six months they had been flying at night, pushing out their performance envelopes, streaking across moonless skies, kerosene fuel powering them to Mach 5, hydrogen injected supersonically into their ramjet engines taking them far beyond to Mach 10. Flight paths carried them over oil production regions, the flames of natural gas burning off at drilling sites helping to confuse infrared detectors carried on board American reconnaissance satellites. Speed and radar decoys did the same for space-based radar sensors. By morning only the crystalline vapour trails hanging high in the atmosphere signalled to those below a recent overflight by a shape which they had never seen and would never recognise.

The two men turned back from the panorama, the Director from Irkutsk smiling in a way peculiar to successful bureaucrats. There was much to be pleased about.

'It never ceases to surprise that one of the world's most environmentally friendly fuels should be produced here at Bratsk.'

'Our advantages have not been fully appreciated.' The plant's manager was sensitive to even the most oblique criticism of his home town.

'Come now.' A hand clamped down on his shoulder in a gesture of supportive domination as they walked away. 'You have done well. The Americans will be caught unawares, their precious military systems rendered obsolete.' Yes, the Americans would be caught, unaware of everything.

The autocratic grip of familiarity was uncomfortably hard. 'An achievement I am proud to play a part in.'

'As we all are.' The Director halted. 'And what you have down there, and what I have in Irkutsk will leave the F-22, their wonderful Raptor, far behind. Back with the dinosaurs.'

The chins bobbed with amusement, the eyes like wet pebbles; slippery, ungiving. The enemy might stumble on fragments, detect the occasional signal or abnormality. But that was not enough. Indeed, that was not enough.

Back in his office, the plant manager slumped in a worn chair adjacent to his desk. Sleep deprivation was part of his life, tranquillisers and stress almost hobbies. There was no relaxation, no free time; his family, when they saw him, encountered an ill, malnourished wreck dream-walking through an existence of crisis meetings and unscheduled calls from technical staff and muddled middle-management. Schedules were constantly revised and shortened, days compressed. At least under Communism, the habit of 'storming' to meet monthly production targets set by the central authorities had occurred in predictable bursts. Here the panic was unrelenting, total. There were few perks. He opened a drawer and levered out one of them – a bottle of Scotch. This and a decent salary made it worthwhile; bonuses ensured that anything was bearable. The neck tipped, alcohol taken in. He wiped his mouth with the back of a hand, steadied the bottle on a filing cabinet and edged round to the office cupboards to check. It was still there, safe in this locked office, protected by the security cordons and patrols ever vigilant on the outskirts of the complex. Even they did not know what they were guarding. It was his livelihood, his future. The metallic case lay covered by papers and surplus equipment. The American had said it contained rough diamonds, requested that he store them for a while. There was no reason to doubt him: Strachan always paid well.

Away from the wire, beyond the olfactory range of the attack dogs, shape white-blended against the landscape, the old man lay in a snow scrape. A mittened hand adjusted the focus, swinging the binoculars to view the guards striding inside the perimeter. The distance was too great to discern their unit: perhaps there were no identifying patches, in which case they were Cheka, NKVD, KGB or FSB, whatever the Secret Police chose to call themselves in their latest incarnation. Their methods never changed – he would not move closer. His bones ached, joints hurt, circulation slowing, numbing his extremities, reminding him of the great age he carried. So many years, so many lives. Some he remembered, some not. He shifted painfully, working his toes to ease the cramp and encourage the blood, concentrating to take his mind from the discomfort. A senior visitor had arrived earlier and then departed; few people came to the location. Tanker vehicles would leave, heading for the rail freight depot, but they were under military guard, impossible to approach. Strangely busy for a city as dreary and depressed as Bratsk. Earlier, he photographed the aerostat, reminiscent of a wartime barrage balloon, which had hovered throughout the night at several thousand feet on an anchor line nearby. The film was destined for London, its frames indicating a new strategic target worthy of close attention. Another sweep of the lenses, searching out details, weaknesses. He pitied those condemned to work here, but they had heating, food, friends. When he was enslaved, forced to labour building the temporary relief railway across the Bratsk reservoir to the Lena-Vostochnaya freight port, he had none of these. And when he hid out west of Siberia's Lake Baikal, a fugitive in the mountains and dense taiga forest, living among the wolves and bears, comfort was eating berries, survival was sleeping in an elk carcass. Activity noted, he stowed the glasses and reached stiffly for his ski poles. Intelligence-gathering did not become any easier.

Dryden had brought in coffee, three tables were now covered in papers and maps. The two men continued to walk and talk around the room.

'If it's a liquid hydrogen project, why not the Angara River dam? It's closer to aircraft production at Irkutsk. Would make more sense.'

'Not if you wanted to spread the assets, camouflage the

work,' Parsons replied, marking a transparency with a pen. 'Bratsk's power station has a reservoir almost five thousand square kilometres to support it, a second hydroelectric plant at Ust-Ilimsk as backup with over 4,000 Megawatts. Everything you need. Be interesting to discover if electric power to the BAM has been affected.' He moved to an overhead projector and switched it on. 'Watch closely.' A picture of Eastern Siberia, Trans-Siberian and BAM railways stretching across it, slid on to the wall. 'You see Bratsk and Irkutsk, the GES hydroelectric station and the aircraft manufacturing plant respectively?'

Dryden drew up a chair and stared at the image, thin face side-lit by the projector. 'I do.'

'The link.' A second transparency was placed above the first, superimposing the wide Angara River which flowed between Bratsk on the BAM railway and Irkutsk on the Trans-Siberian. 'Logistically, it's unbeatable, and we know that vessels have resumed operating again between the two locations.'

'My notes say they stopped in 1993. Lack of business.'

'So what explains the restart? We're talking ferries, not hydrofoils. I guarantee they're strengthened for ice-breaking and will become larger the more LH2 they carry.'

'The Angara is only navigable from May through September.'

'Enough to fill tanks at the oil centre in Angarsk twenty-four miles down river from Irkutsk. In winter, tanker trains can bring LH2 from Bratsk via Taishet.'

'Cold Cut hasn't reported anything.' Dryden was paid to be sceptical.

'I should imagine the last time he linked hydrogen and aviation was when the *Hindenberg* crashed at Lakenhurst.' The third overlay was placed down, a series of symbols dotted onto the original map. 'You want to accompany me with the summary, Hugh?'

Dryden dictated. 'The facilities at Irkutsk – bearing in mind they're operated by Sukhoi, Russia's premier combat aircraft manufacturer – the possible LH2 site at Bratsk, as discussed.'

'Here and here.'

'River and train links, including an increase in rail traffic between Ust-Ilimsk, Bratsk and Irkutsk via Taishet; renewed boat services; potential storage at Angarsk. Ditto.'

'Check.'

'Then we've got a large aluminium smelting and alloy plant twelve miles west of Bratsk and another at the foot of the Primorski mountains in Goncharovo fourteen miles east of Irkutsk.'

'That's these two points.' A hand shadow waved briefly over the screen.

'Relevance?'

'Boys over at the old War Office suspect the plants also develop advanced carbon composites, materials used in fabricating cryoplane structures – hydrogen-powered aircraft.'

'And taken together with circumstantial evidence, cold weather which favours liquid hydrogen storage, a depopulated region that aids a secret test flight regime, the industrial infrastructure, the presence of oil and gas industries . . .'

'With their parallel efforts to develop techniques for extracting hydrogen.'

'The presence of Tupolev bombers as window-dressing and the killing of a low-level agent. The consensus is?'

'That there is no consensus.' Parsons left the projector. 'We know they're ahead with cryogenics, flight-tested an alternative fuel-burn K-88 engine back in 1988; we know they've squeezed everything they can out of their joint-venture relationship with Germany; we know from a small disturbance in French Guiana six years ago that they stole hydrogen-handling systems from the Ariane rocket programme which ships in its fuel by sea container. If they did it there, they'll be doing it with the EQHHPP hydroelectric programme in Quebec which produces and transports liquid hydrogen to Europe.'

'A big effort.'

'I'd concur. We could even throw into the plot the closure of the MAPO-Mig factories around Moscow for most of 1997.'

Dryden had heard the rumour. 'I read the article in *Kommersant Daily.*'

'A clandestine redeployment of skilled aerospace workers to Sukhoi's assembly line at Novosibirsk or to the suspected cryoplane plant at Irkutsk comes to mind.'

'Do we know what types of cryogenic aircraft they might be looking at?'

'There's a suspicion it might be scramjets – supersonic combustion ramjets.'

'Bombers and strike-aircraft?'

'At Mach 10, Hugh, I think military categorisation ceases to hold any real relevance.' Both men remained temporarily silent, consumed by the magnitude of what had been presented.

'The resurrection of the Russian Defence Industrial Complex.' More quietly. 'Hallelujah.'

Parsons sat and pushed his fingers together in a pyramid, a point of precision. 'A miracle indeed. Where's the funding coming from? Why the secrecy? Why the project? Who's authorised it?'

'Are we certain it's not simply a civilian concept study – blended wing-body mockups, laminar flow control models, flying-wings scaled up in balsa wood?'

'If we were certain, Hugh, we wouldn't be brainstorming. But multi-spectral satellites suggest something more solid than chipboard, and more flyable than a mockup.'

'Any precedents?'

A picture of a delta-shaped flying object was produced. 'An early concept drawing by Tupolev of its idea for a future hypersonic scramjet bomber and reconnaissance aircraft.'

'Looks similar to what the Americans were designing.'

'Strikingly so. To produce it would take political will, billions of dollars, and flawless design and production techniques. It was thought impossible that the Russians could leapfrog the West in this manner.'

'They've surprised us before.'

'I'd love to think it was paranoia spooking me. Unfortunately...' Parsons pulled a cassette tape from his jacket pocket and inserted it into the player close by on the desk '... It's not the whole story'. He depressed the switch. A stream of unintelligible squeaks and electronic sounds burbled from it. 'What do you make of this?'

'Nothing. I'm not a mainframe computer.'

Parsons turned the device to mute. 'If you were, you'd realise it's the satellite launch code to the Russian *Perimetr* doomsday system. Picked up from their last ICBM launch by our new stations in Poland. It matches against the library copy at GCHQ.'

So this was how the end of the world sounded. Dryden had his eyes closed. 'Odd.'

'Becoming more so.' Parsons ejected the tape. 'It's the latest in a series of Russian tests checking progress on their nuclear weapons modernisation programme.'

'You'd think their priorities might have changed.'

'This is Russia, Hugh.' True. It could be a red herring, it could be anti-NATO posturing. 'I'm hardly overjoyed when stability – political, military or economic – is not assured, when there's no real logic to these specific projects, and when the means of funding them are obscure.' A looming breakdown in relations between opposing criminal camps was a major variable in the equation: outcomes were almost impossible to call. 'It's still Third World meets weapons of mass destruction. Makes me nervous.'

'Diakanov?'

'Part of the reason. An inexplicable bad feeling about it, the other.' The Russia supremo shuffled papers, tapped and inserted them into a file, and rose. 'We're getting glimpses of capability. That doesn't tell us intentions.'

'Have you informed the Chief?' Dryden stacked and handed over a group of folders.

'Only when I'm certain it fits into our broader picture. It would be tricky persuading anyone with a story of a secret arms buildup.' Tricky understated the task. Exaggeration, over-emphasis on worst-case scenarios, had been hallmarks of Cold War intelligence assessments. The mistake would not be repeated.

'Hitler got away with rearmament.'

'Before the era of signals intelligence and reconnaissance satellites, when men were men, *blitzkrieg* was simple and you could train air force pilots by disguising them as Lufthansa crews.'

'The führer also had a touching belief in miracle weapons.'

'Successful countermeasures always appear eventually.'

'Eventually,' Dryden repeated. 'We'd still have trouble bringing down a V-2. Or a Scud. And a hypersonic aircraft flying at ten times the speed of sound? Would outrun anything.'

Parsons stopped. 'Things are a little different here. Russia's not looking for a fight. Certainly no rationale for some of our wilder conjectures.'

'And yet . . .'

'And yet.' He was standing still. 'If there's a government-in-waiting, or in hiding, with a different agenda or set of ideals, all we can do is wait until they overstep. We'll keep this conversation between ourselves, Hugh.' Dryden nodded. 'For the moment, I'm not ready to face the men in white coats.'

'Which means Purton Senior and Junior are in for a bumpy ride.'

The tea had done nothing to wash away the bitterness of the midday bread and *salo* – salted pig fat – consumed between meetings, its after-taste clinging to the back of his throat with the same obstinacy as the diesel fumes hanging acrid in the goods and marshalling yards. Shouts, the clash of trains coupling and decoupling, the grinding of TEM shunting engines heaving wagons into place, directed by hoarse men yelling angrily into handsets. Lazin picked his way among the images, an outsider, too calm to be part of the tumult: Tynda, the centre of the BAM railway, home to its headquarters, linked by a branchline to the Trans-Siberian railway hundreds of miles to the south, a focal point for trade and transit, for the FSB Colonel's investigation.

Vignettes and fragments of conversation, overlapping, competing. 'For fuck's sake. You know I can't get spares. We've cannibalised every fucking ChME3 we've got. You want me to go to the Czech Republic and ask nicely?' The answer was not appreciated. 'You fucking *pedik*.' Other voices, equally rich in the vernacular. '*Idi na khui*.' Fuck off. 'We need that like a cunt needs an alarm clock. I'm telling you . . . *Poshli yob tvoyu mat*.' A pause. 'Mouth of a whore! Listen to me . . .' Patience was lost. 'Ask the East Germans! They built the fucking carriage.' A wink at Lazin.

He had circulated among these people for days, trawled the Zheleznorozhnikov railwaymen's hostel, listened to the gossip on the dormitory floors of the Hotel Nadezhda, visited workers in their prefabricated Nissen-hut style *bochka* dwellings up on the hillside, sat in uniform rooms with a hundred bug-eyed officials, stares as blank as an Amursk apartment block. And there was nothing. So there was something. Along the BAM, electromagnetic pickups beneath the rails recorded the position and identity of every train and passed it back to the control room in Tynda. There were no discrepancies, traffic flow had been normal and minimal throughout the period of the robbery. The diamond train was tracked, plotted, its halt at Daban shown on hardcopy, as was its subsequent departure through the tunnel. Yet whoever mounted the raid knew everything about railways: how to override the dead man's handle, how to deactivate alarms, remove the black box in the driver's cab, access the three-light autoblocking signalling system. The train might have been shadowed, the gang resourceful enough to remain invisible to the authorities. Some resources.

The railwayman's demeanour and language were under-scored with spleen. Lazin singled him out and approached, standing before him as he howled orders.

'What do you want?'

'A word.'

'I'm busy.'

Lazin held up the identification wallet. 'State Security.'

The eyes swivelled and noticed a scene beyond the FSB officer's shoulder, brows meeting, lungs filling. 'For fuck's sake, move it along! Now!' The practised temper of a professional. His attention returned to Lazin. 'I'm still busy.'

'Then you'll find a cell inconvenient.'

Palms raised defensively. 'OK, OK. Just don't hang around too long. It makes my men nervous.' It made everyone nervous. Many here would have been the progeny of inmates from the KGB-run, Stalin-era gulags. Memories lingered in Siberia. 'I can always smell a Chekist, tell when they've visited,' he grumbled. 'Even if they're plainclothes like you.'

It may not have been a compliment, but the conversation was flowing. 'You're perceptive.'

'I miss nothing.' A break for some frantic hand-signals to an unseen member of his marshalling staff. 'That's why I'm in charge. Thirty years here; there's nothing I don't notice.' Thirty years' imprisonment, without even knowing it. He reached for the cigarette proffered by Lazin and lit it himself. 'Your department is taking an unhealthy interest in my yard, been busy. Why? You think we're smuggling drugs? Timber? Gold?' Undoubtedly.

Lazin pocketed the cigarettes without taking one. He preferred to use them as cash. 'How busy?'

'Night visits, requests for preparing special trains. You should know.'

'Which ones?'

'Snow collectors – CMs we call them. Don't ask me why they need that kind of equipment. It's specialised kit: snow ploughs or rotator-clearers are usually enough. I thought you people concentrated on collecting bodies.'

The FSB's charm offensive had a long way to go, thought Lazin. He did not smile. That would have lent legitimacy to the sarcasm, undermined his authority. Collecting bodies. *Check the sidings*, the voice had told him in the darkness of his room at the military camp. There had to be access to the site of the robbery, and egress. In mountainous terrain, weather predictably spiteful, prisoners to dispose of, rail was the surest way. And specialist trains neither drew attention nor required rigid timetables. 'Have you got log-books for the past three months? Which specialist engines were being prepared or passing through?'

'Destroyed in a fire.' The adjective was 'convenient'. As convenient as the unavailability of files at the nearby BAM administration block. 'Three weeks ago, an electrical fault. Wiped out computer records, notes on conversations with BAM apparatchiks next door, our register of items missing from rolling stock. If that wasn't disruptive enough, we then had militia, accident investigators, Ministry of Transport heavyweights and the like crawling over the place. We're only just getting back to normal.'

'Where are the non-conventional engines kept?'

'You ask a lot of questions.'

'Habit. Do you have a separate depot for the snow-clearers?'

A hand waved vaguely. 'That shed. You'll only find a few ploughs. The rest are out. There's a repair train lying up in unit three. Been there a while.'

'I want to see it.'

'I'll have to ask. We've been told not to approach it.'

'Who by?'

The stance was guarded. 'I don't know. People drop hints, word spreads, you understand how it works. What's it to you? It's probably your office anyway. Heavy build, heavy coats, heavy faces. I don't make enquiries.'

'Is that common – other agencies taking out repair engines?'

'It's not uncommon.' A hasty draw on the cigarette; the

dialogue was becoming edgy. 'Could be Rail Forces, could be FSB. They use them for surveillance sometimes. If you see two of them closer than two hundred kilometres apart, one of them shouldn't be there. Colonel, leave me out of this.'

'I need a walk-round,' Lazin replied unsympathetically. 'We can do it quietly.' He threw the remainder of the cigarettes to the man. 'Or we can do it loud – you in handcuffs, a gun in your back, with a delegation of officials snapping at your arse. You have my authorisation, and it comes straight from Director Gresko in Moscow.'

Reluctantly, surreptitiously, and making a circuitous approach, the man led Lazin to the sheds hidden behind the larger, mainstream depots. Rails disappeared beneath their padlocked doors, the area sectioned off and silent.

'In here.' Plastic sheeting, brittle with ice, and corrugated iron, hid the small side-entrance fashioned into the wall where the steel verticals failed to meet. 'Keep your head down, pick up a flashlight on your right.'

They stooped, shuffled through and entered. The place smelt of oil, droppings – rodent and bird – and half a century of rail history, shrouded in winter shadow. Heating had not improved in the interim. The dozen carriages loomed high, grey sides picked out by the moving beams, a crane perched and overhanging on the rear flatbed.

'The carriages are usually pulled by a heavy-duty diesel. 3TE10 or 4TE10.'

The specifications meant nothing to Lazin. 'When was this last used?' He trailed the light horizontally along the unmarked cars.

The man was checking the bogeys, ducking to inspect the undersides. 'Can't say. There's generally a lot of movement, repairs being called for from here to Taishet. The specialist cabs aren't my area.'

'What would this carry?'

'Spare track, enough to make an artificial passing loop for itself round derailments. The crane you can see. There are sleeping quarters for over thirty men, and a canteen – that's where those vents are. These two box cars,' he indicated them with the torch, 'are carrying either bulldozers or tracked, all-terrain snow vehicles. Ten men apiece.' Alive or dead? The man continued talking, his earlier reticence overcome by enthusiasm for lecturing the uninitiated. Lazin's mind was working in parallel, laying its own tracks, pushing in new directions. The monologue was sustained. '. . . You can go anywhere in this. It's totally self-contained.' Precisely. It was totally self-contained, sealed. Just as the robbery had been.

'Get me in there.'

The grumbling cut in, but the arguments had ceased. The man recognised types who would get their way; it was better to concede control and move on, and get the visitor moved out, as quickly as possible. Put it down to a life experience. The cars were of standard construction, easily accessible. The first contained an all-terrain vehicle, drab-olive beneath its tarpaulin, in better condition than was normal for the BAM.

'Definitely a new gearbox,' the railwayman opined, sliding the doors shut after Lazin had jumped down. 'And the engine's cleaner than Siberian pussy. That's high maintenance. Not worth it in my view.' Unless you could not afford mistakes, malfunction. 'You want to see the second wagon?' A nod. 'Shit.'

The canvas came off, the yard marshaller shaking his head. 'I was expecting to see a bulldozer.'

Lazin peeled the fabric back, joining the man as he attempted to open the door to the snow-vehicle's driving compartment. 'What's the problem?'

'You, Colonel. I said we shouldn't be here. This one's locked, and look. That's a coded seal. We can't get in.'

'You are a defeatist.' He was screwing the suppressor onto his secondary pistol, a Makarov. 'Stand back.' An arm swept round to ensure that the order was followed. He lined up and fired twice into the lock. Instant rupture, holes punched in a shower of white sparks. 'Vandalising state property is no longer a capital offence.' He wrenched at the damaged panel. 'Climb through and open the rear hatches.'

A kick from a booted foot and the steel flew open from the back of the transporter, the foreman crouching inside, shielding his eyes from the torch beam. Lazin clambered to join him.

'Search everything.'

'It's an older vehicle. See.' The light played across the cabin floor. 'Rust in places.'

Lazin knelt, extracted a pocket-knife and scraped with an unfolded blade at a mark encrusted into a corner. Dry and brown, it came away easily. He wiped it onto his palm and spat, the knife used as improvised spatula to mix in the saliva.

'What are you doing?'

'Direct your torch onto the floor, show me the marks.' The railwayman did so.

'Rust doesn't smear like that. They've tried to wash it down. It's blood.' He held up his hand, palm imprinted, vivid with a wet stigmata. 'It's human blood.'

Collar up, the flaps of his hat down, he stepped out across the river footbridge. It was icy, unprotected from the wind eddies gusting above the iron neutrality of the water, and doubtless worse along the depressing main street of Krasnaya Presnya. So, he had found blood. Even if it were DNA-tested, linked to the bodies of the troops from the diamond train executed and dumped in the uranium mine over eight hundred miles distant, it would prove, mean and lead to nothing. Perhaps he was meant to find it, and the radio jammer on the roof of the generator truck capable of disrupting the 150MHz communications system positioned along the length of the track; perhaps he was meant to become diverted, would take himself off on fruitless paths of enquiry. Revelation that was no revelation. The end was a start, the start an end. *Dig around the wound*. Kokhlov might have found something: he liked projects, would build an overview from a pile of corpses, could find clues while his FSB friend scrabbled around on the floor in the dark of a cold, mobile abattoir. But that FSB friend was part of the system, and therefore used by it. Truth, lies, official stances, nuances, power-plays and feints changing points, back-tracking or lying dormant while officers like himself were forced to stand passively on the platform and watch. So many interests, competing, self-serving, the BAM itself run by the central body answerable to the Ministry of Railways, the regional provinces through which the railway ran – Republic of Sakha, Khabarovsk Krai, Amur, Chita, Republic of Buryatiya and Irkutsk Oblast – the mining ministries, the feudal towns and economic zones operated by 'entre-preneurial bosses' including Boris Diakanov. It was Diakanov who had stripped the experimental and inoperable military radio monitoring station at Bolshaya Kartel of up to two million dollars' worth of precious metals and highly classi-fied technical equipment. Another force absorbed into the power-game, another factor. Lazin had never been good at passivity or watching.

Three men appeared at the far end of the bridge and stood, motionless. Lazin slowed his pace. He did not need to see faces to recognise the rougher end of his own directorate. Instinct, training, the way they carried their weight, all alerted his senses. They were hardly rail travellers who had overshot on a winter fishing-trip to Kuanda. A glance to the side, his peripheral vision picking up a further team taking up position behind him; a glance downwards – an impractical choice of escape route. Confront one team? Both? Confront his imagination? And then he heard running.

'You remember me.' Her eyes showed it. She did not answer, for it had been a statement, not a question. 'I would like to come in.'

'Why are you here?'

'I was passing. You have had so many visitors. I did not think you would mind.'

'It is inconvenient.'

Petr Ivanov stared, hands thrust deep into the pockets of his greatcoat. 'Come now, Mrs Cherkashin. Your husband hardly takes up much of your time any more. And your children, well . . .'

'I have nothing to say.' Disgust, defiance. Ivanov did not care.

'Then I will do the talking and you will listen.' He worked his fingers along the edges of the emerald cross, taken from the dying, bloodied form of Empress Alexandra by his grandfather. Such an admirer of beautiful things. In the left pocket, his hand looped around a length of wire knotted with leather straps at either end. It was old-fashioned and an old favourite, tested on the first three double-agents to be exposed by CIA traitor Aldrich Ames in the mid-1980s. The American received two million dollars for his information, Ivanov the opportunity to test his skills as an executioner, called in by Vladimir Kryuchkov, head of the First Chief Directorate and later of the entire KGB. The wire felt cold, the cross warm. Religion and the garotte – the Grand Inquisitor was ready.

'You will get cold out here,' he said, eyes unblinking, weighing the cross and the wire. She would get cold indoors also.

'Please, it is not necessary.'

'I will be the judge.' The hand was withdrawn from the pocket and used to push against the door. 'It won't take long. You have my word.'

She relented.

Lunch had been an extravagant affair, quite at odds with the Foreign Secretary's avowed intent to cut costs, but it was a gloom-laden month and the week needed to be rounded off with an indulgent morale- and cholesterol-lift. Pumpkin soup over which sage oil had been lightly drizzled, dusted with shavings of parmesan and served with warm walnut and raisin bread. Next were scallops with slow-roasted tomatoes and rocquet salad, pan-fried Trelough duck – raised in ancient apple orchards, naturally – served with damson brandy sauce, puy lentils and spinach. The fourth course was molten Vacherin cheese available only at certain times of the year when brought down from the Swiss mountains. It was followed finally by individual moulds of baked chocolate pudding accompanied by prune and almanac ice-cream. Nigel Ferris regretted being unable to sample too much of the 1982 Chateau la Lagune Haut Medoc or '78 Rabaud-Promis, but he was driving that afternoon, had no intention of inadvertently drawing police attention. Reformed fire-brands, born-again as symbols of the modern establishment, enjoyed the perks and the pampering as much as the free-marketeers, perhaps more so: it was part of power, of growing up, of becoming electable. And there was no guilt. The odd token gesture to the mythical 'people', the occasional petty refusal to wear black tie to functions, but elitism and disdain sat well with the left-leaning bourgeoisie. Patronising the workers was all part of leading them. And he shared the disdain. Had he not spent the morning placating the parents of some lumpen oaf who was locked up in a remote corner of a foreign cesspit – and Commonwealth Member – on ill-defined trafficking charges? That's what came from refusing to pay local Customs the standard bribery rate. Why could the youth not use his brain and instead follow the migrating herd to Disneyland, Paris? The parents talked of rights, freedoms, the protection afforded by a European Union passport. Foolish. Ferris talked of ongoing efforts, his personal interest, of dialogue with the different parties, insisted it was no trouble, implied it was a great favour, and checked his watch. His assistant coughed, the couple were ushered out with platitudes and assurances, and Ferris was ready for his gastronomic appointment.

He was pleased, yet not surprised, to be invited up by the Foreign Secretary. He had once been his PPS, served with him in other departments and on countless committees, campaigned and accompanied him around the country. Theirs was a special relationship. They were friends, close political allies, Ferris benefiting from his proximity to power, the Foreign Secretary from the availability of an image-maker and confidante who raised the department's profile and enhanced his ability to duck and dodge during Cabinet brawls. Under Ferris, diplomacy had become media and user-friendly, lapel pins and ties declared a freshness of thought, the stately halls of the Foreign Office were opened to roving television crews and gawping inner-city teenagers promised careers in diplomacy and then, at day-end, returned to their lives serving behind fast-food counters. The Vacherin cheese would never pass their lips, nor the Trelough duck, claret, nor even the prune and almanac ice-cream. But for a few hours they could dream; for a few hours they could provide a public relations fillip. And the Junior Minister was its architect. He was also a gossip and backbiter, a mongerer of rumours without compare who could damage reputations as easily as he elevated his own – always useful attributes in the mêlée that was politics. Quite simply, he was irreplaceable, much to the chagrin of his colleagues.

Ferris slid the car into the centre lane and switched radio channels. Easy listening. Everything was easy – influence, career, making people think they were important or actually mattered. Jackie, his wife, could be a challenge, of course, but she played her part, went through the motions. The price of being half of a dream team, a couple that loved being loved. She thought he was at a dreary think-tank party that evening. He found himself humming along with a nonde-script harmony and looked about. Harmony, he liked the word. It described perfectly his lunch with the Foreign Secretary. They had discussed his proposals for 'Europe Day': fairs, food, circuses, beer, subliminal political messages wrapped up in the European Flag, a palatable whole. *Tomorrow Belongs To Me*. Get the children and you get their parents was the Ferris assessment. *Get the children*. The Foreign Secretary smirked and nodded. They talked too of Russia, of the reception for businessmen at the Kremlin which the Americans had hijacked with policy statements and pledges of support. It was irksome. Ferris suggested a rival initiative which he would lead. The idea was well received. From Monday, officials would begin researching the prime Moscow hospital and orphanage sites at which to appear: those with optimum space to mount presentations to the accompanying media groups. Roving Ambassador, King of Hearts.

He punched a memory key and waited for the hands-free call to connect. It was answered promptly.

'Are you ready?' the Junior Foreign Office Minister asked.

'All set up. How long will you be?'

'Forty-five minutes, max.'

'No sweat. See you then.'

'*Grazie ciao.*' Ferris liked the affectation.

The receiver was replaced. Hire car, hire phone, all through his assistant: it was little appreciated how the communications networks and therefore, ultimately, Special Branch and the Security Services tracked and kept on laser disc the location of mobile telephones. The microchip revolution; Ferris was aware of its ramifications. He turned up the radio, knew the lyrics to the song, mouthed tunelessly in accompaniment. Strange that the rock track's odyssey had taken it from cutting-edge radicalism to middle-aged acceptability. It depended only on how you packaged it. *My Generation* . . .

As socialist-turned-realist, he sought to reach out and touch a younger, dumbed-down generation, a generation stranded by progressive teaching and phonetic spelling, methods he once espoused and now excused as an experiment with the right instinct but wrong approach. Over the years, his own instincts and approach had been refined. He was a former supply teacher and lecturer in Modern History – the Marxist dialectic was quietly dropped – an educationalist with particular interests in problem children. Before politics, where his erudition, presentational skills, relaxed way with youngsters and desire to banish Third World poverty made him a Conference darling, his work had taken him on numerous 'workshop' visits around Europe. He favoured the Benelux countries – they could be so forward-looking, so open to new ideas, and his friends in Belgium were ever hospitable. In fact, his friends everywhere were hospitable: that was the great advantage of the Net, of making technology work to find those with like interests. His mastery of computers and understanding of their use in teaching and communication gave further scope for travel. Opening access to such wonders for the dispossessed inhabiting the planet's remoter parts had become something of a priority. *Pax Britannica*, a young team for a young world. Modernity was the sales pitch, Ferris the salesman, mobbed by children wherever he went. So many people with such similar tastes. The Third Way. Politics was about pressing the flesh.

He turned the hire-car into the driveway and manoeuvred over the speed humps, the headlights catching the reflecting eyes of a fox as it slunk shamefully into the undergrowth crowding untidily along the length of the pitted tarmac. Everyone was hiding something. The building was Edwardian, red-brick, shabby, once a private residence, but since transformed into general purpose institutional obscurity. Cost-cutting, the resort to lowest-tender maintenance, and a variety of owners and uses – wartime rest-home, mental institution, hotel, borstal – had left it unsightly and stranded in grounds given over to weeds. It squatted back in the darkness as Ferris passed and stopped before a featureless modern bungalow built beside a group of huts. Squeak-activation of the car alarm and he approached the front door. It opened before he reached it.

'I see you're worried about security.'

'They're a lot of law-breakers round here.' Ferris replied. Neither missed the irony.

He was ushered in. The room was dimly lit, smelt of cigarettes, stale incense and cat piss.

The Minister extracted his wallet. 'Who have you got for me?'

'Bella. She's eleven, cute, waiting for you down at the cottage.' The man took the notes, counted them rapidly and passed across a key. He was perspiring slightly, a bead appearing at the corner of a retreating hairline. Nervousness was part of the experience. 'She's wearing what you wanted.'

'Relaxed?'

'Very. She's a doll, a real pro.'

'I hate amateurs. Are you sending anyone down from the main house?'

'Michael, if you want.'

'Don't know him.'

'Thirteen. Enthusiastic, a looker, likes poppers.'

'Make it an hour.'

'Fine. Jelly, everything you need, is down there.'

Ferris shuddered as the night air hit him again. It was only a short walk and he planned to warm up quickly. The stars were bright this evening. He heard his footfall crackle on residual frost, an ambitious, determined tread. Power was his compass – it swung him in many directions. And in the cottage a young girl waited.

The man turned back from the front door; two people faced him.

'Thank you for your invitation to listen.' The woman smiled, vividly sexual, all mouth below the fur hat. Astonishingly beautiful, the man thought – if you were into that kind of thing.

'I think you'd better go before my wife returns,' he replied, sweating some more.

'Ah, your wife.' Another owner of a children's home who took a spouse to gain respectablity and trust. It never fooled Soviet Intelligence, nor it seemed the covert unit at the European Commission whose detailed knowledge of a British Minister's sexual predilections were clearly detailed in the records handed to her through a letter-box in a quiet Brussels street by a seconded and suborned French secret policeman. Ferris's visits to Belgium in a previous incarnation were well documented. The woman patted him on the cheek. 'You know she won't be back for two days. And we must stay to collect the recordings from the cottage. Come now, we'll have fun.'

He doubted it, and this female's impassive, muscle-bound companion did not inspire confidence. But they had paid well, and the options were simple: double or quits. Quits sounded a little too permanent, even terminal. He chose the cash. They followed him through, back into the sitting room. 'Don't forget to send young Michael along,' she reminded him. He grunted. Organisation was the key to looking after the young.

The Junior Minister reached the cottage and inserted the key. It was an advantage that his contact could inject variety, supply both girls and boys. Somehow they went together – particularly if you asked them nicely. He pushed on the door, felt the heat from inside, welcoming. A thought came to him, made him smile. He had spent the morning getting a juvenile out of trouble, and by the evening he was here getting juveniles back into trouble. Politics demanded an advanced sense of humour. Thank God for comprehensive – truly comprehensive – education. He was through.

CHAPTER 5

The young priest and the lay member heard nothing. They were busy, one praying before candles, the other cleaning. Few others were awake in Moscow at this hour, and within the gently floodlit walls of the Cathedral of Christ the Saviour, rebuilt since they were torn down and replaced with the Moskva open-air swimming baths in the 1930s, the nightly routine of spiritual and physical maintenance continued as it always had. Here, President Boris Yeltsin had sat dabbing his politician's eye with a damp, doubtless onion- or alcohol-impregnated handkerchief beside the white-bearded figure of Patriarch Aleksi II during the official opening ceremony of September 1997. Moscow reborn, the cathedral a crowning adornment to the capital city which began as Prince Yuri Dolgoruky of Suzdal's modest settlement and banqueting site on the western fringes of his territory in the twelfth century. The new landmark symbolised stability and confidence, a link between past and future, a reaffirmation of the role of this metropolis as the central powerhouse to Russian existence. In the streets there may have been beggars, drunks and prostitutes, but these were the historical adjuncts and sideshow to progress, symbiotic by-products of success. While wealth increased, so did they, as integral as mosaics, icons and chants to the Orthodox church itself.

The hands were those of professionals. They worked fast, smoothly, opening the cold bags, selecting the insulator-jacketed tubes, peeling back covers and easing out their contents. The ammunition, frozen, came away easily, each round placed carefully into a crossbow groove, the graphite composite weapons pump-action cocked, their magnified sights zeroed and sitting disproportionate above the short barrels. Silent. Kneeling positions taken, the unseen impostors lowered the combat bows from vertical to horizontal, rifle-style butts nestled into shoulders, eyes, cross-hairs and targets aligned, waiting for the command tone through the headsets. The ice shards, moulded and polished for precision and aerodynamics, tested in live-fire exercises on pigs, lay twelve inches long on their launchers. As sharp as the head of an anti-tank sabot round, they would penetrate and leave no ballistic clues or residue for an inquisitive pathologist: technology meeting the ice age in the imagination crucible of the assassination laboratory.

The priest ended a catechism, his eyes focused on an icon, nostrils inhaling on the pressing atmosphere of religion and incense. Consciousness slowed, settled on another plane, senses were calmed. Or should have been. He felt suddenly restless, something intruded. The lay member was engaged with the minutiae of polishing; there was nothing disturbing in that presence. Yet the prickling grew, spreading like sweat along the spine and around the collar, jaw and neck muscles tightening involuntarily. He looked around, searching in the gloom for movement, for a jarring aspect to which he was not immunised.

An order came, three pips counting down to the longer tone. Launch. There was no immunity here. A glint in the periphery – that was all – a streak of reflected light, and an icicle as hard as toughened glass impacted, impaled against and through the temple. The lay member glanced up, the hollow thud and splintering of bone a peculiar diversion, grating in the somnolence of the church. An object protruded from the side of the priest's head, its shaft transparent, carving an alternative message path through the black *kobluki* into the brain. Eyes wobbled, the cerebral mass they fronted sliced and cauterised, the face registering unjustified blandness in death before the legs gave and he dropped.

'Oh Holy Father . . .' The lay member began praying

without knowing why. It was brief, the words cut short by a direct hit that threw the torso forward, limbs scrabbling listlessly below a severed spinal column.

'Amen.'

Squads in boiler-suits and balaclavas moved from their side positions, fanning out, following the blueprint of the building, the blueprint of their briefing. Stop-watch rehearsals had fine-tuned the procedure.

'Priests are meant to get closer to God,' one man explained, rolling the corpse with a foot.

His colleague stepped past. 'Glad to have helped.'

Incendiaries were set, thermite charges pushed into alcoves, small packages of sequence-timed explosive lodged against support walls and fire dams, optimising the destruction planned and rehearsed in countless computer simulations. The Moscow Fire Department would find this one a challenge. Too challenging to notice the irony in fighting flames set with the aid of its own illegally obtained floor maps. Primers and liquid fuel went down, men with back-tanks feeding inflammables through hosing into ducts and grilles. A rat squealed and scratched across the flagstones.

'Hey, the Patriarch's getting away.'

The crossbow swung, rodent split by a William Tell shot. 'That's fucking blasphemous,' its firer complained. The weapon was handling well; few moving parts, no sparks to generate unwanted ignitions. Useful in this environment.

A new tone in the ears: withdrawal was ordered. Time to go. The men filed towards the exits. Twenty minutes later, Moscow's skyline was changing. In St Petersburg, the pink mosaic splendour of The Church of the Saviour of Spilt Blood – built on the assassination site of the reformist Tsar Alexander II, restored, and reopened to worshippers in August 1997 after sixty years – was also beginning to burn.

'See anything?'

'Stupid question. Rail troops can't afford night-equipment.'

The two guards pushed their faces to the glass, manoeuvred to attain an optimum view, cupped hands to filter out back-light, and gave up. A patrol would be leaving on relief duty in thirty minutes. Why do their job? It was miserable enough on bridge fatigues – tedious enough covering assigned roles – without expending energy on the thankless task of staying sober, alert, sane in this spirit-sapping, taiga-clad wilderness over four and a half thousand miles from Moscow. There was only one kind of spirit which mattered when trapped in these endless, forested, boreal flatlands of Yeddo, Ayan and Norwegian spruce, Siberian and Dahurian larch, and the whole depressing gamut of pines. It made you forget suffering, the daily drudgery of living within a group of thirty bored soldiers, of being quartered adjacent to the BAM ghost-town of Zeisk and its few inhabitants who clung on with grim anticipation in grim apartment blocks set in unnamed streets, waiting for life, laughter, passion, the opening of the Elgynscoye coalfields up north in the Sakha Republic. That spirit made you forget discipline. And it came in a large variety of glass or plastic containers.

The men returned to their card game. It beat playing Russian roulette with a *Bizon* submachine gun, which one of their number had attempted the previous month. Poor sod, poor odds. The weapon fired at a rate of one thousand rounds per minute. By the time his finger had left the trigger, and the foolhardy nature of the enterprise impressed, the thirty-round magazine was empty, his head contents on the ceiling and unable to grasp the magnitude of the folly. A mind-expanding experience. This was a safer gamble, took less effort than *dedovschina* – the institutionalised 'hazing', bullying of juniors, which came with its own quota of fatalities.

Outside, spanning over one thousand metres, the steel mass of the rail bridge hung above the Zeya river. Nine years in building, an engineering feat of extraordinary complexity and difficulty, it took fewer than two minutes to demolish.

The initial charges barely drew the attention of the card-players, the sound snatched by a snow-sodden wind and gusted down-river. They could not ignore what followed. As supports blew and structures buckled, the lumpen detonations and shriek of distressed metal caused the soldiers to rush, underdressed and floundering, into the piled snow outside the guard hut. An odd phenomenon, the effects of cold on caffeinated blood-alcohol. The two thought they were witnessing a mirage, a trick of light, short puffs of flame bursting and extinguishing about the giant frame. It seemed to be changing shape before them, shaking violently, discarding pieces, dipping, a fairground roller-coaster which had lost its rivets through instant trauma. They wondered vaguely if they would be in trouble. Other men appeared, stripped of sleep, a multitude of yelling shapes contorting, working their way into blindly grabbed clothing. The bridge began its fifty-metre plunge.

Six kilometres away, close to the village of Gorni, the small airport was closed. A week previously, a team of men had landed by helicopter and disappeared into the surrounding countryside for winter warfare training. But their doctrine was economic warfare, and the Zeya bridge their target. Almost eight hundred miles to the west on the BAM railway, across the Vitim River which divided the Republic of Buryatiya and Amur Oblast, another bridge was falling through the ice. The duo standing astonished on the bank of the Zeya were unaware of such details. They could barely comprehend the magnitude of the scene, a vision of release from their days of sub-military servitude in sub-zero temperatures deep in eastern Siberia. Cold ground into them like powdered glass. Nothing to guard, nothing left to lose, and their card game was waiting.

Escalate: to increase or develop rapidly by stages, to cause action to become more intense. Definition, a defining moment. Leonid Gresko tapped the cigarette, applied it to sour mouth, and drew against the flame. Satisfaction exhaled. Ash and glowing embers, that was all that remained of the great cathedrals. They were burial mounds for Russia's hopes and inward investment, the residue from a fiery magnificence, from beacons of despair lit in the great cities. And the torch-carrier and fire-setter remained hidden. Another drag and the orange luminescence of cheap tobacco. Across Moscow, the debris of the Cathedral of Christ the Saviour smouldered, emitting sporadic clouds of cindered smoke, the occasional post-cataclysmic puff of heat, warmed water playing from a hundred hoses, turning to ice-crust – a crystalline sarcophagus – in an instant on the surface of the blackened remains. Death of God. What Stalin destroyed and Russia rebuilt had again been destroyed. Nothing would put out the flame.

A light in the side-office was on, a box of white paper towels and the legs of a padded orthopaedic couch visible from behind his desk. There would be massage and sex that afternoon, perhaps blood would be spilled. He had a tendency – preference – for violence: carnality and brutality entwined, an element of the power equation. The infliction of pain, tension release, was part of the process, as integral as the disposable towels, as integral as disposable humans.

Escalate. Tensions were rising within the mafiya, the Senate of the criminal overlords imploding, fragmenting the carefully constructed control-monolith, producing new alliances that could only collide and create greater friction and violence. The surviving Gribanov brothers fought the St Petersburg Orlovs whom they suspected of backing the deceased Maxim Shelepin to gain greater distribution opportunities in Moscow; Diakanov supported the Gribanovs whom he saw as a bulwark against attempts to undermine him; the Nechiporenkos supported the Orlovs through fear that Diakanov was using the Gribanovs to usurp them in their home territory; the Lessiovskis fence-sat, the fence itself becoming creosoted with the blood of warlords and their bankers. Uncertainty and opportunity, the roots of dispute lost in dispute, and a father's rage at a lost son blinding and driving. The sacrifice of one boy could end a dynasty, end an era. Tsarevich Alexis, heir to Tsar Nicholas II and the Russian throne, had been the same age as Oleg Diakanov when bullets took his life and those of his family in an Ekaterinburg cellar. It finished the Romanov reign, wrenched history from its preordained course. Seized history. It seemed the moment for another empire to die, a new one to grow. *Escalate*.

He reached for the intercom and depressed to activate. 'I am ready.' The acknowledgement came through. He rose and walked from the study, making his way along the art-decked corridor to a conference suite. The Old Masters meant little to him, but if their residence here prevented a claim by other bodies, so be it.

A remote electrical bleat, padded doors opening and closing, footfall softened by deep carpets, and the mahogany parted to allow Colonel Georgi Lazin into the far end of the room. Gresko noted his approach, noted the salute, and remained expressionless, unresponsive. The unimpeachable Colonel, his father a hero from the wartime Siege of Tula. The honest fell the furthest and the fastest; heroes were fools, and usually dead. Perhaps the Colonel wished to be heroic.

Gresko three-quarters shuttered an eyelid in the direction of a chair. 'Sit.' He pulled a file across while the officer followed the command.

'I was taken from the case before I made significant progress, Director.'

'You made progress?'

'I believe so.' The antipathy-stilted conversation was unlikely to improve.

'I believe not, Colonel.' Pages were flicked, the file dropped. Lazin felt the corrosive shadow. 'What have you found of the rough gems?'

'That three men died attempting to prevent me uncovering further information, discovering the bodies of the executed train guards.'

'Four men died,' Gresko corrected. 'A communications

specialist at the Daban camp was found shortly after your departure. He had been strangled.' Lazin kept his gaze middle-distance. So, they had silenced his source, the voice that spoke in the claustrophobic stillness of his barrack-room sleeping quarters. Identity revealed. 'I prevented your arrest and questioning only because the Rail Minister's authority is so undermined he is in no position to challenge State Security.' It was ever unwise to make such a challenge. 'I must commend you on your shooting skills.' Laughter behind the stone? Suspicion? Lazin could not tell. His report had not mentioned the old man who came to his aid.

'Afghanistan had some benefits,' he replied.

'You thrive in war zones. Moscow in its present state will suit you.'

'The Major at Daban . . .'

'Is under investigation. FSB security troops have taken over the camp from Rail Forces and assumed control in their other key settlements. Ministers have agreed that the Railways have plainly been penetrated by subversive and criminal bodies to the detriment of national security.' Meaning that their personal take from diamond stockpiles had been hit, Lazin reflected.

'The destruction of the Vitim and Zeya Bridges must have confirmed this.'

'That is so. It is a strategic blow to the economic viability of the entire BAM region, a strain on the country's resources. We suspect it is the work of separatist bodies in the Siberian regions. We already have Buryatiyan and Amur extremists in our cells for the Vitim attack.'

And how would damaging their own livelihoods, their ability to trade, how would increasing dependency on emergency aid from the central government help their separatist cause? Logic never prevented State Security from getting its man, or finding its chosen victim. Lazin levelled his eyes to his Director's sight-line. You are moving fast, faster than anyone, he thought. An airlift had started to supply the remoter areas with food and medication, but with weather hampering relief work, money short, and the immense cost of rebuilding the bridges and patching up the BAM railway for basic use causing panic-inertia in government and Treasury, the sense of crisis was growing. There were moves to impose direct Kremlin control on the Siberian republics. The FSB would be its tool.

'Perhaps I should have remained in the BAM region, Director?'

'It is not necessary, Colonel. We are reinforcing local coverage to meet perceived threat levels and to replace Rail Ministry personnel.' Not content with travelling incognito in railway repair engines, the FSB operatives now moved into offices. The stockpiles – gold, diamonds, uranium – growing, cut off when the BAM was severed, at the mercy of the Federal Security Service. The Cane Toad blinked. 'I had you recalled because priorities have changed. The President argues that the mafiya troubles and troublemakers must be dealt with to restore confidence at home and overseas.'

'The attack on the American delegation?'

It had provided a downbeat conclusion to what was intended to have been an upbeat trip, grenades and small arms damaging but not destroying Senator O'Day's armoured limousine as he was driven back, post-banquet, to the American embassy. In the brief firefight which followed, a couple of minor criminal gang members were killed. The international press had their prejudices confirmed in an instant, words of optimism from the speeches juxtaposed with photographs in every global broadsheet or tabloid of pitted buildings and sheet-draped bodies. Russia in Fear, Russia in Crisis, Russia on the Run.

Gresko sat – a beached amphibian – and did not answer the question. 'You will be . . .' a pause to add intentional insult. 'More productive here.' And more easily watched. Lazin regulated his breathing, controlled the heartbeat. The FSB Director's voice was like marsh gas. 'You are sensitive to the political problems surrounding such areas. As an experienced investigator, I know that you will tread carefully.'

He knew that the Colonel would be blundering through a minefield; the Colonel knew it.

Lazin sat straight, stiff with the discipline of the KGB Academy, unmoved by the undercurrent of criticism and implied hostility. He had been sent to Siberia to fail, sent to the BAM to find nothing but a frozen, snowed waste devoid of leads and information. But he had found something, the beginnings of a trace that took him to a zone without definition or rules, an area through which others in the FSB has passed before, where Colonel Petr Ivanov had visited, exerting influence, developing agendas and following sealed orders far different from his own. It was a land populated with mangled remains. What are you planning Gresko? He heard the Director's words, heard the standard rhetoric of State Security being above politics, within the law and answerable to government. His inner-ear scrambled the message – they were above the law, they were the government.

Outside, sleet-snow scuffed the windows in wet, multiple, wind-gusted impacts, the depression of Moscow deepening with each shapeless, grey drop-flake. The crisp, white snows of March belonged to the past, to a fairy-tale landscape, replaced by global warming and the dirt-dullness of a city in cold storage. Climatic change had much to answer for. There were other answers – to the incendiaries at the cathedrals, to the bridges lying broken like the rib-cages of mammoths, to the mafiya conflict, to the blood-spattered carriage on a repair train in Tynda, to the armed assault on the Americans, to questions he had yet to formulate – and they might remain as closed to him as his Director squatting low with self-contained malice behind the table. Locked drawers and locked minds were a prerequisite in Lubyanka Square. Few communicated with him; his assistant, Yuri Vakulchuk, was as small and wizened as ever, but more silent, large extra-planetary eyes showing a fear which went beyond the bureaucratic. One picked up the subtleties in a small office, and his was very small, an amplifier for the nuances and in-house gossip, the political undercurrents of a political underworld. Less filtered through in his isolation. More to suspect. And there was a shift, an unseen pressure, grown since his absence: eyes averted, backstage whispers, groups of staff drifting unconvincingly together on his approach, too hasty, too contrived. The canteen saw the radius of dead ground widen between himself and his colleagues. He was singled out, placed in twilight.

The meeting ran its course, Gresko's voice flat and ungiving. 'I have given Captain Vakulchuk authorisation to pick up the necessary files from Registry. I want you working independent from other investigations. If we can detect particular trends in the mafiya confrontation, then we can interdict and contain. It is a priority.'

'Then I require greater resources, Director.'

'You have skill instead.' Plainly not enough to stay on the diamond case, Lazin thought. 'Use it. We are stretched as it is.'

The Colonel had left, Gresko staring after him at the burnished wood. Lazin was no political animal, was not ambitious enough to be corrupt. His responses were as predictable as the movement of the doors: smart, polished and precise, his resting place predetermined. Perfect for what the Director had in mind. That mind was testing, checking, moving and counter-moving, pacing ahead into the future, roving the streets below and above. The future was his, the streets were his. If things went wrong, so be it. There were always fall-backs, surprises. And nothing would surprise more than a Doomsday command system such as *Perimetr*. The voices were baying, howling, strange tongues. *Seize it, seize the day, seize your world.* He clamped both hands to his ears. The clamour rose inside.

A face, as anonymous as any other made morose and wan by several Russian winters, peered about the reading room. He was jumpy, but it went unnoticed by the studious figures seated in rows, heads bowed or talking in hushed academic voices to slope-shouldered colleagues wearing intense expressions and clothes that made not the slightest concession to fashion. Nervous eyes searched for the professor. This was the Russian State Library, the world's largest, an immense edifice on ulitsa Vozdvizhenka, and although an intellectual himself, a regular visitor with an annual *propusk*, the man felt conspicuous here in Reading Room No. 1, reserved as it was for foreigners and members of the Academy of Science. Lucky that he was a foreigner, Hungarian by birth. But he would have preferred the drop to take place in a lavatory – retrieval from a cistern was considerably less public than here. More scanning of the tops of heads. Contact. Easy to miss among the cardigans and grey hair. Strange how committed professors could be to their subjects, even in the whip-tail of the cold season. Three fingers wiped across the forehead, a glance at a wristwatch and the professor stood to go in search of a librarian. The man felt reassured: the information was ready, visual codes checked out, it was safe to approach. A stooped back disappeared from view, would not return for five minutes. Relax like him, the Hungarian commanded himself; you have every right to be here, every right to be brazen, to be stealing Russian strategic military secrets. The small lie seemed to help. Different people had different methods. Experience was what mattered most and he was a relative newcomer as gofer for British intelligence. The professor, by contrast, had years behind him in passing details of aeronautical developments to his masters in Albion. Since the collapse of the Soviet defence industry base, the subsequent drought in Russian military funding and procurement, there had been a fall-off in demand for the insights of the ageing academic. His handlers were retired to golf and garden-fêtes, the espionage effort as a whole curtailed. The Hungarian was a product of that rationalisation and downgrading: cheap and utilised on an ad hoc basis. But recently he had noticed an increase in pace; old assets were being resurrected and reactivated, the SIS station discreetly infused with extra staff.

Independent of the British embassy, and reporting to officers sent direct from London by Guy Parsons, head of SIS Russia desk, the Hungarian was nevertheless aware of the new impetus, but unaware of the importance of this live drop in the library. He walked across to the table and slipped into a seat one removed from the tidy stack of journals marking the professor's work position. A book lay open in front of him. Page twenty. Two microfilms to collect. Fingertips moved along the underside of the table rim, searching diagonally inwards, and connected – a pair of button heads attached to drawing-pins, easily prised away. He palmed them quickly, made the transfer, speed-read a few pages and left to explore the catalogues. In his pocket lay photographic film recording initial Russian designs – and, more importantly, an official 1980s concept study into logistics backup and fuel production – for hydrogen-powered cryoplane scramjets. London was most anxious for the information.

Lazin climbed from Belorusskaya, the warmth of the Metro lost in the wind-chill snapping at his face as he made his way back to the apartment. He adjusted the scarf – the last present given to him by his wife before the separation – and marched on, oblivious to the vehicles grinding in snaking slo-mo, their drivers peering through windscreens of ice, fighting wheels and gears, coaxing protesting engines in an ongoing and daily act of environmental pollution. Vakulchuk had brought in the last of the background reading, a green file perched on top of a hundred of its clones, next to a pile of a hundred more. His office was a store room, a book depository, he its keeper, kept there to study, either to find or to be prevented from finding. So much to think about. It would remove him from the canteen – a blessing. He should contact Kokhlov in Krasnoyarsk, find if the pathologist had uncovered anything new. His friend had been drunk, made little sense, the last time they spoke, had refused to answer the telephone on other occasions. Perhaps he ought to let him be; his Siberian project abruptly halted, he could leave cannibalism and the antics of the post-mortem room alone for a while. Somewhere behind the façade of FSB headquarters, made sinister by history and featureless stonework, was an answer. He was inside and excluded, a stranger in a blood-rusted tracked vehicle stored within a railway box car, a stranger on his rust-carpeted floor at the Federal Security Service. There was no better place from which to start. Yet what intruded was the insignificant, an item small enough to matter, its absence more noticeable than its presence: his tea glass had gone missing.

Key inserted, a return to the bare but heated womb of a Moscow apartment in winter, the short super-warmed, liquid-linoleumed passageway running past the two rooms in which he slept, ate and brought to entertain the occasional female Interior Ministry worker. Occasionality had turned to rarity. Once, they might have appreciated that his reputation as a somewhat dour conversationalist was more than outweighed by a physicality that tested their endurance, the patience of the neighbours and the poor workmanship shown in most Russian housing. Since his position as office-pariah had become enshrined, his prospects poor, association frowned upon, a stint in a city bread queue appeared more enticing to the majority of his erstwhile fans. Perhaps sleepless arrangements on a solitary sofa-couch, residue of a failed marriage, put them off. He did not dwell on such developments. At least the integrity of the chipboard walls was secured, providing a hiding-place for copies of the notes taken of his BAM-zone enquiries. The originals were with Gresko, to be handed on to the replacement case officers. His own case was far from over. Light on, he removed his hat, shrugged out of his greatcoat and hung them on the regulation-issue hooks. Everything was regulation-issue, everything was liable to break. Kettle on in the kitchenette – his wife had left the Indesit cooker, but taken the heavy furniture and glass-fronted bookcases. The unimaginative improvisation of a solo bachelor evening in prospect, he re-entered the corridor and knelt to unlace his boots. The brown envelope, small and camouflaged, pushed upright against the wall by the action of the door, lodged in his field of vision.

Saliva production was low, even with the gum, adrenalin-shot nerves draining the pilot's mouth into a dry wadi state. At least flying a lone ship meant the risk of air interception was lower, but it also meant fewer diversions for a well-armed enemy ambush once the aircraft was on the ground, vulnerable. Turn-around had better be fast; the Yemeni authorities had an unhealthy sideline in cutting off balls. He touched them gingerly, said a silent prayer and slid his hand down to the pistol tucked into a flying boot: if required, it was to use on himself rather than the enemy. His co-pilot saw the action, said nothing, similar thoughts crowding his mind in the silence. That was the trouble with turboprop aircraft. There was more time to think, more time to fear.

'Cockpit lighting down, active white off. NVG check.' A dull red luminescence transformed the appearance of the critical instrumentation as the crew swung night-vision optics into position over their eyes. 'Operating.'

'Roger that. Operating.'

'E.T.A?'

'Thirty minutes. Three-zero,' the co-pilot replied. 'Way-points correspond; Inertial and GPS are OK.'

'At least their Mig-21's don't go out after dark.' Given the spares shortages, it was a miracle the obsolete fighters got airborne at all.

Turbulence bucked the airframe, the engines of the heavily modified Shorts Sherpa growling to regain height. The crew rode it out. Behind them, strapped securely in the cargo hold, were equipment pallets loaded in Saudi Arabia and bound for the secret guerrilla airstrip near Al-Mahra deep in the Republic of Yemen. They contained the intial tranche of weaponry ordered by Purton and destined for the forward stockpiles to be established in support of the planned southern rising. Not a large load on this run – but Viet Cong irregulars had created a vortex of destruction against the most modern army in existence with only seven tons of ordnance a day passing along the Ho Chi Minh Trail. Purton's enemy was poorly integrated and coordinated, fractured by political and religious schism, ripe for mutiny. The Sherpa flights took the chisel deep into the fracture. They would be perfectly adequate.

The pilot switched to manual, feeling the controls respond, sweat forming between his fingers. The chest protector, layers of laminate armour, trapped the heat, trapped his nerves. He wondered what ballistic properties it would have to deal with; please God not tracer or anything heavier than assault rifle calibre. The RCL – reception committee leader – was an old hand, one of Ahmed Badr's most competent quarter-masters, versed in clandestine drops. In and out, nothing flamboyant, fancy, nothing to draw attention. There were procedures for any crisis, yet procedures did not stop a bullet. The moisture spread from between his shoulder-blades and around his neck. These early flights were always the worst. He tried to calm his breathing, make himself part of the somnolent vibration of the aircraft. No use.

'On time. Hitting the mark. Five minutes.' The co-pilot's voice was harsh in the headset.

'Warn the loadmaster. Keep a look out for the sign.'

Systems checks, the panoply of pre-landing routines, tension adding speed to their actions. 'I've got a visual. We have identification V for Victor, one o'clock.'

'I have it. Confirm safety signal is constant.' It shone bright in the green world projected by the goggles.

'I can confirm. Three miles.' The co-pilot would watch that one light, placed midway and to the right of the runway, throughout landing. If it flickered, or was extinguished, there would be mission abort, full power and a steep climbout.

The pilot's jaw was aching, teeth clenched in concentration, but pain receptors were off, awareness elsewhere, as he coaxed the transport through the virtual reality arcade game created by the narrow artificial field transmitted to his eyes. Danger was a green place.

On the ground, they heard the low hum of the Sherpa's props, the reception gathered mute about the leader, behind and to the left of the aircraft touch-down point, adjacent to the runway starter lights. The lamps, pointing downwards, yet discernible from the air with passive-view systems, marked out the length in isolated pairs. They had been switched on for only two minutes. Standard. Any attack and they would be doused instantly. The sound transformed into a harder drone, approaching, growing. All clear. The smooth, baked mudflat of the runway lay out before them in the dark, hidden yet exposed, protected by a light cordon of sentries and outer pickets. Ready.

A roar above their heads, touchdown, a light bounce, gravity's response, rubber searching and gripping, deceleration and the aircraft ground-crawling hurriedly to the end of the strip to turn and move back to its waiting and unloading position close to the landing spot. Another turn, loop complete, and the aircraft came to a halt, engines running, facing upwind in preparation for take-off. The rear loading-ramp came down, reception running to offload supplies, the leader making his way across to swap information with the pilot via a headset link passed through the open cockpit window. Clock check. A human chain passed crates of rifle grenades out to a trailer near-full with a consignment of mines and explosives. The last batch was rolled off. Wire unplugged, the leader withdrew, gave a thumbs up and rotate sign and sloped back low to the figures kneeling among the piled stores. Throttle opened, roll, and the nightbird, free of its cargo, climbed tightly, an ungainly, non-reflecting creature escaping to the blackness. Its mission was complete, the insurgency on schedule.

'Got you.' Howell peered through the monocular, feet braced against the swell. 'I've found the IR beacon. Codes check out; reception's waiting.'

Purton took the proffered glasses and studied the landing point for himself. Al-Fatk, the pro-insurgency settlement some twenty-eight miles within the Yemen border. They were here. Forty years of clandestine beach approaches, all with that one constant imponderable – who would be waiting at reception. And now another, the adrenalin fix, the uncertainty, a friendly fishing village. Friendly until turned, until they fired on you, betrayed you, disembowelled the guiding team on the sand; friendly until they ran screaming for you while your men struggled in the surf. Thirty seconds, the infrared lamp stuttered out its short message – 'Safe to Land' – on the dhow's approach axis, before repeating it at thirty degrees on either side.

'No duress signal. That's a relief. Send confirmation and let's get the Ribs wet.'

A Hayab crane let out a hydraulic-driven sigh as its mouse took the strain of the four lifting strops attached to fixtures on the inflatable's sides. The carrying ring tugged, the laden boat with its coxswains rising steadily from the cargo deck cradle, swinging outwards, hanging momentarily and dipping towards the water. Lines played out to its bow and stern, joining a quick-release tow-rope already bonding the mother and baby in umbilical union. The first group of four men clambered over. One took over a pintle-mounted machine gun replacing the navigation light in the stern.

'Your turn, Nick. Make sure they love you.'

'They follow British SIS landing procedures,' the NCO replied, hoisting his bergen. 'They must do. See you at the LUP.' Once into the hinterland, they would move to prepared lying-up positions before trekking on to the area chosen for guerrilla training.

Last aboard, Howell bent, removed the rod passing through the ring on the bow cleat. Splice cleared, tow-rope released, steadying lines removed, the Rib sidled away from the dhow while the crane ducked to hoist its sister.

Run-in was at thirty knots, the second boat giving cover offshore, Howell's team aiming at the filtered torch of the lone reception committee leader, lifting engines and beaching close by to unload once coded identification numbers had been swapped. Movement. A group of Badr loyalists swarmed from the rocks to assist, carrying munitions away in packs or on litters. It took only one to be an informant, Purton thought. Beach clear. The two craft reversed roles, Purton hitting sand, wincing as his ankle took an uncomfortable angle, and waving out his men. Hands, used to hauling nets, smuggled goods, worked feverishly. No commands were necessary. Offloaded. The Ribs, using the leader's beach-light as a temporary back coordinate, sped for the direction of the dhow. They would return the next night, and the next, feeding the training effort, supporting the exiles infiltrating by land across the border from Oman, carrying more recruits for the special forces camp. Lying behind a boulder on the position's flank, assault rifle cocked, Purton watched them go. The breeze was fresh, stars cold and fierce. He felt alive. Thus were civil wars started, campaigns begun.

Hidden by an earth dune, the Russian saw the churned wake of the Ribs as they sped to the mother-dhow. The Westerners were efficient, understood their work. Understood nothing. He wished them luck.

Max mounted the shallow steps into the lobby on Kuznetsky Most, Gennady, his hulking bodyguard and driver, at his side gently steering him by an elbow. A moroseness hung over the building, hung over Moscow. Losing a cathedral could not have helped, neither did street-fighting between criminal gangs which saw bombings and body-counts rise daily and armed response by *Spesrota* squads continue to frighten commuters as their thundering convoys sped west into the city from the Interior Ministry's First ODON base at Balashika. People were cowed, black-bereted OMON riot police patrolled in their ceramic-armour and grey coveralls, tension and crisis pervaded the senses as depressingly as the dirt-snow. At least paramilitary had yet to turn military, citizens reassured themselves, and cursed the government. Max passed the reinforced doors, aware of cameras, of security men standing back in the gloom-burdened interior.

Boris Diakanov's domain, projecting an image of normality when circumstances were far from normal. The businessman was recently returned from an overseas trip. To this? He was better advised to stay away; rumour had it he was losing ground and influence. But predicting a winner in Russia had always been an inexact science, fraught with surprises and incalculables. Even more reason to make the delayed courtesy call, to pay respects and stand well back to avoid the crossfire. So far, Strachan's haulage venture had proved immune to the troubles – drink, cigarettes and small luxuries remained in demand – but further upheaval and loss of confidence, more infrastructure hit along the BAM railway, a collapse of the mafiyoso-primed and sustained economy, and both government and the underworld syndicates would place an opportunistic squeeze on the American's interests.

Hence this opportunistic visit. There was also the small matter of a client's Junktim bond, setting off the cost of goods exported against those imported. A discrepancy had occurred.

'Come this way, please.' Gennady was left, Max taken through to the side rooms to be searched. Keys, wallet, pocket-book, cuff-links, shoes removed and examined, he was walked through scanner-gates, had metal and explosive vapour-detectors run over him, was hand-frisked, had his collar felt, balls felt. Over-familiar for a first date, he thought. Maybe this was normal, maybe not; maybe it was paranoia. His walking-stick was being x-rayed.

'I guess you'll be wanting a stool sample?' The exploration continued.

He made it to the elevator, accompanied by two burly assistants – presumably taking him for full internal inspection. Floor rose, gravity pulled, stomach dropped. No, they were heading for *tsisari*'s reception floor. His hair lay damp from the hotel shower, wetter from outside ice formation, Zenya's body imprint keeping him warm. She was in bed when he left, exhausted, a 'Do not Disturb' sign prominent on the door exterior. It would stay until his return and into the early evening.

Diakanov sat waiting. So, the foreign gangs thought they could turn on him? The American Gambinos, Colombian Calí cartel, Japanese Yakuza, Hong Kong's Sun Yee On triad, the Turks, the Italians, all moving in to pick over his carcass and take his possessions. Local difficulty on his home territories, and the deals he had struck through his representatives to the Beaune criminal summits meant nothing. He should have known: you could never trust mobsters. They could negotiate or fight, and if they fought they would lose. The Russians had an appetite for cruelty that went far beyond what any number of dapper Dons from New York or Chicago might stomach; the Russians had the manpower, the hunger, the firepower. Potent combinations to concentrate the mind during business conferences. Less potent now. Diakanov's authority was being challenged; the criminal Senate he chaired and championed was in disarray, its members divided into well-armed camps. Bankers were shot, banks demolished, overseas funds raided. Discipline was collapsing. The fools believed he was replaceable.

He stared at the priceless five foot-high stone Buddha serene on its marble plinth across the room. Fifteen hundred years of age, it was China's oldest until its theft in March 1998 from Dong'erying village. He wished he were as calm. No, they could not oust him. He had left too many bloody handprints on his way to the top to make it worthwhile climbing down. He was strong, his interests expanding. It was with him that the Burmese military government in Rangoon linked to traffick high-grade No. 4 heroin into the burgeoning Chinese market, his money which funded the country's main port and Mandalay highway projects, his 'agro-economists' who went to the country's mountainous north-eastern frontiers with China to cultivate contacts and opium poppies among the ethnic Shan, Wa and Kokang guerrilla movements. They took his metamphetamine production expertise, he took their Myanmar alcohol; they disappeared the native opposition in Insein prison, he provided them with seaplanes to service the Andaman coast drug-runs; they gave him the raw material, he refined and trucked it through India's Manipur State and China's porous Guangzhou sector. Trade and barter, barter and trade. They still came to *tsisari*; he could still buy or bury. His mood lifted briefly and then slipped. He could not pretend that things were going well.

A knock and announcement. Max Purton, representative of Hunter Strachan, was ushered in. Diakanov rose to greet the young man.

'*Zdravstvuyte. Menya zovut Boris Fedorovich Diakanov.*'

'*Ochen' priyatno,*' Max replied formally.

Conversation would keep to Russian. He felt the enveloping hand, cold, the grip strong, an impress of power designed to master. In this light, he could not discern the face or eyes, but the stillness of the silhouette, the touch, transmitted enough. The room reminded him of the faith healer's he had been brought to as a child by a mother who sought solace and a cure for her son's declining vision. He possessed the same curiosity now, mixed with reluctance, a sense of sharing a space, a darkened theatre, with a mystery, an eminence who might be proved a fraud.

'So you are blind?' Diakanov asked.

'Getting there.'

'Bring the chair to him,' the Russian commanded. It was placed down behind. 'Sit, please.'

'Thank you.' Max lowered himself.

The diversion is all mine. Diakanov studied the face: American college-boy with college-boy looks and college-boy teeth, but with none of the pampering, the expectation of ease, he decided. You needed heart to peg eyesight loss at the level of medium inconvenience. 'I met your Mr Hunter Strachan in Moldova in 1997.'

'He works hard to spread the business.'

'And to diversify. He was busy transporting Archer infrared missiles and spare parts for twenty-one surplus Mig-

29 Fulcrum C fighters to a collecting depot for the US to fly out to Wright Patterson Air Force base in Ohio.'

'I remember the deal. The Pentagon paid a fair price.'

'Overpaid.'

'The aircraft were wired for nukes. There was concern the republic would sell them to the Iranians.'

Fear generally added value, Diakanov mused. He was in Moldova for another reason – to plan the termination of the five main criminal groupings which operated from its capital Chisinau.

'I admire responsibility in a government.'

'The two aren't generally compatible,' Max replied.

'What is your responsibility, Mr Purton? Coming to me to request that my arguments with business rivals do not affect your trade?' He answered his own question. 'We have existing agreements. That will suffice.'

'Your word is appreciated.' People hung on that word, were beaten on that word, crippled on that word. He wondered if Diakanov had caught the killers of his son or of his capo butchered in the lobby of the Kosmos hotel. The two events were subsumed by more recent atrocity, had slipped from Moscow's collective consciousness and conversation. They remained in Max's head – like the image relayed to him by excited onlookers of the bar stool jutting from a man's eye. For Diakanov it was part of risk-taking, another element of trade. War as diplomacy. Strachan interacted well with it.

Glasses, vodka and thick, yellow lemonade were carried in and laid out on low tables while the conversation continued. Diakanov's mind loitered on the thugs brought back alive from his excursion to the empty warehouse. They were less alive by the day, kept in limbo for the grand example he would make of them. The more imaginative the message, the clearer it might be, the further it should carry. He was certain that they knew nothing, could not have held out. Whoever was attacking him was using freelancers and wiping the prints; no information was reaching him. Yet he spent hundreds of millions of roubles to be informed: such silence was impossible. Unless. Unless they were outsiders, beyond his reach, enjoyed higher influence, could provide greater patronage than he. He could think of no one. Potential enemies were once easily spotted and dealt with. Times changed, omnipotence decayed. His source in the operations room at the Ministry of Railways had uncovered little new on the diamond robbery along the BAM line; strategic bridges were blown, his earnings depleted by the fall-off in traffic – and still no leads – and the Director of the FSB saw fit to bring the investigating Colonel back to Moscow. Cul-de-sacs everywhere. And what of this young American and his boss? They benefited from armed escorts assigned by the Interior Ministry, had government links which bypassed his gate-guardians and watchers. They were backed, and the backers were unidentified. While he, *tsisari*, hid in his city fortress, beset by problems, this Hunter Strachan roamed freely. *Outsiders, higher influence*. And the source at the Ministry of Railways, his own observers dotted throughout Siberia's staging posts, spoke of the American's box-trains making deliveries during these winter months. Months in which diamonds were taken and sabotage occurred. He reached for a glass. Absurd, irrational. Max was talking. It was the Russian way to find scapegoats. If he followed that path anyone, everyone, could be blamed, brought under suspicion, tortured to the point of confession. Next, he would be pointing an accusatory finger at a blind man. Westerners, foreigners, were too obvious, had no stake in seeing his demise. The threat he faced must be home-grown. Yet Oleg had died in the West, a schoolboy coughing bright blood on that muddy playing field in England. Borders were meaningless. He poured.

'Has the room been electronically swept?' Max asked.

Zenya was careful; the only way to survive. Instinct gave her the motive, training the techniques. She had watched the room door for some time, noted that it was beyond the view of the scowling babushka seated near the elevators whose mood and role had long since bombed with the ending of Communism. Spying on guests had fallen to younger, more attractive examples of womanhood, those like Zenya who could cruise a corridor in the garb of a predatory hooker, knocking on doors, apparently knocking up punters, and drawing the attention only of mid-life males with sea-sponge torsos and dicks to match. She took lipstick from the ostentatious clutch-bag, unscrewed the top and put it not to her lips but to her eye as she bent near the handle, a small ultra-violet glow shining out in front. The examination was swift, up along the join, around the carpet seam. No luminescent powder scattered here to trap the unwary and unwanted visitor, no threads or feathers left to warrant concern or extra caution. Satisfied, she replaced the device and withdrew a pair of wire-picks: lock barrels at the Ukraina were never a challenge. Insert, looking for a take – looking each way along the passage – manipulation, thumb and forefingers working gently, methodically, dextrously. Give. She sighed against the door, satisfaction and opening pressure combined, slipped a make-up mirror through the widening gap and rotated it for a prismatic scan of the interior. Two voices approaching, a man and a woman, closing, native Russians, the tone of temporary residents rather than staff. Zenya retrieved her bag from the floor, found a pump atomizer of cheap scent and sprayed it liberally before the couple turned the corner.

'OK, darling. We reach agreement. I make you happy,' she laughed to the client inside, letting herself through.

The two Russians saw a slight, athletic form, pale back set off by the low-cut, high-hemmed cocktail pelmet, smelt the perfumed air that announced the presence of a representative from Moscow's most persistent service sector, and passed by.

Hunter Strachan and Colonel Petr Ivanov saw another side, Zenya's front, as they stood together at a bank of monitors on an upper floor of the hotel. It was a command and control suite, outpost of the FSB.

'Well, well, will you take a peek at that. Makes me wish I was down there, naked, with a hard-on.'

'Consider her yours, Mr Strachan,' the Colonel replied.

The American used the Budweiser bottle to push up the rim of his cavalry hat. 'You have yourself a deal.' A pleasant adjunct to the contract. 'She's certainly a pro.'

'Too professional. I wish to know who trained her.'

'Heidi Fleiss, the way she's dressed.' The working-garb was convincing.

Ivanov's face was stone grave. 'I do not joke when I see an enemy agent searching your room.' As cold as grave stone.

'Loosen up, Colonel. It's the blind screwing the blind. Believe me. They know nothing. I have to hand it to Max, though. The boy-chick's got taste. Yes, sir. She's good enough to eat.'

'That will be arranged.' By now his men had enough experience in counterfeiting a variety of motives – including hunger – to accompany their grisly missions. Strachan swivelled his eyes to the Russian: still no joke.

'I've got a different kind of spit-roast in mind. Cut her some slack, Colonel. She's young, she's pretty and I want her to dance for me.' People hanged themselves faster when given a longer rope.

'And she could be working for your beloved Central Intelligence Agency.'

A generous mouthful of beer. 'They take all sorts. Fuck, they even employ me. Some reflection, huh?'

Indeed. Ivanov knew the history. Beside him was a man whose links with American intelligence stretched back over thirty years, to the day when a decorated, staring-eyed veteran of the Air Cav, still in his early twenties, presented himself for preliminary interviews in Saigon. He became a pilot-instructor in Air America, attached to Taiwan's 'deepest deniability' Tnirty-fourth Squadron, flying modified long-range C-130 Hercs in low-level expeditions to drop remote sensors in China's Lop Nor nuclear test region, and taking Laotian commandos in De Havilland Twin Otters and quietened Hughes Defender-500 helicopters from their PS 44 jungle base on raid after raid deep into North Vietnam. They planted *Threshold* wire taps and relay bugging devices on enemy phone-lines, seismic sensors along the Ho Chi Minh trail, took out surface-to-air missile sites and ground-vectoring facilities to enable President Nixon to launch his massive Linebacker series of B-52 bomber strikes. An operator, a useful ally, Ivanov mused.

'I think it is time we dealt with your blind friend,' he said. 'The sight-impaired are always having accidents.'

'I'm telling you, Colonel, we don't want them offed yet. That's official, from my superiors.'

'What are your superiors' views on light interrogation?'

'By you fellas? Pessimistic. "Lay off" are the words coming down. It'll only draw attention. If they're looking, it means they haven't found.' Strachan indicated the screen.

'If they are looking, it means your organisation is penetrated.'

'By Ray fucking Charles, by a guy who can hardly see? Christ, Colonel – Max can barely pick out where he's pissing. Even the Company's bunch of crap-headed bureaucrats wouldn't use him as an agent handler.'

'They take all sorts. Fuck, they even employ you.' Ivanov repeated Strachan's words, without the accent, without humour.

'When I say he's in the dark, I frigging mean it. RP – it stands for retinitus pigmentosa – and I'll decide when to insert the "I". I'll handle him. Ok?'

For the moment, Strachan, only for the moment. They continued to watch the images.

Zenya was methodical, surgical-gloved hands probing, testing, fingers running lightly beneath covers, around skirting-boards, into side-pockets of suits and luggage, opening, unfolding and replacing. Pen-torch in mouth, she went through drawers, unplugged light bulbs, peered into sockets and felt her way through clothes and toiletries. Toothpaste was uncapped and tested, the screw-top of a whisky bottle removed and explored, writing paper pressed onto carbon scroll and held under filtered spectrum light to test for indentations caused by any previous writing. The place was clean, sterile, as if prepared for a visit.

'I just love that tush when she bends over,' Strachan was observing. 'Sure you can't wire me up Max's room before tomorrow?'

'You will have to rely on imagination and the audio tapes until then,' Ivanov answered. And make the most of them before Max Purton died. The boy, the girl, were a complication. They had to be contained. As head of security for the project, he would choose the method of that containment. He possessed the measurements.

A member of the planning staff detached himself from a group of individuals gathered around the communications consoles and approached, coughing slightly to draw attention.

'Excuse me, Colonel.' He passed two printed sheets to the extended hand. 'These are the latest progress summaries. Three more bankers were killed this morning, two were Diakanov's.'

'Difficulties?'

'None, Colonel. You will note the overview of the bottlenecks developing at the Emergency Ministry. Our FAPSI units are disrupting many of their communications and slowing their response to the Siberian food crisis.'

'I note that the West wishes to send supplies of meat. Get Kalinin and Krivitsky to stir up the press against it; editors should use the Russian pride and sovereignty angle.' There was always scope to massage the national inferiority complex.

'Very good, Colonel.'

'Has the Director been informed?'

'Colonel-General Gresko remains in meetings.'

'Very well. Do not disturb him.' He shuffled the pages perfunctorily. 'How much are we paying the Chechens?'

'One hundred thousand dollars for each assault.'

'Tell Chebotok to offer a bonus, within the existing

budget, if the initial attack produces a hundred corpses or more. I want extra foreign television in the area – encourage the freelancers.'

The man nodded and returned to his position.

Strachan was opening another beer with a corner of his steel triangular pendant carrying the symbolic eye of Caodaism. 'Did your parents ever ask what you thought you'd be doing when you grew up, Colonel?'

The eyes, as warm as the pendant, gave nothing. 'I do not recall my parents, Mr Strachan.' Zenya was still searching.

The gates were unlocked, always were at School N159 on Festivalnaya Street, the ice crackling on the hinges as Lazin pushed through into the basketball playground, boots seeking grip on the silicon-smooth surface. He was wearing body-armour beneath the greatcoat, but felt naked to a hundred cross-hairs in a hundred night-sights, felt the pressure of fingers squeezing on rifle triggers, squeezing on his abdomen. The small flashlight was in his gloved hand: perhaps its beam would flare in the passive-view systems, throw off their aim until he found cover. It was the kind of thought which dark nights and danger – vulnerability – always threw up. Humans were invariably over-optimistic. He aimed the torch to his right, across the marked concrete, and tapped out a single morse identification letter. If it were going to happen, an execution to provide a talking point at the school for months, draw groups of healthily morbid children to the spot during break, now was the moment. He tensed, tightness spreading through his limbs, counting, senses reaching for the subsonic flatulence of a report from a silenced weapon, the last sound before his own guttural shuddering. No impact. A brief flicker. A corner of his brain commanded him to duck, to dive and return fire. The light repeated. All clear; approach. They wanted a closer body-shot. He walked slowly, methodically, in the direction of the source, crossed the pitch.

'You won't win a match at that speed, Colonel.' The bass was muffled, timbre interrupted, pinched by a blocked nasal cavity. Deep Throat required a lozenge. 'Stay where you are. Abide by the rules and you will not be hurt. Are you alone?'

'Yes.' Rules? He had abandoned them as soon as he read the note in his apartment, accepted the invitation to attend this solitary reception in the early hours at a deserted playground.

'Followed?'

'I took precautions.'

'We are talking threat to life, Colonel, not a teenage pregnancy. You are lucky my men are here to sanitise the area.' Luck was open to interpretation. The night shadow, indistinct, made a slight movement. 'At your feet is an electronic device. Pick it up and take it with you. It's American, advanced, will detect if you have tracking devices in your clothes. Instructions are provided. Use it before all future assignments. For now, we will rely on keeping our conversation short.'

'Assignments? You seem certain of my cooperation.'

'You have come to this meeting. It shows, at the very least, curiosity.'

Or madness. Lazin stooped and found the package. He rose carefully. 'The last time I had a conversation in the dark, the man died.'

'The camp at Daban. He was one of mine.'

'Then I am not filled with confidence.'

The shadow was still, had become part of the surroundings. 'He died for helping you. That is commitment.'

'That is lack of judgement.'

'Do you wonder why Leonid Gresko brought you back from the BAM Zone?'

'I wonder why he sent me out.'

'To keep you away from your security routine in Moscow; because there were things to hide; because he needs a fall-guy, someone who can be tainted, accused, used when the Security Council demands action.' The shadow, and Gresko, both used him: differentiation was hard at this hour.

'Action against what?' Lazin asked.

A pause. 'I have yet to discover.'

'My faith is draining rapidly.'

'As are your chances of survival.'

'So, I'm being kept sweet for a set-up? Why the attempt on my life at the mine?'

'Panic, knee-jerk, by a Major who never expected you to find anything. He plainly did not wait for orders. Gresko will be unforgiving.' Lazin was paid not to trust, paid poorly; it was part of the counter-espionage job description. There was no money on offer here. Strange for a deal struck in Moscow.

'It is usually within the first minutes that I decide an informant is either drunk or mad.'

'I am neither, Colonel. You uncovered threads which you are incapable of pulling together, cannot explain.'

'I do not hear answers from you.'

'Only that they all lead to Leonid Gresko, Director of the Federal Security Service.'

'*My* Director,' Lazin added.

'We are talking subversion.'

'Then it could include almost any government minister.'

'Cynicism will be a rare luxury. Do not cover your eyes to what is happening. You saw things in the BAM Zone.'

The shadow was too well-briefed to be anything but an insider. A provocateur? A genuine enemy of Gresko's? Motive, discover the motive. 'I am an officer in the Federal Security Service; Leonid Gresko is my employer.' Keep the shadow talking.

'Your loyalty is commendable, but unrequited. And it is owed to your country, not to any individual.' Lazin stood waiting for more. The patriotism card was always played at some stage of the hook. Often a useful, and cheaper, currency to banknotes. 'Perhaps your view would alter if you knew Gresko sent Colonel Petr Ivanov to murder Mrs Cherkashin the railway official's wife whom you interviewed. I'm sure you will do your research. You will be wasting your time. I guarantee her fate will be as obscure as many others in the

BAM Zone, as obscure as her children's.' She had mentioned Ivanov when he met her. Had the Colonel returned to the dacha outside Tynda, to the overgrown garden, to the desolate interior with its small shrine? Lazin remembered the grief. She wanted to go, to join her son and daughter.

'Mrs Cherkashin? Why?' he asked.

'Again, I do not know. Perhaps you came too close to FSB involvement; perhaps they aim to pin a death on you.'

'You are a fantasist.'

'Then I have gone to a great deal of trouble and expense to play out my fantasy.'

'This is Moscow. Cash can buy any dream.'

'And what is Gresko's? He has the resources; he has gone to the trouble. Look around, Colonel Lazin. You are sent on a wasted mission to Siberia; on your return you are tasked with digging around Diakanov and the mafiya troubles, digging your own grave.'

'The fall-guy theory again?'

'Time is almost up, Colonel. For you, for me, for Russia. I have trusted you to come here; you have trusted me. That is a start. I hope it is not the end.'

It was unlikely to be. Lazin bestrode a chasm of uncertainty, of plot and counter-plot, a potential tragedy in which he was a bit-player or the comedy-chorus. A slip, one slip would be all, and he could tumble, fall from the comfortable vantage of remaining unnoticed, neutral, an outsider. Why antagonise Gresko for the sake of appeasing an unknown crank with an unknown design? But the face of the FSB Director came to him, the hooded pupils, his mission special only because it made no sense, his marginalisation in Lubyanka Square; the thought of Petr Ivanov and murder came to him.

'I need to think.'

'In the meantime, check the tunnels between Victory Park and the nuclear citadel beneath Ramenki District.' They were part of the largest nuclear-proof bolt-hole ever constructed for government and its servants. A palace in which to while away those tedious hours of Armageddon, to practise procreation and inbreeding for a brave and barren new future.

Lazin stared at the spectre, eyes aching with the effort of defining the contours, mind aching at defining the implications of the conversation. 'You realise they are heavily guarded.'

'By Federal Security Service troops, Gresko's troops. You were tasked with revising defence plans for the bunkers and tunnels during their reconstruction from 1997 to 1999.'

'My file will also inform you that I was re-assigned to assess security at other locations of strategic significance.'

'Not before you learned everything about the running of these sites, gained knowledge of how to access them. Use it. No one else can engineer an entry.'

'Why Ramenki?'

'It can house up to thirty thousand men below ground; its secret metro link passes close to the President's underground emergency departure point from the Kremlin. That makes me worried, more worried that Gresko controls everything below street-level.'

'Then both of us are nervous. If I am caught down there, way beyond my remit, I will be executed.'

'So make it worthwhile: examine the Kremlin's clandestine metro link out to the military airbase at Vnukovo-2 also. Twenty-five kilometres and you know every inch. It could be our warrants have already been signed.' Forceful, deliberate. 'Gresko has plans, Colonel. When you reach your apartment, use that detector, run it over your clothing. If you are wired, it means you are on his game-board, it means he is playing you. We will all be taken. You want a return to the old ways?'

'There was job security.'

'And before that there was Lavrenti Beria, there was Stalin. Listen to me, Colonel. Listen.'

Lazin stepped back through the gate, checked the street and set off in a random direction. Deep Throat watched him go. It was going to be bloody, it was going to be close, and he had no evidence on which to act. Five minutes later two unmarked Mercedes drew up at opposing ends of the street, six occupants emerging to saunter awkwardly on ice towards the school gates. They were armed. Ten minutes. The figures re-emerged, professionalism disguising the body-language of disappointment. Nothing was found; Lazin and his hidden contact had escaped the area.

He was pleased to be back in the hut. It had the familiarity of a lifetime, the bare, wooden institutionalisation of the camps. But here he could warm himself by a stove, lie down when he wished, decide life and death for himself. So different to the past. These were the few luxuries, concessions, in being old. The younger man handed over the photographs.

'And you recognised him from previous visits?' The old trapper concentrated on the images.

'That is so, Brodets. Our Tofy friends have monitored a great deal of movement, claim there's a definite military-security element.'

'The others with him?'

'Were following the colonel you saved – Lazin. One of them is identifiable as FSB; he's been a KGB stooge in the Nizhneudinsk area for years.'

'How long did they remain in the caves?'

'An hour. Then they left in snow vehicles, carrying another of the cases. Made to look like a KSO search and rescue team, had all the markings, but heavily armed.'

'And too cautious,' added a bearded combatant in snow-clothing wandering across with a mug of kompot and chewing on a piece of smoked kolbasa sausage. 'Most KSOs go out of their way to be noticed.'

The old man placed the pictures down and pressed his palms together, hands calloused and misshapen by the years of hard labour, fingernails deformed or lost to torture and frostbite. White hair fell across the ice-worn face, but did not soften it, relieve it with the gentle decline of age. Lines were of suffering rather than character, for character belonged to existence before the betrayal, before the gold and uranium mines, before the road and track laying. Before Siberia.

'You say Vladimir Prison is open for business again?'

'Fresh guard details have been assigned. Training has increased.'

'You do not require training to shoot innocents in the back.' The eyes sank into a memory, reached back to the shouts and shots, when cell doors opened and slammed only for beatings or execution. The squeal of hinges – metal on metal – the squeal of prisoners, metal on flesh. Fleeting; a return to the surface, an icing over. 'The reports from our Buryat contacts?'

'Modern equipment has been seen in the hands of internal security units. They're definitely preparing for something. The Yukagir herdsmen continue to talk of their reindeer becoming frightened by strange high-altitude noises at night.'

He had spies everywhere, and none provided better or more willing recruits than the dying indigenous tribes of Siberia whose lives he helped and dialects he spoke. They were the first to aid his escape from the Communist penal system, the only ones to feed, clothe and hide him, and in return he had organised their resistance to a regime which sought to Sovietise and marginalise their entire existence. His system grew, intelligence-gathering and sabotage activities spreading, funds draining from Moscow, siphoned from Russian state-controlled projects, unscrupulous loggers and polluters, bureaucrats and commissars, brought to account or to their knees. In training and building active cells to challenge the government dictat, he had fuelled a growing autonomy movement, demonstrated the means to succeed, to endure politically and physically, giving new edge and impact to small groups subjugated by the ravages of disease, alcoholism and enforced integration. From the hunters, gatherers and fishermen who operated far from the collectives and settlements – the Udeghe along the Bikin River forced out by loggers, the Nivkhi seal-cullers, Ulchas and Nanais of the lower Amur, the Even people found east of

301

the Lena river, Udehes of the Aniui and Kungan rivers – to the native grassland descendants of Gengis Khan's horse armies now squeezed into miserable overcrowded slum settlements, he gained information, respect, gave funding and hope. The KGB never found him: the gulags had taught him the lesson.

'High-altitude noises at night? I am more interested in what happens on the ground. Or below it.' He gestured to two cases sitting on a carpentry bench. They were the same design as that handed by Hunter Strachan to the security officer based at the Kosvinsky Mountain ballistic-missile control centre, to that being stored by the commander of the hydrogen fuel production plant near Bratsk. 'I suggest an examination. Have you done preliminary tests?'

'Sure,' the beard replied. 'I dropped one and it did not explode. Perhaps they are diamonds.'

'Perhaps not. I shall be more careful.'

The old man rose, produced a clasp-knife and approached the nearest. The locks went quickly, knife cutting leather bindings and easing off a catch. There was no hesitation; he had lived too long anyway. The lid came up.

Silence. Then: 'I think we need the camera.'

A fortnight later, an employee of WARS – Poland's state railway – stepped aboard the wagon sipalny section run by his own company on the Moscow-Liege Ost-West express. He was tense, and would remain so long after the train left the city's Belarus station, only permitting himself to relax when, searches and customs checks over, the carriages shunted nerve-wrenchingly past the Belarusian guard towers and across the steel girder-bridge spanning the Bug River into Poland. The trip did not get easier. Arriving at Warsaw's grim Centralny Station, the attendant pushed his way through crowds of waiting passengers. A beggar – one of many, forgettable – brushed by. Ten yards on, the attendant felt his right side coat pocket: the camera films had been lifted. He sighed, burden relieved. They were consistently professional. Several days later the package was delivered by post to a flat *in London's Westbourne Gardens, Bayswater. The place was sparsely furnished, unlived in, and had been operated as a safe address by Britain's Secret Intelligence Service for decades. Longevity of use made it unusual. But the sole and as yet unidentified espionage asset sending reports here was himself unusual. Cold Cut had reported in.*

Morton's was busy, the off-white stuccoed booths full, Washington's power-players at play, the best midwestern steaks in town carried above the cosy clamour to the tables lit dimly by pewter oil lamps and illuminated pictures. On the walls, framed LeRoy Nieman sports prints, colourful evocations of the Olympics, flat racing and America's Cup, suggested informality, diners responding by loosening up and hanging out, consuming Maine lobster and Pacific salmon on an epic scale as a prelude to the beef.

Two men, sober and sober-suited, chatted amiably, alone and anonymous in their near-hidden corner position. Senator O'Day was a regular here, his favoured eaterie for male friends when wives and mistresses were out of town or elsewhere being worthy. A framed photograph of him was placed alongside that of George Burns in the panelled reception area, faces of fellow political colleagues and rivals joining in the grinning snapshot collage of dedicated carnivores. His guest tonight was Central Intelligence Agency, an operator in the field and on the Capitol, a senior figure who worked the halls and prepared the ground for the ever-grateful Director and Deputy-Director appearing before interminable and self-important Congressional subcommittees to explain and plead. The Langley leviathan, that most overt of covert organisations, had spawned many mechanisms and departments to aid its fortunes in a hostile political environment which saw officials, capabilities, morale and even survival chances rise and fall on a whim. While the situation lasted, the espionage lobbyist eating a piled lump-crabmeat cocktail was in high demand.

'Sounds like you had quite a fright in Moscow, Paddy.'

The Senator swallowed a piece of onion bread cut from the circular loaf in the centre of the table. 'Sure, had me rattled.' Must have done, the Company representative reflected. The draft-dodging generation were never very good when it came to facing incoming. 'Hell, I thought they liked my speech. The limo took most of the impact. Lot of dented chrome.'

'And two bodies left on the street.' There had been more red meat than on the Morton's trolley wheeled over to them earlier to demonstrate the cuts of beef.

'Russian security reacted quickly. They were real embarrassed. Brief firefight, we ducked, then it was over. Foreign Minister told me later it was mistaken identity by a criminal gang. Your Station Chief at the embassy dittoed the view.'

'They know best.' came the sardonic reply. His point-man Hunter Strachan was doing well; the crisis would soon be gathering pace. He was staying in touch with Leonid Gresko.

The Senator scowled. 'Criminal gang? 'Bout as useful as a quack telling you you've got non-specific urethritis.'

'I'll keep an eye on the traffic, pass on anything concrete. It'll be quicker than getting it from State.' A nod of gratitude from the politician, an ironic smile from the Agency man. 'Must reassure you about the direction the country's heading, huh?'

'The only things that reassured me were bullet-proof panels and an armoured windscreen.'

A short intermission for food. More crabmeat in mustard mayonnaise sauce disappeared. A plate of Cokenoe Oysters sat naked between them in their half shells. 'How would you react if I told you that Russia was about to collapse?'

'Act surprised, ask how you knew. Why?'

'I'm serious.' The tone was frosting subtly; the Senator failed to notice.

'Where are our steaks?' He scooped hollandaise onto the asparagus and lowered his mouth towards the dripping stem. The hand pressed firmly on his cuff, driving the food away. A look of surprise. 'What are you playing at?'

'Play's over, Paddy. If Russia is on the point of disintegration, what will your response be?'

Irritated, the Senator eyed the asparagus. The Langley boy could be intense, but this was out of place, out of line, in so relaxed an environment. 'I'd say you're talking shit. My visit went down well, business confidence is battered but coming back, and the security situation fluctuates between incompetence and chaos. What's new? But . . .' He held up a hand to forestall further intervention. 'Hypothetically, if things unravelled, I'd say maintaining law and order was a prerequisite.'

'That's what you will say.'

'Was there a question-mark at the end of that?'

'Nope. It's an order, Senator. You have the President's ear; I'm asking that you use it.'

'What the fuck is this? You're dictating to me, to an elected member of the Senate? You're planning a coup or something? Tell me this is a dream, a joke? And get the check.' He rose abruptly. 'I'll have your apology when I get back from the john. Then I'll do you a favour. We'll forget we ever had this conversation.'

'Personally, I think you'll remember it a long time, Paddy. It's no dream, no joke. Go powder your nose – and give your nostrils a long, slow wipe. Gets the charlie off.' The Senator swayed slightly, ego absorbing the body-blow. The CIA man continued. 'I suggest you sit, before you draw attention over here.' A briefcase had been produced from below the table, rested flat on an edge and opened towards the politician. O'Day watched the interior, a small flat screen relaying images silently to him. Dark eyes locked on the picture, furrowed in concentration.

'You're fucking with me.'

'No more than Snow White's going to fuck your career.'

'How dare . . .'

'Righteous indignation, Paddy. I like that in a politician: means they're flawed. It's how voters will react. Quite a habit you've acquired – you can't kick it, so now it's kicking you. They're less forgiving round New England way than Mayor Marion Barry's followers, if you catch my drift.'

'We're friends, Jack.' He said it without conviction, sank slowly, staring at the video-footage. The date and time recording meant nothing. So many deals done in so many hotel rooms, a single memory lost among a thousand encounters. Once more. 'We're friends.'

'Wrong town.' The horse's head sculpted on the lamp cast its shadow on the table.

'For God's sake.'

'He doesn't own a ballot paper, Senator. I know,' a small sip of wine, a full Italian red. 'You didn't take it all the way up your nose; you've no idea what to do with silver foil; you've never had a Colombian rush. And presidents don't inhale. Save it. It's there, the moving picture. I think it'll move everyone who sees it. You're so big in anti-drugs. Do as I say, Paddy.'

Urgency constrained in low, measured tones. 'I can't do it. I cannot attempt to change American foreign policy. No individual could. You understand that; you understand the system.'

'Work the system. Plenty of other Senators do. It's what you're paid for; it's what I've got this tape for.' He rested a palm flat on the case. 'You're heard at State, cosy with the Foreign Secretary, influential with the Treasury Committee, who can squeeze the balls of the IMF. And trust me, that's where Moscow will again be heading when the bottom falls out of its central banks.' He went on. 'All I need is a block on financial aid, a hold-off until there's a new regime for which you and the Chief Exec will make strong political and economic noises of support. You're the best catalyst there is. Respected, trusted. By those who don't know you, naturally. Congress is a bear-pit and it's chewing the ass out of the President's programme. He needs you. He'll listen.'

The Senator tapped heatedly on the table. 'To me and a thousand other advisers.' True, the figure opposite mused. Some were already on side, some would take convincing. He anticipated few problems. 'Checks and balances, Jack. Does that mean anything?'

'You're the balance. Call in the debts.'

'Are you asking me to condone a takeover in Russia?'

'You've just told me law and order is a prerequisite for rescuing a hopeless situation. You want G7 loans to vanish? You want our oil investments to collapse in another Russian Revolution? Nuclear stockpiles to go walkabout in the general turmoil? God gave you an imagination because your fellow Americans weren't blessed with one. So goddam use it, Paddy.'

'If I don't?'

'Candy's bad for a lot of things: health, prospects, marriage. Even if it's cut with vitamins.'

'Chrissakes, Jack.' O'Day adjusted volume as he caught a face turned towards their booth. 'You're creating the Russian situation; you're sure as hell predicting it. And then you ask me to betray my principles?' Rage suffused the whisper.

The crab was delicious. 'I can see you're sore, but hell, that's not morality, that's because you've been outsmarted, outgunned, outmanoeuvred.'

The Senator was thinking, thinking. 'In all conscience . . .'

'You left that with puberty, Paddy. I mean, you knew when Iraq attempted to destabilise Iran by poisoning its crops; our Director warned you that it was spraying the Kurds and southern Shi'ites with carcinogenic aflatoxin and riot-control chemical agents to cause outbreaks of liver cancer. Ethnic cleansing on a massive scale. And you stayed silent?'

'C'mon, Jack. It wasn't the climate, you know that.'

'Sure, it wasn't. We wanted the trade. So Uncle Sam kept on building up Saddam's biological warfare stocks, everyone else joined in, and you and your committees turned a blind eye to what the American Type Culture Collection was supplying.'

'Iraq is irrelevant here. I've told you, it wasn't expedient at the time.' Careful, a man picking his way through the situation, feeling for boundaries.

The CIA officer was leisurely. He had a captive audience. 'I couldn't define political principle better. Doesn't exactly give you the moral high ground in this conversation.'

'Get to the point.'

Eyes narrowed. 'Panic and unrest, Senator. That's what we're about, and that's what we're looking at in Mother Russia. Your chance to call for order, a new security regime.'

'What's in it for you?'

'We'll think of something.'

'I'm not hearing this. You're fucking crazy.'

'Most visionaries are, Paddy. I prefer to see it as method.'

'Who do you represent? The Agency? Pentagon hawks? Defence Industry interests? We left this conspiracy shit behind years ago. No one's going to swallow it.'

'Humans – presidents too – swallow anything when they've got a gun pushed in their mouths. An unstable Russia is too dangerous for the world, Paddy. Fragmentation is what we all fear. Encourage America to be decisive, support the heroic Russian Security Service as it struggles to regain control. Presidents look good when they turn disaster to their advantage.'

'And the Russian people?'

'Fuck them. And if we don't, their leaders will. They're born to die. Give them bread, they love you. Vodka, they love you even more. Oppress them, and they'll offer to bear your children. They appreciate strength; they'll applaud when the robber-barons are put on the cattle trucks, and they're sure as hell used to arbitrary rule by presidential decree. They won't notice the difference.'

'But for the midnight knocks, the gulags, the disappearance of dissidents. I've fought that all my life.'

'Mankind doesn't change, Senator. They'll always opt for authoritarianism if the alternative is civil war.'

The steaks arrived. O'Day pushed his to one side, the CIA representative adding salt and pepper and slicing into the meat. 'New York strip. Melts in the mouth.' Teeth bared in encouragement, triumph.

So, the subject had been broached, the Senator cornered, the culmination to years of preparation and the luring of him into drug-dependency and small-scale dealing among close associates. Trappings of office, personal achievement and wealth, superiority cocooned in the rear of a Lincoln, often made those exposed to them feel immune to the laws they espoused yet flouted. Immunity had gone, privilege and plutocracy made meaningless. Loss of appetite was the least of the politician's worries. O'Day stared at his dining companion, wanted to kill, felt himself reaching for a wooden-handled steak-knife to plunge into the throat of this traitor and captor. It would ruin the man's suit, destroy the meticulous planning. Hopeless; helpless; nemesis; cocaine-paranoia sending up his heart-rate. He needed to get away, escape from the booth. His throat was dry, so dry. Whatever he did, he was caged, bars moving inwards. People saw through the wall, saw through him. He gripped the seat, squeezing, breathing heavily, forced his body and mind to normalise. Lying came naturally; narcotics made it a reflex. Why should he worry about personal involvement in a plot to alter the destiny of a nation, the course of world events? Perhaps it made sense. Yes, somewhere, it made perfect sense. He only had to grasp for it, grapple, work it through, work it out.

'I can see the human rights thing is still bothering you, Paddy.' The CIA officer found the mustard. 'I'll pass it off as shock. It'll wear off.' A generous helping of French was piled onto the side. 'What we're talking about here is your acting as an agent of influence and giving us your views on how people are taking developments. That's all.'

The Senator was feeling faint, light-headed at the loss of initiative. 'All? I'll give you my views. There'll be sanctions; Russia will be isolated; any aid will be linked to political reform; there'll be international condemnation of a coup d'état by stealth. Russia will be cut off when it can least afford it, when its economy can least afford it. You want a scenario? – you have it, Jack.'

The man ate in silence for a minute, two minutes, a solitary diner, providing no let-out for the tension. He dabbed his mouth, sampled the wine and looked up at O'Day, drawn and shadowed in the lamplight, the Senator's face frightened without showing fear, a manipulator manipulated, a controller controlled, a mover shaken. 'Interesting,' he said finally. Whether a reference to the wine or to the politician's outburst was unclear. 'Quit the rhetoric, Paddy. It's touching, but it's horseshit. You know it, the whole goddam world knows it. Remember China? I thought not. Tanks turn students two-dimensional in Tiananmen Square. So what? No one likes students. We pay lip-service to grief, we wring our hands, and then we ring the tills. Whaddya know? It's business as usual. They've even dropped the issue in the Human Rights Committee at the UN, and America provides space and rocket technology to persuade the slants to sign up to the Missile Technology Control Regime.' He would not tell the Senator of the technology passed to the Russian military, filtered into strategic nuclear forces, into the scramjet project, into Leonid Gresko's programme. 'You think there'll be a united world response? When did you last see that? Forgive me – I recall: *Independence Day*, the movie.'

'You're wrong.'

'Two words. Stability and trade, Paddy. They're what we strive for. That's what statesmanship is all about. I don't see human rights in there. If people get unhappy having their teeth pulled, give them Levis, give them Pepsi. It calms them, makes them feel special, appreciate the good things. The American way, Senator. Accept it, act the power-broker you claim to be.'

'I'm not alone, Jack.'

'Neither was Armand Hammer. There are a thousand – ten thousand – tycoons, wannabes out there waiting to do business, wanting to fill his soft leather shoes, queuing for concessions from a future hard-line Russian government.'

'Listen, goddamit.' *Sotto voce* shouting. 'You think the President will accept this? It's not going to happen. You hear me? It's not going to happen. Never.'

'Read my lips, eh?' Power-suit shifted back. 'You blow the President's nose, wipe his ass, procure his women, pay the hush money, fix the hush jobs, raise his Party's funds. It's going to happen.'

'And if it doesn't? If he's not in receiving mode?'

'Then you leverage up.'

'Blackmail? Blackmail the fucking President?' O'Day's energy levels were sagging.

'If it was good enough for J. Edgar Hoover . . .' A discreet adjustment of the cuff-link: it carried a microphone. 'Ten minutes ago you wouldn't have believed in blackmailing a Senator. It's a steep learning curve.'

'I have a duty.'

'To yourself. You're Irish Catholic, there's supposed to be guilt. You're also a politician, so think of perjury and lying before a Grand Jury as an occupational hazard, occupational therapy. Remember, Paddy boy,' he stood and leant in close. 'Ambition can make a man or kill him. It's your call. Thanks for dinner. I'm sure your deep religious faith will be a help.'

'Senator, are you all right?' The waitress hovered anxiously. 'Senator? Sir?' The political figure familiar in a thousand sound bites, the presence capable of radiating seduction from every American television set, sat looking ahead, lost, diminished, motionless. He had been that way for over twenty minutes, the staff were talking, the manager fretting over liability and insurance claims. 'Sir?'

The mustiness of disuse had gone – the first thing he noticed. The shabby sixteen-storey Khrushchev-concrete block remained unchanged, yellowing and stained, an over-budgeted theatre set from an era in which budgets were limitless and waste a way of *apparat* life. It was the same life that the building was designed to play a major part in preserving, for its functionalist structure concealed nothing less than the key components of the ram-air and filtration systems feeding the nuclear-proof bunkers, tunnels and citadels planted deep beneath the streets of Moscow and the city's outlying areas. With some imagination, passers-by might have guessed at the role of the stunted tower: the small opaque windows set high, the use of reinforced slabs the size and strength of blockhouses, the novel design of vents close to a roof which supported a range of bulbous communication domes positioned about a protruding central excrescence. The military's imprint was self-evident to those who bothered to see. Few did. Depressing architecture was common enough, was unlikely to stir the spirit or attract the attention of an inquisitive mind. The designers had counted on it. Occasionally a police patrol – Federal Security Service guards in disguise – nosed around the environs, but they merely duplicated the work of the rooftop omni-directional cameras and there was little for them to do. Even the drunks stayed away. Better quality harassment could be found elsewhere.

Lazin had let himself in through a small litter-strewn entrance situated at the rear between the arcs of two CC cameras rotating unsystematically on a single horizontal plane. Operating out of sync, they provided a temporary blind-spot which the Colonel moved swiftly to exploit. It was he who had once reported the potential danger, knowing there would never be follow-up. The guards could plug the gaps, he was assured. But guards never plugged gaps, only created them. Stories abounded of Russian SVR foreign intelligence agents gaining access to American nuclear facilities through posing as FedEx delivery men: it was not unknown for courteous security officers to hold the doors for the forgettable blue-collar types sweating and lumbering in with their heavy loads. *Never here, never here* – the sentiment expressed in every compromised high-security location. Thank the gods for human fallibility, the FSB man thought, swivelling the goggles into position, activating the infrared torch and moving through to the second set of double steel doors. They were capable of withstanding anti-tank rockets fitted with tandem warheads. To a screwdriver, however, they remained vulnerable. He loosened the armoured plate covering the control panel, inserted the maintenance card and punched a sequence of numbers onto the pad. A lock gave; he placed a key in position beneath the card and turned twice. A low series of pips, a tug on the master handle and the doors slid smoothly back on rollers. They would remain open until his return. Through to a long, narrow corridor, right-angles into further passageways, past firedoors and down a series of metal stairways linking unguarded and silent landings. In wartime every corner, every cul-de-sac, would be populated by heavily armed soldiers, searching, questioning, checking passes, trained to shoot without compunction. But now he was alone, a grave robber working to a map he had committed to memory, an insider who knew the labyrinth and its traps, who could reach the inner tomb because he had helped design its safeguards. *Wholly alone*. He was wearing newly purchased civilian clothes: his uniforms, all of them, carried micro-trackers placed into their linings and discovered by the scanner given to him in the darkened playground by the shadow. It convinced him, gave substance – a focus – to the sense of isolation at Security Service headquarters. They must have turned the apartment over while he was in Siberia. Microchips had been inserted into the fabric of his clothing, the fabric of his life; he was controlled, monitored, captured in an information loop. And he was the one uninformed yet informed upon. Watchers everywhere, dread pressing down. What was going down? Two masters to serve, both unseen, Leonid Gresko and an apparition furnishing a different set of orders. Basic instinct told him to trust neither, advanced instinct to trust the latter.

He was safer down here in the dark.

Blast-proof doors. Beyond, a honeycomb of rooms kept at positive pressure during closed-down situations, when the world was closed down and the policy-makers, the imple-menters, sat snug, if somewhat rueful, detached from the consequences of their actions above. Today was open day, when the complex threw its doors wide to Georgi Lazin. The conventional Moscow metro system comprised over 250 kilometres of tunnel connecting almost 150 stations. Guide maps never gave a clue to the existence of the system that he was entering. He stepped beneath the cameras – operational only when the lighting was activated – past the ballistic-protected glass of the empty guard boxes, and seized the handles on the wheel-lock. The spars spun easily. There was no alarm fitted.

Six storeys below street level and the environment was chill, fans breathing the scrubbed artificiality of decontaminated air in and out through the ducting. The noise was invasive, a contrast to the sense-deadening solitude of the upper levels. Lazin scanned the narrow concrete apron which led down to the walkway running alongside the single track. Power lights were off – the line was inactive. There were culverts set in the walls: pre-positioning crannies for anti-personnel mines. The Soviets had always been world-class urban fighters. He lowered himself onto the towpath and started for central Moscow, the route clear and snaking away beneath a low curving roof, disappearing around gentle turns and past collection sites and ambush points. On the opposite side, reached by under-track burrows, were short bisecting tunnels, storage bays and sudden expanses of platform leading nowhere and placed adjacent to double sidings. He was walking against the tide: in wartime, officialdom in its tens of thousands would stampede for safety in his direction, rats running from a fire, rats in sable and beaver coats, carrying their last shopping from GUM, smelling of expensive soaps and scents, of cheap terror. And he, Colonel Lazin, might once have been among them, part of the *nomenklatura*, the list. He headed on, edging cautiously round the corners, back pressed into the lined walls. Far behind, out at the arrival zone in Ramenki, and closer to the subterranean administration, the defensive placements would be manned permanently. Spot checks were the norm closer to the Kremlin, roving patrols sent to relieve their colleagues and themselves in these hidden corridors of power. Urine was the best indicator of habitation.

He had not anticipated the open car. It glided, near-soundless under its own electric power, overhauling him at gentle cruise speed, flashlights of its crew playing along the tunnel sides and reaching into the recesses. Ambient glare in his goggles, intensified by the night-vision electronics, gave him the first warning. He ran, brightness increasing, catching. There was no time, no point in turning – a torch could easily blind him. A bolt-hole. He ducked down beneath the track, feet splayed absurdly for quiet movement, slithering underneath, waiting for the vehicle either to proceed or halt. Goggles removed, retinas adapting abruptly to real life, optical tricks played without the benefit of military science. *You rank amateur, Lazin.* Too pleased with yourself, at getting in so easily; getting in right up above your head. He cursed, chided himself silently, would kill silently. Suppressor applied, barrel lengthened. A gleam reflected on the surfaces beyond the entrance to his hiding-place, dynamo whir increasing, a rumble overhead. It passed, light receding. Goggles re-applied, Lazin crawled out slowly, ready to meet any stay-behind with a multiple body-tap. Deserted again. He would follow the vehicle.

Twenty minutes and he had caught up, trudging purposefully until a glow spread out from a section lit by a ceiling trail of work lamps. A burst of power-drilling. He shied unconsciously and went low, the harsh drumming ricocheting above and away down the tunnel, rebounding with a hollow tone from a distance. Leopard crawl, keeping flat, using sound as cover, moving seamlessly to avoid jarring in the peripheral viewfields of a sentry. Another drill, an overlapping duet of metallic fury. Static shadows cast by the illuminations; he wriggled between them, had to get close. Pulling himself uncomfortably over a girder studded with rivets, he wedged himself into a corner formed by a steel bulkhead adjoining the wall. The lamps were directed, should keep him relatively secure. Clamour ceased: a final diminishing echo, then footsteps and voices. Lazin peered around, one eye exposed.

'Are you on schedule?' Petr Ivanov asked, bleached face translucent against the background.

The other man was small, wizened in the ill-fitting greatcoat, recognisable to Lazin by stance alone, from hours and duties shared on countless projects throughout Russia on behalf of the KGB's Second Chief Directorate and cloned successor, the Federal Security Service. Yuri Vakulchuk, gnomish assistant, stood – hands on hips – over the work-detail. Resources were stretched, Gresko had said. *So were loyalties; so were loyalties.* Lazin wiped his eye, moisture formed from an unblinking stare, ears straining to hear the shape-distorted acoustics. Witching hour; the spell drew him.

Vakulchuk was speaking. Moonlighting within the Service, Lazin brooded, working for Colonel Ivanov, enemy, symbol of the old ways, of everything he rejected. Seems and not seems; trust formed over a decade and torn out, torn up, in seconds.

'We are completely prepared,' the little frame said. 'The tunnels are cleared, all blockages removed. You may report to the Director that ingress at three points, including the new opening made at Poteshny Palace, is now possible.' Poteshny Palace, Stalin's old Kremlin living quarters. Lazin made micro-adjustments to his position, had to listen, had to witness.

'The trains?'

'Functioning perfectly. Using the holding bays, we can push one thousand men through in ten minutes, five thousand in forty-five.' Vakulchuk, the military strategist, Lazin thought sarcastically. Plainly he had underestimated this scarecrow of a man. Gresko's stooge, Ivanov's lackey.

'I am interested only in certainties, Captain. There will be no dress rehearsal.'

'Nor need there be, Colonel.' The voice was reassuring. 'It will be the calmest region in the whole of Moscow.'

A dry laugh from a mirthless throat. 'Not difficult when

the surface is ablaze. I want people throwing themselves at the Kremlin walls, street-fights drowning out the *kuranty* chimes from Spasskaya Tower, before the Director acts.'

'The mafiya are giving us a taste.'

'Most encouraging. A clean-out without a single loss to ourselves.'

'And enhanced earnings for our black-market and cross-border operations.'

'Civil strife has its winners and losers,' Ivanov replied. And Leonid Gresko plainly wished to be the winner – absolute winner – Lazin ruminated from his insecure hiding-place. Tear down and rebuild, that was it. And done with an unparalleled economy of effort.

For ten minutes the men talked, compared schedules, discussed progress. What had Vakulchuk been promised? Promotion? Had he been threatened? No, this was not the behaviour of a soul in fear, but of a willing collaborator and quisling, a man who would happily present the head of his colleague and commander as a trophy to Petr Ivanov. Small men and savagery were so often comfortable together.

Vakulchuk shielded his eyes and looked into the darkness, beyond and through his nominal superior behind the partition. Lazin shrank from the gaze, aware of his lack of camouflage, his skin exposed without matt blackening. His FSB partner possessed a slyness which suited well these tunnels; they were his domain. Tonight was not the moment to confront him. There would be time, Yuri Andreyevich Vakulchuk, there would be time. He had stayed long enough.

'Be warned.' Ivanov faced the diminutive form. 'The Director has given orders for the highest levels of security to be maintained. Western intelligence is already snooping at the fringes. The greater the instability, the more concerned their governments. Their espionage efforts will increase correspondingly.'

'That is also true for the spying enterprises run by government ministers.'

'Activity has been detected.'

'How do we hold them, Colonel?'

'Close down the opportunities.' Ivanov was thinking of one in particular. 'Proceed with your work, Captain.'

Lazin was back beneath the track when the electric vehicle made its return journey to Ramenki. He crouched alone for an hour before moving.

Above, several kilometres west of the Kremlin on Berezhkovskaya, the Englishman sat in one of the Radisson Hotel's numerous coffee bars. He had shopped, dined at The Exchange, was on his second cup, pushing the hours past, waiting for contact. A group of immodest Russian entrepreneurs talked loudly across the room, staring out lesser mortals, indulging in a seated arms-only swagger that looked absurd but for the obvious menace. New Russians, the Englishman sneered to himself, wished they had been extinguished by the last banking crash. If their posturing grew any more assertive, they would soon be dropping their trousers to spray territorial scent on the furnishings. Unspeakable types. He would stick it out, had already made three trips to the lavatory at thirty-minute intervals to check if the Hungarian were ready with the microdots. A no-show so far. Might as well sit back and enjoy the SIS expense account. Guy Parsons was parsimonious at the best of times, Six notoriously mean. But as a stringer, he had legitimate dealings in the capital which served as adequate cover and provided an entertainment budget far beyond the resources of 85 Vauxhall Cross. The occasional package to take out, political gossip to pass on; nothing too demanding, or dangerous. The Cold War was over – a lecture, wink and conspiratorial glass of vodka were the main sanctions if caught. He was proud to do the occasional favour for the British Establishment. It was more exciting than a round of golf in the Home Counties, afforded ample opportunity to give guarded hints in the clubhouse of derring-do that smacked of reticence and therefore boosted authenticity. Raucous laughter from the Russians. The Englishman sipped.

He knew these people, loved coming here, preferred to stay in the smarter locations.

Few observed the three men in dark coats enter and spread out in a walking line. Those who did turned away uninterested. It was how the leader wanted it to be. They had avoided the security checks at the front; the single ex-soldier allocated to the service door was one of theirs. Final visuals, confirmation and a nod. Hands brushed aside heavy wool fabric, went up to MP5K submachine guns hung from underarm shoulder holsters and tilted the barrels forward on their swivel slings. Target selection. Aiming from the hip, full automatic. Fire. The Englishman flattened himself on the ground, willing himself into a narrow profile, mentally redirecting bullets as marble, glass, porcelain and flesh erupted around. Left hands up to spare magazines in opposing holsters, quick release, change, slap home, continue. Lighting crashed down, a body fell across ornamental flowers, jumping erratically at the impact explosions straddling it. Another slid, marking the wall like soiled underwear. Eyes closed, face pressed down, the Englishman did not see the dark, thickening cascades, the faster streams of coffee, the Russians tumbling unembarrassed in the drop-falls of the dead. He did not see the leader approach, nor feel the kinetic force of the rounds. Just my bloody luck, he was thinking, just my bloody luck. And then nothing.

The leader stepped away. Not as enjoyable as travel to England for a murderous appointment with a schoolboy beside a rugby field, nor as demanding as the laser surgery he performed on Viktor Gribanov in St Petersburg. But fee-paying work, nevertheless, and further success to his credit. On the far side of the room a team member held up four fingers – the Russian entrepreneurs had veered from dominant to dormant in only a few seconds. Mission complete, withdrawal before hotel security or a police rapid-reaction squad felt inclined to tangle. It was inadvisable: as an ex-member of the KGB's *Vympel* foreign sabotage and assassination unit, he had faced worse odds, disliked having his nights out interrupted. It was also unlikely. His friends in the FSB should prevent outside interference. He signalled the two wing-men to follow. Colonel Ivanov would be pleased. A British agent – to the world, a regular businessman – caught and killed in the crossfire at a top American-owned hotel, Russian mobsters gunned down in another twist to gangland violence. Negativity everywhere; a positive start. The microdots were retrieved and the Hungarian carrier, already weighted, pushed alive through thinning ice and left on the silted bottom of the Moscow River.

He had left Jackie working out on her pastel-coloured set of weights similar to the one she had seen in the great hall at Chequers, the Prime Minister's official country retreat, during the couple's pre-Christmas visit. Ferris glanced at the desk clock, nestling among the photographs of him, family, him with family, and him with family and PM. The cult of assumed personality was not dead in this office. All smiles, all sincerity. She would have worked up quite a sweat by now; isotonic expunging of the toxins and stress built up by years in a political marriage of political convenience. It had the charm of a public convenience, he thought acidly. Grin and bear it, then grin again. The fortnightly Saturday advice surgeries he held were a welcome diversion. Meet, greet and love the people: no bad thing for a Member of Parliament. Strangely therapeutic. For most of the visitors, he was a cheap substitute for a priest or psychiatrist. Nice to be wanted.

'Nigel, Janet Sikorski outside to see you.' The long earrings of his assistant swung into view, framing a face devoid of make-up, neuroses displaced into the metallic tendrils hanging from over-stretched lobes. The improvements wrought by Prozac were indiscernible.

'Show her in, please.' The brittle features, topped by their brutalist haircut, disappeared, a parting glare indicating that the visitor was attractive and therefore a mistrusted impostor among the international sisterhood.

She was an impostor anywhere, a vision that stood tall and apart from the everyday, a welcome invader of his concentration and constituency business. A smile, broad and bright, an openness to which he responded with a gauche, damp handshake and an offer to sit. She accepted. Perhaps he should hug her – many of his colleagues favoured this approach. He would get to know her first. Flowers? Dinner? They would come. For the moment, he was content to maintain eye-contact, convinced that his status alone was enough to ensure mutual attraction, that the laws of political power could overcome those of nature and seduction and enable any government Minister to get laid. He was far from the ugliest, so optimism was justified. Even the Yorkshire Ripper had female admirers.

He breathed deeply, uncertain whether the odour from outside had fully dissipated from the previous month. It was no way to greet this Prada-clad pulchritude. A group of militant farmers and animal husbanders, accompanied by huntsmen blowing horns, had descended on the office and used muck-spreading machinery to spray agricultural ferti- lizer over the front of the building. Bad publicity; slickness versus slurry, and slurry had won. One in the urbanite eye. It was so much easier to concentrate on foreign policy, where moralising self-interest could be conducted in elegantly furnished surroundings, expressed in joint declarations, immune from those whose lives they touched. How he hated that country smell. Simple folk, barbarians. Yes, he definitely preferred the sophistication of diplomacy, where cracks were smoothed over, not with manure, but with obfuscation and semantics, where the rural youth were friendlier, poorer, and possessed healthy olive skins.

'I've never met a politician,' she said.

'Some of us only come out after dark.' Some of us will never come out. Laughter, understanding. 'I read your letter, Janet. I'd be delighted to help. If we can find the records of your father's wartime service, I will push the right authorities over pension rights for your mother. I'm glad that you brought

321

the matter to my attention.' That he was, glad *she* was brought to his attention. Veterans and widows were always worth a few votes, a line or two in the press.

'I have the relevant records, Mr Ferris.' Long, tapered fingers brushed through her hair. He wished badly to do the same. Legs capable of a furlong unfolded and swung black leather Pollini boots to the side; bicarbonate smile and lip gloss. Christ, she was flirting with him.

'Please, call me Nigel.'

'I have the relevant records, Nigel.' She opened a bag and handed over an envelope. The contents would never pass a critical examination, but they were stage-props, adequate for today's meeting. Entrapment should not take long. Then she would fly to Washington DC to assess progress with that other mass of human contradiction and fault, Senator Patrick O'Day. News was positive, pressure increasing. Powerful men, predictably weak. Ferris checked briefly, laid the package on the desk, and patted it. 'I will do all the right things.'

'I can see that.'

Small talk followed, casual interchange, mental circling. He clock-watched, aware that, driven by an unsubtle blend of envy and contempt, earrings would reappear to warn him against time-overruns and to check that his priapic personality was not unduly oppressing the female visitor. As if that were possible: her Giorgio scent wrapped around him, stifled him with her authority. They had moved on to the subject of hobbies, Ferris remarking on a fondness for travel and his wish to fly to Poland some day.

'I hear that you like Europe.'

'That's no secret, Janet.' Condescension without being condescending, the *'perhaps you've read about it in the papers?'* expression giving way to *'perhaps you'd like to accompany me?'* It was about to change again.

She was holding up a photograph, then another, a sequence of story-boards, shuffled slowly in front of his eyes. He peered forwards. 'Are these secret, Nigel?' The images gained focus. 'Think of the sound bite, Nigel. European integration. Is that how you'll play it?' He blinked hyperactively, lids running out of dynamism, sinking shut. She went on. 'Under-age, Nigel. Electors don't like it. It won't just be shit they throw at the windows here. Picture the doorstep scene, your wife Jackie standing beside you; you, uncertain whether to place a supportive hand on your child's shoulder. Might give the wrong impression to the voters. Right, Nigel?'

The communicator was not communicating; confusion had interrupted the brain and speech patterns. 'Stop . . . stop . . . stop.'

'There are so many pictures, Nigel, and recordings. Different places, positions. What was your election promise? To bring a new approach to the international arena?'

'Stop.' Whispered pain and panic.

'A new approach. Congratulations. You've achieved it.' He could turn nowhere, to no one. Compliance was assured.

'Stop it. For pity's sake.'

'Your career destroyed, your government ruined. I have to say, Nigel. We've only just met, but I can tell that you're the kind of man who would relish the challenge of turning it around.'

A knock at the door and earrings jutted round, glove-puppet head taking in the scene and bobbing from view. The Member of Parliament, Junior Foreign Office Minister, appeared not to notice, seemed flushed, deep in concentration and conspiratorial conversation. It was disgusting to see.

Behind his desk, Ferris was mutating, a man trapped, assessing escapes and finding none. The man who put the buggery into humbug. *For pity's sake* . . . She could not pity him.

'Blackmail is illegal in this country, Miss Sikorski.'

'And this is illegal in most.' She waved the photographs.

'They will be confiscated and destroyed. The police take a very dim view of your kind.'

'Prisoners take a dimmer view of yours.'

'They're fakes, all the pictures. Fakes. It's done with computer graphics.'

'Then they're most convincing. Sound quality is also good. Those hits you've made on the man–boy love sites, your hidden files, the pass codes which use your family's birthdays. Coincidence? The general public make up their minds quite quickly.'

He regrouped, tried to calm himself. His instinct and purpose were to survive: if she wished to destroy him, myriad opportunities existed to do so. There was flexibility here. It was a question of finding the correct combinations. She had yet to state a price, was waiting for him to make the offer.

'Fifty thousand pounds.' No response. He retried. 'A hundred. That's fair. For everything.' Moving too high, too rapidly, she thought.

'Generous, given you believe them fake,' she replied.

'I don't respond well to bullying, Miss Sikorski.' He had already.

'You may respond to this.'

At her word-processor position adjoining the waiting-room, earrings fretted. Janet Sikorski's appointment was overrunning by twenty minutes and there were a further two individuals waiting to air their current grievances. Like a doctor's receptionist, she did not appreciate filling his schedule with the tedium of other people's minor complaints and obsessions. She suspected that the queues which formed owed more to his appearance on television than to any genuine problems which arose in the area. TV status afforded cult status round these parts.

The deal was struck. The mobility in the Minister's mouth suggested he was in de-tox rather than agreeing to become an agent in place.

'Any questions?' Gresko's representative enquired.

None that could be expressed logically.

When she had left, he sat, head in hands, confidence and future crumbling between his fingers. And then he was sick, the burning stench of the slurry – imagined or real – making him gag, ripping at his stomach. Mud sticking, covering. He was being swamped. Disappearing.

'Load.' A double-click to the stop-watch.

Six men dropped into a crouch at Purton's command, six men presenting a smaller target to an imagined enemy as they smacked magazines into their standard-issue 9 mm Browning automatics.

'I want a semi-weaver position. Like so.' He demonstrated, adopting a feet-apart stance to face down range. 'We're doing pepper-potting – fire and manoeuvre pairs – later, so make sure you're comfortable with the drill. OK. Eight rounds. Target to your front.' Ear-defenders adjusted. 'Go on.'

They sprang up, right arms at full extension, pistol butts resting in left palms, and began firing at cardboard figure targets twenty feet away. Purton walked along the line, the crack of rounds dull to his protected hearing.

'Stoppage!' A member of the team knelt quickly, expelled the magazine, off-cocked the weapon three times to clear, re-loaded and jumped to his feet. Purton checked his watch. Not bad.

'Right.' The shooting had ceased, chambers examined, safety-catches applied, and they moved towards the targets. 'Improvement. That stoppage occurred because your arm wasn't rigid, but your recovery was decent. This here.' He led his gaggle to a display of widely dispersed hits. 'Unacceptable. I want separation on targets of under three inches, magazine changes in under three seconds. Number One, you were fine on the close-in grouping shots, so practise. Squeeze the trigger, don't pull it, and keep both eyes open when you line up on target. Got it?' A nod. 'Number Three, you weren't counting off your paired shots, you weren't ready to reload, so you'd be open-cocked, dick in hand and totally defenceless. Understood?' Sort of.

There was more criticism and advice, questions from among the assembled, before the targets were patched. 'Free-fire session, then it's on to the Sig Sauer 9 mm. Take your positions and reload. I want to see blood-blisters.'

A squad, dressed in light, drab fatigues, ran wearily in double-time past the firing points, hounded by Howell shouting venomous encouragement. 'It's only pain you fuckers . . . give it some rice . . . Move it, you bunch of fucking sackrats or I'll hang your arses out! Are you asleep?' With a command to keep going, he peeled away and jogged over to Purton. 'Talk about getting poetry from motion. Bunch of turds.'

'You're heading for a fragging.'

'Not before I turn them into a decent training cadre first. How they doing here?'

'A couple of limp wrists, a bit of finger trouble, but some naturals among them. I recognise a few from '94.'

'You'll have them shooting a fly off a dog's bollocks before long.'

'It'd be a start. Want to demo?'

'Pleasure.' The NCO beckoned the firing party after him, acquired and pulled on defenders as he walked. 'Gentlemen. You are on covert ops in Sana'a, when a carload of secret policemen swarms out towards you. What do you do?' No suggestions were proffered. He continued. 'You can run, in which case you'll die – probably from lead poisoning. Or . . .' The Browning came out from the cut-away holster tucked into the waistband in the small of his back. Swivelling on the balls of his feet, right arm rising, straightening out at the target, left hand supporting, thumb slipping the safety to fire, he squeezed off twelve rounds. It was fast. He dropped to his knee, magazine ejected, left hand retrieving the spare from a hip holster and slamming it home. Firing resumed, the head of the crouching cardboard figure twenty-five metres distant obliterated in a cloud of dust and charred wood fragments. 'Or you can give them a headache,' Howell concluded. 'Which means you'll live to tell Uncle Nick here the story.'

He rejoined Purton. Long-range pistol-shooting at a hundred metres was his speciality; these were the basics.

The students were plainly awed.

'You kitted out for the demolitions work this afternoon?' his senior officer asked.

A satisfied nod. 'Enough det cord to keep me amused. I'm taking them through improvised switches and initiation, testing them on charges: cutting, borehole, breaching, shaped, frame, platter, bulk-fuel, you name it. Night shooting and mine-laying this evening. You?'

'Sniping, Dry for the moment. Schedule's holding.'

'Stags are signalling.' Eyes shaded, Howell looked towards a moving dust cyclone which contained a Landcruiser rocking across the rough, undulating terrain. They watched for several minutes while it approached, negotiating sharp inclines and dipping behind shallow ridges until it braked close by in a shower of loose sandstone.

Ahmed Badr was in buoyant mood. 'You're making soldiers of them?'

'Giving it a tweak here and there,' Purton replied diplomatically.

'And the time across the assault course is coming down,' Howell added, cigarette perched on his lower lip. 'Want some scran? Food?'

'Tea perhaps. Let us talk.' The NCO gave orders to the units to stand down, sent a runner after the team out on the circuit, before the three moved across to the shade of tent canvas and the sandbags set around a low table. Badr had brought a map, unfolding it, using a mug and a pistol to peg it out. 'We have intelligence from Sana'a. It is a hundred per cent.' Purton focused on the chart, did not raise an eye to Howell. Allegiances, like life, were a commodity here, to trade, steal and swap according to the prevailing political climate. Sana'a, the capital of the north, and now of the entire unified Republic of Yemen, was the chief bazaar. Nothing was a hundred per cent.

'If it's time-critical, we're not ready to act on it, Ahmed,' Purton pre-empted. 'We haven't even made selections for the first full guerrilla course.'

'Ben, Ben.' A slap on the shoulder. 'I know you have worries. But the National Opposition wants a sign, to show our people in the south that we mean business. One incident. It could be the spark.'

'Cue the Charge of the bloody Light Brigade,' Howell muttered, brewing the tea.

'Ahmed, we're only your advisers. But why dilute your efforts? If you've got a long-term strategy, stay with it. We're talking about a war, not a battle.'

Badr rubbed his knees, looked doubtful, rubbed long enough for his features to brighten once again. 'We have to take orders. That is why we are soldiers, not presidents.' A semi-snort and a cup of tea from the NCO. 'Listen, Ben, Nick. I will show you.' He smoothed the paper and traced his finger along the coast to Aden. 'The new governor of Aden, Ibrahim Abd al-Aziz, sent down by the north, is an extremist. It is rumoured he engineered the Islamic Jihad riots against the old Al-Islah party governor to have him removed. He's hated in the south, very feared, very powerful, a member of the hard-line Bakil federation and backed by extremist factions in the Moslem Brothers. He has shot strikers, hanged union leaders, uses torture, sends the Al-Amaliqa brigade to raze ancient holy places and Hashemite tombs he claims are sacrilegious.'

The fanaticism was not new, simply worse. 'A monster who wants to make his mark. Always dangerous,' Purton responded.

Badr had their attention, was eager to capitalise. 'He spends much time in Sana'a cultivating allies, disposing of enemies. His fortified home in Aden is almost complete and he will stay there longer. It will be bad.'

'You want him hit?'

'NATO standard, minus sugar,' Howell declared, passing the tea across.

'It is rumoured that he is working to become the Interior Minister, with all the intelligence services of the Republic at his disposal. That will mean more oppression for my people, more terrorism in Saudi and against the West. You know he has links to Bin Laden?' No wonder Riyadh and London were scared.

Purton looked over the map, picked out his old battle-grounds. He was the fire-fighter or fire-lighter, arriving to douse threats, build barriers and pull the leaders from the burning landscape so that they might live to set a future blaze. Yesterday, Communism; today, Islam; tomorrow, any number of creeds, any amount of intolerance, stupidity or avarice to ignite the region. And he would appear, older, ankles weaker, to advise and fight.

'So, what's your intel?' he asked.

Badr gulped from the mug. 'We know what date the governor returns to Aden and for how long he intends to be at the new residence; for three days next month after flying into Khormaksar. We have his itinerary; we have a chance, Ben.'

'Where's his des res, this fortified palace?'

'In the government complex at R'as Marshag.'

'That clifftop promontory off the main Aden peninsula, where the East Germans kept their little interrogation block?'

A nod from Badr. 'Shit,' Howell replied flatly. Overlooked by Aidrus Hill, and jutting into Fisherman's Bay – where fishing boats were not welcome – it was one of the most heavily defended sites in Aden.

Purton made himself more comfortable. 'Ahmed, I'm all for seizing the initiative, but a high-level assassination is going to cause reprisals, provoke a counter-attack. Your agents in place might get burned.'

'There is a risk of reprisals at any stage of a conflict. The governor conducts them for no reason already. It cannot get worse.'

'That's what the Czech partisans thought when they murdered Heydrich,' Howell interjected.

'I want to think some more on it, Ahmed. And I want you to pass on my deep reservations.'

An apologetic smile. 'The National Opposition Front has

many factions. There's a lot of pressure to act.'

Howell scuffed a stone away distractedly with his foot. 'Hadn't noticed.'

Effusive thanks and farewells. As Badr trotted to his vehicle, bodyguards falling into position to the side, the NCO cupped his chin and watched.

'Christ, Ben. Thought you said there wouldn't be political interference.'

'Conflict's a political act. Unavoidable.'

'The proposal. What do you think?'

'Most positive thing I've heard in twenty-four hours. You?'

'Need the exercise. Might take a few of these schoolgirls along. A field-study outing should broaden their minds.'

'Or get them killed. I want minimum baggage on this one, and I'm thinking seaborne.' Cross-country to Aden held too many hazards; too many hostiles; too many unknowns. 'Ahmed knows a guy with a safe house who can wave us in.'

'Haven't the Yemenis centred their naval forces on the harbour?'

'It's why they won't expect a naval assault.'

'Just so long as we don't share the planning with Badr's mob. Another wet?' Howell offered more tea. 'Think you're right, though. Apart from Palestinian ops against Israel, the towels don't major in beach landings.'

'Or going to sea at night. A three-day window. It's going to be tight.'

'The best things in life . . .' Howell let it trail off. He was pondering that afternoon's training session.

The best things. Purton thought of the family which had left him. Civil war – some substitute.

'I'm telling you, Dmitri. With decent pathology, they might have discovered years ago how Napoleon was murdered.'

'Who cares?' Kokhlov's assistant responded unenthusiastically. 'After all the Russians he killed, I only hope it was painful.' He still bore a grudge over the distant ancestor he believed had fallen with forty-four thousand countrymen during the Battle of Borodino in August 1812.

The duo were alone together in the post-mortem room, Kokhlov dissecting out infarct from a ventricular septum, its original owner lying, face up and covered, on the nearby table. It was a late arrival, the last corpse of the day, and the chief pathologist was eager to ease the backlog stacking up in the preparation-room lockers. His evidence had grown, circumstantial yet compelling, of FSB involvement in a string of deaths throughout Siberia. He had asked fellow-professionals to submit their findings, promised favours in return, the use of Krasnoyarsk's impressive forensic facilities as a chance to improve their clear-up rates. The data was extraordinary: the same bites found on bodies five hundred miles apart, but two different local men accused, hurriedly sentenced and shot, their dental impressions unavailable; marks on cadavers which appeared to lack the random savagery of the dedicated serial killer and serial drunk on whom they were blamed; lesions that could only have been applied after death or as an afterthought; torn fingernails on a victim who fought, but neither were skin samples taken from beneath them nor scratch marks found on the accused. He instead showed heavy bruising to his face and welts on his back, consistent with a police beating. A confession was obtained. Strange too the spate of ritualistic killings in which young wives were murdered and cut up – their belongings either inserted or arranged symmetrically – but with no sign of the attacker's semen or excrement on the victims: the calling-card of most alienated, frustrated, psychotic sexual inadequates. There were deaths in Udachny – there always were – the giant diamond mine close to the Arctic Circle, where temperatures fell to minus seventy degrees centigrade, men remained unpaid for months, and stress was relieved through fights and bouts of manic drinking. An unusually high mortality rate for the previous winter – five foremen had their throats slit and faces mutilated. A rumour spread, its provenance unknown and unquestioned, that responsibility lay with an Uzbech, recently arrived, who did not know the deceased. He was thrown down a shaft. Case closed. For Kokhlov it remained open – facial disfiguration was a favored pastime of those who knew their targets well. Profiles did not fit. The deaths and their subsequent, half-hearted investigation, the former benefiting from greater attention to detail than the latter, haunted him. Surely, the wrong emphasis, the homicides professional, the inquests cursory? Surely an explosion of violent criminality way beyond that expected in even the most heavily overcrowded urban areas? There were blues, winter blues, and there was this. And always State Security intruding where it had no immediate right or interest to intrude, fleeting, cold. The foremen at Udachny were replaced by faceless, traceless entities. But one of the newcomers had been identified, was believed to be the son of a man once employed as manager of a Yakutian mine operated by the NKVD, Stalin's secret police, fore-runner to the KGB. Memories preserved in ice, memories of an Empire, the Terror, recognition of its agents. The republic of Sakha numbered fewer than one million citizens. It was being infiltrated by officers from the police state.

Kokhlov worried. The information was sealed, complaints muted among those on whom the papers were hidden. Discretion was a key advantage of the dead. He found diversions, drank more, barred himself into his undersized apartment at night.

Dmitri was tying the ends of a garbage sack, ready for the evening cleaners. It was a race between them and the rats. Pyjamas poked from the top of the bag.

'So, how did the Corsican dwarf meet his end?'

Parallel thought processes reverted to one. 'I thought you didn't care?'

'I was being flippant, Ilya. Every day I get something life-enhancing from you.' There were few serious contenders in a mortuary.

'And sarcasm you got from your mother. Along with the pox.' He frowned down at his handiwork while Dmitri busied himself with a collection of bottles. 'Very well. It was extremely subtle, so will be lost on you. Guess the cause of death?'

'Stomach cancer. It's in the history books.'

'Try again. He died fat, and there were no symptoms of cancer.'

'I need clues.'

'Name me a poison that's almost impossible to detect unless you're looking for it, is odourless, colourless and tasteless, and produces over thirty different symptoms.'

'Arsenic.'

'The American FBI tested hair samples shaved from Napoleon's head on 6 May 1821, the day after he croaked on the island of St Helena. They found irrefutable evidence of long-term arsenical intoxication. At least six months' worth.'

'Americans always exaggerate.'

'Eye-witnesses to his decline weren't American, Dmitri.' Kokhlov straightened and placed the scalpel in the tray. 'And they mention most of those arsenic symptoms in their accounts. Stomach cramps, constipation, vomiting, terrible thirst, a burning feeling throughout the body, complete loss of hair . . .'

'The man was a wreck.'

'Of course he was. He was slowly poisoned to make it look like natural deterioration, otherwise the French army who remained loyal to him would have revolted against their royalist rulers. At times, the poor sod had fifty-one parts per million of arsenic showing up in his hair.' A whistle from Dmitri. 'And that was just part one.'

'Fuck. There was more?'

'Warm up over, Napoleon sickening, and still two months before his death, the terminal phase. And he was given it as medication.'

'Never trust doctors. That's why people like him,' the assistant wandered round and jerked a thumb at the cadaver. 'End up with people like us.'

Kokhlov was in lecture mode. 'Three compounds they fed Napoleon, all apparently aimed at curing him, all

333

designed to have precisely the reverse effect. It's there in the diaries of his doctors. Tartar emetic – antimony potassium tartrate – to induce vomiting and expel the body's illnesses. Also happens to dissolve the mucous lining of the stomach and makes it harder to vomit later on. Highly toxic, weakened him even further, and made it easier for the final poisons to stay in his body.'

'You scare me, Ilya. Now I realise why you were exiled.'

'Listen, you'll learn. Then they gave him a mix of orgeat to slake his appalling thirst – the arsenic symptom. It was an orange juice with oil from bitter almonds or peach stones in it.'

'Prussic acid?'

'The best. Hydro-cyanic, with sodium and potassium salts. Wonderful stuff: 7.5 cc is all it takes to kill. So they were careful with the dose. That was the thirst dealt with. And they also prescribed a substance known as calomel for his constipation. Unfortunately for Bonaparte it contained mercury chloride and he received up to forty times the normal dose.'

Dmitri shook his head. 'Killed for want of a crap,' he murmured.

'Worthy of the Chekist bastards at the Lubyanka. Hydro-cyanic acid and mercury chloride combine to produce?'

'Mercury cyanide. Creates a huge annular swelling of the pylorus muscle. Fatal.'

Hands thrown up triumphantly. 'The biggest stomach upset in history. Paralysis, unconsciousness and death follow. Ilya Kokhlov and his star assistant Dmitri solve the mystery of Napoleon Bonaparte's murder. There you have it, a political assassination. What do you think?'

'You need more friends. Can I go home?'

'Of course, you fucking ingrate. We have a busy day tomorrow. I'll finish up here.'

The body was returned to its short-stay refrigeration, the autopsy room silent. Kokhlov wrote carefully onto a label, peeling it off and smoothing it onto the side of a jar containing an organ section. Within his chaotic exterior, he was an organised man, proud of his system, fanatical about his subject, bemused at the jocular disrespect shown by friends for the profession. He would show them, demonstrate to Georgi Lazin how useful he could be, that he was a pathologist through choice, not a failed surgeon distrusted and relegated to patients who were already deceased.

It was a presence, unseen, which made him turn. The glass of the observation level threw back the light, darkness behind. It sat over him, blank and watching. He laughed to himself. Proximity to bodies could turn the mind, make one jumpy. There was no room for superstition in this business. Scalpel blade detached from the shaft, he dropped it into the safety container. A quick check around, a change of footwear, scrub-up, and he would leave for a night compressed by vodka and television. The connecting door moved: it was always left unlocked for the late-night team to sluice and disinfect the premises for the following morning. Odour seeped into the walls, impregnated the place with the same permanency as the stains, but they did their best. Today had produced quite an overflow. He was pleased with the productivity; the aprons, waiting to be doused, were racked like pig carcasses, smeared with indications of the labour.

The man stood in the doorway, his face unfamiliar, frame filling the frame. Kokhlov was motionless. A noise behind; locked with inaction, he did not respond. It was hopeless. His nervous system reflected the hopelessness, reflected the lack of movement in his opponent. Silence again. And then the flicker of a strip-light, lightning marking out a shadow figure against the pane of the observation room. He knew it was Petr Ivanov. The intercom cut in harshly.

'A touching concern for the Butcher of Moscow. You always were a traitor.'

'Who is the butcher? Who is the traitor?' The response was raw, enhanced in his ears by fear, his own voice unrecognisable.

'I am sorry to intrude in your place of work. I assumed

you would feel more comfortable here.' And there were three slabs from which to choose. The power caught and held, Ivanov lit ethereally, voice distanced by amplification. 'Your assistant failed to ask the most salient question – *why* did the French Emperor have to die? There has to be a reason. Without it, the life taken is worthless, has no meaning. But he does not have your enquiring mind, does he?'

It did not elicit an answer, was not designed to. The face – white against Kokhlov's grey – tilted upwards, appraising the quarry. The pathologist's arms were seized from behind, the man to his front stepping in and delivering a sharp blow to the stomach. Kokhlov went to fold, but was held upright, the shock travelling downwards to buckle his legs.

Petr Ivanov was talking, still artificial through the barrier. Communicating with a prisoner. 'Do you want your life to have been pointless, Ilya? Your death to be painful? You have two options – quick or slow – and time is a precious commodity. Think, Ilya. We will begin operating shortly. Where are the lies, the details you received from your pathology contacts? Are you working with Colonel Lazin?'

You have killed me, Georgi. For nothing, for a few notes which I could have shredded, for a sense of purpose which I did not need. For a friendship. And where are you now, Georgi? Remember me, Georgi.

'I will never cooperate. Never. You hear? Never. Never.' He was shouting, panicking, each fuelling the other. Let them concentrate on his body, avoid those in storage.

'A challenge. You know how to humour me. I ask again. Where is the information you have gathered?'

'I don't know.'

'Then we will search everything, find everything. Lazin has deserted you; he is under arrest. He has agreed to tell us about your activities. Where do you store your reference material?'

'In my head.'

'And that is where we will first look. Lay him out.'

The index finger tripped off the intercom switch and

Ivanov crossed to the door, repeating the process with the gallery lights. Below, in theatre glare, Ilya Kokhlov was being manhandled and strapped across his own autopsy table. Through the glass, vibrating and dulled by its thickness, the words *Never . . . never . . . never . . .* reached him. A great optimist, Ilya Kokhlov. The Colonel took another glance before leaving to join his actors on stage.

'Have you considered what I had to say?' He spoke from the doorway.

'You have no place here, Ivanov.' Kokhlov was bound. 'You have no place in Russia, in a civilised world.'

'Nor you. But I fear you will leave it faster, and at my discretion. As will Lazin.'

'What have you done to Georgi?' It was a trap, he understood, would test his vulnerability. Yet he wanted news, wished to talk, to summon anything of existence from beyond these weeping concrete walls. 'What have you done?'

'I think you'll find it worthy of the Chekist bastards at the Lubyanka you referred to. But, to concentrate on matters that concern you more.' An order to the men standing around the pathologist. 'Fill him up.' The nose was held, mouth opening reflexively, funnel inserted, the contents of a bottle poured. Ivanov walked slowly from his position at the doorway.

'No . . .' The fight for air. Spluttering.

Surgical spirit flowed, spilling out, gagged upwards and back over the rim.

'This is, I'm afraid, only part one.'

'No . . . ' The fight for life. More spluttering.

The FSB officer picked up the circular bandsaw from its cradle at the head of the adjoining table, checked its electrical attachment, and approached. The drive motor activated. 'Now – like Napoleon Bonaparte – the terminal phase.' It would not take two months.

Liquid choking. 'Dmitri . . . ' The voice bubbled off.

'Has left the building. You were right when you told him you'd finish up here.'

The premonition. Yet he was looking up, not at himself but at a Colonel of the Security Service. Ivanov moved in. Life moved in. He detected motion, a spinning, disc-shaped blur; his ears heard the lower-octave whine of saw teeth which had yet to connect. *There you have it, a political assassination. There you have it.* The alcohol rose from his throat to fill his nostrils, brain marinating. The walls were crying for him, faces wet with tears. He closed his eyes, willing anaesthesia, numbness. But reality and the present stayed. He would never talk. *There you have it.* Ivanov stared down, applied greater pressure to the trigger. Kokhlov would talk.

CHAPTER 6

T he Russian novelist Michael Prishvin, acute observer of his beloved native countryside, wrote of the several stages of spring: first, there was the 'spring of light', when the skies cleared and days grew bright and calm; then the 'spring of water', the ice breaking, snow melting and rivers running fast; next, the 'spring of grass' with its fresh, verdant cheer and the filling out of trees. Finally, there would be the 'spring of flowers'. It had not yet been reached, and, in the Moscow docks, never would. The season had stalled with the grass, the cyclical 'green noise', but the sound here in the back section of the deserted wharf was more disturbing, insistent on the human ear. It had resembled hail, an upwards, unrhythmical clatter from within, revealed as the batting of flies emerging from gorged pupae and expending their meat-derived energy on the task of escaping against corrugated iron.

The militia investigator, a haggard-faced wreck from the six-storey police headquarters complex on Petrovka Street, chain-smoked fretfully, nicotine tingeing the bile smell on his breath. Lazin sympathised. It could not have been easy; in the circumstances, anyone would have doubled over, spilled his breakfast. But it kept the man focused, away from the sparring which habitually marred joint operations. Make them heave, and cooperation was assured. A useful lesson. The FSB were here as observers, to record and report, to keep abreast of mafiya troubles. In this case, demarcation barely mattered. Delegation was what the policeman wanted, his answer to avoiding another foray into the heated ripening sheds tucked beside an intestine loop of the river Moskva. The youngsters he sent in, forensics, fumigators, cleansers, shovellers, came out retching behind their protective masks. Activated charcoal suits, respirators – the technology of nuclear, biological and chemical warfare – offered scant protection for the psyche when confronted with the horrors of human fermentation.

Plastic-lined tents, negative-pressurised, abutted the buildings, erected for the task of analysing and categorising the dead. Drab functionality excluded emotion, suggested order where man-made rules had broken down. Inside, pathologists were busy, Lazin's thoughts penetrating the fabric walls, peering over their shoulders at the decay, wondering at the pain behind the lipless grins, the horrors affixing wasted limbs in foetal displays of self-protection. An assistant emerged for a cigarette, smoke resuscitation, face drawn tight by life fatigue. Epic barbarity evoked many responses; predominant was exhaustion. Lazin felt it too, the weariness of lost nights in his parallel world, reporting to his parallel, unidentified chief, working to Deep Throat's orders, making forays to new territory, into new files, constructing a strategy. And his strategy was to survive. His Director, Gresko, might have other plans. The assistant leant on a frame support, savoured the tobacco, reluctant to release his grip and return through the flap. Colour had fled from him, from the location, everyone moved in depressed monotonal grey. Today's Russia.

The Investigator waggled the hip flask. Lazin shook his head.

'I'm on duty.'

'The best reason of all,' the organised crime man replied, draining the contents in a prolonged still-life pose. Eyes opened, throat guttering shut, head returned to balance.

Lazin was remembering Ilya Kokhlov, his friend, the mad and maddening soulmate, eccentric ally, the liberal refugee exiled to Krasnoyarsk. Killed on his own pathology slab, cut to pieces, that intelligent hairless head split with a circular saw. For what? He was happiest as the outsider, a jester with a new court away from Moscow, far from the past and its elements he feared. Elements like Colonel Petr Ivanov. But they caught him, disposed of him. He had been doing a favour, prying for his demanding ex-colleague Georgi Lazin, complaining with the joyful vehemence reserved only for trusted confidants, when they detected, decided, dissected. *They*. And it was Lazin who was to blame, who should have died. *I ought to have left him; I broke him; I am responsible.* He must have discovered. One man gets pulled back from his enquiries into a train robbery, the other gets strapped down and de-boned in a mortuary room. The FSB officer breathed deep, eyes dwelling on the tent outlines. Imagination drew the smell of death up his nostrils. Perhaps it was not imagination. The interim post-mortems were underway, the technicians performing routines which Kokhlov could do, did do, blindfold. There, in Siberia, an aggravated homicide, perpetrator doubtless an employee of state security; here, in Moscow, multiple aggravated homicides, victims and perpetrators apparently linked to underworld blood-feuds. Savagery and lack of meaning: his fraternity and the criminal fraternity. The differences had blurred long ago. He should have accepted the hip-flask.

The Investigator was speaking, possibly had been for minutes. '. . . I never want to see that again, not in my life. Looked like a brain, a giant, pulsating brain grown too big for its head. It was just a ball of screw worms, thousands of them.'

And the man on whom they were feeding, like the rest, was alive when they started. Warmed by infrared lamps, the female screw worm flies sought out cuts and abrasions in which to lay their eggs. Their warm-blooded hosts were incubators, receptacles for the precious load, and once hatched, the larvae ate voraciously, burrowing deep into the flesh. They reached maturity within a week, the one-and-a-half centimetre maggots dropping from their bore-holes, body orifices and urinary-excretory passageways to pupate on the ground for the three-day transition into adult screwfly.

Their life cycle lasted three weeks, during which they would lay more eggs, breed more carnivorous offspring. Fifteen corpses were scooped from that building, fifteen nests placed at different times, once breathing, sustained with fluids, who had been conscious of their roles for at least a week prior to oblivion.

The conversation, already one-sided, waned. Lazin did not feel much like talking, concentrated instead on calming his stomach. An entomologist approached from a side door, besuited in wrinkled rubber – condom coral – beard straggling in pubic replication above the paper face mask.

'Hold out your hand, please.'

Lazin responded, palm upfacing. They assumed authority lay with those in civilian clothing. The tweezers relaxed. A maggot fell, balled, and straightened out on contact.

'I've seen enough of those things inside. Do you have to take them for a walk as well?' the militia investigator asked, backing off. There was a wide discrepancy between the specialist's enthusiasm and his own.

'Found in the section where the last two cadavers were quarantined from the rest.' The men were discovered, without their eyes or genitals, pinned out in excrement on a sand-strewn floor, their sinuses a teeming feeding channel to empty head cavities. Close by was the discarded box of a miniature cassette tape. Interrogation had been prolonged. Fly expert beamed at the sightless organism. 'In every one, an insect waiting to escape.'

'In every sodding human, from what I saw in there.' The Investigator was massaging his forehead, fumbling for his cigarettes. Lazin wondered how much, what, the larva specimen had consumed.

'And?' he asked. The grub somersaulted, twitching to get out of itself. A natural Houdini.

The mask was pulled down. 'The Congo floor maggot. Amazing little creature. Blowfly plants her eggs in the ground, larvae lie up during the day and come out to feed at night.'

342

'I suppose that's a clue?' Lazin indicated the tent.

'They home in on carbon-dioxide, so they're drawn by human breath.' Visible excitement. 'Fussy eaters. Partial to the soft bits, mucous membrane: eyes, inside of nose and mouth. Suck the blood out.'

The investigator lurched off. Lazin felt the tense, erratic movements of the maggot. It was heading for the darkness of his cuff. He re-directed it. It returned. 'Can we assume the victims survived long enough?'

'Of course. The floor maggot only needs to feed twice a week, maximum.' The entomologist remained oblivious to the effect his words were having. 'Whoever arranged this knows his species, understands how to smuggle and breed the types.'

And would need the resources. These were mafiya hits, of that the FSB Colonel was certain; this was Diakanov territory. He supplied the demand by the country's new rich for exotic wildlife from overseas. If he could transport elephants in-country, insects posed little challenge.

A corpse, plastic-wrapped, was carried out to an armoured GAZ ambulance of the Interior Ministry and slid lightly into the back. The litter contained the mortal remains of a thug paid to bludgeon to death a gangland administrator named Konon at the Kosmos Hotel in north-east Moscow.

'About a week to go and that will be an adult fly,' the insect researcher added, attention returning to the larva flicking aimlessly on Lazin's hand. A week until its evolution to an egg-laying grotesque in browns and black.

Lazin squeezed. It burst, jettisoning blood down his fingers. He never liked experts. 'The best predictions don't factor in chance.'

He would be taking one himself. For these deaths, the unimaginable scenes, provided an excuse to visit Boris Diakanov.

The hills were lost in the night, the eye drawn to the foreshore, to the misted illumination cast by docks and fuel terminals operating a twenty-four-hour shift. Out here, the glare, the activity, was only a hint, a small brightening on its particular patch of the horizon, nothing more. But the team leaders knew where they were heading, cruising at antennae depth, maintaining sweep formation, watching the global positioning updates, listening for active sonar. Their men on the *Protoy* underwater chariots sat huddled behind, passengers on the electric vessels, swathed in wetsuits, masks and closed-cycle breathing apparatus, carried at ten knots without a bubble trail or wake. No need for fins – climbing, not swimming, was tonight's requirement. They had launched earlier from Black Sea cutters operated by the border troops, the hand-picked units answering direct to Leonid Gresko, loyalty assured by higher wages, nationalist tendencies and counter-espionage agents planted by the Federal Security Service within their ranks. Commands were unwritten and unquestioned. The combatives owed their livelihood and future to following orders. On the flanks, snub-nosed, stub-winged *Triton* midget subs shepherded the group forwards, pathfinders, corallers, their two-man crews guarding against interference.

'Twenty minutes to target. Passive sensors show negative detection or tracking. Complete all checks. Time synchro in ten.' The intercom switched off.

In their open compartments, astride the aquadynamic shape of the torpedo-like hulls, and segregated by bulkheads acting as back rests and body protectors, men moved methodically through their pre-attack routines. Hands slipped down to killing-knives strapped to calves, secured access devices more tightly, smoothed equipment pouches buffeted from position by water pressure. Mouths were dry behind the respirators, teeth masticating on rubber to encourage saliva and ease the nerves. Transported to destiny – at this point there was always an urge to release the grip, to float away and down, to stay free and alone in the darkness. A missile hovercraft had earlier hummed thunderously over their heads, a giant mouth skidding above them, too occupied to snap shut, heading off to challenge the Turks on its territorial boundaries. Downwash and panic receded together. Solitude. Not for long. They felt a subtle change in the propulsors beneath them, gentle vibration as the tactical turn-in began. Scrutinise weapons: each man carried a 5.66 mm APS underwater assault rifle, capable of killing both above and below the waterline. At five metres depth, its heavy specialised bullet, twelve centimetres long, stored in a twenty-six round magazine, could take out an opponent at thirty metres. Forty metres down, effective range fell to ten. Enough to scare off most sharks or divers. In air, it was highly accurate to a hundred metres. Strapped to belts were 4.5 mm calibre SPP-1M underwater pistols, loaded with four-round clips of ammunition, which, like the APS, could also be fired from below the water at land-based targets, or from land into water. Submerged defenders were at risk from the gun out to seventeen metres. The balance of power lay with the invaders.

'Look to viewfinders.' The commander's voice was abrupt, strained with concentration and controlled adrenalin.

Faces leant into cushioned panel surrounds to receive intensified images projected from miniature periscopes penetrating the surface. Acclimatisation, situational aware-ness. Framed in the scanning lens, brought artificially close, made shockingly immediate to sense-deprived brains and eyes attuned to blind murk, was the target. Nvovorossiysk. Russia's most important conduit for the export of oil to international markets, the port was an immense complex of pipes, ducting, storage tanks, and pump and generator units, decorated in the white festivity of several thousand arc-lights. It deserved celebration, was the hub of Russia's precarious economic survival in the harsh competitive reality of a post-Communist world in which domestic demand for indigen-ously manufactured products slumped and overseas demand never materialised. Force-fed for too long on Soviet designs and Soviet quality, the Russians had developed an allergy to their own goods. Consumers abroad shared their antipathy.

Oil was safe, oil was needed. This was its manifestation.

'Warhead activated.' The limpet charge, a tandem-explosive capable of tearing with ease through double-hulls, screw shafts, ballast and storage sections, was armed. Abreast, five other chariot leaders replicated the procedure.

'Starting the run. Passing boom defences.'

Sheltered, deep, circled by hills, the bay offered natural protection to ships, both civil and naval. Such intrinsic advantage made it an immediate choice for the redeployment of Russia's share of the Black Sea fleet after repeated rows with neighbouring Ukraine – new owners of its traditional bases – ensured trans-border residency was untenable. Building work was frantic, basic defences were cannibalised and transferred from the oil port, and warships were rotated through before full facilities for surface combatants were available. Strategic necessity was the driver, haste and lack of preparation the result. Among the construction workers, services and control engineers, dockers and stevedores crowding the bars, jostling for employ on the waterfront, were Gresko's men. They were merging with the rest, waiting.

'Stand by.'

The raiding craft fanned out towards the three tankers, two to a ship, the attack leader aiming for an aviation fuel carrier berthed in a loading station away from the main fuelling points. Pumping had been completed that evening, the vessel destined to sail with the dawn, carrying its highly explosive liquid cargo westwards to supply the pride of the Black Sea navy. Anything to avoid reliance upon the untrustworthy Ukrainians. The second tanker, large, conventional, was stationed ready to receive crude, its containers vented, inflammable vapours flushed, emptied for the thirty-hour process. But oil was tricky to ignite to a critical level, harder to explode. Intelligence files from the late 1980s showed numerous examples of laden tankers hit by swarms of Iranian-released Exocet anti-ship missiles; yet even with decks buckled from the heat, steel castles melting, detonations failed to occur. Loading was different. As the tank filled with hydrocarbons, gas spread into the empty spaces; a spark could catch, setting off the chain explosions. And the incoming groups planned to generate more than a spark. The third tanker, over a thousand feet in length, stood outside the port, fully laden and low in the water. It too was waiting for sailing orders. There were other marine vessels in harbour, but they were ignored, their roles enshrined as bit-players trapped by the fire ships, consumed by and feeding a tidal flame that would lap and scorch the surrounding peaks.

The *Protoy* edged bow-forward, collided softly with the tanker hull and released into place its mine appendage. The move had been rehearsed many times in training.

'Warhead attached. Go.'

Figures disconnected from their breathing equipment, slipped from seats and rose gently to break through into a strange night-laden, air-breathing plane from which they had sunk some three hours previously. On the right hand and left knee of each point man were climbing magnets, used by Special Forces for clandestine access and assault of vertical steel structures. Contact was made, the mollusc-like crawl began. Anchor chains, traditional ingress routes, would be avoided. Below, the specialists waited, floating on the gas-filled buoyancy linings inflated around their torsos, nylon ropes linking them umbilically to the furtive mother craft kept in position by automatic manoeuvre systems and lying quiet beneath the water.

On the road south from Krasnodar, above the port, Colonel Petr Ivanov of the FSB stood beside the command truck, Nvovorossiysk spread out, an ocean speckled by street and house lamps. Plankton, that was man. Inside the communications compartment, FAPSI operatives monitored radio traffic and emergency channels. So far, there had been no alert, no discovery or the hurried movement of small boats rushing in patternless search patterns; the mission was on schedule. He glanced at the luminous dial of his watch. The cab door swung, a uniformed officer jumping down to report.

'Delivery should be taking place, Colonel.'

Ivanov swung his head. 'I am aware of the programme, Captain.'

The man wilted. He was uncomfortable, nervous, in such company. This representative from Moscow, Gresko's chosen, had a reputation, brought menace. It was enough to make anyone fearful, to induce guilt and terror, the clumsiness in speech and action of those over-compensating for insecurity. He backed away, apologetic.

'I . . . I am sorry, Colonel.' The voice stuttered, but found sufficient momentum to finish.

'Is the signal equipment ready?'

'Yes, Colonel. If you wish . . .'

'We will rehearse the sequences in an hour. Keep me informed.'

'Yes, Colonel.' The officer saluted and retreated to the cab interior, feeling vulnerable, his psyche stripped by the colourless eyes and tone. Ivanov was a night crow, carrion, a visage as motionless and white-bleached as the bones over which it picked.

The ascents were made, point men rolling onto the decks and dropping weighted lines to haul up the ladders. Slick, rapid, the rungs mounted and unfolded, were fixed into place. Three pulls. Rubber-sealed commandos clambered up behind, small-arms holstered for easy reach. They were not expecting opposition. Automation, by its very nature, entailed undermanning on modern tankers. Port calls, by their very nature, also entailed undermanning: by seamen intending to take on liquid and to release body fluid. Crouching runs to the access hatches, the donning of emergency breathing masks and disappearance into the tanks, port and starboard, as assault weapons – suppressed and scoped – were brought to shoulders by those remaining outside. Five minutes. Across the water, similar activity was taking place.

They were away, the chariots, full complements aboard and free of their mines, gliding noiselessly out past Russia's territorial limits. It had been flawless. A long return journey, scare-free, *Tritons* in attendance. The low-light optics picked out the surface ships, the hull panels opening, the welcoming rattle given louder cadence by the water. These were multipurpose cutters – in Soviet days purpose was often vague, ever dubious, stated roles a cover for unstated capabilities – one aspect of which included the dropping of seabed mines, listening devices and *Spetsnaz* forces near foreign shores. Designed to probe the enemy's flanks, to take the fight to new areas, tonight they took it to their own coast. The flotilla included a fleet intelligence-gatherer, *Primorye*-class, cruising five miles off, keeping watch for electronic emissions, its aerials, bipolar scanners and direction-finders tuned to its nation's military and radar frequencies. Lined up, the chariots nudged into the recovery wells, securing lines were tied and the submersibles hoisted. Vodka, coffee and claps on the back were ready for their crews. A salvage and rescue ship hoisted the *Tritons*.

The moment. It was indicated by the watch face, demonstrated by the filling operations on the main deck of the crude tanker. And it was implicit in the ball-dropping, heart-stopping explosions which erupted on the water, tearing open three hulls, the blows resonating off the high ground.

'Now.'

Ivanov spoke without turning to face the officer. Unmoving, he had maintained his position for several hours. The order was given, a sequence of master switches thrown on a control panel in the rear compartment, the coded signal sent. It would be received by devices hidden in the ships' tanks and among the more vital corners of the terminal. Five minutes to incineration. Ivanov climbed into the cab, staring ahead as the engine caught. Men were racing for hoses and foam guns, rescue tugs press-ganging the drunk and available while power plants churned into life. The only life. There would be little to rescue. Two minutes. Sound was muffled by the incline. Point zero. The windscreen reflected green, atmospheric moisture playing refractive games, world turning the emerald tint of the Tsarina's cross in his pocket. This was his trophy, the *aurora borealis* moving south. It went blue, bordered by electric thunder, expanding, glimmering, taking over the sky. From afar, the patch of brightness above the port had swollen into an aura, no longer a hint, but a statement, reaching out to the sea, consuming the clouds and the water, burning out heaven. The windscreen shook; a roaring force whipped at the sides; the truck left the storm behind.

'We're ready.'

Howell beckoned them round. Aden lay at his feet, represented in sand, the model fashioned with a planner's eye into peaks and valleys, roads and beaches, the litter of a military camp applied in furnishing detail and three-dimensioned authenticity. Numbers were added to correspond with those featured on the ordnance survey.

'I'm impressed, Nick.' Ahmed Badr folded his hands and gazed approvingly.

'Wait till you've heard the plan,' Purton advised, moving in beside the Arab. 'Okay, Nick, take us through it.'

They had spent a month preparing for the attack while continuing to train and assess the core instructor group of covert-ops guerrillas. In that time, fresh intelligence from National Opposition Front sources in the capital Sana'a filtered down, indicating that the Aden governor was intending to spend only one night at his new fortress residence in the government complex of R'as Marshag off the main peninsula. Logic may have dictated postponement, but politics held sway, the assassination took priority.

The NCO opened out a discarded radio aerial for use as a pointer. 'Right, Ahmed. We've discussed the position and strength of the north's occupying forces.' He swiftly summarised. There was an armoured brigade and ground-attack aircraft at Ataq; an infantry brigade present at Mukhalla with detached battalions in Sayun and Bir Ali; fighters, helicopters and transport aircraft at Riyan airbase; a further infantry brigade with helicopters at Al-Ghaydor, and a battalion stationed in the Marib to guard the oil installations. Formidable, at least on paper.

Howell's lecture instrument swept over the downscaled landscape. 'Of course, the nastiest buggers of all, the Al-Amaliqa brigade, are here in Aden. So we intend to get in and out without ever having to meet them. As you know, the southern part of the Aden peninsula,' a pause as the aerial swept down to pick out prominent features, 'is steeply mountainous and largely deserted. The shoreline is made up of a series of high-sided bays and inlets bounded by a lighthouse on the Elephant Back to the west, here, and our target zone, Ra's Marshag – the government complex – here to the east.' He tapped the two strategically placed ration cans. Ahmed Badr nodded as Howell continued. 'The highest point at 553 metres is Jabal Shamsan South. Note the narrow ridge running roughly parallel to the sea to point 474. From here it slopes down sharply to Fisherman's Bay, to the 244-metre-high Aidrus Hill and to Crater town adjoining the government complex. Ben remembers a steep re-entrant running down from 474 here just east of R'as Antuk.'

'It's our first choice as a landing point,' Purton came in.

'And if that's impossible, we'll go wide to this small bay west of Ra's Antuk. There's a wide break in the cliffs.'

'It looks a difficult climb,' Badr observed.

'Hopefully too difficult for the enemy. A thousand metres' distance up to point 474, broken ground, numerous streams, and we'll be heaving packs. Nothing a Marine can't handle.'

Purton produced string and laid pieces out on the incline. 'We've done some rope-training with the four volunteers. Could come in useful for the escape descent.'

'What about naval patrols?' Badr scratched his head. 'The dhow and its Ribs will be vulnerable to interception anywhere from Crater and Khormaksar and out to the north-east. Approaches to Aden are regularly swept, and there are two high-speed military inflatables kept on alert in Holkat Bay.'

'That's what the two pebbles represent, Ahmed.' Howell stepped on them, pushing the stones beneath the dirt.

Purton explained the tactics. 'We've got surprise, fire-power, a large sea to vanish into, emergency lying-up positions along the coast to the east, and another safe house in Mukhalla if we need it. Our two Ribs should be able to outrun most things. They're each adapted to carry a hundred gallons of fuel with the special aft tanks, which gives us four hundred miles. If the dhow is approached early in the journey, it's just another trading vessel on its way to Eritrea.'

'Full of staple products, useful things to barter: mines, plastic – of the explosive variety – ammo belts, and sundry items banned by the United Nations. It'll do good business.'

'Where is the attack to take place?' the Yemeni asked. A success was vital for his military standing within the Front. Howell and Purton felt the tension in him, contained, suppressed beneath the cordiality and enthusiasm. He was an old friend. They were expected to deliver, would do their best. It was understood the details would not travel beyond the three of them.

Howell prodded at the model. 'You see where the high ground acts as a natural barrier to the expansion of Crater town?'

'Yes.'

'There's a section of flat ground surrounded by old fortifications and a single fence defending this narrow stretch linking the government complex and Crater town.'

'I've seen the road running between them.'

'Then you'll also have seen that it bends sharply here, with a footpath running down from Aidrus Hill. The contact in Crater town confirms that it's patrolled, but not at night. So, we go down, work our magic, and wait for sicko Ibrahim Abd al-Aziz to crawl past in his sadly under-armoured Mercedes. Voila. X marks the spot.' He sabre-stroked the cross into the earth.

They went through the timings. Moving down from the Omani coastal town of Rayzut on the afternoon of D minus 5, the dhow would cross into coastal waters before picking the team up from the pro-opposition fishing village of Al

Fatk and sailing at twelve knots towards the drop-off point some 680 miles distant. Here, fifty miles east of Aden, the two loaded Ribs would be launched to make land during the night of D-3. Ahmed Badr's contact in Crater town was to be the sole member of the reception, bringing in the seaborne party and sending them on the hard climb up to their observation and lying up positions on Point 474 at the eastern end of the Jabal Shamsan. Uncomfortable certainly – cover was to be provided by camouflage netting and clefts in the rock, rations were equally sparse – but unrivalled views east over Aidrus Hill and the government buildings on the Ra's Marshag promontory were sufficient compensation. The following day, D-2, would be spent surveying the ground beneath them and around the target area, the night taken up with moving to a forward LUP and conducting close target reconnaissance. A number of fallback attack profiles could be rehearsed and rejected at this stage, and the principal option tested: a stand-off roadside bomb. The day prior to the governor's appearance, D-1, was for intensive observation of the target site and the route into it, before the team slipped back in to plant the devices, cover their handiwork and confirm procedures for planned and emergency withdrawals. Howell and his pair of Yemeni volunteers would remain in the forward observation post to initiate the D-Day explosion, Purton taking his team back to Point 474 ready to fix ropes and secure the landing point for departure.

Smiling broadly, the Yemeni guerrilla commander clapped. 'It is perfection.'

'The governor might not share your attitude.'

'What does it matter? He will be dead.' He turned to Howell. 'You have all the equipment you need?'

'I'm testing the laser. Seems to check out,' the NCO answered. Generally, he preferred to function at the black masking tape end of the technical spectrum, but the situation demanded something different. 'We need accuracy if we're going to reconstitute the governor.'

Simple mathematics. If the limousine were travelling at

thirty miles per hour, its rear passenger door would pass the point of explosion in about one tenth of a second; ten miles per hour, and the average car would be clear within a second. Ample scope for human error, for a bomber to mistime his attack while using a remote-control and manual trigger. Roadside detonations were notoriously inaccurate; many officials, bankers and businessmen owed their lives to the fact. The laser trigger modified the odds.

Purton took over as Howell searched for a cigarette. 'We've factored in an escort car in front, so there'll be two triggers, more if our man in Crater town tells us over the satphone the governor's in the middle of a crowd of trucks.'

'Adaptable software. Beautiful.' The patting of pockets went on.

'Escort car breaks light beam, one trigger down.'

'Then the governor's car breaks the beam. Second trigger down.' Cigarette found, extracted and lit. Lighter cap snapped shut to extinguish. 'Bomb is placed at the precise distance between a Mercedes saloon's grille and the rear passenger door. Car is slowed by the turn in the road, and kept close to the kerb. Optimum position. Boom.' A momentary plume of lighter fuel went up in an exaggerated pipe flame, before Howell shut it down. He allowed himself a satisfied drag of self-congratulation. 'It's amazing what you can learn from spoilt middle-class radicals. You know, it was terrorists using a photoelectric cell trigger to murder Alfred Herrhausen, chairman of Deutsche Bank, in 1989 that gave us the idea?'

'No, I did not know.' Badr replied, bemused by the frame of reference.

'Trust the Krauts to demo test the technology before we get to play with it.'

'And after we've played, we get out fast.' Purton slapped a bug into a smear on his forearm. 'Extraction is a simple reversal of the infiltration.'

Badr was gleeful. 'There will be much to talk of on your return. The attack will mark a significant escalation by the National Opposition. We have four hundred fighters here in the base area. D+1 will see them raiding outposts at Rama, intercepting expected reinforcements from Al Ghadar at an ambush site near Mar'at, and harassing military vehicles on the road between Mukhalla and Sayun and into the Hadramawt from the west. Al-Karab nomads loyal to us have been providing intelligence and carrying supplies into the area from the coast. Pre-positioning is complete.'

'Busy times.' And bloody. Purton contemplated the sand structure. Details had been omitted: it should be festooned with miniature corpses cut down in size, killed to scale. 'I suggest we use the first troops from the training course to hit the MSR's.'

'Count me in,' Howell ventured.

Badr nodded. 'You have my full support. I would be happy if you led the specialist missions. The telecoms tower on the mountain above Mahfidh is a priority.'

'Consider it scrap.'

'Also in the week after D-Day, simultaneous uprisings are planned for Aden and Mukhalla. I will be leading operations in the eastern Hadramawt.' Death or glory. Purton wondered which.

The largest wadi on the Arabian peninsula, running a hundred and sixty kilometres west to east across the stony Jol desert plateau, the Hadramawt was a desolate brown slash, remote, inhospitable and peopled with tribes naturally hostile to the Islamic radicalism of the alien northern authorities. Badr would cultivate such antipathy, use this fortress as a springboard for the resistance, and commandeer the airstrips belonging to the oil companies exploring the East Shabwa concession. His mobile penetration squads were an elite within the National Opposition's eclectic ranks. Yet, so were Saddam's Republican Guard within Iraq during the Gulf War: it had not prevented their annihilation. I'm too old, Purton thought. Just too damn old. He heard Max telling him that.

'What about the bedouin here in the Al-Mahra?' he asked. The region's thinly populated wild east, close to the Omani border, whose tribes spoke in indigenous semitic tongues, provided a critical bolt-hole and operating base for the uprising. It was vital that backing for the insurgency remained strong.

'They have yet to forgive the Sana'a rulers for their stance during the Gulf crisis. It lost them their remittances in Saudi. They are looking forward to revenge.'

'Ram-raiding for grown-ups,' Howell remarked with a half-chuckle. 'Makes me feel young again.'

It made Purton feel uneasy. Governor al-Aziz, count your days.

Different location, different map. The electronically generated display, bordered by smaller screens, dominated one side of the strategic-planning suite at SIS headquarters, Vauxhall Cross. Hugh Dryden and Russia chief, Guy Parsons, sat in soft chairs, clipboard check-lists to hand, heads bathed in directed light from recessed ceiling spots. Before them, vivid in the room's artificial dimness, the territories of the Russian Federation lay outlined and charted, plots in computerised primary colours, flashing symbology, etching out a pictorial representation of unfolding disaster. Alongside, adding to the detail, providing clarification – interpretation – text readouts flicked up and flowed through continuously.

'I have to say, Guy, it's put me off my popcorn.' Dryden was staring at the images.

'I lost any appetite long ago,' replied Parsons, short legs thrust out before him, black leather brogues shining meticulous on the edges of the beam pool. 'The latest from Cold Cut doesn't improve matters.'

'If he's doing a Michal Goleniewski, he's taking his time.' An in-joke. Over two years, and until his defection to the CIA in December 1960 and subsequent debriefing at the Agency's Ashford Farm in Maryland, the Polish intelligence officer, signing himself only as 'Sniper', had betrayed critical Soviet and Warsaw Pact secrets in letters sent direct to

Western intelligence. Cold Cut's letters had been arriving for over a generation.

'He's never going to walk in, thank God. At a time like this, I need him in place.'

'Particularly when Gresko is taking such an aggressive line towards our other operatives.' Dryden gave a knowing glance. 'Pity about the Hungarian gofer and your man at the Radisson. An expensive red herring, Guy.'

Parsons rubbed his palms. 'Theories have to be tested. Proves the old adversaries are rattled.'

'Proves they're using any measure to protect their cryo-plane work. Taken with your stringer being whacked last year while sniffing round Angarsk . . .'

'But, as you say, a high price.' A 'let's not dwell on it' tone tinged the voice. 'There's more to worry about now. This,' Parsons waved a hand towards the screen, 'for example.'

Russia's oil industry was ablaze, a furnace lit beneath the cauldron of an entire economy, havoc spread across the map, each emblem depicting fresh news, a broken pipe, a burning well, a strike, a closed factory, local unrest, greater loss. Here, collapse was illustrated cleanly, distantly, as sifted and sanitised as a weather report, cost calculated without the intrusion of human cost. Small concentric circles, pulsing in red, picked out the destruction at the Black Sea port of Nvovorossiysk, three gutted tankers reduced to miniaturised white silhouettes and caught within the rings. In one attack, the prospects for Russia's main foreign trade activity had been crippled; follow-up actions elsewhere ensured it was moribund; repercussions were expanding beyond calculation or comprehension. Energy – oil and gas – accounted for forty per cent of all Russia's exports, was critical to its capacity to earn dollars, acted as almost the only pull to direct overseas investment. No more. At Nvovorossiysk, in the shattered remains of a once-booming oil terminus, lay the wreckage of an economic future without a future. The Iran–Iraq war had demonstrated the potential to maintain oil flows at the epicentre of bombings and all-out hostility, the ability to patch up and replace pumps, to run out auxiliary pipes to floating pontoons and ships stationed outside the clogged approaches and ruined wastes of a flattened port, to modify, circumvent, improvise and thrive. Situations changed. It would take months to clear and rebuild from this scrap-cum-graveyard: pumping stations were obliterated, electricity generation demolished, berths blocked and large tracts of piping blast-welded into useless entanglements. And there was pollution, poisoned slicks of crude pouring from ruptured tanks, dispersing along the coast, drenching the shoreline and tourist resorts of the west Caucasus. Gelendzhik, Dzhubga, Dagomys and Sochi – beaches submerged in the black gloss of environmental disfigurement, littered with the oiled remains of sightless, flightless seabirds, the stench of a season without visitors rising above the towns and tea-plantations. Tankers would not be welcome, could not be welcome, in these parts for some time. Yet it was not the end. Explosions on the giant twin pipelines passing through the West Siberian oil capital of Tyumen had ripped the heart from the city; a series of detonations on pipes running parallel to the central sections of the Trans-Siberian railway cut supplies from the Tatarstan and Baskir fields; the sprawling plant at Perm was now a crater, and strategic outlets to Ukraine and Finland were heavily disrupted by sabotage. Cash dried with the refineries. *Months to clear and rebuild*. But months were unavailable. Funds were unavailable.

Parson's countenance grew gloomier. 'The Americans and their Defence Human Intelligence Service are working overtime on this one. Our Langley friends are so concerned, they want to send in HALOs.' The unpiloted High-Altitude, Low Observable drones, equipped with signals-gathering and photo-imaging systems, would fly long-endurance missions to cover ground already swept by space-based reconnaissance satellites. It was desperation: evidence had to be out there somewhere. 'Unfortunately, we have to tread carefully. We can't afford to precipitate matters.'

'It doesn't need our help to precipitate.' Dryden side-tilted his head towards the screen. 'Investment programmes collapsed, foreign reserves gone, stampede for dollarisation, rouble through the floor, Central Bank printing money, hyperinflation, xenophobia flaring, city-centre riots, political system diving into an abyss with the economy. Crisis management has simply become crisis.'

A sombre response. 'The blood-dimmed tide. And those behind it won't break out, show themselves until it's too late. It's the Rajasthani desert all over again.'

The intelligence failure of the 1990s – the inability to pick up India's preparations to conduct nuclear tests in May 1998 – weighed heavily on the Western espionage community Detection and analysis: flawed, fragmented, a guessing game, and the consequences became greater. It bore down on them in the planning room.

'Trouble is, how do we find the major elements in play, identify the units involved, ascertain the FSB's grip round the President's throat?' Dryden doodled a note onto his pad. 'Current mobilisation of paramilitary forces, and the enforcement of martial law in key regions, makes it impossible to spot which organisations are manoeuvring on behalf of Gresko.'

Parsons nodded. 'Or whether Gresko is up to anything at all. It's why the Foreign Secretary was so sceptical when the Chief and I went to brief him. We had to reveal more then we intended, simply to get his attention.'

'And that of his sidekick I presume?'

A resigned sigh. 'Naturally. Nigel Ferris is cleared to attend everything – is deferred to on everything – has set himself up as Russian expert. A sound-bite for every tragedy.'

'He'll have his syntax tested by Russia. God help us, Guy.' Dryden replaced a page beneath the clip. 'Secret intelligence meets public relations. And he a former Marxist. It's the final end to reason.'

'Reason ceased to be a factor when the Prime Minister announced the world's ills could be cured with the laying on of hands and the odd air bombardment.' The expression suggested that Parsons might dearly wish to lay his own hands around the junior minister's neck. 'Ferris is the new reality.'

'Liability.'

'Emotion is all. We are its servants.'

'And Ferris's whipping-boys. How did his salesman mentality respond to your general thrust?'

'Claimed our role at Six is to gather information, not to analyse it or dictate policy, that he's sure the Russian situation will work itself out. Insinuated we were being hysterical, adopting a typically Cold War posture.'

'Whose side is he on?'

Parsons' eyebrows arched upwards, uncomfortably close to meeting. 'He has his supporters.'

'Russian Communists, nationalists, anyone in the State Duma or government who wants a return to the old Soviet value system.'

'Order is the watchword. It's what Ferris kept repeating as the Foreign Secretary looked on and smiled benevolently. He's obviously made his mark.'

'I wish it were on your knuckles. How did C respond?'

'He's going straight to the PM. Doesn't expect any joy. Thinks Ferris and the Foreign Office view will prevail. Their argument is simple: a coup is unlikely, strength is preferable to weak government, and any means of shoring up executive authority and centralised control in Russia has to be welcome. They'll make representations, tut tut a little if there's excess bloodshed, but are prepared to sit things out until the trend becomes clearer.' Economics and poorly guarded nuclear stockpiles tended to encourage Western governments towards caution.

'So, they'll back the Russian President at any cost?'

'No one wants total mayhem, Hugh. Chaos breeds inertia, and the Foreign Secretary's gone native and sticks to his Wait and See policy. They like familiarity, even if it's despotic in character.'

'Which is why Gresko will assume control by sleight of hand.'

The two officials had been noticed, tracked: civilian-clothed, relaxed, passing through, but officials nevertheless. Attempts to maintain a low profile were wasted here in the heavy taiga and swamp region at the foot of the Yakan mountains. One visit to the drab, near-forgotten town of Anosovskaya sinking relentlessly into its cracked permafrost foundations was enough to earn the sobriquet 'stranger', two to generate talk of conspiracy. They arrived by Mercedes jeep, turning off from the Amur–Yakutsk highway and heading through uniform streets of two-storeyed squalor for the unremarkable Railway Hostel. Nearby, the station itself was subsiding into dereliction, a waypoint, nothing more, on the single unelectrified 'Little BAM' track running north–south some 124 miles between Tynda on the BAM railway and Bamovskaya on the Trans-Siberian. The place stank of poverty, retained its mantle of winter despondency. Visitors were not always welcome, visitors with papers less so.

Timber was a staple industry in these parts, logging settlements and the faded traces of Soviet-era gulag forestry complexes – Dubrovlags – leading off from a myriad of hidden tracks. Among the settlements were those operated by North Korea, a trade and slave-labour concession retained on Russian soil by the world's most committed, personality-cult driven Marxist state. Glasnost and perestroika, the ending of Communist rule, had bypassed these camps, the decades since the 1950s representing changing years not changing attitudes. Photography around the sites was forbidden, armed guards in Mao suits patrolled, watchtowers surveyed, propaganda was broadcast from tree-top speakers and floated across fences festooned with eulogies to 'Dear Leader' Kim Jong II and the great achievements of his country's serfs. Thus, through government silence or wilful inertia, encouraged by mutual convenience and intelligence-sharing protocols, there remained isolated clearings set in pockets of wooded Russian landscape which would forever be totalitarian in form. Occasionally, escapes occurred. When caught, the 'volunteers' were handed back for execution to the local North Korean administration or carried in chains to the DPRK's consulate at Chegdomyn for 're-education' – and then execution. Some made it to freedom, aided by sympathetic citizens and militiamen, others succumbed in the wild. A few were found and sheltered by smuggling or espionage cells operated by Cold Cut made aware through logging contacts of the latest security breaches and attempted runs for the Chinese border.

There were North Koreans in the team watching the pair. Originally from the lumberjack camp at Seti, they were the first to bring news of UFO sightings in the area to the attention of the man known to them only as 'Brodets', the Wanderer. He duly passed it to British Intelligence who identified the likely cause of such phenomena as early flight trials of the Irkutsk-built military scramjet cryoplane. Sightings increased, membership of Seti's dedicated UFO society grew. Yet attention here was focused on identified things, for the men checked in to the Railway Hostel matched photographs taken and circulated of individuals seen visiting the caves near Nizhneudinsk well over a thousand miles to the west – and still three thousand miles east of Moscow. Distances were vast, Cold Cut's espionage apparatus flexible enough to gather and disseminate the information required. Two men observed in winter with known FSB personnel at a location storing tactical nuclear weapons designed for terrorist attack, since detected in the vicinity of various strategic sites, now appearing in a backwater. Interesting enough for detailed examination, for the order to be given along a telephone line requisitioned from the BAM Railway company, to close with the enemy.

They were off-guard, sobriety fleeing as it usually did in stop-overs devoid of charm or diversions. The bar was full, men and women slumped or lying in stages of stupefied inebriation, or dance-shuffling to internal, intoxicated *rhythms they shared with no one else. Human distilleries, adding to the pungent cocktail of vomit, sweat and alcohol fumes. Only drunks could appreciate it; it was best to be drunk. A woodsman challenged the strangers in competition: goals were vague, rules fluctuating, match rounds equating to refilled container rounds, lost or won to cheers, jeers and a generosity and outpouring of spirit. At the hostel, paying hard dollars, a small group of workers arrived late to book themselves into dormitories. Greenbacks overcame resistance; they were assigned quarters. While one stood guard, kept the manager supplied with nicotine and refreshment, his team-mates gained access to the rooms of other guests. It was slick, lighting equipment set up, document cases found, locks unpicked and integrated ink-sprays disabled. Photography followed, the papers removed, recorded and replaced exactly as they were found. Assignment complete, the space and contents restored to their original state, the operators let themselves out. The vehicle was next. Along the street, a colleague was pouring further shots for two of Leonid Gresko's most trusted employees.*

A remote-controller had appeared between Guy Parsons' fingers. 'I want to show you something.' The image of the radar aerostat balloon sent by Cold Cut dematerialised from the peripheral screen, to be replaced by a photograph of a man dressed in dark coat and fur hat. The face emanated poison, blank domination which spoke of control and cruelty, unaware of its presence on camera. 'Know him?'

'I'm not acquainted with anyone that ugly.'

'You're luckier than those who are.' The figure faded and reappeared, exposed to different angles, the head and body turned frame by frame for viewing. 'Colonel Petr Ivanov, Federal Security Service. One of the nastier elements in the old KGB's Second Chief Directorate. He's graduated successfully to becoming Director Gresko's main hatchet-man. I emphasise the word "hatchet".'

'Résumé makes disturbing reading?'

'Son of a Smersh executioner who in turn was son of a Cheka executioner. He's a chip off the old chopping-block and not averse to showing extreme prejudice towards defectors and their families.' An understated synopsis which belied the extent of the Russian's career. Parsons was not given to emotional subjectivity. 'Rumoured he played the lead in the apparently accidental deaths of Colonel Ryszard Kuklinski's two sons. He certainly captained the KGB squad sent from Moscow to assist in Kuklinski's summary execution. Took the consolation prize, instead.'

Again Polish, and a senior military planner, the Colonel became one of the CIA's most significant Cold War sources before his eventual defection to the United States in 1981. A sad postscript was the mysterious and untimely deaths of his sons, one in a hit-and-run, the other while out boating.

Dryden kept his eyes on the face, mesmerised by its corrupted, demonic quality. 'I wish we had a Kuklinski to reveal Gresko's plans.'

'He would be dealing with someone like that.' Parsons jabbed a finger at the two-dimensional presence. 'You'd better see the rest.'

An annotated biography, transferred from MI6 computer files, rolled enlarged onto a corner display. Dryden read the headings. 'One-time playmate of Qusay Hussein, Saddam Hussein's second son. Doesn't surprise me.'

Qusay, head of Iraq's intelligence apparatus, adviser to the country's Military Industrialisation Organisation tasked with acquiring and hiding nuclear, biological and chemical weapons, was Saddam's lynchpin in outwitting UN enforcement teams. Gaining advance warning of the 'no-notice' inspections to allow evacuation of incriminating material and the shredding of sensitive documents was critical, and at this Qusay excelled. Using his elite *Amn al-Khass* Special Security Service, *Mukhabarat* Intelligence Directorate and *Estikhabarat* Military Intelligence, he successfully protected a vast proportion of his father's secret arsenal. He was aided by information passed on by Petr Ivanov from Russian espionage contacts within the UN Inspectorate.

'Interesting.' Dryden was working down the career report. 'Ivanov even lent Russian FAPSI signals intelligence people to Iraq's *Al Hadi* eavesdropping unit.'

'How else do you think the Office of the Presidential Palace maintained its edge over the UN? Intercepting communications and unscrambling its satellite phones was all part of it.'

'As was the kind Colonel Ivanov, I assume.' Dryden's attention shifted to another part of the text. 'They seem to have been tight.'

Parsons nodded. 'The SSS were there to eliminate any threats to Saddam. On the Lubyanka's orders, Ivanov was an active participant in everything they did.'

'How active?'

'Torture, mutilation, mass killings – bread-and-butter counter-intelligence work for that part of the world. Sweetening the client relationship. He advised Lieutenant General Hazim Shihab – then in charge of Iraq's rocket forces – on Scud concealment. Same story with Syria and its Homs-Hama corridor. The original Happy Valley.' The eyes cued Dryden back to the electronic script. North-west Syria, centre of the country's attempts to develop chemical and biological cluster warheads for its ballistic missile forces. On the road to Salamiyah, a Scud C brigade at Stage 3 alert; east of Homs, a storage and launch facility; south of Hama, a mobile launcher depot and training base built into a hillside; attached to the Homs oil refinery pumping out ethanol, methanol, ethylene and isopropyl alcohol – vital precursor compounds for chemical weapons – a well disguised nerve agent plant. And Petr Ivanov had visited, advised, abetted in a covert buildup of the former Soviet surrogate's military arsenals. Parsons returned to the subject of Iraq. 'We believe he was also present at the meeting of 15 February 1996 held at Mukhabarat headquarters, Baghdad, in which Qusay sanctioned an assassination attempt on Ambassador Rolf Ekeus, Chairman of the UN Special Commission investigating the regime's weapons of mass destruction.'

'Truly one of the saints,' Dryden murmured.

'A defector told us Ivanov offered to supply the time-delayed poison.'

'And the West never complained?'

A close-lipped smile from the Russia section. 'Better to stick with the devil who's been identified. At least we know Petr Ivanov is linked unequivocally with Gresko, specialises in foul play and the running of large-scale dissimulation projects.'

'The man to watch.'

'You'll say the same of this character.' The still photograph of a second individual materialised in the place of Ivanov. 'The Americans handed it to us. It was taken from the Radisson Hotel's security camera, and shows the leader of the team which hit our chap in the random crossfire. Incidentally, the other victims were linked to Maxim Shelepin – deceased star of our intercepted video-conference footage – so it might be Gresko wanting to make it appear as Diakanov's handiwork.'

'Clever.'

'Fiendishly,' Parsons added. 'We've enhanced the picture.'

'Large guy.'

'And probably ex-military. Highly professional. Name a check and it's been done. We've run it against our files; Five has taken a look at it; it's passed through twenty-five million records at the FBI's National Crime Information Centre, and the Phoenix database on the U.K.'s Police National Computer. No matches, even with full facial curve analysis.'

'Pity the Radisson didn't have thermographic filters on the CCTV,' Dryden commented, narrowing his eyes to spark the memory. Thermography allowed comparison and computer recognition from distinctive facial heat signatures.

Parsons punctured the idea. 'Unlikely to help. He simply isn't on file. However ∴ .' Portentous announcements generally came with little ceremony or warning. 'He matches eye-witness descriptions of the individual seen shooting young Oleg Diakanov dead beside a rugby pitch at Hawbreys prep school.'

'Ah, the mysterious Uncle Radomir.'

'Or, so he told the headmaster's secretary. Personally, not someone I'd want in my family. We've spent hours sifting through footage from airports and docks. Got him too.' Another picture, frontal, came up. Dryden rested his chin on a hand. 'Heathrow. Flew out on an Israeli passport to Tel Aviv the same day as the killing. Almost certainly Russian, not a Galilee pedestrian. Shin Bet have identified him as the same man who left for Moscow a few days later.'

'Obviously didn't disguise himself because he's usually domestic violence rather than foreign assignment.' Dryden twisted his balled knuckles in the direction of the screen, the killer's face anaemic in the low-light enhancement of the hotel's camera lens.

'Obviously. And it means we have a positive connection between a fellow who guns down the son of Russia's main crime overlord and dispatches one of our intelligence collectors in cold blood at a Russian hotel.'

Dryden closed the circle. 'Which leads us to Gresko.'

'At the very least, it shortens the odds.' The frenetic energy of a small man had temporarily deserted the head of Russia Division. He seemed awed by the immensity of what was unravelling. 'I could have accepted the Radisson was a Diakanov-inspired cull of his opponents, I might once have conceived of circumstances in which he would want to promote economic collapse to fuel his black marketeering . . .'

'But not when he requires stability for his legitimate front organisations to function, for his political bribery to be effective, for running his scams and rackets throughout the Schengen zone.'

'And not when his son is murdered, and the Senate he established to harmonize criminal antics across Mother Russia is tearing itself to pieces. He's been hurt personally, economically and politically.'

'Could be in need of an ally.'

'If he's up against Leonid Gresko, he'll require the next best thing to the antichrist. Viktor Abakumov, Nikolai Yezhov, Lavrenti Beria – secret police states tend to devour their own. We have to ensure it devours the present incumbent.'

'Any suggestions welcome.'

'I'm going to play my Joker, pass on the pictures to our reliable conduit in the Russian security apparatus.'

'How do we know he's not compromised?' Dryden was tapping lightly on his clipboard.

'We don't. But our hands are tied by the Foreign Office, and they'll get the vapours at the merest hint of direct action. So we have to trust the contact. He handed our intel to Gorbachev and Yeltsin during their tricky periods, and I met him a few times when I was stationed in Moscow. As straight as they come.'

The tapping ceased. 'It's Russia. Forgive my cynicism.'

'This might change your mind. Or concentrate it.' An electronic purr in response to the control pad, and a different shot revealed itself to the room. Exposed, contained in a suitcase, was a technological load at odds with the unassuming style of its container. 'It seems Colonel Petr Ivanov's interest in weapons of mass destruction – and by extension his boss Leonid Gresko's – did not end when he finished his tour in Iraq. The case is from the location he visited. Photography again courtesy of Cold Cut.'

Dryden left his seat and approached the screen. He said nothing, peering closely at the presentation before turning. 'Guy. What the hell are we dealing with here?'

'I can tell you that well over a hundred nuclear weapons, manufactured for the KGB and designed to fit into holdalls and suitcases for terrorist purposes, were never listed in arms control inventories and therefore never decommissioned. I can also tell you that they remain unaccounted for.' Parsons rose and went to stand beside his fellow SIS-officer. 'I don't know what it's about, Hugh. But it goes far beyond any coup attempt I've ever seen.'

They were silent, gazing up at a blinking panorama of confusion, a cheerless constellation from which the spectre of Colonel General Leonid Gresko, Director of the Federal Security Service, might yet emerge in zodiac outline. He was more subtle than that, remained out of sight, relied upon his surrogates. Western intelligence too had its surrogates.

'Happy Easter, my darling.'

Diakanov twitched, mind falling out of troubled sleep disrupted by retained tension from a previous day and anticipated stress of the next. No release – it was morning – the next was here. His eyelids, fatigue-gummed, battled, retreated and struggled open on the kiss. Irina smiled, the look that dominated his heart, groin and senses. He, boss of bosses, *tsisari*, woken, broken, brought alive yet to his knees by this extraordinary girl. Why did she remain with him? The only one whose loyalty was undoubted because it was permeated with love and tenderness. And he wanted her to carry his child, give him a son, bear a new Oleg. He would not leave his wife, but could not leave Irina.

'You make me happy,' he grunted, moving, the ache in his forehead rolling in a mercury stream to his temples. N549 was what he remembered of the night, Prisoner N549. There was never a face, but the number pulsed through his consciousness, crawled from the childhood chasm into the fractured thoughts of a man under pressure. He had reached back to find him once more, discovered only his number, the political prisoner – a '58' in hard labour parlance – who acted as his father's intelligence officer in the camps, was instrumental in securing a power base, outwitted the other murderous thieves, protected young Boris the moment he landed from a death-laden hulk onto a death-laden shore at Magadan. Always an outsider, admired by Diakanov Senior for his quiet bravery, ability to think strategically, beyond the mundane brutality of life within the zek barracks, he became the eyes, ears and counsellor to the spreading organisation. Yes, N549 was so very different: almost too humane to be Russian – a born spy, diplomatic, a winner of minds, a killer when necessary, a self-reliant survivor who disappeared from the track-laying gang in 1960. For him, 'the green prosecutor', as they called escapes, became reality. Perhaps he lived, perhaps not. Diakanov wished he were here, serving him as he had served his father. Instinctively, he would know how to act, care for Irina, foil the gathering foe. A number, not a face – an eloquent epistle to Communism.

The smile was there again. 'I have a surprise for you. But you have to sit up.' The firmness, though mock, was insistent. His senses caught hold of the stronger imagery from the day-world and pulled him after them. He was awake.

'A surprise? They are only ever welcome from you.' There had been enough surprises these past months, too many upsets. He wrestled into a higher elevation on a bank of silk-swathed pillows, their down fillings retaining shape more successfully than the puffed face backed onto them.

Her strong fingers mapped the countenance, smoothing it out, rediscovering its hardness, trailing across the lips and nose, pushing beneath the cheek bones. Tension drained from him, energy received; he wanted to be in her hands, to leave this guarded compound far behind.

The cloth was lifted from the tray, eggs – boiled and painted – revealed, jostling on the crowded surface with a pile of *kulich* Easter cakes.

'So, this is where you were last night,' he said softly, voice pebbled with the residue of sleep. She had banned him from her study for several hours, but he smelled the eggs turning terracotta in their boiling onion water. He selected one for examination, rotated it between fingers, viewed with the intensity of a gem cutter. The design was intricate, a matrix of lapis and jade; the skill of a craftsman, the enthusiasm of a child, her commitment to him represented in each detail, every minute spent creating. 'My Irina, thank you. They are so beautiful.'

'I will never be Ilya Repin,' she laughed apologetically,

sweeping the shimmered strands from her face.

He caught her hands and brought them to his lips. 'I want you as you are.'

She, who countered his darkness with light, dazzled him, was precious because she was like no other, needed no jewels, no luxury, was as unaffected by wealth or rank as on the first day they met. And he repaid her with a cage, with the guarded, jealous claustrophobia, the armed paranoia of an emperor's palace, banishing her from friends, from those she found most natural and enhancing. Instead of freedom, he surrounded her with the glittering hardness of criminality. His form of demonstrative affection – yet she remained, thrived.

Diakanov reached for another egg, its surface marbled in turquoise. This was Irina's Easter. A year ago, she had visited the Moscow Kabaret theatre, taken Oleg to the Lent *capustnik* plays, strolled laughing in the parks, gone to church. A year ago, when his boy was alive, when there was no mafiya war. His eyes were closing, mind and head receding into the bed clothes. Safety.

The men lay flat, had made their approach undetected by the microlights sent out for reconnaissance from the short airstrip within the compound. Engines dipped and droned, metallic gnats wheeling and hovering above the estate surrounding Diakanov's retreat, thermal imagers scanning the ground for body radiation, underslung machine-gun pods primed for follow-through. Occasionally a helicopter would join the aerial antics, dropping patrols at random from abseil ropes, checking on fixed sensors. An impressive display of readiness, eye-catching also. But an army used to domination, to the offensive, an organisation expectant of loyalty, demanding complete obeisance, rarely adapted well to the defensive. The infiltration groups knew the weaknesses, possessed the blueprint of the complex, the plans. Their commanders belonged to the disbanded hierarchy of the criminal Senate, to the Orlov and Nechiporenko clans, a number of whose capos had been gunned down at the Radisson Hotel in Moscow several weeks before. An unpleasant affair, becoming more so. Plainly, Diakanov was lashing out, remained unmollified by the gesture-massacre of Maxim Shelepin's family, would not call a halt until every rival became fertilizer or foundations. Corpses infested with blowfly larvae had been found in the Moscow dock area: nightmare-scapes, product of psychopathic inclinations and imagination, placed few limits on atrocity. *Eat or be eaten.* The chuck meat was in the water, baited. Hunters were circling around the Great White.

A utility helicopter pulled revs and nosed upwards from the compound. They ignored it. Their manportable, shoulder-launched SA-14 missiles could bring down any rotor-craft, infrared-muffled or not. Yet their orders were to concentrate on the central buildings. Peripherals, interference, could be dealt with later. The helicopter dipped and clattered away, hollow whine of the turbines downwashed by the rotors. Below, a face streaked in camo cream ducked for a time-check and spoke briefly into the scrambled radio. Ahead lay the unprepossessing façades of *tsisari*'s lair sprawled in an evocation of Sixties-era industrial architecture. Factories and management blocks, brutish symbols of Sovietisation, requisitioned and converted to the needs of a multinational crime syndicate. Size and ugliness prevailed, but there were other features: the outer coils of razor wire, the electrified matrix fence, a ploughed strip within concealing a minefield, inner perimeter barriers enclosing attack dogs on running leashes, and guards manning rooftop observation posts and entry points. Against the skyline, the stub silhouettes of multi-barrelled cannon, and the awkward shape of satellite dishes and multifrequency aerials attached to a communications tower, could be picked out across the cleared land-scape. To the observers, it meant the vulnerability of a large target, one thoughtfully placed for convenience on a man-made plain, all the easier for zeroing. Diakanov's retreat – secluded, woven with trip-flares, omni-directional and dual-spectral cameras, movement, heat and sound detectors, the paraphernalia of security that would never give security – shortly to become a rout. Everything noted and assessed – the layout, the décor, down to the row of hand-painted Gorodets Rospis children's toys kept on a shelf in the master bedroom. *Tsisari* was becoming sentimental, collected mementos, the playthings of his young. The forces beyond the wire were not deceived; sentimentality and cruelty so often coexisted harmoniously. The watching continued. Every measure had its counter; a stand-off attack was called for.

Diakanov toyed with the painted eggs, ears tuned distantly to the dampened noise of the airborne surveillance sweeps, mind distracted behind the armoured glass of his day rooms. He had underestimated the opposition, lost hundreds of millions of dollars, hundreds of personnel, seen business evaporate, friends turn. The stability he had fought so bloodily to protect, the order he had imposed, gone, taking the joint-ventures, mutual trust, the easy cooperation with overseas groups, with them. Legitimate front companies required a buoyant economy, rising demand to suck out dirty money and renumber it as clean. They were failing, Diakanov's fortunes withering. Few would enter Russia now, fewer wished to negotiate, shake the hand of one who might be deposed. Better to wait and pick up the scraps, make overtures, provisional displays of courtship, in other camps. That was the prevailing view. He squeezed the egg, its shell crumpling between thumb and forefinger, Irina's simple, heartfelt gift bursting into a proteinous mass on the desk. Realisation, brain engaged, the edge of a palm sweeping the sulphurous pulp into a waste-paper basket. Anything he touched, he damaged, even Irina. Instinctively, he looked up, expecting her presence, recalling she was in the helicopter bound for nearby Cheboksary and the Easter service at its golden domed fifteenth-century monastery. She loved its frescoes and icons, the blaze of candles, the profusion – confusion – of pomp during its full Mass, the bells, smells, chants, the curtain drawn back and forth across an altar front secure behind iron gates. To her it made sense, and that was enough. He had to allow the trip, provided an escort of his most experienced bodyguards, a picnic of champagne, caviar, salmon, wild mushroom soup and crabmeat salad for her intended visit to an elderly painter on the eighth floor of a shabby apartment block overlooking the river. If he could not give or buy her the freedom enjoyed by those unacquainted with his world, then a small gesture, a caring thought, might somehow make amends. *The prevailing view*: that he was isolated, spent, finished. He should have stayed in Moscow, at the centre, not retreated here to his fur-trimmed provincial cocoon, to these fir-lined plains rolling down to the Volga. But he had to recoup, regroup, gather his thoughts and strength. They would never find him among the forests. He was several hundred miles south-east of the capital, among his own, close to the birthplace of Ivan the Terrible. A gravitational pull. And he would emerge, like Stalin's armies from behind the Urals, and prevail – *his prevailing view*.

The line of sight took him to a flat roof of an accommodation block a hundred metres distant. A protection squad member prowled the section, webbing hung with radio, ammunition pouches and side-arm, assault weapon slung around his neck. Diakanov's gaze followed the man idly, took in the casual lilt to the step, the friendly exchange with a second guard pacing out the same area. They could afford to be relaxed; responsibilities were minor, dangers diminished out here in the countryside. Not like the city, not like Moscow. The carbon-reinforced thickness of the glass skewed the image, sent the bodies into a shapeless spasm, carried them distorted, leaking colour, across a pane of empty space. The picture stilled. Horizontal, motionless, the pair remained where they were blown, placed by dint of light, by dint of heavy-calibre sniper shell. Skywards, a microlight folded, assumed the aerodynamics of a stone and hurtled from its orbit. Diakanov rose from his seat, hands gripping, indenting the leather rests, and staggered with the drunk surprise of shock to the window ledge. He was in time to see a group of soldiers, his soldiers, clatter down steps, disappear in a balloon of orange-centred light which seared them on his retina, imprints of wire dancers disassembled, sucked up with dirt, and scattered. A second mortar bomb landed close behind, prefabricated walls torn up and apart, portals crashing in volcanic baths of black eruption. The mafiya chief scrambled for the door, the crazed vibration of air cut by high explosive and shrapnel singing loud, peppered with the gathering, deeper crump of walking, falling, rounds, the clattering chain effect of rapid fire, the *tic tic* of lead impact on brick.

He was outside, running, pistol discharged in futility and rage at a distant enemy, his landscape sprouting wild plumes, straddled by earth sprays, by the dark, incessant *Ilandai* pushed up by military science. Fires had taken hold, wind smothering the scene in drifting pockets of acrid smoke, vignettes of battle at once clear and then obscured in a changing shroud: sand bags ripped away, emplacements ripped away, bodies ripped away. The communications tower had been plucked out and discarded, its broken stump jutting from debris. Flame and scorched ground, flame and scorched, fragile dead. He wiped his eyes, emptied his nose. The heat was climbing; the taste lodged at the back of his throat. People would pay.

'This way! This way!' he screamed at a bewildered team struggling to find bearings or shelter, herding them on towards an outer line of slit trenches.

They responded, three by dying instantly, the remainder falling flat and covering their heads. Diakanov kicked them, stamping authority with a steel-capped shoe, dragging a prostrate figure by the collar until, through enforced momentum, the individual found his balance. 'You cowards. Up! I will kill you all.'

Above the thickening fog, flame lanced abruptly from the forty-millimetre mouth of an automatic cannon placed on the reinforced balcony of a storage wing. At least some were fighting, Diakanov thought, wrenching a combat rifle from the claw-hold of a cadaver's stiffening fingers. Bullets flecked out miniature geysers close by. In a meadow towards the city of Cheboksary, a downed helicopter smouldered.

He had considered returning to London to see Adele, but here, now, leaning with Zenya on the rough veranda rail of their wood cabin, awaiting the precise airborne formations of evening birds, enthusiasm grew less, excuse list longer. He telephoned, her resignation echoing with resentment, dialogue drawn out by enforced trivia, neither wishing to tip-toe into emotional marshland, to spark confrontation. She was muted, understood his reasons for remaining in Russia: it must be difficult given the economic and political climate; the business was surely suffering. He asked about her work. She had summarised. The give and take of conversation without real give or take, communication without communicating, politeness, the loss of spontaneity. Possibly, the loss of Adele.

'Look, Max, here they come!' Zenya squeezed his arm, directed him with an outstretched finger.

Low over the silver birches came the whooper swans, honking, necks straining, travelling in magnetic synchronisation. He could not give up Zenya, her childlike delight in nature, her capacity to make him laugh. And would not miss Adele. Three hundred miles from Moscow, he was further from his American girlfriend than he had ever been, closer to the girl who crawled into his cramped bed and guarded heart at the student block in Volgograd.

'Did you see them? Did you see them?'

'Better than the stars you picked out for me last night.' He had not noticed one for twenty years, their light sources too poorly defined against the immensity of space.

'Stars don't make a noise. You can't follow them.'

His hand travelled down to the small of her back and pulled her gently in towards him. 'No problem. Love is blind, remember?' Love was cutting out their sleep.

'Do you think we do it better now than when we were in Volgograd?'

'Dunno. But I'm enjoying the practice.'

'I'm not sure I will marry you, Max.'

He laughed. Her tangential mind could often surprise. 'That's a hell of a leap.'

'I mean it, Max.' The eyes turned grave, large in her thin, delicate face. 'You belong in the West. It's where you should be, with your girlfriend. I don't want to be like those cheap Russian women who find an American husband for a passport.'

'You could never be cheap, an imitation, a passport fraudster, or just another Russian woman.' He kiss-punctuated the statement. The attempt to argue back was suppressed, lips responding and repeating.

'But . . .' Concern melted, replaced by closeness.

'But, we're on vacation.' Honeymoon would be a rank disappointment after this. 'So, I'm not about to spoil it by going down on bended knee. OK?'

She bit his ear playfully. 'Say "Green Card" slowly. It does things for me.'

'Immigration tests are getting stiffer.'

A cough from below them. Hunter Strachan stood, hands on denim, with the wry, twisted squint of a practised voyeur shaded beneath his cavalry hat. 'You kids need a bucket of cold water?'

'A telephone call would have been enough,' Max replied pointedly.

'Foreplay will have to wait.' He swung himself up onto the deck, tipped his hat in gentlemanly afterthought to Zenya and ruined the effect by winking. 'Besides, I paid for you to come to Galich for a rest.'

'We've visited the local Assumption Cathedral. We're doing the rest.'

'Where's your beer?' He was shown, and invited himself to a bottle. They regrouped outside.

'How's Moscow?' Max asked.

'Bad, getting worse. Ditto, the country. No offence, Zenya.' A large swallow. 'More church-burning than Mississippi in an off year. I'd say get out, but I'm depending on you here to plug the gaps. Russian shuttle traders are in shock. They buy on the international market in dollars, but can't afford greenbacks with the rouble hospitalised. Besides, no one's purchasing what they've got to offer.'

He looked unconcerned. The shuttle traders – along with crime gangs, the lubricants of the home economy – were responsible for bringing up to forty billion dollars each year into Russia's commercial banking system. This time they were keeping earnings offshore, nervous at a revenue-starved presidency lashing out at the fattest and most vulnerable accounts.

Max folded his arms. 'We're healthy.'

'Surviving. The shift from luxuries to staples won't help margins, and traffic's down. At least we've never had to convert from the local currency. Big problem is the mafiya. Another convoy's been hit.'

'Casualties?'

'Scratches, peed pants, a Maz rig with a broken axle.'

'They've always been jealous.'

'Sure, but now they're not scared.' Strachan scraped beneath his hat with a forefinger. 'Government protection means squat when there's no government. We're outsiders on their land, eating their caviar, making profits at their expense. Kind of irritating when everyone's suffering.'

'I thought they were too busy sticking it to each other.'

'Never underestimate their appetite.'

'I don't,' Max replied. 'They even used a SAM to knock out *tsisari*'s mistress's whirlybird. It was on the late news last night.'

'Might have dropped her himself. His relationships end messy. Whatever, be assured, the Cheboksary assault was a warm-up. There'll be collateral fallout. Reminds me – I'm assigning Gennady to you.'

Zenya circled an arm round her lover's waist. 'Max is in danger out here?'

'From what I've just seen, I'd say so.' Delivery was as arid as the face.

Max protested. 'C'mon, Hunter. You're overreacting. I don't need a guard-dog.'

'Chill out, boy, it's not a full team. It's just a precaution, and a better barrier than rubber. He's unpacking in the lodge two along. I've told him to stay low, blend in.'

'Low? Blend? Gennady?' The bodyguard would be conspicuous at a convention of flat-faced giants, his own kind. Among ordinary folk, he was a landmark.

'I'm taking three shadows on my own break to Sochi.'

And several young female friends from Moscow, thought Max. 'That's self-importance.'

'Common sense. Though I admit, now that the Black Sea's real black after the oil terminal raid, I won't be swimming.'

'You never intended to leave the hotel room.'

'After taking security advice, naturally.' He cupped a hand on Max's face. 'You'll do the same. I'd hate to lose you.'

'So much for escape. I was expecting to leave Russian troubles behind. Thanks for turning up.'

'My boundless pleasure. And happy vacation. We deserve it.'

'Then what?'

'Relax, kick back. Wait to see what happens next.'

The Godfather, bare-knuckled Russian version: minus the padded cheeks, the method accent of Brando – scarier for it – head of a clan as ready to nail-gun an innocent to a door as fuck one against it. Lazin studied the devastation, Diakanov an unmoving and unmoved presence at his side. But the FSB officer felt the shuddering fury, saw the amber eye spots, and tried to concentrate on the blitzed scene before him. Gelatinous reds and yellows, postscript to extreme-mortality firefights, faded nature-brown in sunlight, had been swilled away by footsoldiers bearing buckets, mops and double-lined garbage bags. To end as scrag in the trash – an improvement for hordes of life's unfortunates. Men filled in holes, rebuilt barricades, collected fragments created from fragments. A bulldozer butted the sagging remnants of a house-frame to submission; on an adjoining structure, maintenance crew plastered the scars, burying embedded bone marrow beneath a fresh decorative coat. Memorial wall, widespread tomb of the unknown mafiosi. Better than no grave at all.

'You come well armed,' the boss of bosses commented. 'A Gyurza nine millimetre. Fine weapon. Powerful.'

'Goes with the job.'

'Eleven-gramme cartridge, eighteen rounds in the magazine, can put a bullet through thirty layers of kevlar or two titanium plates at fifty metres.'

'You know your firearms.'

'Goes with the job.'

Diakanov reached for an inside pocket, the gold cigarette case produced, opened, proffered and refused. Lazin's receptors were overloaded by the melancholic energy – power without peace of mind – of a man whose certainties were gone, of a man reverting to the survival creed of the street and the camps, reverting to type. And this type had fed rivals to bears, used acid as an executive toy. So this was New Russia, what Lazin was pledged to defend? Barely an improvement on the old – Colonel General Leonid Gresko's model, the Soviet model – one more gilded, perfumed, puffed up than the other, bringing the crime market to the free market. Both were criminal, both brutal, arbitrary, lawless, unconstrained by the norms of decency, respect for the Russian people and the printed text of a constitution. And he, Lazin, was its guardian.

A shot cracked, a dog, lighter for loss of entrails, abruptly stopped its thrashing and was bagged up to feed the rest. The mafiya chief withdrew a filterless for himself, snapped shut the engraved box lid.

'I'm told cigarettes will kill me.' Heavy fingers pinched the tobacco tube and tapped a smoker's morse on the precious metal. It went to his mouth, a flame generated by the closest attendant touch-tapering an inhalation. 'If they do, they'll be more successful than my enemies.'

'The attack was not intended to kill you.'

A silence, long, dangerous, while Diakanov nipped the cigarette between tightened teeth and burnt it shorter. 'So, this . . .' The head turned in a measured arc. 'All this.' He stooped and picked up the shrapnel fragment of a *Podnos* mortar round. 'A game?'

'A provocation.'

'Consider me provoked.' Diakanov was thinking of Prisoner N549.

Lazin spoke slowly. He had to hook the man, draw him in. 'Assassination requires information, accuracy. They missed – I assume they had neither. Quite an oversight after so much planning.'

'They murder my son, now they murder Irina, and you claim I am not a target, that a bombardment which destroys my compound is not intended for me?' A hand pushed Lazin in the upper back, patted with subdued ferocity. It felt as if he were marking the spot, picking an aiming point. 'I do not like theories, Colonel.'

'They would have known of your nuclear and conventional war bunkers here. Soviet-era factory design is no longer a state secret.'

'They would not take such risks, without a reward.'

'Mortars and machine guns used at long range? They are hardly surgical, Boris Fedorovich.' Lazin persisted, hoped it would not irritate to a terminal degree. His office offered no protection here.

Diakanov swung to face the Colonel from the Federal Security Service, the tall, uniformed caricature of solid, disciplined incorruptibility. There was the hint of a children's history book here, the Communist vision of how a steel-eyed, square-jawed security hero should look. No one believed that any more. He had seen greater men bought, stronger men beg, could demonstrate the true meaning of surgical. Professionally, the officer was finished, did not enjoy the patronage of Leonid Gresko, was a loner, failed to pass the nationalist or Marxist test, was unlikely to have an agenda or future. More trustworthy for it. Evidently, he had been assigned the wasted and cosmetic exercise of adding to security service files on the ongoing mafiya conflict. Nothing too profound, enough to brief the Director, keep the Kremlin informed and panicked. And then he would be withdrawn, prematurely, as he was from the diamond train case, closing a chapter, admitting through defeat that progress was impossible. Another downwards jolt to his career.

'I pay my own people for advice, Colonel,' *tsisari* said at last.

'Then you are overgenerous. They did not keep your son and mistress secure.'

A blink and he could have Lazin strangled where he stood. The eyes stayed open, wills locked, the moment passed. And Lazin detected grief – choking, raw beneath the anger – compounded by desperation and guilt, the culpability of a woman's lover, a boy's father, who had handed them over to die. He found himself pitying the pitiless.

Diakanov did not move. 'Mistakes have been made. They are being dealt with.'

As was the Georgian, his senior capo who had organised the helicopter journey. The enemy operated insiders. It was the sole explanation for the discovery of his haven, the tracking and downing of Irina's transport. He pushed her death to a discreet corner of his brain, where it ached, adulterated his thoughts. The pain would only end if he tore off his head. How could they dream, dare, to do this to him? To her? They were sending him mad. He would trap them, tear off their heads before he tore off his own.

'I have seen your solutions in the Moscow docks.' They had reduced a hard-bitten team of veteran militiamen to white-faced virgins, vomiting white-faced virgins. So many maggots there.

'This is why you are here, why you sought an interview?

To tell me I am not above the law?' A rasping semiquaver of a laugh. The cigarette was jettisoned sharply, swivel-crushed beneath a foot.

'I am not so naïve.'

The hand clenched on the shoulder. 'Neither am I, Colonel.' Russian tactility was always a power gesture, Lazin thought. 'Why then?'

'Because you are being weakened. Those you cared for most have been taken, your beloved Senate has crumbled, your businesses are crippled and you are at war with former friends. Russia blames you for its troubles, the violence, is searching for scapegoats.'

'And this concerns you, a representative of state security? I asked why you are here.' The pressure on the shoulder was unrelenting.

'I can help you. You, in turn, can help me.'

If the man were talking of a retainer, asking for a bribe, that was understandable, brave given the situation. There were procedures, recognised formalities. If not, and it was merely a rhetorical device, an excuse to speak riddles, the offer of an opinion, he would learn to regret ever making the journey from Moscow. Diakanov observed the face: none of the smug expectation of the self-assured moonlighter, the secret policeman who thought the bulging white envelope a perk, concomitant, a birthright.

Tsisari let his arm fall. 'Colonel, help yourself. Leave in the next sixty seconds, and you will not be fed to my dogs.'

'I know who is behind these assaults. I know why.' Lazin sensed grips tightening on sub-machine guns, the anticipation of men clutching an armoury of *Kedr* and *Klin* models. Close-quarter weapons; close-quarter target.

'You do not notice the trail you leave; you do not find stolen diamonds. But you hold out answers.'

'People I was close to have died. People you were close to have died. We share common ground. I ask you to listen.'

'I ask you to go. Thirty seconds.'

'Then I will leave you with this.'

Lazin reached into his coat pocket. Two men stepped in to seize his arms; a shake of Diakanov's head caused their retreat. There was no risk, the body search had proved that, removed the Gyurza from its long shoulder-holster, the small self-loading PSM 5.45 mm from its ankle position. This was not a suicide-run. A photograph was produced and handed over.

'Explain.'

Guy Parsons, head of Russia department at Britain's SIS, was playing his Joker. 'It is the man who killed your son,' said Lazin.

Lateen sails furled, the dhow butted into the headwind, spray slapping arbitrarily over the black phallus of the stemhead, decks juddering above the Gardner diesels in the engine compartment. Howell ladled drinking water to his lips and rejoined Purton making pencil sketches by the inadequate light of a hurricane lamp. Beyond its radius, among the crates, sacks and net restraints holding the inheritance of a thousand years of Gulf trade, twenty crew members and four of Ahmed Badr's Yemeni guerrillas lay sleeping.

The NCO sat on a teak block and indicated the drawings. 'I got drinking and fighting from my dad. You middle classes get to play with crayons.'

'A key intelligence-gathering skill. Baden-Powell could have told you that.'

'You trust a man who wrote *Scouting for Boys*? Who's it for? Max?' Affirmative cue. 'He won't be pleased you're on the loose from the retirement home.'

Purton put the pad down, a view of sambuks under full sail, identified by their raked sterns and curved trailing wings, half-complete on the top sheet. 'You've done well with the volunteers, Nick,' he said. 'A few weeks ago, I wouldn't have had them down to crap in the correct sequence.'

'If they can handle their irons, I'm unfussy.'

Weapons tests at sea had demonstrated the improvements

wrought in the preceding weeks. It was in the interests of the Britons to drive the men hard: lives could, would, depend on it, always did in small-unit operations. The live-fire assessment was to be conducted against a live-firing enemy.

'They're fitter than the average British soldier.'

'Who the fuck isn't?' came the derisive reply.

'Well, there'll be plenty of opportunity to prove themselves.'

Howell wrist-turned his watch face. 'Pretty soon too. An hour, and we'll get the buggers up to load the Ribs.'

They felt the boat respond to the helmsman's adjustment, the man's face concentrating, reflected irregularly in the flame of an oil wick caged above the compass binnacle.

'Sodding timeless, isn't it?' Howell muttered. 'Nothing's changed since they carried myrrh and frankincense on these routes.'

'Bit before my arrival.'

'Not by much.' Howell smiled, face puckering.

The sharp cry of a lookout interrupted, the scuffle of men moving rapidly from sleep to dazed action rippling out in its wake. A flare went up and popped, magnesium white hanging high above, drifting imperceptibly lower in its own cloud of gossamer smoke, startled faces naked beneath its brightness.

'Christ. Haven't they heard of international waters?' Howell hissed.

'*Everyone stay down!*' Purton scrambled to the edge of the raised poop and jumped a body-length into the deep well of the main deck. He looked up at his sergeant. 'If they're hostile they'll want to close, so we'll take them. We can't afford a shooting match at stand-off – they'll sink us.'

'Want me to keep the helmsman happy?'

Purton nodded and caught the shortened Remington 870 pump-action *Ninja* dropped down with the bag of Number 3 cartridges. The best for close-quarter work: four rounds carried, butt replaced with a soft pistol grip, a vertical fore-grip, a barrel less than ten inches long and finished in military manganese phosphate. With a useful nine-inch spread at thirty feet on a regular choke, it could blow a hole in the best-laid plans of the best-armed opponents.

'I'll send a pair of fighters to join you.' Purton squeeze-tested the switch for the attached tactical flashlight – it flickered briefly in its carbon metal tube – and telescoped out the forks of the extended stock. Locked. Functioning. The boat's master climbed calmly up to Howell's deck.

The NCO tilted his head in the man's direction. 'Nelson died on the bloody quarter-deck too, you know?'

Cartridge loading. 'What do you think?'

'Your sketch?' he leaned down. 'Wonderful composition; classically balanced, clever use of light and perspective.'

'Anything else?'

Howell shaded his eyes. 'Nope. Not even a bow shape. No lights, so odds on it's an aggressor.'

'Pirates. Probably old hands from the headland at Ras al-Usaydah.'

'That ended in the fifties.'

'Civil war, poverty. Might just be a revival.'

'Or the Yemen navy.'

'Wait on my signal.'

If it were a naval vessel, it was here to intercept, to destroy. There could be no other explanation for it being so far out at such a time. They were compromised. Purton worked his way forward, whispering to the guerrillas, taking two of them to lie flat beside the lookout at the bow. The second pair came aft. Howell watched them. His hands moved over the Kalashnikov, checking, feeling.

Another flare. The men huddled down, Purton's group, horizontal, appearing flash-frozen in the searing over-exposure of its candlepower. It dimmed; Howell activated the night vision.

The ship was a merchantman, coastal type, low tonnage, bathed in the delicate artificiality of the imager. No automatic cannon visible. A relief. No identification, no pennants. A real concern. Figures moved real-time, framed in the zoom, carrying field glasses and the short silhouettes of assault weapons. Bandits, gun-runners or security forces in mufti – demarcations blurred in these parts. A carbine swung over the shoulder, casual. Howell blinked, breathing shallow, lungs under-oxygenated. The opponents were taking their time to size the kill, screws slow and churning out a fat wash. His stomach synchronised. Powerplant and emotions in neutral; shadow-play. *Fuck, make a decision.*

The wake changed, narrowed, engines powered up, and the vessel heaved past off the bow at two hundred metres. Howell waited for the parting burst of raked automatic, the sudden turn. Aftermath was drawn out – he followed the ship to the horizon – reality dripping down with the sweat. They were clear. He blew out his cheeks, finger easing on the trigger guard, tightness easing in his head. *The Flying Dutchman* had been close to becoming driftwood.

The Russian economy was in slide from basket-case to casket-case, and Leonid Gresko sat low in the rear of the Zil with the contented demeanour of the mad or the schizophrenic. There were two kinds of queue on the streets of Moscow: those waiting for bread, and those waiting to extricate their savings from the government-controlled Sherbank to buy that bread. As the rouble plunged and the price of a loaf spiralled upwards, the lines for each grew longer. Bartering rose with the tension: medals, toys, washing machines, radio sets, homemade pickles and rusting food cans laid out on every street corner, the haggling furious, exchanges surly, the din increased by the cry of beggars, fights between vendors, between thieves, and the plaintive notes from harmonica and accordion-playing cripples. At Pharmacy Number 1, the elderly collected their prescription drugs and sold them on to teenage junkies; the teenage junkies shot up in the cellars beneath the vacant nightclubs. A hard season. The population's famed *nakhodchivost* – peasant resourcefulness – was not enough.

People were scared – it was reflected in their faces; the president's advisers were scared – it was reflected in their measured talk of stabilisation. Yet Gresko's stabilisation plans remained hidden. He leafed through the morning's newspapers. Bond markets vaporised, GKO notes dumped, stock markets dead. Savings gone, industry gone, the future gone. Five hundred banks had crashed in a month, a thousand more sustained by Central Bank credit alone; interest rates at an unprecedented two hundred per cent. Now the Sherbank was refusing to release domestic deposits and reneging on the government's guarantees. But those were promises made by an administration which no longer existed. Close the banks while the presses printed money: the only way to stem panic. The panic worsened, prices moved to new orbit. Kremlin technocrats conferred with the Germans, the Americans, the IMF, beseeching for loans, appealing that democracy be saved. The response was muted, ungenerous – too slow, as events moved too fast – unable to grasp the magnitude, dwelling on 'confidence building' when there was no confidence on which to build. High-profile legislators and spokesmen, opinion formers, in the United States and Great Britain – Senator Patrick O'Day and Nigel Ferris among them – urged caution, claimed the obligation lay with the Russians to find an answer, claimed it would get worse. They were right. Gresko folded the paper, created a knife-edge.

The previous night, Lubavitch Synagogue and its Jewish culltural centre in the city's Maryina Roshcha district had been bombed for a fourth and decisive time. Neo-Nazis, of course, their act a barometer of despair and the nationalist inter-ethnic prejudices it threw up. He was counting on such stirrings, fissures, to follow the economic collapse, to pull Russia closer to the brink, to involve her in clashes with neighbours that might yet ripple wider into the international sphere.

Armoured personnel carriers of the Second Taman Guards, tank units from the Fourth Kantemirov, were parked along the approaches to the Kremlin. Main gun ammunition was being loaded into the rear of a T-80 battle tank. A novel way to project an image of normality, of a president in control, the Director of the Federal Security Service mused. Each picture relayed to the West would see more funds leave, further the desiccation of the Russian body politic. It was an odd phenomenon: to see international broadcast agencies transmit footage, repeat newsflashes from the Ostankino television tower, which he had made available. This was prime time, Gresko the scheduler.

He passed the troops, failed to acknowledge their hasty line-ups, the sergeants drawing them to attention, the salutes. They were toy soldiers, a model army to be tossed aside in a model putsch. The Zil headed down Borovitskaya ploshchad, cut through the southern end of the Alexandrovsky Gardens wrapping the west walls of the Kremlin, and slowed to negotiate the Borovitskaya gate entrance. It was the President's customary route; fitting for one with more power than the present titular leader. Men from the Presidential Guard Regiment stepped back from the motorcade. They wore combat fatigues. The siege had begun, thought Gresko. The limousine gathered speed into the interior of the fortress, visions of tension – of men from the Kremlin Guard looking purposeful, yet without real purpose – running to orders, rushing past his side window. Black suits of the SBP Presidential Security Service mingled outside, wired ears, wired nerves, glancing around, unruffled professionals who were plainly ruffled. It was as he had predicted, as he had planned.

The Security Council, de facto government since the President's abrupt dismissal of his cabinet and vacillation in appointing successors, was in crisis session. A superfluous term – every session marked a crisis. The venue had changed: in the place of luxury was a committee room of commendable plainness. It suggested focus, application, commitment to solution-finding. To the Director of the FSB, it spoke of a bunker mentality, final days. They would never find a solution, for he was the cause.

'Mr Secretary,' the President asked. 'We all have minutes

of the last discussions. Please outline the key points for today's extraordinary meeting.'

Minutes that would turn to hours, discussions that would end in recrimination and argument, but no cure. Extraordinary had become the norm. Gresko's countenance was grave, his mind gleeful. Everything was going so wrong, it could scarcely be going so right.

The Secretary cleared his throat, nervous at his responsibility for introducing the next tranche of bad news. 'Mr President. I must report that inter-state and ethnic rivalries in our border regions, particularly as regards the Trans-Caucasus, require immediate attention. You will also note items concerning terrorist assaults by Chechen commandos on Russian nationals, the call by Armenia for arms in confronting renewed hostilities in Nagorno-Karabach, and continuing domestic subversion by criminal gangs . . .'

Require immediate attention. The President's own attention seemed lacking, strain provoking lassitude, the narcoleptic drowsiness of a man beyond shock or the reach of poor tidings. Drink may have contributed. Most of those attending were on some form of cocktail. Eyes were bloodshot, fright-tremors affecting speech and smaller movements, the palsy and pallor of officialdom at breaking point. Only the President's Chief of Staff appeared calm. So different to the rest; therefore so threatening. Gresko noted it, was ever aware of this pretender with pretensions of authority, usurper with a private intelligence network and access to the top. The government was in limbo, these men the rulers. National survival was what events had reduced affairs of state to. Yet the Chief of Staff carried the burden lightly, calmly. Inexplicably. Gresko's mood was turning. Debate continued around the table.

'Have you further information concerning the destruction of the Nvovorossiysk oil port?' The Secretary was staring at him.

'All evidence points to the Georgians, with Ukrainian connivance,' Gresko replied evenly.

'Ludicrous.' The Foreign Minister – removed from office, but provisionally reinstated – was shaking his head. In his present position, his reasoning carried little weight. He was a cosmetic, applied to reassure the West of policy continuity, the prettification of ugly reality. 'Mr President, what possible advantage would the Georgians or Ukrainians have in committing an act of war?'

Gresko answered. 'Because, with men like you overseeing foreign policy, they are aware of our weakness, that we would not respond.' He addressed the President. 'The Georgians wish to expand the export of Azeri oil from Baku along their pipeline to the Black Sea terminal at Supsa. It makes sense to undermine our own efforts in this respect.'

'But no sense to challenge us with sabotage,' the Chief of Staff intervened.

'Mr President,' Gresko persisted. He ignored the Chief of Staff, the warning implicit. The man was irrelevant, he would make sure of it. 'The Georgians are eager to see us remove our peace-keeping troops from their soil, to ruin our *miro-tvorcheskie operatsii*. Because we block its advance into territories lost to the Abkhaz separatists, the regime in Tbilisi has paid Svan bandits to attack our positions in the Kodori valley. Hit our economy, and you hit our force-deployment. There is the reason for the destruction of our oil port.'

'The feebler our neighbours, the more racked they become with civil strife, the greater our relative strength and the chances of reabsorbing the trans-Caucasus and Caspian regions into a Greater Russia. I'm sure that crosses the Director's mind.' The Chief of Staff's delivery was measured. *I have you measured for a box*, Gresko thought. 'Perhaps it explains FSB contacts with Mingelian mercenaries and refugees along the Inguri river. Perhaps it explains why the Director arms Cossack irregulars to raid Chechen villages and provoke unrest in Ossetia, Ingushetia and Dagestan.'

'Are you suggesting that I am a traitor?'

'Only that resistance by Moslem warlords, their terrorist actions against Russian civilians and observation posts, suits the aims of our hard-liners, provides an excuse for intervention.' Scorched earth, scores settled, and Russians could cheer, pride swelling while the rockets fell, oblivious for a moment to their own precarious situation. Order restored on the borders, integrity of the homeland achieved. That was what the people wanted, what the world wanted. Gresko would deliver. And this politician dared oppose him, was insistent. 'And the Ukraine? Why should they collude with Georgia in destroying our oil exports?' The Chief of Staff was acting out his role as presidential mouthpiece. *You will be silenced, I promise.*

Gresko's lids were safety curtains; drawn down, gave no hint. 'They are developing closer links to the United States, attempting to draw away from us. We have seen how they collaborate with Georgia to explore alternative supplies of energy.'

The Chief of Staff was dismissive. 'Those are not hard facts. Neither do they amount to a reason for the Georgians and Ukrainians to commit suicide. There would be no benefit in this.' There is no benefit to your contempt, the Colonel General observed to himself. It would not last under torture.

'Come to the Lubyanka. I will show you facts.' Said the spider.

The President looked vague, the details beyond his immediate comprehension. He rubbed his eyes. The clash between his two closest advisers made him uncomfortable. Once, he might have relished the friction, played on it. 'Our enemies take advantage of our predicament. We need solutions, we need unity.' His contribution came with a tired wave of the hand. It was as pointed as he would get.

'Mr President, conspiracy theories will provide neither.' The acting Prime Minister-elect, a technocrat and suspected ally of the Chief of Staff, directed the glance towards Gresko.

Evolution, revolution – both could overtake, overthrow a state before they were noticed. Paralysis was the key, Gresko's key. He altered direction. 'We have seen the open warfare on our streets, the latest fighting at Cheboksary. Are we to let the mafiya conduct a civil war, tear the fabric of our nation, fight tank battles, create carnage, while we stand idly by?'

The new Justice Minister, a Gresko and Interior Ministry nominee, came in on cue. 'If we do nothing, it proves that they are stronger than ourselves.'

'As if we need proof.' The President was contemplating his hands.

'Mr President, I believe we must strike. They are parasites, they feed on our troubles. All the while, the people lose faith.'

'Director Gresko is right,' the commander of the Border troops seconded. 'A major gesture is necessary.' Gesture was one of the few options left to this presidency. The FSB would be the heroes, conducting well-documented raids, riding to meet the threat. Inoculate the population to clampdowns and they would become accustomed, ask for more.

'Mr President.' Gresko was firm, reasonable. His was the reassuring mask of the competent, caring secret policeman. 'The gangs are fighting amongst themselves, their attention is elsewhere. If we move on them, we can win. What better way to demonstrate your authority? You have removed an ineffectual government. It is the moment to follow up against others who care nothing for this country.' Or nothing for the system soon to be imposed.

'Using your interpretation.' The Chief of Staff was caustic. 'And will your measures cure disease, provide clothing and medicines, feed stomachs, help the people?' His finger pointed. Gresko's mind chose the pair of bolt-cutters to employ on it.

'My funding is more limited,' Gresko snapped back, turning to the President for support. 'The Russian nation can tolerate anything except inaction, Mr President. At home or abroad.'

The conversation snaked on. Deep Throat felt aloof, almost exhilarated by the shifting influences, the subtleties, the danger. Gresko would get the Presidential decree, more power, greater influence, the command to move on the gangs and – by extension and association – their political and business clients. He was closing in, quarantining his victims for future disposal. Ends could justify any act, and when the ends had no boundaries, the acts themselves were limitless. But perpetrators of terror feared the most, for it was the chief component of their being: the self-destruction born from their destructiveness. For them, threats were everywhere. Poisoners could be poisoned, murderers murdered, plotters plotted against. Control unnerved them more than lack of it – the great paradox of paranoia. Gresko unnerved would make mistakes. He was calculating, but there were factors missed; the President's Chief of Staff was calculating – absorbing, analysing what sources such as Georgi Lazin were passing him. There were few fallbacks except death. All the more reason to fight.

There was a dread time in Russian history when the oprichniki *ruled the kingdom, when rule itself was euphemism for oppression and slaughter. Dressed in black, carrying on spikes the severed heads of dogs, and riding jet black chargers around whose saddles clattered a mass of human skulls, the enforcers rode at the behest of Tsar Ivan IV 'The Terrible' to spread anarchy and fear about the land. This was his great experiment, his* Oprichnina *– 'separate state' – and millions died within it. Centuries on came Stalin's own version, the police state, dominated by men in black garb, sent out in jet black vehicles to harvest the people. Same experiment, modern techniques and a justifying ideology. And millions more died. On past Communism to another elite set apart, black marketeers clothed in designer black, driven in jet black limousines, dominating Russia and growing fat on its misery. They would fall, they would fall. And the* oprichniki *were again waiting, arisen from the past, summoned by Leonid Gresko, ready to assume the powers that he alone could grant them. History was a fault-line running beneath humanity. Cold Cut could feel the tremors. He had to stop it, had to . . .*

'Brodets, Brodets. Wake up!' The old man stirred. 'I'm sorry. It's important.'

Eyes opened; the rush to consciousness of one conditioned, primed for hiding, flight and the arrival of the authorities. 'My sleep was troubled enough. Have you been through the papers?'

'Every page and every line. Please, Brodets, you must come, see for yourself.' There was respect and concern in the voice, love, sensitivity for a leader.

Cold Cut swung himself to his feet, hiding the pain, internalising, cutting off the gasp with teeth clamped. There was no room for weakness, self-indulgence. That was for later generations, for those who knew peace and peace of mind. He padded across the hut towards the glow of hurricane lamps and the shapes of people part-illuminated, part-silhouetted in a circle. His disciples. The faces represented many of Russia's dispossessed tribes, ethnic and political. They made room for him.

'What have you got?' he asked.

A North Korean spoke. 'Charts, coordinates, directions, instructions, identity papers. Just as you thought. The two men we turned over at the railway hostel in Anosovskaya belonged to Gresko.'

'And their plans belong to us. Show me.'

'One acted as driver, fixer and bodyguard for the other.' The Buryat tribesman pushed across copies of ID. 'The second man is a senior figure in Colonel Petr Ivanov's unit. They were seen together at the storage caves.'

'It means we are dealing with direct contact to the top, orders from the top.'

'He is stationed at the FSB command and control centre in the Urals. His assignment was to check and enter the initial arming codes into nuclear suitcase weapons.'

The silence was lengthy. Cold Cut watched an oily flame climb yellow in its glass. 'Where are those weapons now?'

'According to the map they carried, and letters of introduction to the station security heads, at six strategic locations throughout the country. These include the rocket forces post inside Kosvinsky mountain and the plant you recced near Bratsk with its radar balloon.'

'And if these warheads are primed, what is the step to detonation?'

'A simple series of numbers on the main keypad. They were designed for terrorist use abroad by the KGB First Chief Directorate and follow-on Foreign Intelligence Service. There is an integrated time-delay system for operator escape.'

'Brodets.' Another man spoke. 'Why would Gresko wish to destroy defence assets he is pledged to protect, it is in his interests to protect?'

'Why would personnel at these locations cooperate with him?' The North Korean's puzzlement was echoed in murmurs around the group.

Cold Cut was still. 'Like us, they see only fragments. Perhaps they are unaware of what the cases contain; perhaps they do not comprehend the strategy.'

'What is our strategy?'

'As it has always been: to take the initiative. Do we have the arming sequences for the cases in our possession?'

'They are recorded here with the list of registration and armoury numbers. Once that is done, we might be able to short-circuit the trigger codes. The timer mechanism will be harder.'

'I spotted anti-tampering devices.' The old man had never lost his grasp for detail.

'We must neutralise them before final activation. Otherwise, we are left with a useless container full of radioactive isotopes.'

Cold Cut stood, movement disguised to indicate authority, designed to relieve the worn, arthritic joints.

'See what you can do.'

'And then?'

'Then we return an item of lost property to Colonel-General Gresko and his secret police.'

The tiredness was clearing, replaced by anticipation, the ache for combat that had accompanied him throughout his life. You have entered my realm, Leonid Gresko. Now I will enter yours.

They were left together, doors locked, the Council dismissed, water tumblers and blotters scattered in post-conference disorder. Here, Gresko had the ear and attention of his President. There were no quibblers or questioners, no interruptions. The Chief of Staff had been excluded from the room – his face betrayed less anxiety than the others.

'You say it is urgent, Leonid?'

'And for your ears only, Mr President. It is a delicate matter.'

'The situation is precarious. What matter is not delicate?' He spoke as a leader who had sacrificed his colleagues for political expediency, to discover that he was now exposed. The cladding was falling from the edifice. 'Do you wish to talk of the identity cards? You assured me the technology was ready.'

So it was. The latest and best from America, acquired for the Russian Federal Security Service by Hunter Strachan, ID containing an individual's electronic fingerprints, facial image, iris match, dental and biological details, financial and personal records, antecedents and criminal history. It would be an offence not to carry a card, and retrieval from the database was instantaneous. Over one hundred million cards were manufactured, waiting for allocation; over one hundred million pass keys into Gresko's security state. Emergency necessitated it, the President dictated it. The FSB had installed the system pre-emptively – some might argue presciently – were ready to capitalise. The executive head of state seemed grateful.

Gresko unclipped his attaché case. 'Everything is prepared. It will ensure the survival of all your reforms, of the rule of law.' It would ensure anything but. 'No, Mr President, I wish to hand you these dossiers. You will understand why it demands privacy.' He pushed them across, the cardboard envelopes bulging.

'You think I do not have enough paperwork? With each page there is trouble.'

'It is my duty to bring it to your attention, to protect the Constitution.'

'You do it well.'

The unembarrassed stillness of one who expected praise. 'I would request that you read the summaries now, Mr President. Your concern is appreciated.'

Resigned, the President turned to the top file and edged out the front pages. Gresko waited. *A delicate matter*. Personalisation of the Russian political system made the Constitution a shallow, frail entity, open to abuse, the vagaries and arbitrariness of the Presidential decree. For all the talk of plurality, power was vested in one man, and if the people lost faith, they might lose faith in the whole. Thus was the path of proto-democracy crazy-paved to authoritarianism. The Director of the FSB crouched at its end.

The President's eyes lifted. 'You are serious?'

'With the deepest regrets, I am.' Sincerity trickled.

'Mouth of a whore!' The expletive was heartfelt. 'I need a glass of Armenian brandy.' The FSB Director pulled a small bottle from the case and relayed it. It was uncapped, poured generously, the liquid swallowed. 'It should not be publicised.'

'On the contrary, Mr President. Here are several ministers whom you have recently dropped. To punish them for treason, for their links to the mafiya, with the unassailable evidence which I have provided, is to prove you can take the most difficult decisions.'

'They are out of office. That was a difficult decision. It is enough.'

'Not when the people are penniless, when their situation will worsen, when the mafiya has brought blood to our cities. Your latest purge will be forgotten; the citizens will blame you. Rumours of irregularity have persisted in *Nesavisimaya*

Gazeta for months. The public expect a firm hand. Prolong the disgrace of those you once trusted, and you will be respected. Demand their execution, and you will be respected further.'

'I am old enough to remember show trials. I am not Stalin.'

'If I might speak bluntly, you may not be President for the remainder of your term. We are striking at Boris Diakanov. These members of government were bankrolled by him. Destroy his powerbase, build your own. Demonstrate clean hands.'

'You are suggesting I bloody them.' The brandy bottle tipped.

'Symbolism is vital; the international currency markets illustrate this every day. Renewal, the shedding of old ways – and confidence will return. Lose a few discredited incompetents, or you will lose everything.

'They were a government lacking in dynamism, initiative, new viewpoints and ideas.' The words had belonged to President Boris Yeltsin and used to justify the sudden dismissal of his government in March 1998. Armenian brandy was a contributing element to irony.

'The explanation will be accepted. We are at war against the mafiya, there is a state of emergency. These individuals betrayed us at the highest level.'

'I will summon the Justice Minister.'

He would agree with Gresko; the President, embattled, in turn would agree with them. Executions could be so energising. Gresko's thoughts loitered on the news from England, sent by Nigel Ferris' handler, that the Secret Intelligence Service suspected the FSB of manipulating an enveloping Russian crisis. The name of Colonel Petr Ivanov was even raised in closed meetings. It could not be coincidence: SIS prying into the cryogenic aircraft project, increased activity at their Moscow station, the young woman Zenya filmed breaking in to Hunter Strachan's hotel room at the Ukraina. Somehow the strands were linked, coordinated. A partially-sighted man tapped his way into Gresko's consciousness. Disabled, and therefore overlooked, going blind, going nowhere. Close to Strachan, closer to Zenya, he had fooled everyone. Everyone but Gresko. The Colonel General grunted. How unfortunate that the youthful, charming American could not see what was coming to him. Max Purton's charitable status was about to be revoked.

The President was speaking, but Gresko could not hear, babble in his head drowning the voice. He watched the mime, the charade. *I have the answer*.

'What did you say your horse was called, Max?'

'Glue, if it doesn't handle decently. Should have taken the Steppe horse.'

What was good enough for a Cossack was good enough for him: a *Przevalski* could travel a thousand miles a month through heavy snow.

He was not certain if equestrian pursuits were ranked among his favourite time-killers. Teenage holidays spent working on an uncle's stud in South Hamilton, Massachusetts, had – like the effect of enforced religion on spiritual development – exploded the mystery and therefore any interest in the subject. But he persevered, daily picked out the scavenging wood ticks which attached themselves instinctively and unrelentingly to the human scrotum, and mastered both horsemanship and regular, exhausting sex with the stable-girls. Long hours, a horizontal learning curve.

Zenya leant over and patted the neck of his horse, a black cross-bred Polish Trakehnen stallion given height, muscularity and a Roman nose by tortuous blood-line from the imperial Austrian Kladruber breed. An impressive beast.

'Don't be so cruel,' she admonished, raking her fingers through the mane to reassure the seventeen-hand animal. 'You're handsome, intelligent, and we love you.'

'Perhaps you'd like a moment alone together? I'm obviously cramping your style.'

She reached up, hooked the back of his head, and pulled his mouth to hers.

'Sometimes a horse isn't quite enough.' A second kiss.

'Tell that to Catherine the Great.' A third. Christ, he was remembering the girls of South Hamilton – the smell of the tack room, the horse box, leather, straw, mildew, human sweat among the dung – or at least his hypothalamus was. But Zenya could trigger things which only came from adulthood. He squeezed her arm and shifted back, jeans tightening. Hormones and hard-ons made uncomfortable companions in the saddle.

They had cantered along the shore of the Galich Sea, picnicked in a clearing on bread, cheese and beer, their rides cropping leisurely at tufts of nearby grass beneath the birch trees, and commandeered an untrammelled patch on which to make love. The stallion whinnied and snorted.

'Fuck off. I'm the one having the orgasm.'

'That's sexist.' Zenya had protested from beneath, struggling to turn him on his back.

'I'm sorry, little one. He's probably never read D.H. Lawrence.'

'Have you?'

'Nope. But I know they all make out in the forests.' The charger had flicked its ears and turned away.

The horses walked on among the silver firs, sun slanting intermittently onto the bridleways, sound and breeze muzzled by abundant green. Zenya pointed out plant species, Max nodding, assuring interest, before it became apparent his eyes were aligned on the wrong areas. They laughed. High above, a light aircraft piston-stroked its way on an unknown course, noise reedy, surging and fading unimpressively into the distance.

'You should be a naturist.'

'You mean a naturalist,' she replied seriously.

'I know what I mean.'

She persisted with her lecture, but the class petered out, a victim of Max's idleness and myopia. He felt mildly giddy, the ground rocking, travelling fast across his narrow vision field. The days of the grand panorama were over, life and sight reduced to a tunnel from which he would pay anything to crawl. He could reach out and touch her, replace one sense with physicality, sexuality, but he felt ashamed – at having to scan her face, at having to build her image from partial snapshots, a composite. Blindness would drag him away, and then he would be alone. He could not volunteer her to share that pain.

She reached across and took his hand. 'What's on your mind?'

'Depravity. And pine cones.'

The smile slipped up to her eyes. 'Max Purton. You are mad.'

'Blame my two parts per thousand of Irish blood.' Blame it on weakness, the impossibility of the situation. Humour was no escape. You deserve better, Zenya, so much better. Her grey Orloff Rostopchin mare nuzzled at the lips of his mount, the horses biting playfully. It was a day for flirtation, interaction.

'*Soidite! Soidite! Ruki vverkh!*' The horses reared.

They had not heard the helicopter. It was a Mil Mi-17, equipped for psy-ops – psychological warfare – bursting above the tree-line, the command to dismount bearing down from tannoy speakers slung beneath the fuselage. Max wrestled with the reins, his stallion and Zenya's mare backing neurotically from the creeping shadow.

'What do we do, Max?'

'. . . *Ruki vverkh* . . .' Hands up. The order, hard, unequivocal, decibel-boosted, sent a flight of duck panicking skywards.

'Ask my dad. He's the commando.' He calmed the horse. 'OK, Zenya, listen. We turn on my count, hit the point where the trail divides and split. From there, follow the drill.'

'I understand.' She tensed, ready.

The shape moved to the side. A trio of shots, dirt puffed up in quick spasms ahead. The horses nudged further into untidy dressage reverse.

'Pretend to climb off, cooperate. Stay low, keep to track too narrow for the bird to put down.'

'OK, OK.' Lying forward on the neck, concentrating, infusing the mare with confidence, suppressing fright.

'You go first. I love you. Three, two, one . . . Now. Go! Go!' She loitered fractionally and spun.

He was strapped to the front of a subway train, pushed by fear, directionless, rushing through glades, through thickets of aspen, dodging branches he could not see, torn by them, driven on. The world had speeded, into and past his tunnel view, the engine derailed, charging terrifyingly on its improvised course. Fuck, no hobby for a blind man, his brain registered. He flinched, leg scraped a trunk. And he was whooping, absurdity and alarm feeding the elation. Follow me you pretty helicopter, you pricks, follow me. Stay away from Zenya, burn your fuel. Stay away, or I'll bring you down. He kicked, ducked, urged on the horse. Its charge was instinctive, a product of its Polish cavalry ancestry. Lights were speckling his crippled retina, cells unable to process, diseased rods and cones overcome by formless colour, by images veering from bright to shade. The stallion's head was rocking, hoofs pulsing rhythmically; the rotors intruded, galloping. He was confused.

The breath would not come. He tried again, pain in the chest keeping attempts shallow, summoning nausea. Had he been thrown? Hit? The horse had swerved. The girls in South Hamilton would have found it funny. Where was Zenya? Where was the helicopter? *Relax, wait to see what's next*, Strachan had said. Prone, there seemed no choice. Waggle fingers, toes. Spinal column intact. It had to be, the body ached too much. Couldn't the frigging nag check where it was going? Why was he expected to do everything? He winched back his eyelids, enjoying the dancing fauna, followed the spider on its silken thread, beautiful, abstract. Armed. It landed close, hands – or were they legs on an arachnid? – patting him down, pulling him roughly into a harness, attaching the safety clip. They left the earth together, ravelling up the web.

Zenya hid deep among the trees. She had sent the horse on, careering wildly, wide-nostrilled and foaming, back towards the resorts. The mare would lead her pursuers a frantic chase; her rider could have jumped anywhere. There was gunfire, automatic. Perhaps they were trying to bring her steed down, or firing on Max. Or trying to flush her out. She would stay here until nightfall, venture out and pick up the trails. The log cabin was useless – it would be guarded. But she and Max were bounced, ambushed, in the wild, so the enemy wanted matters kept unofficial, low-profile. That was an advantage, for there would be no field army beating with sticks around her position. If she kept her nerve, she might survive. For Max, estimates were harder. The helicopter was hovering far upwind, decoyed. She crouched down and hummed an ancient Russian folk song. It cracked into a sob.

Max lay in shock on the cargo deck, ribs tight, head and torso hemmed in by army boots, rotorcraft vibrations shuddering through him. He moved his face, short searchlight gaze taking in the flight-deck access, a fragment of gauge and switch panelling, a pilot's shoulder, beyond. The heavy-tread sole clamped on his cheek, opening up the cut, pinioning him to the steel floor. A flight-suit appeared, foot pressure eased and he raised his head again. Hunter Strachan, ravaged countenance wrapped in a flying-helmet, gave a salute and paralysed grin from the cockpit.

Governor Ibrahim Abd al-Aziz sat smug in the rear of the armoured Mercedes. He appreciated the suspension; the road – built by the Chinese in the 1970s – was showing both its age and its lack of upkeep. In front, the escort bucked on a pothole. He braced himself. The limousine dipped smoothly and continued. A satisfying day. He had flown in to the airport at Khormaksar fifty kilometres from Aden that morning, been greeted by men from his spearhead Al-

Amaliqa brigade and taken on a tour of military camps near Kharaz and Taiz. There was a mood of anticipation, swollen by the units of civilian volunteers, of preparation underway. So much to do, to carry through. Excitement was palpable, infectious, the extra *materiél* he brought from the north eagerly unpacked and examined. 'Infectious' described it well. How he would infect the south. The destruction he and his brothers from Islamic Jihad intended to wreak on these unreconstructed, unrepentant socialists, Communists, non-believers and idolatrous Shafi'i Moslem moderates would see him swept into the highest echelons of government office. Today he was governor of Aden – the hard man, the instrument of true north-south integration, the obtainer of full obedience from a sullen population – tomorrow, he was promised the Ministry of the Interior. After that? Possibly the presidency. The regime in Sana'a had long sought to impose its will; there was unfinished work from the civil war of 1994. Now he was to complete it, definitively. His success was the north's success, the final and starting act. Starting, because Saudi Arabia would be next on the target scroll, and the corrupt, complacent rulers of the entire Arabian peninsula were to follow.

Outside, the scrub bushes clung threadbare on the salt-stung rocks, a wasted twilight landscape caught sporadically in the revealing tunnels of the vehicle headlights. The West was so powerless, the governor mused. It could posture, threaten, pass resolutions and send grave-looking, hand-wringing diplomats scurrying to convene conferences on human rights and political stabilisation, but they wanted oil, wanted gas. So they would talk, compromise and ultimately trade. His plans were safe. A few more weeks of fine-tuning in the capital, the shoring up of alliances, and the pogroms could begin. He would return to Aden, to his beautiful, secure palace in the grounds of the government complex, to initiate and coordinate.

A yawn, and the rhythmic tapping of fingers along the window edge. Approaching, city lights sparkled like muzzle flashes. One day soon, the effect would be so real. The governorship was truly a blessed role. He peered out, overwhelmed by a childlike desire to speed his arrival at the completed residence, the sweep up to its grand portals. Cocooned, tyres rumbling, he eased comfortably back, sensing the mountain crags which loomed at the edge of Crater town, deepening the lightlessness, pressing in on the haphazard urban blocks and characterless flat-roofed housing. The convoy maintained its momentum, car beams trampolining on the rough surface, engines powering through streets denuded by darkness and curfew. Few saw the three vehicles sweep by, close-knit, tight around the central pivot. One did. In his hand was a satellite telephone. Not long, the governor thought. Not long.

Not long. The reasons for his being here were lost in the ache of his joints. Howell rocked a little, easing from side to side, a rolling blood-pump. Circulation remained sluggish, confined to the easy areas. Come to me al-Aziz; come to Nick. I'll make you pay for the discomfort. The report – concise, urgent – had arrived on the satphone, confirmed earlier information of the governor's escort procedures. Three vehicles, Subaru four-by-four in front, indeterminate model behind, governor sitting ugly between. Foolish to have so high a profile, to visit your pet troops on your official deathday. Critics had eyes, ears, communications technology, Howell the explosives to make a terminal statement. Another crater for Crater town. Topography was so changeable round here. From this Aidrus Hill position the triggers were armed, laser-activated, software contacted and controlled by the attached satellite receivers.

Purton had departed with two men a thousand metres up the escarpment to wait on the eastern heights of Jabal Shamsan ridge. They could watch the unfolding tableau, cover the retreat of the forward team with a night-sighted heavy machine gun and grenade launchers, and mount a rearguard defence against pursuers while Howell's group leapfrogged past to the escape point. By now, he would be observing the downwards sweep of the landscape, repeating the distant reconnaissance of their first night in Aden. It was a tense day, avoiding the pickets and patrols staking out government territory on the narrow route to R'as Marshag. Unhurried Arab casualness, and all the more dangerous for it, random patterns interrupting intended forays through the cut wire, sudden appearances disrupting the schedules recorded in the assault team's surveillance log from the previous twenty-four hours. But they continued, pressed flat, crawling – frozen inertia as enemy forces passed too close – crawling again, handing equipment through and along the unobserved lizard chain. For an hour, Howell had been isolated on the far side of the road, wiring detonators, optimising energy arcs, while an army four-tonner parked up beside his cover for no apparent reason. Nerves held. It rolled off, the driver not bothering to look hard into the shallow gully running beside his cab. In any cursory inspection, the rock creature blended well with its surroundings; its weight loss over sixty minutes was marked. The Governor of Aden too was marked. The laser and photoelectrics had been aligned.

Howell felt the nudge to his ribs. A moving fluorescence flickered distantly between rocks below and to the left.

'They are coming.' Only to exit, on a white-knuckle ride to nothingness. Cut the official in half; cut his country in half: the mission had simplicity and clarity. A clear shot.

'How's activity at the R'as Marshag gatehouse?' he demanded.

The second guerrilla kept his eyes to the thermal imaging scope. 'Number three has joined the first two. Number four has appeared. There are others in the guard building.'

'They're expecting. Pity their guests won't be making it to the party. Not in one piece, anyway.' He glanced askew. 'OK, time to bin the fucker. Stay alert and get ready to bug out as soon as he's fried.' Nods from the Arabs. They were aware of ongoing assessment; he was a hard teacher.

A pair of headlights bounced onto the promontory road. The Subaru. Next, the Mercedes, separated by two car lengths. *For Chrissakes close up*, Howell cursed. The blasphemy worked, front vehicle slowing into the run-up to the curve, the governor's transport compressing the gap.

'Going, going . . .'

Al-Aziz died quickly, surgically. His mind was engaged – about to be elsewhere – flitting along the headings of his favourite subjects: religion, discipline, authority, political expansion, power and self-advancement. He was not aware that the Subaru had broken a laser beam, switched the first trigger, nor that his own vehicle was acting as the crucial instrument and initiator of his own demise. To his left, a bright flame tongued into his consciousness, sensed but not analysed, orange-white, a coloured shock force unopposed by the ceramic kevlar inlays and treated layered glass of the passenger door. It burst in on him, charging ahead of the sound, directed by fifty pounds of plastic explosive, punching shape and life from the body, a cyclone fury that melted seats and mortality in an instant. *Must get to the fortress, to safety*. A remnant of flickering cognizance reached from the closing redness and focused on a star. So bright, a burning star. The Mercedes symbol faded. Implosion. Darkness. Displaced matter cooked.

'. . . Gone.' Howell's voice remained expressionless. 'Right, you know what to do.'

Thirty seconds, the trio were falling back, Howell leading. Forty seconds, they reached a lumpen boulder squat on the track. He turned. At the rear, the Yemeni hooked his arm up and around, withdrawing it across the throat of his country-man. He stepped aside, let the body go its own way. A low bubbling, fingers patting at a windpipe severed deep by a high-tensile blade, superficial exploration changing to discovery and frenzy. Once dead, the corpse would be booby-trapped with wide area fragmentation grenades. Pursuit deterrence.

Howell depressed a code sequence into the satphone.

Connection made. He listened, night-dilated pupils taking in the scene, at his feet a Yemeni expiring helplessly in self-generated froth, beyond, the wreckage of a bomb-blasted Mercedes surrounded by debris-fields of burning fuel and contorted metal. Brief words. '*Prizrika. Starets. Zadacha vypolnena. Zhdu prikaza.*' The message received was also short. The line was cut. He entered new digits and thumbed the transmit key. At the site of the explosion, the surviving bodyguards, concussed, confused, staggering directionless in a post-trauma trance of unreality, were joined by running, yelling soldiers from the R'as Marshag entrance. Their gestures made no sense; their words were soundless in the ringing deafness of over-pressured inner ears. To Howell, the multiple detonations of his anti-personnel mines, set into the rocks around the roadway killing zone, rose thin and insignificant in the fresh evening air. Rook culling. He worked the cramp from his calf muscle. The high-pitched cracks hammer-fired, cross-fired for a moment longer, blending men that he had never met from existence with a million ball-bearings. Hard to engage in a chase without arms, legs, or a head. Too bad. There was an appointment with a dhow.

Book Three

THE BEAST IS BORN

He is in his chair, curiously unsurprised. But deception is his way. A stand-off, seated. There is no welcome, no *bonhomie*, no jokes, only the neutrality of real hatred. We are facing, studying each other. I see his features, sunk with terminal decline, the raddled alcoholic spite, the violence shading the eyes, and I remember, remember it all. Kim Philby. He was my executioner; I am now his ghost. He moves, leans forward. A wrist is exposed from its cuff, and there are scars. I smile, for he has failed, to kill me, even to kill himself. *Failure*. That is it; that is why he hates. It is the essence of the man, the primer for the pain he feels and once inflicted, the driver of the bully, the persecutor, the inadequate. In knowing, I am victor. Around him, a clutter of objects, trinkets, books and memorabilia, crowd on surfaces, artificial comforts for a place which holds no comfort. A cramped existence for a cramped soul. Confinement. And I have intruded, to remind him of true freedom, of the waste, and of the past.

Words are halting. How to summarise betrayal, the years lost in the horror-white of frozen penal *Lagers*, the friendships and families torn up, bodies discarded, by the creed he served. Served avidly, served well. I have seen so much, and he will never see. There will be no conversion here. But I am reborn, while he is condemned; I am the surviving truth, he the dying lie. His falsehood, the Communist falsehood, is crumbling. I stare at the wreckage. It is ill, self-pitying, crying. It is ignored. I look again at the apartment. He gave up the West for this; he handed me over for this, handed over so many, so much. I expect to see the thirty silver pieces mounted. They must have been spent, on bread, vodka, on airmail deliveries of *The Times* from London. Perhaps I wish he had gained more from my suffering. It would give greater meaning, a higher value. Instead, I am presented with decay; forty years of my life, his life, summarised with decrepitude and the ramblings of a monster grown old. He achieved nothing. We are the same age, yet are strangers, our lives spliced, entwined, spliced, entwined, through destiny, politics and enmity. It is a strange way to end, a strange place to end.

For him, the finale will come soon. He will be judged – the loser. But he peers up, fury-flush to his cheek, and murmurs: *We will see who wins. We will see who wins . . .*

CHAPTER 7

So dark, but there was movement. His eyes strained; no use. He felt excluded, was watched – but unable to watch – participated without being a participant. Perhaps if he stayed still, they would ignore, forget him. He thought of the teenage dances of his youth, the long hours spent standing blind, resigned, a little dazed from the noise and strobes, unable to get a handle or a pair of hips, unable to handle anything, while his contemporaries groped and sucked face around him. Happy days. The comparison was poor: this was far more threatening. A brief light source and the slamming of a vehicle door; Max turned his head towards it. He had been kept in a cell for three days or thereabouts – the bare bulb above his head never went off – was reluctant to leave confinement for this unknown. He shivered. There were other unknowns. It was cold in this period before dawn. Uncivilised spot, uncivilised time – perfect for an execution. The command to kneel would come.

He heard the approach; several pairs of feet, heavy tread, one foot lighter and less rhythmical. Stare the invisible figures out. *They can't see me, for I can't see myself.* Unconvincing. The boots came on. Eyes defeated by the contrast of black against deeper black, he closed the lids. If there were a code of conduct for such occasions, he did not know it. A prayer might be in order, or a rapid pictorial résumé of his life. No, that was too defeatist, almost willing the inevitable.

'Bad face-cut you've got there, Max.' Strachan's conversational and opening gambit.

413

'No worse than your limp.'

'Wounds gained in battle. Isn't that so?' The horse versus the helicopter: a quixotic and unequal contest. Max's bruises testified to it. 'You and your girlfriend taking off like that. Makes me think you've got something to hide.'

'Yep. I lied about my riding skills. Your actions speak a little louder.'

'You got balls. For the moment.'

Stand-off. Vision or imagination, Max detected the cavalry hat, set straight, hovering against the skyline. Below it, blanked out, Strachan. The older and younger man, feinting, dodging each other, dialogue underscored by betrayal. Max wanted to see the expression, knew there would be none. A mouth sewn into a cracked saddle – as flexible as Strachan's features could ever get.

'Where's Gennady?' the captive asked. The company bodyguard, his friend, a stalwart with the arms of a steroid abuser and heart of a giant, must have divulged their riding route. There was no reason for the Russian to refuse: Strachan was his employer, beyond suspicion.

'He's been retasked.'

'You've killed him,' Max stated flatly.

'An ugly turn of phrase. But, hell, it wasn't working. He forgot who kept him in vodka, was caught heading out in a four-by-four to warn you.' Max breathed deep through his nostrils. 'Quite a fighter. Would've put Rasputin to shame.'

'Fuck.' It came from a head hung low. 'He's got a family.'

'Wrong tense. Incidentally, they were easier.'

Max blinked moisture in the dark. Grief, fury, impotence – it was hard to kill what you could not see. 'One day, I swear . . .'

'You'll join them. And so will Zenya.'

'Why? Tell me. I want to know. Why?'

'I'm intrigued myself, truly I am. But I'll have to wait until the interrogators have been at you a while. You're a disappointment to me, Max.'

'And you're a fucking revelation.'

'American boy with spirit. Heartwarming. I like to think I've revealed nothing, bubba.' The art of ease, the studied languor, insouciance of the South. Camouflage.

'Stop jerking me, Hunter. What is this? I'm not a criminal. I work my ass off, stay months over here for you, sit tight during a near goddam civil war. Hotels are shit, pay is shit.'

'Makes you wonder what the incentive is to stay, huh?' Whatever decisions had been taken, they were made elsewhere, set. Max would save his energy. In the unseen distance, dogs barked, savage, discomforting. Zenya had got away, he felt it, was certain. It gave him a connection beyond this drama, a lifeline thrown out past this gathering.

'You may be interested, Mr Purton . . .' The vocals were Russian, hollow like a skull. Max did not recognise its owner – Petr Ivanov – but registered the tone. Until then, he might have scoffed at the concept of being frightened by a voice. His illusion was punctured, safety stripped, adrenal glands triggered. He wanted to run, hoped Zenya would never be close enough to hear this man. 'FAPSI specialists are dismantling your computer, assessing all your international communications, the more specialist service providers you use. You will be analysed with equal vigour.'

'Just keeping you in the loop, Max.' Which type would he end hanging from?

'This is nuts, man. What are you saying? That I'm a kind of spy?'

'Don't you go putting ideas in my head, boy.'

'Cut the lynch-mob crap, Hunter. You're setting me up. Say it's a joke.'

'Humour doesn't travel this far. You gonna say you always trusted me? Thought not. Now, then.' A return to business. 'Take out your lenses.'

The effect would be to remove his remaining useful sight during the hours of daylight. Contacts gone, contact gone. Max could not function without them. It meant total vulnerability. 'I can't, I need them. You know that.' He had kept them wet with saliva for his days of imprisonment; the routine was about to end.

'Refuse again, and I will cut them out.' Ivanov spoke. A spring-blade opened.

'You heard the man, you heard the knife. Do it.'

Max released the lenses into his palm. A guard stepped forward to retrieve them. Could be a formality, a precursor to the harvesting of his corneas once he was dead. *Don't tremble, you fuck. Don't give them the satisfaction.* His stick was back in the log cabin: another comfort gone, familiarity factor reduced. His belongings would be tied in a bundle, piled on a table. It was what gave the deceased pathos.

He translated the tension into disgust. 'And this is the guy who reported corrupt Divisional HQ officers in 'Nam for ordering him to machine-gun elephants from his helicopter for the ivory.'

'I like animals.'

There was a push to Max's back. He shuffled slowly, feet testing the ground. He was disappearing, knew it. 'Where am I being sent?'

'Between you and me? It won't be Patrick's Roadhouse for pancakes.' Strachan's voice shifted. The cavalry hat did not move with it – another false image imprinted on Max's consciousness. He could be wrong about Zenya's escape. Nothing was certain. Tricks were played everywhere.

Another prod, a slight stumble. 'Hunter, I don't know what's going on, but you've got the wrong man. Believe me.'

'I hear what you're saying, Max. You'll be in good hands.' Hard, professional hands. The walk continued. They reached a van, Max's head pushed down. 'I guess employee relations just aren't my thing. Still, sorry to lose you.'

Max was already lost. He fell forwards.

The *Izvestia* journalist perched on the bench, let the sun warm the trace elements of unease from him, the fountains soothe with the falling sounds of water. He stayed worried. Around, people milled in Pushkin Square, but the ambience had changed from the days when open-air debate was common, when every voice, every proto-demagogue, was expected, encouraged, to speak out loudly, proclaim opinions, on this site and on any subject. It was grassroots democracy, bounded on one side by the gold double-arches of Moscow's first McDonald's, the imprimatur of Western capitalism. But the grass was dying, democracy with it, and city-dwellers held silent wagers on the likelihood of Interior Ministry VV – *Vnutrennie voiska* – troops turning up, churning up and parking their tanks and armoured personnel carriers on this particular lawn.

A short step from his newspaper's headquarters on the north front of the square, he came here routinely to think, relax, to gauge the mood of the citizens. And what he discerned was the depressed fatalism of men and women secure in the inevitability that things would only get worse. He unwrapped his *kombi* sandwich – food could always cheer, if the appetite were there to exploit it. The pensioner nearby looked hungrily at it, saliva glands prompting a line of chin-dribble: in this world, fixed state income meant no income. Too old to sell his ass, too poor to sell anything, too despised by the brash demi-aristocracy of New Russians to be in line for cake handout. A group of striking miners wandered past, off down Tverskaya Street, eyed warily by militia squads concerned at their potential to escalate from surly window-shopping to joyous window-breaking. There was little to take, but the miners – camped in protest and in depth outside government headquarters, sending forage parties across town to scavenge and disrupt – stayed immune to urban sensibilities. They were tough men, unpaid men, were here to collect, and their numbers grew daily. Blood-stains on the sidewalk would also grow, for payment came in tear-gas, water cannon, and the overreaction of lead or baton rounds. An improvement on the grinding horror of their mining shifts. More street-theatre and warfare, crackdowns and cracked heads, for the embattled people of Moscow.

The journalist sighed. It was all going wrong; that wrong

was exploited by those with no stake in freedom's survival. Even his own paper, standard-bearer, flagship for liberal reform, had called for 'assertive action' in restoring authority and defending the Presidency. Yes, the Interior Ministry responded – in its traditional manner, obscuring the divide between assertiveness and brutal force. The riots spread. Now, several dismissed and disgraced ministers had been arrested on suspicion of graft, patronage and cronyism, of long-term connections with organised crime, unnamed foreign agitators and overseas interests, and a named Boris Diakanov. Nothing new. What was new was the language of Orwell, the vilification, the presence of those men in jail. Sweepouts generally meant the filth stayed hidden. He squeezed a sachet of mayo onto the sandwich. His reporter's instincts told him Leonid Gresko was involved, manipulating, planning, ousting one power elite in favour of his own. Unofficial contacts were unavailable for comment, which meant pressure, threats, hidden activity. The FSB Director had the grudging respect of international commentators and lending agencies, for he detested corruption, ensured no official stood immune to investigation; his vigorous deployment of the Security Service against the mafiya underworld delighted a downtrodden public sick of profiteering; his efforts to counter numerous internal threats to Russian sovereignty earned applause and gratitude across the political and social spectrum. He was irreplaceable, his stock high. Desperation made it so. And all the while, the position of the President's Chief of Staff, last of the reformers, became less secure. It was Gresko who was taking over. The journalist was sure of it.

A second sigh. During Communist times, when two newspapers – *Pravda*, meaning 'Truth,' and *Izvestia*, meaning 'News' – had served as mouthpieces for Soviet propaganda, there was a common saying among cynical Russians: there is no Truth in the News and no News in the Truth. Perhaps it was still justified. He had been called in by his editor the previous week, ordered to dilute his trenchant views on the role of the security forces in the present crisis. His stance was losing readers, he was told, was ill-timed, unpatriotic, out of touch with public sentiment. We are a commercial publication, the editor said. We have shareholders who are twisting your balls, the journalist thought, but did not say. What about independence, integrity? he replied. What about insubordination? came the response. He continued to submit copy littered with hostile references to Leonid Gresko. Colleagues were turning against him, whispering, advising him to redirect undoubted investigative talents elsewhere, or to leave. The sandwich was ready for consumption. He would save a piece for the three-quarters starved pensioner. They might soon be neighbours on the street.

A large man, middle-aged, rough-dressed, obscuring his athleticism, raw strength, with a studied gait and outfilled torso, ambled by. He might have been a miner, ex-soldier, both. The journalist was aware of immense size, of a short-lived shadow consuming the bench and passing by; memory ended there. The fine aerosol mist enveloped his face, entered the mouth and nostrils, droplets dissolving through the membrane and diffusing into the bloodstream. Many saw their effect. The journalist stiffened, rose, expression changing through shock to pain, hands clamped to chest, feet carrying him in disorderly circles until he fell.

An unsettling vignette, for the assassin, routine, similar to every dry or wet run he performed in the covert killing business. He was a hundred metres away, walking steadily, thinking of the American boy in custody he might have to terminate, the girlfriend – when found – who would follow. No problem, simpler than the hit on Diakanov's son beside an English playing field. Petr Ivanov would deliver the orders in that same deadpan, dead-voiced manner; they would be carried through with the efficiency demanded of an ex-*Vympel* special missions operative.

A crowd gathered, split unevenly between observers and helpers, all useless, drawn by the vicarious thrill of human suffering, a life tipped, and the convulsions of a citizen more distressed than themselves. The doctor pushed his way through, was counter-barged by a grandmother protecting her viewing position – a spot from which she could relay commentary to the back – and knelt beside the blue-lipped, sweating stranger. Pulse and breathing check: racing, all the pathognomic signs, a definite coronary, massive. He worked fast. Mouth-to-mouth, count, two-fingered chest pumping, count, compression, inflation, compression for five, inflation for one, five-to-one – odds on he would expire – a one-handed search in the medical bag for emergency syringes and the mini-ECG. Everything was a risk. Had to get flow. Fibrillation worsened; stabilisation vanished. The man was falling away, arterial muscles in spasm, blocking oxygen supply, starving the heart. A pedestrian knelt, took over while the three leads were attached, injections prepared. The representative trace came up. Still no sinus rhythm. *Try harder, come on, come on.* Needle stabbed deep, chest insertion, plunger depressed. Intracardiac adrenalin to improve blood-flow, save the brain. A second phial, diamorphine – test spurt – application. Veins constricting, blood returning to the heart. Massage continued, lidocaine and bretylium on standby. The doctor keyed a number on his mobile telephone, spoke briefly and returned to his patient. A faint pulse, rhythm steadying, then fade-out. Again, fluttering, catching, heartbeat weak but holding. *Stay with us*, he murmured into the man's ear. Life was crawling back. Screened by a press of bodies, the pensioner sidled to the bench and snatched the uneaten sandwich. He enjoyed the occasional treat, and this one was free. It served the bastard right for eating rich food. Later, savoured privately, the *kombi* was consumed in a side alley. Verdict: not bad, but a bit overdone on the mayonnaise.

The pensioner, doctor and volunteer lived – a consequence of the evaporating properties of an unknown and undetected poison spray. Its victim, the journalist, also survived, on account of treatment received from a senior medical practitioner based at a government clinic in the Swallow Hills and making house-calls that day to elderly, privileged patients residing near the Boulevard Ring. Heart and circulation complaints factored large in such visits. It would take major restorative surgery, several months, numerous blood trans-fusions and *Isolda* ultraviolet irradiation, and a difficult rehabilitation period, for the journalist to reach recovery. Of sorts.

'Will you take a look at those spikes. Gorgeous.'

The correspondent from the *Washington Post* was in better health than his counterpart from *Izvestia*, and in high spirits. He had no interest in Russia, few interests outside his own parochial world of political gossip and domestic scandal. After all, a body of ocean lay between America and the rest; the fifty states contained every facet and manifestation of humanity, so his public's distrust for matters foreign, their ignorance of international affairs, was laudable, excusable and downright understandable. For DC, an infighting power elite meant an inward-looking power elite; back-stabbing and behind-covering, patronage and perfidy, supplied the red-meat staple to feed the broadsheets. No need to overdo abroad when page-space could be given to advertising.

'I think this spells S.C.O.O.P,' a junior colleague stated.

'Spells F.A.M.E,' the man from the *Post* replied. He rewound the tape. 'Let's go through it again.'

Four of them sat at the table, cassette-player centre, stress-analyser and polygraph miked and wired to it, electronic screen display duplicating the peaks and troughs of a hard-copy printout rolling its paper spillage onto the floor. The group listened. It was an off-the-record interview conducted earlier that week with Senator Patrick O'Day. Except that every word was recorded, digitised and logged by equipment which carried the conversation from the adapted pen top of the journalist standing on a bridge spanning the C&O Canal to an unmarked van stationed close to the towpath. An unusual meeting, but one voluntarily attended by a politician eager to maintain close press relations and lured with the promise from a reliable newspaper source of sensitive information on his rivals. That reliability was now turned on him, and the graphic representations etched by the printer needle vividly demonstrated the result.

'Here we go for above-the-line bullshit.'

The lie-detector operator pressed 'play' and leant forward to watch. He and his female colleague – a psychologist specialising in vocal interpretation – gave greater credibility to the developing story, made it too persuasive for an editor to kill. Like many personal and political catastrophes, the tale had started simply. A Senator, senior establishment figure, a longstanding friend and hard-hitting ally of the President, was by chance observed with known drug felons. His anti-narcotics stance and interest in detailed research provided some explanation: he was widely recognised and lauded for his conscience and conscientiousness, for his involvement in social issues, his concern over inner-city inequality. His wife, a legal academic and confidante of the First Lady, Sixties radical turned worthy millennial matron, added to his standing. But it was not enough. Further inquiries revealed oddities: obsessive secrecy, cash withdrawals from banks before meetings, circuitous routes to rendezvous locations, the use of complex disguises and cut-outs. Then a lead spoke of cocaine-sharing and occasional restroom deals struck at parties, a camera was smuggled in, pictures taken. They were followed by agreement with a powder pusher in which details, records of quantities and quality, a history that went back several years, were passed across and checked. The popular politician, a persuasive speaker against aid to a corrupt and crisis-torn Russia, was in trouble. Condemned men loved to talk.

'*I am not a user . . . I'm telling you . . . It's not my scene . . . No, no . . . No . . . Yes . . . No . . . Everyone knows my views . . . Those photographs are faked . . . When I was a boy, going to church every day – did I tell you I was an altarboy? – it was made clear . . .*' The responses – negative or positive, concise or rambling – were delivered with uniform and vehement intensity.

'Strong performance.'

'Stronger smell.'

'Lies, without the blushing,' the polygraph expert interrupted. 'Great technique he's got going. I just wish you'd standardised around a simple yes or no reply to your questions.'

'Wrong profession for a straight answer,' the journalist retorted. A shrug from the specialist.

The psychologist was chewing methodically on a pencil, once in a while extracting to make a note. 'Disney only came up with Pinocchio's nose. We've got the whole package – higher pitch, use of negative statements, short answers where longer ones are appropriate, lack of detail. Sure signs of dissembling. As to the irrelevant, long-winded digressions – classic symptom.'

The older of the two journalists smiled. 'Only of being in Congress. It's enough to go on.'

'What's the plan?'

'Stir things up, spread the muck – for him and the press – leak a vague, unattributed story of insatiable nostrils in high places. He'll run to us to come clean, anything to put his side, stop the witch-hunt before a CNN helicopter lands in his tub. The only splash I want is from us.'

'You're forgetting your editor. He likes the President.'

'Nope. He likes speaking to the President. It's different. Besides, every administration needs uproar, a few casualties. It's why White House staffers get paid. The Senator will make a fine project, easily jettisoned.'

'And the President will look thoughtful and magnanimous throughout,' the second correspondent added.

The professional tore a printout from the machine and re-set. He was beginning to feel sorry for the Senator.

The man had followed him for three blocks. Bearded, amateur, he stopped when Lazin stopped, ducked into doorways, allowed the distance between them to fluctuate noticeably. Even by the haphazard standards of the FSB, he could not be an official pass-holder, Lazin assured himself. Its operatives had their own distinct patterns, particular flaws. Hammed-up private dick charades, product of imagination meeting 1930s American movie genre, were not among them. A freelancer? Possible. The Federal Security Service was overstretched; unsurprising when subversion rather than counter-subversion had been added to its duties by Director Leonid Gresko. Each day, the evidence amassed: of a mafiya war initiated by the murder of Boris Diakanov's son, of killings everywhere, of preparation and planning below ground in the nuclear-proof tunnels of Moscow, of a struggle at the heart – for the soul – of the Kremlin. And still Gresko held back, was waiting; Russia burned. Deep Throat likewise was waiting. *Too late*, Lazin thought, *too damn late to save anything*.

He sensed the man change pace, the angle of observation shift as they rounded the corner towards the gables and onion domes of the Church of the Trinity in Nikitniki. Absurd or dangerous – hard to guess. Tourists no longer came to the narrow streets of Kitay-Gorod, the ancient pocket with its chapels and craft shops east of Red Square, no longer visited Moscow or Russia. It was a trap of a different kind. Pace and pulse rose. His faceless, menacing colleagues might be putting pressure on him, rattling him, warning, or he was mid-sequence of an execution, with himself as the target. It would tickle them, humour Gresko, to do the job on sacred ground: a fresh delivery, the unreliable Colonel transformed into Church property. Then the propaganda, the death of a hero, justification for round-ups of anti-security elements. He ran through their likely itinerary, wanted to run physically. Beard was carrying a briefcase: confidence, stupidity. To the teeming street-thieves, it meant he was employed, meant he had money. Meant he could finish face down with a blade lodged between his shoulders. Lazin hoped they would act faster than the man, hoped fervently. But somewhere there was backup, he had yet to spot it, a second agent for the coup-de-grâce, a third for covering fire, a fourth in a doorway as scout and barrier, a fifth for the outer defence screen. All armed, linked with discreet comms, trained-up and throat-miked. They were not being drawn. Hope was irrational. He turned into a courtyard, double-backed through a deserted alleyway. If they knew of his work for Deep Throat, he was dead; if they knew of the information passed by British Intelligence and handed by him to crime boss Boris Diakanov, he was dead. Conceivable outcomes were depressingly similar. He had been careful, avoided mistakes. It must have attracted attention, alerted the office moles. Or tracking and eavesdropping devices existed which he had failed to detect. Yuri Vakulchuk, his nominal assistant, Gresko's plant, the wizened gnome – it was him, without a doubt, the Russian Judas. He had never liked the FSB Captain, nor trusted him. His presence down in the tunnel that night confirmed every fear. Here was reciprocity, Vakulchuk's revenge. Lazin heard the clattering echoes behind, eased into the darkness of a shallow storage area, listened for other pairs of feet. The footsteps halted, turned, hesitancy in the scrape of the sole. This was not routine, aggressive professionalism.

'Drop the case. Hands out to the side. Slowly. Do it, or your brain's going airborne.'

He could see the body shaking, adrenalin pumping for flight rather than fight. The neck concertinaed into the shoulders, the briefcase fell. 'Please, don't hurt me. Colonel Lazin, please don't shoot.'

A coward. It hardly narrowed the field. 'I need reasons. Who are you?'

'D-Dmitri S-s-hischkin, Dmitri Shischkin, pathologist's assistant. Please, Colonel, I'm sorry I followed you.'

'The dead don't have regrets.'

'My God, Colonel, please. *Please* . . .' The body vibrations were more pronounced. 'I'm a friend of Ilya's. I worked with him.' The man convulsed at the touch of Lazin's hand running along his clothing, the impress of a gun barrel in the small of the back.

'Move and you get a whole magazine. Who are you with?'

'Nobody, Colonel. Nobody.' Too scared, too out of condition to be in the security business. He smelt of the abattoir, the tell-tale hint of post-mortem. It could not be faked.

'Who's seen you?'

'No one. I'm alone Colonel.'

'Two paces forward, towards the wall. Now.' The man obeyed, the fragile totter of fright at imminent demise. Lazin crouched and took the case, withdrawing back into the dark. 'Turn around. Slow.' Dmitri pivoted, eyes closed, beard matted with sweat.

'I was Ilya's assistant. Believe me.' Lazin recognised him. He could be working for Ivanov, complicit in Ilya's murder. But the terror was real – the central nervous system made a poor method actor. Keep it that way. 'I have a letter from him, material, evidence. He hid them . . .' The eyes remained shut.

'Where?'

'On a body. The killers never looked there. They stripped out his office, didn't think of the lockers. I discovered it by chance.'

'How did you find me?'

'He left a note with directions, said I should make an approach away from your apartment. I've been following you.'

'I never guessed.' Mild satisfaction from Dmitri, before awareness of sarcasm penetrated. 'Have you been questioned?'

'By the police and Federal Security Service people. There was a man – thin, sunken face – asked about everything, threatened me, wanted me to keep in contact. Terrifying . . .' Ivanov. Dmitri would not begin to comprehend.

'Get back to Krasnoyarsk immediately. We never met or

spoke. There will be no further communication. Understood?'
Enthusiastic nods. 'If he hears of this, your only immortality
will come when he stuffs your body parts personally into
preservation fluid.' The nodding faltered. 'Now go.'

Sadness and anger rode on the fear. 'Ilya did not die
quickly, Colonel. Stop them. Just stop them.'

Lazin trod wearily up the bare staircase of his apartment
block, sweat-rings spreading from armpits to back in the
early summer haze of heat. In winter the common parts
trapped the cold, at this time of year warmth. There was no
middle way – architecture and its flaws reflected national
character, failings. Both were tested in the street-fighting
and fire-lighting of Moscow, razing and erasing, twists of
black smoke pluming from every district, dereliction discovered on each corner. A week had passed since the
exchange with Dmitri, a week of dreary regularity in Russia's
turmoil and decline. And Lazin did not notice, for he was
reading and re-reading the testimony of a dead man, his
friend Ilya Kokhlov, unlikely hero, sliced into pieces for his
efforts. He continued his study into the mafiya, travelled to
the Lubyanka, sent Vakulchuk on errands, went home at
night, but Ilya dominated his consciousness. Guilt and
immersion were the drivers of his agenda. The career was a
charade, for him, for Gresko: there would come a day of
revelation, of reckoning. Kokhlov's research told him so.
Lazin had passed it by dead drop to his shadow boss, Deep
Throat, the stranger in whom he placed his trust and to
whom he handed everything. Here were records of political
murders disguised as random events or serial killings,
apparent cannibalism, laid bare as lies in autopsy rooms,
shown as precursors to strategic takeover. In their systematic
nature, and in their aftermath, was the FSB, the country's
Federal Security Service. In the FSB was Leonid Gresko.
The life of Ilya Kokhlov the compiler, archivist, exchanged
for a few pieces of paper: it would not go wasted, unavenged.
Lazin promised himself.

He reached the landing; the light diffusing through an upper window was swallowed.

'Colonel Lazin. I suggest you remain still. You understand our methods.'

Petr Ivanov, funereal-suited, black coat draped unseasonably across an arm, stood several steps above, gaze and gun elevated downwards.

'A visit from a colleague. My diary makes no mention.'

'It will be recorded in our case report. Note that escape is blocked from below.' Lazin glanced. His FSB opponent was correct. 'Hands behind your back.' He complied. The door behind opened, a pair of handcuffs was applied tight. Ivanov descended a pace.

They had never socialised before. Lazin doubted this was a break with precedent. 'You were not invited here.'

'Then it is convenient we have become close neighbours. Accept my hospitality instead.'

Lazin was pulled backwards and through. It was pointless asking to where the long-term occupants, an academic couple and their baby, were moved, enquiring as to what kind of housewarming Ivanov had in mind. The FSB were ultimate relocation experts.

The apartment was small, neat, its sitting room dominated by a single, steel chair in which Lazin sat, bound, a wire noose around his neck and held tight by a guard. Ivanov remained standing, facing: two officers, one seated waiting for the other to give a command to strangle. Sunlight patterned the cream walls. The schools had closed, the 'last bell ringing' ceremonies performed, when young first-term girls rang decorative bells in traditional and moving farewell to the leavers. Schools out, anarchy loosed. Moscow's children were away in summer camps, their vacation transformed to evacuation by parents anxious at the urban turbulence, the breakdown in law. Lazin wondered who would ring the final bell for him. He remembered his childhood holidays in Abkhazia on the Black Sea, the smell of the Osman-fortune trees, the taste of feijoa berries, the sight of the glittering subterranean lakes in the Novy Aphon cave. The beautiful subtropical land was now racked by civil strife, war with Georgia, memories overlaid by pictures of blackened dwellings fronted with contorted bodies, family groupings face down or staring skywards. He was sure Leonid Gresko had reignited the conflict, sure his Director was behind the decision to invade Chechnia, behind his country's implosion, behind the tension with China and every bordering state. And he was certain that Gresko had ordered Colonel Petr Ivanov to eradicate him.

'I would ask how much you know. But it is of no consequence.' The look was calm, gave nothing. 'You served with the KGB Second Chief Directorate, yet you make the error of believing you can turn on us and survive.'

'You make the same error with your country.' Lazin was aware of the security service habit of manufacturing taped and faked confessions from computerized banks of digitally pre-recorded dialogue. The more he spoke, the wider the vocabulary from which they could draw. He was past caring, past the point at which they would allow him to live.

'The people will welcome us as their liberators.'

'As the people once did with Pol Pot in Kampuchea,' Lazin responded.

There was no discernible effect on the humanity vacuum. '"An independent spirit given to rogue action and anti-political sentiment." One of the more memorable lines from your psychological assessment.'

'I imagine yours runs to five volumes.' Ivanov ignored it.

'It will explain some of the crimes you will be blamed for. Incidentally, I killed your friend Ilya Kokhlov.'

'Dissection describes it more adequately.'

'I saw little reason to waste my journey to Krasnoyarsk. You will be taking credit for that death also.'

If they could lay the mutilation of a close friend at his feet, there were no limits; they were reinventing Stalinism, recultivating the viral strain of Beria's totalitarian secret police state. His investigation was complete. 'I'm flattered.'

'Not at all.' It was the nearest Ivanov would come to crowing. 'We needed you. You provided a connection between the crime chief Boris Diakanov and the President's Chief of Staff. It will enable a move to our final objectives.'

Lazin's head sank. Play on Ivanov's frigid triumphalism, on the mutual antagonism. 'I do not understand. The Chief of Staff?'

'The man you have been talking to, reporting to, leaving notes to. We recorded the meetings, the *dubok* methods.' He referred to dead drops in KGB slang. 'The tracking devices were a diversion. You were bound to discover them, feel you were safe.' He had never felt safe.

'Your efforts are commendable.'

'Yours will not be so praised.' Ivanov pulled a small, felt bag from his pocket, loosened the draw-string and tipped five rough diamonds onto his palm. 'Among the hoard discovered upstairs in your apartment.'

'Absurd.'

'Naturally. But they are part of several hundred million dollars' worth recovered from a number of surprising locations, from a number of surprising individuals. Surprised individuals. Like yourself, all have links to the President's Chief of Staff.'

'No one will believe it.'

'I beg to differ. Top ministers are in custody for embezzlement and corruption, anti-state activities which we uncovered. Why should the Chief of Staff be immune to such temptation? Revenue-raising was his stated goal. Remember Kozlenok? Bychkov?'

Lazin did. The Russian people had every reason, right, to accept the FSB version. In the mid-1990s, Andrei Kozlenok had swindled 180 million dollars from the Russian government in apparent collusion with the then head of the State Committee on Precious Metals and Stones, Yevgeny Bychkov. Senior politicians, including onetime Prime Minister Viktor Chernomyrdin, were indirectly implicated. The population expected – and got – the worst from its leadership. Crushed, threatened, without money, food, denuded of certainty and livelihood, the *narod* were in no mood to compromise, shouted for retribution. Gresko would throw these fallen masters to the crowd.

Lazin stayed motionless, tried to ease the pressure of the noose. 'The FSB presence will raise suspicions. Conspiracists will begin to search.'

'And they will find conspiracy – grand larceny turned to high treason, a Colonel in the Federal Security Service acting as go-between for organised crime and government servants. It explains our difficulty in uncovering the plot.'

'A plot which you set up.'

'Indeed. The Daban camp commander, one of ours, was troubled by your progress, wanted you neutralised. So many accidents occur in Siberian winters. But you survived, dispatched three of his operatives. I persuaded Director Gresko to allow your continuation.'

'Why?'

'The same reason the Major wanted you dead: because of the approach made to you in the camp by a man from the intelligence apparatus of the President's Chief of Staff. It proved that our rivals were organised, aware of something. Encouraging you would help expose them. I gave you a new career path.'

'Forgive my lack of gratitude.'

'The Chief of Staff would inevitably contact you once his agent-in-place at Daban went silent. We brought you back to Moscow in anticipation of it. A question of simple, convincing stages.' And they were.

Ivanov laid them out. One: Lazin's involvement in the train robbery, proved by diamonds in his possession, by the body of the co-driver found buried in the grounds of his country *izba* beside Lake Plescheevo, by the testimony of the commander at the BAM rail tunnel base near Daban, by the surviving driver, and by FSB records which proved his presence in the area. Two: his attempts to frustrate subsequent investigations, usually through murder. An FSB communications officer seen visiting him in the Daban camp was killed, followed by three soldiers sent to escort him on an exploratory mission to a disused mine discovered to contain the remains of rail troops from the diamonds train. In this act he received assistance from an outside and unidentified party, probably mafiya or an agent from the Kremlin Chief of Staff's espionage cadre. Proof of conspiracy. He further covered his traces by moving on to the central BAM town of Tynda and strangling Mrs Cherkashin, wife of a rail official involved in precious stones transportation. Her children had been slaughtered in an earlier attempt to frighten the husband – in fact it made him insane. Tragedy, ruthless planning, Lazin the perpetrator.

'Along with other objects, a tea glass at the woman's house carried your fingerprints,' Ivanov added. So, they had transferred it from his Lubyanka office to Siberia for later discovery by the local militia. 'Post-mortem examination of the woman revealed traces of your semen in her body. Varied receptacles. Secretaries at the Interior Ministry have their uses, Colonel Lazin.'

'Leading, no doubt, to Stage Three.' More strangulation? The noose bit at his larynx. He kept the neck muscles taut. Useless: they would be severed easily.

'Your links with Boris Diakanov, your removal and copying of our most sensitive mafiya files to hand on to him. Captain Vakulchuk can vouch for this.'

'Director Gresko assigned me to analyse Diakanov and his current operations.'

'But not to abet him, to play a leading role in his theft of diamonds, to cut a former acquaintance Ilya Kokhlov to ribbons on an autopsy table because he raised the matter of political and mafiya killings. Killings orchestrated by *tsisari* and the President's Chief of Staff.'

'I misjudged my effectiveness.'

'As did we, Colonel Lazin. You subverted our every effort to uncover the truth.'

Lazin watched the sunlight speckle the paint. 'Truth? The

word is not one I've heard before in the corridors of the Lubyanka. Your theories will pack a courtroom.'

'A trial is not anticipated.' A slow study of a wristwatch. Sentence was being passed. 'As of five minutes ago, you have become a fugitive, one of the most wanted men in Russia. Director Gresko has called for your immediate apprehension or death. Fugitives do desperate things, Lazin. They are hunted, so they panic, bring forward plans, persuade allies to support them.'

'I am not aware of allies.' He was not aware of friends.

'Diakanov is attacked by us on all sides; he has every reason to wish to strike back. The Chief of Staff – with whom you are acquainted through secret midnight rendezvous – senses the FSB is closing in, decides it is the moment to make history, to change Russia's leadership. They have much at stake: their mutually advantageous relationship, their wealth, their carefully constructed programme to cripple and then dominate our Mother Country. There are your natural collaborators.'

'You intend to assassinate the President? You forget the Federal Protection Service, the Presidential Guard.'

'It is you who forgets, which is why you will fail and die in the attempt. It will be ultimate proof of the country's instability, of the sickness in our midst.'

'I would choose the same words. You play a long game.'

Ivanov's delivery hovered in neutral. 'Only the Federal Security Service can guarantee survival, has the power to dismantle the intelligence organs established by the President's Chief of Staff. He will be destroyed; Diakanov and his cohorts will be mopped up; and the President will remain as our public-relations front to the world beyond the Kremlin.' Until Gresko tired; until he brought his forces into the Kremlin along the underground tunnels.

'And then?' Lazin heard his thoughts, words, amplified by the intensity of a brain anticipating its end.

'Why predict when there are no limits?'

'The only prediction is blood.'

433

'It is what empires, unchallenged authority, are built on.'

'They die. And you wish to resurrect a corpse.'

Ivanov hesitated. 'Your destiny is different to mine, Colonel Lazin. And more short-term.' It was the glacial image seen by chief morbid anatomist Ilya Kokhlov before the blade descended.

There was a dull post-storm drizzle slanting over Washington DC, turning the grass and tarmac of Dulles International a homogenised grey as the scheduled British Airways flight – briefly re-routed via Newark – made its approach. The visitor looked from his business class window, felt the shudder of tyres connecting, the reverse thrust of Rolls-Royce turbofans and rapid deceleration, and stretched. His leg had been stiff on the journey. Safety lights from trucks and aircraft lanced out across the wet concrete in intermittent shards of orange and white, reflected flashes in the premature gloaming, workers cowled in yellow waterproofs moving among them with practised ritual. The control tower taxied past, its concave stem underlit like a sculpture displayed for the travelling viewer, set off by red hazard pinpricks on its roof; luminous blue night-light toadstools picked out the grass verges, guarded ground-level stand directions. Y >, Y <. Why indeed? the visitor mused. Why was he making the kill? Because he was the best; because Leonid Gresko had sent him. A terminal form of crisis management was the aim.

At this hour, the lawyers, lobbyists and beltway bandits would be readying themselves to leave work, spinning home through the cedars and beech woods to their spun-out, spoilt and spoiled offspring in Bethesda, Potomac and Alexandria. Commuters for whom presents substituted presence, where child therapy was an adequate alternative to parenting, attention deficit syndrome the standard excuse for a kick in the pants deficit. The visitor despised the place, its valueless values. Junk food, junked minds. Why worry if your kid failed to concentrate at school when you could pump it full of Ritalin? Why educate when 'inclusive' anti-excellence praised grey underachievement? Why be concerned at junior's lack of morals, when he could grow up to enter law or politics like yourself? Orphans of affluence, the next generation, the decline of civilisation and civility behind the placid, expensive façades of the 'burbs. And all because society wanted to bribe the young to like it, had lost the right to judge. Abuse by its proxy – negligence.

Such matters pressed on the visitor as he caught the transit bus to arrivals. DC, the dirt behind its classical frontages, the sleaze rotting the foundations of its pillared monuments and stuccoed splendour, peopled by urbanised vermin tipped from their trailer-parks, breeding despair and dependency, breeding prostitutes and pizza-deliverers, governed by egos in motorcades. You surely are a Confederate sonofabitch cynic, he thought wryly. He would hole up in the safe house, grand and set back among the trees off Georgetown Pike, meet his contacts, liaise with the small group from the Agency committed to carrying through the process started by the Cuban Sanction. Technology transfer had been so limited an aim; their sights were on a higher goal. They should have anticipated impediments, the occasional upset, leaks which needed stemming – the gradual destabilisation and overthrow of a foreign government was a complex affair. People got hurt, killed. Max Purton may have been an innocent, maybe not, but his life expectancy was under review, about to be modified. The same went for the Senator: one less Capitol Hill legislator to enjoy taxpayers' generosity. The visitor crossed the concourse. Too bad he had missed the city's blossom. He wondered if the bagelry on M Street was still in business.

Across Washington, at the corner of G on 20th, depression and overwork filtered with the light from the uniform windows of the International Monetary Fund headquarters. Men and women paced the grey-flecked marble floors beneath the building's central atrium, expressions grave, footfall rapid – as if driven to a call of nature by the unimaginative step-waterfall set to one side – or sat cloistered in the dining and meeting rooms placed to the rear.

On the twelfth floor, along endless expanses of more grey-carpeted corridors – beyond the great wood seal depicting twinned globes and an olive branch, through an ante-room – the board of the IMF was in restricted session. Around the hollow circle of the conference table were the sober-suited representatives of the lending countries – the executive directors – missionaries for economic stabilisation, engaged in heated exchange from the safety of their high-backed chairs, highbrow point-scoring from behind spike-microphones. Their discussions concerned Russia. Technically, it was a follow-on debate to earlier Article 4 negotiations; a chance observer would have called it a full-blown row.

To the right of the Managing Director was the Mission Chief – a permanent staff director – adjacent to two of the three deputy MDs and supported by the team for Russia immediately behind in the second tier of seats. It was their report which had ignited the dispute, altercations soothed or fuelled in the corridors and annexes, alliances fragmenting and forming on political and economic whims, and spilling back into the chamber. Eight along from the Chair, the British appointee listened gloomily. It was no bad thing that sound-deadening fabric covered the walls. '*This is unacceptable* . . .' Another outburst. He glanced at the net curtains drawn across the room's single window – they needed to be cleaned. There was no money for that; certainly no money for a crippled Russia.

The Russian President had declared a state of emergency. A masterly understatement. He had dismissed his government, placed several of its ministers under arrest, ordered the Defence and Interior Ministries to put tanks onto the streets of major cities, and, in a final move, dissolved the lower house of parliament, the State Duma. Reasons were varied, the will of the people cited, rule was by decree, rubber-stamped by the country's Security Council. There was no doubt that the economic collapse warranted a period of authoritarian leadership and greater stability. Opinion polls indicated support. Elections were on hold, the Constitutional Court suborned, the clampdown begun. In the daily struggle to survive, few questioned the consequences; with direct threats to Russian territorial integrity rising, few would dare. Already, and after yet another Presidential Representative was kidnapped by local warlords while attempting to broker a reduction in cross-border terrorist incidents, Russian military units had re-entered the troublesome republic of Chechnia on 'punitive' raids. This time, there would be no humiliating retreat – every village, town, city, from Shali to Grozny, was to be levelled, every Iranian and Afghan training camp obliterated, every guerrilla castrated, hanged, butchered. The military were out for revenge.

The Managing Director made an intervention, Gallic smoothness calming the Japanese representative. The Englishman made a ballpoint entry on his notepad and poured more water. He respected the Frenchman, graduate of the *grandes écoles*, symptom of France's continuing efforts to punch well above its weight in the international arena. Its success was obvious, illustrated by portraits of former Managing Directors hung on the walls: the majority were confection-box depictions of French nationals. There were few other countries which could champion their own in that fashion.

'Mr Chairman,' the German delegate intoned. 'My government is reluctant to allow the positive aspects of Russian reform to disintegrate.'

'Then perhaps it should seek a national solution,' his American counterpart replied. The United States was in no hurry to extend credit: Congress, led by political heavy-weights such as Senator O'Day, were refusing to sanction the release of additional funding facilities to the institution, and the President had affirmed the mood of caution. Other nations took their cue.

The Managing Director pinched the top of his nose,

nipping a developing migraine arching from his sinuses. 'Russia owes the Fund's shareholders twenty-five billion dollars in outstanding debt from previous provisions. Do we burn that money, or do we recoup a little by providing another chance?'

'A chance costing a further twenty-five to fifty billion dollars is one that cannot be afforded.'

'And that will be the start. We've been here before. Our taxpayers will no longer subsidize Russian profligacy and mismanagement.'

'Russia will exist physically, geographically, whether we like it or not, Mr Chairman.' The German turned to his colleagues. 'So, the question is whether or not we can afford to handle a corpse on our doorstep.'

'Might be cheaper than feeding a dying patient,' the American hit back.

The Englishman cleared his throat. 'The RTS stockmarket is finished, investors have fled. We would be going against commercial and economic logic to intervene. As it is, they cannot service their short-term debt.'

'What hasn't been blown up is falling to pieces. Why go where the banks won't go?'

'They cannot meet existing terms. How can they meet our future ones?' the American added.

Another supported him. 'There are limits to the stability we can provide. Even the head of their Accounting Chamber is against further loans. A professional body! They will only be embezzled, lost, squandered.'

'As everything else has been. Remember 1996? 1998 and '99? They should not be given the luxury of playing politics with our money.'

'The Russians do not do themselves favours with military adventures in Chechnia and sabre-rattling against Ukraine and Georgia.'

'Do nothing and there will be more than sabre-rattling. Economic calamity and militarism go hand-in-hand. Have we not learned anything?' The French emissary stared meaningfully at the German. The subtlety of oblique support and ironic put-down were not lost.

'We have learned to distinguish between common sense and antipathy to Anglo-Saxon economic principles,' came a barbed response from the far side of the table.

The Japanese representative nodded. 'Mr Chairman, we do not exist to underwrite the Russian armed forces,' he stated forcefully. Concern was growing in Tokyo at the risks in diverting lines of credit away from Asia. 'Tension on the Sino-Russian border has grown, Moscow's belligerence is worrying my government. We cannot endorse Russian behaviour by providing extra facilities.'

'Madness. They must be given the opportunity.'

'They have had every opportunity. When their new central banker claims that monetary discipline is less important than saving industry, when they print money to fund its remnants, their scope for reform is finished.'

'What about the anti-corruption drive? The raids on crime interests?'

'Populism isn't the same as sound economics,' the American came back acidly.

'Help them, or democracy will die.'

'Government is by presidential decree. Where's democracy?'

'The discussion is academic,' the Managing Director interrupted. 'We do not have the liquidity, nor the agreement of the G10 for extra borrowing limits. No lifeboat exists. To extend the metaphor, if agreement is not reached at government level, we may have to cut Russia adrift. It will be alone.'

'Mr Chairman, they are survivors. They barter, trade, subsist, grow their own vegetables, whatever the prevailing economic climate. They must find their own future.'

'No, no, no.' The French executive was adamant, a flat palm slapping the ink-blotter emphatically. 'If we sit back, it will blow up. We will regret it, the world will regret it. I am telling you.' The Englishman jotted another note. Histrionics

439

were out of place among macroeconomists.

'You understand the limits to my authority. I can make representations and suggestions, that is all,' the MD replied, sympathetic to his fellow-countryman. The recipient rolled his eyes.

An aide entered and hurried behind the outer circle of seats to the head of the mission team. No one took much notice. A written note was passed, heads bent close for whispered exchange, louder debate continuing around the conference table. The mission director turned and saw the concern, the body language. He gestured for an explanation, the message-carrier and mission chief shuffling forward for impromptu discussion. Among the delegates, focus gradually shifted to the sub-grouping, the sub-plot, triggered by instinct, by detection of repressed hiatus in their midst. The Managing Director became involved, drawn in by *sotto voce* asides. Wider argument faltered.

'Ladies and gentlemen. I have an announcement of immediate import. I must inform that the Russian bank payment and clearing system has collapsed. We will adjourn.'

What he could not tell them, for he had no insight, was that Leonid Gresko, Director of Russia's Federal Security Service, utilising specialists from the FAPSI cyber-warfare and code-breaking department, had engineered the calamitous breakdown. Many of the personnel had trained at the Lourdes base in Cuba, refining their techniques, disruptive measures and electronic viral-logic bombs on the microchip-dependent society of the United States. Their homeland, its safeguards, were child's play. No cheque, payment, financial transaction of any kind, could be accepted, processed or recorded. By comparison, the Y2K millennial bug was an irritant. In a single stroke, the tottering edifice of Russian banking – controlled by the central authorities – with it the country's ability to stay in the modern age, was wiped from computer screens and existence. Through convoluted detection, meticulous research and post-trauma analysis, blame would eventually be traced and apportioned to the economic hackers employed by mafiya boss Boris Diakanov. They were not responsible, but imputation was as easy to shift on the wires as international capital. The market in scapegoats had just gone global. Russia was isolated, a backwards kingdom to be seized by new feudal overlords.

The trucks which growled into the city by night or passed close on long-distance highway routes had vanished. Banditry, the evaporation of business, the lack of buyers, loss of produce, kept them from the roads. Oil was scarce, the price of liquid petroleum soaring. There was nowhere to go, and nothing to go for. Yet this journey had its own purpose. Lazin was pushed onto the floor of the van, blindfolded, ears attuned to the silence outside the radius of his vehicle's engine and that of the escort. He had been in enough Volgas to recognise the latter's heavy travelling signature: the secret policeman's last automobile of choice, and first to be purchased by central funding. A rolling whine and vibration, then another – Interior Ministry troops patrolling in their infantry fighting vehicles, BMP-1s or -2s, guarding the nation's arteries with automatic cannon and *Sagger* or *Spandrel* anti-tank missiles. Lazin counted them, tried to pick out details, mind sifting for information, hyperactive in the claustrophobia of sightlessness, the flat monotony of tyres on asphalt. He could have, should have, predicted this ending. The assignment to Siberia, the brief to investigate the mafiya, was nothing more than an accumulation of incidents crafted, contrived to fit and to fit him up. Once the attempt on his life had failed, they opted to improvise, integrating him into the scheme. The FSB required only implication for a damning case. It was their method, honed on the success of their forebears.

In the Volga, the front seat passenger lit two cigarettes and passed one to the driver. Smoke hung heavy about the four guards and an interior littered with wrappers, small arms and disposable coffee cups. Handover was their sole responsibility, as demanding as outriding on a tumbril. It was a routine delivery, similar to other recent shuttle runs taking ex-government ministers and officials for incarceration at Vladimir. The prisoners would reappear for trial, then disappear for good. That was the way with such packages; those were the orders of Colonel General Leonid Gresko. The man leant forward and adjusted the radio. Reception was poor. Outside, dusk had settled an hour before; it came late – 2200 hours – in these summer months. Bugs, attracted by the headlights, rose over the bonnet and impacted in two-dimensional suicides on the laminated glass. Wipers smeared them away. Behind, the van followed close, three FSB officers on board accompanying a captive to the unknown but inevitable.

Static swept the radio. Passenger seat occupant ducked again to fine-tune, fingers searching for a stable frequency. Quality worsened. He gave up: it must be the aerial, he reasoned. His eyes, level with the dash, detected the shuttered outline of military headlights turned, beams full, in their direction. More checkpoints to deal with – the authorities were twitchy, had every reason. But this prison convoy could negotiate any roadblock: the FSB plates were enough, the influence of Director Gresko's employees enough, to sweep aside the most senior official, the most obstructive official-dom. Emergency rule – the incubus of a police state – and the four men delighted in its natural development.

The man could make out the armoured carriers now, a brace of BRDM-2 reconnaissance types and a BTR-70 drawn across their axis. Soldiers fanned out on either side. Their commander was a diligent sort. The Volga slowed, funnelled into the reception arrangement, driver cursing, gesticulating for clearance. He was ignored. He pressed the horn, repeated, the van echoed back, the two vehicles inching forward with a see-saw stereo klaxon, engines revving, the irritability of those within reflected in the mouthed obscenities, the start of a siren. The troop commander held up a hand. Inside the Volga, there was confusion, fury, a hurried conference producing the choice either to ram or to shoot. Whatever happened, the officer's family would be without its dominant male by the morning. The hand dropped.

There were a variety of specialist munitions in the Russian arsenal. One was known as a barricade penetrator. 37mm calibre, travelling at 450 feet per second, based on a polyurethane anti-riot baton round, it was an unusual low-velocity design, capable of boring its way through doors and windows and clearing the space behind. In this it was supremely efficient, in enclosed areas unbeatable. A hard, spinning 'cookie-cutting' disc in the head did the piercing, the load carried in the hollow body did the rest. The driver saw the brief muzzle flash above the officer's head, a black slug emerge towards him, but the distance was too short, reactions too slow. He was aware of the windscreen turning white, of an impact, white glass, white breath, of air rammed from his body, but that was all. That was all.

The penetrator entered the driver's chest and lungs, smoke and micronised CS dust emitting from its rear, sucked up and through the mouth, nose and ears. A vivid effect, the human sulphur pot filling the compartment with acrid density, three figures choking, flailing from opened doors. Clouds billowed after them, their generator motionless behind the wheel. Controlled bursts of suppressed automatic took the FSB men down. The van reversed, blind, tyres shrieking then shredded on spike traps. A troop carrier slewed across to block, armour crumpling vehicle panels.

Lazin's Security Service guard was impact-thrown, fell on him, punching and clawing with aimless ferocity. They were experiencing, but not witnessing, an ambush, sensory deprivation, imagination, multiplying the hopelessness of entrapment. Lazin balled, protected his head. The man was weeping, pummelling, shouting for help, wanting to murder. Lazin was being pistol-whipped. Panic attack – and he was the target. Keep going, he prayed, almost screaming encouragement; don't pause to think, to turn the weapon and aim. He relaxed into the blows, focused on reducing the internal damage. A short report and the locks went. He felt the strike of bullets into the guard's body, the travelling shock, weight lifting off as kinetic force threw it aside. There might have been a shriek, a short expletive – '*blin!*' – or it was a morbid trick on the ears. Hands dragged him from the van, the blindfold came away.

'We are both hunted, Colonel.' Boris Diakanov stood among a group of his men. He wore black, machine-pistol gripped and resting on a shoulder. The barrel was warm. *Fugitives are hunted, so they panic, bring forward plans*, Petr Ivanov had said. There was no panic here, merely ordered liquidation, in numbers, by numbers.

'You do not have the look of a persecuted man.'

'Because I choose to fight. I have that choice.'

'Temporarily.'

'To pull Russia to pieces, to destroy trade, the economy, the currency, suits Gresko. It does not suit me. Yet I am condemned for it.'

'And you will be shot for it. The nature of the Secret Police state is to divert attention from its own agenda.'

Diakanov adjusted his hold on the weapon. 'He took my son from me. I am a father. I grieve, I have a duty. It is my turn to pull him to pieces.'

'With roadblocks? Small-scale night-raids? Dressing up your lieutenants as regular soldiers? With the chance freeing of an insignificant prisoner?'

'You underestimate yourself, Colonel.'

'I recognise myself, my position. And I recognise your position.'

'Then we must unite.' Blood welled from the open end of the van. They watched it flow above the lip, surface tension breaking, and spill.

'The FSB is already linking us. Through me they connect you to the President's Chief of Staff, to efforts to assume control in the Kremlin.'

'More attempts to draw attention from themselves.'

Lazin nodded. 'Distortion is their only currency. That you saved me proves we are in league.'

'They will get conspiracy they have not yet dreamed of.'

'And you do it for yourself?'

'For the memory of my son.'

'Then you have my support, Boris Fedorovich.'

He had escaped. Plans would have to be adapted. Gresko, Ivanov were not invincible; nothing was inevitable.

'Welcome to the *vory v zakone*,' Diakanov said. Welcome to the thieves.

Purton adjusted the desert goggles, swayed against the roll-bar as the Land Rover again bottomed out into a patch of drifting sand, and held tight while it sought and found traction from a shallow ridge of stones. They had left the track marked by the sporadic appearance of white-painted tyres, opted for cross-country, the hard, baked plains interspersed with dunes, scrub, and ragged clumps of acacia and tamarisk. Solitary flat-roofed houses shimmered far off, isolated and tented nomadic settlements clung in the distance and in defiance to bare, infertile earth. Humanity did not feel permanent or welcome here.

The gunner tapped his shoulder and swept an arm to the right. 'We turn at the water tower. Not far.'

Not far, but the voyage into the harsh, pre-biblical landscape was a journey away from modernity. And all he offered from his own civilisation were new techniques in warfare. He had said farewell to Nick Howell and Ahmed Badr five days previously. While he was to proceed into the old No Man's Land between north and south Yemen to assess the military potential of tribes in the Wadi Bayhan, they remained two hundred kilometres south to reconnoitre the Ataq airbase. The insurgents could move anywhere, strike everywhere, and as the government in Sana'a deployed its loyal troops from the north, so it was left vulnerable to defections and raids by disloyal units in the south. Traditional enmity flared, civil war was re-lit. Create artificially a nation from two separate entities, identities, and there was potential for schism. Purton played the wedge. The governor of Aden was the first element to be dislodged. Others would follow. It might yet earn him a firing-squad or a tribal *jambiya* in the back.

The four-wheel-drive bucked, engine at high revs, and slewed past the stranded porcine shape of an *Adonium obesum* – Bottle tree. Ahead, the grey blandness of a water tower mushroomed up, barely visible against the foothills. It was the driver's cue to tussle the wheel into a new axis, setting the vehicle on a widening arc. They would bypass the dust-infested mudbrick villages and towns with their careering droves of ancient *dhabar* buses, their fonduqs, their groups of *qat*-chewing men, coffee-drinkers and smell of dung, *khubz tawwa* bread and goat *salta*. There were fewer informants and checkpoints out here.

He looked down at the driver and bodyguard, both employed by a grandson of Bayhan's last sultan, Sherif Hussein al-Mahdi. A positive sign that the three tribes of the area – Musabein, Bal Harith and Al-Karab – were prepared to combine and rise against their alien northern overlords. These clans and families, once masters of the frankincense trade, were maintained in an impoverished backwater while oil companies encroached from the adjacent Marib in the west and they were exploited and suppressed by a government anxious to pacify and prospect. Scorched earth overlaid on a scorched earth. Fertile territory for recruits.

The gunner, a bedouin Al-Karab, checked the belt-feed and ammunition box for the cannon. He smiled at Purton. 'Soon, soon.' Until a firefight, or until the tribal gathering? He did not ask.

The Land Rover crawled into the incline and edged along a dry wadi, yo-yoing beneath a disused bridge before climbing onto the far bank. The jolts became sharper, terrain and driving more erratic. A ruined fort dissolved slowly in the heat. Twenty minutes, a move to higher ground, another descent, and the militarised off-roader coasted into a clearing obscured among sandstone boulders. Arrival. Purton swung himself down, mounted a rock for better vantage –

confidence building – placed himself on a plinth for their detailed study. Surprise made people nervous. He hoped their still-life appreciation did not embrace sniping, but stayed motionless, kept the safety off in case criticism turned violent. *Artistic temperament, Arab temperament*. He whistled unsuccessfully beneath his breath, wondering at their lines of sight to his position. An approach would be cautious.

The engine ground into reverse, Land Rover backing off at speed, accelerating away to a slipstream of pebbles and rubber-ploughed dirt. Perhaps they were spooked. The wave from the gunner was not encouraging. Purton vaulted behind a barricade of stones and crouched in the lee, scanning for protected exits. His belt contained the basics – water, compass, knife, wire, spare magazines for the Browning High-Power and AK – though basics so often failed to tip the odds. If Badr's contacts proved unreliable, the odds were poorly stacked.

Heavier vehicles, chassis rocking with the downbeat spring of reworked antiquity, nudged their way into the moisture-starved arena. The North Yemenis were stinting on the search parties, Purton thought: a sure sign of defence budget squeeze. His immediate considerations were different. A tail-flap crashed, a scurry of movement following the staggered motor cut-outs, and silence. He listened, reached out for vibrations, rock fall, the clatter of weapons, scatter of loose debris, indications of an enemy outflanking, closing. Acoustics were impeccable – for the younger man. The gunshot-damaged hearing of an old soldier wasted the advantage. He enjoyed the outdoor life; outdoor death was an extension. Kalashnikov brought close. This was the moment when semi-retirement became permanent retirement, natural selection at its most poignant. There was a time when he had hunted the *Idaaraat* political execution squads sent from Marxist South Yemen into Oman like this, crawled and hidden, ambushed and annihilated among the thorn, wild fig and castor-oil trees. *A time* . . . No nerves: a wistfulness that hand-to-hand, a charge with a sword, would be denied. His ancestors had been luckier.

'I see you are still playing cowboys, Major Purton.'

The voice was unmistakable, accent unmistakably French. It carried above the amphitheatre, carried him back to Africa, the heated putrefaction along the arduous, disease-ravaged route of Laurent Kabila's 1997 rebel advance to Kisangani, the strategic Zairean city on the banks of the Congo River. French-backed dictator-president Mobutu Sese Seko was at bay, his towns falling, his troops looting and frantically scrambling to escape. Mercenaries were sent, initially to fight and shore up *La Francophonie*, then to shred and sanitise documents embarrassing to the Elysée Palace. As Kabila's forces prepared for their final assault on Kisangani's besieged military airport, French Air Force transports landed hastily on the runway and snatched their nationals, agents and remaining contacts to safety. Among them, this man.

'Major Purton.' The same tone, sing-song amorality. 'We have rifle-grenades, LAWS rockets, heavy machine guns. Even your dental fillings will go unrecovered. Throw your weapons over. You will be spared.'

Capitaine Marc Deodat Mouton – 'Foccart's Devil' – for over thirty years the covert military manifestation of France's aggrandising foreign policy in Africa. Directed by machiavellian Gaullist and presidential 'witch doctor' Jacques Foccart, he had spearheaded his country's attempts to keep both Communism and the United States from its zone of influence, and former colonies loyal to Paris – 'La Capital'. From the Camores to the Central African Republic, from Rwanda to Zaire, Gabon to Djibouti, the paratrooper, foreign legionnaire, one-time officer in the *Commandos de Recherche et d'Action en Profondeur*, holder of the Grand Cross of the *Légion d'Honneur*, holder of mine and shell fragments in his body, led coups and counter-coups across the continent, excising threats and humans, terrorising and terrifying at will. Purton had witnessed its effects, heard the screams of torture victims above the roar of the C-160

Transall turboprops as they made their emergency landings and departures at Kisangani.

'A firepower demonstration is warranted.' A pause, shots, and two rocks disintegrated a metre each side of Purton's head. Close, near enough to leave Max without a father, Max's father unrecognisable. Powdered stone trickled down. Mouton continued, tone seductively convincing. 'We have your range and position. You are a professional, Major Purton. Weigh the risks. Any chance is better than inevitable death. I say once again, deliver up your weapons, come out towards us. It is the only way.' He was right.

Purton fed the assault rifle onto the slab, let it fall clattering on the other side, then its magazines, the Browning, the spare clips, and sat disarmed in a searing place a long way from Poole and Bess his Irish Terrier. Delivered up, ready for taking. A shame to have missed the summer in England, to miss all future summers. The neutral smell of heat clogged his nostrils. The Frenchman and his followers could wait, snuff him out when ready, if he moved or if he stayed. At least relinquishing the arms had forced the issue. Nick would tell his son, arrange the life insurance payments. Blindness had its merits – it saved Max from finding adventure, imitating the short lives of his antecedents, kept him from danger, from ending confined and cornered in a foreign land.

'I'm standing up,' he shouted, elevating himself methodically, fluidly. His joints registered pain, age, but he was focused on the trucks – three-tonners – and the man relaxing close by on a sandstone outcrop. The same image, prepared for in his mind and from his memory: an emperor, pristine in desert boots, lightweight and pressed combat suit, gazing from his seat, waiting to raise or lower the thumb, decide on a gladiator's fate. Purton slithered to the ground and approached.

'I think you remember me,' the emperor called out.

'I remember the thirty miners you skinned alive at Kalima, the burnings at Punia, the cholera and dysentery sufferers you shot and placed in the maize supplies at Ubundu, the Belgian missionaries and Hutu refugees you command-wired to grenades in that hamlet.'

'As they say, war is hell.' War was the face of an elderly African gardener in the seconds leading to the explosion against his stomach. Such big eyes – all the better to show fear. 'But this is an exciting theatre of conflict, *n'est-ce pas*?' A pair of armed Bedouin looked on, more behind cover.

'For you, Captain Mouton.' Purton walked forward. 'Run out of African wives?' Run out of villages to raze? His peripheral vision was active, searching for gun barrels, for partially hidden positions.

'Wives, no. But there is a run on conflicts which generate income.'

'French interests don't extend this far.'

A Gallic shrug, inexpressive. 'Paris is making economies, South Africans fill the vacuum. I am more inclined towards an international client base.' Not an emperor at all, but a mutant character from *Gigi*. 'France's traditional enemies remain a hobby for me.'

Machine-gun nest positively identified at ten o'clock. 'Is that my category?'

'Possibly,' came the response. 'To surrender was a wise decision, Major.'

'Why are you here, Mouton? Who do you work for?'

'You assassinate the governor of Aden and ask me that? A little presumptuous. And for whom do you seek to divide Yemen once more, Major, to divide it in two? Is it for British Intelligence, for National Opposition forces, the Yemen Socialist Party, for disaffected Hashed tribesmen, for Taiz businessmen and those who seek to protect their Red Sea trade by making rival Aden inoperable? Or is it for the Saudis?' The Frenchman was well briefed.

Purton did not blink. 'Make your point.'

'I could explain my presence through a love of archaeology – I visited excavations here at Tinma and Shabwa in the early 1970s – but I would be lying. Many people are upset at your actions.'

'You're working for the government in Sana'a? They wouldn't trust you.'

'I come highly recommended.' Mock apologia. 'Though, I confess most of my referees are deceased.'

'Doesn't add up. You're dealing with Islamic extremists.'

'Islamic extremists with oil interests, who want stability in Yemen, instability in Saudi; Islamic extremists who want American exploration and production companies to stay, who want the concessions in the Marib and Masila exploited, the pipeline to Al-Shihr guarded, the liquid natural gas network to Balhaf left undamaged.' A lecturer at peak performance.

Purton shifted his weight, balls of his feet testing the ground, preparing; the situation demanded it. 'So, I've annoyed commercial interests. Theirs or yours?'

'Do not come closer, Major,' Mouton warned amicably. 'You will scare my small army. Take a look beneath the tarpaulin.' The Bedouin had moved, stood easy, rifles slung, revealing the covering pulled across their trophies behind. 'Go ahead.'

It came away without snagging, the sight bad, smell worse, Nick Howell and Ahmed Badr lying dead. A solar-powered cassette player activated beside them. '*Prizrika. Starets. Zadacha vypolnena. Zhdu prikaza . . . Prizrika. Starets. Zadacha vypolnena. Zhdu prikaza . . . Prizrika . . .*' Howell's voice speaking Russian, in a loop. Purton dropped the tarpaulin back, hiding the contorted, blackening shapes. Denied sunlight, the tape cut out. He turned towards the Frenchman.

Mouton raised an eyebrow. 'It is better to be on the winning side.'

You filth, Purton bellowed from deep within. It did not reach the exterior. 'Were they shot in the back or the front?' *I will take you, cut your superiority out with a blade*, he was shouting in his breath.

'It is of no concern to them. Do not trouble yourself,

either.' A hand, held up casually. 'Please, nothing un-measured, Major. There is room for a third under the tarpaulin.' Purton inhaled, fists and stomach balled, guilt and grief rooting him in silence. 'Would you prefer that they were interrogated in the special cells below Sana'a central prison?'

Slowly. 'I'd prefer they were alive. What will you earn for two corpses?'

'Credibility, gratitude, open access to the Moslem leader-ship in the capital. It allows the game to continue.'

'This, a game?' The Englishman pointed to the heap. A stain appeared to seep from below.

'They were indiscriminate in their friendships.'

'While yours are enlightened?' Bitterness and impotence cut into the tone.

Mouton rested his chin on a cupped hand, leant forward. 'The recording you heard was made by the American National Security Agency. It was Howell contacting Moscow by satphone, requesting further instructions after your car-bombing in Aden. He was in their pay.'

Confusion expressed as flat denial. 'Enough, Mouton. You're mad.'

'Mad, yet well informed. Think, Major. You recreate an independent South Yemen, a secular country free once again from the North. In whose interests?'

'You know . . .'

'The interests of its old ally, Russia.'

'Don't dress up cold-blooded murder, legitimize your behaviour. You're worthless.'

'And unlike your former friends, alive,' Mouton riposted. 'They were ambushed together near Ataq while negotiating with a senior officer from the airbase, of whose pro-socialist and opposition tendencies we were aware.'

'So far, nothing unusual.' Caustic, contemptuous.

'Unusual is the Russian intelligence officer captured and taken to Sana'a. Unusual were the plans we recovered for a major building and defensive programme at the base once the southern territories were liberated. They include the construction of immense underground storage tanks for the holding of liquid hydrogen.'

Purton was sweating cold droplets in the heat, energy sucked out, thoughts careering as the French mercenary captain laid out circumstance and evidence. The Saudi diplomat vetted and passed on to him at Poole with the blessing of the Secret Intelligence Service – nothing more than a Russian flag of convenience – Ahmed Badr, a Yemeni trader bought with Russian-laundered dollars and the promise of monopolistic deals when the National Opposition Front took power. And Howell.

'The Yemeni guerrilla killed accompanying you on the raid to R'as Marshag had his throat cut.' Mouton drew out a plastic photograph file from his haversack, flipped it open towards Purton. Colour autopsy prints. 'He was not one of them, so had to die. They were in a hurry to report back to Moscow Centre.'

'Where do you report back?'

Mouton did not reply immediately. The photographs changed to zoom shots of Howell and Badr in conference with a group of senior Yemenis, then standing beside a light aircraft talking to three Slavic-featured men and another individual, back to camera, wearing a black stetson. '1200 mm lens, Major, shot at fifteen hundred metres. Russian intelligence, taken a year ago. Very active again in this area.'

'Where do you report back to, Mouton?' Purton repeated.

'Old soldiers never die. They find useful re-employment.'

'As do inhuman bastards who should stand trial for war crimes.'

'You are quick to judge. We are similar, Major Purton. We share a warrior gene.'

'Not the same power of bullshit. As you said, I'm a professional soldier. 'You're an experiment which went wrong.'

A social laugh, amusement in the expression. 'You read

Kipling, I read the works of Arthur Rimbaud. It is the chief difference. It was not I who started an insurgency in southern Yemen, provoked reprisals, undermined livelihoods. Hypocrisy is an English trait. We French have more to offer.'

Halitosis and small pricks, Purton thought. 'Tell me what you want, Mouton.'

There was no haste. 'Once I worked against the Americans, now I work for them. It is a free market. In Kenya, I aid their arms links to the Sudanese SPLA opposition; from Kinshasa I help maintain their supply lines from the Congo to UNITA forces in Angola. Langley's current request is to turn you in to London.'

'Agency?'

A soft handclap, bigger smile. 'Two masters, Sana'a and Washington. The latter pays more. It is fortunate for you.' Purton could think only of hydrogen tanks. 'Let us go.' A gesture, and an Al-Karab neared carrying Purton's Browning. 'Cooperation ensures you will not be damaged in transit. Move to the far truck.'

The inflection jarred, inflamed demons, buried rationale. Purton made to turn. *Hydrogen tanks?* The pistol was held at waist-level: semi-automatics in that position implied the operator had no intent to fire. A great mistake. Five feet, narrowing. Purton balanced, swivelled towards the vehicles and spun. Sideways on, his arm parried the Browning to the outside, fingers gripping and twisting its body, pressing on the working parts to cause malfunction, thumb inserting in front of the hammer, other hand clawed, raking the man's face and eyes. The scream was pitched high, grip releasing. Purton raised and snapped his foot against the knee, stamped down to the instep, whipping the gun into the head as the Arab fell away. The second guard rushed him, rifle held up defensively, leg arcing upwards. Purton blocked it with crossed forearms, held, pivoted back, unbalanced his attacker and kicked repeatedly into the groin. The face dipped, making a retching sound, and impacted on a rising knee.

A round punctuated the aftermath, spitting earth between

Purton and the fallen. He was panting slightly, covering the two with his reclaimed sidearm, hands and clothing bloodied, spattered by Arabs mewling with pain on the ground. The initial casualties of his transit.

'Bravura performance, Major Purton,' Mouton interrupted. He remained seated. 'Your immaturity is a revelation. The next round will enter your heart. Lead bullet beats unarmed combat every time. Please, lose your weapon, proceed to the truck.'

Purton depressed the magazine release, applied the safety catch and dumped the High-Power. At least he had proved that execution was not at the top of their agenda. He looked again at the rudimentary shroud, the misshapen humps representing Nick Howell and Ahmed Badr. Friendship betrayed, ending rotten. Living, he felt the betrayer, felt sick, denied a place with them.

The Frenchman rose, theatre over. 'The photograph with the aircraft, the person in the cavalry hat? Would it be different if I revealed that the man who recruited Badr and Howell into the Russian camp was an American named Strachan, a Mr Hunter Strachan? Ah, recognition.' There was more than that. 'Your son needs you, Major Purton.'

From the corner of his cell, Max was seeing double, triple, and then forgot to count, how to count. Images wobbled, split, fracturing into pieces that floated up and pierced his raw brain. The headache was making him sweat. His father spun by on a fragment and vanished out of shot. How would he, retired Special Forces officer, cope with this? Grit his teeth, claim British superiority and refuse to succumb? Whistle the National Anthem? Probably backwards after these injections. Whatever the drugs, they felt like chemical worms, submerging him, hollowing him out. They were seeking, following the pathways, whispering and repeating the seductive messages of the men dressed in medical white, shouting out the secrets of the demons they uncovered. *We'll try your mind, fry your mind*, they said. Sedatives, hallucinogens and truth narcotics – the nausea only went when he was tripping, sleeping or concentrating on the questions asked by the relay teams of interrogators. Nightmares overlapped, brought in and on by those million wriggling thought-fuckers. Christ, his head hurt. One of Adele's patients had called her his blue-eyed cunt. People showed affection in different ways. *Blue-eyed cunt, blue-eyed cunt*, he repeated, sniggered. Over-familiarity. The name, Adele, was not familiar at all. He brought his hands up, panicking at first that his ears had been lost. Earlier, he was sure they were walking about his cranium.

The hair had come off on arrival and without ceremony. He was pushed to his knees – anticipation of the mushrooming lead fired point-blank making him wince – the shock of the razor's contact stiffening his body. Then came the strip and internal probe: he put it down to rites of that particular passage. Summer camp had provided no real preparation. The beating was severe, thorough, watched and participated in by the prison commandant and half a dozen warders. When conscious, he heard himself yelling mute that it was wrong to hit a man with glasses. But his glasses were misplaced, contact lenses taken, and the warders did not understand. Pain and memory had drifted away in subsequent semi-psychedelia. Rage remained.

He was in Vladimir maximum security prison, operated once again by the secret police, Leonid Gresko's people. They were proud of its history, their role in it, as inheritors and perpetrators of oppression always were with their own architectural heritage. Ownership reclaimed. The edifice faced outwards on the perimeter of the industrial town, close to the Lybed River, closer to the cemetery, its gates, jail blocks and exercise yards overlooked by guard towers and patrol walkways. No inmate had ever made it alive to the mudflat world stretched out beyond the walls, not even reached the Frunze memorial a few hundred metres off. Those walls contained their ghosts, tens of thousands of them, the disturbed wake of mortals buried by a century of tyranny. Crowding was expected to increase.

His fingers were working, massaging the skull, easing the pressure. An interesting shape, the human head, its contours and peculiarities largely unnoticed and unmapped beneath hair. Smoothness lent a new sensation, dimension, permitted him to roam. What went on within the vessel's shell was the worry. He was rocking, could hear the questions, clenched his jawbones tight. Where is Zenya? Who does she work for? *Must not answer, must not* ... Who pays you? Strachan, Hunter Strachan. Who else? The chemical worm devoured a neuron, its waste fouling his metallic-tasting mouth. A stream of expletives burbled from him in unintelligible confusion. That would show them. His legs were jumping, made his body spasm. He leant forward on the floor, tried to pin them down, but they kicked too fast, blurring at speed. He pressed on them: they were motionless, still blurred without his lenses. The lights were changing colour, and he sobbed.

Laughter in the isolation chamber perched at the highest point of his torso. The hippies had lied all along – this was bad shit, poor karma. He did not want to frolic naked, string beads and flowers, paint caravans; he wanted to vomit, to hide. Across the cramped space of the room, the sanitation bucket overflowed. He could smell it. That made two things they could kick the crap out of. More laughter. Control it, control everything. He had sought challenge, adventure. This was it: premature mid-life crisis, real crisis. Perhaps he was past mid-point, way past, approaching the end. Palms out behind to feel the walls. Dung-brown, the colour and contents of a thousand drums of spilled slop. They were familiar. Sometime, long ago, he had been here before. *Yesterday, last year, in a dream*. It was his refuge, the cell they called the Capitalist Decontamination Unit, on the third floor in the five-storey isolator block of the prison's hospital wing. He was pulled up and down the steel flights daily – thoughts bobbing behind, veering off into side corridors, doing ward rounds, weird rounds – counted the landings, sensed through a myopic mist the archway into the exercise pens at the building's centre. Occasionally, he went beneath it. Impossible – he had not been taken there. The hallucinations, the dream, were making him stray, trailing the questions of his captors from a leaking head. If only the hole were large enough, the chemical worms could escape, miniature phallic mind-screwers unscrewed. But the guards refused to give him a nail, anything sharp. They were busy tipping the shit containers, flooding him with faeces: no other reason for the cell being this hue. He would climb to the narrow, high-set window and shout for help, scream at the sky, smear coagulated porridge around in dirty protest. It was against regulations, the orders in cyrillic screwed above his mattress position said so. The beating might bring him back, inflict sanity. Might let him chance upon a nail. He flattened out on the concrete, prayed for himself, prayed that Zenya was free, would never go through this. His brain accelerated, settled back on sharp objects.

The door opened. Hypodermics could not be kept waiting.

200 Old Brompton Road, London, overlooking the more exclusive address of the Little Boltons, period apartments approachable enough to be anonymous, set back enough to be ignored. Only the twinned horses' heads carved in white stone surmounting the portals suggested discreet affluence, nothing suggested actual habitation.

Hugh Dryden and Guy Parsons, employing a circuitous route from Secret Intelligence Service headquarters in Vauxhall, and arriving by cab several blocks away, climbed the steps to the front door. Top button depressed on the wall panel, video entry triggered, they pushed their way through. A guard watched them vanish from one screen, appear on a second. Another unit displayed the entire frontage of the building viewed by remote camera from a nearby rooftop. Security was unobtrusive, non-intrusive – everywhere. The hall was light, understated in pastel shades and reception foliage, a central cage elevator filling the stairwell. The two men entered, gates closing, mechanism initiated automatically and carrying them upwards.

The muscle was waiting, three of them cling-wrapped in deep-chested suits, unsmiling faces surveying the arrivals, patting them down and ushering them through. A butler, pectorals overdeveloped for a man who served drinks, took over. They passed, conversation suspended, into an ante-room opening onto an expanse of colour-indeterminate carpet scattered with antiques. Rowlandson pen and wash drawings adorned the walls.

'Appalling good taste,' Dryden murmured to his colleague. Money would not buy cultivation, but it could surely purchase interior design.

They were led up a flight of stairs, the route softly picked out by recessed ceiling spots, and shown through a steel-panelled door to emerge onto a roof terrace doubling as a large London garden. Sunlight and the smell of lavender, honeysuckle and clematis montana enveloped the teak decking, bamboo catching the slight breeze, ornamental pots and baskets of fuschias, alyssum and campanula lining the sides, cascading or supporting a profusion of dianthus, japonica and winding strands of ioniceras. In the middle, seated at a marble-topped table, shaded by tea-plantation canvas stretched taut in its stand, was Boris Diakanov.

He rose, shook hands and offered drinks. 'I have several decoys around the world. They look like me, wear my clothes, travel in my jets. Yet now you meet the true Diakanov.'

'I have no doubt.' Parsons was courteous, contrived.

'Field Marshal Montgomery used a doppelgänger, did he not?'

As far as the M16 Russia chief knew, Monty never indulged in throwing associates into vats of acid. 'They can be useful in a war situation.'

'Then I shall continue with them. Colonel Lazin sends his respects, Mr Parsons.'

'He is safe?'

'Russia is not safe. But he has my protection.'

At what price, Dryden reflected. He accepted a glass of

iced-tea, contemplated the incongruity of the Panama tilted on Diakanov's close-cropped head – a head which appeared not to perch on the neck, but to back into it.

'Are you staying long, Mr Diakanov?' MI5's Watchers got nervous when *tsisari* came to town. They had been called off for this particular encounter.

'I enjoy London in the summer.' There was no irony behind the closed blackness of wrap-round shades.

'I assume it's less hot than Moscow.' The ice rattled as Parsons sipped.

A scowl. 'Hell would be less hot than Moscow.'

'We are willing to discuss the alleviation of its worst effects.'

'On whose authority?'

'As you are aware, Mr Diakanov, we are not free spirits, free agents.'

The intercourse drifted through Russian and English, the more restrained tones of the British, their finer points, interspersed with exclamations, a coarser dialect, from the mafiya chief. It was he who had spearheaded the development of new opium routes. Countries appointed drug tsars to combat the epidemic – the United States alone spent twenty billion dollars a year combating the effects of addiction – but the true tsars were the providers, the new trans-global rulers. Antipathy was natural. Their wholesale price for a kilogramme of heroin was over a hundred times the original cost of purchase in Afghanistan or Thailand: profits were astronomical, resources unlimited, marketing methods for the addictive by-product of dried opium milk unequalled. An injected water-soluble Number four white heroin 'hit' or smoked and tooted Number three brown wrap cut with morphine and codeine, both containing less than a gramme, could sell for the equivalent of twenty US dollars. Each season, the hectares of land given over to opium poppy cultivation rose, and a potential figure of 350 metric tonnes of heroin were readied and refined for world use. Overkill. Governments were scared, rightly so.

Parsons placed his glass down. 'Some might argue it would benefit British interests to back Leonid Gresko and his FSB against your varied business activities, Mr Diakanov.'

'Then you do not understand him.'

'We have a pretty clear idea.'

'He murdered my son on English soil, under your protection.'

'How many sons and daughters have you murdered with your heroin trafficking, Mr Diakanov?' Parsons was laying out the bargaining position. 'Narcotics makes three hundred billion dollars profit a year; your share is growing. Golden Crescent produce through Quetta, Golden Triangle produce through Phnom Penh, Koh Kong port and trade centres in Singapore, Bangkok and Nigeria. We understand you perfectly.'

Diakanov's reaction was unexpectedly subdued. 'What are you asking for?'

'It is not common practice for servants of Her Majesty's government to endorse individuals implicated in international violence and crime.'

'However,' Dryden intervened. 'As our Foreign Office interacts everyday with foreign regimes whose *modus operandi* embraces such behaviour, a working framework can probably be established.'

'You want to deal?'

'To negotiate,' came the reply.

'Then our interests coincide.'

'At the margins.'

A heavy finger, fringed with dark hair, jabbed at the Briton. 'The future of my country is central to me, to you, and to the world. That is not marginal.'

Parsons' head dipped in oblique concession. 'Neither of us wishes to see Gresko in charge. We consider him a greater danger than you.'

'Is this why you seek to keep me alive, confine me to my lesser properties?'

'It is why you have been granted entry to this country.'

A smirk. 'I will repay the hospitality.'

'In return for our aid in specific areas, the backup we provide in facing down Gresko's Federal Security Service and fighting off the *Bespredel'chiki* upstarts he is encouraging to move against you, we demand reciprocity.'

'Which means?'

'Guaranteed cessation of drugs smuggling into this country and the handing over of information concerning rival gangs.'

'I deal with my enemies in my own way.'

'Then you will be obliged to deal with Leonid Gresko in your own way.'

Dryden maintained the initiative. 'The bar on narcotics is also to cover synthetic heroin and other opiates including methadone, morphine and codeine.'

'You can add temegesic, pethidine, palfium, diconal and dihydrocodeine,' Parsons concluded. To give Diakanov a loophole was to provide him with a business platform.

'And continental Europe? You wish to dictate to me there too?'

'Not at all.' Dryden swatted an insect. 'Quite the opposite.'

Parsons was admiring a creeper. His own climbing plants were a perpetual source of disappointment. 'I suggest you concentrate on the easier trading conditions to be found within the Schengen area. You doubtless appreciate the open border approach more than we do.' It would teach the European partners the absurdity of ditching Customs checks.

'I have seen how pacts finish,' Diakanov said bluntly, face as still as a brick. The assault on his fortress near Cheboksary, the day Irina's helicopter was shot from the sky: that was how agreements ended.

'You will find us better mannered, Mr Diakanov. It is worth considering.'

The shades came off, and the SIS men were aware of the dark eyes, an amber glow filtering through the irises. 'I consider everything. The question is – what is Leonid Gresko next considering?'

A slow goods train might once have been an unremarkable sight on the Trans-Siberian Railway, but was a mirage in the post-collapse economy of Russia. Here, in the shrivelled landscape of sun-parched steppes, where the scrubby East Siberian wastes stretched down to the immense Amur River marking the divide between Russia and China, light could play tricks. Few lived, or wanted to live in this inhospitable land where summer heat burned remorselessly and winter's freeze left only in May. Outsiders did augment the scattered population: their strange settlements were disguised, ringed with electrified and razor wire, guarded, studded with low-lying concrete structures. For these were the ballistic missile silos and bases of Russia's Strategic Rocket Forces. Their alert state had recently been raised on the orders of the Security Council and High Command: relations with China were deteriorating, probing actions by Manchurian forces increased. At Chita, the region's traditional military centre, Russian headquarters staff reoccupied buildings they had left in the early 1990s, military vehicles accelerated along cleared streets, troops were moved forward and patrols along the tense border stepped up. The markets, the mingling of languages and faces, the steady barter trade had gone, replaced by the surly posturing between two sides divided by paranoia, watch towers and a high matrix-mesh fence. Nothing passed beneath the Friendship Gate, no trains branched off from the Trans-Siberian at Chita to run to the Russian border town of Zabaikalsk and on to the Chinese post of Manzhouli. Closed – track, minds, and the chance to negotiate. Confrontation fed itself with rumour and counter-rumour, with tales of Harbin irregulars conducting pirate raids on remote Russian villages, with the need for a crippled Russian presidency to use the crutch of external conflict to shore up the domestic position and divert attention. Minor artillery barrages had been exchanged, Beijing was resurrecting its old territorial claims; Moscow's press, outraged, interpreted it as opportunism, naked belligerence. Controlled, localised aggression could act as a popular unifier.

The box-cars rocked gently on the bogies, their grey uniformity trailing backwards, interrupted only by three unusually large generator wagons placed at the centre. Throughout the winter months, stored in the closed and adapted tunnel of a disused molybdenum mine carved into the rising ground of the Amur mountains, the locomotive had been prepared, its cargo fine-tuned. Observers might have been surprised at the quality of track laid on the redundant branch line, its level of maintenance, but observation was discouraged and unlikely. Fewer, except those with the highest security clearance, would have seen the compartment interiors. Banks of electronic displays crowded the walls, operators sliding between them on tracked chairs, checking incoming data, watching radar scopes, electronic support and intelligence screens, computer-referencing with signal and signature libraries, testing communications and control equipment. The air was scrubbed, filtered, for the train was closed up, sealed, held on action alert. Seated in the command car, position raised above the bowed heads of the encryption specialists and tactical coordinators, was the still, upright figure of Colonel Petr Ivanov. The locomotive coasted to a standstill.

'Are we linked to the radar sites?'

'Affirmative, Colonel. We have full information distribution.'

'Systems checks?'

'Complete, Colonel.'

'Then we are ready. You have authorisation to proceed.'

He felt for the emerald cross in his pocket. One action could set off others, provoke a chain reaction. It was good that an Ivanov was involved once again in the process. The hum from the generators lent a gentle vibration to the floor and bulkheads, the scattering of lights and luminescence of read-outs bright in the general shadow, bathing the Colonel's face a threatening blue. There was power here, ready to be used.

'Three, two, one ... Decoys are airborne. Say again, decoys are airborne. First two flights. Signature augmentation will be activated at five thousand feet.'

Ivanov jostled the headset into position over his ears. 'Switch me to air command frequency.'

Arcade gamesmanship, and he was looking for a high score. The targets were fighters from Russia's Frontal Aviation regiments and their counterparts in the Chinese PLA air force. For weeks, both sides had mounted combat air patrols along the frontier – defending, deterring, feinting. The decoys were about to break the impasse. Small, powered by miniature 0.2kN-thrust turbojet engines, they flew from launchers pre-positioned on high ground and assumed their attack profiles, singly, in pairs or in larger formations, at a variety of altitudes and velocities. The confusion they could cause went way beyond anything suggested by their size, as each was equipped with a state-of-the-art package allowing it to replicate numerous aircraft types when 'painted' by enemy radar. It was a proven system, derived from work undertaken by America's DARPA – Defense Advanced Research Projects Agency – with its suppression of enemy air defences programme. Russia had acquired the technology. Ivanov waited.

'We have hostiles, heading 185. Border violations executed.' It was the air intercept controller on board a Beriev A-50 *Mainstay* Airborne Early Warning aircraft. 'No IFF response. ESM and radar matches indicate four Chinese JZ-5 reconnaissance types. Top cover six Flankers. They're using their Su-27s re-deployed from Wuhu. I'm vectoring a command Su-30 into sector three.'

Excitable chatter. Radar was being spoofed, the electronic environment cluttered with chaff and spurious signals, communications interrupted and distorted. Ivanov closed his eyes. The fog of war, he thought: the *Shoran* navigation sets on the Flankers were unreliable, led pilots off course; people could get killed. The Chinese would be moving forward to meet their own phantom incursions. How expedient that their interceptors were Sukhoi Su-27SKs, sold to them by a Russian defence industry craving orders, grateful for business. An even match. It made for better sport.

The *Mainstay* operators were busy. 'Picking up Phazotron Zhuk-27 radar emissions. Confirms Su-27 Flankers in use. Carriage of stand-off Vympel R-27 missiles likely. You have approval for Beyond-Visual-Range engagement. SAM sites are standing down in forward areas. Repeat, SA-10 *Grumble* launchers and SA-5 *Gammons* are standing down . . . Multiple tracks. Bandits at 190 K, heading 155 at five hundred knots, eleven o'clock. Sentinel looking, switch to discreet.'

Units travelled towards each other. 'Tracking. Missiles armed. Acquisition . . . Outer envelope. Missile one, two away, homing. Breaking. Fire-and-forget; give me an update.'

Countdown, the report terse. 'Missiles closing . . . Twenty miles . . . Ten . . . Terminal phase. You have a kill confirmed. Survivors oncoming; same heading. Handing off.'

Across the front, the sides met, by accident, by Petr Ivanov's design. A squadron leader, following Leonid Gresko's secret orders, fired his long-range, active-radar AA-12 missiles into Chinese airspace. They scored direct hits. No one was about to run. Dog-fights were breaking out, the growling tone of infrared missile lock-ons, shouted warnings, expletives, the vocal stress of furball acrobatics redoubled by pilots pulling top g's, high Alphas.

'*Break hard left, flares–flares–flares. Check six! Check six! . . . He's on your tail . . . Fuck . . . Have two bogies on infrared search, fifteen thousand feet, fifteen miles . . . Closing fast . . . Tracking . . . Looking for a tone . . . We have it – R-73 missile select . . . R-73 dogfight away . . . It's a splash . . . Flight Four doing a tail slide . . . I'm on your left side . . . Bogey, course zero-seven-zero . . . I'm in . . . Looking, looking . . . I've lost him . . . got him . . . Smoking . . . Helmet cueing, snap-shoot, off-boresight . . . Break now.*'

The encounters pitted the Russian short-range AA-11 missile against Chinese-acquired Israeli *Pythons* and locally built copies of the American *Sidewinder* and French *Magic*.

Casualties grew. '*Bogey in sight, Q-5 Fantan going low. Lead will take the shot . . . good tone . . . Have a tally . . . Roger that . . . Turning right, bleeding airspeed . . . Switching to guns . . . Fuck this pitch authority . . . Nose-slicing; rapid tail deflection; overriding flight-controls . . . moving through the stall . . . Angle-of-attack at sixty . . . Christ, I'm doing a Pugachev . . . clear shot . . . Red Seven and Eight are out . . .*'

Their proximity fuses activated, fragmentation warheads exploded, downing aircraft, dropping pilots – an occupational hazard – the wrenching fear lost in a flurry of speed, concentration, violent manoeuvre and a welter of radio slang. Death by euphemism, colloquialism.

'*There's a missile on your tail-pipe. Cut the burners, cut the burners! Flares . . .*'

Ivanov changed to speaker, allowed the staccato cries of battle to permeate the carriage. It was pointless, with hindsight inexplicable. Russian pilots short on flying-hours pitched against Chinese opposites bereft of tactical training, fighting for nothing, over nothing. While the sky filled with burning jet-fuel, the thunder of Lyulka Saturn turbofans, falling hardware and the smoke-black trails of involuntary descent, the decoy drones would float gently down on automatic parachute to be recovered and returned to base. They were less scathed by their outing than the manned fighters. Ivanov observed the central situation display. The trials of life were more interesting when viewed remotely. In his palm, the cross had left a reddening stigmata-impress.

Unblinking eyes, obtuse with bourbon and trauma, stared upwards, had done so for an hour. The ceiling was as featureless as the rest of the Watergate complex, as blank as the Senator's political future. It gave no comfort, but he was too absorbed to seek comfort, unable to focus, to think clearly. He was here to hide and gain space, to wallow in lost days of drink, room service and the limited protection afforded by several storeys placed between himself and the jackals of the press. From political darling to despair in a telephone call. And they said a week was a long time. Christ, he had blown it, even by Washington standards.

O'Day twisted the cord of the bathrobe between his fingers. Denial, it was the only solution, however temporary, came naturally to a politician; lying was the epidermis of an addict and member of Congress. The pursuers might get bored, back off, be diverted. Summer recess, the emptying of the city, would lower the journalistic metabolism and the pace of enquiry. Then again, the longer the investigative process, the more could be uncovered: testimonies and testimonials from dealers, users, those with whom he shared a bathroom, a clean surface, partied. It would be drawn out, dragged out, his face in the mud and in print, constant reminders of his close association with the Oval Office raked over and over. Descent. And as he fell, the safety nets and friendships would be withdrawn, people running to avoid the slipstream, the impact, the President himself damning with decency and a fraudulent smile, supportive while preparing for escape. Extrication was his art. The wave, the posse of Secret Servicemen jogging at his side, the same image repeated on a million screens, of the leader's pink-white legs, fat and baby-hairless, racing out of danger. Politicians united in cowardice. They would return for the corpse, gather round to say nice things, mourning-black setting off their earnest faces, setting off their earnest mouths. '*A giant political figure . . . a flawed human being . . . strengthened by his faults . . . a man of his age*' : eulogy and cliché rippling on the airwaves. A political carcass was safe, for it had no influence. In passing, he would be forgiven – it made those left feel better about themselves, secure that they too could be forgiven.

Their generosity might diminish if they knew of the blackmail, his work for Russians seeking to overthrow the Kremlin, his fellow-travellers based within the Central Intelligence Agency. He would never confess to that. But it weighed, a conspiracy so fantastical he scarcely believed it. His statesmanlike comments were nothing but the cheap products of coercion, his warnings on the foolhardiness of throwing funds at Moscow the result not of careful consideration but of threats made to his career. And that career was finished. In a sense, he was released, obligation destroyed by press discovery of his involvement in drugs. Without authority, he was nothing to those who controlled him. They would leave him, move on to exploit other weaknesses in other weak men, vampires afraid of exposure through coming too close, exposure to flashbulbs. Yet in ending contact, they were reinforcing the humiliation of his decline. Sheer perversity, appreciation of the power-game, ensured his entrapment had both thrilled and terrified, provided risk and opportunity. If they succeeded in toppling and replacing the Russian hierarchy, he might have played the central role in negotiating with the new order he helped obliquely to establish. He could have shone, shuttled between capitals in dramatic acts of nailbiting, high-stakes diplomacy, strutted, posed, added lustre and prestige to his own chances as prospective candidate for the American presidency. Instead, he was disqualified before the race began, banished, a refugee lurking in a nondescript suite, checked in at his country's ugliest hotel.

He swung his legs, found the floor and levered up. Thoughts were easier in fresh air. Stepping through the French windows onto the balcony, he rested his palms on the concrete balustrade, felt the stored heat. Mary should understand, could hold off the trash-bin scavengers with the ferocity of a lone she-wolf aware of her husband's guilt. She was protecting her position, her corner. He had to stay away from the house in Georgetown, for soon the ladders and the cameras, the mike booms, the on-the-spot interviewers who wished to put him on the spot, the jostling crowd of baying journos, would pitch camp and stay for battle. They had yet to face his wife's acerbic tongue and litigious instincts. A party of small schoolchildren skipped along the sidewalk beside the Kennedy Center, too young to know of presidential mores and amphetamine injections. The Senator watched them, envied their innocence and optimism. Today's press would have buried Camelot, killed JFK long before half his head came away in Dallas. Nixon's head was their first complete trophy, O'Day's their latest, Kennedy's a little shop-soiled, book depository-damaged for modern tastes. Perhaps he should ignore his lawyer's advice, come clean, go clean, appeal to the nation's heart? People were suckers for a repentant sinner, the TV confessional, for a man pursued by chemical demons. Hell, it wasn't as if he had driven off a bridge with a broad, semen-splashed an internee's dress. Book in to rehab, reach recovery, win forgiveness. Indulge, then crave – buy – indulgence. The best reason to be a Catholic. Shit, he just couldn't be bothered. He squinted at the Potomac, his River Jordan, baptismal waterway to a past political life. Paddy, you're getting poetic, retrospective, he thought. Must be the hangover. He was an Irishman, would go down fighting, enjoy the lost cause. Screw the false friendships of the Metropolitan Club.

'Knock, knock.'

O'Day spun. 'What the fuck . . .?'

'Dammit. I reckoned you'd know this one.' Hunter Strachan stood in the doorway, a crossbow elevated in his gloved hand. Light caught the scar dimpling, glanced from the mirror shades. A familiar figure rolled the door wide and joined him in the opening.

'Jack. What the hell's going on?' O'Day seized on a face he recognised. It was the response of one bred to work DC's drinks reception circuit, the response of one abjectly scared. His arm went to steady himself against the barrier. Alcohol was slowing him, confusing, building on the alarm.

'The Watergate, Paddy?' the CIA man responded. 'Grave-yard of a few political careers, as I recall.' An automatic pistol was produced from a shoulder holster, the Senator's eyes widening.

'For fuck's sake, Jack.' Silencer applied. Alcohol burning off. 'Jesus, stop this.' He could not back further. 'What are you doing?'

'Preliminaries.'

Disbelief. 'You what?'

'What, what. You're sounding like mad King George of England, Paddy.' Pistol cocked.

'Put it away, Jack. Come on, put it away. You're a Langley Floor Seven fella, you don't need this.' O'Day appealed to the man's seniority, appealed to anything.

'It's good to come down to earth. You'll see.'

'Look, wait a minute, wait a minute. I've done everything you've asked, I haven't harmed your interests. Please.' He turned attention to Strachan, had to win them both. 'I'm not going to tell anyone.'

'I know.'

'Then, for God's sake, lay down your weapons. We can talk.'

'Uh-huh.' Sunbeams shone brightly off the polished surface. Motionless, emotionless lenses.

O'Day tried to penetrate them, communicate through. 'Let's be calm, OK? OK? Nothing hasty, Mr . . .'

'Dr,' answered Strachan. 'Dr Sidney Gottlieb.'

The Senator caught the reference, but only partially its implications. Gottlieb had been the Agency's chief in-house covert assassinations and poisons expert, head of its 'Health Alteration Committee' throughout the fifties and sixties. A new breed of health-alteration specialist faced O'Day.

'You want cooperation? You have it. Everything you've asked, I've done. I've swung the President behind me, blocked credit extension to the IMF.' Rising pitch, rising tremor. 'Jack, this is absurd. Can we discuss over a drink? It's more civilised.'

'But less effective.' Strachan smiled. This was one Watergate operation which would not be bungled.

The CIA official weighed the gun in his hand. He wondered if the Senator would go quietly. 'You've had your minute, Paddy. Nothing's changed.'

'Chrissakes, Jack, negotiate. It's the way forward from

this.' Sweat emerged in an oil sheen. 'I'm asking. Begging. Name it, anything you want.'

'I was hoping you'd give ground.'

'Sure, sure.' Over-eagerness, propelled by the survival code, not attuned to irony. A weak grin of encouragement, bouncing back distorted in Strachan's silver shades. O'Day turned again to the Langley renegade, working them, sensing his way. The antennae were not getting feedback. Try harder. A bigger smile, greater uncertainty. 'I'll give ground. I'm a politician, remember?'

'It's not endearing. You certain you've said nothing about our little deal?'

'Absolutely. Believe me.'

The officer looked sceptical. 'Hard to take from a man who has White Lady blown up his ass.'

'On camera too. It'll change the face of news reporting.' Strachan was lowering the bow. 'Final question, bonus prize. Did you know that each year icicles kill several Muscovites? It's quite a problem.'

'What . . .'

The CIA acquaintance shook his head. 'There you go again. Always *what*. It's pissing me something.'

'I . . .'

'Take a piece of Russia with you.' Strachan fired.

It was quick: trigger depression, shaft release and strike, icicle entering above the left eye, catapulting O'Day backwards and over.

'You think he liked the prize?'

'Out of sight, Hunter. Out of sight.' The voice displayed a note of admiration. 'In the best traditions of Dr Gottlieb's turn on, tune in, drop out approach.'

'Use it or lose it. The round was melting.'

'So was my patience.' A clap on the shoulder. 'He's made his press statement. Quite an impact. Let's go before the street entertainment.'

Below, outside the off-white rectangle of the Kennedy Center, the skipping had stopped, the screaming started.

The conversation was terse, atmosphere stiff, the formality of a meeting where trust was sought rather than a given. They sat in the claustrophobic gloom of a Cotswold house beyond the Oxfordshire village of Taynton, a smattering of SIS, a senior representative from the CIA, and Ben Purton, the group deposited far from London, distance an indication of the situation's gravity. A Cross of St George drooped lifelessly above the church tower, the graveyard and surrounding fields a scene of bucolic tranquillity, summer lassitude not repeated in the cooler environment of the main dining room.

'Thank you for your cooperation, Major.' The brisk sincerity of Guy Parsons accompanied the pouring of mineral water.

'I'm not here to cooperate,' came the reply. 'I'm here to get answers. You played me for a fool.'

'For a soldier. It's different.'

A shake of the head in disagreement. 'Not by much. I was sent to Yemen on the basis of a lie, told to start a war, told it was a Saudi initiative. I'm the last to be informed it was a Russian plot. You set me up, murdered Nick Howell.'

'Not Six's style, Ben. An Agency decision,' Hugh Dryden ventured smoothly from across the table.

'And you were in the dark, Hugh, didn't sanction it? Come on – offloading responsibility is section one of your handbook.'

Parsons tried again. 'Let's be reasonable here, Major.'

'That would strain your resources, Parsons. I've worked with you people before, remember?'

It was the turn of the official from Langley. 'We understand your anger . . .'

'You don't begin to understand my anger,' Purton rounded on him.

'Perhaps not, Ben, and we're sorry, truly.' Parsons knew it would be tricky, moved on to first-name terms. 'But had we told you Howell was suspect, that we discovered the Saudi diplomat's motives, that the Russians are gearing to re-establish bases from Yemen to Angola, would you have done the job so successfully?'

'I've never let you down.'

Dryden interrupted. 'Naturally, but we're talking Nick Howell, Ben. If he detected a change in attitude towards him, a cooling of your friendship, any behavioural quirk you couldn't hide because of your disgust at his parallel agenda, Moscow would have heard.'

'It's my right to balls it up. I'm an adult.'

'But not an actor.'

'You're black-and-white, Ben – it's a strength for a fighting man. In Yemen it could have been a weakness.' Parsons handed off again to Dryden, maintaining pressure.

'A weakness which might have blown the operation out of the water. It's bigger than the Yemen. The whole future of the Russian Federation is up for grabs.'

'And we're in the line-out,' the head of Russia Department added. 'So, yes, we chose to unleash you with less than a full briefing.'

Purton returned to the CIA officer. 'While you chose to let Nick die. Without a trial, without the chance to defend himself. Why? So that a CIA psychopath called Marc Mouton can ingratiate himself with the government in Sana'a and continue feeding you crap for greenbacks.'

The man in the lightweight summer suit did not flinch. 'We need humint in place, frankly we're scared of Moslem fanatics, particularly when they're sitting across the border from Saudi, and if we can get a handle on this Russian thing no price is too high.' It was the unembellished coldness of a strategic pragmatist. 'Mouton may be a psychiatrist's worst nightmare, a basket-case, but he saved you being force-fed your own genitals in a Yemeni jail. He did the same for Howell.'

'Forgive my sounding ungrateful.'

'It's a harsh business, Ben. Harsh decisions need taking.'

'Slogans don't make it easier, Parsons.'

The church clock chimed in the still air, marking time against an occasional disturbance of rooks and the bleating of diminished flocks of sheep, and Purton imagined Howell and Ahmed Badr disintegrating under a tarpaulin. His friend, comrade, Royal Marine NCO, had lost money, seen debts mount and opportunities for a middle-aged man fade. Yet there was never a hint of the ditching of principle, the adoption of values and causes antithetical to everything for which he stood. Throughout his working, waking life he trained, re-trained, prepared to wage a small-unit Special Forces war against the Russians. Then he went civvy. Disgruntlement and despair turned him, as the American haulier and trader Hunter Strachan turned him, and he signed up, sold out, to an alternative interest. Purton's visit to Molly, his widow, in Denbigh had been uneasy, a combination of fact-finding and respect-paying, neither fully accomplished. There were too many gaps, and the greatest was the chasm torn through a lifetime of trust and mutual dependency between two soldiers. Purton was betrayed, and whatever excuses, explanations, however Howell might have assembled the logic for his behaviour, his commanding officer could not forgive. Max had disappeared, and Max worked for Hunter Strachan: Howell was in league with the man instrumental in the Yemen plot, the Russian plot, his son's uncertain fate. For Max, he would fight unconditionally; against that, Howell meant nothing.

'Ever heard of the Cuban Sanction?' the American asked.

'Only in spy thrillers.'

'Unfortunately it's for real.'

He explained. On 4 April 1993, the Agency had lifted a GRU Russian military intelligence officer from a beach in Cuba. He was defecting from the Lourdes Elint base there, revealed its criticality to Russia's strategic defence interests, its role in nuclear early warning, electronic information gathering, the plundering of American computer data banks and the development of cyber-warfare techniques against the continental United States.

'Had us in a spin, I'm telling you,' the visitor from Langley went on. 'But what worried us most was the detailed evidence he provided on the collapsing state of his country's nuke command and control systems.'

Parsons murmured his agreement. 'Made everyone jittery. Our concern seemed justified when in January 1995 Yeltsin, his Defence Minister and Chief of the General Staff activated their *Cheget* nuclear briefcase unblocking codes because the Krokus early warning mistook a Norwegian sounding rocket for an American pre-emptive Trident missile launch.'

'The frights kept coming. But, by then, we had contingencies.'

'The Cuban Sanction?'

'You got it. A few months after the defection, a team of our senior intelligence people met their Russian opposites at a hotel in the Sierra de los Organos. Resulted in a covert agreement by which we would pump funds, advice and technology across to overhaul and modernise their entire nuclear facilities.'

'Probably made sense to someone,' Purton observed.

'Sure. Might seem warped now, but we set out to stabilise deterrence. As their conventional forces fell to pieces, they relied more on their nuclear. We wanted to make it failsafe, foolproof, for our own sakes.'

'Then I'm the only one who sees a discrepancy between pulling an arsenal to pieces and building one up.' Purton looked around the table. 'Where does Hunter Strachan come in?'

A shuffling of papers, the unspoken shifting of responsibility – the bureaucrat's relay race handover – until it settled back on the American. He coughed. 'A group at the Russo-American discussions in Cuba decided to go solo, unilateral, further than anything countenanced by the Sanction.'

'Not exactly a first for an intelligence organisation.'

'They thought, if we're tweaking the nuclear aspect, why not tweak the lot? Hand over a swathe of technology, allow them to integrate or reverse-engineer it, keep Russia our regional peer, provide something for us to kick against, an enemy for us to design weapons to fight against; support a buffer against the growing yellow menace from China, preserve NATO's *raison d'être*.'

'That was their starting point, Ben.' Dryden commented.

'You mean it gets more depressing?'

'Without a doubt,' the SIS man answered.

A beautiful place, and one left alone. Instead of families taking walks in the countryside, bathing in the streams, picking wild flowers and berries, there were groups of Federal Security Service and Al'fa operatives in unlikely disguise as foresters and animal husbanders. Their hands were too clean, their minds too closed, and their packs carried weaponry and radios. They were outclassed and outgunned by the forces belonging to Cold Cut.

He lay behind a screen of chicken-wire and camouflage netting woven with foliage, observation telescope trained on the hillside. For a week, his scouts had reconnoitred the area, scoured the gullies, defilades and natural approaches for land-mines, trip-flares and seismic sensors, climbed trees in search of infrared devices and moving-target indicators. Preparation was thorough, the plan depended on it. From this elevation, the rising ground gave few indications of what hid below it; topographical clues were well hidden. But they were there: the clusters of rock with faces unnaturally smooth, artificially constructed; communications antennae and aerials recessed into trenches and set behind ridges; the tiered earthworks resembling burial mounds, serving the living instead of the dead.

Panning shot, focus adjusted, and down to a track snaking at the base. Too normal, too sanitised. Instinct and recognition informed him. This was it – Point X, Ground Zero – and he would leave more than a mark. He shifted his weight and spoke briefly to an aide lying up in the adjacent position. The man slithered out, was carrying a message. In front of the telescope, a swarm of midges descended to mob and

*cloud the lens. Brodets, the wanderer, waited. He had waited
a lifetime.*

*An hour. Activity was increasing, the morning trail of
vehicles taking the night shift out, bringing the day shift in,
creating a blue diesel haze to hang above the road. A well-
staffed facility. The sun climbed and warmed his back. He
wondered if the FSB officers whose papers he had
sequestrated and copied during their travels to arm hidden
nuclear weapons in Siberia, were returned. They would regret
ending their excursion: field trips could be so advantageous
to personal health, longevity. He squinted again through the
eye-piece. Significance was suggested by the target's mass,
the frequency of patrols and the lengths to which the FSB
went in blending its features into the varying gradients. It
implied a strategic target, worthy of inspection; during
conflict, worthy of destruction. British Intelligence had his
report, the maps indicating location of bombs planted by
Leonid Gresko's servants. Its response would be limited to
the point of inertia. He was left, all that was left, for this was
conflict, and the West was unaware. There were ways to
bring matters to a head, conspiracies to the attention of
others.*

*The rear tyre blew, the bus swinging unrhythmically,
attention drawn by disorder in an ordered world. It veered
from the road, bounced off side barriers, rear slewing across,
impacting with a fat-tyred technical support van. Mountain
roads were treacherous. Cold Cut knew all about treachery.
He watched, dispassionate, the scene played out silently and
at a distance: memories came like this. Figures were
standing, gesticulating, crowding to inspect the damage.
There were bodies in uniform, flung out, laid out, probably
GVS Government Communications Troops –
Gosudarstvennye voiska svyazi. An officer spoke into a radio.
From the hillside came recovery trucks and armoured
bulldozers, lured out, unearthed from their ant-heap by
outside disruption. Access was blocked, would need to be
cleared. Worker ants, soldier ants, mingled.*

Traffic backed up, people milling, perhaps offering to help. A squad of paramedics appeared, adding to the throng, flashing lights demonstrating emergency, overlapping responsibility. So much for a covert establishment, Cold Cut reflected. Minutes passed, routine suspended. Slowly, the bus was winched round, debris cleared, a narrow passage created for one-way flow. Movement returned. A convoy filtered through and headed for an entry point further up the pass, was joined by blood-wagons and a flat-bed loaded with discarded metal. He tracked them, saw the control vehicles vanish into their underground depot. Most satisfactory. On board, one of them carried a nuclear warhead stored in a suitcase. The device was live.

Dryden was talking. 'The GRU defector from the electronic warfare base at Lourdes was a plant, sent over by a Russian official to get American attention, scare them into giving assistance. The official has since risen to become head of the Russian Federal Security Service – Leonid Gresko.'

'The defector was so keen on his American lifestyle, he eventually came clean. Put us on the trail.' The visitor from Langley grimaced. Purton would soon understand why.

Gresko's plans were ambitious, went far beyond acquiring defence know-how. He was thinking, dreaming, political power, and his select group of supporters in American intelligence were delighted to help. Initially, Hunter Strachan was employed to smuggle in hardware and software to the Russian military, passed back news to his American case officers. But the role had grown. He was absorbed into Gresko's scheme, became part of the conspiracy to undermine and then seize a weakened Russian Federation.

The transatlantic guest scratched his head. 'Destroy the economy, reduce the country to near-rubble, make the Russian population and the West stare into an abyss and a hard-line government in Moscow suddenly seems attractive. Better a safe pair of hands.'

'Better a pact with the Devil you know than a fragmenting

Federation made up from a thousand smaller antichrists you don't.' That Devil could be popular if he destroyed the mafiya, fed the people, weeded out corruption and gave direction. Parsons picked at a cuff-link. Tension brought out different tics in people. 'Something comfortably reassuring about old enmities.'

Purton rubbed his eyes, tired, appalled. 'It's how all despots survive – the rest of us refusing to make a stand. We never learn.'

'Despots survive by disguising the truth,' Parsons corrected. 'And the truth in Russia's case is rather ugly.' He pushed across a file. 'Take a look. It's a summary of a number of weapons programmes Gresko has managed to sustain with a little help from his friends. One of them is the Scramjet project.'

'Should I be worried?'

'Undoubtedly. It's a supersonic-combustion ramjet aircraft capable of speeds of over Mach 10. We're not sure if it's manned or unmanned. Still on the drawing-boards in the Western aerospace community; it's reality over there. We think they've got full-scale flying waverider prototypes.'

'Talks here of turbulent diffusion, shockwave interaction, baroclinic torque, low-density polymer ablatives, and axial vorticity. Meaning what?'

'That the Russians have mastered the outer-limits of aero-dynamic and propulsion technology, created major structural carbon composites years before the rest of us. The aircraft, incidentally, is fuelled by liquid hydrogen.'

Purton's face showed recognition. 'The storage tanks in Yemen?'

'Scramjet is perfect for hitting time-critical targets. Ataq airbase would have acted as a forward operating base for its strategic bombing, reconnaissance and maritime strike roles. Howell and Ahmed Badr were involved in that aspect of the plan.'

'They want South Yemen simply as an airbase?'

The CIA rep shook his head. 'As a regional centre of

influence. It would allow them to circumvent encroachment on their borders by the Western alliance. Leapfrog us. They're doing the same elsewhere.'

'Big bang – political and security rebirth. And secret re-militarisation at home hasn't stopped there, Ben.' Dryden waved a hand in the direction of the file. 'For an *hors d'oeuvre*, they've got stocks of haemorrhagic fever that would make the population of this planet literally sweat blood before it died.'

Parsons joined in. 'They're also studying genetic-targeting, making germs and viruses application- or ethno-specific: designed to wipe out only Chechens, for example.'

'And you know all this?'

'Right down to which particular buildings are used for smallpox research – units 6 and 6a at the Vector Institute, incidentally. Then there are the BioPreparat labs in St Petersburg, the Marburg viruses, the chimera strains. Deadly, untreatable. It's taken time to piece things together. We've lost agents doing it.'

Purton turned the pages, each section detailing another aspect of Gresko's strategy. There was a reference to the tactical nuclear weapons designed originally for the KGB and carried in suitcases. A hundred remained unaccounted for. He halted.

'The suitcase devices – Gresko has them?'

'Strong evidence to support it,' Parsons answered. 'Some in the intelligence community refer to them as RA-115s.'

'I call them pains in the butt,' the American ventured. SIS had shown him the location map provided by Cold Cut. Interesting choice of strategic target. None of those present were about to share the information with Purton. 'Meant to be placed at the heart of the enemy – Stateside. It's why Uncle Sam invested so heavily in its wide-area tracking system. Thank God for Lawrence Livermore. We wanted to detect the fuckers' entry, before they were committed.'

'Current location?'

'We think he's got primed bombs dotted around the

territories of the Russian Federation. We don't know why, or precisely where.'

Purton was grappling with the inconsistencies. 'He wouldn't radiate his own country. He's trying to take the damn place over. Why make it glow? It doesn't make sense.'

'Depends on whose perspective,' Parsons said cryptically. 'The final pages deal with a system known as *Perimetr*.'

'Thought it was a vodka brand.'

A grunt from the Langley officer. 'Does greater damage. It's their doomsday device. They've nicknamed it the "Dead Hand" and it goes further than our own ballistic missile command systems.'

Dryden offered the basic facts. 'Went operational in January 1985 after a test flight from Kapustin Yar. It's designed to initiate a retaliatory strike against the United States if Russia's command system and communications with the top brass have been taken out by American first strike.'

'Inventive.' Purton studied the diagrams.

'Very,' Parsons conceded. 'For activation it requires loss of normal command links to the hierarchy, release of preliminary missile launch sanctioning codes by the General Staff, and actual detonations to occur on Russian soil.'

The American unfolded a pair of reading glasses, applied them and found a page in his notes. 'It's a grudge thing. Essentially, it means Russia can rub everyone out from the grave. Satellite sends low-frequency signal to *Perimetr* launch sites, they send up adapted SS-17 ICBMs carrying UHF transmitters which communicate in flight to missile silos across the Federation. Boom – they launch automatically. Cue, everyone melts.'

'We understand *Perimetr* cannot be overridden or counter-manded,' Purton read aloud from the text.

'It's the prevailing view.'

'And it won't function without nuclear explosions on Russian soil? I take it there's point to mentioning Gresko and the suitcase devices?'

'Ah, yes.' Parsons closed his eyes for a moment. It was a

delicate matter. 'You'll appreciate our concern at receiving psychological assessments which conclude that Leonid Gresko is a clinical psychotic, perhaps schizophrenic, who suffers from ongoing delusions and hallucinations.'

No wonder he wanted to get into politics, Purton thought. 'You're saying the planned usurping of the Russian presidency could go radioactive?'

'If it doesn't end the way he wants, quite feasibly. We've been picking up sequences of *Perimetr* authorisation signals hidden behind commercial satellite traffic. Plainly, he's been able to corrupt the system.'

If he could do that, detonate warheads on Russian soil, and possessed the means to spoof early-warning computers and duplicate initial General Staff ballistic missile release codes, then *Perimetr* would be tripped into going live. Live meant Armageddon.

Purton focused on his interlocked hands, stared with the intensity of prayer. It was an attempt to quash disbelief. 'And you've done nothing, avoided intervention, allowed it to come to a head? Have you informed the American President? The Russian President? The British Prime Minister? What the hell are you waiting for?'

'It's a question of evidence, Ben, fitting the pieces together.' The American peered over his spectacles.

'It's a question of you saving your backsides, not wanting the sky to fall in on Langley when news of the Cuban Sanction gets out, when it's revealed your rogue operatives planned to destroy Russian democracy, reinstate and rearm the Russian military, hand power to a certified lunatic.'

'That's . . .'

'What, unfair? For Christ's sake, one of my oldest friends is dead, and my son is in the clutches of a CIA man who's gone bad, gone native. Russia's pear-shaped and you sit in the Oxfordshire countryside claiming you have to fit the pieces together?'

An extended silence. Dryden leant forward. 'Ben, our governments understand the situation. Gresko's running a tight show. We've seen glimpses, but not everything, not enough. Knowing the Saudi diplomat received payment from him was a break.'

'Observing Hunter Strachan's involvement in Senator O'Day's belly-flop at the Watergate was another,' the man from the Central Intelligence Agency added.

'You could have picked him up, questioned him, prevented him from returning to Moscow.'

'And warn Gresko? Trust me, Ben, after traitors like Aldrich Ames, Harold Nicholson and Douglas Groat, we're itching to whack Strachan, drill a hole in his cavalry hat. There's a team of plumbers on standby for that very purpose. But he might be the only one keeping your son alive. And Max is in enough danger.'

'So's the Russian President. Contact him.'

Dryden's long frame draped across the chair. 'Gresko's head of counter-espionage, he's closed down the avenues. He dominates the Security Council, polices the lines of communication within the administration – or what's left of it – and we're not certain of the identities of those in his employ.' His posture reflected the awkwardness of the overall position. 'Any attempt at influencing the situation from here or contacting the Russian President through conventional channels might alert the FSB.'

Parsons nodded. 'Which in turn might provoke a hastening of the takeover attempt or large quantities of nuclear fallout, courtesy of his personal arsenal.'

'It'll happen anyway if you don't act,' Purton responded. 'What about China? The confrontation there is getting out of hand like everything else – another Gresko ploy?'

'I think we can assume that,' Parsons said crisply.

'I'm sure you'll compose a neat little report to cover it.'

'We were hoping you'd favour a more physical approach, Ben,' the American said drily.

'I think you can assume that,' Purton parodied the words of the SIS Russia head.

'How'd you like to go in yourself?'

The pause lengthened, Parsons feeling obliged to follow up. 'You told us to act, Ben.'

'I don't recall volunteering.'

'We need spoilers. There are anti-Gresko elements who can be exploited, must be controlled. It's our one opportunity to get in on the ground.'

'I bet you had the same conversation before sending me to the Yemen.'

Parsons persisted. 'There's an FSB officer – Colonel Georgi Lazin – who's brave, alone, and could do with our support. Sound man, definitely on side. I met him in Moscow a few times.'

'You want him recruited.' Purton interpreted the official-speak.

'I want him helped. Goodwill now could bring benefits later.'

Dryden was examining his fingernails, avoiding eye-contact. 'More controversially, Ben, we'd like you to liaise with Boris Diakanov, the mafiya boss.'

'I'm not surprised you're tip-toeing here.' The retired Special Forces officer leant on the table. They were easing him into their trap, and he had lost the art of escape. 'To make a point, Diakanov's pirates gutted three of my sea marshals and fed them to sharks in the Riau Straits and off Aur Island, just to siphon petroleum and kerosene cargoes.'

'We're aware of that.'

Parsons attempted to head off the argument. 'Whatever our personal views on Diakanov, at the present he's the only alternative and viable power base opposed to Gresko.'

'You seem confident you're making the right decision.'

'Not at all. But at least we know he's outside Gresko's influence. That's clean enough. It's a marriage of convenience.'

Purton felt the pincer closing. 'Convenience? Smells of desperation.'

'Perhaps it does,' Dryden said. 'Product of a desperate

situation. It will be similar to backing Tito's partisans – giving advice, fine-tuning.'

'They took over the country. Didn't make Yugoslavia a happy place.'

'All the more reason to keep an eye on developments. We don't have a choice.' Parsons was patient.

'Speaking for myself, I think I do.'

The Russia chief spread his hands, palms down. His speech was deliberate. 'Gresko is holding your son, Major Purton. Diakanov thinks he knows where. Are you really willing to pass this up?'

The room seemed unnaturally dark, chilled. The trap was sprung, and Purton caught. Dryden's mouth opened and closed; he spoke far off, of authorisation at the highest level, of the risk, of the potential for successful intervention. The planning would come, but improvisation, intuition, his sacrifice, were demanded. For the Sovereign, for the country. At this level, he would be doing it for Max. It gave the task a human scale – save Russia, save a putsch from going nuclear, save his son. The clock bell rang again, broke him from the suspended state. Retirement was postponed once more. Cruel Britannia.

'It's fortunate you're around.' Dryden gazed distractedly at a point somewhere on the wall. 'Six are rather over-stretched tracking down Irish terrorists released early from the Maze under the Good Friday agreement. A sizeable percentage are now retraining and rearming in every corner of the globe.'

Parsons was precise and trenchant. 'As usual, we and Five are left to pick up the pieces – mostly of women and children. Any questions?'

Too many. His own child was the lure. 'Am I being sent because I'm good, or because I'm expendable?'

'Both.' Vindication and relief hid behind the modest smile. 'It's a rare combination.'

Fair enough, Purton mused. They had inducted him, shared their intelligence, knowing he would accept, expecting him to die. The warrior gene, the common DNA thread between himself and Captain Mouton. Someone had to do it. *Smells of desperation.*

The fly alighted, tripping him from his dream. They were hatching from beneath his mattress, the underside with the smell of a dead man, swarming above the latrine bucket, diverting to examine him. He was alive. His tongue felt obese and dry, too large for his mouth, an obstruction. The insect wished to feed on it, crawled to the lower lip. It left in angry fright as a hand came up to swat, returning to land and scuttle higher on the head. Max let it be. None of them had chosen each other as cell mates; energy was too low to persecute. He remembered the dream, the blackened corpse with its turning head propped up on down-filled pillows. His subconscious state threw up only doom, imagery of decay, this mattress its catalyst. You did not need Jung to tell you that: the rankness was enough. He smiled weakly, the fly jigging with excitement, three of its brothers, sisters or cousins coming down to promenade and stomp excreta among needle scabs on an exposed arm. The joys of life.

Drugs had ceased to be administered, were replaced with a regime of casual battering in which questions were incidental, token legitimising agents for physical assault. He almost missed the laboratory coats, for their presence meant he was valuable, his thoughts – however demented, jab-induced – mattered. The hidden authority no longer cared, no longer wanted to know, no longer wished to extend his term. *Killing time before the killing.* Every day, the vague grey forms of the guards appeared, shapeless smudges, savagely ready to beat and kick, to inflict *pizdy* – the Russian idiom for 'cunts', deep gashes. It was contact sport, proved that his jailers were real, solid, not mere apparitions from his near-sightless existence; their blows brought him back to sanity, the present. Next, he would be thanking them. Cool the gratitude, he warned himself – it was not Patty Hearst and the Symbionese Liberation Army here. A fly meandered and pawed restlessly at the corner of one eye; he flicked it away. Everyone wanted a piece of his sleep.

At home with Max Purton. He pushed himself into a sitting position, upper body heavy, the effort making him pant. Bruises sent aching messages pulsing along the nerve routes, adding to the giddiness. Dislodged, the filth-carriers abandoned him, hovering in low orbit stacks for go-around approaches. His spine felt sharp against the wall, bones and body angles pronounced by muscle wastage and thin, nourishment-free diet. But the cold compress of the painted stone gave some relief. God, his mouth was dry. They might be poisoning him: he felt ill enough. Psychotropics had kept hunger compartmentalised, hidden behind hallucination and alteration. Released, it consumed him, gnawed at his stomach, his being. Yet there was another constant, retained from the hours of syringe employment, the hours of howling, at which he clutched as obsessively as the fantasy of food. The speaker set above the door was covered, unused, his inner ear detecting tinnitus echoes, the sonorous crash of the old Soviet national anthem, blasted soundlessly, deafening, heard far beyond his threshold of neurosis and madness. He was filling a dead man's place, was living out the days of predecessors and predeceased, repeating their pattern, imprinting himself as they were doing indelibly and invisibly on him. They were here, brought forward, or he transported back. Crazy. He slumped, unwilling to trust senses frayed by deprivation and flashback. Others could hardly possess him if he himself were not in full possession. It was illusion, a fertile, fertilized imagination. You used to be such a calm, rational guy, he whispered. Quit the spirit babble, the seance, your faculties are flawed. That was it: use of the second person proved insanity. *They were still here.*

He stumbled to his feet, hobbled to the ledge jutting from the door hatch and groped for the steel mug, its outline disguised by dullness. Connection made without vision, he carried it back to the bed, crab-walking and doubled-up as stomach cramps bit, his fingers running around the rim.

Sharp enough. If the guards checked, he would be stamped on, perhaps just his fingers. They could be picky, liked things just so, liked the cell foul, the bed rotting and the mug in place. Better to give them a reason for violence – gratuitous application hurt more, could offend a man's sense of justice. He knelt on the mattress, knees seeming narrow, unsteady, shaking to achieve and sustain balance. The rules and regulations were at eye-level, lines of them, inscribed in black-brown ink, fading into yellowed paper embossed with the Communist hammer and sickle. A manuscript from the past, testimony to the timelessness of prison routine, the codification of cruelty. The regime in a maximum security prison rarely changed, whatever the change in regime outside.

The screws would not come loose. With touch alone, he tried again, eased the narrow lip into the groove and twisted. Resistance. He pushed down on the mug, levered it round, breath constricted by effort, ribs hurting. Air held, exhaled, inhalation and desperation coming in gasps through ulcerated gums. Rest, resumption. An edge buckled. He had to succeed, shift the rules, nudge aside the regulations. Hardly symbolic, but it mattered, as any triumph mattered; he meant to contaminate their precious Capitalist Decontamination Unit. There was give, or expectation ran ahead of result. He tested the indentation: definite displacement, worth working on. If the bottom screw came away, he could swing the metal frame to one side, leave a mark behind, his final footnote. Parts of the mug were disintegrating. They would break bones for this, add to the hairline fractures. He inserted a newly jagged section of the brim and turned, prayed and turned. The head dipped a few degrees. He was sweating – be proactive, earn the beating, passivity only got you crushed. Throw the rules through the barred window. Now, that *would* be symbolic. Where would his body finish, and how? At the chemical works, or adding a natural touch to the synthetic resin institute on the city's industrial eastern outskirts? Small, agonised grunts; it was on its way. A fly probed his ear, loud as a buzz-saw. He ignored it.

Release, victory sweet enough to weep for. He sank back for a moment, drinking vessel deformed in one hand, rusted screw in the other, the double summation of achievement. Then he rose, gently manoeuvred the board aside, pressing his nose to the wall in readiness for basic prison artwork. The etching would be quick, perfunctory. His eyes focused, short-range vision travelling as he moved his head. Forehead stopped. He stared, mouth opening in anguish. Impossible. *Impossible*. It was the drugs, they were doing this to him, infecting his head as they infected his body. He wanted to scream, fold, die, shatter his skull against unyielding stone. A mirror to his past and to his future was held up, confronted him.

CHAPTER 8

Yuri Vakulchuk was getting drunk, could afford to. He was on the winning side, let it show, leered at the hostesses crowding the bar. They would come when he called them, not before. Their sense of hopelessness was suppressed by professionalism, appetites by habitual drug abuse. Lucky, for food was scarce, business and dollars drying up with the departure of foreigners and extinction of the rouble. Exchange booths – the mark of a distrusted currency – were closed, the economy closed with it. *Fin-de-siècle* hysteria everywhere: suicides, fucking, drinking, more suicides, more fucking, more drinking. Vakulchuk smiled, the response from the women instantaneous – faces lit with earnings expectancy, glossed lips parted and pouted, teeth licked by pink tongues accustomed to the sharp tang of sheath lubricant, to working on a thousand swollen, rubber-coated glans. The prospect of dealing with Vakulchuk's withered member hardly appealed, but appeal was a factor void in the sex-finance transaction. He had money, would come prematurely: the optimum equation. And so they flirted, vying for benefaction, for the chance to straddle and to earn – to eat – contempt hidden by over-rehearsed suggestiveness and skin-flick poses.

The attention flattered him. Motive had ceased to matter. He was a little man, devoid of personality or presence, unsuccessful with the opposite gender, sexual interaction bought rather than earned. They looked to him, a new patron, because power had shifted back to the men of the Lubyanka. He despised them for it, would use them. The glass recharged, the iced contents sluiced down his throat, chilling and warming together. Moisture entered his eyes. He blinked, vision remaining blurred before it returned detailed and sharp. A pair of his FSB colleagues had earlier performed in a side-room with a local acquisition. She might have been a schoolgirl, probably was, her father the pimp. As she crouched on all fours, open mouth hammer-heading against an open fly-zip, one man poured vodka down her angled back while the other lapped at it pooling in the cleft of her taut buttocks. Then she was beaten, badly. A tough life being a tart; harder being a drinks fountain. Another shot, glass placed down over-deliberately; burning, blindness, then clarity. Of course, Georgi Lazin would not have approved, but the Colonel was indisposed, on the run. He had been broken out of his prison van, and the evidence pointed to a mafiya – Diakanov – controlled operation. The project would need to be adapted, but it reinforced the view to be sold to the public of a renegade counter-espionage officer conspiring with *tsisari* and the criminal underworld. Useful, so very useful. It should be easy to round them up: every day, the Federal Security Service announced its latest successes, real estate confiscated, warehouses raided, accounts frozen, treasures and banknotes seized, capos and financiers arrested. Diakanov's empire was being dismantled, his political contacts imprisoned. Without a power base he was nothing. Vakulchuk had played his part, reporting direct to Leonid Gresko and his chief enforcer Colonel Petr Ivanov, preparing the way, ensuring a smooth transition and a final reckoning for Georgi Lazin. Reckoning postponed. A shame, for he had been planted on Lazin for over a year, worked hard to win his confidence, become a quasi-friend in a friendless workplace. Lazin depended on him, confided in him; it made surveillance of the Colonel easier. The escape was inconvenient. Nevertheless, there was much else to do.

A late arrival, she was different to the others, imbued with a vulnerability that was natural rather than manufactured, hesitant seductiveness in the place of brazen assertiveness. The eyes were large, pleading, pale, skin flawless, the mouth glimmering between shy possibility and inviting passivity; demureness shot through with sensuality. He found himself drawn, fascinated, the unspoken resentment of the rest serving to highlight her among a cast of auditioning mediocrities. Perhaps she was transsexual – he appreciated the complexities of the pre-ops, the subtleties of the post. There was strength here, a knowingness he could explore, depth and degradation in which he would lose himself and his inadequacy. Money allowed for that. She was sitting opposite him. He could not recall inviting her over, yet she must have picked up on the signs, the wavelength, understood his needs and his thoughts. It was intuition. He groped for her hand, the bar surroundings homogenised into an indistinct canvas which bore no interest. She engaged his mind, engaged his balls, a shoeless foot nudging softly against his crotch. The pressure increased. Soon they would be tumbling at his favoured-status apartment on Ivana Babushkina street.

'I am Yuri Andreyevich Vakulchuk,' he stated with the precision of a drunk, the self-importance of a short man.

The reply was gentle. 'Lovers do not need names.' Or details. She caressed his hand.

Georgi Lazin had described his erstwhile and treacherous assistant well. Her knee lowered, pivoting downwards, pushing harder. His eyes widened. He was enjoying this; not as much as she. Max would be laughing at the scene if he knew, if he were alive. You will tell everything, she willed.

The FSB Captain was flushed, ridiculous. 'That's so good.'

'I can tell you like it.'

A groan disguised. 'You are full of surprises.'

'I won't let you down,' Zenya promised.

The sound of Cossack *nagaika* whips bit through the wall, the blows unrelenting, grunts of exertion and pain split by the sharper crack of impact on flesh through thin prison clothing. Max cradled himself, stopped his ears, but the

493

brutality overrode such crude defences, conducted itself to an echo chamber deep in his head. He shivered, body tensing at each strike, nervous system sympathetic to the victim, anticipating its own encounter with the lash. He tried to think of a better time, of his student days, of eating crayfish on the Volga with Zenya, but his mind fused her with the beating next door, and he shook himself from the process. He wanted to believe she was alive, safe, far from violation.

He had avoided plans, shunned commitment: under the reaching shadow of progressive blindness it seemed the sensible approach, the only approach. Better to be lonely than to be cared for, cosseted. Career, ambition, relationships, the future, undermined by physical uncertainty, fragility. Detachment was the antidote to being smothered. It had led him here, to a cell, and he would vanish. Perhaps that too was sensible; real freedom, the ultimate avoidance, where none could judge, comment, witness his growing dependency, inability to hunt, gather, feed himself, inability to earn an income, raise a family. Pride had trapped and killed him. This was true uncertainty, fragility – bona fide shit in which to land. He pondered the likelihood of his father uncovering details of the death, of his mother's Boston coffee mornings, charity luncheons, gaining added piquancy from his disappearance. Blame would be apportioned. It was her English ex-husband's fault, filling her son's head with absurd notions of travel, of risk-taking. There would be tears, hugs, support, praise for her bravery and new suit, before grief-fatigue and gossip-acquisitiveness drove conversations on. He could hear them, sense her loss, the desperation of a dynamic persona made abrasive by time and excess pampering, made a bitch through boredom. Yet her heart would tear. And he felt sorry, so very sorry.

The whipping had ceased; he noticed because he shook less. They must have left, but the slamming of doors, tramp of departure, was lost on his shifting reverie. Re-engage, he ordered his softening mind. It slipped into paranoiac mode: they were taking a breather, coming for him, having a cigarette before they began again. He controlled the anxiety – thought green, thought calm, counted backwards – let it diminish with the numbers. He listened, breath held and let out cautiously.

There was a tapping, quiet, nonmetallic, on the disused radiator pipe below his sleeping ledge. Too regular to be a chance reflex, too distinct for the scuttling scratch of prison rats or roaches. He knew the characteristics of the in-house, undomesticated wildlife, of every creature infesting walls and body. This was alien, a fingernail transmitting a weak tattoo, sending a message, breaking the rules. The result could be broken bones. His neighbour was alive, was plainly immune to punishment. He would be lying in blood and post-shock, body racked, every effort strained, a source of fresh suffering. It deserved the risk of response. Max clambered down, stretched out prone, ear pressed against the rusting conductor tube. His instinct was to warn, castigate the prisoner for his folly, behaviour which could draw attention, encourage mass reprisal, involve himself. Weak, institutionalised, the inertia of the oppressed: he had sunk further than he thought, was scared of life, scared of death, was becoming a victim. Worse, a coward. It passed, banished by the promise of human contact.

The breathing was pained, summoned an impression of purpling ribs and battered lips.

'Can you hear me?' Max whispered, mouth to the ragged stonework around the pipe's entry point.

The voice was slow, sapped, mouth functioning without saliva. 'I can hear you.'

'Are you OK?'

'Relative to what?' Humour gave instant outline, depth to the man.

'I'm sorry. Stupid of me.'

'No. It was stupid of you to come to Vladimir. Apologise to yourself.'

'I've done that a thousand times.' It went silent. He thought his partner had blacked out, but the voice returned.

'You're the American?'

'I thought my Russian was foolproof.'

'This place has a habit of disappointing.' The murmured chuckle ignited a dribbling cough. Patience was the only help Max could offer. 'I heard there was one in isolation. Your name?'

'Max Purton.'

Shallow intakes intensified through clenched teeth – spasm control – and then calmed. 'Well, Max Purton. What happens here will soon be commonplace.'

'You seem well informed.'

'That is why they hit me so hard. I am the former first Deputy Prime Minister.'

Max's head slumped. So, this was how, where, Russian democracy was to end: banished, locked behind high walls. 'How many of you are there?'

'The numbers are rising. We are a complete government-in-exile.'

'I've never lived close to important people before.'

'Thank Leonid Gresko, Director of the FSB. He'll allow us to die close together as well.'

'It won't come to that.' It was something to say.

'Look around, Max.' The voice was trailing. 'Certainty and platitudes lose their meaning here.'

He did not care for meaning. 'It's OK, it's OK. We'll be all right. Listen. What do I call you?'

'Vitali.'

'Vitali, you're the first person in jail who hasn't shouted at me. Thanks.'

'You're the first who hasn't beaten me unconscious.'

A friendship formed, mutual trust, mutual need creating closeness, an empathetic bond which overrode superficial acquaintance. They might never meet, but they clung to the conversation, the contact, like separated lovers. Five minutes. The pauses were longer, the Russian's voice fading.

'Vitali. Who has been here before us? Who made up the bulk of the prisoners? I need to know.'

'Tsarist dissidents, Decembrists, Bolsheviks purged by Stalin, political prisoners, spies . . .'

'Spies? You mean foreigners?'

'Of course. I do not know their names. It was way back.'

'When?'

'If you live, tell my family. Will you tell my family?'

Max persisted. The politician's mind was thumbing a lift elsewhere. 'Listen to me, Vitali. When?'

'Tell them, Max.' Vocalisation was harsh. '*Tell them . . .*'

'You can tell them, Vitali. You'll do it.'

'Tell them . . . Be strong.'

'I will. You know that.'

'You sound like my interrogators. Will you force me to sign a confession? I will not sign, never . . .'

'Please, Vitali. I'm asking.'

'No . . .' Choking.

The whimpering was low, another cascade of intolerable agony. Silence. A fluttering on the pipe, a non-rhythmic drumming. It stopped. Max listened for breathing.

'Christ, Vitali. Wake up. Don't do this. You can't. Understand me? *You fucking understand me?* Can you hear me?' The pause was cosmetic, a panic-limitation measure. 'Don't die on me. Please, don't die. Hang in there. Your family need you. I need you. You're a Deputy Prime Minister, for God's sake. Come on, my friend. Come back.'

He had crawled to the cell door, was raining his fists on the steel, shouting for help – for Vitali, for himself. The man had betrayed him, opted out; his human link was severed. Friendship over.

There were two images of the Russian President speaking on the screens: one real, the other artificial, both perfect. Leonid Gresko switched attention between them, comparing, searching for the weakness, a technical deficiency which might betray the fake. He turned up the volume; the computer-replicated words, fully synchronised, matched the sombre features of the electronically generated double. The eyes were red, reflected sleeplessness, nasal passages blocked with a heavy summer cold. A clever touch. The technical staff could add psoriasis to the skin, dandruff to the shoulders, pollupses to the vocal chords if necessary. An optical and aural illusion – the President's health damaged or sustained, regardless of reality, regardless of the incumbent's actual situation. That situation was vulnerable.

'*We must be strong,*' President Number One intoned, '*A crisis has enveloped our country,*' President Number Two said. Gresko hit the mute. Even cyber-Statesmen were masters of the understatement, he mused. The people were living on food coupons and barter, currency exchange was history, and he had the power – literally – to put words into the mouth of the President, into the mouths of former politicians and government ministers whose show trials were imminent. Technology of communication, freedom, so naturally evolved into the technology of control.

This was its cutting edge. For years, FAPSI technicians and scientists had worked in the field of intrusive information warfare, fine-tuning their ability to subvert a potential adversary's command of its population and military. Warping and morphing of video footage, allied to off-line 3D synthetic modelling, were used to provide databases of key overseas leaders to be fed from bases such as Lourdes in Cuba onto national television networks during periods of hostility. It could be achieved and accessed real-time, recorded words and computer-generated phonemes mixed, matched to visuals, to gain seamless, believable human discourse. Congressmen, news anchormen, TV evangelists, all copied and mutated. Seeing was believing: Americans sat with their corn chips and microwave meals in the midst of television culture, saw a great deal, believed everything. Advantage lay with the manipulator, with the side that had plundered the United States' own 'Rapid Dominance' programme.

He reached for a scrambler telephone, punched a button. Its glow turned from amber to red. 'What have you to report?' He listened.

Outbreaks of anthrax and smallpox among rural communities and troop concentrations close to the frontier with China had rapidly pushed the confrontation with Beijing to a critical point. If biological weapons were being deployed against them, then it was proof indeed of Moscow's relative weakness. Foreign opinion-formers talked openly of the need to repair Russian defences, of the long-term requirement to see its security rebuilt against threatened expansionism by its neighbours. Strong leadership was vital – how else could the West construct a buffer against Islam, China and the criminal exports from a collapsed economy and satellite bandit republics? It carried logic, carried the whisky-impregnated words of Kim Philby back into his thoughts. The traitor had been prescient, so right. Gresko would show them strength. He snapped a further question.

'Are the high-radiance ultraviolet lasers in place?' He seemed satisfied with the answer. 'Proceed to employ them in containing the viral and spore fallouts.'

The powerful short-wavelength UV beams, transmitted along fibre-optic cables, would inhibit and degrade the biological agents by inducing thymine dimerisation and molecular faults in their DNA and RNA structures. UAVs – Unmanned Airborne Vehicles – were tracking the location and direction of the eruptions, their task made easier by their having been used to initiate the attacks in the first place. Again, the technical advances originated in America; again, they had been passed to representatives of Leonid Gresko, FSB Director.

'Report back for the next stages.' The handset was replaced.

The President mouthed wordlessly at his studio podium. Gresko wondered how he might respond, look, after the incidents planned for the chemical weapons dumps at Maradvkovski airfield several hundred miles east of Moscow and the Mongokhto base on Siberia's eastern coast. The drinking and make-up application prior to the television address would be heavier, the trembling, sweating and vomiting more pronounced – akin to the early effects of nerve gas on its victims. Empathy was part of a successful presidency. Momentum sustained on all fronts, and Gresko was its driver.

Another kind of leak forced its way into his ruminations: the flow of information to his enemies. It too would prove fatal, had been so already, for those foolhardy enough to seek patterns in events, to speculate, conjecture or to comment. There could be no chances taken – the pathologist Ilya Kokhlov, Senator Patrick O'Day, the woman in Tynda, countless officials and journalists silenced, voices smothered, *omerta* enforced. Yet flaws were showing, could not be tolerated. The British minister Nigel Ferris had warned of CIA-SIS suspicions concerning political, social and economic destabilisation in Russia, of their intention to deploy agents against the FSB to discover the truth and to fraternise with subversive elements. Their efforts would be wasted, enquiries barren, their intervention too late. He had already accelerated the project. Boris Diakanov's role as trigger for the mafiya conflict, instigator of wider collapse, was over. He was to be captured, so too the escapee, Colonel Georgi Lazin, one-time trusted member of the Federal Security Service. While their executions were pending, conditional upon arrest, warrants signed, that of the young American, Max Purton, was more imminent. News of his capture might cause complications. The US State Department were asking questions, complete disappearance, disposal and then denital, the habitually effective answer. Finally, there was the President's tiresome Chief of Staff. With Lazin and Diakanov temporarily at large, Western intelligence making forays onto Russian soil, and the American's girlfriend – employed by unidentified opponents – nowhere to be found, opposition might converge and re-emerge, the Chief of Staff its focus. *Never*. The intention to undermine, smear and eventually prosecute the man had gone, replaced by the intention for a quick kill. His survival was a threat. Whatever patience Gresko possessed, the lovingly created conspiracy to weaken the President by stealth and to pick off his allies in sequence, was finished, overtaken – by events, by the desire to strike and to conclude. Gresko adjusted the speed on the electric fan, allowed the breeze to soothe and cool. Let the Americans and British send assistance, provide succour to the human chaff in his path. Let them try. They would find corpses, only corpses.

A secretary brought coffee, sweetmeats and files. There were papers to sign and stamp, proposals for the Security Council to rubber-stamp. He browsed through pages contained in acetate transparencies, pausing to read the print of a Presidential decree commanding Russian-based Internet users, on pain of penal correction, to utilise home-grown Service Providers. Tuberculosis, rape and AIDS versus compliance: common sense would prevail. Gresko would prevail. Attached to the national networks was the Federal Security Service's advanced 'Soros' – Russian acronym for the *System for Ensuring Investigative Action* – employing high-speed links to feed every communication through FSB sifting computers. A system for ensuring his personal dominance, the ultimate in omnipresent eavesdropping. He would wrap his people with security, trap them with fibre-optics. He could hear them, their whispered conversations, their casual remarks, gauge their fear, for he was plugged into them, they into him. They were babbling, chattering. There was conspiracy here, heating his mind. He turned the fan speed to maximum, but the temperature rose, a panting breath beating his face, wind-licking the sweat. He had to pull the wires, cut the people's input to his brain. The shouts rose like climbing mercury; he was on fire, his head a furnace.

Red warning lights were flashing over on a console. Gresko failed to notice, rushing blood blanking out his senses. An alarm repeated monotonously; it was missed. The Director was rocking himself, internalised, unaware. A chorus of sounds broke out, were overridden by those in his damaged imagination. Something more real was occurring, beyond his comprehension or calculation. Far out in the Ural mountains, set below an unobtrusive hill on the linden- and pine-strewn expanse of the Kungur Forest Steppe, was the FSB's chief underground communications complex. Equipped with command-distribution, satellite and Low-Frequency links, it existed to pool domestic electronic intelligence, transmit encrypted orders and to act as hub for his eventual takeover. The catastrophic malfunction indicators which screamed at him marked the end of its service. A low-kiloton nuclear device, contained in a small suitcase, had at that moment detonated in the heart of the subterranean development. It was not part of his plan, the weapon no longer part of his stockpile. On the monitors, the Presidential twins continued their double mime. Cold Cut had just declared war on Leonid Gresko.

The predator picked out Vakulchuk with ease. Its small forked tongue flickered, triangulating direction with its twin tips, tasting the atmosphere, trapping scent particles of urine and sweat – their trace of fear hormone – and carrying them back to the Jacobson's organ in the roof of its mouth for analysis and identification. The brain, designed for hunting, dedicated to the kill function, was processing input from other sensors. Nostrils detected quantities of carbon dioxide, emissions from a living, breathing mammal. Output was heavy; the prey significant, scared, trapped. There was vibration here, high-frequency, rising above the pulse of a warm-blooded heartbeat. It was a constant, did not belong to thrashing limbs, did not belong at all. The brain rerouted from the neural cul-de-sac, extracted clues elsewhere. In cavities recessed before the eyes were passive infrared receptors, staring, enhancing the heat profile of the target, superimposing its image onto optics working in the visual-wavelength range. The snake could close and strike in complete darkness. When it did, its hypodermic fangs, lying flat and linked to venom ducts, would pivot down on hinged bone and lock into position at the moment of attack.

Assessment performed. Correlation: a human was present.

Vakulchuk gripped his knees closer to his chest, drew himself into a tighter defensive ball, the effort to attain invisibility, to reduce exposed surface area, forcing out the occasional moan or sob. He rationed their output. No need to antagonise the beast, and breath was short. Yet fright did not do justice to the elemental terror he felt, to the natural, primal horror that seized and shook him, which paralysed and rooted every cell and every impulse in catatonic uselessness. The Night Vision Goggles whined remorselessly in his ears, their world lit by illumination undetectable to the naked human eye and filtered through blackout screens taped over ceiling lamps. In that world, coiled and awake, caught in the focal plane of the FSB Captain's two lenses, was a pit viper twelve feet in length. Known as a Bushmaster, native to Central and South American rainforests, it was massive, deadly, and it sat twenty feet from the Russian among the floor litter of leaves and moss.

A tapping on the microphone, amplified through speakers. *'Welcome Yuri Andreyevich . . .'*

On the monitors, relayed by narrow- and wide-angle thermal-imaging cameras, they watched Vakulchuk's encumbered head come up, six-inch metal eye protuberances searching for the source.

'Get . . . me . . . out . . . get, me, out . . . out.' His voice came thin and high over the control room communications link, trauma disrupting the syntax.

'Womanising is a dangerous game, Yuri Andreyevich.'

Vakulchuk appreciated that danger. One moment he had been loosening his shirt, drinking champagne with an elfin beauty who wore sexuality like a silken slip, groping clumsily at her breasts and inner thigh, the next he was awaking to a sedative-raddled headache, a dungeon, and the grotesque surrealism of a nightmare, night-time confrontation.

'Help me. Please help me.'

'Help yourself, Captain.'

'How? Please ... please show me mercy. I will do anything.'

'*An encouraging start.*'

'You are committing a State crime. You will answer to the Director of the FSB.'

'*Check where you are. Do you wish to continue making threats?*'

The switch in tactics had been fleeting, inconsistent; it changed back. 'No ... no, forgive me ... I ... I only wanted ... Who are you?'

'*Tsisari.*'

The effect on Vakulchuk was immediate. For several minutes, terror-fragmented whimpers rose and fell like a whisper. Diakanov released the microphone trigger and looked at Purton. 'And your intelligence people think I have no authority.'

Mistaking power for authority: the definition of all tyrants, Purton thought. 'Our concerns are broader, Mr Diakanov.'

'Your concerns are to do with your stockmarkets, your precious economic growth.' Resentful anger flared. 'This is why they have sent you; this is why they are scared. Let us be truthful. Even Vakulchuk is capable of the truth.'

He returned to the microphone. Purton observed, but remained silent. Diakanov's own acquaintanceship with truth was a passing one – crime did not favour an alliance. His wealth was lodged in safer climes, converted into US Treasury Bills, his interest in Russia merely one of self-interest. Misfortune at home outweighed any personal fortune transferred offshore. Without a domestic business base, he would lose face, ground and leverage overseas, lose out in negotiations. Survival was an x-factor.

The Bushmaster's head was raised, frontal body angled away from the main coils, motionless. It was interested by the intruder, aware of its rising temperature. Vakulchuk was transfixed, his sense of threat growing as the snake's diminished.

'*The Bushmaster is territorial. You have invaded its*

territory.' The statement was bald, indifferent. '*It is possible that the noise emitting from your night-vision aid will provoke an attack. Yet, switch it off and you will not detect the viper's approach. A dilemma. There is a tourniquet and pocket-knife to your right. You might prevent some of the poison spreading.*'

'What do you want? Get me out. Please.' Tremulous, wretched.

'*There are other snakes I intend to release into your room. They will be attracted by the different temperatures. Look at the hatches to your right and left.*' The head was following instructions jerkily, a movie-scene played out on the monitors. '*Start praying when you see a six-foot, black-and-white snake come through. It's a Gaboon viper. Highly venomous. It has two-inch fangs – the largest of all.*'

'Oh God . . .'

'*Then there are the taipans. My favourites. They too are six feet in length, have a bad attitude, and are among this planet's most lethal types. They will attack repeatedly. One will bite you up to ten times – it guarantees a lot of poison.*'

He was fond of his snakes, had relied on them before in depleting the senior ranks of Russia's once-powerful Solntsevo criminal combine and in enforcing the Senate code. Even the arrogance of the 'oligarchs', the country's ruling business elite, vanished with such methods.

Whether Vakulchuk absorbed the information was moot. He was half-mumbling, experiencing every permutation of fear, unable to flee, hide or move. If he betrayed Leonid Gresko, his death was assured, would be as imaginative as the one Diakanov had planned. He knew the way his Director operated, the methods employed by Colonel Petr Ivanov. But the immediacy of the present terror, the unpredictability of a viper and its calculating stare, took precedence; natural cowards were inclined towards short-term profit or loss.

Diakanov spoke again, aggression simmering. Lazin stood alongside at a second microphone, taller, contained, against the mafiya boss's shorter frame and shorter fuse. 'We have antivenin here. We can save you if you wish to be saved. You must talk to us. Or you can try to seize the animals behind their heads.' The joke was for emphasis, not for humour. He looked forward to seeing the pitiful specimen wrestling with a twisting, toxin-filled mass of pure fury and slaying instinct. 'Do you know what a snake's venom is capable of doing to the human body?' Short nods, closer to a spasm, from the figure on screen.

Vakulchuk might have had a notion, heard the mythology. He was hazy on detail. Snake venom was enzyme-based, became active once its own inhibitor proteins were diluted in the victim's body, and was designed to paralyse or disrupt every key function in the chosen organism. There were blood poisons – haemotoxins – to destroy corpuscles and essential tissue; nerve poisons – neurotoxins – to dismantle the central nervous system, breathing capability and heart function; myotoxins to eat muscle; coagulants and anticoagulants either to cause clots and thrombosis or to ensure massive, uncontrolled bleeding. Death was gradual, agonising and multifaceted, a combination of cerebral haemorrhage, respiratory failure, internal bleeding and coronary. Quite a floorshow.

Diakanov completed his description. 'You will be vegetable broth contained in a skin by the time they finish.' It seemed the Captain was already undergoing the transformation. 'The militia will be unable to explain their discovery.'

'As they were unable to explain the ripped and half-eaten corpses found throughout the Motherland over the past two or three years.' Lazin intoned softly, let the words permeate down to his FSB assistant.

It broke the near-trance. *'Is that, you, Georgi? Is that you? I tried to warn you. I didn't want you captured . . .'*

'The cannibalism, Yuri. That was Gresko's idea?'

'Yes, yes . . . absolutely.' Eagerness, born of panic and the contact made with a familiar voice.

'Do better, Yuri. From the start.'

Falteringly, then with an intensified conviction that relief might be close, he told of the systematic removal and murder of officials, reformers, those who would not comply with Gresko's wishes, those who blocked his route to enrichment and influence. The tapes ran. It confirmed what Ilya Kokhlov had uncovered, what he died for.

'We have progress. That is good, Yuri.' Panting could be heard from the crumpled, disorientated human. Lazin leant forward.

He had conducted many interviews and interrogations, never in such circumstances. Patience and repetition brought dividends, were his preferred method. He distrusted the bovine brutality favoured by a certain breed of officer at the Lubyanka, or the chilling application of cruelty meted by Ivanov. In their ways, they too were effective, but Lazin had seen the faces of men broken by torture, made deranged through intensive courses of truth drug therapy: truth suffered, Russia endured, and the legitimacy of the Communist government withered. He never again wished to be silent, complicit, a witness, to feel unworthy and unclean. There were dreams in which the Russian nationals revealed as CIA assets by Langley's resident inadequate, traitor, and former head of Soviet division's counter-intelligence group Aldrich Hazen Ames, entered his consciousness. He could not have saved them from the likes of Colonel Ivanov, but they still haunted him. Their treason carried more than the death penalty, for death was the concluding, releasing stage of a process which had dragged them screaming through untold levels of degradation and pain. It was why he was uncomfortable questioning Vakulchuk in this manner.

'Yuri. You can hear me?' Faint nods. 'We need more answers. I saw you with Ivanov in the emergency nuclear tunnels leading to Ramenki district below Moscow. What are they being used for?'

'A . . . a fall-back. If there's a threat to Director Gresko before he seizes power, he can flood the Kremlin with reinforcements regardless of the military opposition or situation on the ground.'

'So, there are contingencies?' He would ask about Gresko's nuclear suitcase warheads – the ultimate fall-back position – later. Purton had passed on the information from Western intelligence, assured him it was being taken care of. If they did not have a fix on the weapons, their confidence was misplaced. He scratched his chin. There were other layers to examine first. 'Yuri, you set me up.'

'No, no . . . I swear, Colonel . . . Georgi.'

'Now is not an opportune moment to lie. You were working for Petr Ivanov.'

'No . . . yes . . . but . . .'

'No, yes, but,' Lazin repeated. 'I am inclined to forgive, Yuri. I know of the intention to use me as proof of contact between Diakanov and the President's Chief of Staff, to have me die in an assassination attempt on the President, and to cause the downfall of his closest ally.'

Vakulchuk's attention switched. 'Georgi . . . The snake, it's moving! The snake . . . Let me go . . .' The voice was shrill, distorted.

'Concentrate on what I am saying, Yuri. I am alive, you also can live. What will Gresko do with the President's Chief of Staff now that I am not available to implicate him by proxy?'

'Kill him . . . kill him.' The words tailed into sustained, ventilated weeping. The Bushmaster was unwrapping itself.

She sat reading, legs folded in the padded cocoon of the armchair, a mug of dark coffee in one hand. The face, even when neutral with application, focused on the uniformity of print, radiated rare energy, mobility of expression. There was warmth, laughter, compelling seductiveness, a hint both of fragility and strength in the petite athleticism of her body; shapeliness beneath the shapeless drape of a man's rough shirt and baggy work pants. She gazed up as Purton came through, eyes intimating melancholy until a smile banished it to the subconscious.

'Am I interrupting?' he asked.

Zenya shook her head. 'I'm glad to be distracted. How is our poor man with his snakes?'

'He has less colour than they do.' Purton pulled up a chair. 'In England we call it obtaining evidence by duress.'

'In Russia, we call it justice.' Her English was accentless rather than mid-Atlantic, gentler than the business-speak learned in language schools.

'It doesn't make it easier to watch. I hope it's not your country's future.'

'It is certainly our past.' Tired resignation. She put down the book, tried the coffee. Seeking out Diakanov, accepting his protection, was not through choice: she had followed Max's orders, carried his messages. Only with *tsisari*'s patronage and support could she stand a chance of finding and releasing her American lover. For that, it was worth sacrificing principle, anything. 'Too much law or too little – they are each dictatorships. Be careful of Diakanov. Great Whites can turn on anyone.'

'We don't choose our friends well.'

'As fugitives, our choice is limited.'

He saw the sadness again. She emanated so many feelings, signals, fascinated him. Max had not spoken of her. That was neither clue nor surprise. The elements he held dear, important, which harnessed his emotions, he kept the closest. She was a hidden depth. It was a habit inherited from his father.

'What are you reading?'

'*Tess of the d'Urbervilles*. Thomas Hardy.' Max was a fan.

'Wessex, Dorset. It's where I live.'

'I know. Max told me often.' She recognised the amused glint, blushed shyly. 'It was in my saddlebag on our last day. The outcast girl who lets her heart rule her, who ends being hunted. It's pure coincidence.'

He held up his hands in mock defence. 'I did not make the connection.' A short silence. 'He'll be all right, Zenya.' The line was a plea, and the plea was as much for his own sake as for her.

'I trust you.' She took a hand and squeezed it.

'And you love him.'

'I don't know anyone who doesn't.' His captors must be high up there, Purton thought. 'You are not similar looking.'

'Generally, Max is happy with that.'

Teeth were exposed, even, white. 'You are a handsome man, too, Major Purton.'

'Ben,' Purton chided, pleased at the flirtation of youth, envious of Max. 'And you are a flatterer.'

'What was he like as a little boy? Men never speak of their childhood.'

'Stubborn, self-reliant, courageous, a smile which won everyone over. He's always been a one-man charm offensive.' It would be lost on the company he was currently keeping.

They spoke for two hours before Lazin appeared. He hung back, listened – the reticence of a policeman – before he was waved over by Purton.

The Englishman fetched another chair. 'Vakulchuk's talking?'

'Singing. Once he heard that he was to be transferred to the elapid house, winched down to a nest containing a fifteen-foot female King Cobra, he lost most of his reserve.'

'I'd lose more than that.'

Lazin tilted his head. 'Final encouragement came when he fought off a red diamond-back rattlesnake. That was when he admitted Federal Security Service involvement in the rough stones robbery on the BAM railway. Part of the Director's money-making activities. As I thought.'

'How did *tsisari* react?'

'Introduced Vakulchuk to a Russell's viper from Sri Lanka. The medic is giving him serum now. I do not endorse Diakanov's means, but I admire his results.'

Zenya interrupted. 'It's barbaric. He should be restrained.'

'I've seen the files.' The FSB officer sat. 'This is restrained.'

'Then I pray for Russia.'

A grim smile. 'By all means. Place flowers in the gun

barrels too. It might work. Unhappily, we are facing Leonid Gresko and his facilitator Colonel Petr Ivanov. Personally, I am grateful for Boris Diakanov.'

'I meant to ask – Ivanov?' Purton had seen the SIS dossier and photographs in London. 'A Chekist executioner with that name murdered my grandfather after a White Russian battle in 1922. Related?'

'A high probability. They were a select group. Petr Ivanov's paternal grandfather helped slaughter the Imperial royal family at Ekaterinburg. He inherited the same appetite.'

'Let's set out to give him indigestion. What else have we learned from the quivering mass in there?' He jerked a thumb towards the door.

'Enough. He has confirmed that your son and most of the Russian Cabinet are held at Vladimir maximum security prison. He has revealed that Gresko knows of the presence of Western agents – suggesting a leak on your side – and he has also indicated a planned attempt on the life of the President's Chief of Staff.'

'Assassination? How?' Purton could not let Max dominate his thoughts, cramp his judgement.

'Air crash. Investigators are used to Russian machines falling from the sky.'

GTK Rossiya, the presidential and government carrier, lacked the finances to maintain its aircraft and helicopter fleet. Most of its Ilyushin Il-62s and Tupolev Tu-154Ms were grounded through lack of engine parts; Rybinsk Motors claimed its D-30 turbofans were operating well past their lifetime limits; the Mil Mi-8 helicopters had largely been cannibalised or mothballed. Few would question an accident.

Zenya was sitting upright. 'If it succeeds, it will remove the last obstacle to Gresko's influence in the Kremlin.'

'If it succeeds, it will be the perfect precursor to a future air disaster involving the President himself,' Purton added.

'You understand Gresko well.' Lazin looked at them both. 'It is our duty to undermine his programme. If we can save the Chief of Staff, break out the imprisoned ministers and your son, it will put Gresko on the defensive.'

'Worrying.' Purton was thinking of *Perimetr*. *Leave the nukes to us*, the CIA man had said.

'We signed up.'

The FSB officer did not speak of Gresko's standing instructions, repeated by Vakulchuk, for the termination and disposal of Max Purton. Neither did he mention a strange, underlying sense that he had somehow met the retired British Special Forces commander before. He could not place him, identify the reason, but his presence plucked at the outline of a memory, suggested a past interlinked, hinted recognition of mannerisms, traits, of a partnership revisited. Diakanov walked through, wiping his hands and face on a towel. The spell broke.

'Fucking cats.'

Five seconds earlier, a family's adored pet had died beneath the wheels of Nigel Ferris' rapidly moving car. The Minister felt no remorse, checked steering alignment and the rearview, and allowed the needle to twitch higher on the speedometer. There were times for sympathy and embrace: when news teams were present and cameras pointing, whèn a catch in the throat meant a rise in the vote. Frankly, on a deserted road, he could do without a child's accusatory crying and tear-stained face. Fuck the cat, fuck the cat, fuck the cat.

Tension eased slightly, the feline's sacrifice almost cathartic. He was amused at the irony of the press labelling him animal- and people-friendly. Labels were so inadequate, the press so malleable. For months, in spite of being a lapsed Anglican, he had been attending the occasional Catholic church service, taken himself on retreat, talked to priests. It gave him depth, a fresh ethical dimension, showed an ecumenical openness and spirituality which went down well with the chattering classes and New Millennia. Another label, religion to counterbalance the superficiality of politics. Lapse was a turn-on, an aphrodisiac. And he was a sinner, there was no doubt about it. Today, his journey was to eradicate evidence of that sin, a trip to his holiday cottage in Herefordshire in order to blank out computer files and pornography contained in an extensive and well-catalogued disk library. Wipe the slate, wipe the cookies and temporary Internet files.

Jackie hated the place, preferred the coast. Just as well. She would be at home – children offloaded – running or working-out with her personal fitness Amazon, lycra-toning a muscled, teenage-hard body. To her, it fused image-sculpting with an outlet, a stress-filter for a married relationship of exhausting shallowness. To him, it provided an androgynous torso on which to write ambiguous sexual preference. The couple were compatible in many ways, ambitious, professional, modern.

The car dipped into a road section overhung with interlocking trees; 'wishing trees' his parents had called them. He made the wish: that his troubles would ease, his pursuers back off. But they clung as relentlessly as his own devils, compelling him to manipulate policy on Russia, to lie and to influence on behalf of the Moscow controller. Promulgating the deceit was simple. Throughout the 1990s, advanced industrialised nations had poured over $120 billion into Russia's Third World economy, losing much of it to the pre-2000 crash which shattered confidence and ended the Wild East's investment fantasy. Their loans were frittered away, salted away, illegally re-exported to private bank accounts, lost to avarice, corruption and incompetence. Few volunteered for renewed exposure, *déjà vu*; masochism and high finance remained mutually exclusive. Debts were written down, Russia written off. The powers closing on the Kremlin knew this well. With encouragement from opinion formers such as Ferris, the West would stand back, let a different order sweep in.

But powers closed on him also. Intelligence briefings by the chief of Britain's SIS and Guy Parsons, its head of Russia department, had alerted him to the espionage community's suspicions of an orchestrated plot by Leonid Gresko. He listened, cautioned restraint, advised that civil servants and the Foreign Secretary should do nothing to precipitate the situation, and passed the news to his handlers. Daily, his fears grew, reinforced by imagined sightings of Security Service vehicles and an irrational belief that the transport provided from the Government Car Service pool had been tampered with, wired for sound. If the Establishment were aware of conspiracy, of the Yemen, of hypervelocity scramjet aircraft, of CIA moonlighters aiding the Russian hard men, it might further be aware of his own role, spying on him, searching for compromising material. Senator O'Day, a vocal critic of aid to Russia, was dead, suicide the verdict. Fine, plausible, if your senses were not supertuned to the slightest permutation, if panic were not gnawing, your involvement not important. He depressed his accelerator foot, searching for a second cat.

Things would improve, he assured himself. The meeting at Chevening, the Foreign Secretary's official country residence, had gone smoothly, his views accepted, lauded. State your position firmly and repeatedly, and the assumption was made that logic or principle was its motivation. He was an acknowledged Russian specialist, was reflecting current American thinking on the crisis in Moscow. It made absolute sense; he was unassailable. Calm did not follow. He was owned, operated by the political elements of a foreign country, would remain theirs, a tied, imprisoned man for as long as he remained in government. Come the regeneration of Russia, the oppressive, threatening, expansionist nation of old, his allegiance would be expected, his apologias encouraged. Non-compliance, failure, and he might feature prominently in a spectrum of publications with a distinctly under-age supporting cast. People could be absurdly judgemental, politicians redeemingly flexible.

Ruts gave the ride a comforting familiarity. Almost there. He gripped the wheel, body hunched, pulse climbing on exhilaration and urgency. The track wound through a tenant farm, rusting agricultural machinery, plastic sheeting and corrugated iron abandoned along its length, the overspill of industrialised farming dumped among barns and trailers. A useful front to his hideaway, and one that MI5 and the positive vetters had never penetrated. So much relied on trust; he was skilled in its abuse. The caravan was still there, burnt-out, near-hidden in undergrowth, its role changed to unofficial beehive, marking a left fork through the unkempt coppice. The car downshifted automatically into first and took the steeper gradient, chassis scraping on bramble and uneven clumps of rough grass. He had stayed away – was warned off – since the encounter in his constituency surgery with the blackmailer. She mentioned this place, was aware of its purpose, forbade him to visit, to tamper with its contents. That was her hold. Defiance felt good, snatched the initiative. *Empowerment* was how Jackie might describe it in pop-psychology terms. Yes, he was empowered. A furtive thrill prickled over him, invoked by memories. The tree house was visible to the right, adventure assault-course to the left. Youngsters loved it here; he loved it here. A pity to have to eradicate the twenty thousand stills, but peace of mind had no price. It had slipped the day a designer-finished female punctured his life and his certainty.

Weeds garlanded the exteriors, shrubs erupting in profusion across the pathways after months of rainfall and non-attendance. But the blended greys of the stone were the same, the feel unchanged. A few months' absence – it could have been years. He climbed from the car and stood, protected, alone in the clearing, taking in the cottage and nature pushing inwards. A creeper had grown up and swallowed the garden swing, the garden itself submerged in green thicket. It felt right, here, even when he was committing wrongs. He wondered if the hot-tub was functioning.

'God damn . . .'

The lock refused the key. He tried again, varying subtlety and force, selecting another on the ring, failing, returning to the original. This was ridiculous. His unease rose, expressed with impractical kicks to the door, a heave of the shoulder against its heavy wood. There was no give. He worked the tip of the key, cursing, oxygenating anger and fear with shallow breaths through his nostrils. The cottage was challenging rather than welcoming him. It was cold in the shadows. He dropped to a knee to examine the lock, to apply greater precision in his efforts. The lock was different.

'Mr Ferris. You will regret breaking your word.'

She stood over him. *Fuck the cat.*

'You are nervous,' Gresko said. Observation without sympathy, a contained fury which clung as glaze to a stone. It made Vakulchuk's trembling more pronounced.

'I am concentrating on my duties, Colonel-General.'

The FSB Director gave no response, savoured the awkwardness. So, Vakulchuk was concentrating on his duties? He resembled a man shitting his pants. The undersized frame was stooped, pigeon-chest lost in its jacket, arms too long for their sleeves, Gandhi-wrists overshooting the cuffs. A pathetic specimen, but with a loyalty built on the sure foundations of self-advancement, financial gain and fear of its master. The feeble collection of bones could always be disassembled in emergency.

Emergency it was. The discharge of a nuclear weapon at his Urals command centre had, in an instant of indescribable destructive release, reduced to ash the hillside, his ability to coordinate events centrally. *Yantar* photo-imaging showed a crater, high ground turned to low ground, a landscape changed, a schedule changed. Much of the radiation was contained: it was little consolation, environmental issues of marginal concern. He could blame it on saboteurs, the Chinese, on other hostile neighbours, use it to sustain a prevailing sense of doom. But he had no need – fate, finality, consumed the minds of his countrymen. Destiny was fickle, undermined so much, was weakening him. Base destroyed, methods switched. Secrecy was a prerequisite for takeover, and it was being compromised. Communications were now rerouted through Defence Ministry and Intersputnik ground stations and transponders on their secure *Molniya*, *Strela* and *Potok* government satellites. Secure? Nothing was secure. As head of counter-espionage, he would know. It was the highest guiding principle, the only principle, proven. There were enemies secreted in government bodies, in the military and its GRU intelligence department – agents of the President's Chief of Staff everywhere, anywhere, listening. He was exposed, forced from offensive to defensive, left with incinerated wildlife and a radioactive pile. An unforeseen nuclear event. One act. His knuckles tightened. It was only Act One.

And *Perimetr*. To activate the system, to trigger the automatic upwards release of hundreds of nuclear-armed ballistic missiles, there had to be a correlation: the simultaneous detonation of enemy warheads landing on Russian soil, launch evidence that they were American in origin, and a severing of communications links to the military and political leadership. Then would computers take over, then would there be Apocalypse. Gresko could simulate it all, initiate the process. His operatives at the Lourdes base in Cuba would generate false launch signatures for Russian *Oko* and *Prognoz* infrared early-warning satellites indicating missile release from the Continental United States; they would back this with falsified electronic and signals intelligence returns demonstrating American orders and intentions to strike. As his men closed down the data and voice highways to Russia's high command, the 'failsafe' protective mechanisms preventing unexpected computer-controlled, man-out-of-the-loop firings would be bypassed – primary authorisation codes sent to missile complexes – and the suitcase nukes set off by a telephone call to their caretakers. Bribed to cooperate, owing allegiance to the FSB and its chief, the individuals believed that the cases contained nothing more than diamonds. They would not discover the truth. As they unlocked the containers to retrieve the precious stones, punched in the numbered sequences sent to them by Gresko, their atomised humanity was to become the epicentre of vast explosions. Detection made, calculations undertaken, algorithms aligned, a single *Perimetr* command signal transmitted from space – lift-off, bird away. Simple. Not any more. It would take longer to organise, orchestrate, to pull together the complex fragments. A last resort, admission of failure, that was what going for nuclear holocaust meant. He preferred success.

He was absorbed in his own thoughts, unsettled at the pace dictated by the actions of an unseen enemy, an unknown quantity. Only the President's Chief of Staff would stand up to him, could muster the contacts capable of launching such an operation. How petty. Yet it showed a level of cunning, of knowledge, proved his own wisdom in accelerating counter-measures. The man would soon be dead. Seize the moment and the presidency, save the planet: there was a neatness to the concept.

He noticed Vakulchuk. 'Are the preparations ready?'

'Yes, Colonel-General.' The Captain nodded, visible anxiety rising rather than dissipating. 'I will be part of the FSB unit escorting the President's Chief of Staff and his officials to Vnukovo 2. Presidential security service teams will also be on hand.'

'Watch them carefully and report. I want live commentary on the whole sixteen-mile journey to the airport: any deviation, any indication they suspect.' More nods. 'When do you leave?'

'An hour, Director.'

'I see you are wired.' The electronic sweep, anti-eaves-dropping device set into his desk indicated the presence of microphones.

Vakulchuk was more than wired. 'I did not intend to break regulations, Colonel-General . . . I . . .'

'You intended to save time, showed initiative. We are short of both.'

'Thank you, Director Colonel-General.' A nerve oscillated.

'The President has lent his jet. He has attached great

importance to this trust-building trip to China by his personal representatives. After the border clashes and air battles, it is understandable.' The fingers, sausage-thick, rested on the desktop. 'At the Federal Security Service, we also attach importance. And a bomb.' Transient levity, without humour.

Vakulchuk was hesitant. 'The technicians verify its readiness, Colonel-General.'

'Then we can expect catastrophic fuel tank explosions somewhere above the Yablonovy mountains.'

As the aircraft climbed out over twenty thousand feet towards cruise height, the barometric trigger would go live. From there, the Ilyushin's inertial-navigation and GLONASS global navigation satellite system receivers were to mark out the precise way-stations to destruction. There would be no arrival at Harbin, China, no return flight, and charges linked to the fly-by-wire system would guarantee a rapid, non-recoverable descent. Flight recorders were removed. Evidence removed.

'Ensure that the targets climb aboard the aircraft.'

'Of course, Colonel-General.'

'You are certain that the Air Force Chief of Staff still intends to travel?'

'The car is arranged.'

'A pity. I like Yanov. But the President deems it wise that he speaks to his Chinese counterpart. He can be replaced.'

The senior figures within the military establishment were Gresko loyalists, grateful for his support in financing and protecting their clandestine research projects. They were aware also that half of Russia's manpower-under-arms belonged to internal security agencies answerable to the Interior Ministry and FSB. Those forces were better equipped than their own; their own could not protect them against a fatal fire at the family dacha or turbine and gearbox failure on a helicopter flight.

Vakulchuk swayed slightly, his leg throbbing where it had received the viper's bite. The swelling remained, a memory flash inducing the pain, jump-starting the nerves. Clipped inside his collar was a wire mike, imprinting the conversation onto the turning spools of a miniaturised cassette. Perhaps it detected his heartbeat, picked up the blood-pulsing fear through his body. Surely, his Director could do the same. The faintness generated more unsteadiness. He was caught between the twin fangs of Leonid Gresko and Boris Diakanov, both poisoned, pressure unrelenting. Failure to comply with *tsisari*'s wishes meant selected moments from his confession arriving in an unmarked parcel at FSB headquarters. Gresko would not show understanding: disseminating information was betrayal, punishable, liable to lead to the appearance of a second package, heavily marked. He wanted to admit, come clean. A small head wove urgently, unpredictably, in a green mist before his eyes, tongue flicking, and lunged. The image receded. He would do as Diakanov asked.

The Director heard the intake of breath. Vakulchuk would never let him down. There were advantages to frightening people.

'Extend my regards. Wish them a pleasant flight,' he said.

It was a low-profile affair made furtive by night, without lights or sirens, black limousines heading westwards for the secret government airbase of Vnukovo 2. Few wished to draw attention to their links with the Kremlin or to lifestyles unaffected by economic disaster. Shiftless rage impregnated the population, could be directed at a passing cavalcade as easily as at a filth-smeared vagrant. Influence, a posse of soldiers, meant nothing when power was draining to the gutters. They were close to those gutters now. Paratroopers in escort trucks watched the curfew-cleared side streets, security men sat close to their principals and spoke into lapels. Tension, within and without.

From the FSB command car, a handset clamped tight to his ear, Vakulchuk reported to headquarters, liaised with the flightline destination. Ahead, traffic lights – they were ignored – speed maintained, bunching avoided, motorcyclists moving up to protect the flanks. His vehicle cruised three behind the leader, equidistant between armoured automobiles. He stared about. The route was left neither to chance nor assailants. There was cause for his panic, more profound than the generalised concerns of his companions: Diakanov must be out there, Lazin with him, biding their moment. Rescue operations, an attempt to save the President's Chief of Staff from his appointed date with a high-altitude inferno, could still get ugly. He concentrated on the conversation and nudged lower in his seat.

Relaxation did not come with arrival. The cars slowed for the first time, waved individually through the checkpoints, moving among staggered guard positions and zig-zagging between off-set barriers out onto the tarmac. Ahead, the two-tone bulk of the Ilyushin Il-96-300 presidential jet reflected in the apron lights, national flag prominent on its tail, the legend 'RUSSIA' picked out in red cyrillics against the sides. An impressive sight, and meant to be. It was one of the few airframes in the fleet still flightworthy, and in the world of diplomatic face and symbolism, would carry to the Chinese not only the President's chosen mouthpiece, but a clear indication of the importance he attached to the mission.

While service trailers scurried and nuzzled beneath the hull, the paratroop trucks deployed in a wide circle to the perimeters and faced outwards. Closer in, *Rus* commandos in black patrolled on foot. A state television crew was setting up as Vakulchuk walked, pensive, to the mobile steps. On a signal, it would film the purposeful and grave expressions of the presidential representatives debussing to the aircraft. There would be a ten-minute delay: worth it for the coverage on that evening's news. Vakulchuk gripped the handrail, eyes swivelling, mind accelerating towards every possible scenario, and ascended. Above him, raised up on hydraulic platforms, boiler-suited figures checked the refuelling probe and added the obligatory Chinese and Russian pennants beside the cockpit windows. Diakanov and Lazin could not get him now, not here. They would wait for him back at his apartment, demand the tape. Little could be done for the Kremlin Chief of Staff.

A group of Presidential Security Service operatives followed him up the forward stairs: byzantine politics, lack of trust, competing agencies with overlapping duties, ensured a surfeit of bodyguards. The Defence Ministry, Interior Ministry, FSB and Federal Protection Service were all represented here, a show of strength as much to each other and their patrons as to any external challenger. Walk-through cursory and complete, they exited, again speaking into hidden radio harnesses. Service vehicles edged away, limousines rolled forward, the go-ahead was given.

Blinking in the glare, remembering not to shield his eyes from the cameras, the President's Chief of Staff emerged and strode for the front of the plane. His premature greyness and grim features were no act: keeping Russia and its Constitution alive was serving to reverse his personal health. Makeup and make-believe were for easier times; reality was crueller. The head of the Air Force accompanied him, a retinue of senior aides and Foreign Ministry advisers falling in to climb aboard. A brief wave, departure from shot. Vakulchuk stood apart, alone in self-pity, willing destruction on his enemies. He saw the Air Force commander's token gesture to camera, witnessed him enter. This was history. The footage would next be of wreckage and of search teams.

'Captain?'

Vakulchuk's head snapped towards the voice. A young Air Force aide smiled apologetically.

'What is it?' His response was sharp, aggressive. He was contemptuous of those outside the closed sacristy of the FSB, despised anyone with a physique improved on his own. That was foremost.

'You are required on board to discuss security arrangements for the return trip.'

'It will be taken care of.'

'That is an order, Captain.'

The man was confident. To Vakulchuk, it translated as

impudent. He would be gracious, concede to the offer. Outright confrontation could wait, as would the flight. It was their funeral. Short, bureacratic delays were inevitable with large-scale cremations.

Pre-flight cabin lighting was subdued, bathing the furnishings in a soft glow of exclusivity, the subtle tones and expensive fixtures reaching throughout the wide-bodied interior. Design was everywhere, luxury in the lack of uniformity. Vakulchuk appeared in the doorway and was beckoned across to a group sitting and standing in a conference recess. The President's Chief of Staff was among them.

'Captain. Thank you for the FSB's excellent work in ensuring our safe passage to the airfield.' The politician charmed for a career.

'I am pleased to have done my duty.'

'Have you contingencies for our return?'

Small plastic bags and a military band to play funeral music. Vakulchuk assumed his air of subservient cooperation. 'Director Gresko has put us at your complete disposal, gentlemen.' Director Gresko had given orders for their complete disposal, gentlemen.

'You have something for us. A tape.' Vakulchuk could not speak. A hand was held out. 'Your recorded conversation with Leonid Gresko. Please.'

He fumbled in his jacket, ejected the cartridge and delivered it up. Unease was tumbling into craven fear. There were games he knew nothing of, in which there was no certainty but that he was the victim.

'Captain Vakulchuk.' The Chief of Staff pocketed the cassette. 'This evidence will be secure with us. Do you think I am over-confident in assessing our chances of survival?'

The beginnings of a voice. 'N-no.'

'Or do you think we will escape before the aircraft disintegrates?'

'I . . . I should be leaving.'

'And miss the opportunity to travel in such first-class

comfort? Captain, the Ilyushin can carry up to three hundred people. There are only thirty of us on board. Join us, make up numbers. Enjoy.'

'Director Gresko . . .'

'Will not miss you.' There was the short whine and damp thud of a door closing mechanically. 'If you do not accept my invitation, then at least listen to a colleague.'

Lazin stepped from behind the partition. 'I'm afraid we cannot leave you behind, Yuri. You might be tempted to renege on our agreement.'

'How did you . . .' The sentence lost its energy.

'Through the cargo hold. The Kremlin has a powerful intelligence apparatus. You should know that.'

'I've told you everything, I've told you!' Vakulchuk was shouting, self-control abandoned to frenzy.

They waited. 'May I show you to your seat? Refreshments are complimentary.'

'There's a bomb. Let me go. I've warned you, I've given you . . . Please, the bomb.'

'In-flight entertainment. Nothing like it.'

'But I've cooperated. We had a deal. You have all my information.'

'This might jolt your memory further. Give a big wave from the window.'

Positions were taken, passengers strapped in. Alone, disarmed, and manacled, Vakulchuk sat slumped in abject defeat and disbelief. Lazin raised a thumb in encouragement. The turbofans powered up, brakes released. Timing.

It was all to do with timing. The executioner pulled the pin, wrenched open the food-delivery hatch, and rammed home the grenade. '*Kushai*,' he whispered. Eat well. He let the flap drop, lock automatically, and stood to one side, mouth open, ears covered. Detonation. Five cells down – many more to go. Sometimes there was scuffling, shrieks, the formless sound of human desperation. Or there would be silence, the inmate too dazed, weak, confused, to react with anything other than mute horror or acceptance. Then the explosion, shrapnel and over-pressure bulging the door outwards, smoke and after-blast leaking through buckled metal. Dragging the ordnance box in its canvas sack, he would move on.

He peered through the spy-hole, wiping his watering eyes free of the acrid particle matter billowing down the corridor in ever higher density. The man had his back to him, was gripping the window bars, screaming to the world. Anticipation was all. The *Vympel* killer watched awhile, an abattoir worker standing back from his trade, pausing before a pig-slitting. He did not care for excessive squealing. Such noise was irksome, but understandable: it must be daunting to listen, cower, as one's friends and colleagues were tenderised with high-explosive. Variety was needed. He would think of something unusual for the American on the upper floor; he even carried the boy's spectacles and contact lenses to aid ritual and preparation. Creativity and destruction together, the young Bostonian blinking, scared, before truth registered, a full appreciation of detail and irony, an appalled dawning before the end.

Inside his cell, the man was taking hysteria to an unexplored plane. It was infectious. Others in the block responded, shouted back, calling for information, clemency, bawling out prayers or curses. The night-silence of prison life replaced by a night cacophony of prison death. Little point in wasting a grenade, blowing another light bulb. Not so long ago he had terminated a Russian national's son in England; this evening he would do the same with an English national's son in Russia. True symmetry. He drew one of two pistols – a suppressed, six-round PSS self-loader – unlocked the door and entered. A former government minister was howling.

The steel cover flew away, propelled at velocity with the sharp accompanying crack of a frame charge to ricochet off the dank concrete walls. Operatives emerged, fanning out to cover the approaches, or standing by to haul others and equipment after them. Purton clambered through and removed his respirator, the stench of Vladimir's ancient sewer system following him. Underground, it had been hard to differentiate the freshwater flows of the Lybed from the excreta-green ooze of the prison disposal tunnels. Perhaps there was none. It had taken six hours to reach this point: quarter of a day of motion within motion, wading through lakes of phosphorescent scum and waist-high effluent, avoiding tunnel collapses and teeming colonies of rats. Here were rodent concentrations of pure organised aggression and anti-human sentiment, bred on human waste. The knives, gauntlets, NBC suits and waders were no afterthought. Anything fed on that diet was bound to display unsociable tendencies; they were true prisoners of Vladimir. The group had lost one man, carried off down a curving sluice channel to an uncharted destination, his slide ushered by scampering feet, the scurrying flick of a thousand naked tails, and the welling sound of excitable chatter informing and massing life forms below. Pay-back. The screeching lasted for some minutes.

Purton stepped out of his protective clothing. He would gladly have traded up to a pipe and slippers. Behind, a boot kicked a trailing rat back into the shaft.

'On me, men, gather round.' He unfolded the line scheme of the prison interior and waited while two team members spread and held it to the wall. 'Okay, you've got your turd-surfing medals. Now, it's the hard stuff.' His interpreter communicated the broader meaning.

Nineteen faces focused on him, concentrating, Diakanov's young, hardened elite, well remunerated, superbly trained and heavily armed. They had all served in GRU *Spetsnaz* – Special Forces controlled by Military Intelligence – and maintained their units' inherited and intense hostility towards the successors of the KGB. This night, they would get even.

The briefing was short, the combatants aware of their individual roles and collective responsibility. Purton summarised. There were nods and no questions. Watches were synchronised.

'Make it slick, and make me proud. We're exactly where we thought we'd be in the bath house. At this hour, night staff should be light. I want them taken down. No fuss, no delay. Get the prisoners to the rendezvous: that's what matters. Simple enough. Let's move out. Good luck.'

A Slav with the delicate bone-structure of a bullock was gesticulating, muttering loudly.

Purton turned for translation. 'What's he saying?'

'He wants you to follow, claims he's found something.'

They were led through the warren of linked trunk-heating and shower rooms to a solitary unit approached on rubber matting, equipped with a single spray nozzle fixed above crude gutter outlets. Set in the wall were restraining hoops and rusting crocodile clips attached to heavily insulated wires. Electrocute the prisoner, wash down the body. Another reason for prisoners to hate taking showers. Years of secret police activity had refined most torture techniques.

'If you had any doubts . . .' He left it there, left it wondering if Max were alive, had been strapped into position, had rent this silent corner with his pain. They would have to move fast.

The FSB trucks sat in the lay-by, lights off, men in uniform or leather jackets stretching their legs and smoking. In this outfit, tobacco and drink were inexpensive, heavily subsidised, paid for with absolute loyalty. These were not the only perks: holidays, cash, girls, and the opportunity to inflict grievous harm on rivals added to the attraction. Yet their way of life was under threat, impunity was not assured, and on those grounds they would fight.

A low whistle. The men stubbed cigarettes and jumped back on board. In the second vehicle, Boris Diakanov loaded a magazine into his Makarov and winked at Zenya. His face was too well known to lead the entry to the prison – stealth, disguise were the operational bedrock – but he would accompany the mission. If a sixty-year-old Englishman could take his finest team through the sewers to save a son and

Russia's politicians, he would be there to extract them. It was pride, principle and the need to be in at the kill. Engines started, wheels turning to manoeuvre into the column, *Tsisari*, his regional *Avtoritet* – 'authority' – commanders, captains, and troops heading for battle, circling a darkened Vladimir.

'I would rather be flying with Pratt & Whitney engines.'

The Chief of Staff returned his gaze from the darkness beyond the aircraft window. He was echoing the sentiment of many passengers who did not fully trust the Perm PS-90A turbofans. Reliability was hardly a byword for advanced Russian engineering. Politically, a set of Western powerplants on the Presidential jet would have been contentious.

Lazin studied the man. 'I would rather be flying without incendiary devices beneath my feet.'

'It puts the danger in perspective,' the politician admitted. 'How is our schedule?'

'An hour until air-to-air refuelling. Standard contingency procedure.'

'Even though there's no cash to pay for it. Gresko wants us filled up. Makes for a better fireball.'

'We should be able to oblige.' Lazin shifted the chart on his knee. 'The Air Force people with us are begging the cockpit to let them watch the tanker hook-up.'

'At least their thoughts are on other things. An advantage we do not share. I trust discipline will not crack when they're given the briefing.'

Lazin doubted it. They were on the flying bomb together; panic would not help, nor fury at being kept uninformed. Self-preservation and training should channel energies elsewhere. He regretted the deceit, but few would have volunteered – sustained the charade – if told beforehand of what they faced. And Gresko had to believe, had to be fooled. The Chief of Staff poured himself another coffee, emptying the pot. His hand trembled, then steadied – nerves, caffeine, or both. A brave man, attempting to be braver.

'So, Colonel.' He looked up, eyes direct, human. So unlike Leonid Gresko. Lazin had made the right choice in switching allegiance. 'What is going through your mind?'

'That we have come a long way since our meeting in the children's playground.'

Deep Throat sipped from his cup. 'I am sorry it has led here.'

'Better than to the prison in Vladimir.'

'Let us hope that Diakanov and his friends succeed. Otherwise, the deaths of my old colleagues could be more realistic than our own.'

'He will try to exact a high price for that success.'

'Criminals always do. We can be vigilant.'

Lazin nodded. Around, voices were muffled, dulled by spaciousness, by the fabrics and padding, the chill hiss of air-conditioning absorbing conversational tones and content. The individual he once knew only as a shadow sat opposite, whose word he took on trust in those sub-frozen nights of a Moscow winter, whose orders he obeyed in digging below Leonid Gresko's defences, in visiting the tunnels. The Deep Throat who operated an espionage body to challenge the FSB, who clung to office tenaciously, who should not be underestimated; the schemer to whom he had reported, passed every scrap of information. The Chief of Staff – identified to him by Colonel Petr Ivanov during the encounter in his neighbour's apartment – with whom he regained contact through a series of dead-letter drops and coded signals to warn and to plan. It was strange to be in the open, out in the light, thrown together. They needed each other.

The politician toyed with the cup. 'Have the *Zvezda* seats and escape canisters been readied?' The issue sat heavy on both their minds.

'The circuits and firing cartridges were replaced and ground-tested.'

'I am more troubled by the air test. Of course, my wife claims I would have made a decent fighter pilot.' A rueful smile. 'From here, I'm less convinced. Considerate of

Director Gresko to sabotage them as final insurance.'

'He has most contingencies covered. Except for our survival.'

'I suspect he would chase us into hell to make sure.' The coffee was drained, a search begun for something stronger.

Lazin picked up a Western magazine – glossy, trite, less compelling since the death of Soviet censorship and taboos, less attractive. It sold lifestyles which Muscovites had once craved, trends they emulated, fashions to which they adhered slavishly. Pornographic commercialism, a new bondage: conceptually as ridiculous as it made them look. This was meant to be freedom. An article on tantric orgasm fell open. He was a passenger on an airliner about to set fire to the clouds, and he was reading a piece which promised to change his life forever. It proclaimed 'a spiritual dimension you've never known'. Events might carry him there faster.

He let the magazine fall, concentrated on a closer future. There was no margin for mistake. Ifs crowded in: if they ejected successfully, prior to the main explosion, the debris might fool military radar that the aircraft was breaking up; if they exfiltrated the area rapidly, they would have a start on Gresko's search teams; if they judged it correctly, they had a chance. If not . . . The Chief of Staff leant across, offered a shot of vodka. Lazin shook his head.

The flask was thrust forward again. 'It's an order, Colonel. If we die, we die with the spirit of Russia in us.' He could drink to that.

Gresko was sunk physically and mentally in thought, body deflated into an armchair, legs propped on a footstool. He was closing in on the President, yet felt encircled, pressure on all sides, the insecurity of plans uncompleted, of an enemy outmanoeuvring. Were they closing on him? Nuclear weapons – *his* nuclear weapons – had gone missing from the caves near Nizhneudinsk, one of them almost certainly used in the destruction of the Urals control centre. His foes could bite. It would not save them. He also could deploy weapons of mass destruction. *A last resort, admission of failure.* Certainty was fraying, doubts corroding the monolithic ego, diverting his energies, distracting him from the ultimate goal. That goal was close, clear, more real than sanity. How were they doing it, undermining him? Was it foreign assistance, the agents Nigel Ferris alluded to? They would be hunted, as Georgi Lazin and Boris Diakanov were being hunted.

His own reassurances failed to reassure, weakened by the hour. Vakulchuk, it was reported, had entered the aircraft to join the President's Chief of Staff. Vakulchuk, willingly committing suicide? Senseless. Unless the intended victim already knew of the bomb, had kidnapped the FSB Captain or arranged his defection. There were solutions.

He selected a telephone, stabbed abruptly at the numbers, and waited.

'You are aware who this is.' A pause while he listened to the act of obeisance. 'Is a *Molniya* ready to fly?' He made no movement during the explanation. 'I want it up on a training mission. Ground radars will be switched off along its corridor . . . It will make an unobserved interception.' He gave the flight positions and details of a presidential Ilyushin jet flying towards Harbin, China. 'You have the necessary details. Report to me by secure datalink. Do not let me down.'

Self-preservation, the struggle to live: when allied with human ingenuity, could conjure such interesting permutations. It made the struggle worthwhile, any death worthwhile. His mood improved. He was expecting news on the disposal of politicals at Vladimir prison.

In a hardened bunker near Irkutsk, a startling-white airframe was being prepared.

It was tonight, he knew, for they marked their progress towards him. Reverberations came up through the hospital block, the dull palpitation of grenades and ringing aftermath echoing through stairwells and corridors, reaching his adrenal-soaked senses. There was nothing covert in these murders. A man's screaming had been cut short, but the shouts of others took his place. Questions, no answers, and a terror which moved before the plodding work of the executioners like a bow-wave. He wanted it to end, would not hide when the fragmentation egg bounced through the slit. Better to lose the head than the legs, to have five seconds in peace than five hours in pieces. Who were the butchers – Strachan, the chill FSB officer who accompanied him, or unknowns? It hardly mattered. Fear had gone: its source was uncertainty, and he was certain, accepting. His body geared for flight, but his mind was settled. Without lenses, he was sightless; sightless he was detached, set apart from others, from reality, pending in a darker place. Death would end the wait.

The tapping on the pipe. Max crouched. 'Vitali. I'm here. Be careful.'

'Why?' His unseen friend had survived the beatings, the trips to punishment cells and interrogation sessions, remained in illicit communication. 'The KGB never left. They still torment us before the final act.'

'You're bigger than them, Vitali.'

'No.' One word; it was a vehicle for despairing finality.

'Pray, Vitali. You can do that. Pray.'

'My countrymen have prayed for centuries to the Icon of Our Lady of Vladimir to save them. Instead, she shuts us in her jail. Now, she dynamites us.'

The explosions were closer. A hint of burning carried through the narrow window. 'Help me out here, I'm dying next door to a cynic.'

'And I to a superstitious holy man.'

They laughed, but it was laughter suffused with pathos that could ease its way to tears. There was no correct manner to meet the circumstances. Max preferred the selfishness of solitude, of not having to share. Contact meant sadness, a reminder of life, of having to care. He had travelled on, eschewed responsibility.

'Our Father, who art in Heaven . . .' His words came with ferocity, proving a point, overriding the wider prison soundstage. The Lord's Prayer, an instinctive gesture, reflex of a condemned Episcopalian who wished to find and give comfort, who had to say something. He was already on his knees; it was the only prayer which came.

'Amen . . .' Vitali finished.

'Amen. And God be with us.'

There was a pause. 'Max. I want to ask you a question.'

'So long as it's not too deep. I haven't got all night.' He might barely have ten minutes.

'Why did you come to Russia?'

'You think I haven't asked myself that?'

'Why, Max? To spy? To penetrate Hunter Strachan's network?'

'What . . .' He began, before cognizance broke through. Oh, sweet Jesus. He fell back, scraping skin, his feet pushing wildly against the floor. They wanted a deathbed confession, had used him, used this man.

'Please, Max. Understand. I have to ask.' Wheedling, the voice distorted by wall and aperture. 'You have nothing to lose, Max. You are dead. We are both dead. Help yourself.' The warmth of shared experience had vanished, the bond, the trust replaced by betrayal. Max stared blindly in the direction of the words. He wanted them stopped, covered his ears.

'Stop talking, stop talking . . .' he shouted. Reality intruded, execution advanced. He was no longer settled.

Filtered headlights swept up the approach ramp, engine-tunes altering, the trucks slowing beside the guard house. An FSB soldier stepped out, routine suspended, adjusting his cap above a look of surprised irritation. He could tell the visit was official, yet the night-officer had failed to warn him. Such things happened, he supposed: a secret organisation forever behaved irregularly, wrong-footed the unwary. He would prefer to be on leave, however, confronting nakedness and sexuality than a bureaucrat with shoulder-boards, service medals and an ego. These arrivals seemed unusual, their escort too numerous. Colonel Petr Ivanov was not due to inspect until the morning. It was feasible he was early, wished to join in. His reputation within the service suggested the possibility.

A general of the Federal Security Service climbed from the cab, acknowledged the salute. He carried the brute forcefulness of a man who got his way, who hurt those obstructing it. The soldier recognised the kind: career bully, an interrogator from the Federal Security Service's central administration or Counter-Intelligence Directorate, the UKR – *Upravlenie kontr-razvedki*. A hard-hitter in every sense. For him, Vladimir prison was simply a workbench.

Pass and identification documents were proffered, the general baleful, the soldier attempting to balance procedure, diplomacy and appreciable limitations on the officer's temper-control mechanism. He should call the Captain, but that would earn fatigues for a month, and further delay this threatening *apparatchik*. A search was unavoidable. He scanned the papers. Not UKR, but UKB – *Upravlenie konstitutsionnoi bezopasnosti* – Constitutional Security Directorate. He would hardly have credited the sort with an interest in highbrow affairs of state. Thugs attained all manner of positions. He nodded; the general embarked on an overbearing lecture concerning security and correct conduct. Flustered, the guard apologised, offered to telephone the Lubyanka for ratification. It met with surly agreement, an invocation of Director Gresko, and a demand that the call be supervised. Illegal, for sure, to have anyone in the guard house, but choice was as elusive as self-confidence when faced with assertive seniority. They went inside. The reaction of his colleagues to this authority-stamp would be memorable.

Memorable, it was. The general reappeared as the armoured electric gates slid open. He gave a double thumbs-up. The soldier had been right to display caution: the officer – a capo in Boris Diakanov's mafiya organisation – was role-playing. He pumped an arm, rejoined the front vehicle and led the group through.

The guards never woke, so had not officially surrendered. Alive they could fight, struggle, raise the alarm, and the operation made no allowance for distraction, rear-echelon duties. Purton's team were front-line combatives, went in with knives. As one approached a steel bed, his foot knocked empty bottles, sent them scattering. But the contents had worked their soporific alchemy, the noise of slumber unbroken even as the glass broke. A hand found the mouth, covered it, the blade swipe-cutting the throat, before its point traversed the ribs and pressed through to the heart. Small air-bubbles formed and burst from the nostrils, the body quivered and then subsided. A hand patted the forehead and withdrew.

A warder, keys rattling on a chain, patrolled the corridor. His colleagues would be sleeping soundly, untroubled by the dull thud of execution and overkill on certain floors of the political and hospital compounds. They would not question ethics or orders – orders were to keep their heads down, beneath a pillow if necessary. Excitement was for the prisoners. The visitor, Leonid Gresko's appointed specialist, had arrived that afternoon. A nice man, freelance, large in physique and character – relaxed yet businesslike – enjoyed crude jokes and a drink, liked his profession. Apparently, he once served as instructor and section commander with the *Vympel* sabotage and infiltration unit, had transferred from Intelligence to Internal Security. That impressed the prison commandant, it was evident in his face: connections with Special Forces had that effect on minor-league types. They went over the charts together, marked off the names against a list carried by Gresko's emissary. It was followed by walk-round. All present, correct, ready in their stalls. Yes, a nice man.

The warder inspected a lock. It was new, replaced for the waves of prisoners expected to enter and exit the jail in rising numbers. This evening's death-row would be refurbished just as soon as the executioner's paint-stripping programme was complete. He straightened, strolled on, the way lit by fluorescent overhead strips. Night did not enter the wings; twenty-four hours of artificial and disorientating daylight were maintained throughout cells and corridors. It wore down prisoners, pacified them. He whistled a snatch of Ukrainian folk song, turned the corner. A colleague sat at the far end, head slumped chin-to-chest, one leg bent, the other straight. An uncomfortable pose for a sleeping man. Lazy oaf, constantly reprimanded. Impossible to get the staff. He drew himself up, indignant, superior, would wake him, report the matter in the duty-book.

'He's too tired to argue.' The words were whispered. A wire noose tightened on his neck. 'Do you want to be tired like him?' The smallest shaking of his head. 'Fine.' Hands detached the keys, pressure stayed on his larynx. 'We will now converse.' He heard the blood pump in his ears, another distant detonation. The missionary from Moscow was entertaining himself.

He had come for Max. There was smoke, drifting stronger now, chasing, drawn in beneath the cracks. The level-plan was memorised, but the institution was large, the floors and cells uniform. This was it, the patched linoleum and flaking walls that absorbed and announced the smell of a latrine, that marked the paces to the Capitalist Decontamination Unit. A few yards, historical footsteps set with a thousand experiences and permutations of human misery. He walked towards the door.

Max waited. He heard the footfall, the key, the initial protest of the hinges, and found himself in a defensive bubble of amniotic silence. Threats were out there, but he was safe inside, cushioned by the invisible screen. He was curious, interested in the enemy's moves, by his responses. It had the dreamlike quality of an abstract, a detached ambience only the condemned could generate. Comforting. Death was comforting. The door swung, he saw it as a moving haze. A shadow separated from it, an organic blur.

'Max, my Max. You're alive.' Sound was an incoming

tide, rushed in on him. He needed more. 'I knew I'd find you. I have been searching the entire prison block.'

Gennady? The voice that made Topol sound a falsetto eunuch, the infectious pleasure, boomed in the confined room. Max placed his hands on the ground, supported himself as he peered towards the indistinct dimensions of his bodyguard.

'I don't understand, Gennady. Strachan said you were dead.'

A rumbling guffaw. 'For a ghost, I have a big appetite.'

'This is unbelievable.' He was sitting, motionless with excitement and relief.

'Fate is like that, Max. Of course, my wife is not so pleased.'

'How did you get here? What's going on, Gennady?'

'You'll find out.'

The questions were tumbling. 'Have you got backup?'

'There is no need.'

'But, the FSB . . . Hunter . . .'

'You cannot believe what Strachan says. He is not *dzhentlemen*. I will take care of you.' He was removing an object from inside his jacket. 'I have your spectacles.'

'*Put it down!*' A shouted command, intrusive. It came from somebody else. Gennady must have turned, his colour cloud shifting. Two shots.

The muzzle reports blast-froze the ears, the senses, burst the protective membrane. A wetness released itself over Max, occipital and parietal brain lobes evacuating from a skull before the body crumpled. Another mass stood behind, filled the vision field: a living, upright replacement for the fallen dead. It seemed to pause, consider its aim. These people were cruelty perfectionists.

'He killed my son,' Diakanov said. 'He killed my son.'

Purton searched deadened eyes and traumatised faces. It was the image of twentieth-century persecution that stared back: the bland depersonalisation of shaven heads, the shuffling feet of inmates in shock, the physical and mental confusion of liberation. Automatons, mannequins, victims. He looked for a spark, expression, the smallest sign of recognition. They filed past. Horror was so mundane.

'Dad. You've broken into the asylum. That *is* fucking nuts.'

Max stood before him in changed form, thin, prison clothes and spectacles ill-fitting on a frame that had lost bulk. But he wore a smile, its impact multiplied by dirt and blood on grey skin against a greyer background.

There was not much to be said. They embraced, Purton caressing his son's head, the prison stubble, holding him close.

'Is that your blood?'

'Wrong Group. I'm AO.' He was trembling slightly.

'We're getting you out, Max. We're getting you out.'

Diakanov appeared. 'There's a report of trucks and helicopter escorts heading this way. The funeral party.'

'Let's move out, before it becomes the Alamo.' Eyes levelled, two fathers acknowledging the moment, their roles. 'Thanks.'

'You would have done the same for my Oleg.'

Exodus.

A stretcher-party went by, body crudely draped in a prison blanket for which a use had been found. Distribution to inmates was almost unknown. Petr Ivanov ignored it, face dispassionate, immobile, while he viewed the night's wreckage.

An aide coughed, made a superfluous mark on a clipboard. 'What do you suggest, Colonel?'

A minute passed. 'I suggest that we return rapidly to Moscow.' The reply came as empty as the echoing wing. Soft matter, a piece of it, clung stubbornly to the sole of his shoe.

'Take your positions. Activate independent life support systems. Twenty minutes.'

The pilot's voice was calm, exuded normality, excluded the possibility of cataclysm. It was an illusion. Lazin, attired in a flight suit, paced towards the rear of the aircraft, past others, similarly dressed, descending service ladders to the cargo deck, and the communications crew making final adjustments to the electronics suite. There was no bigger adjustment than this. Procedure lent an air of rehearsal, but there was nothing artificial in the countdown. The Colonel sensed hurry in the unhurried manner, urgency constrained by military discipline. An Air Force officer folded a travel blanket.

Vakulchuk was bound – and wound tight. He shrank from Lazin, fear and hate, outrage at the injustice, reducing his capacity to observe, to notice the clothing.

The face contorted. 'Director Gresko will not forget this.'

'I think that is guaranteed.'

'I am being held against my will. It is a State Crime.'

'I'm sure you'll come after me.' A small joke, but Lazin's grave demeanour rarely altered. 'Did you hear the announcement?'

'Independent life support systems – what does it mean?'

'If you find yourself falling, flap your arms.' Vakulchuk's chances of staying airborne were limited.

The FSB Captain was dwarfed in the chair, dwarfed by his vulnerability. He tugged at the handcuffs. 'You've got to let me go. I know people, I have funds. Anything, Georgi. I will plead on your behalf.'

'Plead on your own.' Lazin extracted a key from a zipped side-pocket and unlocked a pair of the cuffs. Vakulchuk stretched his freed arm, flexed to restore circulation, and scowled.

'What is going on? What is happening? You have defused the bomb?'

'No.' The key was replaced.

Incredulity, represented strongly in the face. 'We must get out, we must escape!'

'We are. I am here to say farewell, Yuri.'

'But . . .' Progressive realisation, the voice changing pitch. 'I only have one hand free.'

Lazin slapped the side of the chair. 'That is all you require to work an ejection seat, Captain. It's a variant of the Zvezda K-36 model. Better than anything the Americans have. Has to be – our aircraft crash more.'

'You cannot do this.' The struggle was committed, Vakulchuk jerking wildly at the restraint. He stopped abruptly and vomited.

'You do not enjoy air-travel, do you Yuri?'

Liquid breaths. 'I will see you in hell, Colonel.'

'You'll be bored waiting. Enjoy getting there.'

He walked away. Vakulchuk was making noises behind, entreating him to return, but the words were unclear; there was a schedule to keep. The cabin was almost empty as he followed two members of the diplomatic staff down to the pressurised holds containing the one-man exit pods.

'Have all the Search-and-Rescue beacons been destroyed?' he asked a crewman helping a female translator into a capsule.

'Yes, Colonel.' An oversight would allow Gresko's forces to track them, to uncover the deception. He moved on.

'Where's the Chief of Staff?'

A nod towards a container in its launch tube. The hatch remained open. Lazin approached and peered over, a face hidden by an oxygen mask, surmounted by a dome helmet, turning upwards to greet him.

'Comfortable?'

A gloved hand pulled the mask away. 'If feeling like a ballistic missile on a *Typhoon* sub defines comfort.'

'Remember to hold on to the grab handles when you drop.'

'Remember?' came the response. 'I'm not letting go.'

There were twenty-four pods carried, considered sufficient to protect the Russian President and his key government advisers in case of emergency. The rest were expected to fight for their places on the eight ejection seats available in the main cabin. Musical chairs, and the losers could pray and die, content that their senior colleagues had got away.

Lazin swung the lid up. 'It's the moment. We'll meet on the ground. You have the map, compass, terrain-matching photographs and global-positioning?'

'All here.'

'Then you are ready. Lock yourself in. Good luck.' He brought down the cover.

A storm front was coming. Reducing speed to Mach 5, the hypersonic scramjet aircraft codenamed *Molniya* – Lightning – streaked towards its destination. It flew at eighty thousand feet, descending from ninety thousand, in the thin atmosphere of the planet's periphery, the frontier with space, observed by no one, overhauling everything. Below, the curvature of the earth floated like dark marble, its subtle textures and black-crimson shades transmitted to the cockpit by electro-optic link. The pilots, lying almost prone, garbed in cos-monaut suits, watched on monitors. Their craft was capable of flying at ten times the speed of sound, could cross the Pacific in thirty minutes, strike unchallenged, anywhere. This was global warfare, complete supremacy.

The gloved hand of the co-pilot tapped cueing commands into the arm-rest multifunction keyboard. Sensors slewed – laser radar, infrared, visible and invisible spectrum seekers, Elint support – electronically scanned and received, arrays staring. Passive and active detectors embedded in the airframe reached ahead, cameras primed, aligned, readied by computers for the known position of the Presidential aircraft almost fifty thousand feet beneath their heading. Waypoints flashed up on a matrix-crystal screen, the *Avionika* flight-controls making automatic adjustments. On-time, on-target. Precision was vital, error had no margin. It would take five hundred miles for the aircraft to turn after a missed pass. The world remained motionless against the man-made object screeching high, catching the chase.

Contact made. The pilots concentrated. Air encounters were inevitably tricky.

It was easier to eject from a disintegrating aircraft. Without fire, smoke, the natural propellant of terror, Lazin felt drawn to stay. The cabin was quiet, the faint trace of classical music audible through his flight helmet, comforting. So, this was the *Titanic* as calamity struck. He imagined Vakulchuk crying, trapped at the rear. Steerage class always suffered.

'*Two minutes. Ready for full depressurisation and egress . . .*' Cockpit delivery remained disinterested, remote.

He checked the harness and oxygen flow, felt shielded in the insulated, self-contained environment of the ejection seat. It would be quick: just a few seconds between pulling the firing handle and being hurtled into space on a rocket-chair. Better that than the cramped darkness of an escape pod, falling through the night in a device as crashworthy as a tin can. There was nothing noble in giving up his place to another. It was pure self-interest. Five of the remaining seats were occupied at their stations adjacent to the emergency exits, men and women counting down, dummy-running like himself through evacuation drills. He had never seen flight attendants provide advice on this particular method before.

'*Sixty seconds. Remove safety-pins.*'

He extracted the ring from the base of the central stick and tossed it on the ground.

'*Fifty seconds, pressure equalisation underway . . . Forty seconds.*'

His ears were blocking, a sharp ache jabbing into an area behind his molars, He swallowed, opened his mouth wide behind the mask. The tubes cleared, dental pain stayed. A tingling coldness enveloped his feet – there would soon be distance between them and the floor. He blinked, forcing moisture into his eyes. The visor and aerodynamic surfaces of the chair should protect them on the outward journey.

'*Thirty seconds.*'

So much for the enjoinder to switch 'doors to manual'. These were to be blown away. He rested his head back, listened to the breathing, the sound of a death-row inmate waiting to be plugged into the prison generator. Five thousand volts would be simpler than this. The aircraft was oscillating in a slight bucking motion. He tightened his stomach, fastened it down to pre-empt further leaps.

'*Twenty seconds. Stand by, stand by. Prepare to evacuate . . . Ten, nine, eight . . .*'

The inflation pads were squeezing him, compensating for the loss of cabin pressure. He tensed, adjusted his fingers on the trigger loop.

'*Eject, eject, eject.*'

Reality was elsewhere, replaced by a vivid dreamscape. Pieces blew out along the length of the Ilyushin, solid-fuel rockets bathing interiors and sides in bursts of roaring flame as occupants were flung along guide-rails and scattered to the atmosphere. They slowed, miniature, inconsequential figures propelled, dispersed in every direction, pitot sensors extended, drogue parachutes stabilising their flight, tipping them from seat pans and into free-fall before main canopies opened. The aircraft was less controlled. The autopilot overloaded, flight controls shorting – too many demands – cockpit, cabin and cargo holds eviscerated by departure, underbelly ripped apart by spawning capsules jettisoned pneumatically.

Lazin was taking in oxygen, building the impulse to leave. Heat, intense light, washed towards and over him, then reversed in a blizzard of decompression. The floor was heaving: he was riding it, riding out. Ahead, the shape of a seat jumped upwards, disappearing at an angle through a gap left by the detached door section. Another passenger transported away, air carried out behind, plucking at Lazin's flight suit, vacuum-sucking his body forward.

Go. He brought his elbows in, pulled up on the handle, was launched – time, brain and torso compressed by acceleration and gravity – thoughts frozen with speed, systems paralysed through the blinding flash of explosive bolts and the impact of instant thrust pitching him from normality to abnormality. A force was pushing him, flicking him to oblivion, his head a plunger on a spinal spring crushed against the uplift. Then release and exhilaration, freedom, tumbling, a mind confused but catching up. He was alive, away from the aircraft, spread-eagled for descent. Projected inside his visor were satnav cross-hairs and changing tabulations for gliding himself to the parachute-deployment position. The Presidential plane commanded a full equipment complement, this aspect designed to allow high-altitude insertion of Russian Special Forces into Chechnia. Tonight, it would aid his own clandestine return to earth.

Vakulchuk was half-unconscious, buffeted wildly in the seat, his hand alternating between hauling feebly on the firing mechanism and pressing the oxygen mask to his violently shaking face. The aircraft was breaking up around him. He wrenched again at the lever. No movement, no spark of ignition or the chain reaction that might send him swiftly beyond his present circumstance. It was a trick, he had been duped. The knowledge spurred fresh and frantic efforts, the wasted, irrational behaviour of pre-death. But the primary and secondary cartridges were removed; he was not destined to fly solo. The Il-96 banked sharply, compensated – bleeding height, speed, contents – wings rolling, turbofans howling in their attempt to claw back altitude. Nose pitched up, dipped, angle increasing to a dive. Terminal phase. In the cabin, only emergency lighting was left, studding the way to exits opened and abandoned. Oxygen masks streamed on tendrils from the ceiling, waving, dancing for Vakulchuk. He was pressed in his seat, chained, far from the doorways. Cold, so very cold. His head bent towards the frosting window, eyes narrowed. Reflected back was an imminent ghost, pale, making contact through the glass. He reached hesitantly out to touch.

The explosion appeared to split the layered cloud base, a sun-storm intensity that picked out the pin-prick drops of the white parachute silk floating below a larger canopy filled with the orange-red rage of mid-air devastation. It lasted a minute, and faded, a false day eclipsed by returning night. Lazin was awed: Gresko had not stinted on the size of the intended funeral pyre. He would be burned as FSB Captain Yuri Vakulchuk was burned. Ten thousand feet, ground oncoming. It occurred to him that he was out of one fire, might land in another.

Cruising high, many miles on, the Lightning cryoplane was preparing for descent and return to base.

'Incredible.'

'We have another word for it,' the American replied. 'Hyperwar.'

They were in an annexe of the CIA's Langley headquarters, the satellite imagery played in a repetitive loop on the monitor placed at the far end of the conference table. Guy Parsons and Hugh Dryden sat on one side, hosted by their US intelligence cousins, the meeting opening with footage taken of a Russian *Molniya* cryoplane tracked while overflying the burning presidential Ilyushin. The passenger jet was represented by a weaving, slow-moving silhouette shedding parts of its structure, the Lightning a delta-shaped blip scudding past and out of shot at a breathtaking rate.

The DDO – Deputy Director (Operations) – blanked the film by remote. 'Gentlemen. The Loch Ness monster does exist. It'll scare the shit out of our military.'

'It had the same effect on us.' Parsons maintained postural correctness, neat, alert in a summer suit. The American contingent, and Dryden, had opted for shirt-sleeves.

'Without your man Purton sending us the results of Vakulchuk's interrogation, we wouldn't have known of Gresko's attempted assassination of the Kremlin chief of staff. Allowed the National Recon Office to get their space assets in position to watch the show. The cryoplane was an unexpected bonus.'

'Unexpected, certainly. Bonus? I reserve judgement. It means, of course, that Gresko will now realise his attempt failed.'

'Sure.' The thin-framed spectacles caught the light. 'And if it's true he's aware we've sent in direct action agents to counter him, it also means he'll be mighty pissed, and you're mighty penetrated.'

Parsons eyed the man's red braces, applied a snap psychometric test. The official was as bullish as a Wall Street trader, dressed like one too. It was possible that the moment had arrived to prick the self-esteem, diminish the big-budget, big-office, big-dick syndrome.

'After your experience with the renegade Cuban Sanction teams, I'm certain you'll be able to advise.'

'Touché.' An unembarrassed smile, recognition at being caught. Business as usual. 'You've got a point, Guy. There's no question that American technology is flying that baby.' He indicated in the direction of the empty monitor. Almost a hint of pride. 'Too good to be true that they were stuck with the all-metal, neutral-stability Migs and Sukhois they sent to the Paris and Farnborough airshows in the nineties. Should have seen through it.'

'A mistake we all made,' Dryden volunteered tactfully.

'Yep, but even now we're looking in the wrong places. No activity at the LII air research centre in Zhukovsky; nothing happening at the Russian Air Force trials centre in Ahktubinsk. So, what happens? We assumed their research was over, their capabilities were zilch. Jesus, we blew it.'

Parsons concurred. CIA employees had been instrumental in transferring know-how to the opposition: a hard one to explain away to a congressional committee. That was before any admission of individuals with Agency histories abetting a hard-line overthrow in Moscow, pitching a major-league Senator from a balcony at the Watergate. The shredders would be at work on Hunter Strachan's personal file.

He turned the subject back to cryoplanes. 'Take us through the Hyperwar concept.'

'Jeff . . .' The DDO signalled to the white-collar who had attended the briefing of Ben Purton in Oxfordshire.

The case officer cleared his throat and took over. 'The United States Air Force talks of Global Engagement, of parallel operations to wipe out the enemy's entire strategic infrastructure anywhere, anytime, simultaneously. That's the problem – it is just talk.'

'And with Russia it's not?'

'Demonstrably. You saw the pictures. It's torn our projections apart, changed escalatory dynamics forever.'

The DDO removed his glasses, used them for emphasis. 'In 1943, the US Eighth Air Force prosecuted twenty-five strategic targets. That's twenty-five in an entire year. With their Hypersonic Air Vehicles – cryoplanes, scramjets, call them what you like – the Russians can prosecute hundreds in the first sixty minutes of hostility. The advantage is decisively theirs.'

'Troubling, when Gresko is Pretender to the Throne.'

'You said it.'

Dryden kept his relaxed poise. 'What's their lead on us?'

'Twenty years, we reckon. Conservative estimate.'

'I hate to inject a note of scepticism.' It was exactly what Parsons wished to inject. 'But I note the US maintains a twenty billion dollar-a-year spend on its classified black programmes; Area 51 has been expanded, enjoys a new runway and larger hangars; unidentified covert airframes fly daily over White Sands ranges, and high levels of activity continue at Tonopah Air Force Base, former home to the F-117A Nighthawk stealth fighter.'

'What are you stating, Guy?'

'That there aren't many areas of military technology where you lag, where you have allowed the Russians to break out.'

'You're well briefed.'

'I'm in intelligence.'

'Then you'll understand that the Russians moved from the lab, while we stayed in it.' The DDO leaned back defensively, hooked his thumbs behind the braces. 'Their trick was to engineer, fabricate, apply many of the techniques we developed. Don't forget, we rolled out the XB-70 Valkyrie in 1961.'

'Where is it now?'

'On static display in the Air Force museum at Wright Patterson. Russians have had several decades to overtake it.'

The Valkyrie was revolutionary, its capabilities unprecedented and unchallenged. Flying above seventy thousand feet, it could cruise at Mach 3 by riding on its own 'compression-wave lift' supersonic shockwave, had intercontinental reach, boosted acceleration with specially developed zip fuels, and would have recast air warfare. Yet only two were ever built, and the programme was cancelled in 1965, victim of MacNamara's defence reforms and a prevailing view that combat aircraft would soon be obsolete against Soviet surface-to-air missile advances. Other projects were slashed: the Bell X-15 Mach 8 scramjet venture, the hypersonic X-20 Dynasoar, the Lockheed YF-12A Mach 3.5 Interceptor, fading through lack of funds, technical difficulties with flight-control and heat-friction, and their poor manoeuvrability. Speed was out, agility in. Some elements from that era survived – including the Lockheed SR-71A Blackbird strategic-reconnaissance aircraft – but for the most part, visible signs of American hypersonic research were rare. In the 1980s, the X-30 National Aerospace Plane – NASP – development was launched, cancelled in 1995, to re-emerge as first the HySTP and then the HyTech in much diminished form. This, in turn, produced the Hyper-X subscale test-vehicle which was to fly in the early part of the twenty-first century and carry with it the future hyperwar plans of the United States.

'On reflection, we've been too damn leisurely,' the DDO grimaced. 'Even accounting for black *Aurora* research. High-speed, high-altitude – it's the future.'

'And Gresko holds the future.'

'Politically and militarily. He plundered everything we had, cherry-picked from our technology locker. Lockheed Martin's Skunk Works, Boeing's Phantom Works, NASA,

Hyper-X studies, DARPA: their work handed over on a plate.'

'Or in Hunter Strachan's trucks,' Dryden added.

'Correct.' The expression was not congratulatory. 'Software was even easier to transfer. Remember those two British computer nerds, *Datastream Cowboy* and *Kuji* in the early nineties?'

Dryden nodded. 'They penetrated your Command and Control Research Centre at the Rome laboratory, crashed computers and planted sniffer files at NASA, NATO, the Pentagon and Wright-Patterson. Caused mayhem. It's hard to forget.'

'We call them asymmetrical threats, and we're damn vulnerable. Trouble is, the bodies set up to counter them contained persons connected to Hunter Strachan and his maverick Cuban Sanction contacts.'

Parsons ran a finger along an eyebrow. 'My guess is the software slipped out of the GRU Sixth Directorate and FAPSI men at their Lourdes Elint base.'

'Easier than wiring money,' the CIA's liaison officer intervened. 'From Lourdes it would have been up and downloaded to the Mother Country for analysis and replication, fed into the favourite programmes.'

'And funded by?'

'Us, indirectly, Where do you think most of the IMF loans went, Western bank investments disappeared to?'

'I take your point.'

The DDO's knuckles whitened, fist and jaw tightening. 'The oligarchs and politicians salted it away, mafiya re-exported it, but Gresko always took his cut. Add to that the rake-offs from his border troops, smuggling operations, gemstone and precious metal scams, pearl harvesting in the Belomore Sea, protection for Diakanov that gave the FSB complete knowledge of *tsisari's* weaknesses, and you've got yourself a tidy cash sum.'

They had been duped on an heroic scale. It was an uncomfortable admission for any intelligence professional, and the ensuing silence was a reflection of that discomfort.

Finally, Parsons spoke. Bloodless, accepting. 'Quite a feat. They kept it well hidden.'

'Better than our *Senior Trends* programme test-flying stealth fighters around Groom Lake in the 1980s. We were lulled to sleep, forgot about Moscow's capacity for deception and expansion. Perfect.'

'Gives the US Defense industry and the armed forces something to beat.'

'And it gives the Agency a new Cold War. It's a benchmark. Real heart-warming. You can't improve on a scare for winning resources, paying our salaries.'

Another CIA official spoke up. 'That's why it appealed to the hawks. It was kinda neat.'

'Blurring the line between patriotism and high treason is always neat,' the DDO came back. He returned to Parsons. 'Death of O'Day was our signal to start rolling them up.'

An economic smile from Parsons. 'I like to see politicians being useful.'

'It'll put pressure on Gresko, and things are getting hot as it is. Hopefully, we can push him more. We've reports of a sub-surface nuke detonation in the Urals. Wasn't on Gresko's target map. Purton on a frolic?'

'He's no loose cannon. That's the advantage of using his age-group.'

'The advantage of letting him concentrate on saving his son. Nice to be seen doing something.' The cynicism was institutional, inbred. 'You plan to pull him out?'

Parsons tipped back his head. Thinking pose – it was only pose. 'I believe we should determine what happens with the takeover, with *Perimetr* and the suitcase bombs, don't you? Purton has been committed.'

'We're the ones who should be committed,' Dryden observed laconically. There was laughter.

America and Britain, the Special Relationship. Enduring, strong, common interests, shared goals, greater than any individual. Greater than Ben or Max Purton.

* * *

Helicopters searched for them. They would be carrying thermal-imagers, nosing into valleys and behind ridges, landing near villages to disgorge Federal Security teams to turn out occupants and turn over houses. Lazin had taken a reconnaissance group further up the valley, seen the patrols establishing checkpoints and response positions. He and his band of air-disaster survivors were being pushed towards them, herded for five days ahead of the wide-area sweeps conducted by the forces of Leonid Gresko. Tonight, solo, he would try again. It was a smoky moon.

He crouched and listened, ears attuned for the mechanical repetition of rotor-blades, the crackle of undergrowth. The drones might be flying high, the helicopters downwind: silence was no indicator of security. He tightened the draw-strings to his hood, slipped the treated mask higher up his nose. Exposed skin would increase the heat signature, lower the effectiveness of a battle-smock designed for anti-infrared operations. Ready. He planned to work his way along a fissure in the valley's side and up on to higher ground. From there he could scan for alternative exfiltration routes, a circuitous path to take them to the next waypoint. Their stepping-stones were rough shelters constructed in high pasture. The leaps between them were becoming harder.

'You attract trouble, Colonel.'

The voice came from behind. Lazin recognised it, the authority and timbre derived from years in the Siberian wilderness. They had met in a winter landscape near a mine, when his life was in jeopardy, when this wanderer had eliminated a threat without hesitation. Two meetings, separated by months and distance: irrational, yet overcome by a tone of confident rationality. It was impossible that the old man should pick up his trail, materialise, when the entire group had so far evaded detection or interception.

Lazin spoke over his shoulder. 'Trouble? For a simple trapper, you seem drawn to it.'

'In Siberia, unusual occurrences are noticed.'

'And a jetliner crash acts as a beacon?' He was having

difficulty comprehending the taiga-dweller's extraordinary omnipresence. 'I must be in danger if you appear.'

'That is true. My soldiers have been tracking your progress. Unfortunately, so has the FSB.'

'Do you have intelligence?'

'Their deployment suggests you will be surrounded by morning. There are heavily armed detachments everywhere.'

'I have seen them. And you? You think you can hide?'

An arid laugh. 'After many decades, it is a possibility.'

'Will you lead us out?'

'Better. I will provide you with details of every base Leonid Gresko is operating east of the Urals, the facilities to which American technology is flown, the airstrip where a US helicopter pilot is camped.'

'Hunter Strachan?'

'His name is familiar.'

Lazin eased himself from his haunches, turned in the direction of the dark silhouette. He had asked too many questions, but questions were all that remained. 'Why do you do this?'

Cold Cut hesitated, as if self-analysis were alien territory. 'Because of Kim Philby,' he said eventually.

Rape – every which way – was an adjunct to tension, blood an adjunct to rape. And Gresko was tense. He shut the door and lumbered to his desk; sobs followed him in racking gusts from the side-office. Bleeding had been heavy, but it was nothing that pain-killers, dollars and the darkest fears instilled by the FSB could not staunch. She would keep quiet: no authority existed to whom she could complain. He was the highest authority, interpreter and transgressor of law. That the girl lived was a favour, patronage. She might so easily have ended as a fatal accident, an unimportant statistic, a half-eaten corpse minus breasts or a face. Life was cheap, sex free. It happened.

He eased himself into the chair, but unease sat with him, a stress he could not banish. Violent coitus tended to divert rather than solve, and as solutions crumbled and diversions became ineffectual, the quotient of violence increased. The digest was bulky, a weekly compendium of reports from the FSB regional offices, a snapshot of progress towards totalitarianism. Arbitrary arrest on the rise, denunciation of friends and neighbours commonplace, the vast *seksoty* informant networks of the KGB re-established, the roots of oppression spreading. Gresko's foundations were secure.

Meaningless. He slammed the dossier shut. Each day, Russian citizens in their hundreds telephoned the FSB's double-agent hotline – Moscow 224–35–00 – to inform on those they suspected of collusion with the enemy, with foreign powers. Spite, patriotism, xenophobia: the motives were varied. Yet neither the Russian populace, nor his officers, could lead him to a foe dancing beyond his reach, mocking him. The President's Chief of Staff was alive, his death postponed; the American Max Purton and members of the former administration had broken free from Vladimir; intelligence troops were under attack; Diakanov's forces on the offensive. Everywhere, his plan, his schedule met resistance: Lazin was out there; Western agents were out there. News had come of American contacts from the Cuban Sanction, his technology and financial conduits, raided and rolled-up by the FBI. They knew. There was coordination, an undermining. The Urals command post destroyed, he was obliged to send communications on the government's *VCh* Very High Frequency and *Sistema* links operated by FAPSI. His adversaries had engineered it, would listen in, could outflank.

Gresko pounded the desk, fist hammering out frustration, the heavy repetitive fall an expression of disordered thoughts seeking order. Seeking explanation. There was none. So much information, but he was blind, deaf, losing the initiative. And if the President discovered ... *It could not be, could not*. He clutched at the desk and stood, heaving at it, toppling it with impulsive speed. The impact resonated, wood splintering, drawer and surface contents crashing, spilling across the floor, telephones and electronics flailing wire. Smoke and disconnection; destruction. He trampled the debris, crushed it beneath his feet. No one made a fool of Leonid Gresko. His opponents were sending a message. They would receive a reply.

In another room, the crying had stopped.

Marlboro Man was waiting, slouched in the open cargo-deck doorway of the Mi-8 helicopter, hat tilted, snakeskin boots resting on a stub ordnance-pylon, torso against a crate of beer. It was a vision of Air America: ironic, unconcerned, the privateer who could wheel, deal, fight and fly another day in another theatre. A way of life and a state of mind.

Max's shadow reached Strachan before the pilot-cowboy acknowledged a presence. He stared back from the makeshift stoop, eyes narrowed and calmly quizzical. 'Beaten by a blind guy. What kind of shit is that?'

'Affirmative action, I guess.'

'You've come a long way. Makes me feel like Private Ryan.'

'It's not a rescue mission.'

'How was prison? Anyone drop anchor in bum bay?' He went on. 'You look like fuck. Beer?' Max shook his head. 'Don't mind if I do.' A hand went into the crate, extracted a bottle of American import, the cap removed between teeth and spat into the helicopter interior. 'I've got to admit, I'd be less surprised to see Barney the freakin' dinosaur.'

'I'm big on surprises.' Max stood still, arms by his sides, neutral.

'Takes courage to come and confront me, seeing's your eyes don't work an' all.'

'I don't think so, seeing's you're covered by Zenya an' all. She trained to marksmanship level with the KGB.' Delivery was methodical, without emphasis, mimicry understated.

'And you'd be Agency, right?' No response. Strachan drew from the bottle, lip smacking on lip. His vision was travelling across the near and middle distance, taking in the fire-positions, searching for Zenya. 'I'd never have reckoned. S'ppose that was the point. I have to hand it to them – Langley was cleverer than me in taking you in.'

'You should have killed me.'

'Tried to delegate. Never works. You realise we'd have removed your arm without anaesthetic if we'd found a satellite micro-tracker in your elbow joint?'

'We figured it'd be fatal.'

'Is that why you're here – to zip me up?'

'It's an option.' Max subdued the trembling. Fatigue clawed at his brain, hung weights on it. He felt slow, heavy, could lie down here at Strachan's feet and sleep. 'I want to know why, Hunter.'

'Why?' A pull on the bottle, a soft laugh. 'That's good, real good.' The beer sluiced. 'Hey, what do you think of these *Shturm* rockets?' He kicked a pointed toe at the weaponry slung on the pylons. 'Fine fellas, aren't they?'

'I'm sure they do their job.'

'That they do. Used, abused, discarded. It's how we felt in South-east Asia. And we were just doing our job.'

'You're reaching back over thirty years to a jungle for justification? Don't insult me.' Anger was beginning to replace the weariness.

'The jungle's stayed with me, Max. When I was your age, I'd be sent out to find my missing friends in the elephant grass. Know how I traced them?' He paused for an answer, initiated his own. 'By waiting till they ripened. Two days, maybe three. Then I used my sense of smell.'

'What do you want me to say, Hunter?'

'Admit it's all rotten. Have you ever flared a Huey into an NVA ambush and seen your door-gunner disintegrate, watched a squad of grunts disembowelled and screaming?' Silence. 'Or watched the growing pile of your comrades' body parts stack up and wondered if your head would be there the following day?' He put the bottle aside, eyes fixed on Max, intensity growing. 'Or been so hypnotised by tracer the size of baseballs rise towards you, you don't notice the brains of your number two spray across your chest protector from a hole in the side of his flight helmet?'

'Experiences that passed me by. Like betraying my country.'

'Because you're so totally damn convinced your country hasn't betrayed you. Think hard, Max. Try. They realised you were in danger. Did they lift you?'

'Eventually.'

'E-v-e-n-t-u-a-l-l-y.' Smirking emphasis rounded off with an emphatic smirk. 'And now you're acting as some kinda executioner, playing your part in their alternative plot. Funny they let me drop the Senator before making their move. That give you the moral high ground? Them? Does it allow you to judge? We're both trigger-men, bag-men, Max.'

'I'm taking orders. You ignored yours.'

'I took them from a different interest group. That's what it is, Max, interest groups. In the Agency, in government, everywhere.'

Max could not disagree. The Cuban Sanction had seen the CIA committed to the modernisation of Russian strategic nuclear weapons and rocket forces, to their improved effectiveness and credibility. Enhance their ability to incinerate the planet, restore and ensure the continuation of mutual assured destruction, and peace would benefit. Against such logic, attempts by Strachan's mutant intelligence friends to build up Russia's conventional arsenal, to place a worthy foe in command at the Kremlin, seemed reasonable, excusable.

'Washington's a piranha pool. Presidents screw interns, put Monte Cristos in their pussies. There's bureaucratic infighting, covert policy shifts.' Max's voice was becoming louder. He could not let Strachan better him. 'It's a fact of life; I don't need 'Nam thrown in my face. You broke the law.'

'Boo-hoo. I bent the rules, did what I thought was right. It's a misjudgement because I lost, not because it's wrong.'

'There was no remit.'

'America needs an enemy it can see, Max. Not the VC,

liberals, fifth column, conchies, bearded Islamists, but the real thing, a reason to police the world, have the best weapons, the finest servicemen. Russia's the greatest, most useful threat we ever had.'

'Threats are created by people who lack legitimacy, Hunter.'

'Then I'm the original bastard.' Max looked about and ran a hand through his hair. From the hold of a cargo helicopter parked beside a hangar a thousand metres off, Zenya would have the sights of the 7.62 mm Dragunov sniping rifle scoped on the encounter. She could hear every word through her earpiece. Strachan cocked an eye, facial scar tissue stretching. 'Telling her to go for a head-shot?'

'Body.' He was telling her to stay alert.

'A looker and a shooter. I like that in a girl. Not bad for Volgograd.'

Max turned back to face him. 'You still haven't said why you did it.'

'Nothing personal.'

'Bullshit.'

'OK, straight.' Knuckles cracked, Strachan working through his finger joints. 'Mexican gangster, Lord of the Skies, rapes my daughter, forces her to OD on heroin, thinks it's funny; I don't. He dies. He's got strong links to Boris Diakanov, they're of a kind. So, I figure I'm doing the world a favour helping Gresko to bury the dude, secure Russia's boundaries. That personal enough?'

Max was disbelieving. A fraction of his feelings escaped through the peeling mask of self-restraint. 'You take the word of a professional liar, of a KGB man from the moment he left Leningrad State University, who headed the Central Control Department of the Presidential Administration, who knows every political trick there is?'

'I know a few myself.'

'Then you'll appreciate how far you've screwed up on this. There's fallout you can't even imagine. What came first, ego or stupidity?'

'Yeah, I went against standard policy. But if you want something done, you gotta do it yourself. That's what I carried from the jungle, Max. Everyone wastes everyone.'

'Chrissakes, you're an American citizen, not fucking Nietzsche.'

Strachan was unconcerned, cool. 'Out there – Vietnam – Montagnard mercenaries murdered their South Viet ARVN officers because they were bored in rest periods; Chinese hired-guns did the same with US Special Forces advisers; our troopers terminated their platoon leaders for a bet. Slaughter as therapy – seemed to work.'

'I'm tempted myself. But I obey the rules. I'm here to make an offer.'

'If I refuse?'

It would take one bullet. 'My hand goes up.'

'And your high-minded principles disappear. I was never going to grow old getting fat and feeding marshmallows to pet 'gators on Hilton Head.'

'Want to fly a whirlybird?'

'Beats driving a golf-cart.'

End-game. 'Russia doesn't need a Beria or a Leonid Gresko, Hunter. It's over. You come on side, or you join the losing team.'

Hunter studied his toecaps, wordless, life and death considered no more profoundly than the choice to take or leave a beer. The face came up abruptly, carried a half-smile: part chill, part warm.

'Guess you've just tapped in to my winning instinct.'

CHAPTER 9

The moment. Chandeliers, marble, the palace interiors of the Kremlin stretching before him, Gresko strode towards the meeting. On his return, these corridors, these treasures, the government that went with them, would be his. Federal Protection Service staff parted to allow him through, held doors, made their signs of deference. Their commands would come from the allies he had inserted into the central administration. They would obey. There was no room for the miscalculation of disloyalty, of failing to back him. He was the winner in the race for the Presidency – Russian style. Colours were brighter, actions magnified. He smiled benevolently. A guard bowed his head – he would not be the last.

The mood was as black as ever in the Security Council conference room, a morose assembly of those who could no longer pass the blame upwards. It stopped with them, for they were rulers of the land. That land was in darkness, bereft of coal, food, medicines, and the world had renounced its interest. Even aid convoys sent by their charities had slowed to irrelevance. Gresko was elated. So, his enemies scored partial successes: Vladimir prison broken open, the Kremlin's Chief of Staff outliving mid-air disaster. Mere diversions. He was at the seat of power, would remove the incumbent, on it place himself. And the weak men at the table would stand to give their ovation – five minutes to demonstrate respect, five their relief, five to illustrate acceptance, and a further five of spontaneous applause to show their will to live.

Doors were closed, the ongoing crisis trapped within four

walls. Gresko had initiated and controlled every step of it. This was the logical step, the final one. He eyed his watch face. 10.00 hours. Colonel Petr Ivanov was leading the front elements of ten thousand elite FSB troops along tunnels from the underground nuclear-proof centre in Ramenki district. They would emerge into the Moscow fortress from its cellars and secret passageways, neutralise the rump of the Kremlin guard and the officers who failed to switch allegiance. Resistors would be in a minority, token: lists of likely candidates had been drawn up, were either off-duty or destined for a bullet from colleagues bought, inducted, ready. Beyond the walls, hard-line Interior Ministry forces and ODON – veterans of Chechnia – camped in number. Gresko's Defence Ministry allies had agreed to keep the Taman Guards and Kantemirov in barracks. A large demonstration was planned that day, hundreds of thousands of pensioners, students, miners, communists, the hurting and the dispossessed, descending in protest on Red Square. They were not the responsibility of the army; the Interior Ministry would police. Milling and marching crowds, confusion, anger, the perfect human shield. With such masses facing them, army units rushing to save the President would be delayed, prevented from reaching the Kremlin, from doing battle against the VV. But there was no cause to rush, nothing to save, and the demonstration was coordinated by Leonid Gresko's Federal Security Service.

He stifled the triumphalism, remained deadpan. In his head, the celebration had started, wave upon wave of cheering and tumultuous roars. His Security Council colleagues stayed oblivious. Perhaps he should stop his ears, block the sound from leaking out. To give clues was premature, would spoil the entertainment. Briefing papers were handed out. There was a proper order to these things, a beginning, middle – an end. They could not tell, had not heard the voices, the call, which he heard. His excitement grew.

Words were being spoken, the President – ashen and overworked – conducting proceedings. A reference was made

560

to the late Chief of Staff, his contribution to stability, his attempts to negotiate Russia from the quagmire. Hypocrites and liars looked on, for they envied the man his apparent death. He was a martyr; they were barely footnotes. A wider choice of cells awaited them at Vladimir.

Commander of Border Troops, a trusted conspirator, gave an update, provided spurious figures to back his presentation. He did not mention the real facts: hidden accounts, the cross-border trade and trafficking, the black-market staples sold on to pacify the people, to profit Director Gresko. The head of the FSB again thought of the Chief of Staff. Capture was inevitable, would correspond with release of footage to State television of the politician's airborne ejection, his attempted flight from justice. The FSB was closing in, and he had panicked, faked his death; a patriotic Federal Security Service officer, one Yuri Vakulchuk, suffered the consequences. A terrible crime. The Chief of Staff's execution would be a turning point, an example. President Gresko was intolerant of treason and corruption.

'Colonel General.' The incumbent President shot cuffs, leant on his forearms, expectant gaze directed at Gresko. 'In these troubled times, is it not dangerous to be separated from your chain of command?'

An odd comment. Gresko was unblinking. The chorus in his head faltered. 'There are always contingencies, Mr President.'

'Share them.'

'With respect to Council, it would be wrong to discuss operational detail.'

'Then discuss broader strategy.' There was a challenge in the President's eyes. Why? Motive, direction, were hidden.

'Council is aware of our crisis procedures.' Gresko spoke slowly.

'You have learned from past mistakes.'

Gresko detected undercurrents, latent hostility, mockery; from around the table, a shift in mood. He had been too

561

absorbed to notice, too sure. And the sureness belonged to the President.

Careful. 'Adaptation is how institutions survive, Mr President. The FSB is no different.'

'I disagree.' They were mentally circling. 'You learn, but you do not reform. It encourages enemies.'

'None that the Lubyanka cannot handle.'

'Director Gresko, you are in the Kremlin, not the Lubyanka. Do you recall the tale of Daniel and the lion?'

'It can hardly be relevant, Mr President.' Ex-Mr President.

'It is not. Daniel emerged alive.' A fragile silence, passing calm. Recognition. Action.

'Guards!' A second time. 'Guards!' Rising, Gresko glowered at the President and his cohorts. It was here, now, and they knew, they knew. His expression softened to a beatific smile of victory. He must savour the historic act, immerse himself, be proud. The destiny of his nation was seized in this room, altered forever. Transformation complete, transfer achieved. Behind him, armed men joined to back his edict, enforce his will. 'The Council is suspended. I take full responsibility for arresting the President of the Russian Federation.' The day deserved a trophy.

'Is that a confession?' Georgi Lazin held the Gyurza low, barrel aimed at Gresko's centre.

The President folded his arms. 'It seems that an impromptu tribunal is called for. Once you are searched, Director, you may retake your seat. The charge is high treason. I will call the first witness.'

His Chief of Staff entered, placed a cassette machine on the table, pressed the 'play' function. Gresko was sweating, stared at the entrant. The words he heard were his own, had been uttered in his office, recorded by Vakulchuk.

'*Then we can expect catastrophic fuel tank explosions somewhere above the Yablonovy mountains . . . ensure that the targets climb aboard . . . wish them a pleasant flight . . .*'

The tape ended and cut out.

'Thank you for your warm concern.' The Chief of Staff's

smile was sympathetic. 'And for the warning.'

Contrived dismissiveness. 'The words are faked. It is a simple exercise, easily achieved.'

'But utterly convincing,' the President added.

'It can be explained.'

His Commander-in-Chief shook his head. 'Explained? By a man who deals in conspiracy? Your actions in this room – an optical illusion? Your orders to the heads of FSB regional directorates – spurious transmissions?'

They thought they had caught him, were infected with the virus of self-congratulation. There were the greedy glances of individuals edging to wrest his power, the worried faces of those who committed early to his cause. Each one misguided, calculating. He was far from trapped. His reinforcements were on their way.

Lazin spoke, banished such hope. 'I regret that Colonel Ivanov has been detained.'

Eyes closed and opened. 'You will regret it.' How much, they would discover to the cost of the planet. It left him no option. There was slight disappointment, but relief too that their inheritance was to be an atomic wilderness born from war. They were ants, scurrying, working without a grand plan. He had the plan. Ants were so inadequate for re-establishing the evolutionary process.

'Where are the nuclear weapons, Gresko?'

They should be concerned, would have seen the effects of a single blast on his Urals communications centre. And they were asking him, praying for deliverance. Instead, he would deliver them *Perimetr*.

'The suitcase bombs, Gresko. Tell us.'

I will show you. Ants, that was it. The voices goaded him, their tone accusatory, demanding. He had let them down, must make amends. Atonement. Immortality beckoned.

The FSB Special Operations *Vega* units came on, kneeling in the open cars of the subway train. They were heading for Moscow's Victory Park and the tunnel complex which led to the Kremlin. Ivanov travelled with the second echelon, squads which had practised the assault for months. They would move through access points secured earlier, mop up resistance and ensure Director Gresko's complete control of government. The Interior Ministry was pledged, could deal with any defence formations foolish enough to stand in the way. An unlikely occurrence: experience showed that in periods of instability, troops preferred to stay on base or on leave, their officers preferred to wait. Caution took precedence over commitment. By then, it would be over, the result accepted. Army morale was low, NCO cadres utterly depleted, conscript discipline tenuous, the influence of the FSB's military counter-intelligence department pervasive. Inaction was guaranteed. The winner offered strength, stability, a better deal for those in uniform, and the winner would be backed. Leonid Gresko for President. *Fait accompli*.

The opposition stayed low and silent. They were outside the chain of command, an eclectic group which owed nothing to Gresko and whose fighting prowess remained a matter of pride and competition. Diakanov's foot soldiers lay in position alongside men from the Ryazan Higher Airborne Troops Command School, air assault specialists loyal to their senior officer – a personal friend of the President's Chief of Staff. They were defenders of the Constitution, about to be tested.

Tsisari depressed the radio-trigger and spoke into the rubber mouthpiece. 'Drop the pickets.'

Silenced weapons fired, muzzle-flashes suppressed, velocity reduced, forward guards brought down and cleared from view at approaches to the side passages. The carriages rolled towards their position.

'Pick your targets. Take the officers first. Maximum chaos.' Underground routes favoured the few, created a shooting-gallery with depth. Diakanov pulled the respirator down across his face: the CS placed in alcoves would inevitably drift in their direction.

Displaced air blew along the tunnel. Pressure on the ears, on the psyche. The rumble came near; the mafiya chief prepared. He would show no compassion, allow no concession to mercy. Among the enemy might be men who launched the raid on his Cheboksary fortress, shot down his beloved Irina. At the very least they served the chief of the FSB, instigator of such crimes. A tear formed in his eye duct, watered behind the gas-mask. Emotion made him murderous. The uninitiated would learn the true nature of a mafiya vendetta, be pursued, harried, cut to pieces. That he promised, could deliver on. The track was vibrating.

Engine lamps rounded the corner, were extinguished by bullets in a puff of erupting splinters, the pattering of automatic fire. Ricochet and bolt-action provided the main sound, then the impact slap of open palms on wet paint as rounds found their human mark. Warning shouts, screams, the rattling and aimless return of small arms, the bursting of a phosphorus grenade bleaching white the confines in aching horror. Figures were struggling, burning, caught in the killing-axis. A body hung limp on the front casing, buffeted and torn by lead, reddening like those sprawled about it. Ripe enough to fall. More explosions – the pre-positioned shrapnel mines – a grating shudder, and the train emergency-braked against a barricade of girders. Momentum stalled. Soldiers were jumping or crawling from its sides, retreating, taking cover behind steel barriers and wall struts, their progress and hiding places picked out by showers of flash sparks. A smoke-screen was laid down, blew outwards, engulfed the tunnel, confusion and noise eddying off the walls. Through the fog, a shadow pulled himself from an open rail car. The legs did not follow.

Lighting went, illumination replaced by thundering darkness, the individual stab of flashlights underslung on Kalashnikovs, the brief and violent shimmer of gas expansion from gun barrels. They appeared and disappeared through a mist.

'They're into the side-tunnels!' came a cry.

Diakanov raised his mask. 'Hold them.' But his voice was lost here. He ducked, felt a volley of shots fly warm above his head.

Accompanied by a select band of mafiya equipped with radar torches and close-quarter weapons, Purton was roaming the labyrinth ready to prevent break-out or escape. It was important to keep the enemy contained and funnelled, away from running-creeping battles on the periphery. Hand-to-hand was bloody enough without a chase through a hundred unmapped and underground chambers. The Englishman would be busy.

Enemy were leapfrogging forwards in short scurrying movements, then faltered and vanished beneath the fusillades hosing the narrow field of fire.

'Drive them back, drive them back.' Diakanov waved his arm. 'Don't let them regroup.' A grenade went off close by, deafened him, rearranged the formation and posture of three of his lieutenants.

Another counter-attack. It was repulsed, a platoon of *Vega* troopers flushed out with flame-throwers while they attempted to access a sealed service corridor. Smells of gasoline-cooking joined the cordite. Diakanov threw aside the mask, kissed the gun breech, bobbed, squeezed the trigger, sank and shifted position for a further three rounds. These people were tough, would not give up. He was tougher. It was time to lead from the front. Room-clearance could be a rewarding occupation.

As a child Max had played murder in the dark, always won. He hoped that in this situation the instinct, the developed, alternative senses, would not desert him. Stakes were higher – real life, real death. The footsteps were soft, paused occasionally, conveyed a message of one aware of another's presence. Silence, the self-discipline of the armed stalker. Max heard the cocking of the weapon, could not fire prematurely, expose his position. The art of blind duelling, and he preferred to be elsewhere. Zenya hid behind the crates.

For both to tackle the intruder would increase the risk of blue-on-blue, disturb the concentration. He had volunteered with a quiet kiss to her hand and crept away from her location. She could be a hundred miles distant: he was alone, exposed, the lure.

A clatter of empty cartridge cases. He almost turned to challenge, but stilled the reaction. An old trick, guaranteed to catch the unwary. He was not an amateur, would not be caught. The beyond-visual state was entering his consciousness. He felt it, awareness expanding, a pricking sensation in the ears and jaw, a change of condition to the sinuses. Directional antennae were working, ones which warned at night of the proximity of a tree, a building, how to negotiate a crowd. Below ground, placed for safety by his father away from the streets, he met laboratory conditions. The body-mass was to his right, exuded threat, heat. He had to fine-tune, home in. Gently, he crouched, pistol arm extended, supported. There was no movement, but his opponent generated a hostile force-field. It pushed on Max's corneas, alerted the optic nerve. His damaged retina had over-sensitised him in a different plane.

Five shots, the crash of a heavy fall. Threat extinguished. Zenya called out; Max was shaking himself from the trance. Adult murder in the dark.

There was a single return on the monitor. Heartbeat, respiratory activity, all the indications of human presence beyond the wall. The man was feeling his way around the room, methodical, unhurried, hands travelling over vertical surfaces in the darkness. Purton watched the electronic display on the hand-held radar. Whoever it was remained calm, unfrightened, could function in a high-stress environment without the corresponding stress. It showed: normal metabolic rates, normal pulse. Therefore abnormal. A digital reading gave cardio-vascular information in numerical form. Resting pulse, heart-rate at sixty – a cool, bloodless customer, so unlike the FSB quartet they had detected and dispatched

567

five minutes previously. You could not fool this system. Meanwhile, the spectre's colleagues were dying in the remote din far back in the main thoroughfare. He must imagine he was beyond danger; his body stabilised accordingly.

Purton maintained the frequency-modulated track, swept the slender beam around the room for others and came back to the apparition. It seemed to know its way, by instinct or rehearsal, edging in the direction of a flight of steps, avoiding the narrow entry point to a cul-de-sac. With pre-programming and data input on a suspect's known medical and personal details, the equipment could provide full biometric identification. Useful for a hostage and terrorist situation. Here, it gave location, showed bones, organs, metal accessories: adequate for an intercept.

'That's far enough.'

The flashlight shone into Ivanov's face, threw the skull into relief against the black jacket and polo-neck. Purton kept distance, spoke in English.

Thin lips opened, a colourless gash against white skin. 'We were aware of Western saboteurs operating on Russian sovereign territory.'

'We were aware of saboteurs operating against the sovereign Russian government.' The face was recognisable from photographs, explained the radar signature. A floating personification of directed hatred, it seemed detached from its circumstance, from its body, at ease in this night habitat. Purton would be careful. 'Hands open and out to the side, palms facing me, fingers splayed. Nothing hasty.'

As the radar showed, too small to be a grenade. The cross glittered emerald green, hung suspended from the fingers. An operative circled the motionless Colonel, snatched it, plucked the detected pistol from its shoulder-holster, the switchblade from a pocket.

'Lost your way from the Lubyanka, Ivanov?'

'You are inconveniencing me.' Bland statement of fact.

'I forgot you were searching for Ivan the Terrible's lost

library. Mistook you for a coup-plotter.' Purton examined the cross. 'Didn't take you for a Christian either.'

'It is a family memento, a souvenir.'

From whose family? The two faced off, Ivanov blind in the glare, Purton considering the latest generation of a bloodline which killed for the state. Son of a Smersh and NKVD executioner, grandson of a Cheka, GPU and OGPU executioner, an inheritor of their values and techniques and himself a product of the secret police in its succeeding incarnations as KGB and FSB. Only the titles changed. The Englishman stared, thought of his own grandfather, brains blown out in the snow at Volochaevka on 14 February 1922 by a pistol held in the practised grip of Colonel Petr Ivanov's close ancestor. Role reversal, fate reversal. An end to the cycle.

'Kneel,' he ordered.

The black clothes, empty eyes, neutral soul – absence – reflected the past, the image of a man who had unleashed shot after well aimed shot into the Tsar and Tsarina, their children, their maids, bayoneted and clubbed without compassion, who had snuffed out Piers Purton as just another anti-Bolshevik traitor. Ivanov the descendant sank to his knees.

'You are making a mistake, foreigner.'

'I know. I've been in too many Russian tunnels.'

Delivery was monotone. 'Director Gresko is not a forgiving man.'

'Then we share something.'

The silenced Welrod pistol was steady. One round. One target.

Closing in. They had been polite – the Establishment always were – but with the savage civility reserved for a politician whom they knew was compromised. Sheer enjoyment for them; for him, sheer hell. Somewhere, there was a leak, they said, somehow Russian counter-intelligence was expecting Western involvement in a counter-coup. Did Ferris have any views on the subject? the flat-faced, deliberately flat-footed, inquisitor asked. Simply procedural, a routine matter, and they were deeply grateful for the Minister's time and assistance. He was, after all, a busy man. Disingenuous, designed to rattle – effective.

The pager hummed in his breast pocket. He had switched off the mobile telephone, but there were a thousand ways for the saccharine authoritarianism of his Party and government to reach him. They prided themselves on control. He would be a great disappointment, for he was currently well beyond control.

Then there was his Russian handler, the Prada-clad she-devil who operated way ahead, taunted him, lay in wait. He should kill her, send a signal that he was not scared. Moscow would send a replacement, the torment begin afresh. Whatever he did, wherever he turned, he was cornered. Admit the guilt? Wait to be discovered, for a trio of dark cars to draw up outside, for Jackie to be questioned, for the invitations to dry up? Try to run?

He paced the flat, a Westminster pied-à-terre with all the charm of an over-priced cupboard under-designed in dated minimalism. It looked as tired as he felt, as empty as the slogans and sound bites he crafted, as jaded as the to-be-seen-in restaurants he frequented and 'experienced'. This experience outdid them all. The place had seen intrigue, acted as bachelor- and launch-pad, cosseted and carried him from opposition to high office. It was cold, failed to comfort. He slammed the door to the kitchen unit, his search for a jar of instant coffee unsuccessful among the herbal teabags. Obliteration started with small setbacks.

Ferris slid down the doorframe, body crumpled in the opening. A politician without conviction, who faced conviction. He imagined the Prime Minister, blow-dried hair and blow-dried brain, trying to extricate himself from this one, wondered at the smoke-screens, excuses, the diversionary stories to be slipped to pliant editors. Reciprocity was the name and the game, favours traded, called, press barons and multi-media tycoons relegating news, providing support, in return for concessions and licence. A complex affair, a calamity. Treason and illegal sex: it would challenge the most experienced image-manipulator. Pity he was not around to advise. The laughter rose in volume and pitch, reached the frayed edges of hysteria. Nigel Ferris, Foreign Office Minister, was thinking of Russia.

'Phone for you, Major. Secure line Two.'

The security officer of Kapustin Yar Air Defence Weapons Test Centre groaned. He was seventy miles south of Volgograd where nothing ever happened, and the Moscow chiefs still found reason to disturb him. Sure there was pilfering, and the FSB could not stop it. There was little for the men to do but barter components, trade surplus inventory and claim it was expended. No one believed them, nobody had to. The calls were merely a formality, variations on the theme of bureaucratic butt-covering. Trouble was about as likely as a satellite launch from the local cosmodrome. Its rocket towers were long vacant: perhaps he would wake one morning to find them sold as scrap. Anything was possible.

He stretched for the handset, waited for the scramble and connect tone. Most of his commercial activities were conducted along this link. He checked the wall calendar. Rather early in the week for his colleague at Air Reserve and Personnel Training Command in Samara to be in touch. The man, a contemporary of his from military counter-intelligence and FSB Academy days, had grown rich retailing surplus Military Sports and Training Association Yak-152 aircraft and Mi-2 helicopters on to grateful recipients in the Commonwealth of Independent States and elsewhere. With the patronage of their Director, Leonid Gresko, and for the surrender of a percentage royalty, they could grow as fat and prosperous as they wished. North Korea was proving a lucrative marketplace.

He picked at a stray thread on his uniform. Contact. 'Klishin, here.' He listened. The voice was not one he recognised, but the password and codes were correct. He reached for a pencil, scribbled down numbers. '. . . Yes, yes. I have them . . .' He repeated them back. '. . . I understand.' The receiver was replaced.

For a minute he contemplated the request, reclining in his chair. An order from a personal representative of Colonel-General Gresko to remove the diamonds from their storage container and have them ready for collection in an hour could not go ignored. Particularly so, when there was promise of a bonus. He wondered what it might be, started calculating. The Federal Security Service was a generous paymaster, and nothing beat dollars to make him happy.

The case was heavy. He had not examined it since handover by the American helicopter cowboy who seemed to have connections at the Lubyanka. The aviator was the most confident individual he had ever met, pushed bricks of currency on him as readily as though they were cigarette cartons. Perfectly legitimate, for it had the blessing of the Director of the FSB himself. He heaved the suitcase by its handle from one of five wardrobe-sized safes built into the wall and dragged it on to the desk. The doors of each blast-proof mini-strongroom were five inches thick, and there was much to guard: cash, alcohol, black-market luxuries, scientific instruments and computer hardware for resale, files and security dossiers on the centre's personnel. It was right to be aware of the potential commercial competition.

He unlocked, flicked the catches and opened. The keypad and display were as the telephone-caller described. His task was to disarm the anti-tampering, enter the combination details and transfer the merchandise to a holdall. Hardly a challenge. A technician sent by Gresko had visited recently to examine the contents and their security. He appeared satisfied; the remuneration was substantial. Russia could burn, but several storeys below ground in this military complex, there was wealth and peace of mind to be found. Referring to his scrawled sheet of numbers, the officer let his forefinger travel across the keys.

The mushroom cloud was visible for many miles, its billowing white plume climbing, turning grey and black, bulging outwards as it sucked the vaporised particles of Kapustin Yar behind. Ground tremors rippled from the epicentre, shockwaves travelling concentrically to demolish buildings and roads, to turn the land to rubble in a series of answering quakes, a howling wind, sent by an inferno. Telegraph poles fired like porcupine quills; secondary and tertiary explosions swept a scene already devastated. It was witnessed by electronic sensors in extra-terrestrial orbit.

In that same hour, from the Urals to northern Siberia, there were other nuclear detonations. Kosvinsky mountain, Space Defence and Strategic Rocket Forces command post, was almost levelled as it split apart; the annihilation of its sister-centre and backup at Yamntau was equally spectacular. Combined and Corps Headquarters of the Siberian Military District at Novosibirsk disappeared; the Arctic air base at Pevek was flash-fried. The underground scramjet development centre at Irkutsk came next – airframes, engineers and infrastructure consumed – its hydrogen-fuel facility outside Bratsk joining it within minutes. Never had such scale of loss been inflicted in this way, Russia's critical operational centres and defence-industrial assets eradicated in a strike which came from nowhere.

And *Perimetr* was ready for its doomsday role, to launch retaliation. Computers analysed the incoming data, measured the destruction against priority lists and models, found a match. Launch code levels shifted. The enemy had chosen carefully, struck hard. Communications between the High Command and silo outstations were cut. Launch code levels again changed. Initial authorisation commands had been picked up on UHF link, their partial activation enough to provoke a further rise in pre-launch status. It was out of human hands, beyond human comprehension. Software conducted the war, gave its response.

* * *

Off the coast of Cuba, an armada of specialist electronic warfare ships had gathered. While the continental United States permitted an unprecedented release of signals emissions to demonstrate the stand-down position of its nuclear preparedness, the naval vessels were embarked on heavy directed jamming of the Russian intelligence base at Lourdes. The American operators knew their function: to prevent faked transmissions of TACAMO command aircraft and artificially created imagery and intelligence suggesting ballistic missile launch from being beamed to Russian satellites. It was a delicate mission. Too much jamming, and the *Perimetr* computers would identify it as a hostile act, commensurate with a pre-emptive nuclear attack. Too little, and enough contrived early-warning information would seep from Lourdes to indicate the same. A battle ensued, spread across frequencies and power-ranges, displayed on screens and scopes, countermeasures and counter-countermeasures deployed and redeployed, bandwidths and side-lobes penetrated, communications spiked and blanketed. Finally, the *Perimetr* launch order, stored and sent by commercial satellite to a ground-station near Moscow, listened to by a team of frozen-faced NSA officials in Washington and their GCHQ counterparts in Cheltenham. There was no reaction, no release of the single missile with its transmitter to tempt the nuclear birds to flight. Men and women relaxed. They had succeeded; the criteria for automatic launch of the Russian arsenal had not been met. Leonid Gresko was out-tricked.

Nigel Ferris remained where he was, pressed in an open doorway of his apartment. They would come for him.

She soared, found an updraught, spiralled higher and climbed towards nine hundred feet, a diminishing speck of sharp-set ferocity gaining height, hunting. Diakanov watched, heard her telemetry blips on the receiver hung around his neck. At her apex, she would wait on, transmitting from the tracker attached to her tail, circling on thermals, searching below.

Then the stoop, a two hundred-miles per hour vertical dive to punch the prey from the sky, perform a dead drop. Even in level flight she could overhaul the fastest pigeon or partridge, the power and agility of her gyrfalcon-peregrine-barbary cross-breeding providing air superiority, air dominance, allowing her to bind on and bring to earth. There she would break the neck. *Moskva*, byword for a capricious, wild killer. He loved her almost as much as he did *Krista*, the gyr pure-bred retired since Oleg's death. There was freedom here, and memory, and anguish.

Diakanov tipped the hip-flask to his lips, wiped his mouth and adjusted the pigskin hawking glove. Behind him were his falconers with their wooden cadges, hooded birds – Lanners, Sakers, Barbaries – sitting blind and passive, bells silent, attached by jesses and ready to be taken out and exercised. Beside them were three bodyguards in hunting clothes, muskrat caps, rifles unslung. More were with the command vehicles and Land Rovers carrying the bagged-up game for later release and short-lived suicide flights.

Moskva dropped, invisible at speed, her trajectory ripping the air, displacing it with the tell-tale sound of imminent contact. Telemetry signals accelerated as she fell, closed, shredded the wind. Diakanov shaded his eyes. The target must have jinxed, the huntress's stoop bottoming out, for now the blips were slowing. A chase was underway. He swung the aerial to fix on her direction: the tone was fading. It disappeared. *Tsisari* swore, shook the electronic device. Returns had ceased. The bird was in low ground or conducting a rat hunt. He would have to find her before she ate her fill, forgot that he was her primary source of food, her guardian. Man–falcon loyalty was at best tenuous, kept alive with a ready supply of refrigerated day-old chicks.

He picked up the lure, a twenty-foot cord with its leather meat-pouch. 'Never trust a woman whose eyes you can't look into.'

There were nods rather than smiles. To gaze into the eyes of a falcon was to issue a challenge, pose a threat. It was

575

inadvisable, the kind of respect that Diakanov too warranted.

The blips again, but on a different bearing, steady, constant. She was a tricky one, *Moskva*, would be mantling over her kill, guarding it suspiciously against all comers. Defeating her greed and natural anger was the challenge. Binoculars showed up nothing, but she was there, disguised in her blue-grey plumage and speckled brown front, her face with its hangman's hood markings staring about, intent. Diakanov started out, motioned to the others to stay. They would only stress her, encourage escape. He worked his way through the gorse, around tussocks, brushing aside the long grass and scrub, moving towards the thicket of cedars at the edge of a sloping dry meadow. The electronic pulse indicated a thousand metres. He leapt a stream, pushed forwards, removed himself from the line of sight with his men.

She would bait furiously on her return, extend wings, flap, up-end herself on his hand. The irritation was mutual, but her flight pattern and performance made up for the inconvenience. She was worth the search, special. Most of his falcons kept to five hundred feet. He slipped, cursed. Complaints should be reserved for his pair of golden eagles, the birds of prey he used to hunt young musk and roe deer, hares and bobaks. The Mongolians had started the sport, a hobby of warrior-emperors, adopted enthusiastically by a modern overlord. Serious work, major effort. By contrast, this was pleasure, he reminded himself. He thought of Oleg – the boy had relished the outings – and pleasure went, replaced by pain.

He eased himself down a stepped line of rocks. The signal was strong. She would be ten metres away. He studied the vegetation, focused into the shadows, anticipated the proud head raised from its vantage point. The erratic telemetric beat ended, but concentration was elsewhere.

An aged man stood to his left and front, frailty and firmness coexisting, had appeared through a screen of bushes. He carried a package beneath his arm, the other raised, holding a small metal capsule between finger and thumb. Diakanov noticed the missing fingernails. The ancient had the look of the camps, a hardness that could overcome years, ill-health and maltreatment, a fearlessness tested in the harshest regimes on earth. Instantly understood. *Tsisari* had spent his childhood surrounded by such people.

The capsule fell, was crushed beneath a heavy boot. 'Telemetry signals are easily replicated.'

'My falcon?'

'Safe, and eating its prey on dead ground five hundred yards from here.'

Diakanov was wary. Technical interference implied a trap. Yet this was no assassin. There was honour, intelligence in the ungiving eyes.

'You came to see me?'

'You came to see me.'

'I could have you killed.'

The self-assurance of one who knew otherwise. 'I survived Beria.'

Diakanov was still. A spectre of his youth crept, uninvited, into his mind. 'Should I know you?' He plucked at the fingers of the hawking glove, felt vulnerable, uneasy. But it was the insecurity of confrontation with authority, not the appreciation of a physical threat. The man touched his subconscious. 'Should I know you?' he repeated.

Cold Cut looked beyond him, added to his sense of transparency. 'That would be impossible.'

'Do you have a name?' Instinct responded, but recognition stayed aloof. Diakanov's fusiform gyrus worked overtime at the rear of his brain, stimulated the memory. It was ineffective.

'I am only a number on a patch of cloth.'

'Tell me.'

'Prisoner N549,' the wanderer said.

It was a trance, an illusion. Diakanov had forgotten his falcons, forgotten *Moskva*. On the ground before him lay a package. *Tsisari* was bowed, the old man gone.

* * *

577

Three weeks, four, he could not tell. Below ground, days or seasons would pass without being seen or counted. He was entombed, expected Russia to join him, spent the hours breathing filtered air, calculating and recalculating. This is the day, he had thought. Then the next, or the next. His country must be molten, the world on fire. Yet no one spoke. The guards were silent, pushed food through and walked away, avoided contact. He looked for nuance, despair at existence swept to destruction, doomed by *Perimetr*. Disappointment each time. Not a flicker, on their faces, on the walls. He watched the light bulb: it was constant, power steady, undisrupted. Nuclear exchange would lead to dimming, a surge or blackout, before emergency generators cut in. He sighed. How long since the vans rolled from the Kremlin with him bound inside the centre vehicle, how long would it take for vengeance?

Thoughts of Lavrenti Beria came to him, displaced the invisible counsel who discoursed in his head. It was 26 June 1953 when the architect of Stalin's Terror attended a meeting with Khrushchev following the dictator's death. A trap. He was arrested by a squad of fifty elite Red Army troops, taken to a bunker hidden beneath Osipenko Street and, after secret deliberations lasting six months, was executed in his cell. Air Force Chief of Staff Major-General Pavel Batitskii fired the first shot, four other senior officers joined in, and the body of the former secret police supremo was carried to Donskoy crematorium for final and ignominious disposal.

Gresko shaded his eyes from the bulb's intensity. Still no sign. They had stripped his decorations and insignia, removed his belt, buttons and bootlaces, left him while they conducted their own covert trial. Yet they were weaklings, would have no stomach to sentence or condemn. The President and his prodigal Chief of Staff required the moral high ground, needed to differentiate between themselves and the behaviour of an unreconstructed FSB. That was their flaw – a slavish adherence to liberal democratic values, Western economics. Greatness grew from strength, from servants of Russia prepared to shed blood, accept responsibility. It had been thus for centuries. The people absorbed these lessons, these values, made them instinctive. Flirtation with alien socio-political experiments meant nothing, for Gresko dealt with an absolute truth. National destiny could not be altered.

Footsteps – sharp, assured – the pace breaking routine, extending beyond the sound envelope of his changing warders. He listened. A military man, a messenger from his allies, or a courier sent by the leadership. He knew they would negotiate. The rules of Kremlin court life, competing institutions, nationwide insurrection, made his presence and preservation inevitable. Influence was never buried by a few metres of earth, by a prison cell. Civilisation had either come through its apocalyptic ferment, or *Perimetr* and the nuclear suitcase bombs were malfunctioning. He would have to analyse, improvise.

Lock barrels rotated loudly, the door opening to reveal Air Force Commander-in-Chief Colonel-General Nikolan Yanov. He remained outside. The eyes were direct, unforgiving. Was this how they stared at Beria? A nod of the head, gesturing for the FSB Director to follow, to step beyond the threshold. Friendship was unlikely from a high-ranking armed forces officer pushed to eject from the presidential jet at thirty thousand feet. Gresko was untroubled, friendship irrelevant. It was all a matter of coercion. The men who sat on the Security Council were scared of him, terrified by the consequence of causing offence or inconvenience. They would crawl, apologise; they would suffer. Strange that Yanov should be their emissary. Absurd to draw parallels with Beria's fate, Gresko reminded himself. Stalin's protégé was replaceable, whereas he held the modern elite in his thrall.

The van shuddered on a line of potholes, Gresko's face slapping painfully on the metal flooring with each jolt. A soldier's boot pinned him to the deck. His anger intensified, confusion riding hard on it. The treatment smacked of bureaucratic zealotry, petty ambition, was inexcusable. It was their way of undermining his higher cause, his authority. He would shut them out, these cowards, refuse to speak or to listen. If they had conviction, by now he would be broken; if they wanted evidence, by now he would be tortured. If they wanted death . . . He tried to hear the air-raid sirens, the shrieks of the irradiated and the damned, but his Armageddon seemed far away. In his head, the search for scapegoats began, defence and prosecution shouting each other down, everyone judging, seeking retribution. He threw himself into the argument.

The shot, when it came, blew out a fragment of van panel, an ear and part of Gresko's scalp carried with it. Voices stilled. Lazin retrieved the spent cartridge and holstered his pistol. Ten minutes, and the vehicles entered the crematorium compound. They departed shortly afterwards.

History was a fault line.

EPILOGUE

Two days passed before Purton remembered the package. It had been left at the back door, unmarked, unposted, partially obscured by waterproof sacking, and he was too focused in writing up notes of a Mexican kidnap and ransom case to take notice. Eventually, Mrs Massey the occasional cleaner commented. She did not approve of clutter. To placate her, he agreed to remove and examine the delivery.

Bess, the Irish Terrier, followed him through to the sitting room. She liked a project, would involve herself enthusiastically. Old age had not diminished her enjoyment of paper and string, of making a bed out of wrapping. Unstinting good company, inheritor of the virtues and happy vices which made her canine ancestor, Finn – his portrait proud on the wall – so popular on the Western Front during the Great War. She settled expectantly beside the chair while Purton felt the object, ran his forefinger into the creases to check for wires. A habit, and hardly effective. There was no reason for it to be a bomb: the coastal town of Poole came low on the list of potential war zones. He could have lost his life or limbs in a score of different places. Yet he sucked in his breath, held it, as the penknife dug into the protective padding, its blade carving down the edge. Adrenalin was more necessary than caffeine.

The book eased out. It was leather-bound, thick, marked with mildew scars and the dog-eared raggedness of time and travel. He flipped it over, inspected the cover, its bulk which suggested a journal, before removing a sheaf of loose pages folded and inserted inside. A letter. He began to read.

581

They called us 'snowdrops' then, escaped prisoners whose bodies would not be found until the spring thaws came to Siberia, when the snows cleared and the winter crop of the desperate and the mad would be returned to camp for permanent re-planting. But I was never found, never brought back. There was a saying among the *zeks*: five things could kill you – the weather, the hunger, tuberculosis, the guards or the inmates. If you survived, you were unlucky. I was unlucky from the moment of my capture.

I was betrayed by one man, the Judas who pretended friendship, the wartime colleague and Cold War intelligence officer who made a pact with the devil, spied for the Soviets, who used the heads of his associates and agents as a stepladder for advancement and greater betrayal – Harold Adrian Russell 'Kim' Philby. Each rung of his career marked further deaths, meant midnight visits, brave men and women bundled off street corners by anonymous thugs in unmarked vehicles and never seen again. They did not go gently; their destruction was accompanied by indescribable suffering and pain, loneliness, by questions, questions, questions. And behind the rack, standing by the generator, watching as they were held beneath the water, laughing and drinking whisky as their fingernails were pulled and their feet beaten, was the shadow of an Englishman and double-agent.

We were both born in India, he on 1 January 1912 at Ambala in the Punjab, myself a few weeks previously on 28 November 1911 in Calcutta. I was premature – due also at the beginning of January – and from the start we were laughingly viewed as 'half-twins' by the two families. Kim was quiet, self-contained, an introvert who developed a stammer; I was louder and more boisterous, the leader, causing mischief and getting us into trouble in the back streets and markets. It was I who taught him to swear in Hindi: our ayas were mortified. But while I was indulged by my father, a young army intelligence officer answerable to my grandfather in Indian Political Intelligence and serving in the wilder and more remote provinces to pacify the tribes and counter Tsarist influence from the north, Harry St John Philby – an eccentric and extreme disciplinarian attached to the Indian Civil Service – would birch Kim at every opportunity. Grandfather always said he was insane – I never doubted his assessment. In the meantime, Harry St John alternated between ignoring and terrifying Kim and leaving him to be brought up by his mother Dora. She and my mother became close friends, depending on each other: the war years of 1914–18 saw their husbands disappear on operations around Persia and Mesopotamia and return only intermittently. Then my father left for Russia. It was rarely spoken of. Mother wept a little, but with all three uncles killed on the Western Front, family grief was accepted, coped with in private and suppressed. Duty was all. My grandfather, who had lost his three sons, told me that father had been sent by the King himself on a secret mission. That mission was to save the Romanovs. He came home once, briefly, in four years, before travelling back to organise White Russian resistance to the Bolsheviks. I never saw him again. He was executed in 1922 by the Cheka secret police after the Siberian battle of Volochaevka, his personal effects – what there were – smuggled out to us in India. Six months later, his four sons killed serving their country, grandfather died from a heart-attack.

My mother took me to London to live with her sisters in Templewood Avenue, Hampstead. There, once again, I met up with Kim who was staying nearby in his family's house in Acol Road, and – reunited with the other's half-twin – we spent the seasons walking dogs on the Heath, holidaying in Frinton and Corfe and playing practical jokes against Kim's three sisters. School saw us at Westminster together. Kim, although a King's Scholar, never excelled or stood out, but was conscientious, a hard worker, a boy who got on not through natural flair, but simply because nobody noticed him. His reports said as much. In 1929 he went up to Cambridge to read history at Trinity College; I went to do the same at Magdalen College, Oxford. We moved on, grew up and apart. Occasionally we would write with news, mutual friends would keep us informed; we even spent a student holiday taking our motorbikes to Austria. He was fascinated by the politics, seemed rather pro-Socialist – a phase, rites of passage many of my contemporaries were going through. I thought nothing of it, was too busy with my own rites, drinking beer, chasing buxom, ever-friendly and enormously accommodating local girls. I suspected Kim was still a virgin, a Communist – never. I suspected still less that his history tutor, Maurice Dobb, had already put him in touch with the Soviet front organisation 'The World Committee for Relief of Victims of German Fascism', who in turn passed him on for assessment to Moscow Centre's Vienna *Rezidentzura*.

Back to our respective universities and the promise to keep in touch. But the separation of distance also meant new diversions, different lives and a dilution to our old camaraderie. The excitable undergraduate letters grew less and then dried up; there were no more carefree holidays. I was told that he had fallen in with a 'rum' Cambridge crowd, a term that covered all manner of sins and which I dismissed as idle gossip and a symptom of inter-varsity rivalry. It was nothing of the sort: his friends – Anthony Blunt, Guy Burgess, Donald Maclean, John Cairncross, Leo Long and Michael Straight – were busy establishing secret Communist *fuenforgruppen* cells; all were to become paid-up members of the KGB. Their tutors, including Dobb and Roy Pascal, and students such as James Klugmann, were talent-spotters for Soviet intelligence who kept in regular contact with the two main KGB 'illegals' in England at the time, Arnold 'Otto' Deutsch and Thomas Maly, and later the Cambridge Ring's key handler Anatoly Gorsky. I was such an innocent.

We next met while taking the Civil Service exams, before Philby left for a two-year sabbatical teaching English and conducting political research in an unravelling and increasingly dangerous Austria. Upon his return, fleeing from street-battles and violence which had developed into civil war and seen the brutal crushing of the Austrian socialist opposition, he appeared changed, ever more serious, aloof. Perhaps it was maturity, gravitas; he had, after all, witnessed people die, been under fire himself. He won instant respect and admiration among his London friends, was fêted as a hero by his more callow peers, and his reluctance to speak of the experiences only fortified the mystique and the aura. Stammering Kim – always watch the quiet ones, they said. Hidden depths, they said. I never guessed, none did, that while mixing in liberal Viennese artistic circles and proving himself on minor missions, he had finally been approached by the Hungarian Communist refugee Gabor Peter – later to become Stalin's secret police chief in Hungary – and by the agent Edith Tudor–Hart, and recruited into the Comintern. He was tasked with penetrating the intelligence organs of the British Establishment and effecting the Soviet Politburo's dictat to eliminate traitors to the revolution and countering espionage against Russia. Unfortunately, I was to find myself as one of those who stood in his way.

Throughout the rest of the 1930s, I worked for the Indian Civil Service, monitoring the growing independence movement and performing intelligence assignments which both my father and grandfather had undertaken in an earlier part of the century. It was wonderful to be back on the subcontinent among the unchanging sights of my childhood. Philby was by then a journalist, first for the monthly journal *Review of Reviews*, next as editor for the distinctly rightwing *Anglo-German Fellowship* magazine, and, in a final transformation to conservative-leaning establishment figure, as foreign correspondent for *The Times* reporting favourably on Franco's fascist side during the Spanish Civil War. Wounded by a Republican-fired rocket in the village of Caude, personally awarded the Red Cross of Military Merit by the Spanish dictator himself, and in conducting an ongoing affair with an expatriate Canadian divorcee supporting the Royalist cause, his cover became impenetrable. With war in Europe approaching and a dearth of qualified personnel at its disposal, SIS was delighted to welcome into its embrace a new, trustworthy and proven recruit who had already shown his worth and his colours as a Buchanesque freelancer overseas. A real find, was the received opinion. Among the crooks, rogues and drunks being hastily plucked from among the gentlemen's clubs of St James's to populate the secret corridors and expanding covert departments, H.A.R. Philby was a symbol of virtue, sobriety and competence. He was expected to be a high-flier, marked for success, and I, unwittingly, paved the way by adding my endorsement and arranging for his initial interview in June 1940 with Marjorie Maxse, head of MI6 political propaganda, at St Ermin's hotel in Caxton Street. For him, for Soviet foreign intelligence, the wait had been worthwhile.

When Philby arrived in the rapidly growing Section D of SIS in the summer of 1940, I had been there a year, transferred from the Indian Civil Service under cover of the Diplomatic Corps and requested to build up the sabotage, subversion and European anti-Nazi 'stay-behind' capabilities of the department. It was a surreal, chaotic environment: amateurish, factionalised, outdated, full of bureaucratic in-fighting, politicking, petty jealousies, office empire-building and asset-hoarding, riven by a clash of egos between mutually suspicious senior heads. Brought in by Colonel Sir Claude Dansey, an old India hand and friend both of my father and grandfather, who as Deputy Chief of the Secret Service was responsible for offensive espionage operations, I found myself in one distinct camp. Philby, a protégé of Dansey's arch-enemy, the refined SIS Director of Security and soon-to-be Vice Chief Secret Service, Colonel Valentine 'Vee-Vee' Vivian, found himself with a motley collection of thinkers, aesthetes and intellectuals in the other. We were the pirates, they the modernisers. It was a culture clash which was utterly destructive, that the Chief, Major-General Sir Stewart-Menzies, could do little to prevent. He probably enjoyed the conflict. And Philby exploited it, the voice of reason, the man with friends – such as myself – across the divide, the conciliator, counsellor and defuser of tension.

Yet he was only there a few months when D was disbanded by order of the Cabinet, its remnants and roles transferred under the aegis of the Ministry for Economic Warfare and integrated into the independent and newly formed SOE, the Special Operations Executive. Both of us became selectors and instructors, moving from Station XVII at Brickendonbury in Hertfordshire to the Montagu estate at Beaulieu in Hampshire, training the French, Poles, Czechs, and other displaced Europeans to infiltrate enemy-occupied territory and mount sustained resistance campaigns across the continent. Many men and women passed through the courses – committed, astonishingly brave, with complete trust in their British handlers. Post-war, they would become the nucleus for anti-Communist activities in Eastern Europe. Until Philby exposed them.

Dansey pulled me back to SIS to work personally for him in Department Z, shoring up his own position, dealing with foreign espionage units and arranging hits on senior German military figures. In 1941, briefly seconded to the Director of Naval Intelligence, Rear Admiral John Godfrey, I drew up plans with his assistant Ian Fleming – who I believe went on to write spy thrillers – to persuade the Americans to establish a centralised operational intelligence department. They did not appreciate the pressure; Americans rarely do. Yet, eventually, our arguments prevailed. We had, after all, won the signals intelligence war in 1914–18, developed our capabilities through Station X at Bletchley Park, and stood alone against the Nazis since 1939, so had some credibility. The United States agreed to establish first a Joint Intelligence Staff and Committee to collate information from across their fragmented espionage bureaus and finally an Office of Strategic Services, forerunner of the Central Intelligence Agency. It placed me in prime position to liaise between the two organisations, and – unknowingly – was to make me a more significant obstacle to the career prospects of Kim

Philby and the ultimate goals set for him by his masters at Moscow Centre.

His star was in the ascendant. In early 1941, his patron and mentor Valentine Vivian offered him an executive position in Section V, Vee-Vee's personal fiefdom back at SIS. Philby had made it, was on the inside, working for the counter-espionage section of British intelligence, running the Iberian subsection which combated those German spies who watched allied shipping movements through the Straits of Gibraltar. He was remarkably successful, and gained a reputation for being a sound operator in this highly complex field of bluff, double-bluff, the planting of false information and the 'turning' of foreign agents. On my infrequent returns to England from specialist missions overseas, I would visit him at Section V's Prae Wood country house headquarters in St Albans. Something troubled me. I wanted to be sure, to test my instincts: I could not act on intangibles, on doubt alone. And in his reserve, in the cultivated stammer and the charm, the heavy drinking, and in his inability to engage a childhood friend in anything more than a superficial conversation, he marked himself. I knew. And he marked me.

I was sent on more foreign assignments, taking part in SBS and SSRF reconnaissance raids along the Dalmatian coast and throughout the Adriatic and Aegean, acting as SIS representative during commando missions into Albania and Yugoslavia, coordinating diversionary attacks with partisan groups against Nazi Germany's contracting and vulnerable southern flank. The brutality seared my mind, the nightmares never left me. But I fought on, month after month, small unit action after small unit action, before being recalled in early 1944 to work in the Cabinet War Room controlling special European intelligence for the invading allied armies. Special meant more sabotage and the targeting of pro-Nazi elements who might slow our advance. I worked closely both with SIS and Department X, the German Section of SOE, on ways to accelerate the enemy's collapse. Operation Foxley, the encompassing title for plans to assassinate Hitler, grew from this. It covered schemes to fire exploding bullets at the Fuhrer while he strolled to breakfast at the Teehaus along Mooslaner Kopf from his Berghof lodge on Obersalzburg mountain, others to destroy the *Fuhrezug* train inside a rail tunnel, or to attack his car en route to summer headquarters at Schloss Klessheim. They were vetoed – Hitler alive, incompetent, and in charge of the military campaign, was more use to the Allies than Hitler dead.

June 6 1944, D-Day, and the battles leading up to eventual German defeat. Section V had installed itself at offices in Ryder Street, London, but without Philby. Having engineered the dismissal of his section head, he was now rewarded with his own prize as chief of a new department: IX. Its remit – anti-Soviet offensive operations that went well beyond the limited official directive of 'studying illegal Communist activities', and which sanctioned an all-out clandestine effort against a different enemy. And Philby was that enemy, their agent against whom we devoted ourselves to fighting. He asked personally that I, a more senior and experienced figure, should be temporarily re-assigned to him in a consultative capacity. The Chief agreed – 'you're his trump-card' was the argument, team spirit was invoked – and I accepted. I was indeed his trump, part of his winning hand. He played, sacrificed me to improve his credentials in Moscow, to show loyalty in a period when Stalinist paranoia decreed that ease in climbing the British hierarchy could mean only that the Communist spies were compromised, or double-agents working for MI5. By sleight of hand I was offered up.

It was my role in helping to found offensive counter-Soviet operations for SIS in Eastern Europe towards the war-end that singled me out for inevitable betrayal. Philby planned to set me up, wished a potential rival dead, a voice from his past silenced. Had any of the department's schemes achieved their aim – the overthrow of recently installed pro-Moscow regimes in 'liberated' countries under Russian occupation – the Kremlin's ability to impose its will over populations dominated by its puppet totalitarian rulers would have been undermined, the historical inevitability of Marxism questioned. That could never be allowed to happen. Philby ensured it did not.

I was instrumental in reactivating agent networks and contacting underground groups in countries such as Poland and Czechoslovakia, many of them consisting of old friends from the disbanded SIS Department D or SOE with whom Philby and I had met, trained and worked earlier in the war. Loyal and unquestioning, profoundly anti-Communist, and desperate to regain freedoms for which they had suffered and fought so hard, they readily joined our cause and our secret armies. They were identified, signed up; Philby passed their details to the Russians. Most were tortured and shot, and I was the instrument used in drawing up their death sentences.

But I was unaware, too busy performing my own executions. While Philby was temporarily posted in the summer of 1946 to Istanbul, ostensibly as First Secretary with the British Embassy, in reality a cover for his role in establishing cells throughout the underbelly of the widening Soviet Empire, I was hunting and terminating lower-tier German war criminals. The orders, unsigned, oral, came from Churchill and were clear: the de-Nazification process, if fully implemented, would take too long, damage the delicate rebuilding process of a new and allied-orientated Germany, might even encourage Communist sympathies in disgruntled sections of the public. Democracy had to be constructed from point zero, from the devastation of a shattered physical and political landscape. Further court trials would delay that recovery and entrench the lasting bitterness of defeat. The victors' mistakes of the Great War could not be repeated. Yet Nuremberg scraped away only the top layers of the Nazi hierarchy; many of the most savage war criminals – the trigger-pullers, the active and proud participants in retribution killings, SS-led massacres and wholesale slaughter of civilians – were free and hidden. Justice had to be brought to them, swiftly, violently and secretly.

Our brief was to target those who were known to have murdered British agents and servicemen in cold blood, and to do unto them what they had done to us. Justice? Revenge? In those days, in that environment, and knowing what we knew, it made no difference and we felt no remorse. I was honoured to play a part. The Nazi weakness – once its strength – was to record precisely every activity of the Third Reich: nothing could be achieved or carried through without orders being written, stamped, and files being kept. They provided their own evidence, pages and pages testifying to their guilt. In the military records captured in Strasbourg, we found their names, serial numbers, units and details of their involvement. And so we acted. Attached to 2 SAS, often disguised as Military Police, and operating from the village of Wildbad set in the Black Forest near Stuttgart, we travelled the country, removing the criminals from prison camps on the pretext of taking them away for further questioning, and executed them. It became routine: their arrogance when we collected them, their anticipation of easy interrogation, their questioning when we appeared to take a wrong turn, mild alarm at our silence, and then realisation. In the forest clearing, the killing ground, we read them not their rights, but their past. SS Captain Albert Kempff, who castrated Special Forces soldiers and left them hanging from telegraph poles to bleed to death; Major Egon Wendler, a skinning enthusiast; Hinrich Gerle, a Hitler Youth leader and specialist in roasting captured British agents over open fires; Otto Krieger, who impaled captives on town railings – these were the men whose souls I sent to hell. Their numbered SS identification tattoos were cross-checked and they were made to kneel. Denials, rage, screams, weeping, cries for mercy by those who had none, the protestations of innocence by the guilty before death. And then the single shot from the Luger P08 pistol, abrupt, final, through the mouth, scattering the birds, spattering the brains. Another Nazi suicide.

I had killed twenty-five men before I was recalled to

London in 1947; the team continued for a further year before disbandment. Philby reappeared – he and I were both sent down to Gosport and Whale Island for an intensive SIS refresher course in subversion and sabotage – and even now I remember that he had lost none of his strange combination of detached sociability and aggressive competitiveness. That was Kim, his manner. He was already heavily involved in running the Albanian operation, supporting the royalists loyal to the exiled King Zog and sending in supplies and trained insurgents to destabilise the newly installed communist dictatorship of Enva Hoxha. Civil war here, SIS reasoned, could all too easily spread to the rest of the Balkans: it only needed one success, a single spark. I was sent to bolster the effort, approaching old friends including Hamit Matjani and other leaders of wartime Albanian anti-Nazi resistance groups, establishing camps in Malta and Cyprus, flying to Washington to persuade the State Department to lend American backing. Philby encouraged the process, demanding more funds, more recruits from among the displaced native population living as refugees in Greece and Egypt, pointing to initial successes in damaging the Kucova oilfields and copper-mines in Rubik. His enthusiasm was catching. When the operation was finally wound up in spring 1952, it had grown into a vast covert British-American campaign, swallowed millions of dollars and led to the deaths of hundreds of our Albanian agents. The Russians were always waiting for them. Among those shot upon landing, his precise mission known in advance by the enemy, was Hamit Matjani. The concept of secret involvement in the Communist Bloc lay in ruins, a blueprint for further sabotage campaigns never materialised, and the Soviets consolidated their political and military hold on their acquired territories. Philby was consolidating his own hold on SIS. By then, I had been a prisoner for four years.

The traitor's career flourished. 1949, and he became SIS liaison officer with the embryonic CIA in Washington, an extraordinarily privileged position with unrivalled access to, and influence over, trans-Atlantic espionage efforts. He held the post for three critical years, filling a dead man's shoes – my shoes – using my friendships, my goodwill, my memory, building on my links with 'Wild' Bill Donovan of OSS and the CIA's first Director, Roscoe Hillenkoetter. In cultivating cordial relations with Hillenkoetter's successor General Walter Bedell Smith and Deputy Director Allen Dulles, he could plunder every significant American intelligence secret and hand them on to his Soviet controllers. He did more. By being granted top-level clearance to the 'Venona' project, the US Signals Intelligence Service operation based at Arlington Hall west of Washington DC, aimed at cracking Russian communication codes, Philby could monitor American achievements in identifying Communist agents referred to only by their codenames in Russian diplomatic radio traffic. 'Homer' was Donald Maclean, 'Hicks' was Guy Burgess, 'Stanley' was himself. The codebreakers were closing in.

My suspicions started long before. He had been so clever, so accommodating, a manipulator without compare, an office politician who feigned a cool objectivity and distrust of politics. Yet he was too clean, his swing to the right during the Spanish Civil War over-cunning. On their own, as fragments of a fragmented personality, they meant nothing. Together, the elements jarred, drew my attention. What of his brief marriage to the Austrian Communist Litzi Friedman in the mid-1930s, conveniently annulled as he made his transition into Establishment circles? What of the way in which he blocked my 1943 report which pointed out serious divisions within the German High Command and the need to exploit anti-Nazi sentiment in the Abwehr, Admiral Canaris' Military Intelligence? My agent networks passed back conclusive evidence of a plot against Hitler – a plot which culminated in the Wolf's Lair bomb attack on the Führer – and we never acted to back it, were not sanctioned to do so. Philby prevented the paper's circulation, buried it: he was a Section V counter-espionage officer, claimed that my sources were compromised, my analysis based on flawed evidence and over-optimistic assumptions. Years on, I understood the motive. He and his Kremlin commanders could not allow a brokered peace between the Western Allies and a militarily still-potent Germany that might lead to a combined assault against Stalin. He smiled when I objected, that distant, detached smile.

Had I confided my fears, I would have been laughed at, accused of envy, told that my wartime exploits were making me irrational. Was I not originally one of Colonel Dansey's acolytes in Department Z, Philby a counter-espionage man from Colonel Vivian's Section V? Old rivalries would have been cited, my reasons for concern dismissed. I did not even fully comprehend those reasons myself. Besides, Dansey had died in 1944; I was short of allies. Any investigation would be a solo one. I determined to watch him, to get close once again, had already been persuaded to join his department. My advisory role provided a perfect excuse. There were glimmers, inconsistencies, irregularities, reflections from his unreflecting soul. I noticed them all, assembled the dossier, shadowed his career and movements until 1948. It was not enough – mere suspicions rather than evidence. These I confided to a friend, independent of SIS, in the Security Service. He, in turn, sounded out the opinions of a mutual acquaintance from wartime MI5, a university 'talent spotter' for the intelligence services and once involved in counter-espionage among exiled resistance groups. The man had since returned to academe. His name was Anthony Blunt, a long-serving Soviet agent from the same Cambridge University hatchery of treason as Philby, Burgess and Maclean. My private investigation was reported back to the target.

In those days, Western agents were constantly snatched or murdered in Europe by squads answerable initially to Russia's Smersh and then to the MGB and its successor, Department V – the assassination bureau – of the KGB's First Chief Directorate. I was simply another victim of the early, ragged and confusing stages of the Cold War, albeit marked by my seniority and knowledge of SIS networks in the Soviet sector of Germany and beyond. It was in that sector that I was caught, making contact with a reliable source who had promised a comprehensive list of Wollweber team members on condition that I dealt with him personally. SIS could not afford to ignore the offer. Since 1946, Ernst Wollweber, the German ex-seaman and docker and fully paid-up Comintern agent, had been 'Director-General of Shipping and Transport' for Germany's Soviet zone. His organisation was dedicated to one task – sinking and sabotaging as much Western shipping, especially tonnage under British flag, as possible. And it was highly effective. If we could identify the key operatives, and its methods, not only would we be able to create a more effective counter to the fires and explosions which were occurring regularly on our merchantmen, but we might also have the opportunity to discredit the Director General from within his own department. This hugely over-weight, balding psychotic – 'the walking pancake' to his contemporaries – thwarted, British intelligence would get the credit. That was the reasoning, the prize, and I was sent. I became the prize: Wollweber met me personally, tipped off by Philby's handlers, and put into practice his team's favourite expression. *Willst Du nicht mein Bruder sein, so schlag'ich dir den Schaedel ein* – If you don't want to be my Brother, I'll smash your skull. The German was tickled, beat me with a chain to prove it, inflicted a level of agony so great that my heart stopped on two occasions and he was ordered to hand me to more subtle practitioners. In keeping silent, I hoped to allow our remaining and uncompromised assets time to disperse before their cut-outs and false trails were exposed and their escapes blocked. I did not learn their fate. In 1953, at Moscow's behest, Wollweber was appointed as head of MIS, East Germany's Ministerium for State Security, charged with overall responsibility for the foreign intelligence work of the HVA and internal repression by the police and SSD *Staatsicherheitsdienst* security police. My own career had finished.

The British people knew of the Nazi death camps – the appalling images of walking bones freed by victorious allied armies, the piles of starved corpses too numerous to bury. The newsreels had lingered on these horrors. But the cameras were not there when I became an inmate, and the British people this time were unaware. Sachsenhausen and Buchenwald, names of the Holocaust, and my new home. Every day I saw men, women and children battered to death, butchered with kitchen knives, taken away to be hanged summarily by order of a brave new totalitarianism; every day I witnessed sights that made me pray to die. If this were humanity, I no longer wished to share its planet, the sewer it had created. I was tired; of war, of a freedom which persecuted the free, of existence. I was tired of pain and of hearing my own shrieks, of bullets being chambered and fired into the wall above my head in countless mock executions. And then the man from Moscow, an 'Administrative Measures' specialist named Konstantin Ivanov, arrived, and I was transferred to the dungeons below the Hohenschoenhausen meat factory for further and special interrogation. We called him *Totenkopf*, but he was a different death to the one I sought. There was no peace, no release. And in my torment I swore that I would survive, and in surviving that I would have vengeance on those who betrayed me and those who made me whimper with fear in the corner of my cell at night. God had abandoned me, turned his face in tears from what he had made, and in the void and in the darkness Ivanov became the life-giver and life-taker, the Supreme Being. And he saw there was no light.

I was brutalised, my senses pulled out with teeth and fingernails to confirm the information which Philby had already passed to them. I became a guinea pig, a corpse on which new practitioners could learn their pathological trade. And finally, I was sent east for disposal, my mind and body altered, my past and being stamped out. I got my revenge: Ivanov I killed on a cruise of retired Party faithful around the Black Sea in July 1990. I was a bona fide member of the group – my papers said so – and I dined with Konstantin, swapped stories, played cards and drank vodka with a hero torturer of the Soviet Union, a monster who had reduced me to ash. And I did the same to him, setting him alight, watching him scream, plead for help. The smoke detectors and alarms did not function, a loud party covered the noise. He was no longer my God, but an old man and the offspring of a Chekist who had shot my father in cold blood on a Siberian battlefield in 1922. And he saw, remembered, fire burning through the drunkenness, who I was. He did not ask why.

Philby had been different, wanted to understand why I let him live. 'Because you are not alive,' I replied. He was clinging on, an insomniac, a drunk, watching as the ideal for which he had worked shook itself to pieces, confronted by a wasted past and a future in which he and his kind would play no part. He had no meaning. In his apartment off Pushkin Square I sat opposite him – this sick, lost, chilling man who had erased me as easily as he betrayed so many others – and I laughed. For I was victor, and he had the scars of attempted suicide on his wrists. Here were his mementos, there a picture of the Hotel Normandie in Beirut, his books, the Bedouin coffee service, the ancient transistor radio with which he could listen to the World Service and cricket test scores, the trappings that would always make him an Englishman and an outsider. And I was part of the system, a survivor, which he could never be; free, which he was not. I wanted him as witness, to his own failure, to my success. He died a month later, on 11 May 1988. His Russian wife said how kind and considerate he was, a charmer, a perfect gentleman who would stop to help pensioners with their shopping across the street. I dare say.

Lavrenti Beria himself, former head of Stalin's NKVD – People's Commissariat for Internal Affairs – and now Deputy Prime Minister responsible for all state organs of terror, met me at the Lubyanka Prison, Moscow. I remember the dead eyes behind the steel-rimmed glasses, eyes which had witnessed his own signature on a million warrants of execution, which had overseen atrocity and murder on an epic scale. Against that, I was insignificant, a subject crawling across thousands of miles of mass graves. He kept me there for six months, visiting my cell periodically with Viktor Abakumov, his security chief, to see how the 'soft' capitalist was being broken and readied for further Bolshevik justice. The shootings were no longer mock: weekly, I was led out to the special wing and forced to kneel with others near a punishment wall, our backs to the killing squad. In time I learned to keep my eyes open, to stare forward, not to recoil with each gunshot. But in the early days, in those early hours, I would clench my fists, teeth and eyelids tight, smell the fear about me of men and women waiting for the infinite, hear the suppressed whimpers and whispered prayers, and spasm at the violence of the reports. Some would cry 'Long live Stalin!', in a final and futile act of supplication as the revolver was put to their heads – a display of faith in the very demon who had sent them to this fate. *Fire.* Loyalty repaid; the pistol travelled on, its wielder stinking of vodka and eau de cologne, drunk and worn to steady the hand and blunt the stench. Lead impacting with flesh, bone and stone, cordite in the nostrils, the slump of lifeless bodies, the tread of the executioner working methodically along the line, footfalls of professional murderers. They were famous in their way: the bespectacled Latvian – Pyotr Maggo – the deranged Shigalev brothers, and long-serving Ernest Mach who shook so much he was liable to miss and take off an ear. Decent, worthy psychopaths, and my daily company. And I was alive, left kneeling there with the blood and matter of innocent strangers on my face and prison pyjamas. Corpses dragged away, more prisoners would join me, die, fall and exit. I was the only one walking back to my cell, deafened, nervous system shaking with trauma, my brain processing the ricochets and echoes long afterwards while I sat alone on the silent, cleared floor of the Lubyanka. Another week – daily rituals of one bowl of thin soup, one mug of weak tea, one lump of sugar and one piece of black bread, interspersed with beatings, interrogation, beatings, interrogation – and the process was repeated. I existed in a netherworld of greens and browns, the colour of my cell, of the torture rooms, the colour of evil and normality, evil and reality. Greens and browns, splashed red. The colour of routine. It filled day and night: the sounds, the odour, the dying, the bulb always on, the radiator always off, light, terror and cold occupying every corner and every hour. *Philby put me here; an Englishman put me here*. Beria introduced variations. I was allowed on to the roof to walk in one of the exercise pens overlooked by the guards on their wooden platform. It was a space, twelve feet square, surrounded by high brick walls and topped with barbed wire. I would circle slowly, staring up at the sky, reaching silently out to freedom, before a second inmate was introduced into the enclosure to join my circuit. A short burst of automatic fire, clouds of stone dust and chippings, and a further bloodied heap lay warm on the ground, its wetness coursing over my canvas boots. I dared look at no one: those who came close were sent to die. I stopped reaching out to freedom; I stopped looking out from myself.

Beria had tired of my presence in Moscow. Approaching the winter of 1949, I was pulled from the metal slats of my bed, made to dress and taken through the silent streets of the fearful, traumatised city to be pushed onto a Stolypin prison train. A change from the routine visit to the execution basement. Sentence had been passed, *Ssylno-Katorzhny* stamped on my form, slow death was demanded and granted, and I began my journey into the darkest heart of totalitarianism and its frozen chambers of justice and humanity. Beria and Abakumov did not bid farewell; they had complete faith in their bluecaps. Destination was the Siberian gulag for *katorga* – forced labour – where bodies were so plentiful that, even when dead, they were used to build foundations for the roads and railways. Disappearance. Yet there were stages, procedures to follow. All dictatorships require them.

First, the Secret Police prison at Vladimir, the processing centre. I remember mostly its screams: similar to those at the Lubyanka, but here their owners were further along the line to insanity and hopelessness. It gave the cries a different pitch. My head was shaved again, I received a beating – a buckle tore off part of my ear – was handed the louse-infested pyjamas of a previous inmate and thrown into an isolator cell in the hospital block. They dubbed it the capitalist decontamination unit, a place where I could not infect others with my dangerous Western thoughts: a place where excrement overflowed from the steel drum in the corner before I even arrived. That was my latrine, the smell that invaded my day, pervaded my nightmares. At least it stayed semi-frozen. My mind dwelled in the past, for I had no future and could not bear the present. Every day there were shots, every day the dulled thud of bone being hit, teeth being broken. And I sat in a hospital wing which cured no one, where patient care was not a pillow tucked behind the head but one pressed over it with an interrogator's knee.

A printed confession arrived, a blunt pencil to sign it. I drew a portrait of my guard on the back. It earned me a kicking, the soup was thrown into the shit bucket. I retrieved the bread. But the governor had seen the picture, sent me paper and a sharper pencil to sketch him for his wife. The work of dead artists tends to increase in value. I did the work. Extra commissions arrived, paid for in lumps of bread, a respite from the pummelling – I drew the man's family from photographs, his favourite guard dog, his elderly and less appealing mother who slavered more than the hound. Sometimes I held the pencil with both hands to stop it shaking. And in the meantime, using what little energy I had reserved from the twenty-four-hour act of shivering, I employed the blade of the sharpener to loosen the bottom screw attaching the prison rules and regulations to the wall. It took a week to prise away – damage to state property constituted a capital offence. Small act, big crime, the way Communism stood everything on its head, distorted the slightest form of self-expression. It was worth the risk. I wanted to leave an epitaph, was driven by the urge to prove my existence, to myself, to those who came later. I was the condemned prisoner making his mark, the individual reclaiming individuality. If they discovered it a day after my departure, a fortnight or a year, it meant I had touched another mind, reached out beyond anonymity, established a wake behind me. It became my obsession. And when the board shifted, revealed was the name of Raoul Wallenberg, heroic Swedish diplomat and saviour to a hundred thousand wartime Hungarian Jews with his brilliantly conceived *Schutz-Pass* system. Snatched by the Soviets, as I had been snatched, he vanished on 17 January 1945. Perhaps they thought he was an American agent; perhaps they were making an oblique threat to neutral Sweden; perhaps he was taken because he was there. Kidnap and murder rarely needed a rationale. He must have passed through my cell, gone before, scratched his name as a prayer and as a memory, handing on to the next in line, linking with those who for the moment lived. My turn. I wrote my name and sketched Finn, an Irish Terrier of Great War fame whose picture hung in my family's home. I spent furtive minutes, disproportionate minutes, capturing his eyes, reflecting their fire, warmth, indomitable spirit. They stared back at me, stayed with me, humanity from a canine form, understanding, banishing the loneliness and the shivering, sharing the hardship. I replaced the board, slid to the ground and wept.

I do not know how I survived the winter, but the spring came, without heat, and I was pulled from my ice-bound corner to be thrown back onto the prison wagons for the terminal stages of the eastwards journey. Finn travelled too in my mind, the eyes steady, unwavering, unconditional. He was my imagined companion, the one I trusted. And Philby stayed in my head, in the recesses, a focus for my hatred; while it lasted, summoned energy, I had reason, I was conscious. Blackness contained its own kind of light. I arrived after a week in my own filth and that of others on the

Pacific seaboard of the Soviet Union, Siberia's Far East, at the Vtoraya-Rechka suburb of Vladivostock. From there I was placed on a prison ship to the transit camp of Vanino, feeder port for the horrors of Magadan, Arctic capital of the northern Kolyma territories. I lived in the open, ragged, starving, surrounded by armies of shifting convicts – women, children, the young, the old – selected and processed for slavery and expiration, marching and marshalled in all directions, flanked by guards, heading for labour colonies in Kamchatka and Sakhalin or the uranium mines of Primorski. Representatives from all the branches of Stalin's state terror would come among us, gathering up their quota to work, their quota to shoot. And the thousands would shuffle in, replacing thousands who had shuffled out. The transfer to the death barges remains vivid – the sea fog enveloping the misery in a chlorinated mist, the shrouded lines of prisoners trudging into holds for a destination from which they would never return, the bark of dogs, whips slicing down on invisible targets. And I was invisible also; I was nothing. Many lay motionless in the slop, drowned voluntarily or succumbing to maltreatment and temperatures of minus forty degrees, adding to the void that was our existence. We wanted to be with them, alone with private destinies we did not have to share. There were ships on which convicts were pacified with water hoses; ice blocks containing human forms would be chipped out at the destination. After ten days, my barge arrived and I came ashore standing.

Magadan, a desolate planet. Administered by the NKVD Secret Police through their *Dalstroy* organisation, and located in Nagaeva Bay on the barren north shore of the Sea of Okhotsk, it was the centre of the security empire's precious metals extraction programme, proof that their influence touched the furthest reaches of my known universe. In this universe, guards watched the guards who watched the prisoners; columns of pipe-wire men were raked with machine-gun fire to make room for newcomers; gold came from the mines and human flesh was thrown into them.

Marched along the 'road of bones' to a lager a hundred miles inland, there were sights for which even the liberation of Auschwitz and Belsen had not prepared me. I saw teenagers have their faces eaten by patrol dogs while the greatcoats laughed; I saw bloated figures tied to stakes choking and moaning in obliterating clouds of mosquitoes. In winter, we were plucked at night to walk the generator wheel, producing light for the guard barracks, our fellow-sufferers behind or to the front often sighing, slumping dead from cold, slipping to the sides. The lights would dim, a substitute prisoner be sent for. By morning, an untidy pile of corpses littered the floor as we maintained step. Man – the cheapest form of energy known to man. Next, roll-call, an additional smattering of the deceased – professors, teachers, disgraced commissars, petty thieves, liberals, decorated yet denounced High Command officers, boys who had stolen a bottle of vodka for a prank, boys snatched arbitrarily from the street – their frozen forms slapping weakly on the snow-packed earth. We went on calling our numbers, ignoring these railway sleepers thudding insignificantly at our feet. I was Prisoner N549.

Prisoner N549 inhabited a wooden shack, over-filled with two hundred zeks. Two hundred stinking nonbeings eating air, drinking frozen urine, shitting their bloody innards, clawing at the nether end of their lives. The dead were pushed into rafters, their food claimed. You could be killed for an ounce of coarse *makhorka* tobacco, killed for breathing space, killed for being in the Soviet Union. The reason did not matter, result mattered less. We were the *katorzhane* – condemned to corrective labour – and that correction was terminal. For fourteen hours a day, we toiled in the earth, attempting vainly to fill the quotas set for gold extraction. Failure meant a cut in rations, reduction in the one piece of bread and two bowls of cabbage water soup supplied each day. My body was consuming itself. I was placed on 'first cauldron', the punishment level, my daily bread intake lowered to three hundred grammes. The stronger prisoners stared, waiting, ready to move in and snatch what was wasted on this *dokhodyagi* – a goner. We were all goners in the *katorzhane* section, the NKVD encouraging the thieves who ran the kitchens and delivered the mess tins through the hatch to disrupt and befoul the supply. Occasionally, bars of soap were passed through – they were eaten; occasionally, politically educational newspapers on which we would be questioned – they too were eaten. There was no water, no real light, and no human energy, besides, to wash or read. In temperatures of minus forty centigrade, we were taken outside and strip-searched for smuggled contraband or hidden supplies. When displeased, and that was often, the chief security officer – the *kum* – would choose a group to starve to death, all contact ceased, and the moaning ebbed for three days before silence.

In the four hours given for sleep I turned on my platform to the wall and willed again to die. It should have been easy, a simple matter of redirecting the will to live, for each morning we found ourselves frozen to the bunks. But a man passed bread to me in the dark, lumps of fat, and life energy stayed. I neither saw nor identified him, but he saved me, without reason or explanation. Nothing had reason or explanation here. My mind fixed him as a Communist agent sent to extend my agony, and I hated him, as I hated everyone. I was pushed nearest the hatch, the coldest area of the shed, but it was a position from which I could palm bread passed through for the rest, utilise the skills learned in British intelligence. Tobacco was traded, I took a cut, negotiating for 'miner's rations', bartering for pieces left from the fourth and fifth cauldrons unused in the camp hospital. Our own hospital was the shallow mass grave hacked out behind the barracks. My strength grew.

It was night when they came for him, crashing through, heavy boots scraping, hut filled with shouts and the acrid smell of burning paraffin torches. He was a wasted figure on the sleeping platform next to mine, a louse-infested skeleton sunk in the self-absorption of malnutrition and impending death, could put up little struggle. Two of the raiders seized him, another two providing light, as the executioner approached with a log axe. It rose to a cheer, the hut inmates crawling from the light and into the darker recesses to avoid inclusion. Their eyes, big with shock and lack of food, glimmered nocturnally on the fringes. The axe drew back, started the upwards section of its descent curve, the victim's face tensed in anticipation and acceptance of the finale. I provided it. The move was classic SOE, one hand striking the rolled copy of a *Pravda* newspaper into the blade-handler's exposed throat, the other tearing the axe from his flaccid grip, back-handing in a swing against the skull of a participant and scything it into the forehead of his opposite. I wrenched it free, was stamping on the body at my feet, battering at the dead, heel onto stomach, steel onto bone. The intended sacrifice was as still as a knight figure on a tomb, lay crying, the blood of his abusers guttering over him. Circling eyes kept their distance.

The torch-bearers fled, to be replaced by the guards; I was taken away and chain-whipped beyond consciousness and recall. When imagination ran dry, hanging was the general, multi-purpose solution in the gulags. But having been condemned by the Cold War, my life was now extended by it. I was cheated. The nuclear arms race was in its sickly infancy; Stalin required bombs, and bombs required uranium. The members of our hut were called to parade, beaten into double lines and dragged off further into the interior. It took a week, and less than half of us arrived at the *gorlag* mountain camp. There were no wooden shelters, only tents: our shifts were spent tearing at radioactive rock with inadequate tools, often with bare hands, our short breaks convulsing with cold. I witnessed humans – or their nearest mutant equivalent – break and be broken, jump down shafts, throw themselves beneath the wheels of loaded trolleys, entreat to be decapitated and pulped with shovels or picks. The madness afflicted all, destruction and self-destruction in harmony, meted out and accepted gladly. In the place of pity, hope, friendship, emotion, there was radiation sickness, tuberculosis, dysentery and rage. Conveyor belts ran ceaselessly, feeding out rock and body parts from the mine. I remember only numbers – not faces – the cyrillic patches sewn to front and back of uniforms stamping out personality, stamping the person for burial. Their bodies were laid out to the horizon, and I was not among them.

A foreman sent me to the surface, his tone saying nothing, his eyes betraying an indifferent farewell to an indifferent soul. Recall on a shift meant chastisement, the likelihood of being held down by a bluecap and bludgeoned for an imagined misdemeanour, or selection for cabaret: clambering up and down steep, uneven steps with a boulder on the head until exhaustion, resignation or a clumsy foot caused the inevitable and fatal fall. It made the guards laugh. The Revolution allowed for jocularity, for involuntary contributions in sustaining morale. That day I was aware of a difference – not only a new sport, but a new destination. I was hooded up, thrown into the back of a truck and driven off. Occasionally the vehicle stopped, rancid water and stale salted bread forced into my mouth, and the journey re-started. After two days, I was given soup gruel. And I felt euphoric, that I was picked, discovered, my anonymity blown, that my lack of courage in forcing the end was out of my hands and laid with others. Things would be swift.

I stood in a wooden hut, numb, the sack pulled from my head, and a heavy-set ogre sat across from me. He looked, did not speak, stroked his beard with tattooed fingers. It frightened me – lack of comprehension did that to a prisoner. We preferred the normality of known, pervasive, uniformed terror and state criminality to unknown encounters with unknown sub-state criminality. I was a political, I was zero; only the mercury tumbled lower than that. Mass murder in all its startling mundanity was our comfort zone. Existence was defined by prisoners crucified into diagonal stars at the front gate with bayonets, by watch-tower guards forcing convicts to pick up dropped bullet casings then shooting them for gunnery practice. It was defined by beatings with iron pipes when the camp authorities wished to mark us, with mallets struck on plywood planks laid across our bodies when they did not. That I recognised, not this.

'Stalin is dead.' He spat on the floor. 'Long live Comrade Josif Vissarionovich, wise leader of the Communist Party and friend of the Soviet people.' Later, I noticed the black flags around the barracks.

March 1953. One life, twenty million deaths, summarised with a gobbet of phlegm. It was a slight on my gulag existence. My confusion gave way to tears, welled from the guilt and the agony, from the sense of loss for myself, for the innocents and for a ruler who had condemned us to epic suffering. We depended on him, and he had left us; our reason was gone. We were complicit in the torture. The response would be inexplicable to those who never experienced it.

There was no embarrassment. I had exceeded the average two-year life expectancy of the camps, earned the right to a hunger-bloated body and wrecked emotions.

'Cheese?' It was held out to me on a knife. I took it, chewed and swallowed. Stalin was gone. So many had died before the war – farmers, intellectuals, officers, Trotskyites, Party members – so many during it. So many died after: crypto-capitalists, those guilty of 'cosmopolitanism'; infected by foreign values, having been captured or seen their lands occupied by German invaders. They were dust, remembered by no one. And I was devouring cheese.

'I have had you brought here. You killed two of my men.'

I stopped eating. He was the crime leader who had sent the murderers into my hut, whose wish I thwarted. It earned me banishment to the uranium mines, and he was not yet finished with me.

'It was my obligation,' I replied.

'The target was an *Uporovtsy*.'

I pointed out it made no difference had the man been *Makhrovtsy*, *Fuli Nam*, *Pirovarovtsy*, *Crowbar-belted*, a *Little Red Riding Hood* or from any other of the multitudinous

607

subsections in the criminal fraternity. I would have done the same.

'A '58 who fights in the gutter, who can strike with a rolled newspaper. Useful trick,' he said. 'You have my respect.' I did not care. 'You speak languages?' I nodded, admitted to fluency in German, Spanish, English and French. 'Then you are a bourgeois nationalist, a recidivist intellectual.' At least he thought I was Russian.

My first meeting with Diakanov, feared underworld boss, king of thieves, master of many in the camps. In a land where guards wanted comfort, commanders wanted quotas filled and their population passive, and where corruption and oppression overlapped, this figure held the answers and the threads. We talked. He predicted a general amnesty for the thieves – the Communists required their cooperation, a successful black market to stem Russian discontent, to repair Stalin's damage – but he planned to stay. Overnight, his rivals would be removed in mass exodus from Siberia, and he could consolidate, extend his power base, his interests and opportunities. He wanted me in.

It was my chance. To refuse was an expression of intent to die. To accept was to gain protection, influence, an improved likelihood of one day emerging upright from the penal colonies. Until that moment, the possibility was as remote as the location. Before me was Diakanov, my future, the swapping of one tyranny for another. I switched allegiance, chose to put off extinction. Logic overcame self-recrimination and reproach. I was a professional intelligence officer under the deepest cover of all: banishment and sentence to certain death by Lavrenti Beria himself. I was Prisoner N549, a nameless Russian; I was alive, and I would use it. Throughout the war I had liaised with partisans, smugglers, brigands, employed them for my own ends and for those of SIS. This was no different. I could piggy-back on an embryonic Russian mafiya empire, operate in two parallel worlds, create two parallel networks, report to two parallel authorities. In fomenting dissent, inciting revolt among the vast armies of slave labourers, I would sabotage the Soviet revival, weaken its threat to the West, while serving the interests of Diakanov. In gauging the response of the authorities, the stance taken by Internal Affairs to a rash of mutinies and uprisings, I could gain insight to the post-Stalinist mind-set, whether reform or reaction was in the ascendant. Espionage was once again my cause.

Diakanov was right. The Voroshilov Amnesty came, released thousands of hardened zeks and gangsters back into a society traumatised by war and the Terrors. He filled the vacuum – with recruits, with bodies – and I was instrumental in projecting his influence. We moved fast. I established consultative councils to liaise with other nationalities, to tip the balance of power in favour of the prisoners. Next, I initiated a campaign to cleanse the camps of the loathed *suki* – 'bitch' – element, the stool-pigeons who poisoned every element of existence, gave the authorities complete dominance, who led even to young girls being shot for whispering 'anti-Soviet slander' in moments of shared and quiet desperation. The 'bitch wars' were bloody. As a solitary warder did the early morning rounds and unlocked the huts, my men crept in and stuck their improvised blades into the collaborators. There were many choppings. Some bitches were pursued screaming through the camp, others were butchered with axes in the bath house, the rest fled to seek protection in the Disciplinary Barracks away from the main compounds. The bluecaps lost their eyes and ears, their primary source of intelligence, did not know whom to target. Prisoner morale rose, our influence with it.

The gulag system was the economic heart of Soviet Russia, and Diakanov's ability to dominate its mood and rhythm, to slow or stimulate, block and unblock, was spreading. Our enforcers from among the ranks of captured Lithuanian Nazis and the Organisation of Ukrainian Nationalists were a potent foil to the security apparat; our messengers within the politicals disseminated information backwards and forwards along the chain of transit camps.

Every time a group of 'troublemakers' was dispersed to corrective prisons, Magadan or to the grim Dzhezkazgan mines, our agents travelled with them. When Germans were 'bought' by their government and repatriated in exchange for Chancellor Adenauer's gold, when Poles were permitted to return to their homeland, we inserted our representatives, provided their livelihood. In return, we gained forward operating cells and data on the Warsaw Pact which I could pass to London.

Efforts were made by State organs to re-establish authority; insurrections were brutally crushed. In Vorkuta, protesting slave coal-miners were machine-gunned, riots were put down in Taishet, Mylgi and Karaganda, hunger-strikers shot at Peschany, strafed by aircraft, fired on by tanks at Elgena Toskana, Norilsk and – after the infamous forty-day siege – at Kengir. Yet the bloodshed and savagery fuelled resistance, both passive and active, and won us recruits. We were costing the Soviet system dear.

I became protector and tutor to Diakanov's son, Boris. He had been brought to live in the juvenile camp for his own safety and under the eye of his father. Murder attempts on the boy were numerous. I countered each move, responded in kind. My reward was to become his father's most trusted confidant. I was not always needed. A prison trusty from the Production Planning Section threatened Boris – he suffered a fatal accident beneath a dislodged pile of timber logs. A privileged barracks elder refused to hand over a canteen of roast potatoes and pig fat – he disappeared into the cement works. The guards noted the incidents, appreciated the difficulty in pursuing enquiries, and went no further. I knew the truth, that the mishaps were engineered by a businessman and violent criminal below the age of fourteen. He was cutting his teeth. Innocence and childhood did not exist in this medium, or in that mind. He never learned that I had my own son, had my own agenda. I was his Walsingham: obedient, loyal, discreet, an adviser and bodyguard, sage and bullet-catcher. What I defended was as rotten as the labour camp itself.

In 1956, Diakanov arranged for my transfer to rail construction and I was sent westwards to work on a section of the Circumbaikal branch line near Lake Baikal. It was an important step, for I was consolidating my boss's grip on the Siberian transportation networks and the labour which would man them. I travelled, observed, wrote reports, photographed, stole documentation, made copies in my capacity as criminal and spy; made plans. By 1958, I was labouring on the temporary railway for the 'Fiftieth Anniversary Great October' Bratsk hydroelectric dam, putting down different kinds of sleeper: those to support track, and the human kind to support first Diakanov's empire and then my escape. Fiftieth Anniversary – I felt as though I had spent half a century in irons. It was already ten years.

The Bratsk area was a giant concentration camp, one of Communist Russia's great industrial ventures. Diakanov senior plundered it, ensured that his men received preferential treatment, demonstrated to local commanders how they might get rich at Moscow's expense and without discovery. Productivity improved. Everyone was happy, except the convicts, except me. I cut through the *Ozerlaq* wire at Taishet on Russian New Year's Eve 1960, the night drunken guards took sniper-rifles, dropped flares from their watch towers, and picked off six inmates. No one saw me. They would have thought it a hallucination. I believed I was mad, but measurement of such had ceased to be valid. It was freedom. If I died, it would be outside a perimeter fence. I trudged south-eastwards in the snow, following the route of the Trans-Siberian railway. The patrols, the trappers and loggers would be inside at this hour and in this weather. I could not feel my limbs, visibility was a few feet, but I blundered on in sub-freezing conditions, the layers of quilted clothing and the bag of pilfered provisions weighing me down. Many times I fell into drifts, stumbled off pathways, became lost. I kept on, planned to make contact with a band of partisan *zeks* whom I learned had escaped from the Cheremkhovo coal

611

mines and settled in forests around the town of Zima – 'winter' in Russian – over two hundred and sixty miles from my position. Their reaction was an unknown: I could be killed or welcomed, but I placed faith in the advantages I could bring with my training and contacts. One of those contacts I intended to use now. My immediate destination was a disused railway service hut set back in a clearing. There I was to sit until the snow-plough operator I had bribed would pick me up and transfer me a hundred miles along my route to a group of indigenous local hunters. To forewarn them was to increase the risk of discovery, of a government informant leading me into a trap. It was well-known that a bounty was paid for every escapee handed over. I prayed that tribal rather than government loyalty would prevail. Out here, we were all oppressed – a bond of sorts.

After ten hours, I found the abandoned cabin, tried to keep warm, lay curled on the floor, eked out my food. The man never came. For two days I waited, until awareness of my situation, exposure to cold and near-discovery, forced me to move on. I covered my tracks, swept the traces, doubled back and pushed forwards. Search teams were an inevitability; I had to outwit them. Living in snow-holes and scrapes, I zig-zagged through the forests, avoided settlements. A convict gang collecting firewood under armed guard ventured by while I huddled beneath an improvised shelter. The branch came away: I was staring into the eyes of a young man grown old with hardship, stupefied by fright and surprise. My head slumped; I made no sign, was prepared for the panic and shots. When my eyes opened, I was alone, the wood replaced. Further branches had been added.

I was making progress, or so I fooled myself, aware of advance rather than slowing. Then accident, the breaking through ice, submersion to my chest in water. As I scrabbled desperately up the bank, hauled myself over the lip, I was encased in a crystalline suit of ice armour. My heart, body systems were in shock, closing down, skin burning in an intense glacial fire; I could barely function. Remaining strength I used to crawl, face furrowing the snow, instinct not energy driving me in a senseless mission to get away. I forget details: they merge into the whiteness without form or outline. My next recollection was of heat. I shook, for it reminded me of a freeze, the body's thaw reversing the process, taking me back through the agony. There was flame and colour, the pain came in waves, and I was a mortal once more. My ears picked up an unfamiliar language; the smell of animal skins and meat broth hung in the cave. This was no gulag, no Stalinist regimen.

My saviours were the *Tofy*, a dwindling band of native taiga-dwellers whose livelihoods and independence were threatened by the edict of central dictatorship, the intrusion of slave colonies on their lands. They had found me comatose and near death inside the rotting carcass of an elk, carried me to one of their storage caves, cared for me. It was decency, dignity, a respect for fellow-man which I had not experienced in a decade. Weeks went by before I could trust them, trust myself, lower my guard. They persevered, expected nothing, smiled, came to sit by me when I wanted company or left when I was tired. In their acts, and in their kindness, I found humanity again, warmth. The contact revived me. But the *Tofy* were few in number. Spot checks by the authorities might uncover me, consign them to deportation and eradication. It had happened to millions; a population numbering merely a few hundred would pose scant difficulty to the 'resettlement' specialists. So, I chose to leave. I had stayed two months. In that time, news had come of the escaped miners near Zima: liquidated to a man. I was handed on to new hosts.

The departure was heart-breaking, the sadness and risk profound. I vowed to return, to reciprocate their selfless gesture, little realising that my future path would bring me to them – and they to me – for the next forty years.

'*Brodets! Brodets!*'

I dismissed it, blamed it on mistaken identity. The old woman was insistent, kept pointing at me, placing her hand over her mouth, removing it to chatter excitedly to her family. They were shaking their heads, plainly sceptical. She continued, addressing me as 'Wanderer', breaking into Russian to claim that I was a reincarnation, prodding me to convince herself I was real. That I was. Yet I was as bemused as she. The others drew closer to inspect, there were murmurings of the date '1920'. Obviously, I was someone of note, a hero returned. They were patting me on the back now, the grandmother kissed me; the enthusiasm was almost infectious. Simple tribespeople, Buryat descendants of the Mongol hordes, and I was being treated as a demi-god. Disturbing. If they were so easily won over by the cult of personality, then there were those among them who might be won over by cult of Soviet leader. I would be watchful. We talked, their eyes wide, the grandmother asking questions. The truth emerged: she was mistaking me for my dead father, an intelligence officer who forty years before had operated with the White Russians in the area, befriended the Buryat and smuggled thousands to safety as the Bolshevik armies advanced. They were his scouts, his spies and his retainers. In this small Siberian village outside Ulan-Ude, I was told how in 1920 the city had been held for seven months by a combination of 'Whites' and American troops, how a British officer they called only *Brodets* had helped construct the defences, led sabotage and kidnap raids, disrupted the enemy's progress. He must have been an inspiring figure, had fought throughout the Great War, carried the battle into revolutionary Russia, attempted to save the Imperial family, and was to die two years on, victim of a Communist executioner's bullet.

I walked where he had walked, talked with those to whom he had talked. It was a strange, almost spiritual experience, the retracing and reliving of my lost father's final years, humbling because of his quiet and overpowering dedication, breathtaking because of such sudden revelation. I was confronted by sacrifice, duty, by a collision of our destinies. In making his journey, I was making my own, and in finding his past, I was laying down my future. It exerted a hold which I could not explain and from which I could not extricate myself. I became *Brodets*.

The Buryat asked that I stay. I accepted. They subsisted on the poorest margins of the Soviet system, were treated as scavenging dogs, mistrusted and oppressed by Stalin's servants. For me, they provided friendship and cover, became – as they did for my father – a core group of allies and agents. I used them to carry messages and supplies, their horsemen smuggling goods over a thousand miles, their women and children infiltrating the settlements to steal and gather information. All the while they were being 'communised', their traditional way of life banished, their people forced into the stark Siberian tenements that created another gulag. I encouraged their combative Mongolian spirit, taught them modern espionage skills and techniques which I had developed in the camps. We formed cells with other indigenous populations, grew rich on theft and illicit trade, monitored the activities of both Diakanov and his gangs and the KGB, and kept our distance. At a time when travel and movement for individuals within the USSR was heavily curtailed, we crossed the land freely, rode the railways. I reactivated the Belarusian, Ukrainian, Baltic, Polish and German networks I had originally established among the political prisoners repatriated from the prisons. The Soviets were the enemy, I a spymaster, Siberia my fiefdom. As the Cold War matured, and military technology developed with it, my task grew and the information I sent covertly to Britain increased. Radar sites were photographed, ballistic missile silos mapped, rail movement recorded, troop concentrations observed. I forwarded codebooks, transcripts, documentation and field manuals, military components, news of the Pacific fleet, of the state of armed readiness along the Sino-Soviet border, anything which might improve the readiness of Western forces to counter the Reds. The Soviets expected overflights of U-2 reconnaissance aircraft, were aware of developing American spy satellite capabilities. They never anticipated the extent to which, for decades, I penetrated their entire defence complex.

I could have fled, boarded a train, boat, aircraft, gone anywhere to escape the land of my incarceration. After all, I had amassed a fortune, developed sophisticated channels for evasion and escape, employed the world's finest counterfeiters, raised an army and extensive counter-espionage apparatus. The passes and paperwork I collected would have gained me access to a heads-of-state meeting at the Kremlin. But history held me. I was an intelligence operative, had been betrayed, suffered at the hands of Konstantin Ivanov and Lavrenti Beria, endured the weight of the camps. I wanted vengeance, for myself and for my father, remained in a realm echoing with my own screams. It was comforting. In Britain, they had given a knighthood to the traitor Anthony Blunt, a reprimand to KGB spy John Cairncross, shrugged when Burgess and Maclean defected, sighed with relief when Kim Philby eventually slipped across the Iron Curtain. Loose ends tied up, Moscow's bedfellows revealed and debriefed, the Establishment complacent and secure. I could not return and be a part of it. Would they have wanted me? I doubt it. The cosy assumptions would have been exploded, their explanations seemed ridiculous. I was a forgotten survivor who should never have survived. Such unpleasantness, such untidiness – and Whitehall was full of tidy minds.

If the past is a foreign country, then I can but stay abroad with the ghosts and memories. They are familiar, a link to sanity, a connection with who I am and what I was. In the labour camps, in the torture cells, in the mines and on the railways, I died a thousand times – saw people with lovers and families die a hundred thousand times – and was born tormented with each new dawn. Rage, pure rage, was my life force. That is Man. I had seen, fought, the two great industrialised evils of the twentieth century – Nazi Germany and Soviet Russia – experienced the end of civilisation, the corruption of the human spirit, perversion of the human soul. Enclosed is my journal of that time and of this, a record of the seeds of poison carried and cultivated by men such as Philby, a chronicle of attempted resurrection by the FSB of the old ways. My role continued. I had crossed not the Rubicon, but the Styx, and could not go back, had no right to re-emerge from the underworld. And in that foreign country I left behind a wife and young son. I visit them in my sleep; they exorcise the nightmares.

I entrust this history to my former charge, Boris Diakanov, to be handed to my son Ben if he can be found and if he is alive. I will complete my life in the land where my father completed his, be buried where he was buried, unmourned and unrecorded. I ask only that it made a difference.

I trust I have done my duty.
Tom Frederick Purton.

POSTSCRIPT

Leonid Gresko was awarded a posthumous medal For Services to the Fatherland, Second Class. It was rumoured that he had suffered a heart attack.

Western Intelligence had been informed of the precise target locations selected for nuclear annihilation by the Director of the FSB. It chose to avoid passing details to the Kremlin and instead concentrated on sabotaging *Perimetr* to prevent retaliation. Destruction of the sites meant an immediate end to much of Russia's remaining strategic military effectiveness. A result achieved without loss or expense to either the United States or NATO.

The butchered remains of a human male were discovered by a caretaker one morning in the hallway of the French Cultural Centre in Aden – *Espace Culturel en Poetique Franco-Yemenite* – former residence of the nineteenth-century poet-adventurer Arthur Rimbaud. In the victim's mouth were stuffed the torn pages of Rimbaud's prose poem *Une Saison en Enfer*. Ironic, for hell, or its earthly manifestation in the form of interrogation cells sited below the central prison in Yemen's capital Sana'a, was where the deceased had spent the last agonising months of his life. He was the Frenchman, mercenary and intelligence hireling, Captain Marc Deodat Mouton.

Several Interior Ministry and FSB strongholds with elements loyal to Leonid Gresko were attacked by Defence Ministry troops under direct orders from the Russian president. One such, a base situated near the Siberian city of Tomsk, experienced particularly heavy fighting. Dug into underground redoubts built originally for Soviet military manufacture, the defenders held out for a fortnight against concerted aerial and ground bombardment. It was estimated that during this period up to twenty thousand *Uragan* and *Grad* multiple-launch rockets fell on the location. In the final night assault, a number of helicopters preceded the advance fitted with American-supplied dual-mode infrared laser and hyperspectral devices for stand-off detection and mapping of hidden minefields. Hunter Strachan led. He had volunteered, contesting that Leonid Gresko misled him and other CIA Cuban Sanction colleagues over the precise nature of the plan. Nuclear weapons and global destruction had never been mentioned. He was at one thousand feet when a CO_2 laser gun – understood to be derived from the US-Israeli *Nautilus* directed energy research programme – illuminated his craft for three seconds. A catastrophic explosion resulted. There were no survivors.

Jackie Ferris trudged disconsolately back in the rain, reminded herself that dogs were good for families, families good for votes, and votes good for her husband's career. Nigel should be the one taking them out for exercise then. Instead, he was locked in his office above the garage, preparing a speech or glib statement concerning international aid which he would rehearse on her later. She might make suggestions, add the feminist or New Age angle, claim that veganism or crystals were the answer. There was no answer. Political wife, political life, and she hated it all, hated him. That was the trouble with a perfect match backed with perfect publicity: ugliness grew in the emptiness.

The dogs were pawing at the electric doors, whining. She scowled at them. They were stupid, vacuous-design canines, a breed suggested by Party advisers for the clean-cut, large-eyed look they lent to Christmas cards. She was bored of their pinched faces and pinched brains. They were yelping now, sniffing compulsively around the base. She drew near and heard the car engine, muffled behind the steel shuttering. Strange. The fumes reached her nostrils, heavy, petrol-laden. She saw the dogs running, heard herself scream.

The funeral came replete with politicians, TV personalities without personality, and soap micro stars from central casting and the D-for-desperate invitation list. Nice things were said: Great Communicator, Great Charisma, Great Guy, Great Loss. The Prime Minister gave an address – emphatic, emotional, damp – advised by his media handlers that association with vulnerability and suicide could benefit his humanitarian appeal, illustrate his depth, his lack of interest in image-manipulation. As useful as referenda for the cloying dictatorship. Tears were shed, cameras were present. Nigel would have liked that. His widow was dignified in her grief, won the respect of the nation and – more importantly – of the gutter press. Jackie gained her own parliamentary seat in the following general election.

The Cessna performed a neat, unfussy landing on the airstrip and rolled, props turning, to a bamboo staging-point beside a row of oil drums. Within a week, the base would once again be overgrown. It was sensible to avoid offering targets long-term to American espionage and direct-action agencies. Three men descended from the aircraft, the obvious leader wearing a pale blue cotton suit, face shaded by a broad-brimmed Panama. He did not like the sun: it irritated the skin grafts.

Two figures emerged from the hide to greet the arrivals. They were ethnic Chinese, unarmed, casual. Here in the Wa hills of Burma, south of Kokang, nothing would disturb them. Jungle and a narco-army of several thousand guerrillas stood between them and the authorities, and the authorities were paid to stay at home. They nodded; there were smiles. One proffered a hand. Their guest reached to take it, found his wrist twisted, body turned and knees kicked from behind as he sank in to an arm-lock. He was secured.

The bodyguards stood back and watched. They had delivered their package. While a reception team member roughly pulled back the captive's head and held the nose, the other inserted a dental plate and clamped the jaws tight on the plastic putty cement. The man struggled, face reddening, was pacified. He was allowed to breathe, hyperventilation again cut off as the plate was removed with a stream of saliva and invective. It was carried behind the screen. A tape went over the mouth, the adhesive roll wrapped round until the lower part of the head became obscured. Then the wait.

Minutes passed. The man in the pale blue suit spent them face down in the dirt. Eventually movement, the appearance of a tall newcomer in tropical fatigues and a bush hat, a reconstructed model of upper and lower teeth in one hand, a sheaf of photographs and x-rays in the other. He might have been stepping onto a veranda to study the tobacco or tea crop. Instead, he was delivering a verdict.

'Mr Diakanov. It *is* Mr Boris Diakanov.' Hugh Dryden looked down at the prostrate form. 'I'm afraid that your very expensive plastic surgery has gone to waste. We have a positive ID. You have reneged on your intention to cease supply of Class As to the United Kingdom, and we cannot be seen to endorse a major trafficker and exporter of crime. The present Russian government has also tired of your influence and activities. To prevent embarrassment and future complications, you will appreciate I must inform you that our earlier understanding is void.'

The British SIS officer turned away. It took 135 seconds for Boris Diakanov to die. His body was loaded back on to the Cessna and later air-dropped in to a deep gorge set in densely foliated and near-inaccessible terrain.

It was a rich, overwhelming scene, resonant with history and poignancy, the uniforms and vestments of two nations, of Church and State, mingled in a glittering pageant and set off by the magnificence of the malachite-patterned reception hall. The National Anthems played, a fanfare from the Royal Trumpeters followed, and the British Sovereign stepped forward holding a scarlet cushion on which was placed the emerald cross of Tsarina Alexandra, murdered in the House of Special Purpose at Ekaterinburg in a previous century.

Among the invited audience, watching as the President of the Russian Federation bowed solemnly and took the newly named Cross of Joy, was Ben Purton, now in his seventies. His suggestion for the precious object's title had been eagerly welcomed by both sides anxious to encapsulate the feelings of optimism and completion surrounding the artefact's return, and to mark publicly the warm and cordial relations between the countries. In the pocket of his jacket was a photograph of his grandfather Piers Purton, British agent, fighter for the White Russian army, intended saviour of the Russian Imperial family. He was holding close a spaniel called Joy that he had found at a place of slaughter.

The formal ceremony over, Colonel-General Georgi Lazin wandered among guests and participants, acknowledged the nods of recognition and wary allegiance from his fellow-countrymen. Max Purton stood in a corner, blind, laughing, his wife Adele – an American like himself – talking in his ear, doubtless describing in vivid and imaginative detail the sights and action around them. He still refused to carry a white cane, Lazin observed. At their feet a young daughter played happily, oblivious to protocol, unimpressed with occasion. Zenya would have liked her, but Lazin had re-tasked her elsewhere. The President, a former Kremlin Chief of Staff, walked by with a retinue and winked at the Director of his Federal Security Service. Beside him was his striking, intelligent mistress, a blonde with the health of the country-side in her skin and the quickness and control of a survivor in her eyes. Irina was back with her master and handler, had faked her death in the helicopter crash near Diakanov's base in Cheboksary. The assignment was over. She smiled, position secure. Lazin smiled back. He had *kompromat, kompromat* on them all.

* * *

On an unremarkable day in an unremarkable year, and for no particular reason save one of bureaucratic and periodic efficiency, the files were collected from their safe and taken down to archive. They would never be released for scrutiny. Cold Cut had ceased to report.

AUTHOR'S NOTE

Perimetr is an operational system. Many of the Russian nuclear suitcase bombs designed and produced for use by the former KGB are believed still to be missing. The Moscow Aviation Institute and Tupolev aircraft design bureau continue their research into cryogenic fuels and hypersonic scramjet technology.

Dead Headers

James H. Jackson

Officially the British Intelligence organisation known as Executive Support doesn't exist. But for its far-from-innocent victims it is all too real. Its aim: to terrorize the terrorists, to eliminate them before they can act. Its nickname: the Dead Headers.

When a sadistic mortar attack turns the streets of Paris into a charnel house, no group claims responsibility and there are no clues to the killers' motives. But the attack is only the first piece of a terrifying jigsaw that leads the Dead Headers from a secretive German pharmaceuticals company to an Iraqi biological weapons base in the Libyan desert, from a gruesome sex-murder in London's Hammersmith to a power struggle at the heart of the Iranian revolutionary regime. And by the time the final piece is in place, the fate of millions will have been decided . . .

'Tense, well researched, fast-paced and hard-nosed'
Frederick Forsyth

'Hair-raising' *Guardian*

0 7472 5771 X

HEADLINE
FEATURE

The Locust Farm

Jeremy Dronfield

Carole Perceval lives alone on a remote Yorkshire farm, trying to forget a traumatic past. Her life is one of tranquil routine, until one rain-swept night when a dishevelled figure hammers on her door.

Lost and confused, the man has no memory, no idea who he is. His only certainty is that he is being pursued, that he has to flee at all costs. Exhausted, desperate, the farm is his final refuge.

Both of them dream of escape. Of change. Of redemption. And both are about to step into a nightmare.

'A tense page-turner . . . dodging between serial-killer thriller, psychological suspense and full-on action drama' Val McDermid

0 7472 5947 X

If you enjoyed this book here is a selection of other bestselling titles from Headline